Selected Stories

Vincent O'Sullivan

Selected Stories

Edited by Stephen Stratford

Victoria University Press

TE WHARE WĀNANGA O TE ŪPOKO O TE IKA A MĀUI
VICTORIA
UNIVERSITY OF WELLINGTON

VICTORIA UNIVERSITY PRESS
Victoria University of Wellington
PO Box 600 Wellington
vup.victoria.ac.nz

First published 2019

ISBN 9781776562886

A catalogue record is available from the
National Library of New Zealand

Printed in China by 1010 Printing International

For Dominic and Deirdre

Acknowledgements

'Grove', 'The Boy, The Bridge, The River' and 'Palms and Minarets' have appeared previously in *The Boy, The Bridge, The River* (John McIndoe Ltd/ Reed, 1978); 'The Corner', 'That's the Apple for You', 'The Witness Man', 'The Professional' and 'Dandy Edison For Lunch' in *Dandy Edison for Lunch* (John McIndoe Ltd, 1981); 'The Club', 'The Last of Freddie' and 'Survivals' in *Survivals* (Allen & Unwin, 1985); 'Billy Joel Her Bird', 'the snow in spain', 'Putting Bob Down', 'Closing the File' and 'Terminus' in *the snow in spain* (Allen & Unwin, 1990); 'Hims Ancient and Modern' and 'Coasting' in *Palms and Minarets* (VUP, 1992); 'Recital', 'Picture Window', 'One Ordinary Thursday', 'Photos, to Begin With', 'Not Always, Mrs Woolf', 'Waiting for Rongo', 'Still Life', 'Family Unit' and 'Pictures by Goya' in *Pictures by Goya* (Penguin Books, 2006); 'The Families', 'On a Clear Day', 'Mrs Bennett and the Bears', 'Fainting and the Fat Man', 'Daddy Drops a Line', 'Pieces', 'Getting It Right' and 'Luce' in *The Families* (VUP, 2014).

Contents

Grove

Grove's face wasn't injured, as far as you could tell, but it curved in on one side, so that his left temple and jaw were at least an inch further out than his left cheek. Whether he talked or smiled, his lips on that side stayed straight and together, and the right side of his face moved by itself. And there were two deep lines that ran from beside his nostrils almost to the end of his chin. He wasn't scarred or hideous or funny. You didn't want to laugh at his face and you didn't want to say you felt sorry for him. But I can't remember being in any company with him when people didn't tend to look at him rather than at anyone else. They wouldn't let on, but they were absorbed by his dent.

'You can't take your eyes off it can you?' Mary said. She was McCaffrey's daughter, and used to come round to the flat on Wednesday nights, on her way home from CYM or whatever she called it. She'd come in on Saturdays to get my lunch, and of course I'd have to go to her place whenever I took her out. Her father insisted on the old niceties, sitting there with his Scotch in his hand in front of one of his own latest TVs. He'd led his wife a dance with his drinking but he never offered me one because of his daughter.

'Well you can't either,' I told her. Grove had been in the flat two months, and Mary was still as fascinated by his face as when she'd first seen it. We'd asked him to share that weekly dinner on Sundays, but he ate with us only twice. Then he told us a lie and said there was a small group he blew with at one o'clock. I found out later that the group met at three, yet he left shortly after midday, and must have bought a hamburger in town. When I told Mary this she told her mother and her mother said that it showed how delicate he was. I didn't think the word gelled with the bent face and the long awkward silences and I said, 'I think he's scared of women, that's the real reason.'

'No fear he isn't,' she said.

We seemed to talk about him a lot, about what we didn't know more than what we did. 'He likes music, all right?' Mary said, ticking off the little finger of one hand with the forefinger of the other.

'Right,' I said.

'He's polite, and he's clean.'

'Right again.'

'He's always punctual.'

'And that's about it.'

'It *can't* be,' Mary said.

'What else is there?'

'What else should there be?'

I said, 'If there's nothing else why do we think there is?' Mary laughed and said, 'As long as he keeps playing wherever he is for the next hour, anyway.' We'd been lying on my bed talking about him and I began unbuttoning her blouse. We always seemed to have our eye on the clock.

'Just a minute,' she said. She took a chain with a medal on it from round her neck. She leaned across me with it closed in her fist, and put it beside the alarm clock on the chair by my bed.

'Think it's not so bad if you take that armour off?' I asked her.

'Never you mind why I do it,' she told me. Sometimes I thought of old McCaffrey when she looked sly like that, her lips slightly apart, her hair brushing my face as she came back from depositing her medal. I thought how he'd need more than his bottle of Scotch a day if he knew how his little lady ended her Wednesday nights and Saturday afternoons.

*

One day I said to him, 'Why do people always call you Grove?'

'They always have,' he said.

I was rinsing a shirt in the bath while he stood before the mirror, shaving the straight side of his face. 'I didn't mean that,' I explained to him. 'I mean why don't you get called Graham like your parents called you?'

'They've always called me Grove too,' he said. 'It's no problem.'

It was like that when you spoke to him. He gave you the feeling that it wouldn't matter what you asked him, or that it made any difference to him whether you liked his answer or thought it was nonsense.

'It's like he can't imagine needing to stress anything that's the truth,' Mary said. This was another time, when she asked him one afternoon if he ever danced himself at the places he played at, and he said, No, that if he liked a girl it was better to talk to her than dance, and that if a girl didn't like him it wasn't fair to bail her up, she might say yes she'd dance with him because she felt sorry for him, or because he was in the band and some girls liked the band to make a fuss of them. 'So there's no point is there?' he'd said.

When Mary said the bit about truth I said, 'That's all very well but he lies about Saturday afternoons doesn't he?'

'That kind of excuse's got nothing to do with it,' she insisted. 'It's not the same thing at all.'

I hardly saw Grove except at weekends and breakfast. Mostly in the mornings he'd be finishing in the kitchen when I came in. If we were there at the same time he'd chat about the band, or occasionally about work, where he'd just been put on some union committee, I think he said. On Sundays he would do his washing and read. He had no preferences when it came to reading. He'd pick up any kind of book and seem to enjoy it. Mary brought him a couple of novels once that he said he liked, but he said the same about some Plymouth

Brethren thing a fellow at the milk factory had given him, and about a book he'd found in the bus shelter. It was a study of Mexico and must have been left there by a student.

'But you can't like *everything* you read,' I said to him. I'd looked at the Mexican book, and it wasn't accounts of battles and peaces that didn't last but about growth rates and projected development and there were pages of graphs and figures.

'I don't read so very much,' he said.

'But what you do read.'

'There's reasons for books,' he said. 'Even not very good ones.'

'What's that got to do with it?'

'I mean the reasons are always interesting,' he said. 'The reasons why they write them.'

He had his hollow side towards me and I thought for a minute is he having me on? But Grove didn't ever joke, so there was no point thinking he didn't mean what he said. A couple of times he had seen me with electrical books, and he stood perhaps two or three minutes looking at the one diagram, although he didn't ask what it meant. One time the diagram was of a radar system that theoretically dispensed with antennae. The other was in a fifty-year-old book that I'd picked up for curiosity, and it explained positive and negative charges in a way a child could understand. He looked at both of them carefully then put the books down and began on something else.

I'm certain McCaffrey thought his daughter could do better for herself than take up with me. He was hardly in a position to say it, seeing the maintenance work depended mostly on my efforts, so he just said to Mary had she ever thought of a trip overseas? He'd give her half the fare if she saved the other half. And he never mentioned her to me at work. He was out half the day, at golf if the weather was all right or along at the Commercial, in the private bar where he had his own private tankard on a peg near the Johnnie Walker ad. A couple of afternoons he might sit in his swivel-chair going through orders and catalogues that sooner or later he'd pass on to me.

I was glad often that it was his daughter I was having a go at. It kind of evened things, although that had nothing to do with my liking her, I mean, that was an extra. I'd seen her in the workshop several times and was thinking how to speak to her before I even knew who she was. She was about an inch taller than I was, and if she wore her hair up she could look unapproachable. Then once I was meeting her after work we'd go for a drink before walking over the bridge. I'd leave her at the corner of the park beside the river and keep on, up past the ugly grey church and the statue with its arms raised as though it were in a line-out. The old man wouldn't let her out more than two nights a week, and as often as not if we went to the movies her younger sister would come too.

'You're nearly twenty,' I said. 'Tell him to get lost.'

'That wouldn't help,' Mary said. She looked at me as she did when she wanted to tease me and said, 'It'd scare you like hell, wouldn't it, if I left home to live with you?'

'That wouldn't be fair on Grove,' I said, to make a joke of it. 'Ladies' things in the bathroom and all.' And then I said, 'You know, I wouldn't mind going down to the Arcadia one night.'

'To listen to him?'

'And watch him,' I said. 'I can't imagine what he'd be like when he's playing and in public and that, can you?'

'Wait until he asks us,' Mary said.

'God,' I said. 'Imagine old Grove with strobes on!' Suddenly I could see him there after all, with his bell-bottoms and the medallion he carried in his pocket until he was in the hall and the light sliding up and down his trombone and his head like a dented kettle.

'Don't be at him all the time,' she said.

'Rather stay home for a treat then?' I asked her.

'That'd be nicer.'

When we did get home that Saturday, after an afternoon up at the park, Grove was sitting on the sofa with a woman who must have been pushing thirty-five. He stood up and said very formally, 'This is my friend Ruth.'

'Hello.' She smiled and I could tell her teeth weren't her own. Her breasts were huge inside a pink blouse and silly pale blond curls were licked down over her forehead. Her skirt was short although Mary said that length had been out for months now.

'Hello,' Mary said. Grove asked her would she like to sit next to Ruth?

'No, you stay there Grove,' she told him. She sat in the armchair near the window. She looked very good like that, the pale curtain just stirring behind her dark hair.

Grove was dressed up in his suit and glitter shirt and string tie. I thought how ridiculous he looked next to that tart, his jaw longer than ever in the way the late light glanced over it. I could tell he was pleased that we'd come in time to meet her.

'Ruth works in the TAB,' Grove said. 'Her husband grows strawberries along the Cambridge Road.'

'That's when I'm there, that is,' Ruth said. She smiled knowingly at Mary and Grove smiled quietly on the other side, pleased to see the two women taking to each other.

'She doesn't get on with her husband,' Grove explained.

'The other way round, more likely,' Ruth said. Her tongue came out and ran along her lips, making the pale lipstick like a wet lolly. I thought for God's sake Grove haven't you any idea at all? Mary said she would make a cup of tea and Ruth said yes, that'd be lovely, she was dry as a sandpit at the moment. I followed Mary about thirty seconds later. I went up close to her but she put her finger on my lips and said in a loud voice that was meant to sound ordinary, 'You can rinse the teapot if you want to help.' I tipped the old leaves out beneath a scraggy hydrangea and stood in the back porch. Mary kept making signs to me from where she leaned against the bench. She said later that she thought I'd break out laughing or say something Grove would hear and be hurt by.

From the kitchen I could see through the door crack into the sitting-room. Ruth had opened a metal powder compact and was rapt in the little mirror. Grove touched very lightly the hair that curled above her pink collar. It was a shy sort of touch, as though he were brushing the skin of a baby. He didn't speak and she smiled at him before she clicked the compact shut. Mary had told me once that compacts like that look like the things priests take with them to accidents.

Mary became impatient with my prying at them. 'You can take the tea things in,' she told me. 'Then you can put some biscuits on a plate for us.' As I took a cup and saucer in each hand she added in a whisper, 'Don't stay in there longer than you have to. We'll go round home for tea.'

We sat in the room with them for ten minutes. It was long enough for me to have a quick second cup, and for Ruth to tell us what must have been half her life story. The climax was that old pig who was the father of her two children, who was becoming more objectionable all the time. 'You wouldn't believe what he says in front of those kids.' She clicked her tongue, to give us some idea of how vile he was.

'How old are they?' Mary asked.

'Peter's eight and Bronwyn's six,' Ruth said. And then, carefully, 'We've been married just over nine years.'

'That's where the children are now,' Grove told us. 'Their father's looking after them.'

'Not for much longer, he isn't. Not if I can help it.' I poured more tea rather than say anything. It amazed me that Grove just didn't see what was obvious as the day. I mean, she only had to hitch at her bra strap through her blouse, or uncross her legs so that she could ease down the heel of one shoe with the toe of the other, for you to tell what a bag she was. You didn't need to get as far as her teeth or her gritty hair or the ladder that began in a small hole behind the crossed knee and disappeared somewhere in the lump of her thigh.

Grove actually spoke to her as he'd once spoken to Mary's mother, when she had called in to say Mary had flu coming on and would I like a lift round to see her? She had tried not to stare at Grove and I think he knew this, yet he asked her to sit down, and in a few minutes he had old lady McCaffrey telling him about the time she'd lived in Eltham, years before Grove's family had settled there. Her eyebrows were cocked as much as to say you wouldn't think me that old, would you?

Even now Grove looked solemn. He sat with an elbow on the arm of the settee, his fist knuckled into the hollow side of his head. I made the usual allowances for women not being as affected by looks as men are, but he still struck me as pretty near impossible. I said this to Mary later in the evening and she said, 'You're getting obsessed with him. You should look for a new flat if he's getting on your nerves.'

'He's all right to flat with,' I said.

'Then the rest is his business, isn't it?' She had to agree though that Ruth was a bit rough round the edges. When I'd almost finished my second cup that afternoon and Mary was waiting for me, standing in the doorway with her suede jacket already pulled up at the collar, Ruth had said, 'You'd think he'd make more effort with the children though, wouldn't you?'

'Won't he let you have them?' Mary asked.

'Oh, I haven't left him. I mean, when you've got a young family well you've got a young family, haven't you? But I feel like a few nights off *sometimes*,' she said. Her appeal was very simply to reason.

'He doesn't even cook for them properly when she's not there,' Grove added. He was looking at her although he spoke to us.

'Cook?' she said. '*Cook*? That's not half of it.' She leaned towards Grove, her hand resting on his knee. Her cigarette was burned down almost level with her stained fingers. 'You mightn't believe this,' she said. 'The kids' own father. But the other morning I went in about breakfast time. I'd been at my girlfriend's for the night, and I can't ring him to let him know because he's too stubborn to have the phone reconnected. So I walked in just as they were all sitting at the table, no cloth or anything, just their plates of Kornies, and he said right across the kids as if they weren't even there, "Been out rooting again, have you?" Can you imagine that in front of kids? "Been out *rooting*?"'

I looked to see how Mary took it. I was always careful what I said in front of her and I felt embarrassed, but she simply said, 'I suppose he was worried about where you were.'

Except for a few pale spots where a camellia tree stood, it was dark at the side of the house when we came back from Mary's. We'd told her parents we were going on to a dance. It was only nine o'clock. I held Mary's hand until I'd crossed the kitchen and felt above the fridge for the light cord.

'We've got four hours,' I said.

'At least four.' Mary kicked her shoes off and moved her feet backwards and forwards over the lino the way a bull paws. We'd been impatient to get away and back to the flat, only it was the one Saturday in a dozen when her father had come in early. He'd had more than his share, Mary's mother said, which meant he kept pouring himself a third of a glass of Scotch and sloshing water on it while he kept up this spiel about the shop and the retailers and the rest of it. He had taken me into the lounge, to talk in his uneven slurred voice about the business in Frankton he was going to take over. 'He's had the place for two years and hasn't made a cracker out of it. He thinks there's no money in TVs! I thought haven't you heard of colour, mate, but if he wants his funeral in black and white we won't be the ones to stop him, eh?' Mary came and put her bare feet on my shoes and her arms round my neck and said, 'Get along then.' Her weight pressed where the laces of one shoe went crooked into my foot and I wanted to tell her to get to hell off, it was hurting me. I was half way across the sitting room, my hands holding the tops of her legs under her dress to balance her, when she brought her arm around and spread the palm of her hand flat across my mouth. I licked her palm but she said 'Shhh!' against my ear and nodded her head at the sofa. Ruth's purse and her scuffed white shoes were lying on it.

'What're they there for?' I said.

'They can't have gone out. They must be in Grove's room.' I let her down from my shoes and swore. 'And what are we supposed to do?'

'Just keep quiet,' Mary said. She took my hand now, and led me on tiptoe to the open door of my room. Grove's door was closed. It seemed ridiculous to think of him tucked away in there with a woman.

Inside my bedroom I said, 'Well there's no need for us to go sneaking about. They must have heard us come in.'

'Be nice to them,' Mary said. She wouldn't let me put the light on, then told me not to let my shoes drop to the floor. To make sure, she knelt down and took them off for me. I'd already unzipped her dress and I unhooked her as she squatted in front of me. With only the street light from up the road her breasts were like two pale bowls.

'Hurry up,' I said. I wanted her to think I was on edge to get to bed but I disliked her in front of me like that. Her shoulders looked rounded like an old lady's and she had forgotten for once about the chain and medal around her neck. Later on when I lit a cigarette her fingers were moving round her throat and touching it, although she said nothing.

She took my shoes and put them at the end of the bed. We made sure the bed didn't creak in one corner as it usually did by putting a pillow between the wirewove and the wooden beam you get in those old-fashioned beds. Mary already had my cigarettes in her hand when I went to lean across her, in case I tipped something off the dresser. I lay propped against the top of the bed, with one arm under her head. Suddenly she raised her head and pressed my hand. There was an odd sound from the other side of the wall. I wasn't sure at first if it was an animal or what it was.

'What is it?' I whispered to her. We lay without moving and I could hear the blood threading through my ears.

'Grove's singing to her,' she said.

The sound was more distinct. He must have been moving within four or five notes, yet it wasn't a song, or like anything I'd heard him trying around the flat. Only those few notes, a kind of deep soft swell, but so little difference between crest and fall that it was there, but hardly there. It was a sound that wrapped round and touched softly and was never meant to be overheard.

At first I wanted to laugh—Grove with his thirty-five-year-old mother of two curled in his arm as Mary was in mine, Ruth's dyed hair brushing his dented side as though the hollow was there deliberately for her to nuzzle into. And to think he'd thrown away his evening with the band, and very likely his job as well, to catch what was probably the easiest lay around even for a man ten years older than he was. I tried to think of them only a foot or two from where we were, but it was too much, Grove and his naked woman! For a second I thought what if she sings back? She didn't though, and I'd left it too long to laugh. I could tell Mary was serious by the way her fingers lay against my cheek when she meant to be keeping them over my mouth. Sometimes it was like a hive of bees behind the wall, on one note. Then he would run notes together, quickly, for maybe thirty seconds, before the humming sound again, and I thought we can't listen to this any more, it's like being a peeping Tom. Then Mary surprised me for the second time that night, and more than the first. She had gripped my arm tightly then thrown the blankets back and her tongue was working over my chest and down to my stomach. It seemed that Grove was holding that sound of bees in a box at my head, until I didn't notice exactly when the sound stopped, only that it was silent again when Mary came back to lay her head on my arm.

'He's stopped singing anyway, thank Christ,' I said.

'I know,' Mary said. 'They've just left.'

McCaffrey sent me to Wellington for a month when a branch manager had peritonitis. This was the Thursday after Grove first brought his lady home, and a fortnight, exactly, before he died in a car crash on the way back from playing at Ohaupo. The band had left the hall at two o'clock and Grove had sat next to the driver. Mary said Ruth must have had a crisis of conscience, because she was usually with Grove, but that night she was home again next to her strawberry-grower, ready to give the children the breakfast they deserved.

Mary put through a toll call the next morning. At first I took it for granted that he must have died of head injuries. It seemed the obvious way for him to die, as only his head ever occurred to you when you thought of him. But then later that week I heard how his chest had been broken up, that he had died in the narrow speeding confines of the ambulance, minutes away from the hospital. At first he was conscious and when the St John's man asked him did he want anyone he said, 'No, it'll be all right, thank you.' I could see him very easily like that, not letting on much as the ambulance sped back between the hedges and through the country, the red light flashing and even the lean of trees and sheds and the front porches of houses lit for a second as though a fire was moving past them. And Grove there silent and polite and his head caught too in the red flare and then in the darkness and the siren growing thin as a thread as Hamilton came up from the right, but too late.

I wrote a letter to Grove's sister in Eltham and to his brother in Gisborne. Only the sister replied. She said she hadn't seen much of Grove over recent years, and if there was anything in the way of records or books I'd like for mementoes, to take them by all means before his gear was packed off to her place. I passed that message on to Mary, but as far as I know she did nothing about it. Then, no more than three weeks after, she wrote to say that seeing her father was leaving me in charge of the Wellington shop, perhaps we would be wiser to let things cool for a while? She'd see me at Christmas when we'd both know how she felt. Of course by then she was in England as she must have known all the time.

When I did drive through Hamilton soon after New Year I wanted to talk about Grove. (He had been cremated so there wasn't even a bit of ground I could look at.) But Mary wasn't there and no one else I knew had known him. So I went to the TAB beside the Riverina and asked for Ruth. A neat man spoke to me through the grille.

'She left a couple of months ago,' he informed me.

'You don't know where she's gone?'

The man looked at me more attentively and said, 'She wasn't here that long you know.'

'I wanted to see her for family reasons,' I told him. 'Could you tell me where her husband lives then?'

He called a woman from another window and spoke to her. Then she came to the grille where I was waiting and said, 'She didn't have one.'

'I thought he grew strawberries or something. A kind of gardener.'

'She lived in a flat off Hood Street somewhere,' the woman said. 'You're welcome to any gardeners you find up that way.' The neat man smiled over her shoulder and held up his palms as he must have seen in movies. 'If we could help,' he said.

I thought if I could track down his band that might throw up something, at least someone who could say a few sentences about him, but only the bass player was with them from Grove's time, and he was away on holiday. I spoke about Ruth again, on the off chance. The pianist I spoke to tried to think of her, but then he said, 'That's not enough to go on, is it, thirty-odd, randy, falling apart a bit? There's quite a few like her round.'

I'd tried to do something for Grove and I left it at that. The notes of his Ruth song have almost come back to me once or twice, although it's a good thing they haven't. All that does come back is a blonde with plastic teeth who thought she had to lie to him. And a siren that grows thin as the city lights lift above the swamp.

The Boy, The Bridge, The River

I

It was four kilometres along a straight road from the village to the barns, and six kilometres coming back, if one took the looping road that diverged to run beside the river. The poplars were high on one side of the road and the movement of their leaves, even on a night so still as this, sounded more like a river than the river itself, that sluggish expanse of water turning slowly with the sandy road. The cart held to the centre of the road and its rubber-rimmed wheels kept up a steady soft pouring between the muted stepping of the horse. There were several bags of grain in the cart and a six-year-old boy sat on top of one of them, and leaned back against the others. The boy watched his uncle's back, so dark and unmoving except when one of the arms would rise a little to flick at the reins. The boy wore a black sailor's cap with a stiff peak which he believed made it the captain's, and when light from a farm house touched the river or the cart moved over the bridge as they came near the village, it was for him the sea that glimmered and passed beneath their deck.

'Shall we get to land soon?' the boy asked.

'Soon enough,' his uncle told him. They drew on to the bridge and the sudden clopping after the padded stepping on the road slowed and slowed until the cart jolted slightly and was still. The river slid between the supports of the wooden bridge and a continual broad hissing rose up from beneath them. The few lights from the village were a thin string to their left. There was nothing in the darkness to tell where, between that house beside the church and here on the bridge, the land might begin and the water end. You knew of course that even a boy could almost throw

a stone from where they were stopped to the other bank, but that was not now, there was water and water the child thought until those lights beside the church could be the wharf. The horse and the man and the boy were silent above the slow push of the river, its thick sibilant washing against the piers. Then one of the lights from the village winked out as a window was closed or a lamp extinguished.

'All right?' the man asked quietly, without turning his head. Yes, the boy said. He turned one of the lugs on the sack he sat against and adjusted his captain's cap. 'I'm just fixing this lever here,' he told his uncle, and the man said, 'Tell me when we're ready to cast off then.' There was another moment while they heard the sea curling against the bows, the gushing pliancy of the sea which was three days travelling at least from the village and which the boy could see stretching, widening until there was nothing and nothing for half a year, and then America that would lift up very slowly and would look from the distance like the thin row of lights he could see across there now, while he tugged again at the sack and tapped against the side of the cart with a stick to let the engine room know. Yes, he told the man, You can go full ahead now. The horse's stepping was again very loud on the wooden bridge, then the soft pouring of the wheels against the sandy road. The man turned and saw his nephew's small shape against the pale sacks, the stick still tapping against the side of the cart, the face he imagined absorbed with the business of berthing as the hooves suddenly rang on the stones of the small square. When they turned into their own street the light from the house at the corner moved right along the tackle, down from the glint of brass at the horse's mouth until all the light seemed to push along into the man's fists and snapped there for a second on the plain ring on one of his hands.

'Those are bright lights from the wharf,' the boy said. He was glad those sacks were there behind him, he was tired now that they had arrived.

'They have to be,' his uncle said, 'or we wouldn't know where to tie up would we?' And when they had driven into the small yard behind the house his uncle hooked his hands under the boy's armpits and swung him high over the side, so high that the boy could look down on his uncle's head and along the horse's back that shone like it was polished when his mother opened the door and the light spilled over them.

'The captain brought us back safely,' his uncle called out and laughed, and so did his mother, who took the boy and pressed his face against her own and said 'It must have been cold out there. Are your hands cold too?' She put both of his hands inside her own and closed her fingers round them and then blew down between her thumbs.

'We stopped on the bridge, you know,' the boy told her. Then his father came out but he was not smiling, he ran his hand along the horse's neck while his uncle bent underneath the animal to unbuckle a strap. His father took the gear from the horse's head and said while he was doing it, 'The news has just come through. They have reached the capital already. They will be here in a couple of days.' Then his father went to the cart and carried two sacks at once, one resting across each shoulder, and took them into the house. His uncle carried another in front of him like carrying a calf, the sick calf they had inside for the worst part of the winter and his uncle used to pick it up like that. You could tell by feeling it and then watching it when you put it back on its legs how it was getting better. And one day he had taken the boy's small hand and made him press where the bones were bumps stretching the skin and said 'See how she's getting fatter every day?' And then for a joke his uncle had made him put his hand inside his own shirt and tell him which of them was growing faster, because those bumps were there under his own skin as well.

'He's asleep is he?' his father said. Then they had stood in the yard together before they went inside, and the man had looked at his nephew and his sister and his brother-in-law's long tired

face against the light thrown up from the lantern. He could smell the urinous reek from the stable. He had taken the cap from his nephew's head as it tilted up when the boy sank against his mother, and noticed the red line where the brim had pressed into his forehead. He had touched the line with his thumb.

II

He waited for the bus at the small collection of shops at the end of the street. It was almost seven o'clock and the morning was cold and bright, the grass verge at the edge of the road stiff with frost. The regular passengers nodded to each other or if they spoke their voices were unexpectedly clear in the freezing air. A girl stood by herself in the doorway of the dairy, beside the stacked crates of milk, a cigarette in her black-gloved hand. Latty watched her stamp on her cigarette butt and pull her coat higher round her ears, her blond hair billowing into a puff above the collar. When the bus approached she picked up a pair of white boots from beside the crates, and stepped ahead of the men. One of the men put his tongue into his cheek and looked across at the friend he was standing with. 'Not too cold to think of it though,' the other one said.

Latty waited until the rest had boarded the bus. He answered the driver's greeting and smiled at one of the other men who winked as he moved to the seat he always took, beside the middle door. Whenever the bus stopped and the folding doors hushed back, the early morning air would flood into him, the cold air of frost on a morning like this, or the smell of hay in January, or depending on the stop, the scents from the Dutchman's orchards or the drifting pungency of pig shit from the long low grey sties. Latty liked to sit where the differences of air and temperature and smell would most easily reach him, a few feet above the road, behind the curved tubular railing at the middle door. A simple young man with a narrow pale head always sat on the other side of the aisle. He watched Latty with open-mouthed surveillance, or would swivel to gape at the girl who sat behind them, who this morning carried her marching boots and kept her collar high about her ears. Latty knew she marched in the team that his friend Len sometimes mentioned to him. She was one of the girls who on summer evenings manoeuvred and wheeled and marked time so precisely and pointlessly in the park beside the cenotaph. But it was autumn now, Latty thought, they had disappeared like birds who sought some kinder climate until the frosts and rains and winds of the next few months had iced or fallen or blown themselves out. Another season he thought until the smoothed and rollered lawn received again those children at their strange rite of obedience and drill and swishing skirts, the accurate falling of their boots.

After it crossed the high bridge that spanned the river, the bus stopped first at the post office, and again at the corner where the white wooden church sat handsomely among the splendid oaks. The sun splintered through their branches on the other side of the road. There were few other stops for this early bus. The cold fields, some of them recently harvested of their maize crops, flowed past the window. Several brown hawks drifted low above the sliced stalks of the maize. Latty supposed they were after mice. The hawthorn hedges were whiskered with the greyness of the cold, and he noticed in the dip before the outskirts of the city, how the puddles were frozen beneath the blue strutting birds with their bright beaks. Then the bus no longer moved between paddocks and sheds and milkstands, for the houses were closer now, long low bungalows or peaked beamed structures with careful gardens and curved drives, the ten-acre people he heard Dryford talk about at work. These were the dentists and accountants and land speculators who had made havens of ease on land that should be worked and laboured at. Latty was amused at how he always thought it, *I am a peasant still*, but land should bear crops or support cattle, it ought not be given to these ornamental shrubs, not the weak-boughed acacias and clumped camellias, the children's pampered horses behind white-washed fences. After the dip with its last lovely crowding of willows and poplars along the edges of a creek, the bus rose to the neatness and the pastels of the suburbs, not country and not town, the ugliness of local brick and dull slatted wood. Latty wondered at how much could be spent on what looked so drear, these houses which *again to my peasant mind* he thought did not seem like homes, which had coiled electric tubes instead of open fires, where kitchens were for eating as quickly as possible and lounges for television, where there was no one space where young and old might come together for food or talk or singing or grief, for the closeness that was life. *Yet this is not my country, I do not understand.* He thought of the toss of chance or history or design that had set these quiet deliberate people in a place so fine, and then as if with malice had deprived them of so much that he remembered from home, where the land was dull and hard and the winter enough to kill, and sufficient to eat had been the constant goal. Yet here whatever fate you liked to call it had taken joy and exuberance and the delight a people come to in the simple fact that they were born to this one place, together. Then as frequently, once he had thought such things, Latty was ashamed. How many of these people here, he asked himself, had betrayed a neighbour in the way the river engineer had betrayed the owner of the bookshop, that mild man behind his rows of faded volumes who married a girl the engineer had once pursued? And twenty years later to the day, the father of four children, he had faced rifles at the side of the church because an old rival had lied of his sedition. How many, like his own cousin, would permit their daughter to leave each night at nine to go to the barracks of invaders?

To stay until dawn with the tall captain who later sent off to camps the women who at last had taken the girl as she left her home, scarred her and shaved her and thrown her back at the barracks' gate? Latty looked at the dull houses and the undemonstrative people taking in their morning papers or their milk bottles from their gates, walking on the clean deep pavements. He thought of those he worked with at the office, and grew confused. He had been here now for nearly half a lifetime and there was no answer to these things.

Dryford was the boss. He paused for a moment at the side of the desk, the shadow from his thick body falling and covering the papers in front of this foreigner whose job was to check the figures and the returns from the buses, to set these against the sheets the drivers handed in.

'Forget your English numbers or something did you?'

Latty took the sheaf held out to him. He saw that a circle had been scored in red biro around a figure on the top page. The error was no more than a slip of the pen, a three where a two should have been entered.

'I'm sorry,' Latty said. 'It is of no consequence.' He took up his pen and leaned forward to correct the figure.

'Oh?' Dryford lifted his head and looked vaguely ahead of him, like a beast that has detected what it cannot yet define. 'Of no consequence?' he repeated, as though the words were a novelty to him. He turned to the woman at the next desk, a widow who checked the catering accounts. Dryford spoke to her in a quiet, reasonable voice.

'Would you say, Mrs Cleary, that it's of no consequence that a two is mistaken for a three?'

The woman pressed one dimpled fist with the pencil she held in her other hand, so that a little circle of white shone round the point. She knew too much of Mr Dryford's oblique humour to offer her opinion. 'Well you, Shirley,' he asked the girl who was passing through to the ticket counter. 'As your elders who work so much with figures are reluctant to commit themselves, would you mind telling me? The difference between three and two. Would that be of no consequence, would you say?'

The others in the office had stopped working now, they were prepared for the entertainment that made their boss the almost single topic of conversation which they shared. Shirley looked at the broad shoulders, the close-cropped hair. 'Depends,' she said carefully.

'Depends, does it then? Whether you get a two or three bus home, for example? Have two meals a day instead of three? No difference to speak of?' Mrs Cleary felt how the voice was rising. She watched the thick forefinger, hardly longer than the curiously elongated thumb, tapping on the edge of her own desk to the rhythm of his words.

'Two or three children or wives? Or arms or legs?' The girl herself and Mrs Cleary and the two other men in the office were smiling, the boss was in full spate now, there was no spin-off likely in their direction. He had taken the papers with the mistake in order to fan them out, to shake them, in front of the foreigner's nose. '*You* might come from two or three countries and *that's* of no consequence, you can put your money on that,' Dryford said. He thrust the papers on Latty's desk and ran his square thick thumbnail along the lines scored with his pen. 'That mightn't be,' he repeated, 'but this bloody is!' He knocked his closed fist on the papers and passed through to his own desk behind the panelling and the frosted glass. He knew the performance had gone well, that the rest of them were looking to their own business and that Shirley would let them know at the counter, they'd all know within minutes that he was on form. He had left the desk and the knuckled papers without so much as looking at the man he was putting down. He knew that those eyes with their brownish lids like some kind of suede would be looking back at him, no sign of fear, and none of insolence, but looking as though at something on a screen. The others would know that too, that was the trouble. Later he would say, 'The bugger's too thick-skinned for anything to get through,' as he had said it at least once a week for a couple of years. He would say it as he stood at the lowered tray of the cocktail cabinet, beneath the large reproduction of Tretchikoff's swan, that dying erotic slab of colour which he had bought his wife for their twelfth anniversary. And he would say again, 'I'm damned if I know where this stuff goes to, people seem to forget it doesn't come cheap as water.' His hand would move down among the bottles for the almost emptied quart of gin, a reflection of his hand lowering in the greenish-tinged glass panel behind the bottles. And as for the sticky rings on the lowered tray, even a slattern, he had remarked two nights ago, would keep things a little more agreeable and hygienic than that.

'You're the only one who uses there,' his wife said.

'The only one when I'm at home,' he corrected her. He took his gin and tonic and handed his wife a sherry as he crossed to his armchair. From the landscape window he looked down on the streaming traffic along the Drive, beneath the glaring orange lights that made his wife think of aquariums, of orderly deadly rows of metallic fish. She knew she saw too often the threat of daily things, the reflections in firetongs as suddenly intense and sinister, a cutlery drawer too like a tray of dubious instruments. The fear would brush her mind for no more than seconds, as though this other world, this domain of secret threat, withdrew as soon as it was observed. She knew too that it would need to last so very little more than those few seconds for panic to direct her, for perhaps the innocence of curtains and sofa and the cold sides of the tea-service to cross that line as well, to join the other world. Yet to talk of it was nonsense, it was to invite from her mother the advice to take a holiday, from her doctor another note for the masking veil valium.

This evening Dryford took a large mouthful of his drink, washed the soft fizzing against his tongue and throat. 'That's better,' he said. There was a respite in the traffic he overlooked, no sound in the room they sat in.

'He's at it again,' he announced to his wife. 'That bugger in the office.'

'Yes?' she said.

'He's got just that knack for getting under my skin.'

His wife waited while he drew again at his glass, made the smacking sound of satisfaction after he swallowed. 'There's one of the drivers, see, a half-caste or something,' he began to tell her. It was a story like many she had heard before. She thought of her boy who was now at gym, whose father forced him she was sure against his natural grain so that he might do the things that must be done, grow to the pattern that was already set. She also heard how dollars were missing, how ticket numbers failed to tally.

'Was he taking it?' she asked, and, 'Very good,' Dryford commended her, inflecting his voice like a teacher's. 'Mind like a razor sitting over there.' He finished his drink and rose to mix another, taking his wife's glass with a kind of swoop as he returned to the cabinet. She noticed the soft splashing behind his voice, as he poured and kept on speaking. 'The old case of tickling the peter, as you might well think,' he went on. 'Old Hori salting a bit away for next pork and puha day. The figures come in each morning after our Polack checks them and three days on end there's this gap—tickets say one thing, money another.' There was a heavy chink as the sherry decanter knocked against its neighbours. 'Take it,' Dryford said, returning his wife's glass. There was a long pause while he crossed to his chair, eased himself into its comfort with exaggerated pleasure.

'Where was I?' he asked. He watched his wife as she said simply, 'They didn't match.'

'Very good again,' he told her. Then he said to cut it short, anyway, he had called the driver in. 'I was just on the verge of scaring the living shit out of him when he says oh didn't Latty pass it on? Didn't tell you about old Gray's eggs?' Dryford's wife remembered old Gray whom she hadn't seen for years, the owner of the company who had no interest in buses apart from what profits they brought him, who spent his declining years breeding Siamese cats. 'This driver see had run into him and he said how he kept his own chooks out there near the pā where a bloody hen'd have the time of its life, it's all one great fowlyard. So he drops these bloody eggs off each week at Gray's drive out past Te Rapa and he just takes the money from the fares. And I'm supposed to run a business like that.'

Dryford's wife thought of the lean pampered creatures the old man drove about with him in his car and carried at least one of wherever he went, their vile frank eyes staring at you she remembered. She had said to Gray—was it five years ago?—'Those awful eyes!' and the old man had pressed his fingers close against the animal's neck so that its purr must have vibrated against his own flesh and he answered, 'Ah, they know everything.' He had offered her one hadn't he, said he would be delighted to give his manager's wife one from the next litter? And she had told him, No, she couldn't think of taking one, they were worth a small fortune. And she thought now of the seething newborn kittens, blind and indecent as fat pinkish maggots butting against their slack-bellied mother. Her husband had stopped talking and she knew that it was her cue.

'And where's your foreigner come in?' she said.

'Him, for Christ's sake,' Dryford said. 'He comes in because he knew all the time, that's all. Would you credit that? The driver had told him and instead of passing it on like any normal person, not on your life. He just keeps putting in the takings and the ticket numbers and I'm supposed to find out by clairvoyance or something!' Dryford tilted his glass and jogged it, the drink lapping towards the rim. He forgot his irritation for the moment and thought of Shirley's arse when it moved against the side of the chair this morning and he had touched it, surprised himself that he was doing it, and she had turned and looked at him without amazement or concern and held his eye, simply waiting until he had taken his hand away. He would play his cards pretty carefully there, he thought. He saw his hand against the denim of her skirt and remembered looking up at her tallness, the swelling of her tits and her hair falling to one side as her head tilted to look down at him, by God that was lovely.

'So you spoke to him?'

'What?' Dryford turned from the window to look at his wife. He took in her careful hair and her small upraised face, the boy's mother all right, there was so much more of her came out in him. He was a good kid and he was keen but he didn't have the build, that was the trouble, Dryford couldn't imagine him making the first team in anything. His wife spoke again but he left her question unanswered, he made a grating noise with his sinuses and stood facing the highway, the streaming lines taking the broad curve of the gully. He thought again of Shirley and then of the club, of how much time he put into it and how you had to keep yourself in the clear, you couldn't afford a wrong move there any more than you could at work, not if you wanted to keep up with the play. Dryford's wife watched him stand there against the night and the reflected glow from the Drive. She thought what she had never said, that her husband was dominated by this man at the office for a reason so obvious and so sad, that it was the foreigner's last care in the world whether his boss smiled at him or raged, favoured or reviled him. And mustn't a man who could go untouched by her husband's selective spite hold some centre of balance, some certainty of himself, which was a simple richness she could scarcely put a name to?

III

In his lunch hours Latty liked to visit the public library. There were several magazines which he looked at, like the illustrated French monthly which he read no more for its articles on expensive furniture and art and elaborate dwellings than for its stories of the rich and the beautiful, their world of reflected profiles and Mediterranean coastline. He read it for the sake of the language, which he knew imperfectly yet better than he suspected, the language of a country he had marched into in the grey uniform of the Germans and where he stayed on, once he had deserted, in the blue overalls of a labourer. Often, in these past few months, he found himself going over those years, recalling some isolated event which until now had lain embedded in that block of his life which for the greater part had been fear and hunger and cold. And between the fear which a dozen times had turned his guts to water, and the hunger which he had carried like a heavy dead unappeasable child month after month, were those acts which had lifted him it seemed on a crest. After decades of remoteness they now came into his mind when he did not expect them, and he felt in them neither pride nor shame.

Before he walked down to the library, Latty would eat in the lunchroom the small stack of sandwiches he prepared for himself each morning. Sometimes there would be a slight exchange with the others at work, a rare attempt to draw him into chat, but there was no expectation that he would take up their offer, no belief for a moment that there would be anything more than the customary polite murmur, the mild withdrawal which was decisive as a grill lowered between them. He once heard Mrs Cleary declaim as she scoured her cup at the lunchroom sink, her back towards him as he entered, 'It's not as if he can't talk English properly, is it? It's as if he just doesn't want to be sociable.' And the girl standing beside her, a slight angular child who had left to marry a Mormon, said in a way which had touched him, 'He must have his own things to think about anyway, mustn't he? Everybody has but you don't have to go on about it.' Then Mrs Cleary, who thought the girl an upstart quite apart from who she was going to marry, said, 'I wouldn't know about that. I believe in being open myself.'

'Well I'd rather have him than anyone else here,' the girl persisted. 'He's not always trying to be smart and that, you can tell he likes people.' Latty had stepped back quickly along the corridor so that they would not observe him. He knew the girl would be embarrassed, and Mrs Geary angry. She had told him before, a couple of years ago when he began at the office, that he should have been a burglar the way he moved so quietly between the desks or came into the room. 'You're like a cat,' she said, and he had looked back from his eyes which never seemed properly open. She watched his podgy face which she thought was like off-white putty, and that stupid little black beret thing which was what really drove Mr Dryford mad. He looked and smiled and said nothing, of course.

'You've pissed him off now,' one of the others had said.

'I wouldn't say so,' she answered, and that skinny thing who wouldn't drink tea any longer because of her boyfriend said, 'He wouldn't give twopence what any of you thought, anyway.' Mr Dryford was in the office for the last bit of it and he had put her in her place nicely, he said, 'Probably he's a religious nut too, then,' and young Miss Bones as they called her had gone red as a beetroot.

Latty would take his magazines and mount the stairs to the second floor, to a gallery where one could sit at a small desk and look down into the life of the library. Frequently he would place his hands side by side on the smooth opened pages and look at the activity on the floor beneath, at the figures moving between the steel shelves, at the librarians in their odd frocks which made so many of them look pregnant. Or as he read, the French words would rise to him from the page, words which he believed he had forgotten and which did not so much invite as force him back to the grey towns which he remembered almost always as under drizzling or snowing skies, although he had spent two summers there as well. The grey sky and the line of trees like pencil strokes against it. He thought of the farm kitchens and the small apartments where how many times, he wondered, he had sat opposite a man dressed usually like himself, whose real name he was never to learn and who addressed to him a few words which at first he scarcely understood.

There was no light when they had left the farmhouse in their peasant clothes and their thin canvas shoes. The cold, not long before dawn, was intense. The stars were chinks of ice turning and glittering. His companion he sensed rather than saw in front of him, he followed him along a ditch and then through a wire barrier which accomplices a few minutes before had severed. At the edge of the village where two sentries stood guard at opposing corners (or so he had been told and must believe) he had left the other man and moved against the roughcast walls, towards the soldier who stood invisible a few yards ahead of him. He pressed against the wall until he heard the light fall of a stone which he awaited, and the sudden alerted attention of the guards. A voice now only feet away spoke in German, and was answered from the opposite corner. The guards relaxed and exchanged a few words, there was the stamp as the one so close to him moved his booted feet against the frost. And Latty was filled he remembered with his own ice-cold concentration. He drew out the thin piano wire coiled in his sleeve and tugged briefly at the wooden peg on either end of its short span. The wire gave its odd almost living vibration as he drew it taut. His hands rose like a priest's he had thought at the elevation, delicate and confident, and fell over the helmeted head, the crossed pegs biting against his straining fingers. Latty looked down at the moving figures in the library, the young girls and the ageing men, the women with pushchairs and the student taking notes at one of the tables. Those human lives whose names he did not know, who passed his own in the endless indecipherable web of drawing breath, of breeding, of hope and distress, and for all of them that moment waited for and yet denied, the weakening of some artery wall, some ravenous cell, *the hands failing and crossing, the single width of wire.*

For twenty years those memories had not touched him, and now they returned to him almost every week. They were more clear to his mind than the events of a month ago. And more often too he experienced those dreams which had come to him intermittently for years. Dreams of the flowing river on the last night of which he had any memory from home, the lights when they had halted on the bridge and the boy was sitting behind him, commanding from the high deck of the grain sacks. And as he woke, as he saw the lightening sky through the squares of his window, he would sometimes find himself calling out, or beginning to raise his arms to swing the tired child from the back of the cart.

Latty's bach was a converted toolshed, with a small kitchen added at one end and a bathroom at the other. The room was carpeted and lined with hardboard, and a double-bar heater made it cosy in the winter months. There was a window above the heater, and another had been fitted at the side of the door. The furniture was a large bed and two armchairs, a table covered by a plastic cloth patterned to look like lace, and a bookcase which for the most part carried folded newspapers, and a few books drawn from the library. There was nothing, not so much as a folded shirt or a pair of shoes, which lay casually out of place. The room's one brilliant feature was a red and white Greek rug, which lay over the bed as a cover. The landlady's niece had sent it to her as a gift, and the woman had passed it on, believing that as a foreigner Latty would appreciate what she thought garish and crude. Those thick double threads of wool could have been worked, she said, by a child. And there were two preserving jars which served as vases, one on a shelf behind the door, one on a carefully folded square of paper in the middle of the table. Both jars were filled with clumps of holly from the hedge in front of the house. The small sharp leaves glistened as though oiled. His landlady had seen them and said, 'Might as well put weeds there,' and was glad to return to the taste of her own front room.

Once a month Latty would go across to the house with his rent book. She took his notes and counted them, and on the large oval table she would open the book and enter the amount in one column, the date in another. 'Thank you,' she would say. Light slid across her spectacles as she raised her head, and Latty would look into her unwell eyes, their scaled pinkish rims and the mucus in their corners. At the last payment before Christmas and once or twice through the year, on some day perhaps whose significance she chose to keep to herself, she would offer Latty a glass of blackberry nip. They sat on opposite sides of the table with its white bowl and the clump of plastic flowers, large yellow-centred pieces with inflamed lashes, and raise their glasses. 'Season's greetings,' she would say to him at Christmas, and at other times, 'Your good health.' Latty thanked her, and his heavy pale face smiled towards her. Her hand with discoloured tan spots trembled very slightly until the glass touched her lips. Neither she nor her brother had married.

'Likes her drop, I'll tell you that,' Len said. He was a shortish man who had spent a lifetime with the local borough council, and now in retirement he lived with his one sister. He would walk beside Latty with the slightest depression of his left foot. It was injured by a baler when he was in his early twenties, a few years before the War. 'That's luck for you,' he told Latty. 'I'd have been up and off and out of this lot with the first volunteers if it hadn't been for the old leg. Two toes, that's all, but it put paid to any gallivanting I might have got up to.' He moved his hand generally towards the town, to the unspecified lucky ones who had got away. 'All those other buggers over Italy and Greece and what have you.' Or he would laugh another time when his injury was raised, and the War he was deprived of. 'Probably wouldn't be here now anyway, so what's the odds?'

At the weekends the two men frequently shared their walks. Their walking together had begun by chance, after Latty had rented the bach for the best part of a year. His landlady's brother had nodded to him whenever they passed in the street. Then one weekend they met, by taking different routes from the house, at the corner of the bridge. Together, they had begun to cross the high span over the dark heavy flowing of the river.

'My old man remembered the day this thing was opened,' Len offered. 'That's going back a bit for you.' They had stopped when they were at the middle of the bridge. The river was almost black as they gazed straight down on it. Thirty yards upstream a thick column of water fell and broke against the current. 'Seepage,' Len said. He leaned against the white wooden railing. 'The odd kid still walks across this ledge for a dare, they reckon.' Latty stood beside him with his hands in the pockets of his gabardine coat. He watched the stream of water from the bank impacting on the moving surface of the river. Two large fern trees projected from the damp tangle of the bank, two green wheels with drooping spokes. In places the clay of the bank showed through like a wet heavy skin.

'You never get tired of this view, you know,' Len said. 'Like looking straight back there, between those banks where you can't see any houses and that. Must have been like that for hundreds of years, except the water's a darn sight dirtier now.' He pointed to several clots of brownish foam, some of them strung out over several yards, that moved downstream with the current. 'Top-dressing or factory stuff or something,' he said. He leaned forward so that his heels were off the ground and his chest rested on the railing like a schoolboy's as he peered down into the river, at the slight lifting and crosshatching of the surface where wind moved across. After that first meeting they always stopped on the bridge, and Len's remarks were very often the same. He liked to think this view of the banks, the stretch where houses were hidden, had been like this before any of them came, before the land was cut up into farms and the farms cut up into sections, maybe even before the Maoris had slipped down through the bush to the level of the river.

The weekend walk became as certain as the weekend itself. In the summer they would stand on the embankment where the road divided, and look down on a swimming pool and its throng of splashing, shouting young bodies. 'Does you good to see them enjoying life like that,' Len said. Or if they came across a wedding party at one of the churches further up the street, where the grand spread of the oaks and chestnuts gave the wooden buildings an air of charm, Len's view of things would again come out.

'Wonder how much of this they'll remember in thirty years?' he had said one morning. They were watching a heavy, solemn girl standing for her photograph. Her husband of a few minutes ran one finger down the sides of his moustache, his other hand signalling to a cluster of his mates. 'If only they all got what they were hoping for, eh?' and he had sighed rather like his sister, Latty thought, when she set down her glass on one of those rare occasions, and said as she carefully refilled first his glass and then her own, 'It's like a key, of course, we all know that, don't we?' meaning the slowly rising sweetish liquor, the flood of memory rising with it. Latty smiled slightly. He watched his friend's absorbed interest in the young couple and thought how lucky perhaps a man might be to have lived so simply. Len's life had been spent only in this town, his schooldays and his working life, the death of his parents, the long closeness with his sister. That, and maybe a hundred or so friends and acquaintances who were the full range of his life. He had once told Latty, 'There's not much happens anywhere that you couldn't see here if you kept your eyes peeled.'

At times they would walk in silence, Len's slight limp and Latty's soft stepping beside him. Except in the warmest days of summer, Latty wore his gabardine, his hands deep in its pockets, his black beret set above his round face.

'You look foreign, you know that, Latty? You can tell by just a look I mean that you're not one of the locals. Not one of us.' Then he had said, 'I don't mean any offence by that.' Latty had smiled at him, looking down at the reddish grey hair which was level with his own shoulder. There was a saddle of freckles across Len's nose that made his face boyish and pryingly eager, although the men were much the same age. At times they covered miles in silence, at others Len would talk as if taking breath were something of a luxury. Usually he would be unwinding an intricate account of some gossip or event which that year or twenty years before had stirred the town. One morning he pointed out a man who had killed his wife with an axe because she had left their canary out in the porch during a frost. The man had done fifteen years and had come back to the very same house, where he now had what you might as well call an aviary, finches and budgies and Indian whatever they were, brown birds anyway with a red tuft like a little crown. 'We don't have too many to match him mind you,' Len said. Another morning he touched Latty's arm as they passed the broad doorway of the Post Office. He edged his head discreetly to a woman in front of the wall where the private boxes were like small cells in numbered rows.

'You won't believe this one Latty but get a load of her when she comes out to her flash car over there.' The men stopped a few yards further on, supposedly engaged in the land agent's display of houses and properties, sections and farms. Latty looked at the meaningless figures written below the photographs, sums as remote to him as the prices that might have been asked for palaces. Then as Len directed, he turned to see a handsome middle-aged woman step briskly across the pavement to a sleek emerald-coloured car. Her large breasts stirred at each step and two teenagers riding their bicycles on the pavement yelped at each other at their sudden luck. One of them held huge imaginary globes in front of his jersey while his mate doubled between his tall handlebars with delight.

'Well her,' Len said. He watched the woman ease the car from the kerb and as she drove past them Latty could see the diamantes on her watchstrap shiver against her arm. 'She used to be married to a bloke who managed the dairy factory on the road out to the hydro, the road up from us. He was away quite often and the whole town knew she was a player, but this time it came out in the maddest way. No one ever worked out quite what she was at, mind you, but she was actually taken off to hospital—ambulance and the whole works—with a french letter, you know, *a frog,* stuck in her throat like a fishbone or something. It as good as choked her.' Len's own face showed surprise as he told the story, a boy's face amazed at what adults can bring themselves to do. And his eyes followed the car while he was talking, it was not a dirty *story* he was giving his friend but yet another segment of what made life rich and various and endlessly of interest, and the car turning there now at the cenotaph, drawing over and pulling up at the wine-shop, was freighted with glamour. 'She's got a nerve living here after that,' Len said.

They paused again at the nursery shop and examined the plants that were in the window. Len had known the chap who ran it when he didn't have a penny to his name, now he had this shop and another two in Hamilton. He spoke of him while they walked on up the town's main street. Then suddenly, 'Look,' Len said. He held his friend's eye and said, 'You just tell me if I ramble on a bit won't you? You will, now?'

Latty touched Len on the sleeve. 'I like this walking with you,' he said. 'I like you to tell me things.'

'Well I mean I can listen too,' Len said. 'You don't seem to need to say much Latty but don't forget, if you do.'

Latty's hand still shook as they waited for the stream of traffic near the park. The football season had begun and several games were under way on the large square with its rim of trees. He did not understand why he was so affected, why a life which had given so much of itself to control and dissimulation, to discipline and will, should at this very moment, this late in the day, reveal something new. He was glad that his strange talkative friend had gone on ahead, was now stepping up the slope to watch the game. Latty's eyes were confused. He saw the branches of the tree immediately in front of him run together in an unexpected blur. *This is the first time,* Latty thought, *this is the first time in this country where I have been for half a lifetime, when I have touched another person not by necessity or politeness or accident, but as a friend. I have touched him as a friend because words were not enough.* Len already was rapt in the game, in the player who moved the ball over half the length of the field before he passed it across in a deft confident lift. 'He's got the makings all right,' his friend was saying, 'he's a cut above the others.'

IV

There was half a year of which he remembered nothing. There was the journey with the cart, the darkness and his talk with the boy, and what the boy's father had said when they were back home, unbuckling the horse while his sister carried down the lantern and placed it between the men on the cobbled yard. He thought of before that, of waking in the morning, waking and walking to the kitchen, to the long broad table and the barrels in the corner and the open fireplace which had warmed them since his childhood. Waking to his brother-in-law silently gazing from the window, across to their farm which was the first on the edge of the village, while he plucked at the large chunk of bread he broke each morning from the loaves in one of the barrels. Woke to his sister who sometimes sang, who so deserved he thought the man she had and the child at the table with two fat books on a chair to raise him high enough to eat. Mostly he remembered his sister in the kitchen and in winter, the reflection from the broad flat expanses of snow thrown up on the beams and ceiling at that hour of morning. In his memory Latty himself was mostly sitting at the table across from the boy, his sister moving from the hearth to the table, a bowl steaming in her hands, and the light lifting always from the snow, the cold pure radiance that seemed without source, the very quality and permeation of the air itself. The light showed against her face, lightening the firm handsome line of her jaw, and the scar which he noticed especially at that time. And further back they were children on the riverbank, it was spring. Their father managed an orchard whose owner not only they but their father too had never seen. There were row upon row of pink blossoming trees. To walk along the spaces between the rows at this time of year, to walk there when the wind stirred, was to be in the constant slow flicker of falling and turning petals.

The children played in the orchard as in the middle of a story, his sister saying once she was the queen, her bare arms held out before her and the trees spreading and packed behind her, a hall of spring and colour. And she had said that day the forbidden thought, 'Let's climb the tree, let's shake the blossom down like a real storm.' The boy was younger than his sister and afraid. Their father had thrashed a visiting cousin for so much as shaking a branch. 'You are killing fruit each single petal you make fall,' he had told them. 'Whatever you touch this time of year, you kill.' But she had climbed the tree and sat in its gorgeous branches, her navy smock showing between the masses of delicate flares. She had braced her feet on one branch and taken hold of another, slightly above her head. He remembered standing in the tall grass as he watched her grey serious eyes looking directly at his, implicating him while his own hands were limp beside him, and she began to shake the tree. A thin shower of the blossom, so much paler when it was falling than when it was on the tree, began to descend on him. And then what seemed a smother, a thickness of the drifting weightless fragments until his own call, surging in his ears before he realised he had called it, 'Father! Father!' Latty recalled nothing of his father's approach, of the shouting or the anger which must have followed. The memory finished with his sister's falling, the attempt to leap from the tree and her foot catching in the notch of a branch. She fell into the grass beside him, and lay for a moment so still that he had grown afraid. And when she had raised her head her hair was stuck across her mouth. A stone had opened a gash along her chin, the blood coursing down her throat and small petals from the blossom adhered to her skin, some of them curled and drenched in the flow, like the thin papers he had seen men use upon their chins while shaving. It was that scar from the orchard he saw when his sister's throat and jaw took the reflection from the snow, the thin line he had seen for the last time when she raised her head in the yard, raising it to rest the tired boy against her shoulder.

In that half year which he had lost as permanently as an amputated limb, Latty learned and pieced together that he had crossed three borders and been recruited for an army before he woke on a striped filthy mattress in a basement not only in a town but in a country he did not know the name of. His head was bandaged and for a month he could not see from his left eye. The uniform he wore was Russian and the officers were Russian, but at least half of the men he saw, the other wounded and those who cared for them, spoke his own language. They said his village was no longer there, that it had been won and lost and won again, although neither victors nor losers were the people who had lived there. They said there was nothing left, there were craters formed on top of craters, only the levels of bombardment. The journey which had led him from the yard and the family, from the child and the cart, to his waking on the sodden mattress and his wounded head, was a dark corridor which was never to lighten. It was one life ended as it seemed simply by a blink, another begun with the opening of his eyes. He was not a man with one continuous life, but lives that were like the broken tracks of a railway, lines that ran towards each other until where they met was in fact where they did not meet at all. The fracture gaped irrevocably in those images of his hand last seen raised in the soft light to touch the sleeping boy, that same hand next seen lying across the canvas mattress in a country he did not know. Armies had merged and pressed against each other like a matted entanglement of maggots, one filling the space where another had been, wavering across a map which covered a third of Europe. The undulation moved above him as he lay in the basement, while this town like his own slipped beneath alternate armies. Latty had lain there in a fever while the man on the mattress beside him died, and men in other uniforms came and dragged away the body. He remembered that the man was gross and that the two uniformed boys were incapable of lifting him. Latty's mind had gone back to the farm, to a beast which had fallen into a canal. 'Drag him,' he said. Each soldier had taken a leg and hooked it at the knee beneath his arm, then lurched the weight across the concrete floor. Briefly, the body wedged in the doorway. One of the soldiers forced it through with his boot, like shoving at a sack of grain that had stuck. Then there had come the steady thump, seven times he had counted as the man was dragged up the seven steps and his head jarred against the ascent. He looked at the broad slur the body had scoured across the filthy floor. Then he had slept until the soldiers returned and he was carried to a clean bed, his head freshly dressed by a doctor whose hands were soft as gauze. He was interrogated, cured, assigned to a division of men who like himself were the derelicts of war, the sweepings of smaller nations. They were the salvageable flesh from the writhing lines of combat.

And now as autumn sank into winter, as the frosts gave way to winds and days of rain, Latty thought frequently about the War. He walked as usual each weekend with Len, and one night a week his friend came to the room in the converted toolshed. Together they would share a bottle of sherry which at first Len had offered shyly, and which then they took it turn about to buy. Len would talk on, of the town and its people, his parents, what he had heard and half believed of his great-grandfather, the Maoris, the whores from Auckland who were supposed to have come down this far for the regiments stationed at Alexandra. Latty sat on a wooden kitchen chair and insisted that his friend take the cane basket chair which he had found at the Shakespeare Street dump, and carried home through the streets.

'You just lugged it along in the open?' Len had asked.

'Of course,' Latty told him. 'Like this.' He mimed his carrying the chair by its two arms, the seat above his head and the back falling behind his shoulders like a stiff cape.

'No wonder they think you're an oddball,' Len laughed. He liked looking at Latty's face. It hardly changed its expression no matter what he was listening to or talking about. You could only just see his puckered eyes as they looked from above his broad cheeks. It wasn't still so much either, it was—Len felt about for the word he wanted, and found one which he had never used he supposed in his life before. It was *repose* in his friend's face, that was it. It would take a lot to change it, Len thought, that was what he really meant.

The two men would sit and sip slowly at their sherry. Sometimes Latty spoke of work, very occasionally of something he may have done or seen many years before. But always it was of unspectacular things he spoke, of nothing that might have proposed how much there was between their lives. One man who had killed and killed and crossed the world, who had not known friendship for over twenty years, whose mind returned to a road at night and a small boy in the cart behind him; another who several times had travelled the hundred miles to Auckland and twice the three-hundred-odd to Wellington, who as a young man had caught his foot in a machine and then worked in one job all his life, who lived as though his small town and all that took place in it were extensions of himself. 'And why Latty anyway? Why that name?' Len had asked him one night.

'When I first come to here,' Latty said. 'First come soon after the War, I mean, and I am working in the timber camp where I stay as a logger and when I am too old for that, in the office, right until I come here. And in those days I did not know much English and they say, "He's from Latvia or somewhere," and so they call me that.'

'And you don't mind?' Len said. 'Don't mind not having your real name?'

Latty stood to refill his friend's glass for him. He looked down at the freckles, at the forehead that stored like the files of a newspaper the lives and deaths of the town. And now Len had asked not as anyone else would *where were you from then?*

but *don't you mind?* instead. He said, 'All right?' when the glass was almost full and Len told him, 'Lovely, that'll be lovely.'

I am learning all the time, Latty thought. *There is nothing which is what one expects, nothing I have the right to predict.*

V

It's not as though marching were only a pastime, Shirley thought. It was that of course, but it was posture as well, it was discipline and rhythm and team spirit, it was as she remembered from the Governor-General's speech both aesthetically rewarding and physically fulfilling. She remembered too the phrases from the last social night of the season and the way her cheeks had burned when her own name was called out. She had pushed past Gary and Lynaire and the others and gone up on the stage to receive her trophy, the most improved girl of the year. Her face had felt as though there were hot cloths laid across it. And as well as the cup the club president had pinned the badge shaped like a small shield on to her and put his hand on her shoulder *and kissed her on the cheek!* She could have died she admitted later. When she came back down the hall Lynaire had said, 'He's a bit keen on you, Shirl,' and Gary got that mad! He had sulked the rest of the night. Then afterwards they sat in the car down on the flat near the swimming pool. It must have been two o'clock and she was worried about her mother carrying on if she was back as late as that. He had just sat there, his hands opening and closing on the steering wheel until she had said *for goodness sake, Gary* and touched his trousers until he let go of the wheel and held her and started unbuttoning her, and then it was OK again. Mum had said a couple of years ago, when she first went out with boys, *there's one thing you don't want Shirl and that's a boy who's jealous,* and she knew now from Gary what that meant, didn't she just.

'It wouldn't have been so bad if it was just the presentation,' Lynaire said later. 'It was all that laughing at supper that did it.' There was a lot of fooling round and no one was quite sober and Shirley had been talking to the president's wife. She was a sort of sad woman who just smiled when her husband said those embarrassing things about Shirl being the best looker in the team. Lynaire said, 'She looks a bloody hundred years older than him anyway.' But she was nice though, nice in the way she listened when you talked to her and covered up for her husband when some kid in the juniors with braces on her teeth and flat as an ironing board came up and looked at Shirley's medal and then spoke to the president, and it was Mrs Dryford who remembered the kid's name. But even when Shirley was talking to her Gary had been surly. He had gone off when she spoke to him without hardly answering. Then later in the car he had kept on sulking, even when she was moving her hand on him and he was lying back with his eyes closed, when she was moving him like that and she leaned forward and kissed his neck and his throat and told him *you know there's no one else I give a stuff about* he hadn't answered her like she wanted him to. As soon as it was over and they had made themselves look respectable he had said they should be getting back, he didn't want to be too late. He had told the boys he'd be out at the lake by nine, it was no good getting up on the skis if you felt poked. She had been pretty hurt at that, he must have known she would be in for it with Mum, yet she hadn't gone on about it had she? He hadn't even passed her his hanky after she had done it for him.

'You're well rid of that one,' her mother said when Gary was transferred down to Palmerston North. 'Anyway you're only eighteen, there'll be plenty more.' That hadn't been much consolation, not for the first few months. Gary had come up and she had gone down a few times, and once she had said she was going to Taupō with Lynaire but in fact she was meeting Gary, they were going to have the weekend together at a motel. *She must have been a child*, Shirley thought. She had taken the Road Services bus on the Friday after work and when she arrived there was Gary sure enough, he was waiting and grinning and he waved as the bus drew round into the depot. She was carrying the white imitation-leather overnight bag she had bought just for this. The bag had a mirror in the lid when you opened it and compartments for cosmetics, and gathering and tucking round the inside so it all looked like a piece of lingerie. Shirley had thought about their meeting on the way down through the open country that the moon had made look so gentle and smooth it could have been moulded, and then through the long road with the pine forest on either side. The moon kept appearing and disappearing between the whisk and blur of the trees like something that was keeping pace with them. It would be like being married in a way, she had thought, as she sat with the square leather case on her knees and her hands folded over the handle on the top. Inside was the nightie she had bought yesterday at lunchtime in Garden Place, and the face cream she hadn't touched yet, a kind she knew nothing about but smelled divine, fitted into one of the compartments. She stepped from the bus and Gary had kissed her. She tasted the rum on his breath and laughed when he told her, 'Can't wait to start feeding you a length, Shirl.' He led her through the depot to the street where she could see the stretch of the lake.

'There was a moon all the way down,' she said.

They walked to the hotel on the corner. 'I've booked here instead of a motel,' he said. He opened the door to a house-bar and Shirley squinted her eyes against the pall of cigarette smoke. He took her to the bar with its line of leather stools and to a man she had never seen, several years older than Gary. 'This is Jay,' he said. 'He drove up with me for the weekend. We're all booked in together.' Gary laughed as he said that and Jay smiled without laughing. His teeth showed between the lips which kept level as he smiled. His eyes looked directly into hers and Gary stood back a little, watching them and laughing still and saying, 'Here, Jay's got you a Kahlua.' As she placed her heel on the chromium rung of the stool and then lowered herself to the seat she felt Gary's hand beneath her, his middle finger raised, and the man she had just met smiled jointly, it seemed, at Gary and herself. He leaned forward and slapped Gary's hand. 'Here,' he said, 'we won't have any of that thank you,' and both watched Shirley as they were laughing. Much later they had all gone to bed together drunk and before the men had woken Shirley took the overnight bag she had not opened and walked out into the empty road. She saw the lake there under a dull sky, the water lying like a broad sheet of perfectly rolled lead. She had looked at it for a moment, at the dark blue line of hills or mountains they might even be, right across, on the far side of the water, then stepped to the edge of the footpath, her thumb extended to the first car that approached her, and hitched back home.

After that she had moped for a couple of months. Her mother had come to her one morning, one Saturday when the rest of the family was out and Shirley sat in her dressing gown on the back porch, in the sun. Mum brought her a cup of tea and carried a cup for herself as well. 'That's nice,' she said as she took the cup and held it carefully between her two palms, almost as though she expected it to break and the pressure of her hands was holding it together. Then, 'Listen,' Mum had said, so matter of fact that Shirley had nearly died when the rest came. 'You're not in trouble or anything are you?' She felt herself going red and put her face closer to the steaming tea. As far as her mother knew she mightn't even have kissed a boy properly, and she felt awful when it came out like that. 'What on earth are you on about?' she asked, and Mum had said it again, 'Well are you?' she said. Her mother touched her on the knee, it was awkward the way she leaned across and opened her hand and for a few seconds let it lie on the quilted dressing gown. There was no weight as it lay there and then the hand was taken away, as though her mother too was embarrassed by what she had asked. There was a silence and Shirley said with her head only inches from the cup and the steam wisping in front of her. 'You needn't worry about me, you should know that, Mum.'

'Then you need a tonic,' her mother said. 'You've been so down to it lately.'

'I'm just tired from work I think,' Shirley said. She thought how her mother was sharper than she had realised. Since that awful time at Taupo she had hardly spoken to the family, or she was scrapping with her brother. Then as if her mother was thinking about that too she said, 'I know Wayne can be a little bugger but he's at that age. He'll be all right in a year or two.'

'Oh, it's not Wayne, Mum,' Shirley said. 'I think I need a change or something.'

Then everything came right without her having to try. She had been up at the clubrooms as they were called, that old cricket pavilion which was going to be pulled down until someone said why not get it for the girls, why not let them get changed there or talk in there if it rains during practice. It was only a few days after Mum had raised that business about thinking she was in trouble.

'It's no good trying to get a new job out here,' Lynaire was saying. 'You have to go into Hamilton whether you like it or not.' Her friend was a tall girl with thin legs, and was always a problem in the team. No matter where you put her she would look out of place. Shirley liked her because she knew she looked a fright and didn't make a thing of it. She was always the last to get a boy when they were away with the team and she would sit next to Shirley on the bus coming home and say, 'I'll tell you this, Shirl, if I had looks like yours you wouldn't get me going back to a dump like this.' She meant the town they were born in and had gone to school in and would probably marry in as well. 'No way,' Lynaire said. 'I'd be off like a shot up to Auckland, the Pink Pussycat or somewhere and I'd be shaking them in their faces every night. I'd make ten times the money I get in this hole and I'd get a few decent bites as well.' She couldn't care less what she said, Lynaire. The chaperones told her to go easy sometimes, they said she had a mouth like a freezing worker, but even that wouldn't stop her. 'Freezing worker my arse,' she had said. The chaperone for that weekend was furious with her, and the team had been in an uproar. They all knew the old bag was a wowser anyway and watched the girls like a hawk. 'Still thinks you get pregnant from rubbing noses,' Lynaire said, and when she christened her the Nun the name had stuck to her.

'Well I'm sick of working in that bloody garage out here anyway,' Shirley said. 'It's just a matter of finding one in town that pays you something reasonable. Then there's all that drag of the trip across every day remember.'

Mr Dryford had come in and was pinning notices about fixtures and so on to the board. The girls hadn't known he was listening. He was often in the clubrooms, he or his wife, and he was so easy to get on with they more or less forgot he was there some of the time. 'If it wasn't for his whistling you'd be dropping your daks before you knew he was in here,' Lynaire said once. Now he asked her, 'Ever thought of the Bus Company, Shirley?' and it was as simple as that. She was taken on as a kind of office girl, but she did a lot of messages and driving about in Mr Dryford's car for him. Then in the summer she found that half her time at work just about seemed to be spent on marching business, or things to do with one of the half-dozen other clubs Mr Dryford was tied up with. Of course he had a sharp tongue at work that you would never have suspected if you only met him with the team. He was more like a good-tempered father with all the girls. But Shirley grew used to that, it was never at her expense so it wasn't for her to worry, was it? And as Dad used to say, No one ever thought work was supposed to be fun anyway.

Shirley caught the bus at the same stop each morning as the foreigner. She had noticed him before, walking about the town with old Len who did odd jobs round the club rooms, but it was at the office she first took any notice of him. Or rather, the new job made her see two things at much the same time. One was that he was quiet and polite and a bit pathetic, with his large face and little beret affair and his eyes squeezed into the folds of skin so you hardly saw them. The other was that Mr Dryford hated his guts. On her first day for instance her new boss had taken her and introduced her to the staff in both offices and in the garage and the cafeteria as well. *The dream girl from the marching team* he had called her when he took her into the lunchroom for the first time. He had been very kind and repeated everyone's name except for the large quiet man's who was putting on a raincoat in the alcove near the lockers. Mr Dryford led her past without saying a word, and she had asked 'Who's that?' and he had turned to her and said loud enough for the man to hear, 'That? He works here too but there's no need for that to worry you. Not like it worries me but then I'm the one who pays him.' Shirley had seen the man looking back towards them as he buttoned his coat. Well there must be a reason for it, Shirley thought, Mr Dryford wouldn't have it in for him unless he asked for it. That used to be another of Dad's favourite sayings, that it took two to make a quarrel. Though after she had been there for a few weeks she couldn't very well imagine Latty making one, he was about as argumentative as a pudding. She had never known anyone who minded his business quite the way Latty did.

'Look,' Mr Dryford said one evening. He had to drive out to a meeting with some of the club officials and he was giving her a lift home. She mentioned how she and Latty caught the same bus in the mornings and Mr Dryford asked her if they ever talked together. Not talk, she said, they nodded though after a couple of weeks but Latty sat in the same seat every morning, the one near the middle doors, and she always sat in the high seat at the back, above the wheels. Shirley said, 'We're not bosom pals, you know.' She had laughed at that but Mr Dryford hadn't. It was then he said, 'Look, you can't give them an inch, Shirley. I've been round longer than you have and I've seen them all, Dutchies, Eyeties, you name them. And there's not one of them you'll ever get the length of. They mightn't all be no-hopers but they're different from us, you can't get past that one.'

'I think this one's pretty harmless,' Shirley said, and Mr Dryford had snorted at that, he said 'We'll see how harmless he is one of these days.' He let his hand fall on her knee then, just for a moment. 'Still, he needn't be your problem,' he said.

Later when she told Lynaire, she said, 'It could have been like an uncle or something, his hand just touching me for a minute.'

'Only uncles don't as a rule, that's the difference,' Lynaire said. Well she didn't mind that much anyway, Shirley thought to herself. And one day when she saw the old bloke walking up past the cenotaph with Len the caretaker, she pointed him out.

'That's him, that nice old foreign joker at work.'

'Probably plays stink finger with little boys if you ask me,' Lynaire said.

'Oh, stink finger yourself!' Shirley had said, and Lynaire opened her eyes very wide, like a comedian on TV or something, and said 'Wouldn't be the first time would it?' They were still cracking up at that one when they arrived back home. Mum was in one of her moods and she said to them,

'You've got about as much sense now the pair of you as when you were fourteen.'

'We're laughing about that foreigner Shirl works with, that's all,' Lynaire said.

'I've got enough to think of here without foreigners,' Mum had snapped.

VI

Latty and Len sat on one of the wooden benches above the lake. A little in front of them the ground dipped then fell sharply in a steep bank. Through the branches which carried the fresh leaves of early spring they could see a distant corner of the lake, the greyish water, the massing of clumped reeds. Latty had been off work for a fortnight, and now it was Friday morning. They were the only people in sight.

Latty looked up to the clear sky through the newly living trees. 'I have not missed my work before, not one day since I come to this country.'

Len smiled as he sat with his hands, palm downwards, tucked between his legs and the bench. 'You're not letting that upset you?' he asked. 'I mean, you're not one of those roosters who thinks it's a black mark to be off crook?'

The two men had walked slowly from the house down to the bridge, over the high spanning of the dull sliding river, and up through the town. 'It is quite different you know,' Latty had said, 'out here on a workday.' He had never thought of it before now, the women with their parcels and cartons, pushing their prams or crossing the pavement to the cars parked slantingly towards the kerb. It was good to see the women, the colours of their clothes, on these early days of sun. He had been in his room for almost ten days, with Len or Len's sister bringing him his meals, the dull pain the size of a tennis ball behind his ribs receding until now there was no sign of it left. The doctor twice came to the bach, and this morning in his surgery had said, 'An X-ray and a few tests, I think, just to be on the safe side.' Latty had come from the doctor's surprisingly cold hands and the neatly trimmed head caught against the sharp light of the window, and his friend was sitting in the waiting room, cross-legged and leaning forward like a boy, a magazine opened on his knee. He felt a tenderness for the row of waiting people, not only for Len his friend, as their eyes raised and looked at his own while his hand moved to his pocket for the black beret. His friend stood up and as they stepped from the waiting room to the concrete path, into the warming sun of a new season, he said, 'I am quite well, Len.' Without surprise his friend answered him, 'Of course you are, Latty, you're right as rain.'

They had walked at an easy pace among the mothers and the shoppers, past the butchers and drapers and grocers Latty had not seen at their work as he did this morning, but knew only by the words painted on the windows and that dullish empty reflection, the hollow shine that shops give back at weekends when they are closed. Latty wondered as he always did at the children, the firmness of their limbs, the clear simplicities of food and peace. Ah, to be sick, even with this mild brief indisposition of his own, and then to walk out on a day when there is sun and moving drifts of cloud and wind that stirs against the new leaves, against your own face as you sit here above the grey ruffling lake . . . What was it, a kind of lightness, an uncomplicated pleasure in looking and breathing and sitting for long spells of silence beside his friend? It was as though the clarity of the day, the muted light from the lake and the constant papery shiver of the leaves against each other, had entered into him. Then his mind was taken by a strange image. He saw the bright streaming of the day between the banks of his own life. What he had lost was on one side and what he now made do with was on the other, and yet he stood contentedly enough above it, as though on a bridge, a man he imagined above pellucid water on a day sharp and bright as this, watching his own shadow thrown out across the stream.

'I don't need to see him again,' Latty said. He spoke of the doctor, of the fact that these last weeks had been the only time in his life he had placed his body before one, apart from the examination when he had come here not long after the war. *He did not count the injury to his head which somehow had taken him from the yard at home and woke him in the cellar that stank of decay and urine. That was not true sickness, not something within himself. It had been a fragment of that large dark force which destroys and erases, eliminates and forgets. It was like a roller, like a tank. A man's own illness, even his own death should it come naturally, come suppose as that warm pain the size of a tennis ball inside his chest—that is something very different, Latty thought. That is the second and enduring obsession one has with one's own body. That is the successor of love, which is the first.* Latty looked ahead of him, between the branches of a tree whose emerging leaves reminded him of gas flares, pale against the sun. There was gaslight still in France, he remembered. *A night in France and he was very drunk, he had not cared for that night whether he was taken or not. He was dressed as a farm labourer and had ridden in a high creaking wagon into a village of grey-walled, stiffly angular buildings. The driver slowed without speaking to him and he had dropped quietly to the unpaved road. He walked to where he had been directed, to the two-storey house which was unlocked and empty. Whoever lived there, whoever had sat at the long refectory table and last lit the fire which held some remnant of heat as he scraped and prodded the pile of grey ash, had run. He was to wait there until he heard, that was all he knew. Wait until a tap upon the window or a soft scrabbling at the door would signal him and take him as it had before then and would a dozen times more, lead him from a kitchen or the sacristy of a church or the cellars of a chateau, and deposit him again where his hatred and his gifts would ensure as much protection as could be offered. His hatred which came to him so oddly when he thought of it now, above the slightly shifting water, like the sound of a far-off cry hardly recognisable as his own. And the gift, his curious deadly knack, for which men and women risked their lives in order to move it wherever it might work to its fullest. His hands, the soft priest-like fingers, dedicated and deadly, resting now in the mottled light upon his gabardine as innocently as those of his friend, the man whose world was a few miles any side from where they sat. That night he had drunk two bottles of wine he discovered hidden behind a stack of empty crates. He drank the bland red liquor then shattered the bottles against the wooden door, and laid his head against the long table, shouting and weeping for his own village that was a pocked scrap of mud. When he woke to the two men pouring water on him, he saw the gas flare one of them lit rise delicately and transparent against the window behind it, against the first greyness of the morning. The light came through the pale flare*, as now through pale leaves. Len was speaking, Latty realised, his friend was looking at him and waiting for him to answer.

'I am a long way away,' Latty said. 'You must say it to me again.'

'It's just that blazer business,' Len said. 'Remember I mentioned it quite a while ago, right back near the end of last season?' Yes, he remembered that. It was the day they had watched a football match, when the skies had opened in the second half and they huddled beneath the huge naked trees. Len had pointed at the shed-like building with the small pillared veranda, and told him yet again about the marching teams. He had said what a good lot of kids they were, how he enjoyed the odd jobs he had done on the club rooms for them. It wasn't something he was paid for, he wouldn't have taken money if they had asked him to, just to see the kids happy with his bits of painting, with his putting together the odd bench and a row of lockers, that made it worth doing. He had knocked up a sink affair for them even, they could make themselves a cup of tea if the weather turned ugly on them. And now he was glad that Latty mentioned the things he had told him so many months before. He said, 'Well you might remember too how Mr Dryford said after I'd done that bench job that he'd have to get me a club blazer like he and the others wear? Remember I said that to you and how I'd just laughed at it? Well anyway he was dinkum about it after all. He told me a couple of nights ago when I was up there putting the second coat on the new lockers. He came in and he said what's your chest measurement, Len?' He was smiling quietly while he told his friend, he was like a boy talking of something he had wanted and now knew for certain he was going to get. 'I thought what's he on about, I didn't click for a minute. And then I saw he was really waiting for me to tell him. He said, "Look, it came up at the committee meeting about all you've been doing for the club and we said how chaperones and managers wore club blazers and you've done a bloody sight more than some of those bludgers." That's exactly how he put it.' Len paused again and looked down through the trees, at the line of shadow gradually receding from the water. He had joined his hands between his knees and was leaning forward, one thumb slowly stroking across the other. 'I wouldn't have hoped in a hundred years for something like that, Latty.' As he leaned forward his head had moved into a spot of direct sunlight, his hair for a moment was red as it must have been years ago, an aura that blurred and shone and then disappeared as he again sat upright. 'I didn't mention it through the week when you were crook,' he said.

Latty asked him when he would get the blazer, when would he be able to wear it?

'This weekend,' Len said. 'He'll bring it out this weekend. He wanted a presentation when the teams were there but I put the kybosh on that one. Bad enough strutting round in the thing without all that.' He laughed softly and Latty thought yet again how his friend had kept so naturally, so easily, his simplicity and his delight in things, in gossip and warmth and the easiness of sitting talking like this, as if it were a young bird he had carried for all those years in the breast of his coat.

'You know what it looks like?' Len asked. 'The colour and that?'

'I've seen the girl on the bus wearing one. The girl who works at the office,' Latty said.

'That sort of lovely blue colour? You don't know really whether it's light or dark.'

'That's the one she wears,' Latty said.

Len raised his right hand and rested it against his chest. 'And the monogram?' he asked. 'Have you seen the monogram?'

'Not up close,' Latty told him.

'It's all worked in white on the pocket. A Māori club affair sloping one way and a spade the other, and they're sort of roped together with little fine flowers, like a chain or something.'

'I have not seen all that,' Latty said.

'You need to look pretty close otherwise you miss it.'

The men were silent while Len smoked a cigarette and the light altered about them. The day was gusty still but so full of brightness, Latty thought, it's as if the light itself was being buffeted and blown about. And then there were long minutes when there was no wind at all, when the branches and the new leaves were motionless and the scraps and stretches of light at their feet grew focused and clear.

'It's an emblem for the district,' Len said. 'The flowers growing over the war things and the farming and that, it's supposed to mean peace.'

'That is a good idea,' Latty said. His broad head nodded at his friend.

Suddenly the sun was above the lake beneath them and its reflection flashed up as from a mirror. Latty squinted against the glare and Len laughed again as he saw his friend's heavy face fold up so that his eyes quite disappeared. You'd swear he had no eyes at all sometimes, Len was thinking. You'd think he was a Chink or something. They stood up and he said perhaps they should be moving back. 'You don't want to wear yourself out and that,' he told him. 'Not your first day up out of bed.'

VII

There had been only once in seven years when the weather wasn't fine for the Lions' Fair. 'Old Hughie knows who his boys are all right,' Mr Dryford joked.

As the day approached most of the women in the office were pressed into some kind of service for the Fair. Anyone who volunteered for baking or sewing or novelty goods was allowed off a couple of afternoons. The two men who sat at neighbouring desks in Latty's office had offered themselves, one for the wheel and the other for the stall where you aimed pingpong balls at the plaster heads of clowns with great gaping mouths.

'Just as long as you make it clear what people are aiming for,' the boss explained to the office. 'If you didn't tell them they mightn't know, like,' and he had winked very broadly and moved his head slowly from side to side, his mouth gaping. The young chap who had volunteered for that job wasn't the brightest, so they all saw the point of *that* one. Then on the Friday before the Fair Mr Dryford stood with one hand pressed against the doorway to his own office and his other hand caught by its thumb in his belt.

'Right,' he said. He nodded his head as he glanced from one employee to another. 'That takes care of you all, I reckon.' And as a final joke he added, 'Anyone with too much stuff for their car need a company bus laid on?' A couple of women sniggered and he said, 'There's no back seat in this one, love, so you can rule that out.' There was a roar from the men and Mrs Cleary, who did not go in for the risqué, shook her head and smiled very slightly at the same time.

'Right,' Mr Dryford repeated after the amusement died down. 'That takes care of most of you. Ones who know what a community's supposed to be about, anyway.' His barb was directed at Latty, who had not looked up from his papers while the entertainment was taking place. The large foreigner with his florist's hands, Mrs Cleary thought, you can hardly blame him for not knowing what a Lions' Day's about. She glanced across at him, prepared to offer a sympathetic raising of her brows, but he was engaged at the long roll from an adding machine which was unravelling between his hands. His right hand held a thick white pencil. Between those pale, slightly puffed fingers it was like the stem you saw in St Joseph's hand in certain statues. Only that was a strange and irreverent thought, surely, she considered. Again she coloured slightly and wondered what put such things into your head. She was glad, anyway, that she had done her share for tomorrow. She had telephoned Mrs Dryford who was in charge of the sweets and home bakery stall and asked her what it was she most needed, Mrs Cleary was willing to take on anything. She had hoped for sponges, but over the phone she heard that quiet voice say anything *but*, there were so many of them promised. So she had ended up with half a dozen things, toffee apples even, and butterscotch, and caramel fudge. She had packed them neatly into shoe-boxes and tied them with coloured tape. Mr Dryford had called her a treasure. 'Of course my wife will take all the credit for these, you know,' he said. She had thought he was hinting perhaps that she should take a stint on the stall, and she explained, 'You appreciate my circumstances don't you, my caring for an ageing parent . . . ?' She had left Mr Dryford his opening to say something consoling, but what he had said hurt her rather more than perhaps he intended. He had spread his arms and it might have been no more than an expansive movement, but she couldn't help taking it personally, not with her weight problem, could she? He had opened his arms up like that and said, 'Not for a minute, Mrs Cleary. You've done enough making them, surely. We don't need you there eating them as well.'

Mrs Cleary eased herself between the desks and moved the papers spread out on her blotter. She hated people to see how sensitive she was. She searched her top drawer for the tin of paper clips and thought how you couldn't say that even one of them in the office was *delicate*, you could never use that word about them. It was why these days she took a much softer line with Latty here than the rest of them. You couldn't be sure how much of it got through to him, mind you. How many of the jokes about his beret and Mr Dryford's jibes and the way some of the younger ones doubled over and pretended they couldn't abide the smell of garlic if he opened anything in the lunchroom? And now when he looked up from the strip of figures moving slowly between his fingers and settling in loops on his lap, she made sure she caught his eye. He was a gentleman anyway and she had a soft spot for that, who couldn't have in this place? He met her glance for a moment, his eyes closing as it seemed, his own smile slighter than her own. It seemed as though he had taken his time and yet his fingers had not stopped moving, he had looked up from the strip of paper and acknowledged her and returned to the column of figures without losing his place.

There was nothing he could do, Latty thought, *that was always the story.* He accepted Mrs Cleary's kindness and wished that he could do more than this simple folding of his slab-like cheeks, this bunching of his eyes. He understood how this woman beside him, in her late fifties and wearing her tasteful fawns and greys and today a scarf which he believed was called cerise, wished to stretch out her hand to him, to say how she longed to share his own quietness there in his corner desk. He recognised that as he knew too that Shirley was his friend, and yet he had spoken how seldom to either of them? He had known Mrs Cleary's embarrassment when she returned from giving Dryford the boxes of her baking, when she searched about for the paperclips but also for the tissues she kept in her top drawer. He had wanted to speak to her, to say—but what was it he could say to her? What words in this foreign tongue which he knew better than any of them suspected, or in French which he loved to read or in German which he disliked and yet found still came to him at times when he lay awake in the mornings, or in his own language so far now behind those others, his own speech like a secret well—what word from all those to ease that gross ageing woman, to comfort her? Or to speak to Shirley, with her exquisite fall of pale hair and the grace she carried in her movements? And at times he was ashamed that he had thought of that girl as he awoke from sleep, her breasts and the colour of her limbs. He had observed how Dryford looked at her, his joking to make her mouth open with laughter, to see her tongue held softly between her teeth. *I am an old man*, Latty thought, *there is nothing in these, in this quietly hopeless woman who sits day after day beside me, in this child whose body I cherish and envy, nothing for Christ's sake is there which I understand?* He kept his attention to the papers in front of him, the accumulated trivia for which he was paid and tolerated by a man who detested him, for whom he represented, in a way which again he did not comprehend, both threat and malice. *Yet to him*, Latty thought, *I am a mirror, I give him back what he demands to see.*

For almost a month Latty had heard talk of the Lions' Day. He hoped with the others that it would be fine, that the record of favour or luck would not be broken. 'It means so much to them at the office,' he said to Len, and his friend answered, 'Not only to them, Latty. It's the first day the kids are marching again so it's pretty important all round.'

'It had better be good weather then,' Latty agreed.

'You can put a ring round that,' Len said.

There was nothing to disappoint any of them. Saturday began with an early sky that lay as though painted, so still were the broad flat layers of cloud behind the town. Latty looked, as he did every morning, through the window opposite his bed to the rise of the hills. In three hours' time that cloud would disperse and the sun break over them. By nine the men would be up at the park, by ten the booths and tents and stalls erected and in place. It was a strange thing, Latty thought, this day when money was raised for charity, when people whose houses were filled with convenience and clutter would rifle through old clothes and stacks of books, tap dilapidated furniture, test rejected radios and third-hand sewing machines. His landlady would be picked up by one of her friends at eleven o'clock. At two she would return with her two string kits stretched with jam and fruit she did not require, a painted gourd which would gather dust in the wash-house, a purple tea-cosy which a few months later would be included in a Christmas present to the friend who drove her home. She would carry sword-fern wrapped in damp newspaper, an elegantly potted begonia won in a raffle. And Len would be down at the park even earlier in the piece. The first team was marching just after noon, between the pipe band and the lolly scramble when the Liontamer, in his frayed and weakly leonine fancy-dress, rode through the park in a jeep, hurling into the air the papered toffees donated by a firm in Frankton. Len would need to check that the club rooms were A-1, he would be there at ten and sweep the already dustless floor, switch on the newly installed Zip heater, open the windows so the rooms were fresh when the girls arrived. He would be wearing his blazer for the first time.

A week ago Latty had inspected the new garment which was pale and soft, with almost a plush feeling when it folded and one's hand sank against it, as his own had been invited to do. 'You like it then, do you?' Len had asked. He shook it out under the light from above the table in the bach. The monogram was pure white against the blue, the threads neat and careful and taut. 'I like that,' Latty said. 'I like the colour and the feel and this bit especially,' and his fingers lay against the embroidered crest.

Len grinned across the table as he slipped his arms into the sleeves. He checked that the collar was lying flat, then placed his hands in the pockets. 'Good fit?' he asked. Latty nodded and Len said, 'Feels pretty right anyway.' He had left the blazer on while they drank their bottle of sherry. They had joked about it and even when they were not speaking of it, it remained the centre of the room, the living colour against the drab walls. Latty surprised himself by thinking *he is like the open doors of a church or something.* He supposed he had not been in a church, not in a way which was real, since he had gone with his sister at home, and then it was a habit like his brother-in-law's standing at the kitchen window, a thing so often done it did not make sense to stop it. *He had stood near the font at the baptism, the boy was turned over and his sister had undone the little bow at the back of his gown, and the priest's oiled thumb had moved in the creases of the infant's neck. And why that,* Latty put to himself, *why remember that now?* A child's dedication to divine providence and his people's church, a child dead for over thirty years, a church which no longer stands, *which I perhaps am the last person in the world to remember, as I look across the table, to the blue arm of my friend lying along the plastic cloth?*

'I'm wearing it Saturday if it's fine,' Len had said. The bottle was empty between them and he stood doing up the buttons which were a matching blue. 'I wore it into town today but I had my plastic coat on as well. You don't want them thinking you're swanking about in it.'

'You'd see the colour through the plastic coat though,' Latty remarked.

'Ah, well,' Len smiled. 'That's still not really wearing it, like.'

Latty switched on the radio and lay back, his fingers laced behind his head. He supposed this was the best part of the week, on Saturdays and Sundays, awake and ready to get up yet still lying there, listening to music and the news. It was good that he was no longer feeling ill. *Not since I have been in this country have I been sick*, he had told the doctor. That was a good thing a man could say after so many years. The doctor was looking at the card he held between his hands where he had written all the answers Latty had made to him. He smiled across the desk where the stethoscope lay and the bit of wood he had placed on Latty's tongue and the little silver wheel with the black tyre of rubber which he had used against his knees. He had wanted Latty to stay away from work for a little longer, 'Make it a month,' he had said. 'No,' Latty answered him. 'That will be quite enough, two weeks is quite enough.' And for that time he had lain each morning like this, his hands behind his head, watching the sky through the window which was really four small windows together, happy that he could lie and think of nothing.

On Saturdays he made his breakfast at eight o'clock and read slowly the paper which Len's sister left folded for him on the step. For two hours he would read the stories from different parts of the world, and then the pages which told him about the country where he lived, what crimes were committed and what clubs had met, the things which took place in farming and teaching and sport. Latty enjoyed such details, surprised that so much happened where what he saw himself was no more than the habits of peace and work, the occasional surfacings of love and hate. It was more interesting to read a paper than any book. He had explained to Len, 'It is like it is in a story, you know? And then you say to yourself but this is not a story, all this is for a fact, and it is where you live. It is your own story that you read, and yet you don't know it until you read it. That is always strange.'

Len said, 'But it's only the *Herald* after all.' And what pleasure there was on a day like this, to leave his carefully tidied room and stand in the doorway of the bach, such colour and freshness to the morning, to the new fruit trees in early leaf. At the end of the section there was a row of citrus trees. A few weeks ago the lemons were plump and large, they glowed like yellow globes among their shiny dark leaves. Later in the day he looked across a heaped tray of similar fruit, six or seven hours later when the declining sun was tangled in the freshly emerged oaks at the park, and he stood before an almost depleted stall. There were as well a few pots of jam on the trestle table, their grease-proof paper tops stretched like small tight drums. The sun shot through the trees and picked out flags of brightness on the grass, and tipped the row of jars.

'I couldn't tempt you?' a voice asked him. Latty smiled and shook his head. His hands were deep in his overcoat pockets and he turned to move from the stall, to where a man stood on the back of a truck, shouting to the crowd milling about that this was definitely the last of the hams, there wouldn't be another chance after this one. The man's hand was on the wheel with its narrow strips of colour, the numbers painted near the rim. There was a crush of buyers round the ticket-sellers in front of the truck. Latty handed across a fifty-cent coin and was given a piece of board with the number 2 written on it. The man barked on from the back of the truck and then the wheel was spinning with a soft whirr above the uplifted expectant faces. The wheel stopped and a teenager who already stood with one leg of ham balanced upright between his feet called out, 'Right, I'll have that one too, thanks.' Latty felt his own card taken from his hand and again the man on the truck was shouting his encouragement, this time holding a box of groceries level with his chest. 'Take it or leave it,' he was telling them. 'Don't want this lot for twenty cents then just keep walking.' Latty moved on, brushing against the rope that enclosed the used-furniture mart. He saw Len leaning on one of the long iron pegs the rope was threaded round. His friend was talking to a woman who crouched to examine the scratches on a small dressing table.

Len called across to him. He waved his hand at the jumble of dismantled beds and misshapen sofas, tables and dulled mirrors and nests of chairs. 'Offered my services for the afternoon and got lumbered with this lot,' he said. 'Either this or leading a donkey round with kids on its back for a couple of hours. So ask yourself.' The woman spoke to him and Len leaned forward again, one hand crossed over the other on the top of the iron stake. Then he took a school notebook from the pocket of his blazer and wrote down the name she spelled out to him. As the woman left he said, 'Missed my calling, Latty. That's the second dressing table I've got rid of, and that tallboy over there like a coffin, that one with the old-fashioned handles.' He patted his side pocket where he returned the notebook. Then, 'See the girls?' he asked.

'When I first come over,' Latty said. 'They march like an army, eh?'

'Don't know if that's what they had in mind,' Len said. He supposed that if you had been through the War and that then you wouldn't be likely to watch any marching in the right spirit. He said, 'Everyone seemed pretty pleased for their first showing this season.'

'They practise up and down a lot,' Latty said. 'March, march.' He moved his arms slightly and smiled at the notion of it, those girls from offices and factories and schools rushing their tea two nights a week, then up to the park, to wheel and stamp and obey like sheep dogs the whistling and the shouts of their instructors. There was something Latty simply did not understand in their pounding one spot of grass, swinging from the shoulder, raising their knees high at the precision turn, swishing their skirts against their thighs. It was so unlike the elation of sport, there was not the pleasure of making music as with a band. The delight he guessed must come from group response, the precision of the obedient unit.

'Of course the uniforms give them a hell of a kick,' Len had told him. 'And there's the admiration bit, too. There's always a line up of young bucks when the teams are out.'

Latty walked again around the park. The Lions' Day was coming to an end. The last raffle tickets had been sold and the gambling wheel on the truck was now lying flat. One of the boys from the office was dismantling the white faces and scarlet peaked hats of the plaster clowns who sometimes swallowed the lobbed celluloid balls. The young fellow waved across to him and Latty gave back his greeting. There were ladders against some of the large trees and the steel-meshed speakers were unhooked and carefully handed down. The crowd had thinned out, litter lay strewn across the grass. It was like wreckage after the receding of a tide. A few gangs of young boys kicked through the cartons and the screwed papers and discarded cones, hunting for bottles. The only activities which kept on were the large platform with dodgem cars, and the donkeys at the corner opposite the bowling green. The children waiting for the animals were smaller than those who queued for the cars. Latty strolled towards them and leaned against the trunk of one of the trees. As he watched the children mount and clutch at the man who led them, he broke into fragments a piece of loose bark he lifted from the trunk. The scent was faint and pleasing, the bark springy against his fingers. He watched a boy who had been waiting quietly by himself now take his turn at the head of the queue. The boy stepped into the man's cupped hand and swung himself on to the donkey's back, and took the thin reins into his hands. As the donkey carried him the length of the short track the boy was oblivious of those who still waited or the man who walked beside him, holding the bridle. The child looked frail as he sat absorbed and stiffly upright on the animal's back, his hands closed tightly around the reins. 'Give him a belt,' one of the other boys called out. Another said, 'Go easy, he's nearly crapping himself as it is.' The boy seemed not to hear. The animal turned close to the edge of the park, where Latty stood against his tree. The ageing man saw the thick vein in the boy's pale neck, the excitement pulsing as he disregarded all but the beast beneath him, the fact of himself straddling it. As the man led him back the boy laid one hand along the donkey's neck, leaning far forward, his hand small and white against the broad muscular arch. At the end of the ride the boy threw his leg across the animal's back and jumped to the ground before the man could help him. He moved through and past the other children without speaking and without disturbance, as self-contained as when he had sat with the reins in his hands. His dark hair fell straight forward over a high forehead. He began to walk across the park, through the litter and the dismantled stalls. Latty felt for his loneliness, for that and for the small precious private world he carried with him across the grass, to where his mother waited for him at one of the park benches. Latty recognised her from where he stood, that woman who came to the office on the past two Christmas Eves, each time as Latty, after his one glass of beer, was about to leave before the party got under way. Mrs Cleary said last year, 'Stay a bit longer surely, won't you?' but he had said, No, it was better that he went now. He had stepped back from the doorway to let the boy's mother pass into the paper-streamered lunch-room and the chatter which hushed as she stood there. Then, 'Ah, the little lady,' Dryford had called out. 'Better *roll* in another couple of dozen, lads,' and the laughing had started up again, the boss had broken the ice.

Latty watched the boy go up to his mother, her laying her hand briefly on his shoulder as he turned to her and spoke. The woman smiled and she tapped the boy lightly on the side of the face. She then pointed to a large paper bag which the boy took up and raised his knee to balance, before carrying it across to a car. He saw the boy sit in the car beside his mother, speak to her again, and buckle the safety belt he drew down across his shoulder. The boy's forehead and his hand raised to brush against his hair made Latty think of the other boy, *his face pale in the light from the lantern, the pool of light they stood in and his sister holding the tired child, his brother-in-law speaking quietly across the horse's broad and shining back, the capital had fallen he was saying, they cannot be far from here.*

'Just give us a lift here will you, Latty?' Len called out to him. He went quickly to where his friend and a younger man were dragging a wardrobe up a short ramp on to a large covered truck. Most of the furniture from the second-hand mart was already loaded on. A few of the better pieces were muffled under scrim. Latty stepped on to the ramp next to Len and dragged at the wardrobe. The driver who would not have been half their age lifted the lower end. 'Right there, grandad?' he asked.

'I'll last you out, you young bugger,' Len told him. Then the driver said, 'You might as well come for the ride if you like,' and flicked his thumb towards the cab. He said he'd take the truck down to the plant where it came from and leave it there for the night. The Lions' blokes were going to help him with delivering the stuff in the morning. 'I'll be bringing my own car back so I'll drop you here if you want.'

'Might as well,' Len said. 'Ages since I've ridden in one of these.' Then he said, 'How about you, Latty?'

'Not since the timber days,' Latty said. 'Then I drive one, oh, for years all together.'

'They've come on since then, though,' Len said. 'Just get a dekko at that.' He tapped his fingers against a large radio attached to the dashboard. 'Everything except sheilas eh?' he said as the driver swung himself in behind the wheel.

'What do you think's under there?' the young man joked. He nodded his head back to the space behind the seat, to a long folded tarpaulin. He eased the long truck across on to the road. They drove three or four miles out of town, to large corrugated iron sheds where fertiliser and coal were held in bulk.

'Be worth a bit,' Len remarked. 'All they keep in there.'

'Take a lot of men to flog it anyway,' the driver said. He backed under a roofed section of the yard.

'Old Harvey's come on all right,' Len said. He pointed to the name on the sides of the other trucks in the yard. 'I went to school with him and you mightn't believe it but he was as thick as they come in those days. Talk about slow.'

The driver laughed good naturedly and said, 'Still is, Len. Thick as pig-shit.' Latty was glad that the driver enjoyed talking with his friend, that beneath his crude bluffness there was a warmth towards the older man. 'Anyway we'll have a drink on him before we head back.' He winked at Latty as he spoke and led them to a shed in the corner of the yard. He opened the lock with a key he singled out on a keyring that was shaped like a hula girl. He pulled out a couple of chairs from a bench that was strewn with papers. 'Don't spill your piss on them,' he advised them. 'They're the dockets from last week.' He crouched down and lugged a carton from beneath the bench. 'Treat ourselves on an old schoolmate, eh Len?' the driver said. He placed a bottle of Scotch in a space he had cleared among the papers. He brought out three glasses which he rubbed quickly with a soiled towel that hung behind the door. The bottle was less than half full, and the young man emptied it as he poured into the glasses. Len looked up from beneath his untidy hair, an ancient schoolboy delighted at the adventure of it. 'Makes a nice change,' he grinned.

Latty said, 'Thank you,' as he took the carefully handed glass. The driver himself sat on the floor, his head leaned against the support in the middle of the bench. He raised his glass to eye level and said, 'Here's mud in it, then.' Len chuckled as he sipped at his glass, his eyes closed for the unexpected pleasure. Latty's broad face turned from the younger man towards his friend who had now opened his eyes. 'Here's good luck,' he said.

When the driver dropped them back at the park it was almost dark. You could make out the shapes of the trees against the sky, Latty noticed, but only just. The strong drink was singing slightly in his ears and he closed his fists in his overcoat pocket. There was a kind of joy in the evening. He looked directly above him, to the few stars he could see stirring between the delicate leaves. It was like they were chips of shining glass on a soft rich cloth. He braced his feet firmly as he leaned back and looked up, he felt the freshness of the air and the simple goodness of standing here, slightly drunk, beneath the clean falling of the night.

'I'll wait here shall I?' he asked Len.

'What on earth for?' his friend said. 'You walk over with me.'

Their feet scuffed against papers and rubbish as they crossed the damp grass towards the club rooms. 'Sorry to drag you over Latty but there's that bag of stuff my sister left for me to take back. She'd go butchers if I left it here.' And then he said, 'The walk'll do us good anyway, after that young bloke's hospitality.' The wooden pavilion took shape in front of them. Len had given the veranda its second coat earlier in the week, and the odour of paint came to them above the smell of the grass. There was another scent too, mingling with the others.

'There's laburnum or something near here,' Len said. 'Must be from that boarding house across the road there, it's all down one side of it.' Latty did not know if it was the same flower but he thought of hanging purple clusters, dying almost before they had fully blossomed. They had been in one place, hadn't they? He tried to remember where it was. He saw himself hidden in a barn, that sweetness carrying through a gap between the boards as he sat in near darkness, in the dry catching odour of piled sacks. The memory came into his mind with a strange clarity, the sacks, the gloom, the sweet heavy flowering somewhere outside. He remembered that a bottle had been given to him when his food was brought, and each time he had raised it to his mouth he lowered it carefully on to the pile of sacks. There must have been some danger he no longer recalled. *Not remember if he waited to kill or be killed. Only the raising and the replacing of the bottle, the intermingled smells of life around his darkness and his fear. And yet not where it was, not why or for whom he waited.* That is strange, Latty thought, to remember and to forget at the same time, *the sacks and the perfume which were nothing then and now are all that is left.*

The sound of the traffic carried over from the main road. This side of the park, under its high spreading trees, seemed withdrawn and quiet. There were lights from most of the houses across the street, but no noise. A blue television flicker showed behind several of the drawn blinds. Latty looked across and stood on the edge of the veranda while Len took a Yale key from his trouser pocket, fitted it to the lock then felt for the switch inside the opened door.

A widening carpet of light fell brightly and suddenly across the veranda and out on to the grass. Latty saw the sheen on the newly painted boards, the cartons stacked at the end of the veranda, the pair of white boots one of the girls had left tucked beneath the seat that ran the length of the wall. He saw these things and heard the cry and the shout from inside the room. At once he had taken several steps and was behind his friend. Len was as though struck into the position he held, his hand resting still on the light switch, the other hand raised and holding the key in the opened door. Across Len's shoulder, past the large freckled ear and the reddish hair tufted above the blue collar of his blazer, Latty saw the girl's breasts swing as she turned, the dark smear at her thighs blurring as she moved from the light, the opened door, the two ageing men. Her blond hair arced out behind her, settled across her shoulders as she crouched and grabbed at the clothes untidily spread across a chair and partly fallen on the floor. Latty removed his eyes from her lithe animal panic to the man who stood facing them above a coat spread out on the boards of the floor, exposed as he fumbled into his trousers, his shirt and net singlet rucked at his waist. He was shouting at them, threatening them incoherently. His face strained so that from the neck of his opened shirt he was like a throttled man. One hand now held the top of his trousers as he rushed towards them, and as he raged a thread of spit leaped from his mouth and fell across his chin. His free hand was raised and his fingers grabbed at the pocket of Len's blazer, there was the quick rip of stitching and Latty's own hand came up towards the straining throat. His spread hand waited there without in fact touching flesh, the two men separated by no more than inches in the absurd silence, the girl faced to them now, her clothes partly on and the rest held in front of her while she shivered, as though she had come from bathing in icy water. Dryford's eyes were on Latty. 'I'll get you,' he was telling him, his voice lowered now and unsteady. 'I'll get you, you wop cunt.' But he let his hand fall from the pocket he had ripped, from the cloth he had tugged at as the emblem of all he would have shredded and destroyed. He knew as he stepped back that he had cowered before the older man. Latty touched his friend's sleeve and said, 'We must go now, Len.'

For the first time since the opened door and the flooded light, Dryford spoke to the girl. 'I'll drive you back,' he said, and the girl told him, 'No, I can walk back from here.' The three men stood and waited as she pulled a sweater over her head and turned again towards them. She looked at Latty and he said to her, 'You need not be worried. No one will know we came here.' She looked at him still as though his words were not clear to her while she sat to pull on her boots. Then she brushed between the men, she began to run as she stepped from the veranda on to the grass, her white boots flickering when nothing else was visible, and the gasping of her breath came back to them until the flicker too was gone. Latty turned once more to his friend, he said again, 'We must go now.' Len took a leather bag from the corner of the room and passed in front of Dryford. Then he and Latty followed across where Shirley had run, over the dozen or so yards of the broadening fading wedge of light thrown from the opened door, and then across the darkened grass to the other side of the park. The headlights of the traffic were picking out the trunks and branches of the trees.

Len said no, he could manage all right, when Latty offered to help him with the laden bag. They walked without speaking past the quiet shops and the cinema and the bank with the large pillars on the corner. Each place they passed had drawn a story from Len at one time or another, the crockery shop whose owner had lost a fortune on horses, the hotel with the haemophiliac barman, the gardening and hardware store where incest was not only verified in court, but incest that was knowingly and encouragingly observed by the town councillor next door. The two men walked on, across the pedestrian crossing and in front of the Post Office whose tower had been removed after an earthquake scare more than fifty years before, its graceful structure reduced to a squat hulk. He stopped to change the bag from one hand to the other. 'Well that sort of took the shine off things Latty,' he said.

There was nothing Latty could think of to say, no word he could dredge up which might alter the truth of what his friend had said. The shine which had rubbed off not from today simply but from so much more as well, the disenchantment and the abuse which Len was now too old to have remedied, ever, the end of a time which he had thought as solid as the building they now passed. They walked from the spread of street lights into the cavern, as it seemed, beneath the large trees further down the road. They emerged again beneath the naked skies as they came to the incline towards the bridge. And as they stepped from the pavement to the bridge Latty raised his right hand from his pocket and slid it between the broad lapels of his coat. There was a sudden uncomfortable heat inside his chest, a glowing which was also pain. 'Wait,' he said to Len. He stopped and breathed the cold black air from the depth beneath them, the quiet slipping of the river between its banks. He leaned forward against the rail then, 'Over here,' Len was saying, 'over here Latty.' He was leading his friend to the other end of the bridge, holding his arm as he sat him against a concrete pole.

'Take it easy for a minute eh?'

The feeling in Latty's chest expanded, he felt the altering of his pulse. *Ah* he was thinking *we are near the river*, and he must have spoken aloud without awareness, for Len sat beside him now and had his hand across his back, 'Of course we are,' he was saying, 'we've just crossed it, Latty.'

Near the river he was saying and then he said it in words his friend no longer understood. *He was listening for the voice behind him, for the boy's voice to break the monotonous soft progress of the cart, the tapping of the stick against the side. Soon they would notice that light from the surface of the river which was not reflection, an eminence scarcely less dark than the night but which spoke the broad presence of the curving water. And then the gushing against the wooden supports of the bridge.* 'Not far,' Len was telling him. 'Not far once you've got your wind back.' Latty kept his hand between his lapels, his fingers now on the smooth fabric of his shirt and the button he was attempting to undo. Len leaned above him and, *'All right?'* Latty asked, *the boy had not answered and he supposed he was nodded off against the sacks of grain. There were the lights already across to the left, the river beneath them now its washing against the piers. The boy with his sailor's cap pulled down, imagining the fullness of the sea curling against the bows, the line across the pale forehead when Latty raised and lifted and handed him to his sister, and the cap fell back.*

Palms and Minarets

'You're the one who will have to decide. You're the one who knows whether you're run down or not.'

My wife sat under the lampshade made from a sheet of old monk's music we had brought back from Spain.

'I'll decide,' I told her. 'I'll decide before next weekend.' Her needles clicked while she knitted. The shiny pages of a pattern book lay open on the sofa beside her, and even as she spoke her eyes moved from the needles to the instructions in the book, then back to her work. I looked past her to the red lines drawn on the curved stiffness of the parchment, at the heavy black squares to tell a monk's voice where exactly to go, where in the huge cool greyness of a church his voice was to rise or fall, the light from a high window over the shaved heads of the monks. Because I saw that once in Spain. My wife was looking for a shop that sold filigree work, the kind she had seen in Toledo and decided not to buy, and had then thought about and spoken about for the next three days. We were in a town whose name I forget, where we had not meant to be. She lay down in the afternoon and I walked through streets which were high white walls and stiff shadows. Then late in the afternoon she had decided to go after her filigree and I walked into a church, into the rise and fall of the voices behind the heavy leather curtain at the door, the black squares on the red lines behind my wife's head.

'If you don't decide to take a rest now who knows where we'll finish up?'

There had been a smell in the greyness like concrete, like water spilled on concrete. There was a young monk with a beard who looked like a movie star.

'I told you I'd go next week.'

'You know very well with a specialist you need to make an appointment well ahead.'

'I'm sure I'll last that long,' I said. My wife's needles clashed, they were steel and clashed softly but she may also have been cross that I kept putting things off. Her hair which once I had thought so lovely was drawn close against her head. It was red in the light from the monks' singing, from the music which had no tune to follow, no notes I could read although I had learned the piano for several years. My mother had said, *He'll never be a concert pianist but he sticks to a thing.* She had said it to my aunt while she stood at the kitchen sink. She wore pink rubber gloves which almost made me feel ill if they touched my skin. *You can play that piece you did for the examinations* she told me, *the piece you played last night for your father.* But it was for *him*, I thought, I am not playing it for anyone else.

I'll play it when she comes round next week I told her. I watched her pink gloves shine each time she raised them from the water and their pale dry insides when she peeled them off. *Next week, auntie. I'll be better at it by then.*

Only a few times, once or twice in the Army and another time in a church group, have I been with men who talked about their fathers. I do not mean the way one reminisces with friends, because it is likely they would have known him or heard about him anyway. I mean the times when men try to tell others what their fathers were like. That doesn't happen very often, and I think that when it does, most men will tell lies.

My own father was short, his features as sharply fine as if clipped from paper. In these past months I have thought of him a great deal. I believe I remember the first time he walked down the street with me. He held my hand as I stepped across the dappled footpath through circles and patches of brightness and moving shadow, when I was still too young to know that the pavement wasn't shifting but the flickering was from the trees that grew right along the street. We would come to a puddle of light and when I paused he would take both my hands in his and say, 'Over we go, digger.'

I am the only person I know whose father was a dandy, a man who failed at almost everything except keeping his shoes polished to perfection, and at a kind of kidding all the time that he was more melancholy than anyone understood. He loved standing on the back porch with his jacket off but his white sleeves rolled down, the cuffs held with slender jade cuff-links, his waistcoat buttoned and his watch-chain shining across his lean stomach. He would stand with a book open and resting on one palm and in the sunlight (it is never winter when I remember him), from the distance, he was lithe and solitary, a kind of figure from a western who held a book instead of a gun. But he would take books up and lay them down as though there were something in them which roughness would spill.

My father's single hobby was pool. Several nights a week he went out after we had eaten our dinner. My mother would say it was all very well having an interest but it would be nice if it was something that put food on the table. One of the delights of my childhood was to be taken to the saloon which was across the road from the library. Children were not meant to enter the bluish darkness with the great pyramids of light from the lamps above the tables, but my father nodded his head to the man at the doorway and said, 'He's keeping an eye on me.' He looked down at me and said, 'Don't you break the place up, do you hear me?' The tables were so brilliant and green that my hope for weeks was simply to touch one. It was my fourth or fifth visit before I asked if I might, and my father surprised me. He gave a quiet laugh and pressed my shoulder and said, 'You just go ahead and touch it if that's all you want.' He spoke as though it was nothing at all that I had keyed myself up to ask, and I ran my hand along the side of the table on the smooth varnished wood, then on the table itself, backwards and forwards on the pliant crushed firmness of the felt.

My partner is the one who really makes the money. He brings ideas to me for new lines and especially for new promotion methods and at the board meetings he always begins 'We've decided' or 'We came to the conclusion' and the board believes that when he says 'we' he naturally means the two of us. He is loyal because ten years ago I brought him in against opposition. He had no official qualifications and he is as ugly a man, I suppose, as you are going to get. At the staff barbecues (it is there, I mean, one most notices it) he wears a short-sleeved shirt and his guts sag over his belt. His arms are fat and pale and hairless, his hair has receded from a forehead which shines always in a slight glaze of sweat. One looks at him because one must. There is no way of working with a man, of sharing with him the responsibilities of a company, and avoiding his physical insistence. Nor would one ever call his wife attractive, but at least she is not gross, she does not make you want to reach out your hand to remove plate or glass, to spirit away both food and drink because one knows how it will sag and weigh against the strained belt, puff those disagreeable arms. She is a smallish woman and when he stands beside her she seems less than half his size. The lines of her clothes hang parallel from her shoulders to below her knees. It is of no consequence of course what she looks like, whether she is all rotundities or a breathing pencil, but I notice because she is so incongruous beside her husband. They are each a kind of distorting mirror to the other. She lays her thin fingers on the cushion of his forearm, he sometimes rests his arm across her shoulders, his hand hanging loosely in front of her slight breast as though to protect it. Perhaps because her skin is so sallow, so much the colour of a kind of tawny soap, I am reminded of an Eastern woman, perhaps an Indian

I may have seen in *National Geographic*, with a plump snake relaxed about her neck. Yet I admit one has so little right to be fastidious with the lives or the choices of others.

Sometimes I see his eyes slightly puckered as against a drift of smoke, and he is taking in my wife and myself. I wonder why he is so meticulous to present me favourably to the board, to share with me what he has a right to keep for himself. Or why when he speaks to the staff in his joking way does he pretend it is my way as well? There is nothing more he can get from the company, he is my full partner although I took him in when the board said quite openly did I know what I was doing? Even then he was fat and smiled. When he covered his eyes with one pale hand at the very first meeting, opened his fingers and looked at them like a child to see if he was going to be attacked before he explained his figures, they had laughed and they had loved him. Several times over the years they have said they have me to thank for him. And over and over when he begins in those meetings 'We decided' or 'We think it best', he is saying over and over too that he has me to thank for them.

I sat on the bench in the hospital corridor, leaning my head on the wall behind me. I wore one of those shapeless blue-towelling hospital gowns and sat cross-legged, while nurses pushed at the noisy swinging doors of the X-ray rooms. An old man sat a few yards from me in a wheelchair. His eyes were receded and his hands constantly smoothed the blanket across his knees. I feel uncomfortable among the sickly, but I continued to watch him. I was wasting the better part of an afternoon to satisfy a doctor I had visited because of occasional digestive pains in my chest. ('We don't know however that it's nothing until we see these,' he told me a few weeks later. He slipped a large negative from its brown envelope and held it against the window so we both could inspect the overlapping of shadow and outline, an aerial photograph it might as well be of a city I did not know, taken through cloud and gathering darkness.) I looked down at the incongruous shoes and socks which the attendant had told me I could keep on, and across to a young man opposite me who sat with bare feet, in a gown identical to my own. Again I glanced at my watch, I suppose with some impatience. A woman beside me said, 'Would you like this to look at? It might pass the time.' She held towards me an *Australasian Post* which had become dog-eared with handling by the bored and the ill. 'No, thank you,' I told her. I saw her own hands joined together on her lap, the band of a wedding ring on one of her fingers. Beneath the sleeves of her gown the bones of her wrists stood up like little domes. I went back to looking at the old man, at the gleaming lino along the long corridor, hearing the squeak of rubber soles as the nurses came and went. The woman beside me was Eva, and for as long as I was to know her that was her way of sitting, knees together and the fingers of her hands interlacing as they rested across her skirt or her paisley housecoat at home, or her naked legs during the summer.

We would joke that we met in a hospital corridor, in our ill-fitting gowns among the clattering of metal trays and the constant swinging of the doors. Later when she went for other X-rays or for tests, I would wait in the larger room at the end of the corridor. It became so much easier to take time away from my office than ever I had thought. I would leave at ten or at twelve or at three, whenever I wished, and I felt the freedom of a boy deciding simply to walk away from school. We would drive to Cornwall Park to the grey constantly stirring olives which Eva loved or to the kiosk in the Domain and once, on a flawless day in early September, we crossed the harbour bridge and walked on sloping paths between the dark green of native trees, above the glitter of the sea. Or more often, and what I preferred, was to sit at Eva's home, a small state unit on the other side of the city to where I lived. In our one winter we would sit on a settee in front of an open fire, burning thick lengths of pine which her brother had sent down to her from his farm. The ends of the logs hissed at the oozing sap and gave out a clean delicate scent. In the part of our one summer we sat in deckchairs at the back of the house, on the small square of grass, protected from neighbours and from wind by a screen of corrugated plastic sheets I had erected for her.

When I think of us it is seldom of one particular time, hardly at all of what we spoke about. I think of that simplest of things, the closeness neither of us needed to work at. It is as though when we were together we moved always under a canopy of content, like some ikon in a procession (which again I saw in Spain). And always Eva's physical stillness is in my mind, her voice which was almost harsh, which knew and carried more of life than any other I have heard. Yet she had not even been to the South Island, where her husband had settled with another family.

For the past eight years, since she came to the city from a small town in the north, she had worked at a warehouse I drove past every day. From the window behind her desk she could see our factory, with my name along the side.

I have said to my wife that I do not want to go out in the next few weeks, not to dinners nor parties nor to the Old Boys' Ball she has mentioned several times. 'You go by all means,' I tell her. 'We have gone with the same group for ten years, you will know everyone there.'

'I wouldn't dream of it,' she says. She smiles to let me know that her disappointment will never show. My partner has said to me several times, 'She's a brick, that woman,' so I do not fuss when she is heroic. I say simply, 'You may change your mind. You may want to go when the time comes.' She smiles again and shakes her head and there is the faintest of metallic sounds from the movement of her earrings.

My wife is the kind of woman everyone says has charm. The last time we were out together, the week before last at another company's social, the woman I was dancing with said, 'Your wife's got him eating out of her hand.' She meant one of the directors who wore a hairpiece and who slid his spread hand over my wife's buttock when they turned into the shadow at the further end of the hall. She took the hand and raised it back to her waist. I danced with this younger female because I was obliged to. She was the wife of one of our up-and-coming men, a boyish petulant man who sat drinking in one of the booths at the side of the floor, his leg out stiffly in front of him in the swathed bandages of an ankle sprained while skiing. When his wife spoke she smiled at me and shook back her hair and I presume I was meant to be a little taken with her charm too. 'Oh,' I said to her, 'has she?' And the young woman I held and turned with and was bored to death by said, 'There, every man with a lovely wife likes to play it down.' She gave her gay young executive wife's laugh, and it was like a stick being run across a child's xylophone. I thought as I glanced at the young throat and the breasts raised up by her dress and the folded lace handkerchief affair tucked like some small animal between them that Eva, without looks or charm, was all that mattered in my life after even fourteen months.

As on that night, dancing with the young wives of my staff, or at any other time I think of, alone with my family or going through the hoops with my equally well-trained guests, it is all much the same. I look at the faces in front of me as though at cardboard and plastic; I think of a woman who is nothing and nowhere, and she is more real to me than my own hand. Always as I think of her I am tapping my thick square nails (which Eva liked to play with, to snick her own nails against or press the bands of cuticle towards their base) on whatever happens to be near me. The vile marble thing on my desk at work or on an ashtray at home, until my wife says, 'I don't like to nag but would you mind stopping that? It gets on my nerves.'

'So would breathing if you could hear it,' I answer her. Or once when she asked me if I did it simply to pass the time I said no, it was more than that, it was hearing time pass as well, and she and her daughter looked across at each other 'significantly', as I suppose they would think it. Their look is to say, Observe how husband and father is over-strained, is in advanced depression, when in fact I am bored, bored. Recently I dreamed of myself fishing a lake. I was sort of trawling with several lines from the back of the boat as we moved along. There was no water in the lake and the hooks dragged at the bottom like the teeth of a plough. As far back as I could see were the neat parallel lines of the dragging hooks. But while I tap my nails against ashtray or table or the wooden arm of a chair, my wife turns her head and raises her hands when she speaks, and her rings and earrings sparkle and her voice 'tinkles', as she likes to be told. I see her standing in life and splashing as a child in the shallows of a river. That is where she speaks from, and I answer from the dry floor of my lake.

My father stopped with me one afternoon at a house much finer than our own. I had been with him at the library for the whole morning. At two o'clock he slipped his jacket over his long white sleeves with the jade links, and the dark waistcoat he did not take off when he worked. I liked to be with him in the room where he did his tasks, and breathe in the odours of glue and ageing paper and the shiny leather chair. His job was to sort out all the papers which came to the library, and put them in the wooden frames that held them together in bunches. There were brass hooks in the frames and the frames hung in rows, and between the rows it was like being in a tunnel of papers.

He took his hat from a high shelf and turned it as he always did against his sleeve, while he held the edge of his sleeve in his hand. Sometimes on Saturdays we would go to the snooker saloon where I watched him play, or sometimes to the afternoon pictures. What I remember are stories about the desert and sheikhs in long flowing robes and headpieces which flapped behind them as they galloped their horses in a smear of flying sand. There were often clumps of palms where they spoke to women inside silken tents, or cities with wonderfully white walls and high thin towers. After the pictures I would hold his hand when we came onto the street, and everything was so grey and ordinary and dull after what we had seen. But this day he said, 'Nice afternoon to stretch the old legs, wouldn't you say?' Often I did not quite know what he meant. Yes, I would say to everything. He took up a parcel of books from the table where a stack of folded newspapers were still in their brown paper wrappings. We walked up the long street to the bridge and then across the tops of the trees. I looked down on the gully through the flicker of the gaps in the concrete fence. Towards the end of the bridge he lifted me right up and I held the small squares of wire and pressed my face close against them. I could look down to the rounded crowns of the trees, and in the bright summer light some of the leaves were shining like glass.

We walked until we came to a house with a veranda around three sides. A lady opened the door and when we stepped inside it was like going into a deep cool cave. My father placed the books on a small table in the hallway where there was a leaning white tower she said was carved out of one tusk of ivory. My father and the lady sat in a large room with heavy curtains folded like in a picture theatre. They sat in there and drank tea from cups which had little flecks in them that you could see through when they were held against the light. The lady took out to the veranda a little tray with a glass of lemonade, and cake I did not like with seeds in every mouthful. I walked round and round the veranda and put my hands through the spaces between the railings, and pulled over a stool from where wire baskets of trailing ferns and creepers were hanging from the roof. I knelt on the stool and leaned against the railing as though I were on a ship. I could look over the gully we had walked across, see the whole span under the bridge like part of a huge hoop. And far down was the harbour, so brightly blue I am sure I remember it as more brilliant than it was.

After our visit to the lady we walked back across the bridge and it was back to what was ordinary. We would just say we had been for a walk when we got home, my father said, this would be our secret. We waited on the safety zone for the tram to take us home. Usually my father let me sit on the thick curved end of the platform while I held on to his arm, but I remember that day we only stood. When we were walking down the small hill towards our own house my father said, as we came near the gate which always snagged for a second because part of the catch had come away, 'Mecca, eh, old man?'

'Yes,' I said to him. I knew that was a kind of secret too, long before I knew whatever else it was.

There is a marble inkstand on my desk, a present my wife brought me back from Mexico two or three years ago. I find that I tap my nails against it most of the time I am sitting at my desk. The lump of marble is off-white and yellowish on different sides, the veins merely darker unattractive streaks. It is like snow when it begins to thaw, that seeping and trickling and discolouration you see in diminishing banks stacked against the side of a road, when it is eaten at the edges and irregular and stained. This is what Zelma's present has reminded me of since the moment she placed it on my lap at home and said, 'This is yours, señor,' while the children pranced about in their broad-brimmed and sequined hats. She had loved Acapulco even more than she had thought she would, miles more than Spain on our trip before we had the children, when we had pretended to ourselves that we would return there to live.

'More than Honolulu?' my son asked.

'You don't have to compare things, silly.' She tipped the boy's hat forward so that the brim rested against his shirt front. The shirt was a present too, blue linen with eagles embroidered on the shoulders.

'I almost bought you a shirt, you know,' she said to me.

'Almost?'

'Would you have worn it?'

I looked at the bright embroidered wings and lied. I said, 'You just never know.'

'Of course he wouldn't,' my daughter said. 'He'd die if he wore anything with colour in it.'

'You can see him with this hat on too, can't you?' The children held their arms stiffly and strutted as we used to for marching as wooden soldiers, but they were being their father. The boy put his head a little to one side as I suppose I do and gave the curtest of nods several times, his father acknowledging the neighbours. He and the girl and their mother became quite hysterical, 'The idea of him in that gear!' My wife had to sit back and flap herself with both hands until she said, 'Now that will do, you've all had your joke.' I put my folded hands beneath my chin and watched them, the eagles moving when the boy's arms moved and the hats flashing as they turned.

'Did you see a bullfight?' I asked her.

'Do you think I'm sick or something?' she said. 'He says did your mother go and watch those barbarians torture a bull to death?' she exclaimed to the children. She closed her eyes at the thought of it and the girl said, 'I'd certainly hate to see one, I know that.'

'What about you?' I said to the boy. 'Reckon you could face a bullfight?'

The boy was turning the hat in his hands now, his thumbs edging the brim round and round. He shrugged when I asked him what he thought about it. 'Not interested enough to even know?' I said, and my wife and my daughter looked at each other and each raised her eyebrows at the same time. 'We'll leave it there shall we?' my wife said. 'Before we're fighting again.'

I have noticed time and again that they are so close they do not have to speak. I have seen them at parties, they circle and move about like two animals you think are unaware of each other, and yet once they get home each knows exactly what the other has done, to whom the other spoke and when. As they sit together and talk of something again they are feline, precise. They sit above whatever they speak of and nose it, as it were, prod it about with swift careful taps.

One night very recently they were discussing bridal patterns when I came into the lounge before dinner. They were speaking rapidly together, unaware that their husband and father had come into the room until they heard me at the bottles, and I asked them why there was no ice. 'There's ice all right,' my wife said. She moved to stub her half-smoked cigarette.

'Don't you go,' my daughter said to her. 'I'll get it for him.' While she banged at the refrigerator, inserting her arm behind the frozen vegetables and the television dinners to where the one small tray of ice was stuck fast against the back wall, my wife placed her hands palm downwards on the arms of the leather chair, and closed her eyes. She was like an Egyptian statue, something at the door of a monument.

'You'll have to get it for yourself,' my daughter called out. 'It's stuck too hard for me to move.'

'It must have been back there a long enough time,' I said.

'Hard to see how that could happen, the way you go through ice.'

'Well?' I asked her. 'Is that leading up to something?'

'The carving knife's there if you need it,' she said. I chipped between the wall and the metal tray while the girl went back to her mother. As I tugged at the tray to edge it free my hand slipped and my fingers caught against one of the sharp fittings inside the icebox. Suddenly on the white encrusted ice I saw the small blooms of my own blood, splashes that opened like minute flowers. I looked at the drops for a moment, at the close sequence of stains across the ice, and felt my stomach lift with a kind of disgust. I must have stood for quite some time, fascinated at those vivid splashes that were myself. The others picked up the silence after my chipping with the knife and my daughter called out, 'Managed, have you?'

'I've cut my hand,' I said.

'On the knife?'

'On the fridge.' I waited because I thought one of them might move. I pressed my finger in my handkerchief but there was no depth to the cut. Yet I still expected one of them to come across to say is it all right, even to take the tray out for me and put the cubes into my glass. When I turned towards them I saw that both of them were looking at me.

'There's plaster in that drawer,' my wife told me. 'That one right beside you.' I opened the drawer and moved my other hand through the jumble of papers and stamps and rubber bands and tins.

'Manage?' she called again.

'It'll be all right,' I told her. I had found the spool but when I took it from the drawer it was not plaster but masking tape. I left my finger wrapped in my handkerchief and attended again to my drink. I ran the hot tap on the frozen tray, the ice cracking under the stream of steaming water. Neither of the women—for she is that, too, I suppose, my daughter—asked me how it was when I went back into the lounge, my hand concealed in my pocket. I sipped at my gin, the ice cubes nudging and clicking against one of the thin Danish glasses which my partner had given us last year for a Christmas present. 'Not that I believe in Christmas,' he had said as he gave the box with its gay seasonal wrapping to my wife, 'but I believe in presents.' That was the first night—last Christmas Eve—when I knew how clearly I was watching something on a screen. I have thought of that comparison many times; each time I feel more strongly that what I watch does not really have much to do with me. I now watched the two women and turned my glass slowly to hear the ice. They spoke of whether my daughter's hair would need to be cut if that style were to suit. I watch them as if there is an audience between us, like a man who wonders when he sits in a cinema what those actors must be like once the cameras stop filming, is there any small movement, any inflection in their voices, which tells him what they are really like? There is no one I know who is not behind make-up, not across a deep pit. I try to think of people who are not on a screen, and I think only of two, of my father and of Eva.

I have said that my partner's strength is that he can get on with people, whether he knows them or not. He tells me that is what selling is about. It is a way of putting your arm around someone's shoulder, talking to him so that he knows you're his friend. I have heard him explain this several times, to the staff or to the board. His hands open and close while he speaks. His face eases into its broad smile or he looks at whoever he is talking to quite solemnly, sincerely. When he opens his hands and shows his palms he has let out the dove of confidence and intimacy. It hovers over the heads of his audience and they feel its presence too. They look back quite as solemnly. Then when his palms meet and close and his thick fingers interlock or rub over each other in a kind of love-making with themselves, the bird has returned, it has disappeared into the magical hands, and those who have listened smile back, or laugh at his own laughing. It is like a man performing in front of a mirror, and his mirror is people.

Once my partner said to me, 'I know you think my methods are brash but they are also twenty-six per cent better than those anyone else in this outfit would think of using. That's not a bad return on brashness.' He sat opposite me while I tapped my nails against the marble inkstand. His hands were folded across the rise of his guts, as they usually were when we spoke together. He is far from being a fool and I believe he knew very early on that I did not believe in the dove. He had just delivered his latest advertising thoughts onto the broad unstained blotter of my desk. What he had placed there was a coloured photograph of a foetus, the tiniest veins in the creature's disproportionate head quite visible through its surrounding transparent sac. There were words typed beneath it. *Nobody packages more carefully than we do.*

'I can't claim it's my own idea altogether,' he admitted. 'I've seen it in an American magazine, but no one here's to know that.'

I looked again at the glossy photograph and the words on a narrow strip of paper gummed beneath it. The hands in the picture were like small fins.

'It's a logical extension, though,' he went on. 'Remember that one we used last year of a girl sealed in cellophane for the new Airtex Lunchwrap? Remember that?'

Yes, I told him. There was still a lifesize enlargement of it on the wall of the staff cafeteria.

'We're all a lot more ecologically aware now than we were even twelve months ago,' he said. 'That free advertising we did for the beech-forest buffs on our food cartons for example. People associate our name with caring about such things.'

'The public?' I asked him.

'People,' he repeated. 'That's why we can't go wrong with this one.' He leaned forward on his thick thighs and a length of pale pink cuff was exposed as his hand spread above the foetus. 'You don't use a photograph like this lightly,' he told me. 'It's something pretty important, after all, pretty delicate. People would know we were serious because we're serious about what we market. Serious the way nature is when it wraps this up, if you like.' The features on the oval face were obscured by the square jut of his index finger. 'We want them to know we take packaging as seriously as that.' I continued to look down at the photograph when he removed his hand and settled back in his chair. His legs were crossed and one foot jerked slightly as he waited for me to speak. I was amazed at the clarity of what I looked at, the fine detail of the utterly vulnerable and trusting curve of the uncompleted body. I had read once how an embryo goes through the whole of evolution, through various stages of fish and other life before it reaches the fully human. I remembered how appalled I had been twenty years ago when the doctor had called me into my wife's room and shown me my newly delivered daughter. The nurse was washing her with a wad of dampened cotton wool, and there were streaks of blood and foam over the tiny chest and legs. The doctor had said *Well aren't you pleased with her?* and I watched the wad move under the mottled arm, the look of discomfort or even pain on the tight screaming face.

'We'll go ahead then?' my partner asked.

'You'll go ahead anyway,' I told him. 'Everyone else will think it's splendid whether you kidnapped it from an American magazine or conceived it yourself.'

He laughed broadly and said, 'But you think it's shit?'

'You know what I think of it,' I said.

'Like a bet sales are up fifteen per cent at a minimum on this line within three months?'

'I'd rather bet we'll be into glass coffins before the year's out,' I told him. 'Your concern for the living and the unborn can be carried further than this.'

He stood with one hand on the handle of my door and his other rubbed the back of his neck while he clucked and shook his head. 'Don't know what we're going to do with you, pardner,' he said in a drawling voice.

Before he shut the door I called to him, 'Don't you need the photo?'

'I've had half a dozen run off for Friday's meeting,' he said. 'You're welcome to it.'

I slanted the photograph towards the light to examine it more closely. There were even little fingernails on the hands, branched veins in the sac which enveloped the body. I wondered at the minute and intricate being which in time would become one of my partner's people, one of our tenfold profit increase for total additional production costs of maybe five per cent. And then a curious feeling stirred in my stomach as I realised that of course the thing was dead. There could not be a photograph like that unless the child had been removed from its mother. The idea disturbed me, and yet I was amused at my partner's self-congratulation that our care for the people was a huddle of human meat perhaps an hour or two from the first workings of decomposition.

As I said, I watch them. And now they are watching back, even addressing me, which people on a screen or stage should never do. And I remember once I said to Eva when we were in Wellington together, standing at the window of a hotel from which we could look across the clutter of streets beneath us, would she like to go to a play? I had seen one advertised in the *Dominion* we read together in the taxi from the airport. The paper was spread out over our knees like a sheet, and her hand rested on mine while she leaned close to the page to read it, because she would not wear glasses. I had kept the play for a surprise. Through the afternoon, between two meetings, I found my way to the theatre and bought the tickets. We could never go out together like that in Auckland and so now I said, as though I might have asked it any night, did she fancy the theatre? *Love,* she said, *let's not waste our time together.* I said nothing about the tickets and instead we simply walked about the city. She held my arm and we strolled along the finely curved road beneath the hotel. Every few minutes she would press my arm, bring us to a halt as she pointed or remarked on something which held her eye. When it was dark the lights twinkled up and down the hills. Right above where we stood, as though supporting itself, was the large cross illuminated on the wall of a monastery. I began to say something about religion. Eva said nothing and we were walking on, her hair lifting and blowing across her face and touching my own cheek. She raised her hand to draw back and smooth her hair, and her skin seemed so pale against the darkness. A little further on she said, *Do you mind if we rest a while?* She sat on the wall which ran along the seafront, and now we were drenched in the orange glare from the lights along the Parade.

'Tired?' I asked her. And she said to me, *Never, I just want to soak it up.* The harbour was streaked with the broad flowing band of a moon which had risen above the hill across from the city. It seemed almost exaggerated, like an enormous backdrop. I sat beside Eva on the wall and I said we would never be more contented than this, which of course was true, but at the time Eva said, teasing me, it was because like so many rich people I am sentimental.

'Not that rich,' I said to her. The sea slapped against the wall a few feet beneath us and Eva sat with her head rested against my shoulder. A little later I said that it was turning cool, and although she said she did not notice it, when we stood she asked, *Could we take a taxi back, love? is that all right?* At the hotel she lay on the bed and told me to switch on the television, it was the night of a programme she knew I usually watched. She lay there with her hair spread across the pillows. *You'll wake me if I nod off?* she demanded. *I don't want to miss a minute of this.*

Eva's brother was a tall man about my own age, his face lined and weathered, with the same grey eyes as his sister. He waited on the top step leading up to the foyer and reception desk, and he moved down the steps as I came towards him. It was eight o'clock in the morning, March the twenty-third. There was a cool wind coming in from the mudflats which lifted the soft corners of the man's checked collar. The girl at the reception desk was standing and looked down on us. She must have pointed me out to him as I left my car in the carpark on the other side of the road.

'I'm Eva's brother,' he said. 'I don't want to spend any more time with you than I need.' He looked at me with the hard stare that some men who work the land seem to take on, a hardness that dismisses all divergence as weakness, other ways of life as directly hostile to its own. I have seen his face a hundred times at football matches and on the streets of country towns. Eva had told me, when she first spoke of going to stay with him for a few weeks, that he belonged to some small religious sect. His wife was his only help on the farm, they worked difficult land with the singleness of prophets. She had felt the rest and the country air would help her pick up some of the weight she had lost in the last few months. I said I would drive her north but she had demurred at that, she said her brother wouldn't approve of us, it was better if he didn't know. 'I've come to see you because I could not avoid it, because Eva is dead.' I saw the blue-checked collar rise with the wind and lean back against his jaw. I saw the girl still looking down at us from behind the shine of the plate glass, and Eva's brother cleared his throat. 'The service and the rest of it is over,' he said. 'She wanted to make sure I saw you.'

'She knew?' I said. The words were like dry flakes in my mouth, they were colourless sounds.

'She knew she was pretty sick,' her brother said. 'I'd have thought you'd have known that much. I thought there was more between you than sin.'

'She didn't say that?' I asked. His tongue moved quickly along his lips, he turned from me to look over towards the sea. 'She said nothing very much,' he told me.

There was nothing now I wanted to say to her brother, nothing more for him to say to me. I walked up the steps and through the doors with their gentle hushed closing and into my office. I sat among the routine noises of the morning, looking out between the various factories and across the open patches of land to the slight caps of foam on the shallow inlet, the mud-brown shoreline. I watched the odd movements of wind from inside the stillness of a closed room, watched the rocking of an empty drum in the yard behind the factory. There was the stretched emptiness of the sky above the buildings and the low slope of the hills. 'Eva,' I said. *He would scoop the coloured balls into their wooden triangle and then lean at the end of the table for only the slightest moment, because he seemed always to know what to do, while the other men waited and took practice shots and stooped until their chins were tucked back and quite disappeared, and their eyes were level with the table. His cue was back resting upright in his hand before I had seen it move, the packed balls were scattered and brilliant and flowing across the cloth. Then he would pick them off one by one, tock and tock, then the soft catching noise as the first fell into the pockets, and the different kind of click as one after another bulged out the nets in the corners or in the centre of the table.* As I said Eva's name I stood for a second in the intensity of what never comes back, in the curling bluish drifts of smoke and under the bright pyramid of light which I had not thought of for years. And yet now I seem to think always of two things at once, or of one person who immediately brings to mind the other. They are not ghosts, they are what everything else is seen by, is paled against, until what I look at in front of me is not even a film. It is a negative hung at a window, I see by the light from the other side.

They have come to look at me and so to sympathise, to take my elbow on one side with the wifely hands of concern and duty, my elbow on the other with the feeling and the intimacy of having spoken with me daily for a dozen years. I am part of their rights, I am what they have worked at and are entitled to. I am their guarantee that *they* are sane. I let them take me across the yellow earth to where my daughter's fiancé holds open the door of the car.

My daughter with tears in her eyes and my wife who does not wear make-up because her paleness is the marking of her grief, now sit one on either side of me in the back seat. My fat partner accelerates and the white line in the middle of the road disappears beneath the long shining bonnet of his car, an endless ribbon he devours. I sit quite calmly and consider how I am branded because I have stood for longer than usual in one place among the machines and graders of the extended motorway, looked down into a hole where a beautiful house once stood. There was a veranda on the house, and leaning on its rail, my knees supported by a stool, was like leaning over the rail of a ship. I stand on the wet clay and remember my father, and a woman I loved, who are also gone into smaller but identical holes. To think of that seems to me the very best of reasons to stand so still, to wonder what there can be to make moving a matter of any consequence. I have looked things in the face because they are not there.

Yet my wife and my daughter, my partner and my daughter's boyfriend, for all their love of things, their touching and their endless talk and their hating to be alone, do not believe in what they see. All *that*—the bodies, the cars, the Mexican ink stands—is for them no more than a sketch of what is real, of what might be. They believe that reality is something they shall make from all these things, not these things themselves. They now look at me from either side, in discreet glances in the rear-vision mirror. I am smiling slightly which confirms all that they suspect. I am smiling because I am with four people who think that our travelling at forty miles an hour along Great North Road, in the silence of tact and apprehension, will make some difference to anything at all. They are like those mad saints of centuries ago, men who would not believe that the world is what it is, but a distortion from its true shape that love and charity and worship could somehow wrench it back to.

We are now travelling past the used-car marts with their bright strings of flapping plastic flags, with words spelled out in little metal discs which shimmer endlessly against the light and wind. We are coming towards the turn where a church sits high on one's left, a tall grey finger of stone against the sky. I consider for a moment with some amusement that we are a procession from that old time I was thinking of. My partner who is like St Francis opens his thick hands and the doves of fifteen per cent hover at his shoulder, move with their strutting walk along his extended arms. My own wife with her eyes cast down, my daughter like a novice, my devoted son-in-law of two months' time, beside and behind that Franciscan flesh as he leads me to where I shall be questioned, dressed in a special robe, touched and tampered with by men who will work towards that miracle, to turn my world to theirs. They shall give me the cool pastures of a private room, the quiet waters of their choice. And on the green slats of their garden seats I shall be silent as a boy who walks from a picture theatre holding his father's hand, who looks at the bald streets with eyes fresh from palms and minarets.

The Corner

The woman sat at the kitchen window in her corner fifth-floor apartment. Through the foliage in the small park on the other side of the street she could glimpse the streams of traffic across on Broadway, hear the endless playing of horns and the sustained acceleration of engines. It was August, and the night so hot she felt even the heaviness of the cotton robe she wore over her underthings. Her husband sat in the next room, his bare feet on the table with the row of empty beer cans beside the TV guide. Damn them, he had just called out, not a decent can worth drinking in this whole city because those goons over in Milwaukee or wherever got themselves running at what their union boss tells them, whatever little Commie comes along and tells them how about us just messing up this country, boys? He tilted a can to his mouth and when he returned it to rest on the rise of his stomach he said, 'Should be a law, you know that? Stop people selling stuff like this?'

'I got the only ones I could,' the woman said. 'And it's not them out there it's the transport here in the city. The ones over Milwaukee got nothing to do with it.'

She leaned forward to the sill. What was going on down there, she wondered, down on the corner across the way? Round into the avenue a small crowd was suddenly forming and shoving on the sidewalk. It was after twelve now and the walkers from downtown should be thinning out, yet in a few seconds there must have been a hundred people down there. Usually this was when things became quiet for a while. An hour or so later the transvestites would begin their stand over at the same corner, their shouting and their dirty talk and dancing to the blared music from their transistors until three or four in the morning, hot nights like this. Right out there on the street, *cha cha cha* and their elbows close against their bodies as they turned and snapped their fingers. Sometimes the woman was entertained by the get-up, the piled wigs and the artificial breasts, the rather lovely calves tilted above their high heels. Her husband would get into a rage when she talked about them. He had yelled down from their bedroom window one night when three of them were screeching and smacking at each other with their handbags, he called, 'You don't get off this street I'll come down there and kick your rocks off.' They stopped their brawling and screeched right back up at him, the black one who seemed to jig endlessly while he stood there, his inflated breasts wobbling under his shiny satin blouse and his large earrings tapping on his cheeks, he yelled back up to her husband that he just better try, he just better come on down and that ass of his going to eat a lot more than boot, feel like coming down? When her husband came back to bed the woman had gone through into the kitchen and poured him a large glass of the rye he kept in the cupboard above the sink. She could see the strain on his face without turning on the lamp, see it in the glare from the streetlights outside. The transvestites kept on calling up at the tall apartment block with its rows of darkened windows. In every bedroom there must have been someone lying and hearing the noise but no one else looked out or shouted down. Maybe two hundred people lying there and being kept awake and saying to themselves what's it got to do with me? Her husband shook as he took the glass. And they don't want jails for them! he said. They want to bring more of them up here and give them our taxes so they can powder their butts right down there in front of us, Holy Christ!

She watched the crowd pressing close to the middle of the sidewalk. A tall man, who might have been one of the insane boarded out by the overcrowded hospitals in local run-down hotels, stood at the centre and his hands moved rapidly while he spoke. When he thought the crowd ignored him he spoke louder, moving his hands more wildly. The woman made out only the rising pitch of his voice, and the drunks and the drifters around the small patch of green with the statue of Verdi in the middle picked up the agitation going on across the way. Some of them dodged or swayed between the traffic and stood at the edge of the crowd.

'Something going on down there all right,' the woman said, and her husband asked her, 'Some guy drop his tits?' There was the whine of brakes as one of the drunks stepped into the stream of traffic. A taxi swerved to avoid him and horns blared back along the line of cars.

In a sudden movement of the crowd the woman saw something lying at their feet. She said, 'Someone's dead or something.' She held her hand flat to the top of the robe where one of the buttons had come off, and leaned forward on the windowsill. She heard the springs of the settee in the next room as her husband stood and crossed to the window in there. He belched loudly as he stooped between the hanging pots with their trailing ferns. 'Knife each other at last, huh?' he said.

The woman said, 'It might be an old person with a heart attack,' but her husband said, 'What's an old person doing down there this time of night? Unless it's one of them loonies,' he said, 'could be one of them loonies.'

The crowd was constantly reshaping. People would stop and edge towards the centre until they could see. The tall man was at the outside now, still talking, still waving his hands. There was a younger man she saw then, he might have been black or Puerto Rican, it was difficult to tell from here. He seemed the centre of whatever it was, he stood without moving while the crowd flowed and changed. The group always wheeled slowly to the left, with the direction of most of the walkers. The drunk who had almost stepped into the taxi was now back on the other side, near the park. A friend who had not moved from the bench handed him a bottle in a brown paper bag. The man removed the bottle and threw it across the back of the bench, at the marble opera characters who stood beneath the composer. From where she sat the woman could not hear the smash, not above the noise of the traffic, but she saw the falling arc of the bottle and then its springing back again in fragments, in brief glittering shards against the sides of a statue.

'The cops are here now,' her husband said, 'they'll sort it out.' A blue and white car had pulled into the kerb. The officers walked quietly into the crowd, one with his hands on his hips and the other waiting at the kerb, his hand flapping at his side. The dark young man spoke to the officer and the woman leaned further from the window. She could see it now, a still huddle like a coat that had been thrown down.

'My God,' the woman said, 'that's a dog. That's a dead dog down there.'

Her husband grunted from the other room. His bare feet slapped on the kitchen floor as he went to the icebox and took out another beer. 'Did you see that?' the woman asked him. 'That's a dead dog.' The strangeness of it excited her. She had expected to see a person lying there, an old man or a woman with a crumpled skirt like the epileptic who had thrown a fit in the deli once, in front of the imported cheese counter where she worked. There, she could see more clearly now. The officers were moving folk on. She could see the dog was a large Alsatian with a pale head. The legs stuck out from the thick dark coat, thin and very straight. It hadn't been hit by traffic, she thought, she couldn't see any blood. It just lay there bang in the middle of the sidewalk where it must have dropped down dead. Somehow it seemed worse than a person lying there even. You would *expect* to see a person, there were always old ones taking sick or something, or drunks bowled by cars, but she had never heard of a dog just dying, dropping down so it lay as if sleeping, only a crowd watching it, and police.

The dark young man who owned it was kneeling now, he was taking the collar from its neck and the long chain he led it by. He stood up with the collar in his hand and slowly, while he talked to the officer, he wound the chain round and round his fist, until his hand looked swollen and gleaming when he moved it. The other policeman now squatted on his heels and took the dog's feet. He staggered with its weight when he stood up. He hunched and half ran with it to the corner, to the side of the drugstore where he laid the dog against the wall. But it no longer looked as if it was asleep. One front leg was hooked right back under it and the tail instead of lying out behind it had been folded back and was held under the body's weight. The woman couldn't take her eyes from it. She couldn't think how a dog could be trotting along a street and die so suddenly, just falling and lying there while its owner must still have been holding the end of the lead, thinking perhaps the dog was in step behind him before he felt the tug at his arm, and in the mystery of the animal's body the heart had already stopped. She spoke again to her husband and raised her voice when he failed to answer, but he had gone through to the bathroom. She heard the cistern flush and he called through to her from the bedroom door that there was enough to keep him awake most nights without dead dogs, he was going to bed.

She switched off the light and knelt down on the floor, her arms flat along the sill. There was a little movement of sweat in the hollow of her throat that she rubbed at with the collar of her gown. She looked down and wondered what was there for the young man to do now? When the officers returned to their car one of them spoke into a microphone and then they turned across the top of the narrow park, into the traffic going down Broadway. For a few moments the man stood there above the dog, before he knelt beside it, raising it slightly to straighten out the tail, to set the front legs side by side. Then he stood again and leaned against the wall. He folded his arms and looked now at the animal at his feet, now along the quiet street to his right. The main roads continued to carry traffic but here between the apartment blocks and the brownstones there was nothing but a few late strollers, the black plastic bags of garbage stacked in piles or placed singly beside steps. He waited until a grey sanitation truck moved along the street and pulled in beside him. Huge wire brushes pushed out from the front of the truck like carnival moustaches. Sometimes they swept the street at five or six in the morning and the noise was enough to wake you up, the way the brushes whirled and scraped. When that happened the woman would lie very still, hoping her husband slept too heavily to wake.

The driver jumped down from the truck's cab and walked over to the young man. He was in overalls, and perhaps twice the young man's weight. The owner said something and crouched beside the dog while the older man stepped back. He slid his hands and then his arms beneath the dog as though he were going to lift a sleeping child, while the driver went to the back of the truck and pulled down the metal lip. The woman could see how heavy the dog must be. The young man's face was fixed with the lips pulled back and his teeth showing, the dog was rolled in against his chest and the legs flopped at each step he took. As he stepped from the sidewalk the driver grabbed the back legs, and together the two men swung. The dog rose and was balanced on the metal lip above where the garbage was tipped, where the huge blunt blades of the cruncher thing dragged in and crushed whatever was thrown in. The young man saw or only then remembered the blades. He held firmly to the front legs as the driver heaved the rest of the body across the lip. For a moment it looked as though the dog was reaching over a wall, its head rested on the ledge and the young man clutching at its front paws to help it across. And then an elderly woman shouted from the other side of the street, from directly beneath the woman at the window. She had stopped her slow movement along the street as she saw the men heave up the dog. She shouted as she might have done at someone stepping in front of traffic, a rising strain of panic in her voice. 'Get it out of there!' she ordered them, 'Get it straight out!'

The driver already had jumped on a supporting bar and was straining to heave the dead hulk back up, so the whole of the dog's weight tumbled back onto the young man. He grabbed at it but the paws tore from his hands and the woman at the window heard the thud as the dog smacked onto the ground. The driver was shaking his head like he couldn't do anything more, it was all too crazy for him to cope with. The elderly woman was now stopped halfway between the opposite sidewalk and the truck. She waited there in the middle of the street and seemed lost in her agitation. She kept calling, 'Don't you go touching him you hear?' The driver was now at the side of the truck, sliding back a doorway that opened onto a dark space several feet across. He returned and grasped one of the hind legs. He dragged at it until the animal bumped over the kerb and lay beneath the opened door. Then quickly he had hoisted it and thrown it into the dark.

The young man was no longer watching the driver but the elderly woman who continued to call to him. Then he was shouting back himself. 'You get out,' he yelled at her, 'You the one get out!' He spoke like a foreigner, like he was Spanish or something. 'That my focking dog,' he shouted. His hand was pointed to where the driver now had closed the door in the side of his truck and already was climbing back behind the wheel. 'That my focking dog I do as I like!' He stepped back and knocked against a fire-hydrant as the truck moved off. He took up the chain and collar from where he had placed them beside the wall and stood there, drawing out a length of chain then pressing it together between his hands. The elderly woman had gone back to her own side of the street and up a shallow flight of stairs. She was turning a key in one of the doors. Then the young man bent forward as though he had been struck in the stomach, he bawled along the street at her before she disappeared, 'My focking dog, you hear that?' Then once more he wound up the chain on his fingers, like winding up a ribbon or a ball of wool, and laid it with the collar on the papers and junk that rose from a trash can at the corner. He pressed them down carefully and watched that the rubbish did not rise up and throw them on the ground. He then turned and walked in the other direction, until the woman at the window lost sight of him.

There was a pause in the sound of the traffic. There were no cars beneath her nor even there behind the trees, over on Broadway. The drunks on the benches were sleeping and there was only the tick in the fluorescent tubes of the sign at the side of the drugstore, a tiny tick she could hear for once from up here where she knelt. There was nobody in the street for a minute, five minutes, while the woman looked down on the well of light and stillness. Then she heard the tap of heels beside the trees across the way. She saw the shimmer of the red jacket the transvestite was wearing. The figure came over and stood against the wall, above where the dog had been put down and then picked up. He took a tiny transistor from a sequined bag, and held it up against his ear.

That's the Apple for You

Joe ran an off-the-hook fashion store up from the rail station in Bridgeport, and lived with his partner above the shop. Every Tuesday he went down to New York to see what seconds were going among his Jewish friends on 38th Street. 'You don't look for yourself,' he said, 'you don't get the pick of the bargains.' His partner said, 'That's what the telephone was invented for, Joey, so people don't have to visit the Apple.' And Joe would say, 'Look, only kids call it that. Tourists. Smart-ass guys who buy their shirts with fancy French labels. Far as I know I'm none of those. So do me a favour, will you?' One Tuesday after he'd seen a woman knocked down right by the taxi stand at Grand Central he crossed further along the street and went into a small bar. He would say when he got home, 'OK, people get run down every day, I know that. But I don't see it every day, do I? So I go into a bar.' But then each week Joe went back. He took the train half after eight, instead of the one he used to get a little before six. His partner would say, 'You're too late for that show you like about the cops, Joey,' before he had hung his old-fashioned hat on the peg inside the door. 'I been busy down there,' he told her. 'You want to try that crazy town sometime.'

There were never many people in the bar, that was one thing he liked about it. The bartender minded his own business, rubbed glasses with a white cloth, held them up against the light like it really mattered to him, you know? Like it was really something to have them that polished. But if you did speak to him he was friendly. He'd rest the cushions of his palms against the edge of the bar and the greenish light from the fake Tiffany lamp shone over his balding head, like he had just gone under water. That's it, Joe thought, it was precisely like that, as if he had just gone down and was coming up again and that's why those strands of hair were slicked down so smooth on his broad head. And he thought isn't it weird the way you think like that? And everybody must do it. Everybody in every bar from down at the Battery right up to those spic bars in Harlem you wouldn't be seen dead in, everyone sitting with these ideas going on, no one else ever really knowing what's happening in someone else's head. And there was this old broad sat along the bar a bit Joe used to look at. Suppose someone comes up to you and says, She a hooker? you wouldn't think twice, you'd say, Sure, what did you think she was, Queen of the May or something? She sat on a stool down the far end near an advertisement with Mount Rushmore and those big carved heads right over her shoulder. Her skirt was up above her knees, she was selling something make no mistake. But the only time Joe saw some guy approach her she burned him off. So he had his doubts when he saw that, he thought, You can't even tell about people's outsides, let alone their minds. But if she ain't a pro, he thought, she's the best reserve he'd ever seen.

About the third week he came in he said to the bartender who had told him to call him Buck, 'Hey, you got a match there?' Next thing a folder slid down from where this broad sat. He lit one of his stubby cigars and turned to give them back. 'Keep them, mister,' she told him. 'Make like it's your birthday.' And she went back to looking straight ahead where she must have caught herself in the mirror behind the spirit bottles, and turning her glass in front of her like she always did, round and round, very slowly. Sometimes there was this other guy who came in and sat between them. Boy, was he weird. He wore this GI's outfit, green and dirty like fatigues he'd kept wearing since he was shipped home. Because he must have been a Vietnam veteran all right, he had a metal disc round his neck and a name tag sewn on his jacket, although it wasn't any real name he wore but 'Ask me again, Uncle' sewn there above his heart. But that was nothing. He had a crew-cut and blue eyes that made Joe think of Montgomery Clift in that movie about a soldier loving a girl in Hawaii, and sometimes this kid talked crazy, did he ever. It didn't matter a damn if Joe turned to listen or the broad just looked ahead or if Buck kept wiping those glasses and holding them up, looking for the pure light through the pure glass. Didn't matter one bit. This guy would tap the edge of the bar, tap, tap, like he was going into some routine with a drum. He'd close his eyes and click his tongue and when Joe looked at Buck the bartender held out his opened hands, like he was saying, No good asking me, buddy.

Joe got so he used to look for him. And when he came in on Tuesday night if the broad wasn't there he would think, Wonder what's keeping her? Or when only the other black bartender was there Joe asked, 'Buck OK is he?' The black would say, 'Sure, he's OK.' He went on with what he was doing, which usually was leaning back against the bar with his arms folded, looking up at TV. His bow tie was on a piece of elastic. He kept drawing it out a little and easing it back, all the time he was watching a football game. Buck said to him once, 'Reckon you never have to eat, huh? Or even breathe. That box up there does it all for you.' The black guy just laughed at that, showing his front teeth where one overlapped the other and said, 'You jivin' me, man?' but he said it somehow like a comic, not the real black which he was. 'I'm not jiving you,' Buck said, 'I'm just telling you one of these days they're going to switch you on and off, not that thing up there. That's all I'm telling you.' But this black guy wasn't listening because he was watching the game again, he was shaking his head low over his folded arms and saying, 'Where those teams out there ever get the idea they could play this game?' He looked along the bar briefly. 'Anyone tell me that?'

But if the young guy wasn't there Joe missed him more than the others. Wow, as Joe said once while Buck was talking with him, that boy was something else again. Still wearing his gear like that you took him for one of those veteran heavies, lost because he had no shooting left to do. But in fact he was so polite he could have been a six-year-old talking with his teacher. 'Sir?' he'd say, if you nodded and spoke to him. Sometimes he would talk out loud to himself, or as if he was having a conversation but it wasn't with anyone in particular, it was like a sermon, like a piece of a play. One night he said while he was looking between Joe and Buck but never straight at either of them, 'I been exercising this Descartian gamble for so long it don't matter, see? Though I look through to the interstellar spaces and think like our literary fisherman from Arrowhead that while I watch the Milky Way, I am stabbed in the back with annihilation. I neither believe nor disbelieve. Reckon that's some place to get at.'

'Come again?' Joe said. And the young guy looked sideways and said as though someone had broken in on his thoughts, 'Sir?' He looked so goddamn forlorn sitting there, that young boy look yet the face kind of wizened too, but not with age, just pure misery if you can talk about it coming that pure. Joe felt it so sharply he said to Buck, 'Give him a double bourbon.' And the young man turned again when the glass was placed in front of him and he said, 'I appreciate that, sir.' Other nights he would sit in his usual polite silence and then perhaps break out into talk about music, about jazz of which Joe knew not one thing apart from the fact that it was black music, not white. And the kid—because that is what they all called him now, Buck did, and the old broad, she'd say, 'OK kid?' when she caught his eye—he would use technical terms that Joe could not follow, he referred to groups, to combos, to the best bass player who ever lived, he said, who was now dying, dying of you know what? He tapped the bar softly and started this snapping with his fingers and began to half chant over and over, *amytrophic lateral sclerosis*, until the tears began to move down his cheeks and the broad said, 'Buck, give him a shot of something, will you?' The kid smiled when she said that. He looked at them with his soft grin and said excuse me, and a few other words too, but in some foreign lingo, probably in French, Joe thought.

The next Tuesday Joe gave the bar a miss. His brother was visiting across from Springfield, the brother who still made firearms believe it or not, in the town that won the Civil War because of the quality of its guns. (That anyway was what Joe had always believed, what his father had always told him.) So he sat with his brother and his brother's wife and he thought at eight o'clock I know where I'd rather be now, damn it. So next week he was early. He walked up from 38th Street in a bright and pure evening, the silver leaf on the top of the Chrysler Building like it was minted that afternoon. There were kids climbing on the stone lions outside the Public Library, there was spring in the air, imagine that, spring on 42nd Street in the middle of all that garbage, all that filth. The bank building with the curved glass front slid with the evening light. All that dirt, Joe thought, looking along to the cinemas lit up and garish with their porno advertising. He stepped into a small store to buy himself cigars. Then he lit up in the doorway before stepping back onto the sidewalk. That smell too, on this kind of night, Joe thought. Funny how smells peeled the years away, like lifting a veil, that same smell when he was a boy and holding Pop's hand and he looked up for the first time at the Empire State . . . Well no point thinking back, Joe thought. No one gets nowhere doing that.

He turned into the bar. The coloured squares of glass in the lamps were bright against the gloom. He removed his hat and placed it down on the bar, beside the packet of cigars he was carrying still in his hand. The others weren't there yet. There was only Buck who had his back towards him, checking off some list.

Joe said, 'Nice weather out there.' Buck turned and looked at him and raised a glass to a spirit bottle without waiting to be told. 'Have this on me,' he said.

'All righty,' Joe answered. 'I'll just do that.' He lifted his eyes to the TV screen. The president was walking along some guard of honour but the sound was turned too low for him to catch what was said, there was only a distant drone from a military band. Then Buck put a square flat parcel on the bar beside his glass. 'That kid,' he began. 'That kid comes in here Tuesdays sometimes while you're here, remember? Sits over there?'

'Sure I remember,' Joe said.

'Well he comes in last Tuesday, see. He asks me, Where's that old guy drops in here regular? So I tell him I serve people liquor, I'm not a private agent, am I? And he says, OK, just give him this, will you? Make sure you give him this.'

'For me?' Joe said. He lifted the piece of tape at the top of the folded plastic bag and took out a record.

'So I told him, Yeah, I'll give it to him,' Buck went on. 'Then we thought the kid had gone. Mary who sits over there, she thought he was gone. I did. The other bartender did.'

And Joe said, 'Huh huh', and read the writing on the record. It wasn't the original cover but one the kid must have made himself, pieces of cardboard clipped at the corners and written across it in large letters was MINGUS, and in smaller letters below that, 'Goodbye Pork Pie Hat'.

'That a joke or something?' Joe asked.

Buck kept telling him. 'We thought he was gone, see, then this customer comes hollering up from the men's room, he says, Christ, there's someone dead down there.' Joe looked at the man across the bar, the shiny green light on his moist head, the thread of frayed cotton at the side of his collar. 'Who's dead?' he asked him.

'The kid's dead,' Buck said. 'He's got this bit of thin cord tied to a pipe and he's just leaning away from it. Not even hanging, got that? Just *leaning* so he kills himself.' Joe put the record back in the bag. He emptied his glass and said, 'Better have another one, eh?' and both men tipped glasses before they drank. After a pause Joe said, 'Mary not in then?' 'Hasn't showed all week,' Buck said. 'Her health—you know?' He put his palm level in front of him and tilted it a little from side to side. 'Everyone's got problems, huh?'

On the train home Joe looked out at the lights in the high tenements and the refracted shimmer when they crossed the river. He watched through his own reflection in the window so the glaring freeways and the occasional glitter of water and even the roseate sky above the distant towns seemed inside his head, behind his face, as well as out there. He laid the record across his knees, opening his fingers and smoothing them across the plastic bag. Then again he looked out of the window, watching the oval of his ageing face, the dark and the scattered lights of the moving night.

When he stepped from the train he dropped the record in a trash can. Take that home, Joe thought, how was anyone going to understand that? He could see himself trying to explain it and he knew it wouldn't work. Just his partner looking up as she heard of it and then saying like her goddamn dumb phrase explained everything, 'That's the Apple for you, Joey.'

The Witness Man

While Clem ate his sardines and toast he also fed the cat, handing down crusts dipped in the oil at the bottom of the tin. 'You old thing,' he said, 'you'd scoff on until you burst, wouldn't you, eh?' He scraped at the corner of the tin with his fork and tipped the flakes of fish, as well as what oil remained, onto his own plate. Nan would have had something to say about that now, wouldn't she, using the same plate for himself and puss? The cat hummed like a small engine as it rubbed against his trousers, then raised itself to tap at the plate with its paw before the food reached the matting under the table. The elderly man ran his fingers in the thick fur at the animal's neck. There used to be a collar there but it had worn thin with the years and the randy old blighter had probably lost it in a fight. He might be twelve years old but he still came in some mornings with scratches on his face, or a chunk torn out of his ear. 'Real old soldier, aren't you?' Clem told him. The cat licked the oil from the plate and moved away from the man's hand. He's a cool one, Clem thought. Wouldn't miss me for a second as long as someone was giving him his tucker.

It amused him to think of how he sometimes waited for the cat to come in and the darned old thing didn't give a damn one way or the other about him. Nan used to tell him he was a softie about it, about cats, about everything. They almost rowed just after the war when her brother had put up with them for what at first was meant to be a fortnight but lengthened out into four months. 'You can't turf him out like that,' Clem said. 'We don't know what he's had to put up with, do we?' Dear old Nan, she couldn't see softness had nothing to do with it, it was what you owed a bloke. Yet if it was sentimental you were talking about, well Nan was the one there, all right. She'd cry up at the pictures at the Britannia on a Saturday night even when the story had a happy ending. Her favourites were the ones with soldiers saying goodbye to girls on bridges, or the women waiting and looking up while squadrons flew away above them, and you knew by the music that was that. And he'd say to Nan, 'It's only a picture, remember.' She would tuck her hand in the pocket of the heavy coat he used to wear then and he'd squeeze it tight in his own as they crossed at the Three Lamps then took their time walking down St Mary's Road. The light always seemed softer, the night more fresh or something, when you had just come out from the pictures. And walking round was safe as a church in those days. You'd see a group of young fellows walking towards you and you'd never think of crossing over, not even if they were smart-alecking about or drinking from bottles. And now here we were, Clem thought, no wars or anything to set people off, and you thought twice about going up the road the moment it was dark. The other day he heard two women talking about it on the steps of the Leys Institute. One of them was saying, 'His head was caved in like a pumpkin or something.'

'They must have been after his money, were they?'

'Like hell they were. It was just for the fun of it.'

Clem picked up the plate and ran it under the hot tap. He put out his hand to stroke the cat again but the old beggar raised itself from the chair it was lying on, and hopped down to avoid him. 'All right,' Clem told it, 'I'm not going to maul you.' He opened the door and stood there above the cat for a moment, looking across the small sloping lawn with its one tree, and on down the sharp fall of the street towards the motorway, the sea, the arc of the harbour bridge. Must be getting on for twenty years since that was built, mustn't it? Since he and Nan used to sit out here in the late afternoons. They had watched the whole thing, from when the bulldozers first came in and started ripping up the beach beneath the park until the two steel arms narrowed the space between them, and at last they met like that, in that arch he liked to look at, the lovely easy line that took the traffic up and flowed it down the other side. And across the grey web of the bridge he could still make out the Chelsea sugar works, his eyes weren't doing too bad were they? Before the bridge was even talked about Nan needed her glasses to make things out on the other side. He looked across now to the clutter of buildings against the blue bush on the hill around them. He wouldn't mind a tanner for every time he'd crossed that stretch of water.

The first day on the job over there one of the lads called him colonel because of his neat clipped moustache. The name had stuck with him, right until he retired. He never let on that it covered a scar from when he was a boy, from the day the old man pushed him out of the way in the shop and he'd caught his face on an opened biscuit tin.

'Here's the colonel,' one of them called out when he came into the lunchroom. 'Left the bloody horse outside, have we?' The clerks weren't the most popular blokes at the best of times, but Clem made out all right. The thing was you didn't try to have them on in return, that was the answer. Come at that boy and you were a goner. They'd never let up if they got a rise out of you. There was one bloke there, for instance, he used to read the Bible at lunchtime and he would answer them with quotes, this mild almost silly smile on his face even when they asked him which way the missus liked it, talked to him like that. Or another one, an Italian, they never gave him a break. So when Clem had first turned up they naturally worked on him for a bit and then they let up, there wasn't enough sport in it. 'Once they know they can't get at you the penny drops soon enough.' He had explained that to Nan soon after he started there, when someone had filled with sugar the leather bag that he carried his lunch and the odd book in. She was in tears about the mess it made and he had tried to tell her, 'Look, they're always doing someone over. Don't create about it and they'll lay off.'

'They sound like animals,' Nan said.

'They're no worse than anywhere else,' Clem defended them.

Funny how those days came back to him more strongly since the trouble began. It had stirred the past up, Clem thought, like shoving a stick into a swarm of bees. When he looked across now to the distant works he could smell again the hot sweetness he took months to get used to; and the odour of the sea, when he had leaned over the side of the ferry and picked out their house, and Nan was a speck on the veranda with a tea towel waving in her hand. Even the smell of their bedroom—that came back too some of these nights, Nan's own smell and her way of clutching at his shoulder when they were man and wife together. As if I'm not a bit past that, Clem thought, as if with his dicey ticker and all he shouldn't be taking life pretty quietly, instead of waking with the old memories disturbing him. Then thinking of that led him on to other things and sometimes it was hours before he slept again, the old sadnesses about Nan's illness and even years before that, when they still thought they might have a family.

The cat had returned from scratching beneath the tree. 'We can't do much about it now, eh boy?' Clem said. 'Just two old cobbers getting along quite nicely.' This time the cat allowed Clem to finger the deep soft fur of his chest. Right under the doubled front leg he could feel the cat's heart going nineteen to the dozen, although the blighter just lay there, rolling on its side.

Clem hadn't spoken to a policeman since before the war. The last time was at a safety zone in Queen Street, the night the Labour Party won its second election. Earlier that night he and Nan were sitting over their tea, listening to the wireless and talking about how it had been only ten years ago say, what a different world it was now. The way Nan had to call people Sir or Madam when she opened the door of the house in Mountain Road. The retired dentist she worked for gave her a fiver at Christmas and a glass of sherry and then got her against the fireplace, his hand trying to go up under her dress and even while he was doing that Nan was saying Sir to him. 'Don't be silly, sir,' she kept telling him. She knew if she lost that job there wouldn't be another and Clem had been laid off only a few weeks before. She hadn't mentioned it to him for another two years, until he was working again and she was off sick herself, sick for the first time. She was sitting up in bed reading the paper and she saw the name of the people she used to work for.

'See he's dead,' Nan said.

'Someone we know?'

'That poor old sod who tried to handle me that Christmas.' She told Clem the story like it was a joke. At first he thought, By Christ, I wish he was still alive and I'd fix him all right. But then he was angry with Nan. She said, 'Oh, don't go on about it. I hated it more than anything in my life.'

'But you felt sorry for him didn't you?' Clem insisted.

Nan had shrugged at him as if it didn't matter. 'Well I suppose I did.' And that was in Clem's mind as they sat there the night of the election. It had been raining earlier and the earth outside the opened window smelt alive and wet. The leaves of the lemon tree near the clothesline glittered when he moved the curtain back and looked out at the yard. He was thinking of Nan pushed up against the carved mantelpiece she had told him about, that the old bitch at the house used to make her clean with a special tiny brush. Well the bugger was dead now and he supposed it didn't matter. But he thought of how he had got away with it because of his money and how Nan used to get up early and walk to Epsom sometimes before the first tram, to be there when they had special visitors staying and they wanted their breakfast early. He had looked out at the November sky above the house next door. 'By God they'll never come at that again,' Clem said.

Why didn't they walk down town? Nan asked him. They might as well get the excitement of it when Savage got back in. Everybody said 'Savage' in Ponsonby, rather than 'Labour', because you were talking about the same thing, about the ordinary people who wouldn't be kicked round any more, about better things than money to judge life by. Clem had never been that shook on crowds yet he didn't want to miss this one. He was glad Nan had suggested it. So they walked from their cottage on the corner to the end of the convent grounds, then down the little lane to Jacob's Ladder. 'Who on earth had called it that?' Nan used to say. And Clem would tell her, 'Those nuns, don't you reckon?' They owned half the land between here and the Lamps, they gave the streets those saints' names and the Bishop's Palace still rose up among the workers' houses like something in a history book, turret and all. Anyway, it seemed a good name for that long flight of steps. There were a hundred of them, he supposed, dropping steeply down, close to the face of the yellowish clay cliff. At the bottom you could pick your way round the rocks or you could walk the other way, to the broad park with the tall oaks all round it. And fifteen minutes after that you were in the middle of the city. 'It's mad this, you know,' he said to Nan. They had turned to the left at the bottom as they always did, because Nan couldn't pass the water without dabbling in it.

'What is?' she said.

'Living like we do in the centre of Auckland nearly, the tram along the road and that, and here we go picking our way round rocks like there wasn't any other way.' Nan laughed and looked out over the harbour, across the stretch of mud where the tide had fallen back. 'I love that smell, don't you Clem?' She stood awkwardly on a slab of soft crumbly rock. He thought how she loved the beach yet she never looked quite at home away from streets and kitchens and things, she looked as though she would lose her balance any minute and tumble forward. But God she looked lovely standing there all the same. She wore her coat with the fringe of imitation fur at the cuffs and a hat that came right down over her ears. It was nearly dark by now and he looked at her raised above the little beach, the lights over the other side twinkling away behind her, across the water that was now lighter for some reason than the sky. 'Come on,' he said. They had gone across the park with the leaves freshly out on those great trees and the racket from the birds, a city of birds just settling down. And funnily enough Clem had forgotten the rest, wasn't that just the oddest thing? Not a thing about the crowd in front of the newspaper office or the cheering when the results went up like the results on a totalisator or the noise when they saw how they had put Savage back with the biggest lead in the country. He had forgotten those things although he had talked about them enough and not so long ago there was a display of pictures of that night up at the Institute. The pictures were in a glass case and there were political books with their pages held back like birds' wings and Clem had thought, Well it's just about like that now, it's all pretty near museum stuff for what it matters any more. He had watched while a couple of young women came up and glanced at the photos then turned away, their faces as blank as though they had looked at a wall. And the once or twice he had talked about those days to clever young people he had felt it was lost nearly as much as it was with those two women. 'You must remember something about that night, you must have sensed its significance?' one of them had pressed. He had sat there in his grubby enough clothes for a clever young bloke.

He had a notebook on his knee and it was like Clem had to answer charges. 'Well I don't,' Clem had said, 'I don't remember a thing, I wish I could help you some more.' He was blowed if he was going to say about Nan there standing on the rock when the sky was almost dark but the sea was silvery like an old mirror, or about the poor devil they'd seen after all the excitement was over outside the *Star* office, and they came on this other crowd gathering round the safety zone. He and Nan were suddenly among the closest to the low concrete platform. A tram had stopped halfway across the intersecting streets and they saw the conductor jump down, his bag jolting in front of him and the loose change jangling as he jumped. The conductor ran back towards them and picked up something from beside the shining grooves of the rails. At the same moment, he and Nan had noticed the well-dressed man who was sitting on the safety zone, one leg across the other, his knee supporting the ankle that he held in both hands. When the conductor stooped down he picked up a boot with a foot inside it. He carried the boot in both his own hands and knelt down beside the man, as though he were a salesman showing it to a customer. The man looked at him without speaking. Clem remembered how there was no expression of pain on the youngish, surprised face. Then someone broke from the crowd of watchers and started shouting, 'Get the ambulance, will you.' A woman screamed and Nan had pressed against him, her hand holding onto his. And before two policemen came running and thrusting through the crowd Clem watched the black stain spreading on the knee of the man's grey flannel trousers. With a kind of careful modesty the man's efforts now seemed to be to protect his wound from those who watched him. Both his hands were cupped over his ankle, he hardly moved his head when the conductor put the foot beside him on the platform. Clem heard the conductor say, 'I don't know what the hell

I'm supposed to do.' But he kept kneeling beside the man and put his arm across his shoulders. Even as he watched Clem was thinking, Why do I notice such unimportant things when a man is bleeding to death? For he saw how the street lights shivered down the leather strap across the conductor's back and the way the boot was standing by itself, a flat lid of shadow across the top, and so highly polished there was a pip of light winking on its toe-cap.

That was when Clem had last spoken to a policeman. Because he and Nan were at the front of the crowd it was assumed that they had seen it all. 'But we didn't even notice the tram until it stopped,' he said. 'Until we saw the conductor getting off.'

'We'll still need your names,' the policeman said. That was a few minutes or so later, after the chap had been taken off in an ambulance and the driver had lifted up the foot and placed it inside, beside the stretcher, with a towel draped over it. That long ago and Clem had never really spoken to a cop since, not like that, not about questions and times and where exactly he stood. Now this young rooster who looked as if he still didn't know what a razor was had flicked his book open while they sat at the kitchen table. When this boy policeman said, 'Where would you like to begin then, eh?' he suddenly saw that other book opening, all those years ago, the hand slowly writing their address down while the crowd still milled round.

'I'd better begin when the girl first went past me,' Clem said. 'Is that the bit you want to know about?'

The policeman said, 'I want to hear about all of it. Sooner or later it'll have to come out in court, won't it?'

They asked him the same questions over and over. How could he be certain about the time? Surely his sight must be extraordinary for an elderly gentleman? And his observation, too. Wasn't that out of the ordinary?

'I can't say what ordinary is,' Clem said. 'I can only talk about what I saw for myself. I've always had good eyesight so I just sort of take things in.'

'You see what a perceptive witness we're dealing with, your honour,' the police lawyer said when the business had got that far, when Clem stood with both his hands resting on the polished wooden ledge in front of him. He felt that the man didn't like him, it was not just a matter of doing his job. He wanted to trap him somehow, he was trying to say one way and then another that because Clem was old they could hardly expect him to get things correct. He asked him questions about what work he had done before he retired, then he made it all seem so unimportant, being a tally clerk for most of his life, working in the Corso store for the last few years. Clem was annoyed with himself when he said, 'My wife was very ill for a long time then. I had to get a job where I could come and go more easily.' The lawyer just looked at him when he said that and he was left standing there, as though he had said something foolish. Clem had raised his hand and passed it across his neatly clipped moustache and a voice from beneath him told him he could step down. As he turned and left the box he knew he was right about it, knew in the way you sometimes do by intuition, that the lawyer had disliked him because of his moustache, because of his careful answers. He wasn't dumb and senile the way the lawyer wanted him to be, that was what the pleased-with-himself bastard had been hinting at, wasn't it, with his shrugs and hitching at the folds of his gown?

Why on earth would he be inaccurate about it? Clem thought. It wasn't properly dark anyway, there were lights halfway up the steps as well as directly above where he had been standing. There was nothing so extraordinary about noticing two figures who stood at one of the landings halfway down, a man and a woman arguing together. He had seen the man's high fuzzed hair and he had thought why do girls go round with them in the first place? He had never seen what men saw in dark women either, all that nonsense you used to hear after the war from blokes who had been up in the islands or over in Egypt or wherever, and they'd say you couldn't beat them, there wasn't a woman back home who could touch them when it came to the dinkum thing. Nan laughed when they spoke about it, there was nothing he couldn't talk to her about then. 'I bet the Japs'd be saying the same things about us, if they'd ever got here,' she said. 'You don't have to know much about men to know that one, Clem.' The dark man had put out his hand and rested it on the girl's arm. Her head tilted back as though she was trying to look straight up at the stars, because Clem saw the whiteness of her throat before she tried to break free from the man who held her by the wrist, who tried to move towards and over her. She strained away from him and was drawn back again. Clem saw the girl's own hand come up slowly as if she intended stroking the man's face. Then he heard the man call out, he shouted at her obscenely as she lunged away from him, falling against the steps as he freed her wrist. She scrambled up and then began scaling the steps to where Clem stood back against the railing at the top to let her pass. Her face was raised towards him. When she saw him she stopped running and walked past him at a normal pace. ('How do you know what a normal pace is for a young lady?' the lawyer smiled.) She was breathing heavily and her eyes turned again to look at him, but she said nothing as she went by. When she was further along the alley towards the street she began to run again, a clopping awkward run, her wooden-heeled shoes loud against the surface of the path.

You're quite sure she didn't speak to you? both the lawyers in due course would ask him, as the policeman had the next morning when Clem answered the knock on the glass panel in the front door. *What did you see?* I saw a dark man about thirty talking to a young woman who was twenty say, or twenty-five. *How long did you watch them?* It wasn't so much watching as that they just stayed halfway down the steps while I was standing at the top. It is where I stand most evenings if the weather's fine. I like the view from there over the yacht harbour and I used to stand there with my wife. *Would you say you saw anything unusual occur?* I saw a man and a girl talking and then arguing, I saw them struggle with each other for a little and move as if to make up and then the woman must have scarred the man's face, although at the time I thought she was touching his face and not scratching it. I just saw what men and women have been doing for ever, I suppose. The lawyer turned and smiled at the jury when he said that too. And the questioning went on and on, over and over. *You didn't realise something more serious was taking place?* I thought both the man and the girl were serious. *We mean did you realise it was something criminal?* No, Clem said to the policeman, No sir, to both the lawyers who asked him that as well. And when they asked him what did he notice about the girl he said he noticed she ran up the steps, he guessed she simply wanted to get away from the man. The man called her bitch several times as she ran away from him. He continued to shout words of that kind and probably in another language also, even after she had crossed the road and was gone. She wore something, a medallion or a cross or a locket, around her throat. It glinted in the light and it jumped up and down in front of her as she ran. Clem went over most of what he had said as he sat after his tea, and thought about the court. It was all so clear in his mind but he hadn't been able to get the feel of it through, had he? Not so they saw it as he did. She had simply run away from the man and there was no terror in it, as the smart lawyer wanted him to agree, no fear nor panic as she ran up the steps, her breasts moving inside the tight jersey thing she was wearing, and the chain rose and fell at every step she took. *She looked at the witness?* Not directly, no. But her eyes sort of slid across, they were shining but there were no tears either, that was another thing the lawyer had wanted him to say. She was no more than a few feet from him, how could he be wrong? The down on her neck beneath the close-cropped hair was touched with light, he could see that even, that's how close he was. She couldn't have been crying without his noticing it. Because later it was so obvious the man was.

But you didn't wait for the accused to walk up the steps? I was back near the wall where the convent playing courts are, when I heard the man behind me. He was wearing sandshoes so I didn't know until he was nearly right beside me. Then when I turned I looked straight into his face. No, he did not speak to me, no, I don't think he even saw me. And the lawyer said to him then, You thought? Shall we confine ourselves to what you *know*? So Clem had said nothing. He felt his hands slip against the wooden edge of the witness box and the flush, the warmth, rise at the back of his neck. He is wanting me to lose the thread of what I have to say, he is making me seem an old man who cannot remember what he has seen.

There was no way of telling the court so they might see it as clearly as he had himself, the broad dark face with tears streaming across it, glazing in the light from the lamp-post on the other side of the street. Not that, nor the smear of sweat and tears and snot that spread on his upper lip and at the corners of his nose, the three seeping lines dragged across one cheek by the girl's scarlet nails. For they were scarlet when he looked at her hands in court, when he heard her say that she marked the man in self-defence. 'It's when I scratched him like that he let me go. Up till then he was saying he would do it again. He would drag me back to the side of the steps where he had done it before.' The court was shown a grey plastic raincoat the accused had been carrying when he passed Clem, although the older man did not remember seeing it.

This, the lawyer said. He held up the coat for them to see. It was creased and smeared with mud, and the prosecutor asked might he draw their attention to certain other stains?

Clem's confusion grew as the day moved on, as he heard others stand in the box and the judge warn them to take their words and weigh them, and for a moment he saw that too in his mind, the ancient image of scales in perfect balance, then one pan tipping slightly, those could be his words that made it tip. He looked carefully at the girl when her own turn came to be questioned. She answered very clearly in a voice he nevertheless leaned forward to hear. And then the man. He spoke so quietly Clem missed some of what was said. Twice the judge halted him to say that he must speak up. The second time he instructed him to look up as well, there was no point mumbling down at his chest, the court was over here. There was another Islander who stood not far from him, who sometimes translated phrases for him when he was not sure of what was asked. And the translator spoke to the court when the man once answered at length in his own language. That was the one time he seemed confident. He raised his head and gestured with one hand, he turned to where the girl sat and turned again towards the judge, coming back to English as he said, 'You listen to him again.' He pointed to where Clem sat. 'You ask him, you ask the witness man.' The lawyer smiled and said, 'But we already have. Surely you must have heard him?' The man's face became passive again, he looked down at his hands, one laid across the other on the railing in front of him. *The jigsaw*, the lawyer said. He stood in front of the jury. *You must piece it together.*

So the court put together its picture. Its figures were the man and the girl who worked together in Fanshawe Street. They cleaned offices after most of the staff went home. They had worked together for three months, and sometimes, because they both lived in Ponsonby, they walked home together. The girl said, Well it was natural wasn't it, she felt safer when he walked with her. If she was by herself she would never think of taking that short cut up the steps, she would go home by bus. Her mother said, Yes, that was true. Her employer said she was a good worker, the lawyer read a letter that told how last year she gave a month of her time collecting for Telethon. And the girl herself then told them how once or twice after work the man had wanted to kiss her. The girl had laughed and told him don't be silly, he was married wasn't he? And then he had begun to get heavy.

Heavy? the judge queried. And she answered, 'Just pushing his luck a bit.'

That night, then? she was prompted. That night when they were on the asphalt pathway between the motorway and the steps, the man had dragged her from the path, between the clumps of toi-toi. The traffic sped past them twenty yards away and no one else had walked along the path. He had grabbed at her and struggled at her clothes. The girl told them in that same clear voice how he had put one foot behind her leg and forced her back onto the coat he threw down beneath them. And how could she call out when she knew no one was round? That he carried a knife? Then the court was shown that as well, a dull horn-handled pocket knife. *He carried this*, the lawyer said. He passed the knife to the foreman of the jury. Some of them touched its edge with their thumbs and turned it over in their palms before passing it on. But he had not taken it out, the other lawyer said, he had not even mentioned it. Ah, the smart one smiled. He hitched again at the shoulders of his gown and said, 'Ah, I doubt if one needs to remind a young woman about a knife when she is undergoing assault.' The girl spoke out at that, she said, 'He told me at work once he never went anywhere without his knife. He never knew when he would need it.' The man's own lawyer tried to answer. That could mean anything, he said.

'It could mean he liked peeling fruit?' the prosecutor said. In that stagey way of his he simply held the knife up again and for once he said nothing. And somewhere through it all—because he could not remember the day exactly, that was half the trouble, Clem thought—a doctor said there was no doubt what had taken place. There was bruising on the girl's wrist, and contusions on the leg Clem had seen knock against the steps. The doctor confirmed that the marks on the man's face were clearly from the girl's nails. Yes, he agreed, they were the kind of wound a woman might well inflict who was defending herself.

He was dog-tired after the day in court. He had not looked forward to it and then it was worse than any expectation. He now kept coming back to the one thought, that somehow he had let down the man who had passed him, who had never noticed him. And yet for God's sake he couldn't do much more, Clem told himself, there were all those others as well, they believed them and not me. Yet it was two people fighting in distress or regret or in anger after sex, it wasn't what the court believed. He remembered the sly movement of the girl's eyes as she saw and at once dismissed him at the top of the steps. Yet in court she was like a child almost, as she looked down when the doctor asked her questions, when she went back to sit beside her mother. While the man had looked like a liar or at least a fool when he took so long with his answers and refused to face directly at the court. His hands washed over each other while he was questioned, his shirt had been tucked up with the collar of his suit coat so that he looked untidy as well as dumb. He was like a man who wanted to say he was guilty, Clem thought, while the girl stood there well-dressed and confident, she was one of our own. Her mother held her hand much of the time. And further back in the court among the Islanders there were two women in bright long dresses. One of them was elderly, her tight springy hair changing colour, neither black nor reddish nor grey, so that it made Clem think it seemed singed. Beside her sat a much younger woman, perhaps her daughter. He watched that woman at the recesses during the day. When she stood with the group of dark men by the patch of lawn outside the courthouse there was such quietness about her. Then it came to him that she had the look of people who are balancing something, alert yet self-absorbed, while the older woman leaned against one of the men and cried. Her hair was smooth and drawn back with a clip at the side of her neck, then flowed out again across her shoulders. When she moved the light glanced off her hair and Clem wondered if she was the man's wife. He wanted to go and say to her, I've told the truth even if it's not enough, even if he made love to her it was only that, it wasn't more than that. The woman raised her eyes and looked at him and then looked past him.

That night before he slept Clem lay with the cat on his chest, his fingers moving in the soft fur. The animal's body vibrated with contentment. Clem was too tired to watch a programme he usually liked, too shot for anything. But next morning he awoke too early, and felt unwell. The unhappy time with Nan had kept returning to him in broken yet realistic dreams. There were those days again at her bedside when she would no longer speak to him, and the night not long before the end when she had turned, suddenly conscious and alert, watching him with her bright sunken eyes. She had said to him as he covered her thin speckled hand with his own, 'It doesn't matter in the long run you know.'

'Matter?' he had said.

'Whether we had those years or not.' And there was a pause then, he had leaned forward so his head was close against her own.

'Not mattered.' She spoke lucidly and quietly, and he had sat there at her bedside appalled at what she said. A nurse who was in the room said to him, a few minutes later, when Nan's eyes were closed, 'It's all confused with drugs. You mustn't think she knows.' The nurse even touched his shoulder, she was trying to cover up for the dreadful clarity of death. He sat on with his fingers meeting around Nan's wrist. He knew that what the nurse had said to comfort him was wrong. He knew Nan had never spoken so surely to him in all their lives together. And what held him then was *that* was her final truth, the fact he must sit and watch with until the machinery stopped. For that is what we are, he was thinking, we are machines for pain, for these last days of dissolution and denial, as though the sun had never shone on us, as though everything we ever took from music or family or God or whatever it might be, must now be paid for with words like that, the indignity of denying what we always loved.

He had sat on with her until she stirred and asked for water, which he gave her from a teaspoon. She then lay back and watched the corner of the room, and then her lids again were lowered. He had sat until an hour later when the nurse again had touched his arm and led him from the room, because in his thinking of Nan he had not noticed when she left. Then like anything else, as he liked to say, Clem adapted to the silent house, a new routine. There was then a life of shopping and library books, watching TV and taking walks. Once a week he had a meal at his sister's, he visited a friend at the hospice off Shelly Beach Road, he fed and talked with his cat. Those things too were mixed in his dreams, the night after the court. Then he watched the sky lighten, and from the greyness of the first light he saw the day pick out the gilt frame of Nan's old-fashioned mirror, the bright towel at the end of his bed. He closed his eyes again and this time he slept comfortably. When he woke for a second time his mind was calm. He thought without distress about the people he must face again in a few hours' time, the girl who he knew was lying and the Islander who was like a wild thing caught in a light too strong for it. It was so clear now that he thought of it. He would ask the Islander's lawyer to question him once more. If the lawyer drew him out, that was the thing, the way you saw them doing it all the time on TV. Then that dark young woman in the long coloured dress, he would watch her face when it began to dawn on all of them in the courtroom that the man had told the truth, and that it was Clem who made them believe it. If he could only watch that.

How odd it all is, Clem kept thinking as he moved about the kitchen, tidying up after his cup of tea and his piece of toast and his glass of Ribena. Odd how our moods can change even at my age, how much in these past couple of weeks I have passed through, feared, remembered, been ashamed of . . . He shaved and looked at himself in the bathroom mirror. He snipped at two loose hairs at the side of his neat moustache. The scissors were Nan's, something she had kept from her girlhood, from the years before they had met. There was a paua-shell inlay along the flattened grips for your fingers. Clem tilted the scissors for a moment and watched how the iridescent greens and blues ran against each other, merged into a kind of soft remote fire below the smooth surface of the shell. He snipped again at hair growing from his ears. You had to watch yourself all right, you could see it with some of those elderly ones he spoke to up at the library or swapped a few words with in the shops. Suddenly you noticed how they had let themselves go, there were stains on their cardigans or they weren't properly buttoned, and there were others even worse, the ones people moved away from. As long as you watched yourself, Clem thought, you were probably all right.

He was dressed and ready well ahead of time. He could stroll up to the bus stop and even walk round Queen Street for a bit, before he took a second bus to the courthouse. That hill was past him now, although he liked it as much as anything in Auckland. The big palms in the park, the clumps of flax-like leaves with the orange flaring blooms like flying birds, and further up those trees with the huge grey roots lying along the ground—he would come back that way this afternoon. Along past the university and the floral clock that used to have begonias set out to make the numerals, he wondered if it still had those? God, it wasn't so long ago either before the clock was even thought of, and he walked along there with Grandma. When he remembered that he could almost smell the warm fusty odour when the sun fell on her black skirt and he walked along beside her, his hand stretched up, clutching at her own. 'Don't snip your nails on my rings, love,' she used to tell him. And at the corner where once there was only rough grass he had stood looking up to a woman she spoke to, then at the great fat iron lady over there on her stand. She was as much the Queen of New Zealand as the Queen of England, didn't he know that? And the woman had given him a white lolly like a tiny satin cushion and asked him, 'There, won't you talk to me if I give you that?' And Grandma had puzzled him because he didn't have any money of his own and yet she said while she jiggled his arm, 'You'll get no change out of this one.' Clem enjoyed the walk up to the bus. After yesterday's fleeting patches of sun, it was now clear and fine. From his gateway he looked down towards the water. The bridge and the yachts in the boat-harbour were softened by a skein of mist. But up here one was above it. Mornings like this he used to lean on the rail of the ferry and watch the cliffs and the houses slide past. Days like this the colours seemed more vivid, even the brick sugar works lifted up its yellow walls like—well, something more than you expected, somehow, and the sheet of water between the ferry and the approaching wharf was that deep green that slid off into blues, tilting and shimmering like those handles on the scissors.

Groups of girls from the convent passed him. They walked properly like young ladies and there was no swinging their bags about and hollering to one another the way you'd see with some of those other kids up on the main road. He liked it that the older ones wore gloves when they walked past his house on Sundays. If he was on the veranda some of them would look up and say Good morning to him. Some of them made him think of horses, or of foals, rather, that long-legged grace a few of them had. He began to walk up the road and was caught up briefly in their current of youth and litheness, the sudden breaking of laughter from a group on the other side of the road. And then he knew there was a grey car slowly following him, drawing in towards the kerb. It stopped when the policeman caught his eye. It was the same young chap who had come that morning several weeks ago and questioned him for the first time. Only then he had worn his cap down over his eyes, and now he sat with his blond hair combed high, a kind of puff above his forehead. He beckoned Clem over as he opened the door and stepped out. Clem thought they must be giving him a ride to court for some reason. The policeman nodded up past the library to the main road. 'Got you just in time, eh? Saved you a trip.' He spoke while the old man watched his mouth so closely that he saw the way one of his bottom front teeth slightly tilted back, out of kilter with the rest, and there was the grey filling he could see in another tooth further back. The policeman said again, 'Saved you the trip.' He touched the sides of his tie, carefully. 'Our rapist did himself in.'

When Clem said nothing the young man explained it again. 'Cut his wrists,' he said. He moved the side of one hand against his other wrist. 'Had this razorblade tucked somewhere and that was that.'

'Last night?' Clem heard himself ask.

'Last night, early this morning. There wasn't a chance

when they found him anyway.' Then the policeman gave this kind of laugh, his breath caught in as though he were going to cough. 'Shows he must have done it all right. It's one way out of facing it.' And now Clem was looking at the shining metal number on the uniformed shoulder and the slight golden growth of beard along the man's jaw-line. The man must be finishing work, Clem thought, he can't just be starting or he'd have shaved. Then the policeman rested his hand for a moment on Clem's shoulder. 'Don't you think about it any more, Pop. Nothing we could have done.' He stooped back into the car and placed his cap on his head. He glanced up for a second into the rear-vision mirror and made sure the cap sat straight. 'Right,' he said to the driver. As the car edged from the side of the footpath he spoke again, leaning from the lowered window. 'Not to worry now, OK Pop?'

'No,' Clem was saying. 'I won't.' He had no idea why he said it, or why he repeated it when the car had gone. A woman going towards the shops saw him speaking to himself and looked away from him. He continued to walk up the road, up the little distance to the post office and the green slatted seats near the taxi rank. The first time he knew Nan was crook was when she had said, 'I'll have to sit here for a minute, Clem.' It was pension day and they had just left the post office. And now Clem sat there again and looked past the brown iron railings at the top of the men's public lavatory and across to the corner opposite, to the Islanders near that travel shop that advertised Pacific flights. One of the men wore a deep collar of flowers round his neck. There was a woman with them too, he could see her mouth open from here while she laughed and for a second rested her arm against the shoulder of one of the men. Cut his wrists, the policeman had said. He had moved his pale hand like that, like a saw, against his own wrist. The blood and snot and tears on the man's face running up the steps and passing him under the light at the end of the street, and now this, that movement at his wrists—it's as if there was no time between that pain and then this, Clem thought, that man breathless and crying because of the girl, waiting in his cell, taking the blade from where it was hidden. And he must have been thinking of her when he did that too, and of the woman with the face that looked like it was carved, the one stepping onto the grass outside the court, turning from the men, the bright patterned skirt pulling tight against her body. His wrists and that would mean waiting too, Clem had read once how many minutes. And in the dark he supposed he would only feel his bleeding, it would have no colour. Does a man keep his eyes say on a light outside a window, on a corner of a room, until these things ebb, until they waver maybe, waver as though they are dipped in water? Or lie with his eyes closed so that the last thing is not the ordinary things, the table, the chairs, but the last thing you decide on to fill your mind, the last gift to oneself? Can one bring that off, Clem thought. And he said aloud as though he was at home and not where people moved close to him, up and down the steps of the post office, 'I want to know that. I've got to know it.'

The Professional

I decided pretty early on that if the only way you can survive this tangle we call 'life' is by telling lies, then you can't be too careful about the lies you're going to tell. Before I was ten it occurred to me that the kids who were great liars, who were caught and thrashed and stood in corners were the lesser brotherhood, they were bad liars. They were fabulists, fantasists, they in fact wanted a different world to the one they existed in. They wanted a lie to be like a cowboy film that they suddenly lived in, as if their doctoring truth would set them on the dappled horse, make the pearl-handled guns blaze in their hands. They are the ones who never knew what the true point of lying was—that its gift is balance. It is carrying across a room a glass with the water not only to the brim, but a little above the brim, while everyone expects it to spill. A lie is that meniscus. It's the arc where you control the appearance of things.

Let me start with a story.

Zeta Adams was a girl in my class at primary school. She was at least a foot taller than any other girl, and her face was nearly flat. I mean her chin was level, exactly, with her forehead, and her broad nose rose only slightly from the plane of her face. Freckles crowded on its bridge then spread out more sparsely across her cheeks. She had a younger brother called Leo in another classroom. He used to foul himself occasionally, and his sister would be sent for. It was a kind of sport for the rest of us, when the crisis arose, to line up along the windows of the standard four classroom, above the school hall, and look down on the pair of them. Tall Zeta, her legs shapeless and dead white beneath the gymfrock which she wore without the plaited gold girdle that the girls were supposed to wear; and beside her, holding her hand, her young brother walking awkwardly, comically, towards the school lavatories, where one supposed the crisis somehow would be attended to. When she came back to class she would grin at the calls that went up. If she was provoked too far, she would pick up a book, an inkwell, a pencil case, and heave it towards whatever angered her.

Of course, Zeta was several other things besides her brother's keeper, and as tall as a grown-up. She was also dumb, and fairly dirty, and the skin on her neck tended to flake. Anyone who sat next to her moved over towards the wall and called out, 'Snow storm. Watch it!' She was always worth provoking because her temper could run to teachers quite as much as to her fellow pupils. Once she threatened to jump out of the window, to leap twenty feet to the asphalt playground beneath, if the bitch of a teacher, as she called out, took another step towards her. And so she was sat finally by me.

I was the smallest, and the cleverest, and perhaps the best-behaved in the class. I think the teacher thought I was the last chance of shaming her into some kind of couthness. Zeta took her books, and a ruler with the figures almost totally hidden beneath layers of red ink, and shifted in next to me. I made a point of helping her, which no one else would do, and I believe that marginally her pages of grubby confused schoolwork improved. I told her what the simple words were that she baulked at, and once when the message came through from the other block of classrooms that Leo needed his sister, I offered to go with her. The teacher insisted it wasn't necessary, there was no reason at all, she said, why other people should be roped into a family concern. So Zeta once again walked from the classroom, her broad face silly and flushed with the attention. A few minutes later we looked down on the pair of them, Leo bow-legged, clutching his sister's hand. But she had heard my offer to go with her, and from then she was as attentive to me as a pet dog. She would have torn anyone apart had I sooled her onto them. And knowing she was at heel like that pleased me, I suppose, more than actually using her. The less she could do for me, the more she wanted to do. A few times she picked up imaginary slights, and jumped to defend me. She would stand between me and the supposed enemy, a wall of defensive and stupid flesh. 'Leave them, Zeta,' I would order her. And as the minister who used to talk to us about religion recently had gone over Easter week with us, and explained that strange part of the story where Peter cut off the soldier's ear, and Christ joined it on again, even though that soldier may have been the very one who scourged him a few hours later, I felt a sense of virtue when I restrained her.

There's nothing more interesting to say about Zeta Adams once those few facts are told. The point of her story is that about six weeks after she became devoted to me, I stole a green propelling pencil from Irene Duffy. It was a present from her aunt who had travelled round the world, the kind of souvenir that could be bought for a dollar, but was a thing of exotic beauty to the whole class. There were tiny holes near the top, and when you held these close to your eye, and turned towards the light, you saw St Mark's Square in one, and the Houses of Parliament in another, and in the third an avenue in Paris, stretching on and on, trees in leaf along its sides, a great stone arch in the distance. I had never coveted a thing so much. I thought of it when I was at home, and walking to school, and years later when I first saw those places for myself, there was an excitement that went back to Irene Duffy's pencil, held up against the light. After a week, when its glamour was wearing thin for everyone else, I saw it lying on her desk while the class was at the windows, watching a truck dumping earth for the new playground. In the same second I saw it, and knew no one else was looking, I took it in my hand and slipped it under my desk. I then joined the press of children at the window, watching the earth on the raised back of the truck begin to slip, slowly, then gather force, then rush in a brown rapid arc from the tray. The teacher said, 'Go back to your desks now,' and a second later the cry went up that Irene's pencil had disappeared. We all had to change rows and search each other's desks, and the pencil was found between Zeta's books and mine. There was confusion for the next few minutes, the class turning and pointing and accusing, the teacher calling for silence, demanding that Irene stop bawling, for goodness sake, the thing had been found, hadn't it? We were told to go back to our places, whoever was responsible would be properly punished. This long after, I don't remember what that was. What survives is the feeling I had while I stood and faced the teacher and said nothing for Zeta, nor against her. It was a feeling of great clarity, as I saw what power there was in saying nothing: a feeling that control and indifference are perhaps the same thing, as the plane of Zeta's face turned towards me, and I saw the afternoon light fall across her paleness, her eyes a little distended like an animal's in panic, her new and sudden confusion because she did not know whether I lied or not, whether I should be defended or not.

I could tell you three, four stories like that. One would be about my husband, a tall, gentle man who forty years ago had to hold onto the rail of a veranda to cover the trembling of his hands when I said to him, 'No, Desmond, I am sure about it. I know it was from that weekend.' I was twenty-six, he was a year younger, we were on his uncle's farm and I didn't look up when I told him but wound a thread of clematis stalk, I remember, around my finger. 'Who else?' I asked him. 'Who else could it be?'

That would be one story, say.

Another could be about Desmond's friend, the partner in his firm, and the man he sailed with half the summer. He was a widower, and my lover. And Desmond asked me once if it was true, and I said, 'Ah, poor Tom. Why did he have to spread stories like that about us? Because our life is something he doesn't have?' There are one or two others. If I want an image for them it would be something like a boat running before a breeze on a splendid day. You move the tiller to make your course a little finer, you don't do it to overturn. You do it for the excitement of control.

The children come to visit me, my dark son, my fair daughter, my grandchildren who prop their children on the foot of my bed, and I pass the young ones the grapes they have really come to see me for. There is a girl like Desmond in early photos of him, who looks down and doesn't know what to say when I ask her does she like me best, or me and my big bowl of fruit together? And a boy, a little younger, who is my favourite, who tells me, 'Oh, you don't have to say you like one thing more just because you like something else as well, do you Gran?' The staff here tend to fuss me because I'm a 'good' patient. That means I'm not senile nor dirty nor complaining. I know there's not a thing, in the long run, that can alter things by a jot, so why perform about them? I've never been one to ask for that dappled horse, for that blazing pistol, so to speak. But there's a young man who used to call once a week, who now pops in every day because, as he says, he just happens to be passing. He puts his Bible on his knee and smiles at me, he works on the principle that a bald man couldn't sit with a wig salesman every single day and not hint at the little bag of samples, could he?

So I tell him, 'Yes, do come again,' and, 'It's very good of you to drop in.' And when he says a short prayer just before he goes, I close my eyes until it is over. One of these days we may catch each other in the right light, the way one had to turn Irene Duffy's pencil. If I'm that impressed again, if the trees look as leafy and green and the lagoon shines still just as brightly as it used to, then I may well want this little window to peer through too. I may want the young man to talk on about what he's waiting, of course, to tell me. Hold my hand, I may ask him, help me to cross the room without spilling a drop.

Dandy Edison for Lunch

You could tell the Edisons were somebody not simply because their name made you think of the old geezer in the encyclopaedia (and of course they said they were relatives) but because Dick who was the father wore a little RAF moustache. It was because of that everyone called him Dandy. There wasn't another man within ten streets who wasn't as clean shaven as a bread board. And by the telephone table in the Edisons' hallway—we called that bit at home the front passage-way—there was a set of Winston Churchill's war histories, with gold writing on their fat blue spines.

The mother was taller, paler, than anyone else's. She kept to herself, and every evening she walked up the road, and round the top of the park, leaning on her husband's arm. Dandy smiled if you spoke to him, but anything he disagreed with made his mouth purse up as though he'd tasted a bit of lemon. The neighbours liked to say he reeked of sarcasm. This was a phrase I waited to hear when they spoke about him. Two or three women would sit round the kitchen table and the Edisons would come up. Then I'd sit with my hands beneath my thighs, pressing them flat against the chair, and look from one face to another, waiting for it to surface. 'Sarcastic though,' one of them would say at last. Another of the women would turn her cup about on her saucer or give a little snort. 'Reeks of it,' she'd say.

There were two children. There was a boy called Davie who was my age, and a girl five years younger. Another thing the neighbours said was that Janice was the apple of her father's eye, he couldn't see past her. The family had shifted next door while we were all at primary school, and I remember Davie because of two things. One was when he came round to our back porch and waited for me to open the high lattice gate to let him in. I was playing with a cousin so I told him he could get back home, he could scram. Then he began to bawl. I had my arm raised up to the metal catch on my side of the gate and kept snipping it as though any moment I might let him in. So he waited there and when he bellowed through the squares of the lattice I saw his opened mouth, and a pink lolly resting on his tongue. I watched him take from his pocket a white paper bag with the top screwed tight. I knew then he had come over to share the bag with us and on the way across he must have put one in his mouth. He handed the bag through one of the gaps in the gate. But he said nothing and he kept up his crying and I watched the pink lolly with the spit welling round it. I kept saying, 'You'd better get out of here, hadn't you? You better get back home.'

The second time was down the end of their yard. There used to be a creek running there before the State houses were built, so the grass was lush and tall. Davie's father also had this vegetable garden that made my own father say, 'Can't that man think of bloody anything else?'

But there was this strip between the garden and the wire-netting fence where he let the grass grow.

'What's he do that for?' I asked Davie.

'He likes the look of it. He likes the colour and the way the wind moves it. Something like that.' So we used to sit in the grass and talk, and one day I told him he would probably go to hell. The next day his mother came over to see mine because Davie had been too afraid to go to sleep the night before. He was scared of burning forever the way I described it to him, how the flames are never burned out and when it seemed like a million years had passed it was only beginning, it was as if it hadn't yet begun. The nuns shied off that kind of stuff by my time. I think I must have heard my father talking about what he had heard himself when he was a boy back home. But Mrs Edison stood there at the back door while my mother kept drying her hands on a tea towel.

'It's not what we believe,' Mrs Edison said. 'We'd rather not have your son instructing ours.'

Things were tense for a little, but then blew over. Dandy gave us a bag of nectarines and my father arranged to have firewood dropped off on the Edisons' front lawn. When the wood was piled there, the end-cuts and the scraps my father had spent ten minutes tossing from the back of his truck, Dandy walked down the road wearing his little cloth cap that would make anyone know he was an immigrant. He looked at the wood then said to Dad, 'All we need's Joan of Arc now, eh Jim?' That night none of us spoke while we had tea because the old man was so mad. Last time he'd do that sod a good turn, he kept saying.

'He mightn't have meant it,' my mother said. 'He needn't have been getting at Catholics.'

'Meant it!' Dad shouted. Then he began to cough and his breath caught and while my mother was holding a glass of water for him she said, 'I don't know why these things always have to come up.'

I remembered those things at my father's funeral as we came out of the church and I saw Dandy Edison standing at the back. I hadn't seen him for over twenty years. He was leaner, his hair was a touch greyer, that was about the only difference. And he had shaved his moustache. With my arm round my brother's shoulder and the coffin resting between us, I glanced up and he looked across at me, and then nodded as though we were passing on a street. I remembered in a kind of flash as they say, the pink lolly in the dribbling mouth, and the way Davie looked at me while I told him about hell, he couldn't go away from me although he had wanted to, he squatted in the long grass beside me while I gave him terror for the first time in his life. And what he had given to me was the fact that words hold power, that saying 'No' to someone, 'You can't come in,' saying, 'Yes, there's hell all right,' is to put him in a cage, to be outside it oneself and run a stick along the bars.

We shook hands outside the church. The undertaker moved behind us, taking the wreaths from the church porch and arranging them on top of the coffin. We talked about Dad and the old days in Westmere and I said why not come round for lunch one Saturday? There was more to talk about than we could get through then.

He said, 'Yes, that would be nice, sometime.' I told him, 'Let's make it definite then. Let's say Saturday week?'

Karen demanded, 'Why in hell did you ask him?'

I said, 'He's a decent old bloke. He's probably a bit lonely.'

'Oh Jesus. Aren't you just the little chap for sentiment the moment you start sniffing the old incense.'

'He's not a Catholic.'

'Who said he was?'

'He's an old man. He turned up at my father's funeral. What's the crime in asking him to lunch?'

'Why not feed the multitudes as well?' she asked. 'Cure a few lepers for afters?'

When we get this far I can tell precisely where my wife's next thrust is going to be. As predictably as sunrise she said, 'Why not throw in your bit about the stars turning with love? You know, your little swotted-up quote from that old dago? He was one of your boys.' She raised her hand and moved her fingers and rolled her eyes while she recited how divine love sets in motion such beautiful things. She had done languages at university and told me those lines before we were married. I had asked her to write them down for me. Then a year ago she found a letter of mine that said something almost the same, but to someone else. It was about love enduring anyway, about how it moves the spheres, etcetera. She had said, 'Nothing oils the odd screw like a bit of cultcha, eh?'

This is the last flourish that is supposed to take my breath away, the magician producing rabbits from his hat, a hippo from his arse, or whatever. I'm so used to it now I sit back and applaud when she brings it up. '*Very* good,' I congratulate her. 'Clever little read of a private letter and now all this as well.' As likely as not she'll go on then about secretaries without a brain in their heads and turning it on for the boss and I simply wait until she winds down, which she always does. She hasn't the stamina to be a total bitch. And it amuses me while she rages that I've never, but never been so bored with anyone in my life as I was with that little scrubber she is fuming about. *Raylene*, if you'd believe a human being could be called that. She was separated from her husband, she had blue eyes and curled blond hair like a child's doll, and she believed, as she put it, that true love was for keeps. She actually said so! (She went further down the line after I'd burned her off, down to one of the junior copywriters and she said exactly the same thing to him, after their first bash on the very same office couch. 'Love isn't just something you do for fun, is it?' she said. Ker-rist! I lushed up her beau with a touch of company Scotch and it was like hearing the same record played over again. I said to him, 'She's a cross-section of our market. Look at it that way and you might as well charge the company for overtime.' He was more pissed than I was and he thought he had to pay me a compliment in return. He said, 'If you'd written the press release for the first Easter there'd have been no doubting Thomas.' Then he said, 'Good tits though, eh?'

So Karen raised Raylene's ghost until she tired of it, then went back to Dandy. 'Why just him?' she demanded. 'We could always advertise. Old neighbours. Old school friends. The milkman when you were three. Your first Plunket nurse. Sister Mary Sanctuary Lamp from primer one. Get them all together for Kevin's M.S.P.'

She was sitting at her desk, working on the next morning's script. As she spoke she jabbed out the initials in the strong block lettering she uses these days. (Five years ago it was intertwining italics in purple ink.) I knew the game too well to ask her what she meant. 'What the hell's M.S.P.?' I was supposed to ask. It was an old trick on her broadcasts and her interviews. She would drop in some privately invented initials like that and throw someone completely. R.F. for Royal Family, that kind of brilliance. 'Top marks for S.E.,' she had complimented an ageing visiting actor after his third marriage.

'S.E.?' he stumbled.

And Karen said 'Sexual Endeavour' and brought down the studio audience. She was ticked off by the Chairman himself over that one. She said he had sat there in his dark suit with his silver boyish hair glinting in the subdued lighting and his hands joined in front of him, as though he intended inviting her to prayer, or was simply waiting for the dove to descend.

The trick became a hallmark that viewers would wait for. You would hear her latest *mot* repeated at parties or in the pub. Once one of our brown brothers with a beard and the compulsory whalebone pendant, who didn't know me from the Maori Queen, orated as we waited at a bus stop, 'Call this a bus service? F.A. of that round here, as Karen would say.' Baby, I thought, that's fame! But when she came at it domestically I didn't rise to cue. 'There, there,' I told her. 'Back to letters, is it? Whole words too big for little Karen's tongue, is that it?'

We're good at being vile to each other. Often our sniping works up into something quite demanding—a kicked door, a poster ripped from the wall. Once I threw a rug on the fire and once Karen took my John Lennon spectacles, when they were the in thing, and folded them round themselves so they looked like some kind of perverted insect. I describe her outbreaks to her as a kind of emotional menstruation. Once a month, every six weeks at the latest, we simply have to brawl. Then we make it up and ask people to dinner who may have thought we were unhappy simply because they watched us slang each other at their place a week or so before.

Naturally, then, there was no asking her, 'Now tell me what that means, Karen.' Instead, I walked across the room and shut a window. I explained over my shoulder, 'The neighbours' children, you know?' Then I went to the bar beneath her McCahon. (*Lord, what shall we do in this darkness?* and other sundry slogans in a white, black, rat-grey mix. If the government could only commission posters like that, I say to visitors, we'd go back to candles overnight. We wouldn't waste power, we'd pay not to use it.) I opened a bottle of Russian vodka a client had given me and added the requisites. 'Real drink for you?' I asked her. 'Or your usual sherry?'

But Karen wasn't losing a good line because of my distractions. 'Where were we?' she said. 'Yes. Kevin's M.S. bloody P. Menopausal Senility Party.'

'Confusing me with your hack politicians aren't you?' I said. 'Your geriatric stickmen?' I stepped aside when I saw her shadow raise its arm. The pad she heaved at me skidded across the top of the bar, then fell at the other side.

'N.F.M., that one,' I announced. 'Near Fuckin' Miss.'

'Oh, piss off,' she said. She ran her fingers back through her long hair, raising it like a heavy mane.

All this, then, because I had told her Dandy Edison was coming to lunch. When Karen asked me the night before he came if we had to wear our Salvation Army hats, or was it permissible to have our old men's dinner in mufti, I smiled at her and said, 'Quite fancy a bit in Sally gear, actually. Don't you?'

*

On the credit side of our marriage is that we look so good together. I have very pale skin and dark straight hair that flops forward a little over my forehead—the same side as Hitler's did, Karen likes to point out. In a dark suit, and when I move my pale hands as I speak, I'm sometimes rather taken myself when I catch a glimpse in a mirror, in a reflecting window. When I'm with Karen, who even in winter looks as though she has just come in from the sun, we're the kind of couple people like to fuss over. 'Let them,' I always tell her. They recognise her voice first, because a lot of them hear it every morning of the week. Then after the voice there's her teeth, her figure, her sense of fun—they can't resist her. She is good with men in much the same way as we say some children are good with pets. She doesn't know how *not* to be. She has also had surprisingly few lovers, although she likes giving the impression that she knows the score, has been around, roots like a rattlesnake—whatever your patois is.

Last year she was tied up (literally, one wonders?) with a senior politician whose motto, as I told her, was if it moves, screw it; if it doesn't, tax it. And when she tired of trampling him, or whatever their number was, she repented and confessed to me with a few genuine little tears. She told me as she knelt in front of me in a long frock, after a champagne supper we'd been to. We had come home early and lit a fire. She told me while the pine logs flared and her head rested against my knee, and we both sipped Scotch. It was pure *New Yorker*. (It actually came out later in one of my commercials. A similar fire, blond woman, dark man, crystal glasses, on a rather crappy brand of carpet we were putting across. 'I've a confession to make,' she says. 'So have I,' he answers. Then together, 'We both love it.' A bar or two of melting Mozart, and the voice-over declares, 'We sell it by the roll.' A bit *risqué*, a bit cheap even, but we got away with it. I expect by now half of Otara spills its Kentucky Fried over inferior shagpile, thanks to Karen's line.)

'Why are you telling me?' I asked her. 'I'd never have found out.'

'Because it was wrong,' Karen said.

'Silly, don't you mean?'

'No, wrong.' So I patted her head and was understanding about it. We were caring and forgiving because that, quite simply, was what the role asked for. That's a feeling I have about our best times together, when we have the odd weekend away or we stroll through the Domain some quiet Sunday and I snap off a rhododendron and slip the stalk into her hair, it's as if we're watching a movie of ourselves being happy. Perhaps it's because when things go well between us it's like we've been scripted by a real pro. 'If life's not performance, then what is it?' I say some nights when we talk by ourselves, and I'm being what she calls especially H.P. (Heavy Philosophical). When we work as a team there's not much we're after that we don't get. It was teamwork for example that linked us up with California, the one LA–NZ connection that's not only viable but actually fully operative. We had already cut into the Sydney commercial market where they least expected it, you could hear the squealing from here. Then Hersch himself dropped down from LA and I told him, 'You'll only tell where the opposition is from the corpses before long, Herschy.' He's an overweight tit of the Hebrew persuasion who wears magenta sports jackets and calls the tune in half the advertising we have. My kind of confidence makes him smile right back to his gold-stopped molars. Then when Karen got him on her morning show he was chuffed as a haemophiliac with a foolproof razor. She took him to lunch and when she introduced him to people in the corridor outside the studio she began with, 'You'll have heard of Mr Hersch, of course?' Later in the year when we got the call to LA I think it was as much her efforts as mine. As I tell her, when we dance in step, kid, you've really got footwork. When we were over there

Herschy palmed us around like Beautiful People. (One night we drank with Jon Voight, among others, in the revolving bar of the Bonaventure. We saw the city sparkle out as far as your eye could reach. I remembered the nuns' story about J.C. up the mountain and Satan offering him the lot, I thought if it was anything like this and he didn't buy it, then they didn't have the right copywriter.) We picked up exclusive rights to one of their biggest cosmetic outlets. Back home I did a male deodorant clip shot in the changing rooms at Eden Park, the first commercial from here ever to sell in California.

'It was that parcel of lovely bum-meat that did it. Don't get swelled-headed,' Karen reminds me. 'That and my boobs in Herschy's face in the lift.'

'It's your way with old men,' I told her.

So I thought now, even if Karen didn't care for Dandy, he would take a shine to her. He'd see I did all right for myself there.

I phoned Dandy and offered to drive him round, but he insisted, No, if a man was too old to travel, he was too old to arrive. He dropped these wise saws into his conversation like saccharine pills into a coffee cup. So he took a bus to the bottom of the hill, then walked up. When Karen opened the door he stood there with his cap held in his hands at fly level. He wore a wine-coloured shirt, a pearl-grey tie, and a cinnamon-coloured suit that was a little tight under his arms, a shade too loose at his waist. I thought he's had that handed down from someone.

I stood behind Karen and for a moment Dandy could see only my wife. He did this incline as though he was one of our Asian neighbours, a little bow because he was meeting a lady.

'Mr Edison, I presume?' Karen said.

'Do they still say that?' he asked her. 'Perhaps I'm not as old then as I thought.'

Karen turned to lead him in and I saw her eyebrows raised. I stepped forward and shook hands with him. I offered him a drink which of course he refused. This isn't going to be easy, Kevin lad, I told myself. Karen already had whipped off to the kitchen. I heard the blender suddenly burring, the clicking of plates.

'We'll have a look outside, shall we?' I proposed. 'Before the rain beats us to it?' There wasn't an earthly chance of rain, but one had to say something. I thought it was worth looking outside anyway, unless old Dandy's eyes were shot. The glimpse of sea we had down the end of the valley, the dip of the native trees beyond the edge of our section, there was nothing wrong with that, even if my old neighbour wasn't with it enough to admire how on one side our house hung out across the bank on poles. I mentioned the architect on the off-chance he may have heard of how class was actually spelled.

We had had the patio done a few weeks before. Karen dredged up some gifted little foreign chap from Parnell who worked wonders with old bricks. We had heard about a hall at a local convent that was going to be demolished, I was down there like one of my old aunts on Indulgence Day. I fed the good sisters the right line and next thing the yellow bricks were piled at the side of the house, at half the price I'd have got them anywhere else. ('You know I'm getting a bargain, now, don't you Sister?' The nun's lips did that classic convent moue. 'I'm sure you wouldn't offer us anything that wouldn't be a fair price, Mr Grant.') Once Karen's man got to work he chipped and fitted and buffed and we now had our own yellow brick road, as I tell her. I said that at the party we had to christen it and my senior partner did the whole bit, the Judy Garland routine I mean. 'He's pissed out of his tiny mind,' someone said. Anyway my partner did this take-off and all of us except my lady wife were in fits. Leary was so pleased with himself, the pathetic old bugger, so egged on by the clapping hands and the shouts from the rest of us under the fairy lights strung out between the trees, that he did this little dance where the bricks whirled into a circle. He made like he was going to undo his belt, to treat us to a down-trou, and someone shouted out, 'The Wizard of Ass.' Precisely where I stood now with solemn Dandy.

I said, 'We had a little party to launch it, a few weeks ago.' He kept up that smile which seems more for himself perhaps than for whoever he's talking to. I explained how by the end of summer we'd have a punga fence round the whole yard. Dandy was still looking down at the bricks. 'Made a nice job,' he told me.

'Come off it. You don't think I did it, do you?'

The old man tapped at the beautifully levelled bricks with his shoe. 'Pity,' he said. 'Do your own jobs like this and you get twice as much pleasure from it.' He walked across the lawn to examine the brickwork round the barbecue. He ran his palm along the sides. 'That's all right too. That's pretty good.'

Karen came and stood beside us for a moment. She said, 'I'll set the lunch out, shall I?' Then before she went in, while Dandy was still above the bricks as though he were looking like a detective for some kind of clue, she said in a whisper, 'Polonius Mark II, eh?'

'A thousand bucks in that lot there,' I said. 'Pay through the nose for anything like that these days.' He was now touching the metal shield at the back. He seemed not to believe things until he had touched them with his hands. I'd noticed that when he first arrived, when he stepped inside and one hand moved along the brocaded back of a chair. He'd never have recognised it for what it was, of course, a new Belgian weave Karen had picked up in Sydney. And he told me now, as he left the brickwork to face me, 'It'll last you out, Kevin.'

That's rich, I thought, I wouldn't go in for too much of that talk if I were you, old cock. But I laughed to jolly him along. 'Not like that fence in Westmere, then?' I meant the one my father had put up at the end of the yard. It was a bush-carpenter's shambles, bits of wire that sprang loose, uprights that leaned off-centre from the moment they were driven in. It was supposed to keep us in our own place, away from Dandy's nectarines, away from his lettuces where the ball kept falling every time we played cricket. There was a permanent sag in the wire where we balanced for a moment before leaping down to the other side. I brought the fence up now because I thought he'd like to be reminded of back there. (The line to play the oldies with is always the sentimental one.) I didn't tell him I drove down that way after Dad had died, the first time I'd gone back since we moved out. The State houses looked smaller, the streets drearier. The patch of park that used to be at the corner was gone, the big gum tree that stood at the end of the street and that I could see from my bedroom window, its grey strips of bark hanging down like unravelled bandages, that was gone too. It had grown at the end of Carpenters' section. The Carpenter girl had died of polio in the summer when we couldn't go back to school. I used to look at the tree in the night-time and it was the street's death tree, it was the closest I ever came I suppose to reverence. Of course it was bullshit, it was the dark regressive stuff our old mate Freud made light work of once and for all. But Christ, at the time I used to kneel on the bed and pull back the edge of the brown roller blind, and look at the spread arms, the tufts of foliage at the branches' ends. I could hear my parents talking in the kitchen and there was a bar of yellow light under my bedroom door. When someone moved in the kitchen the strip of light was broken. There was one night in February, a night when it was so hot that my father stood at the end of my bed in only his pyjama pants. I had woken up with pains in my legs and I had called out. My mother was crying and pretending not to, I knew they thought this was how it began with Doris Carpenter. Of course it was something else I had, I don't now remember what. But I told my father to make sure the sides of the blind were flat against the window. They thought my telling them that was some kind of fever, but it was the reality of the tree out there, dark against the sky. My father went in next door to the Edisons' and telephoned for a doctor. I heard his steps on the concrete path pass outside my window, and then his steps coming back. And now old Dandy was stepping across the patio and in the drift of my thinking, for the slightest fragment of time, his steps and my father's were the same.

He didn't answer me about the fence, so I presumed he hadn't heard. I stood closer to him, looking at the tuft of hairs that sprang from his ear, catching the light like a spray of fuse wire. I reminded him again because I thought at his age what else can there be except nostalgia? But he didn't rise to it. He turned quietly to look at the white-painted garden furniture, the hard lacy patterns in the cast iron.

'I think of those days quite a bit,' I told him. 'Isn't that curious? And the other families down the street, the Stoddarts, the Jeffreys, all that crowd.' I told him I'd seen one of the Jeffrey girls lately.

'Oh. Which one?'

'Valerie,' I said. I had seen her a month before in Queen Street. I was walking with one of the artistic design people from the office and I had turned almost full on towards him when I saw her coming. I didn't want her speaking to me, I didn't want her looking at me and perhaps not speaking either.

'She was the prettiest,' Dandy said. She had been tall as a girl, with lovely English skin. The sisters had long hair and a drunken old man who was mostly out of work. And their silence, that was it, their way of looking without answering back when most of our mothers thought of excuses why they couldn't play with us, had made them seem wild, defiant. They were the exotic ones among us. Davie Edison had crouched under the house with me one day, in the mixed odour of dry earth and firewood and a rotting canvas tent, and told me Valerie Jeffrey did.

'Did what?' I asked him.

'You know.' And in our newly learned jargon he told me she Father Uncle Cousin Kinged with the oldest of the Stoddarts, one of the other boys had told him down at the reef. The reef was the narrow strip of lava rock pushing out from the mangroves, across the shallows and the sometimes bitterly reeking mud where for some reason one always wanted to talk bad things, the territory of disorder and excitement behind the slope of houses, the tilt of streets, where the suburb leaned down towards the sea.

'His brother told me,' Davie repeated. 'Down the reef.' I thought of the two boys crouched and confiding while I waited for Dandy to speak, to step back towards me and to Karen who was at the opened doors. She watched him with arched amused eyebrows, tapping the front of her blouse just between her breasts, signalling me to note his jazzy tiepin with the red inset stone. I thought if you could only hit on some image to set people off as I had been, some slogan to dredge up instantly the old emotions, what you couldn't sell with that!

I now examined his old man's skin, that bloody awful pink tenderness around his eyes, the skin at his temples so thin you could see the soft blue branching of veins underneath. You're as good as dead when you're like that, I thought, your hands speckled and dry and already cold too, cold because I'd felt it when we had shaken hands, it's as though life is already drawing back. Then from my own little nostalgia gig I went into something darker, an unexpected anger with that careful old man who was now watching me. The feeling swept me so strongly that for several seconds I wasn't able to speak nor even hear him although I saw his prim mouth begin to move. At last I asked him, 'What? What are you saying?'

'I don't,' he said. He faced me with his bland level gaze as though I were under inspection. 'I don't think very much about them, those Westmere days.'

'I suppose a lot slips your mind,' I said. I knew that might sound offensive.

'No, you remember all right,' he corrected me. 'I mean you don't go out of your way to dwell on it.' Then he laughed, his new teeth grotesque in that dry, papery face. He put his fingers around my arm. We walked inside like that, pretty much as he led me round the side of the old house when Davie and I cut up his daughter's doll, and the sawdust guts spilled out on the apron of concrete near the underhouse door. He now surprised me by saying, 'Live in the past, Kevin, you're good as dead already.'

As we came inside he did an odd thing. I hadn't noticed that he had picked anything in the garden, but he now opened his hand, holding it out towards Karen. There was a twig that branched into two or three pinkish tips. I didn't even know we had something like that growing. But Karen took it from his hand and raised it to her face. 'Yes,' she said, smiling at him. 'Daphne.' Then she was talking to him about that, about how it must be one of the loveliest scents there was.

'And verbena,' Dandy said. 'Daphne and verbena.' Karen told him how she had loved it when she first found out what that kind of bush was called. 'I was reading this book of Greek stories, you know, myths and things? It was a book I thought I should hide from my mother anyway because it had photos of statues that showed ladies' bosies, you know that kind?' Dandy was laughing with her, enjoying her casting back to when she was a girl. 'Anyway it had this story in it about

Daphne. It was written in that stilted old style, *Apollo loved her, and as she would have none of him, pursued her.* I had only an inkling of what it was about, but once I knew she turned into a tree instead I thought well *anything* would have been better than that.'

'*Almost* anything,' Dandy wisecracked back at her.

'Exactly.' She was flirting with him now, she tapped her hand on his when she said that. I thought, Shit, you can't resist it, can you? See a corpse with a smile on it and you'd come on strong.

From then it might as well have been Karen who had lived next door to him when she was a kid. A couple of times I tried to bring the lunch back my way, he was eating my food after all, he was on a chair I'd paid for. When Karen went to bring the soufflé from the kitchen I said, 'Davie doing all right is he?'

'Still with Air New Zealand,' Dandy said. 'But I've told you that, you asked me earlier on.' He began to build a little tent from his table napkin and set it upright between his hands. He tapped at the side of it, balancing it, then took his hands away.

'Advertising doesn't have quite the same—well, the same thrills,' I tried to joke. 'I mean it has its moments but there's not the same glamour, is there, as flying those jets around?' I wanted him to say at least that we looked as if we were doing nicely too, to give some flicker that he saw you didn't buy furniture like ours in some bargain store in K Road, that the big picture with the writing on it probably cost more than he'd ever earned in a year at the Electricity Department. ('An inspector,' I'd explained to Karen when she asked what he used to do. 'Got trouble with your connections and old Dandy'd sort them out for you.') I knew even as I thought this that it was a bit vulgar, a bit downmarket. I don't mean that I wanted him to feel our gold, as my partner likes to say.

Not quite. But I wanted him to know we had taste, and that taste wasn't cheap; that our imported glass-topped tables and Swedish lamps and Karen's collection of paintings were a far cry from Taihau Crescent. I wondered what sort of stuff Davie had. I expected that for all his wings and his flying hours he had wooden salad tongs from Fiji and carved Singapore tables. I suppose I didn't give a stuff whether I was crude about it or not, I wanted Dandy Edison with his Churchill histories and his prissy voice to know that I wasn't playing in the backyard of a State house any longer, scoffing a bar of chocolate before my sister came home. Because he'd seen me do that, fuck him. He'd come round with a phone message in those days before we had a phone of our own, and seen me ferret off into the wash-house with my mouth crammed. He had pushed open the door and looked down at me with his high quizzical stare.

'Mrs Mississippi wants your mother to phone sometime.' I looked up from where I stood edged in against the curved concrete surround of the copper. I felt my cheeks bulged out and the heat of embarrassment prickling up from the neck of my shirt. 'It's important she knows the name,' he said. 'What is it?' I remember how I repeated it, breaking up the word into its slippery syllables. He told me, 'I need to know that you get it right.' So I had to say it to get rid of him.

'Mississippi,' I attempted. A dribble of chocolate saliva leaped in a dirty arc, I could feel the oozing at one corner of my mouth. Then Dandy laughed as he took a piece of paper from behind his back. 'Here, the number's on this.' The paper had some name on it as well, a name like our own, or like his, something as simple as that. I slammed the wash-house door and the tears danced in my eyes. I said whatever I could lay my tongue to.

I had that in mind now, watching the fastidious movement of his lips as he smiled at whatever Karen said, as he dabbed at his chin with the corner of the napkin he had unfolded from its temporary tent and laid again across his knees. They were onto cooking now, on how he managed by himself, the kind of dishes he found it most convenient to make. 'Time's never a factor you see,' he confided. 'I can take the whole afternoon preparing it, for all it matters.'

'More soufflé?' Karen was holding the dish in front of him, the server ready as though she were about to feed a child.

'No, I think I've had sufficient.'

'Go on,' she teased him. 'It'll build you up.'

'That's never worked before.' He raised both his arms from the table and his sleeves fell back. He showed her his skinny wrists, and the inch or two of thin forearm below his cuffs.

'But I love a challenge!' Karen opened her eyes wide so her eyelashes stood out like spokes, then they were goofing off together again, old mates, Jesus! I thought why push this little number any further, I've done my bit. I went and poured myself a decent-sized gin and clanked in ice from the fridge. Karen glanced across at me while she continued to dangle her geriatric fish (as I'd tell her later). Just to see if her lines still worked, was that it?

'Janice,' I interrupted when I returned to the table. They were talking about desserts by now, how to eat crap and save five dollars a year, that kind of recipe swapping.

'Guavas,' Dandy was telling her. 'So few people eat them and yet they're a joy. They're exactly that. A joy.'

'And the colour. That lovely deep pink.'

So I threw in, 'Janice.'

For once my spouse was startled at what I said. I had told her there was some kind of tragedy there somewhere, I wasn't sure of how the details went. But apparently no one ever spoke of it, it was something Dandy himself would never mention. So we wouldn't either, I had warned. Ask about Davie as much as you like, but leave Janice out of it. 'Oh,'

Karen had said before Dandy arrived, 'but that's the only bit I want to know.'

'You haven't mentioned Janice.' I stirred the ice about in the glass and smiled across at Karen, then at Dandy. 'Or have I missed it?' I waited for what she calls the N.U. on occasions like this, the Nasty Upshot.

'We're onto recipes, love,' Karen pointed out. There's nothing like a touch of affection to show when she's close to panic.

I continued to smile at them. I lifted the glass and tapped it against my teeth. 'Funny,' I said, 'I seem to have kept up with Davie's movements over the years, but not Janice's. I met one of the Jeffrey girls lately, I think I told you, and she seems to have got through her net too.'

Karen was driven back to asking gaily, 'Janice?'

'Kevin must have mentioned her,' Dandy said. He pushed his plate away from him slightly and laid his dry speckled hands side by side on the cloth. I noticed one of his nails was dark blue, as if it had been jammed. When he looked up he held Karen's eyes, not mine. 'She was my daughter, you probably know that much.' Then he said, 'She used to be a stripper.' Without moving his hands, and in a voice that might still have been talking of guavas, he told us that she took her clothes off first in Wellington, then in Christchurch, because it was the easiest way she could make money. From time to time he smiled slightly while he was talking, when he said, 'She was lazy, you see, but she was also intelligent. I mean she could see the moral objections someone like myself might raise, but she could also talk herself out of them.' Then again, after telling us she had crossed to Sydney, he explained, 'They seem to pay more there for the same thing.' He went on with her career, almost laboriously. Although she was lazy, he repeated, that didn't mean she wouldn't rather do something else than have men look at her. So she bought a massage parlour she called 'Tropic Palms', and then another that was already named when she bought it. Finally there was one that we would probably call V.I.P. It catered only for the rich and was named very simply 'Lolly'. 'And so she led a life of what we call vice. She told me her one weakness in the business she had chosen was sentimentality.'

'What did that mean?' Karen asked.

'I don't know the details.' But he told us other things about her. That she wrote to him often, for example, and that he always knew, more or less, what she was doing. They agreed not to let her mother in on it. 'She always thought Janice had some office job over there. She knew she was doing well.'

'Davie,' I said at last. 'What did Davie think?'

'Oh, he wouldn't speak to her. Not even about her. Did you think he would?' And again there was the slight smile, and the odd feeling he gave that for all his frankness what we were witnessing was only on the surface, some stirring of what went on far off. I felt I had been outmanoeuvred by the old man owning up that his daughter was some kind of seedy call girl. I could tell Karen was moved and that somehow Dandy was untouched, that saying all that filth about his own family seemed almost incidental to him, that because it was Janice it was somehow not so bad, was that it? I was unsure of everything about him. And then he was tapping the red stone in his tiepin and saying, 'She sent this over to me once. It's not imitation either.' He moved the pin slightly for our benefit, so the light streaming in from the window opposite him glanced across the stone. 'Ruby,' he said. Then the old bastard threw his trump card, the one he can never be forgiven for because he must have known all the time he was setting it up, that Karen would go down in front of it like some whore in front of a customer with a hundred bucks, oh mustn't he just. Because Karen already had an expression on her face that I had never seen, not simply shock nor surprise nor wonder. It was like the look on some of those old women who used to go up to St Joseph's when I was a kid, who knelt during the long hours of Exposition when the host was stuck up on the altar in a glass disc and from the edges of the disc gold spikes rayed out. It was like they were gazing into the centre of a dulled sun. And these old hags would stare on and on and the look on their faces was this crazy mix, as if they saw and yet were blind at the same time, that what they looked at was a kind of veil and what they sought was on the other side. It bewildered me that I'd ever think of Karen like that, that I'd put her in that same clutch of mutter and superstition. I sat now without speaking, without any of us in fact moving until Karen tapped his hand and said, 'Is she dead?' And Dandy said, 'Yes, of course.'

We gave him coffee and got rid of him just after three. I'd put away a few more gins and thank Christ we'd got off the morbid line, we'd left the late-lamented Janice stroking the koozers of eternity and the last half hour was Karen's usual fund of chat, travel and work and a touch of politics about which she knows B.A., by which I don't mean Big Amount. But the moment he was gone and I stood beside her and my hand moved across her arse she said simply, 'Don't,' and she went out into the yard. She opened the door to the garden shed and took out the shears. Then she attacked a hedge at one corner of the section, a shaggy mound of a thing that I'd been meaning to ring someone to come and trim for weeks. She was so inept she was comic. I thought, she'll be inside in ten minutes, she'll want me to put Band-Aids across her angry little blisters. I was wrong about that one too. I don't know how long she worked because when she came in I had nodded off, I was sitting in the La-Z-Boy chair with the headphones on, listening to the Who.

'Time to dress up,' she told me. 'Not that I feel much like party times.' But of course she managed. Her gay station manager announced half way through the night, 'Our Karen's nothing if not an old trouper.' He leaned within inches of my face to tell me, his breath rotten with halitosis. I know now why studio producers sit behind a pane of glass. And at midnight when we said we would have to go there were calls of 'Piker' and 'Off for a bit, eh?' and a general sigh of regret that I was depriving them of Life and Soul, as the fat hostess chided me.

'You'll survive without it,' I told her.

Karen put her head on my shoulder during the ride home. We covered the four or five miles without saying a word. Later when she leaned over me her hair fell across me in one broad brushing swathe, a kind of golden tent. It must have been all that old Westmere stuff being churned up earlier in the day, because I raised my hands to run them through her hair, I spread it to either side of us and said, 'Tabernaculum Dei.'

'Some of your old mick talk?' Karen teased. I lowered my hands from her hair and moved them to her tits.

'More a trade name than anything else.' Then I told her, 'Blame your visitor this afternoon.'

I felt her weight move across me, her nails run lightly across my neck. She said, 'Good old Dandy then.' Her hand stretched out and groped for the switch on the bedside lamp. Then it was dark as when we first pushed open the door to the Edisons' under-house in the summer evenings, when we'd hide from Janice, and Davie would tell me 'Shhh!' We'd crouch until we heard her walk past, then begin to talk about our secrets, about the Jeffrey girls and the Stoddart brothers and the things we heard down the reef, and sometimes Davie opened his hand and gave me a badge, or some stamps, or once, a foreign coin he had taken from his father's desk upstairs.

The Club

He is sixty-seven, which makes him perhaps the youngest person in the room. The trouble is he looks no more than in his late fifties. He feels that he is out of place. For when he enters the Club it seems to him that the large central room is full of old people. He is also very nervous. For a moment he remembers entering classrooms as a child, changing sheds on Saturday mornings when he played rugby as a boy. There was the same shyness as he feels now. It is as if all conversation stops, and all those eyes turn to take him in. He is the new boy. The new old man.

A woman whose teeth look to him as though they have been soaked in tea smiles and comes up to him. She says to him, So you're the gentleman who phoned? He tells her, Yes I am. She continues to smile at him and he feels obliged to add something else. He says, I mentioned I was recently bereaved. Then there is another woman beside the first. This one is taller, and smiles with her lips. She also holds out her hand, which he takes. She must be English, he thinks. This one holds his hand firmly. There are sessions she tells him on bereavement some Thursday afternoons. There is a minister and a psychologist who are quite informal. It's remarkable the way reservations fall away and people are willing to speak quite openly about their grief and just everyone benefits from it. That's the point of the whole thing. The woman said all this in so quiet a voice he had to lean forward to catch her words. He is close enough to tell that she smells of peppermint.

The first woman then says how she had occasion to benefit from those sessions over the last eighteen months. She shows her dark teeth. Say what you like, she says, a shoulder to cry on is half the battle. Only then did she say she was Mrs Weston, and the other woman was Mrs Boyer. But for the moment he must of course meet some of the others. If the Club wasn't social then it might as well be nothing, she says. She takes his arm and turns him towards three men who sit and watch him. He thinks of the picture that had been pinned to the kitchen wall for years. A picture by a Frenchman who made his paintings look like stained-glass windows. There were thick black lines of lead between his figures. That picture had been called *The Judges*, hadn't it? Lou in any case was the one who put it up, on the wall between the fridge and the door into the hall.

The three old men look up at him. Then one of them holds out his hand and tells him, They'll be bringing the tea round any time now, it's as well to be in early if you want your pick of the cakes. He tells them his name is John. The others are Stan and Dick and Leo. Mrs Boyer is the wife of Leo. Then John sits on an old armchair with the mock leather flaking away from the canvas beneath. The chair smells sour. He thinks of waiting-rooms in a hospital, the dog-eared magazines. All those articles he had read on Queensland. Lots of girls in skimpy clothes.

The old men have gone back to the game they were talking about. Is that Stan or Dick talking now? It's so easy to get things wrong when you are first introduced. Then he has to say No, he didn't watch that game. Nor the other one they mention. He doesn't know Essendon or Collingwood or Carlton or anything else. He never watches football. He does not say so, but he finds the whole subject boring. Brought up here though were you? one of the men asks him. He has to answer Yes, he was. Christ, one of them says. In pure amazement.

The cakes come on a trolley, and the tea in a big pot that one of the volunteers, a woman with firm brown arms and a word for everyone, pours into cup after cup. One of the men snips a little container and drops tablets into his tea. But there is a lady beside him now talking to him. She laughs and he smiles at her. He is feeling almost panic. He looks about the room, at the old people and the three volunteers. The woman explains to him that once every month they are taken for drives. To the Botanical Gardens or sometimes out to the coast. Sometimes there are theatre parties although not as many as there used to be. All this gloom she says and dirty talk even on the television. I haven't got television, John says. Well I don't want to miss out on this, the woman tells him. She means the plate of strawberry cake that was being handed round.

He is standing then by himself. He notices that the room smells of clothes. Clothes and soap and when the women move past him there is the odour of scent and powder that he turns away from. He watches the eating and the soft pink mouths, the crumbs that some are so careful with, dabbing at their chins, brushing briskly across their chests and stomachs, but that others are not aware of. He is uncomfortable at how easily he finds it all distasteful.

Then another woman speaks to him. For a moment John believes that she is speaking to someone else. Until she touches his arm. With one plumpish hand, one finger pinched in by its broad gold ring. I'm sorry? he says to her. She says simply but in the tone of saying something for the second time, are you all right? Excuse me but I thought you mightn't be all right? Her face has broad cheekbones and her eyes are blue. She wears a black coat with an astrakhan collar. It makes her look old-fashioned, even here. But she watches the tall man she has spoken to, and he knows it is not mere politeness, her asking that. She gives him the feeling that there is no hurry at all, about anything. She is slow and certain as she waits. I'm simply new here today, he says, that's why I'm quiet.

*

He was there because he found the house too painful sometimes to be in by himself. He would try to read or to spend an hour in the garden or to prepare his evening meal in that leisurely, careful way that had been Lou's custom for years. But he would find he had read a dozen pages and barely a paragraph had sunk in. Or he would stop with the secateurs poised in his hand, the reddish-green stems of the rosebushes, the exquisite fine curve of the thorns so vivid. The garden seemed to pulse at him. Even the heap of cuttings at the end of the yard seethed with its rich rankness, those small things moving through it if he leaned forward to inspect the mulch closely. And he felt his own blood churn more clearly. Like seeing the cat one morning with a tattered but living finch tapped from paw to paw, the fine teeth so careful not to pierce it as she saw John step towards her. The bird's eye a pip of reflected light, the cat so elegant as she slipped past to the side of the shed, the billowy fur like trousers on some exotic dancer. She had once left the remains of a rabbit lying in the hall, the ears and the tiny legs. The dark pink veiny ears that felt cold and slightly waxy when he picked them up, like tulip petals. He had said, You're better at this kind of thing than I am, and Lou had taken the pieces from his hand. He had never bothered all that much with what you call 'nature'. Lou was the one for that too. For pointing things out. Arranging flowers. Watching from a window and calling him to look at the beads of rain on the olives in the yard, at their silvery dry flashing when a big wind tossed them. So now it puzzled him at how much he saw. The breaking of trunks from the earth for example, that urgency he had never noticed. Or the gape of some of those flowers he didn't know the name for—a sort of hibiscus, were they? Their mouths turned towards the sky, funnels that could never be sated, that drank and drank at light so desperately, so briefly. He found that he was so often standing, merely looking at such things. It was all like standing too near a flame. Yet Lou must have stood there always. That upset him more. That only now, this late, he saw as Lou had seen all the time. He thought of the white small fangs holding the bird, the coursing white flakes that eat a bloodstream, a human body. John felt an anger that oddly pleased him as he looked at the rage out there in the yard. Which had always been there, as he now knew, while he had seen only the flat planes, the two dimensions. He thought of how he had gone off to work at the library and come home pleasantly tired and they had eaten their meals together, and listened to the radio or read, and gone to bed some nights to love but mostly to lie and drowse together, their hands at ease across each other's bodies. He had lived he thought with someone who was so ordinary. He remembered that design of a bird nested in flame on the back of a red set of books in the literature shelves. Ordinary as a phoenix, Lou was, in its ordinary fire.

The woman who calls herself Joyce watches the new visitor carefully. It is the second or third time that he has come, and she knows how nervous he still is. Because he does not fit in at all, does he? He finds it difficult to talk with the other men, for instance. He sits this afternoon in front of the television. He is the only man in fact who does not speak while he watches the game, although he smiles when a fat man beside him raises his arm and shakes it at one of the players and calls out, A pansy or what are you? Another man shouts across not to be hard on him Fred, can't he see the poor bugger's never handled a bat before? The banter goes on along the rows of chairs around the screen. Joyce thinks how they are like a caricature of a classroom.

She gives half her attention to a funny little thing who has perched beside her. A marquisite brooch bobs up and down as the smaller woman flings herself about as though words alone can't manage, there had to be this 'body language' as well—isn't that the phrase she has heard her daughter use? If there's anything in it then it goes for him too, of course. John, that new man there, in his tartan tie and his suit, stiff there among the open-necked and blazered old blokes shiyacking each other. He'd rather be miles away from here, that's what *he's* saying. Yet Joyce decides he must prefer even this to something, this raucous and ageing equivalent to the yobbos out there on Brunswick Street some nights yelling and revving their motors and making their girls squeal out.

He's bereaved, of course, the other woman says. In her special voice, so the word slips a wreath around his neck. It is like the oval at a country show, Joyce thinks, the red and green and blue sashes handed out for prizes. There are different words with their different colours, but bereavement is the best. That kind of exultation—yes, it is even that, she thinks—each time at the club when a new death ripples among them. *Only last week in that chair beside me. Only Sunday and we were playing bowls. A great bloke, all right. A proper lady.*

The wind shaking the shrubs outside the window quivers the light inside the room. The winking brooch beside her says no one in the district knows him really, that's a bit odd isn't it? He must come from somewhere further out. You'd think there'd be places closer to home he could go to, wouldn't you? Her own husband mind you says he's too stand-offish ever to get on anywhere. Makes the other lads uncomfortable, just sitting there like a no-hoper. There are people like that, the woman keeps on. There are wet blankets by nature and nothing's going to change them.

Joyce sees past the little face beside her to the spiteful girl in grade four, the young wife jealous of a neighbour's car, an old bitch whose only surviving weapon is a husband who is supposed to say the words she gives him. Joyce tells her I don't know anything about him. I'm not interested in guessing. She goes to the counter where the large pot of tea squats between the cups and saucers. I can manage, she tells one of the volunteers. She wonders, without being disturbed by it, why women like that have always grated on her so much. Why their common femininity irks far more than it gives—as her daughter says it should—a sense of sisterhood. Dear Delia who carries the world on her shoulders, so solemn beneath her banners, and would sell her soul to make the world a better place. She tells her mother there can be no future unless we give ourselves to caring and concern. There is also a male force and a female force, but the female must always triumph. Apparently, the woman is replete when the male lies exhausted. Joyce remembers her own mother with her novenas and spiritual bouquets, the Lourdes water sprinkled for whooping cough and Our Lady on the front lawn the night before her wedding. Sure enough the sun shone out and the wedding photos were perfect. They are closer together, Joyce thinks, mum and Delia, so much closer than I am to either of them. Sisters holding hands across my head while I stand too sceptical to take up what they offered. There is no self-congratulation in her thinking this. She lifts the heavy enamel pot and pours the steaming tea.

She says to the new man, You look as lost as I feel myself sometimes, and hands him one of the cups. He says with a wry frankness that pleases her, I didn't know what hard work social life could be. They sit together on a form against a wall. He tells her that he came to the Club in the first place because it became intolerable at home. So it didn't matter really whether he enjoyed it here or not. The important thing was that when he looked at the kitchen clock and closed the door to go out, it was one o'clock. When he opened the door and saw the clock again it was six. At least an afternoon had gone.

How recent was it? she asks him. He tells her, Four months. It is worse now than it was in those first few weeks. Joyce says, There is nothing to say, really, is there? Nothing much helps. And John, blowing softly on the scalding tea, says No. There is only the hollowness. And the distaste for time. Then he looks at her and smiles, You know what it's like too?

Joyce's Andy had been a clerk in a bank. When he was a young man he wore his dark hair sleeked back so smoothly that she thought of a currawong's brilliant sheen. He was tall and lithe and as he grew older his angular features made her think again of a bird. His leaning above her chair, his swooping on bits and pieces the children left about, snapping them up, demanding tidiness as evidence of parental rule. He lived with the regularity of those figures who come out on the dot on ornamental clocks. The season altered on the morning he took out his blazer, or reached for his twills at the back of the wardrobe. He smoked his pipe each evening at seven o'clock. On Tuesday nights they went to the movies. They made love twice a week.

Andy collected recordings of Eddie Cantor and Fats Waller and especially of Al Jolson. He liked to sing the words softly as he did jobs around the house.

And when it's raining, have no regrets,
Because it isn't raining rain, you know, it's raining violets . . .

Joyce liked to hear him singing. He didn't attempt to imitate the intonations from the records, but sang in a light tenor voice that made him sound young.

He was kind and bought her lovely presents for her birthdays and for their anniversaries. He liked to be quiet and warm in the way Bing Crosby was in some of the films he enjoyed so much. She knew although Andy never said such a thing that he would have loved to be an American. The last time they went out before he became ill was to *Easter Parade* at a festival of old-time movies. Judy Garland looked like a doll someone had dressed up. And Joyce had thought how that world with its comfortable houses and blatant accents had nothing to do with their modest home, their flat diffident voices. It all might as well have been in a foreign language. Yet in a sense it was the last time that her husband had been to what spiritually you might as well call home; to where a man who did not believe in God, and who found it difficult to put his tongue to words that carried emotion, might go and return refreshed, where his life opened into brighter lights and warmer sounds than the brick house in Gallipoli Avenue could ever have offered him. She thought how sad it was, even sadder than the slow encroachment of his death, that the vitality and flaming colours there all the time in the world around him, came to him only through tinselly movies, in songs that grew from lives that were nothing like his own. And when the disease did come they were the deepest things.

Her sister tried to tell her how his humming those tunes, those snatches of song coming to him sometimes when he had said nothing else for days, meant that he was happy in himself. And the specialist explained to her as well how the mind's connections jumble and cut out, how what does emerge may seem random and fragmentary, yet there is no reason to believe that people with that deterioration either suffer, or are aware of their own condition. She said, How can we know anything like that for certain?

The boys dutifully sat with their father in front of television and Delia made him scones even when he refused to eat them. Stephen brought cans of beer for when they watched the football, until Andy's hands would jerk and the beer slosh away from his mouth. Then above the mopping of the sofa, the whispers of how their father was going downhill. The light is drawing back from him, Joyce would say, everything he loved is being lifted from around him. Oh mum, Delia said, do you have to go on?

Thank God he had slept for so much of the time. And when sometimes she led him by the hand into the small garden at the back of the house, along the path between the scratched earth where for years he had coaxed up lettuces and radish and skinny sticks of corn, down beneath the big peach tree where she placed the cane chair for him, his face would glimmer with fragments of comprehension. He would try to rise from the chair to embrace her, to call her over to him if she knelt at the weeds that had moved into his garden. It's called Alzheimer's, she explained to the man at the Club. What Andy had.

They sat near a dried fountain in a stiffly formal park, where Joyce thought of people in old-fashioned clothes. John was beside her on the concrete ledge. Over the past weeks they had become friends. Then they met by chance in a delicatessen. Joyce said she would wait outside the shop for him. With their shopping bags they had walked along to the park. It was so much easier talking there than at the Club. That picture of the Queen and the Duke to begin with, John said. Joyce liked him for that too. She kept telling him the story she had begun at the Club, while his fingers ran against the smooth cracked concrete where the water had once played. She said Andy took two years to die. He would go for a month without knowing any of us, then stand in front of me and mumble words from a song. What kind of song? John asked her. In a clear voice she picked out the notes for him.

Rock-a-bye your baby with a Dixie melody,
When you croon, croon a tune from the heart of Dixie . . .

He watched the woman beside him. Her eyes were so like a young woman's and now her voice as well, while her old hands fidgeted in her lap. A man reading on a bench looked up from the paper he held in front of him with widespread arms. He lowered the paper and raised it again at once as soon as he took in the old codger with his natty tie, the crazy woman next to him singing clearly enough for it to float across the clipped lawns, the raked pathway, past the bed of recently turned earth where one good rain would release the frail plants into colour. John saw how her skin was soft and creased as crumpled calfskin gloves. She said quietly, looking straight ahead of her, her heels like a girl's tapping at the concrete wall, I hated my husband before he died. Andy who was the kindest man, the only one I'd ever given twopence for, I hated him. His songs and his silences and his slobbered food. When he died I was in the room with him alone and I sat at the window and looked out at the pure sky for oh I don't know how long, say twenty minutes before I phoned the doctor. There was a clock ticking on the dressing-table, one of those little square travelling clocks. And each tick was like a fragment more of a huge weight being taken away from me. Then I had this oddest picture in my mind. It was of rows and rows of trees, like a forest you see in photos of England or somewhere. The trees had been quite bare only now the leaves were falling back up, do you see what I mean? It was like autumn in reverse. The leaves beginning to rise from where they lay on the ground and then simply pouring back up. I knew it was all inside my head but I saw it so clearly while I looked out at this cloudless sky. Until the whole forest was full and swaying and I could even hear it then, like every leaf was moving in the wind and the leaves were the ticking of the clock as well. Do you see all that?

John was watching the traffic on the main road while Joyce talked on to him. He felt such tenderness for her even as he thought yes, she is a bit crazy, a bit off-centre. He had never heard anyone go on like that. And yet what she said also made its lovely sense. He could imagine himself and Lou looking out there at the same trees she told him about. Then he surprised himself by saying Lou's arms were branches towards the end. I'd see them lying along the outside of the quilt and I always thought that. They were so thin and brown and were like old thin branches.

It was time for them to make a move, Joyce said. We've been sitting here a couple of hours, know that? The man with the newspapers had gone off some time ago. An old Greek lady was on that bench now. Her eyes were closed and her hair was held down tightly with a black scarf. Joyce said as she looked at her, If you're one of them you might even have loathed your husband from the word go, and you've still got to wear black like that forever. John felt how the woman beside him covered her own guilt as she said that, denigrating the love of forty years which after all meant so much more than her feelings at the end, her natural animal distaste at seeing another die so badly. But there was no way he could put that into words. So he joked, he pointed out to her, You're wearing black yourself. He touched her astrakhan cuff. Ah yes, she said. But this is the oldest coat in the world. I had it dyed years ago because it was frog-green once and hardly ever worn, it was faded so much you wouldn't believe it. I got it for our honeymoon, that's how old it is. It can't be, John said. She said, Oh yes it is. To go to Tasmania where I'd heard it was so cold you even needed a coat in March. They both laughed when he asked her, Was it then? As cold as that? And she told him, I can't remember wearing clothes for the whole two weeks.

It is the Thursday in the month when the chaplain and the social worker join the group that gathers in the special lounge. The small room is called special because the furniture there is better than in the larger clubrooms, and there are flowers arranged in a vase shaped like a swan, the stems tucked in between the wings. There are seldom more than a dozen people at these meetings, only those who reasonably come under the heading of Recently Bereaved. The social worker is skilled at weeding out the voyeurs, and the chaplain speaks discreetly if someone becomes upset. There is also a special trolley, and sandwiches brought by the volunteers, for those who sit down to hear the chaplain read briefly from the New Testament. The social worker then holds up a book with many photographs, an American book called *Living Through*. It is a book about terminal illness and how, unbelievable as it may seem, there can even be joy at the end. Well there's nothing wrong with hoping for it, Joyce supposes. She thinks of the dead man in the bed behind her and the leaves, the teeming seconds, the purity of an immense sky outside the room. It is still beyond her to make the two events connect—that afternoon only six months ago and that other day far back, her veil snagging she remembered on the outside safe as she walked round the side of the house, Andy turning slightly as she walked towards him in the church, his face pale and smooth as soap. Yet she knows there is a line between all things, a connection she must work towards. She smiles now as John comes into the room. She can tell that he is tense, that normally he would hate such a place as this. She knows that privacy is a jewel to him, and yet here he is this afternoon, about to make himself public. His eyes move about the room, his hand touches gently, rapidly, at his tie. They look at each other, the youngish old man and the dowdy woman in her black coat.

John raises the tweed sleeve of his jacket and sees it is a few minutes from two o'clock. They will hate him of course, he knows that. They always do when they know. But he has no more choice now than if Lou were there beside him, telling him he must speak for them both, as he had done that other time at a meeting for civil rights. His legs that day had shaken against the back of the chair in front of him. There were nudges and turned heads round the hall. There always had been. In shops and from neighbours and at work in the library, as if the world waited to bestow its one certainty, its sense of anger at them both. But the social worker is leaning forward now, his hands clasped round his knee, talking to them so calmly. He is explaining as he does each month that they are friends together. There is only sympathy in this room, he says, we have all felt the same things, we are friends who will understand. And John finds that he is speaking. He knows his voice is steady and that they look at him with interest. He says I want to talk about my own loss because the words to say it out publicly are the words that help it heal. He sees that the minister and the social worker are both surprised at how he speaks. He knows that some of the others in the room will think that his voice is snooty, that he is educated and so at once to be held in doubt. He says, We were together for over thirty-five years. From soon after the War. We met on the steps of St Paul's during the Victory celebrations. Half the people in London that day seemed to be Australians. And the room stirs because they like that, it means that all of them could cast back to the massive crowds outside Flinders Street Station and the hooters and sirens in the smallest towns even throughout the country, the flags decked across the streets and the bars chocker and the singing late into the night. So they begin to warm to him while he went on, while he said, We have to say the truth because that is the last thing really we can do for the dead, the last and most enduring thing we can give them. As he speaks he is looking at Joyce's placid face. It is as much for her in fact as it is for Lou, this truth that no one wants and that none of them will thank him for offering. He feels the prickling discomfort beneath his collar and the heat at the back of his neck. How Lou used to have him on about his blushing when they were first together. But it was only Lou who had given him confidence in so much—to go to library school, to finish his degree, to sit at last beside that bloody hospital bed for days and then into weeks and to be able to say finally how that was a privilege too, to see how death wins of course but that is not the point. That mere brute massing of the dark. The victory is in defying it, in saying to the last breath you may take this body but never me. He knew how his words would seem wild now. He sees how the minister is softly tapping a ballpoint pen against his thumb. And for Joyce's sake now he will tell them. It is his gift to her for what she has given him, that awful honesty about the husband she had loved and then hated, and now that he was dead, could love him again. I lived with a man, he is telling them. He feels the sweat gathering beneath his eyes. I slept with a man for nearly forty years and it was as true as anything any of you could know, although you will not believe it. He is only able to say it now because his eyes are on Joyce, on the slight smile that remains there while already there is a stirring in the room, the minister glancing at the social worker beside him. Already a couple of the men are on their feet. The cleric says to them benignly, opening his hands in that practised gesture of acceptance and blessing, Shall we break here for tea? He quickly carries a cup to John, and asks the woman at the trolley to pass over the sponge-cake. He is deliberately jolly as he places the tea in front of the recently bereaved. Something to perk you up, he says, thinking this one's going to take some smoothing over, the poor old sod. He is glad to see how the social worker is covering the other front, speaking expansively to the group around the trolley, anxious to hold them there, to delay if only for minutes the word that shall spread out to the other room, among the rest of the Club. That the new geezer in there with his tartan tie if you please and his tweed jacket and his la-di-dah voice he's a poof would you believe it, one of them flaming arse-bandits as Fred Weston will say when the women are out of earshot, shaking his close-cropped head, honest to Christ would you credit that? With the Queen and the Duke on the wall and half of them ex-servicemen and now that kind insinuating himself into a club where there'd never been a pervert of any kind. Out on his jaxie that's where that bugger belonged. For a whole afternoon attention would waver from the TV set in the lounge, and the air shimmer with the odours of the hunt. But that will come later. As the chaplain now keeps up his carefully off-hand remarks and the woman who carries over the sponge wonders if she has actually seen one of them before, one of those queers close up as this, Joyce crosses to her friend. She puts her hand on his arm. Come on, she says to him. He sets down his cup and follows her to the door and across the TV lounge and through the tiled entrance to the shallow fall of steps, out to the main road and again towards the park where already they have sat, the open spaces that are always there as Joyce is telling him, talking to him quietly but without pause, the pure sky is there that you can fill with looking, where time is a great tree shaking through never mind what season, it is now and it's part of ever, it has to be. He is not sure what the woman means but he says to her yes, as they pause to cross the street, yes again when she says, You must know how good it is, don't you, being brave enough to say it? Her black coat bobbing beside her companion's tweed. And when she is not talking to him she is humming one of those songs, one of those tinselly things that Andy liked to think were the last word.

The Last of Freddie

When he went at sixty-four his friends could hardly believe it. Indestructible old Freddie! They all knew his paintings had not been up to so much these last few years, but as for dying—if Freddie played that card, then who couldn't? Although that was said discreetly. Critics liked to say—now he wasn't there—what a gap he was going to leave. On *Kaleidoscope* Bonnard would be mentioned as his master and a constant influence, as a quick comparison of selected canvases confirmed. Bonnard of course through the eyes of the Moderns. But that same preference for intimate domestic scenes, the shortened perspectives, the delicate sense of colour. If the phrases came rather too easily, as Maddy suspected they did, this was not the time to point it out. Oh yes, she thought—he painted, he screwed around, he drank himself to death. Caesar's neat little triplet hardly matched that as an epitaph. But it was a limb lopped off, wasn't it, hearing his death announced that morning over the nine o'clock news? She had poured herself a stiffish drink and switched the radio off. And she thought at once, oh won't they be swarming now, the academic maggots. Not even waiting until the meat had time to go off.

When June phoned her a little after ten she said that to her friend, although she knew June's son was at work on a *catalogue raisonné*. A few weeks before she had said, 'You can't *raisonné* before someone's dead, for God's sake.' She had been amused. But now she was angry, and a little drunk. She thought of Freddie wearing a green paper hat and not a stitch else as he lumbered down on her after a party at the old place in Kelburn. Angus already was out to it in the lounge, a gold cardboard crown slipped over his forehead as he lay squashed into the piled cushions of the sofa. It was after Freddie's finest show. They wore silly hats because it was Angus's birthday as well. Earlier in the night they had blown whistles that unfurled long paper tongues. They had danced to a Glenn Miller record and Maddy livened up her husband's drink with something somebody had brought in a black stone bottle. All it did was tumble him like a tree trunk. Then the artist had raised his long pale arm and groped for the glass-bead cord, like a row of raindrops, beneath the yellow shade. 'Painting be stuffed,' he told her. He said it vehemently. Then he had collapsed on the bed beside her.

'So you've heard?' June asked her.

'I heard it on the news.'

'When you think how well he was looking.' Then after the slightest pause, 'Had you seen him lately?'

'Not for a while,' Maddy told her. (*Madeleine*, Freddie used to enunciate back in those days. Why the hell can't people call you that, why that ridiculous abbreviation?)

'Last time he was that frisky. You'd have thought any of us might have gone before he did.' June reminded her how Freddie of course visited every second Friday. Surely she couldn't have forgotten that? 'We always had such *rapport*.'

Maddy could see her friend, red-eyed and big-busted, sucking at grief like a child at an orange. She thought, you ridiculous old cow, Freddie was into anything. But she said the required things until June had to tell her, 'I can't talk about it now. Not this close. I'll have to go.'

'Take three or four Disprin.'

'As if that'll help.'

'They worked when John went missing, didn't they?' Maddy thought, I'm a bitch saying that, aren't I? June had told her time and again how she hadn't shed a tear when the police came to her after the accident. It had taken weeks before it sank in. She had taken all those Disprin and simply gone to sleep. But this morning she had drawn the curtains and cried until she knew her face would be puffed for days.

'You never know how death will strike you,' Maddy said. After they had talked, she sat by the window that looked out across the valley to the irregular line of hills, her comforting glass beside her. She stroked at the glossy cover of a book she had for review, as though it were a cat. Each of them had forgotten to say so on the phone, but the women took it for granted Lydia would drive down for the funeral. How could she not? The three of them together again, to put their man away.

They met in the porch of the crematorium chapel. A northerly blasted along the valley and across the gravestones, driving people into the porch. 'How he'd love those hills,' June was saying. She nodded to the darkened slopes, the cloud shredding along their tops. 'If he could see them he might,' Maddy said. Why, she thought, do people have to talk such damned rubbish? Then at the same instant she and June called out, 'Lydia!' There was a brief trio of embracing among the mourners.

'We'll talk afterwards,' Maddy said. 'We're late as it is.' She took the smaller woman's arm and directed her to where they should sit. June walked on her other side. 'Oh,' she was saying, even as they stepped into the pew. 'Our meeting up like this!' Lydia smiled without looking at either of them. Then they sat, two tallish women with a shorter between them, listening to what was being said about Freddie, who lay on a slightly raised platform, a few inches of stained pine coffin showing beneath the flag that draped him. Maddy thought of him lying in bed, watching her dress, with his feet extended outside the bedclothes. Once her clothes were back on he would say, 'A gin'd go quite nicely for afters. Know where everything is?' She heard the minister talk of his war service and his art. Then more importantly in the eyes of God, his generosity, his lack of malice. 'Balls,' she thought. In over thirty years, how often had she heard him say a good word about a painter younger than himself? Although he could be very open-minded with the dead. 'Weekes was brilliant,' he used to say. 'He was so very close to being good.'

Lydia heard June sobbing beside her into a handkerchief tugged from the top of her frock. It was one of the handkerchiefs Freddie had made in that period when he used to say, in his best proletarian voice, 'What are us buggers painting pictures for anyway? Why don't we make things people *use*?' This had meant at different times curtain fabrics, wooden toys, neck-pendants with local polished stone. And that spate of handkerchiefs—coarse linen made by a friend in Levin, then treated by Freddie with his own vegetable dyes. Lydia wished for a moment that she had brought hers, a sombre green that Freddie insisted was as natural a dye as it was possible to get. No one could mistake them for anyone else's work. Their size, their big hems that the artist himself had stitched on an old Singer treadle machine. Then she saw a woman at the end of the row in front of them—a woman in a fur coat and with heart trouble it must be, the way she panted, breathing through her mouth. Or asthma. She was dabbing at her throat with the same kind of coloured square, only dun brown. Freddie had given Lydia a tablecloth he must have dyed at the same time. It had been on the table the last time he visited her. He had taken it between his fingers and said it wasn't lasting so badly, the colour had kept quite nicely too. Must be twenty years, he said, since he made those things. Nineteen, she remembered. The year she went to Sydney.

'Get on with it,' she heard Maddy say beside her. Lydia felt confined between her friends. She looked straight ahead, at the pillar of sun that fell from the windows high in the wall. It picked out the line of powder on the sweating woman's throat, and made the ears of the man next to her quite transparent. The tiny veins and splotches seemed unpleasantly naked. What was that story about June and Freddie on the riverbank or something? A light shone on them by surprise? She had an image of their white limbs, of June's rotundities and Freddie's lankiness, caught in the flicker of a policeman's torch. The torchlight falling then and the sunlight now. June's wedding ring blinked where she crushed her handkerchief in her lap. Then Lydia noticed too that Maddy's fingers drummed on her crossed knees, a sign of irritation.

After the prayers and the eulogy a curtain was drawn across so theatrically that a bow would not have been out of the question. Then there was a hymn chosen by Freddie's wife. Everyone sang the words from a printed sheet, and the chapel swelled.

There is a blessed home beyond this land of woe
Where trials never come, nor tears of sorrow flow.
Where faith is lost in sight, and patient hope is crowned,
And everlasting light its glory throws around.

'He'd be bored shitless!' Maddy said at the end of the verse. June looked over sharply, her eyes interestingly pink, as Freddie might have thought, against the dark linen held at her cheek. Lydia continued to gaze ahead, at the stirring in the front pews as the family prepared to leave. That odd little smile of hers, June thought. I wonder if she quite knows what is going on? God knows none of them were any younger. It was senility with some, that was simply the way things were, just as it might be a weight problem unfortunately with others. Though the last time Freddie grabbed at her he had said for the umpteenth time, 'Can't stand these bloody women with no upholstery to them.' He had nuzzled into her as eagerly as at the University Extension weekend all those years ago.

It had been a life-study class. Rather a pert little woman sat partly draped on a desk in front of them, her breasts as small and sharp as the last inch or two of ice-cream cones. That was exactly what she had thought of then, and it came back to her now. It was so silly, June smiled. And the way life goes on, she thought. She watched Freddie's wife walk down the aisle, her arm linked with her son's. What a gift, a wife as innocent as that had been! You'd have thought, though, wouldn't you, that a relative or someone would have told her the little cap thing she'd been wearing for years wasn't quite the thing for a funeral? It made her look like a jockey. And years ago when her own husband took her to the races, June had noticed the little men used to carry their saddles in the birdcage rather as Jos now carried that big old leather handbag across her arm. She wished she had thought of that while Freddie was still alive. He had liked her flair for putting things.

'Outski,' Maddy broke in on her. She jerked her head in that rather masculine way of hers, as though it was simply the movies they were leaving, or the end of a concert. Then for the first time since coming into the chapel together, Lydia looked from one friend to the other. She smiled shyly at both of them. She was thinking how they had all lain and sighed with and been loved by Freddie, hadn't they? There were times when June at least had become unfriendly about it, having to share him around like that. Although Maddy always laughed when they met and his name came up. 'He's fun the old wretch, isn't he? If you want more than that of course you go to someone else.'

They moved slowly from the chapel, the man with the thin pale ears shuffling in front of them. Perhaps a stroke, each of them supposed. There was something wrong with everyone, if only you knew about it. In a few moments they would be in the porch, then out again into the pelt of the northerly, the dappled scudding of the afternoon. There would be a quick embrace with Jos and others in Freddie's family, and words with people Lydia had not seen for so long perhaps she would have forgotten their names, and she would feel awkward because of it. Then the laughter that always began soon after a funeral. She and Maddy and June would separate, come back together, observe at more leisure the encroaching signs of age that marked them. And a man in a vaguely imagined room at the back of the crematorium would turn a jet—she supposed it was something like that—and flames would leap up, a bright engulfing calix with Freddie at their centre. While they were talking, glancing out of windows. It struck her as very strange.

Lydia was a widow as her friends were, but the widow to nothing spectacular. June's husband had quite a name as a surgeon, then drowned a few years ago when he fell from a yacht off Banks Peninsula. Maddy's became a big wheel in theatre design. He had dramatically up and disappeared because of some homosexual flurry just after the War, and died before he was fifty. In other company Lydia perhaps would mention Cliff's Cambridge degree and the edition he had been working on for years when he died. Compared with the others, she supposed, Cliff didn't cut much ice. He now seemed so far away in any case.

'All of us widows!' June said rather gaily, just as Lydia was thinking that.

Young Richard came up to them and said, 'I'm glad you could make it. It's nice so many of his friends could be here.'

'As if we wouldn't have!' Maddy said. As if we'd miss out on seeing how the others were taking it.

Richard was the only son. He was tall like his father, with the same hank of hair falling across his brow. It had always made the self-portraits look lop-sided, that sheet of thick ochre slapped across the thinnish face. The young man smiled at the three elderly women, saying enough for each of them to think yes, what a charming boy he was. They could quite see Freddie coming through in him.

'That same profile,' June said. 'Can't both of you just see it?'

'At the same age!' Lydia said. She had been the first to know his father. 'You'd swear you were twins.'

'You knew him that long ago?'

'When we were students, would you believe that?' There was a vivid memory of swinging along with a group of friends, their arms about each other's waists, across a Gothic quadrangle forty years before. It was late in the evening, after a party. Between the cloisters and the ginkgo tree in the middle of the quad, Freddie had put his hand under her skirt.

'You saw him recently, did you?' Richard's question was to all of them. 'Saw Freddie?'

June hesitated then said, 'Oh, not so long ago.'

'I hadn't seen him to talk to for a year or so,' Lydia had to admit. Then she asked herself aloud, 'Would it have been that long?' Richard had taken their wine glasses to refill, holding them between the fingers of one hand like a clump of transparent tulips. Maddy said, 'After our last *contretemps* it was probably better for everyone if we kept our distance. After that portrait.'

A couple of years ago Freddie had exhibited a nude, the female figure ageing but attractive in a butch, chunky way. And anyone with half an eye could recognise Maddy. The figure was sitting cross-legged on a chair, in a splash of greenish light, starkers except for a pair of long suede boots. Silly old bugger, she had said when she saw it. He hasn't seen me like that for ten years! It still made her hot to think about it.

'Well, as if you didn't have reason to,' June said. She was thinking thank God the one he did of me was *The Pink Hat*, the one the National Gallery had snapped up. It was impossible to guess who that one was. The tilted plane of the hat was all that interested Freddie that day. He had come in the morning, painted, had lunch, painted, then even after John came in he turned down a gin to get it through in 'one bash', those were his very words for it. Until, 'That'll do,' he said. Then he sat down in front of the telly and went to sleep. It was romantic though, June considered. It was how artists should work. She could have paraded about that day in boots and suspenders and it wouldn't have mattered twopence to him. She had reminded him of it only a year or so ago. They were sitting in the garden, it was in the early weeks of spring. They had been there for an hour and he had not even suggested that they go inside. 'Fancy a bit of the old one two?' was what he usually said. It always amused him that June would have liked him to put it more delicately. 'Christ,' he used to shout at her sometimes. 'Your whole life's like those bloody pink doo-dah things you've got over the spare dunny roll in the jakes. All frills and puff and cover-up.' But this day he simply sat in the white cane chair under the lime tree and tapped first the sharpened end of a pencil on the table, then the flat end, over and over until June had said, 'I was just working it out, Freddie. It's exactly fifteen years since you did that picture of me in the hat. That was October too. There's that same light falling across you now.' Freddie had looked at her, surprised. 'You've got a good eye,' he complimented her. Then he told her something else. 'Fifteen bloody years since I've done a decent picture in that case.' But as though saying that was a door he had partly opened and at once regretted, slamming it before June had time to enter, he leaned forward and pressed the swell of her thigh beneath her new wrap-round skirt. 'Still there, is it?' he asked her. He threw his head back and bellowed when she slapped at his hand and looked across, quickly, to where a neighbour's window might have given someone a view of her entertaining.

With the same slight smile she had kept throughout the service, Lydia said now, 'I don't know how I'd feel if it was me. I mean a picture like that, Maddy.' Then she added, 'I suppose as long as people are only thinking of it as art.'

Maddy looked at her friend, at the neatly parted grey hair and the grey suit and the benign fey expression like an ageing doll's. What the hell Freddie ever saw in *that* one. But here came Richard with their glasses again, there was no need to answer her.

'You *are* a darling,' June told him.

'There we are, ladies,' Richard said. Carefully he handed each of them a brimming glass. 'I know they're not supposed to be that full. But it cuts down on travel.' There was such a press of people around them that Lydia wondered how he had carried the glasses so well.

'You'll be all right?' he asked them.

'We won't go dry,' Maddy promised. She gave him one of her broad rare smiles, showing the perfect teeth that had made his father sometimes call her the Piranha. June watched her friend and the young man who now laughed with her about something that was lost in the hubbub of the wake. No wonder Freddie had that nickname for her. Here she was devouring Richard, drawing him off so that she and Lydia were simply left standing there. That'll make her day, June thought. Although not quite a victory like the old days, not like that writer's funeral in Auckland when a much younger Maddy had waltzed off with the dead man's brother onto the side of One Tree Hill. She had come back inside without even brushing the twigs or whatever from the back of her dress.

'Oops!' Lydia broke in on them. Someone had jolted against her arm, so that half her wine leaped from its glass. Richard was with her at once, mopping at her skirt, telling her he didn't think it would stain, in fact he was quite sure it wouldn't. Red might but not white. Then the man from behind the bar was there as well, handing her a dampened cloth. June raised her eyebrows as she caught Maddy's glance. But Lydia was turning from one friend to the other, asking 'Why me?', her face crinkled comically, her little-girl voice that hadn't done so badly for her over the years either, Maddy thought.

They had not met so often over these last five or six years, but Freddie always used to tell her, 'By God you're the one who matters, Lydia.'

'Oh yes,' she would smile.

'You are,' he insisted to her.

'And the others?'

'The others?' He would raise his arm from where it lay above the bedclothes and snap his fingers. He always did that about 'the others'. It made her think of a bank teller, contemptuous of the notes he was counting out.

'You believe me?'

'Yes and no,' she used to say. She said it about liking pictures or people that they knew or in this case what she meant to Freddie. And he so easily became angry when she answered him like that. 'There's not a mind inside there,' he would tell her, pointing at her head. 'There's a bloody see-saw.' He told her she was like the whore he had heard about during the War, who had 'Mild' tattooed on one breast and 'Bitter' on the other. 'You try to please everybody, that's your trouble.' He was so jealous. Then she would put on a face like the one when the wine spilled and Richard sweetly made such a thing about attending to her. 'I please you, don't I?' she used to ask. She would draw herself across him and Freddie always spread his hand across the back of her neck, gripping her as one might hold down the head of a kitten so it couldn't move. 'I love that,' she would tell him.

June broke in on her with the coffee she placed on the table next to her.

'I was just admiring this,' Lydia said. She tapped the marble table beneath her cup.

'Florence,' June said. 'John should have been an auctioneer, the stuff he picked up.'

Maddy took her coffee and said, 'I hope this isn't the strongest drink you're giving us, June?'

'Scotch then? Glenfiddich?'

'That'd do nicely,' Lydia said. Then they sat without switching on the lights, the three women facing the broad window that commanded half the harbour.

'Even on a dull day like this,' June told them, 'it's worth watching.' The northerly still pushed the clouds in ragged packs along the hills behind Eastbourne. The harbour itself might have been made of pewter.

'It depresses me,' Maddy said.

'What does?' June asked. She was kneeling at the gas heater, adjusting the bright whispering flues.

'This view. This weather.'

'Freddie used to say that if we could remember things exactly, things like colour tones and the movement of shadows and the rest of it, there wouldn't be more than half-a-dozen days in a lifetime probably that were exactly the same.'

So the talk came back to the man who had died. They spoke of him warmly, without envy of each other, as the evening darkened outside. Maddy at least was thinking, he is never going to exist so fully as this again. Next time we meet we may talk of him, but not with this ease, this intensity. Our talking is letting him go slowly, slowly. The last time a man is spoken of is when he finally dies. Then she clucked her tongue sharply. It annoyed her that the vague pool of dimming silver in the mirror behind June's head, and that luminous lift that comes to the harbour when the sky itself is all but completely dark, were making her sentimental. How much she disliked June's own love for 'atmosphere', she thought. Her friend's finicky arrangement of camellias and looped Italian candlesticks and such. Those frothy blouses and pastel shades that June wore because they were the 'kindest' to her years. The moment you give way to sentiment, Maddy had always instructed herself, you blur the present as much as the past. You lose the lot. For a moment she held the hot swill of malt in her mouth. Then she asked, 'Can't we have the light on?'

'Is this making you jumpy?' June said. She liked the way the panel in the gas heater glowed there in the darkened room, while outside the night came down. 'There we are,' she said. She had touched a switch beside her. Two carefully angled lights were thrown across the paintings on the large expanse of wall. Only one of them was Freddie's, a gutsy still life of simple brilliant forms. What treasure that is, Maddy thought, after sitting in the gloom. Coming back from Hades. She thought of those favourite lines of hers, the great hero unrecognised in the swirl of fog, the twittering voices as remote as birds.

'The way he gets that orange,' Lydia said. 'Doesn't he?'

'The whole thing's *alive*. That's what matters about it.'

'Drinks again all round?' June offered them. She went to the kitchen for ice. Lydia knew she should refuse if she was sensible. She looked up at the painting and saw the fruit was already slipping when she tried to focus. The orange kept losing its roundness, smearing towards the bottom of the frame. She took a handful of nuts from the dish Maddy held towards her.

Lydia thought what a pity the light went on when it did. She had liked the sense that they were suspended somehow, as though in a transparent bell with the outside world pressing against its curves, a place where their voices came to each other clearly yet mysteriously, where surfaces ran with shadows and the last silvery core of light. There was no way she was able to put it, really. And she had almost made the mistake of confiding in them. It was good that hadn't happened. To have almost said, 'When I woke on Friday morning before it was light I knew he was there with me.' *Who?* she could hear them say. Who are you talking about, Lydia? *Freddie*, she would have had to say. They would not say much back, how could they? 'I opened my eyes, I often wake just before light, but the moment I woke I felt his weight.' Because it couldn't be anyone else. And they might ask her then, 'You'd already heard he was dead?' And she would answer them, 'How could I have heard? He wasn't even dead then. He was dying.'

'You're a quiet lot in here,' June said. She carried through a tray with sandwiches as well as the bowl of ice with claw-shaped tongs lying across it. She placed the tray on a table at the end of the room. Then before she attended to their glasses or handed each a plate, she briskly drew the curtains. She snapped on other lights, the room lifted into a glare of colour, of vases, bookshelves, more pictures on other walls, a brilliant clump of proteas.

'My God!' Maddy said, when she saw the flowers. She stretched out her hand to touch the stiff waxy blooms. With the press of dark leaves that backed them, they made her think of a burst of skyrockets, frozen and held against the night.

'They are lovely aren't they?' June said.

Yes, Lydia was thinking, what a lucky stroke that she hadn't tried to tell them that.

Then June went on, 'He never painted flowers. That's odd, isn't it?'

'It's because he couldn't draw them,' Maddy said.

'Couldn't draw them?' June looked down at her friend. 'But he drew beautifully.'

'He said he couldn't ever do flowers the way he wanted to. They don't have dimension the way fruit does.'

They certainly wouldn't have believed her. June would have become puzzled and flustered, her hand running along the chain of her gold Victorian locket. *There was this weight, how could she explain that?* And Maddy might have said, But isn't it only a coincidence anyway? That she had this feeling and thought of Freddie which was natural enough for *her*, she had hardly played the *field*? Then later that morning she had heard. It was curious, but not so much more than that.

June was adjusting the wall-lamp, directing it more clearly across the painting of the fruit. 'Haven't I seen that jug?' Maddy asked. 'I'm sure I remember it.'

'That one?' June looked more closely at the canvas, at the few brushstrokes that gave the shape of the jug, a dab of whitish-blue along its rim that made you think all the light in the picture was gathered just there.

'It's the one he kept his brushes in,' Lydia said. 'Isn't that the one?'

'As if it matters now.' Maddy spoke quietly, her impatience tailed off. But Lydia was looking at her own hands, thinking again that it was not a thing to tell to others. How her bedroom had been completely dark when she had closed her eyes. Then after—how long, five minutes, ten?—the weight was withdrawn and when she looked again the morning already had come with that feeling of such stillness, and yet such energy too. The furniture and the mirror and her clothes across the chairback near the window, the frames on the photographs even and that oddly sad painting he had done when they spent an entire week in Akaroa, her red dog in grass as stiff as spears—how they had all been steeped in life, immersed in it. Full of that exuberance she had lain there and thought of him. *Dear Freddie*.

'Come on!' June was ordering her. Her friend stood in front of her, holding the fresh glass and with her other hand offering a plate of sandwiches. Maddy was standing too, one knee supported on the arm of a leather chair. She rooted about in her handbag, saying she was after a photograph she had brought to show them, the three of them in summer clothes outside the Takahe, three young women Christ knows how long ago.

'Dreaming, eh?' June had always teased her about that. Lydia smiled up, the 'drifting' smile as Freddie used to tell her, that bloody batty look as he had joked about it to Maddy and to June, there was a screw loose somewhere, there had to be.

She took the glass and an anchovy sandwich. 'Yes and no,' she said.

Survivals

It was November. In the afternoons the paddocks shimmered under the early summer heat and it always seemed at one-thirty, so he thought, at two o'clock, as if his watch must be at least an hour slow. He used to think, 'I can quite imagine dying on an afternoon like this. It's the time when it seems that death could slip in with less flurry about it than at any other time.' The roofing and the walls of the house snapped in their expansions beneath the sun, small clear explosions inside a well of stillness. The poplars across the paddock were bars drawn stiffly against the sky. In front of them lay a narrow stretch of water, a swamp which in certain lights could look as beautiful as a lake. Beyond the trees there were further paddocks stretching flatly out, a few far houses, an occasional car distant and small as a toy, raising a smudge of dust on the unsealed crossroad. The poultry gathered in the shade beside the barn, the rooster with its fall of bronze feathers occasionally scraping out its mechanical cry.

In mid-afternoon, as the woman's motor-scooter passed Dutchman's Orchard half-a-mile down the road, he would pick up its sound and then lose it again where the highway passed beneath a stretch of pines. When the bike emerged from the other end of the windbreak its engine beat more strongly. Another quarter of a mile and it would turn into his drive. Then she would burst from under the boughs of the apple trees at the corner, her foot already stretched out to take her weight when she cut the motor. Everything about her was as decisive as that. On a fine day she rebuckled her safety helmet when she had taken it off, shoved her gloves into its dark crown, then slipped it across the higher of the handlebars. When the weather was bad she carried it to just inside the door and put it on the varnished boards near the Turkish rug. It rocked there for a moment like the half of some huge egg.

Sometimes when Richard picked up the even throb of the approaching bike he pushed the papers in front of him to the centre of the table and piled his books together. When he walked back up the stairs with Monica she would ask him, 'How's it going?' Each time he would give her the same answer, 'It's coming on.' She knew after several weeks this wasn't true, but that in any case it hardly mattered. It was only someone else's story, it had nothing to do with them. They would stand in front of the wall-length windows and look right across, past the pines and the Dutchman's neatly ordered acres and the distant line of English trees. Beyond all that, to the greyish smear of the town. And again Richard had the feeling of looking across at miniatures, a profusion of models set out on a board. That feeling was even stronger from the bedroom that was reached by a ladder at the side of his desk. Only in the bedroom there was no large span of glass but a circular window surrounded with black painted metal. Monica said looking from that, at the top here of this crazy house, always made her think of looking from the window of a space-ship. She said, 'The swamp could be a great sea from up here.' From the bed there was nothing of course but the sky to look out at.

Monica had been in the last intake for the Children of Mary before a new post-conciliar priest, replacing the Irishmen who had run the parish for years, came and put an end as he said to all that old-hat stuff. 'Or should I say old biretta?' He talked of trimming the Church back to its Christ-lean essentials, phrases that embarrassed most of his parishioners who didn't care a rap what tremors were coming through from the European theologians. But they missed the comforting details that to them were inseparable from the one apostolic church. So Monica had worn the silver medal on its broad blue ribbon no more than half-a-dozen times, standing in front of the Fatima statue and reading in unison the vows of the sodality. In the next few years, habits her parents' generation had been used to since their childhood were bundled away in the spiritual spring-cleaning. First there were no purple cloths across the statues during Holy Week. Then the Holy Name Society relinquished the gold-rimmed shields on their long poles that used to be set at the end of each row of dark-suited men, the insignia stacked under the convent hall with the backdrops of the nativity plays. The screen was removed in the confessional so that instead of getting the pepperminty breath of the old priest through the mesh that reminded Monica of the outside safe at the bach, there was the face in full daylight of the new priest chatting away to you. Her father said why didn't the fellow give up the whole shooting-box and call himself an agnostic, at least you could admire him then for being honest. 'You have to keep up with the times,' her mother said. Her father told her irritably, 'He'd rather talk about milk-biscuits in Africa than the Holy Ghost.' 'Spirit,' her mother said. 'These days you call him the Holy Spirit.'

Monica was not what the family would call religious, and so the swing of the tide did not matter to her a great deal. But on the Sunday after the Epiphany, in midsummer in fact when the pohutukawas were in full bloom along the low clay cliffs above Shelly Beach, she turned at the Sign of Peace to see a tall man leaning towards her from the seat behind. She noticed a trace of gold along the edge of his front tooth. He held her hand for the brief time it took to say, 'Peace be with you.' She repeated the phrase back to him.

The man's name was Tom Winton. He came from what everyone called 'a good background', which in his case meant his family's holding a block of land somewhere in Hawke's

Bay in a line of descent that led back to the original purchase from the Maoris. A deal made, so his mother used to say, on a July day between a wall-eyed chief and the however many grandfathers back it was who had some vague but profitable relation with the first Minister of Maori Lands. But the memory of the local chief with the bad eye had stayed with the family for a hundred years.

After Mass, when Monica was introduced by her friend Margaret Stein, she thought two things. It struck her first that the tall man she spoke to was both attractive and oddly reserved. And she knew from the minute he looked down at her that he liked her in a way that had more to it than just wanting to reach his hand under her dress, although it certainly would include that as well.

A year later they were married by the new priest who had gone a bit over the odds, both families felt, by telling them in his homily to make the most of physical love. At the reception Monica's family had felt they were under scrutiny. But Tom's people to their credit could not have made it clearer that although they may have issued in a broad prosperous stream from the day the chief held the deed of sale against his good eye and then carefully placed his name in broad missionary script, there was no landed gentry nonsense about *them.* One of Tom's uncles, a bachelor with a striped regimental tie, said, 'You won't find any of that Canterbury shit in our outfit.'

Her father said afterwards that their all being Catholics together was obviously the thing that saved embarrassment about one side having so much, and the other so little. 'Which wasn't quite accurate,' Monica explained. 'Our side had nothing at all.'

They had been married for only a month when her mother was in a car accident and Monica returned to Auckland for the next six weeks. When she came back Tom went with the first New Zealand farming team invited to China, which took another month and a half. Then it was straight back into lambing, and the farm next door came on the market and his family decided it should be bought. And at the start of the summer holidays, her mother had a 'relapse', as her father called it on the phone. In fact it was a heart attack that may or may not have had something to do with her car ploughing along the culvert outside Tuakau several months before. She died the week before Christmas. Monica stayed on with her younger sisters until it was time for school to begin again. Much later she thought what a good well-trained girl she had been, believing you didn't let go of your family—or them of you—just because you married a man to begin a new life three hundred miles away. When she looked back to that year she felt contempt for what she had been, for the sloppiness of her feelings as she drove back and forth across the Taupo Road and through the bland Waikato farmland. She had tried so hard to fit everyone's conception of what she ought to do. But had she told Tom how since adolescence she was bored and irritated by everything her mother thought and said, he would have been as hurt as though she were getting at him. She had told Richard though, who said very little, and stirred his coffee, and touched her hand as she spoke.

They sat in a coffee shop above an area selling unpainted pine furniture and cane chairs from Singapore. There were piles of bright cushions and a rack of Indian scarves that a couple of teenage girls turned round and round. One of the girls drew the scarves out across her pale forearm or slipped them through the ring she made from her forefinger and thumb. They laughed and fooled about and when they walked out onto the footpath Monica said, 'She nicked one of those scarves, did you notice that?'

'Yes, I saw that,' Richard said. 'Was she one of yours? The thief?'

'Come off it! They'd have spotted me and scarpered, my lot.' She grimaced at the thought of the school where she taught, the enclave of privileged mums and dads tucked into the hills behind the town. Then she laughed, resting her hand against her friend's. 'Nothing like seeing a thief to test your social responsibility though, is there? Both of us watching it and not doing a thing.'

Richard said, 'I've been involved in two political acts in my lifetime. One was being patted on the head by Peter Fraser at the Empire Games when I was a kid. The other was in Athens.' He told her about a café near the hospital in Kolonaki. He used to sit there and drink cup after cup of sweet grainy coffee and watch the fashionable women raise their dark glasses onto their hair when they stopped to look at the displays of confectionery in the window. From the same table, by turning his head but not needing so much as to alter the angle of his chair, he could look to the side entrance of the enormous yellow hospital, and occasionally see the poor lugging their unvarnished coffins to the back of waiting trucks. But the point anyway, he said, was that he sat there one day and saw the jokey little proprietor give a smart young bastard the change for a hundred drachmas when it should have been a thousand. 'The young man slapped the keys of his Lamborghini on the counter and shouted abuse. Then he turned to me because my table was only a few feet away, I could be his witness. No, I said. I used one of the few phrases that I knew. *Then zero tipote*. I know nothing. I have no idea. I'd turned into a sly little peasant in a matter of seconds.'

'Were you playing at Robin Hood?' Monica asked.

'A lie for the workers against the bourgeoisie. Then the man I told it for was the first bloke in the city to stick up a photo of the Colonels after the revolution.'

'The right thing for the wrong reasons. We all do that.'

'It tells you about my nose for social realities.' And he

thought then of one of the last times he had been in the café. He had just walked up past the tanks outside the Royal Palace, past the flower stalls which had been boarded up for the first few days in deference to military power, then returned to normal, to the banks of geraniums and potted oleanders and the huge wreaths an armspan across. He passed the closed doors of the Byzantine museum before he took a turn into a narrow modern street shaded like a canyon, with fingers of trailing vines from the iron balconies. He had let himself into their basement flat. The steps down to the door were made from marble that the landlady told him came from the same quarries as the Parthenon. 'That's no big deal,' Jane had said, 'the whole country's one great fucking quarry.' He opened the door and saw that the Samos rug had gone from the back of the settee and the transistor from the table. Both of them were hers so he knew before he walked into the dark bedroom that Jane had gone, that the muslin dresses would not be hanging there and the poster of some saint who was dressed in heavy vestments but had the head of a dog would be removed from the wall. 'Don't tell me that isn't Anubis in some new gear,' she had said the day she pinned it up. 'Just don't tell me that.'

Monica asked him now, 'Watching the time are you?'

'He's never on time. He's always apologetic and red in the face when he gets to surgery. Rushing in from golf.'

'More then?' She rapped the pot with her knuckle.

'Not for me.'

She stirred in half a spoon of sugar and said, 'I've a chart at home that says I need to walk ten minutes to burn off that many calories.' Richard's hands lay on the table in front of him, the fingers laced together.

'Now you look like you're praying,' Monica said.

'I was brought up to believe that if you had the right disposition and were in a state of grace, everything you did was a prayer. *Laborare est orare*. That was my school motto.'

He played with the strap of his watch that rode loosely round his wrist. 'I'll have to make another hole in this thing.' Then he said, 'I've read girls are having bangles welded on that are too small ever to slide over their fists. You have to wear them for the rest of your life.'

Monica said, 'Archaeologists of the future will think it a significant religious shift.'

'A change from bracelets of bright hair,' Richard said.

'Oh,' Monica laughed. 'That. I used to think that was the loveliest poem I'd ever come across.'

'If only you knew what pits of gloom you dig for your young ladies every time you teach them that.'

'Nothing the latest heavy-metal recording won't atone for. Or a quick grope at the weekend.'

'You're not getting cynical?'

'Donne doesn't mean a thing if you're actually screwing your boyfriend.'

'Culture is anticipation, you mean?' Richard said.

Monica took her cigarettes from her handbag. Richard moved his chair to allow a couple from the next table to ease past. He pushed the ashtray from the corner of the table to the centre, and looked down into the well of the shop. There was now an elderly lady touching the scarves where the girls had thieved, and a tall man stretched out his hand and let it run along the scrollwork of a cane chair. Monica lit her cigarette then snapped the dead match into smaller and smaller pieces. The last section she split with her thumbnail.

Richard asked her, 'Is it a free period this afternoon?'

'My mob are doing a UE paper for practice. The HOD'll keep an eye on them.'

Richard laughed, which pleased her. 'You sound very military when you say that. Like HQ and DMZ.'

'What's that last one?'

'Just journo talk.' He was playing again with his watch

strap. The looseness seemed to bother him. He said, 'Of course I could get one of those expanding ones, you know? Like a garter so it still fits even as you get skinnier.'

'You're not losing weight though,' she said. 'You're holding your own.'

'Just,' he answered. He went to move back his chair as Monica smothered the cigarette that was not yet half-smoked. She asked him, 'Wait a minute, do you mind? It's no great hassle if he does see us but I'd rather he didn't.'

'Who?'

'That man looking at the chair. He's my husband.' They waited until the man had left.

'It's an odd time for a farmer to go shopping,' Richard said.

'Sale day if you remember.' She saw the Stock and Station Agents calendar held at the side of the fridge with magnetic clips, the red and blue and green circles ringing various days of the month. There was another circle Tom had drawn in yellow crayon. It marked her birthday, between the last sale day of the month and the date for car registration.

She was speaking about him to Richard for the first time. She said lightly, 'There's the enemy for you surely, if you're still hitting the bourgeoisie.'

'That's a basic contradiction. People on the land can't be middle class.'

'That's only Europe you're talking about.'

'What are we here, then? If it's something different we haven't worked out what it is.'

'If only you knew his ideals,' Monica said. She spoke kindly, and with exasperation.

'Tom's ideals?'

'Would you believe that? Bred with all the care of a Charolais you might say and then this desperate desire to get in among the Jerseys. I mean, a socialist from that crowd!'

'You know what Zhou Enlai's background was?'

'I'm not mocking him,' Monica said. 'He's actually a very good man.'

Without cynicism, Richard thought how women almost always say that, about the man they are being unfaithful to.

They lay together in the room with the circular window. A scraggy sky streamed past the glass. Richard's head rested in the cradle of his hands. It was the second time she had asked him what he would do when it became too difficult to climb the ladder. 'Put the bed downstairs,' he told her. 'That may be the last and the most difficult decision I have to make.' She thought, how long do you have to know someone to tell how sardonic he's being? But she was wrong. He was being quite level with her. He stretched out his hand and ran his fingers across the smooth cap-like fall of her fringe, and admitted how he sometimes didn't feel like the climb even now. But there was no problem in the long run.

'Problem?' she said.

'There's no pride involved, I mean.' He liked this room and he would stay here as long as he could. And when he couldn't, he would shift. He looked at the sky as he told her.

'You know you never take your eyes from that porthole thing when we're here in bed,' Monica said.

'You wouldn't be in bed with me if that was true.' She slapped her hand lightly against his arm. 'Don't talk bawdy.' And he laughed properly then, as he rarely did. He told her, 'You don't know what bawdy is, do you?'

'Is that a disappointment?'

'It goes for me too, I suppose.' He thought, if Jane's word was anything to rely on. It would have been on *that*, anyway.

Monica said, 'It's always seemed a bit out of my grasp. Gymnastics or whatever.' There had been only one lover before Tom. She supposed it must show one way or another.

And she thought of the night of their first anniversary, she and Tom at a restaurant in town, the curve of mock-Spanish arches in the dim lighting. She had touched his hand on the red cloth and said, 'You know the way this first year has gone, love.' She pointed out to him how in twelve months they must actually have slept together about a third of that time. She didn't think much of that—did he? Tom drew back his hand and slipped it along the sides of his glass. 'Oh,' he asked her, 'did that matter so much?' He didn't look at her as he spoke, he didn't return his hand to hers as she had wanted him to do. She had been as shocked by what he said as by anything in her life. She went over it so many times. Her own hand had stayed resting on the cloth, while her spirit drew back. That was the only way she could think of it. But something altered between them in the restaurant, among the tourist posters and the hard, insistent music getting on Monica's nerves.

'You're not upset are you?'

'Upset?'

Richard jogged her head in the hollow of his shoulder. She brushed her mouth against the side of his body. The raised outline of his ribs behind the flesh reminded her oddly of the supports in a tent, their bending and pressing against the strained canvas when they were at the beach as children, her father always dickering with the tent-pegs he found so difficult to get right. 'My mind's all over the place,' she said. 'Did I look vacant?'

'Withdrawn.'

She shook her head shortly. 'I always look like I'm at a funeral when I'm thinking.'

'Not of me then, I hope.'

'Oh, don't joke like that!' She closed her eyes against the warmth of his side. She could hear the pump of his heart, the silky even push so close to her ear. Yet her mind went back to it, to the shame she had felt and tried to cover when Tom said that about their love-making. They drank champagne and drove back to the farm with his hand occasionally touching her knee. They had made love, and when she woke at two in the morning she heard her husband in the next room. She went to the door and asked was everything all right? He looked at her from the desk where he sat in his dressing-gown, papers spread in front of him. He had smiled at her and she thought how touchy she had been earlier in the night, she was so wrong to take his words as she had. 'Come back soon,' she said. She lay expecting him any moment. But when she woke again at six the bed was empty beside her. At breakfast he told her, 'You were so sound asleep I didn't want to wake you.' There were worse things, she said, than being woken by your own husband. And she asked him, 'What was all that paper anyway? It's not time yet for tax, is it?' And he explained no, they were family papers as a matter of fact.

'*Family*?' She tried to say it lightly, as Tom spoke himself when he mentioned his mother's harking back towards some pure source. But she could not stop herself saying, 'I didn't know you took all that so seriously. To get up in the small hours with it, I mean.' Then for the second time that night—or that night, and the morning after—her husband surprised her. He said how of course on one level it didn't matter, not in the absurd way it did for his aunts who lived in the fiction of their breeding, the 'Merinos' as he called them sometimes, fat-throated, dull-eyed, happy at their grazing. 'But on another?' Monica had prompted him. Yes, it mattered there all right. Because it was fact, didn't that count for something? There are lies all about one, he went on, we live in the thick of them. 'You must know that from school as much as I do from politics. That's why I enjoy looking over these. I might even turn them into some kind of book.' His hand brushed at the array of papers and documents and dark-bound diaries his father had collected and annotated for his last half-dozen years, the family stuff that his son now stood beside at the desk. Monica did not ask, although she felt the urge to do so, why aren't there lies in there too? He watched her and smiled as he had last night when she came from the bedroom to see what he was doing. She thought of him in photos as a boy, as a first-year student in a football jersey (still on his mother's wall), or as he stood on the steps at St Joseph's with herself leaning on his arm, her veil billowing across both of them. Something is happening, she thought from the breakfast table. I am beginning to see him for the first time.

Richard now moved again, and she took her weight from his shoulder. 'Do you want to tell him yet?' he asked her. 'You know. Tell Tom?'

'I will soon,' she said. 'Not for a while yet.'

The affair had begun six months ago.

Monica sometimes rode out to Dutchman's Orchard on the way back from school. There were other places closer to town where she might have bought fruit quite as cheaply, but what she bought and what she paid were not the point. For one thing there was the long row of pines with the afternoon sun cutting down not in bars so much as in constant streaming flickers that gave her a deeply sensual pleasure. She had read once that people with epilepsy could be brought to the brink of seizure if they passed through strips of light and darkness, if they sat in a car say as it drove through late-afternoon woods. Such people were taken as far as she was, she supposed, with what must seem a similar elation, then hurled so much further than she could go. She thought always of that as she entered across the first dapple and mix of light. And then there was the old foreign man with the heavy cheeks, weighing out the asparagus in September, the peaches at Christmas, the apples sometimes as late as March. His hair was clipped to a grey stubble across his high narrow head. He wore lengths of string around his neck which he drew off to tie the sugar sacks for those who ordered in bulk. When he stood in the doorway to his shed the shadows lapped across his face and he reminded her of the book in the school library which fascinated her so disturbingly that she set it on the top of a shelf where none of the girls would find it. It was a book of photographs, detailed and morbidly beautiful studies of bodies taken from Danish bogs, the Bronze-Age corpses lifted from the long preserving night of their interments. Some of the bodies still wore in such awful detail the folds of their capes, the caverns of their hoods, one of them the rope that had killed him. Monica thought how they held their fascination forever, they were so like ourselves, the hooded man and the girl chosen to die, confronted with those final rites that must have been only moments ago for them. They were there still for us to gaze at as closely as at the faces of our friends. She watched the old Dutchman's face and thought of the photos in the book, the long glass cases in the museums that must be in darkness while she watched this man here in the light. Then she would go back to her motor-scooter and turn south as she left his drive. The road home took her past the pa at the corner of the main road, its sharpened stick fences and the carved figures at the gate.

She would begin preparing dinner as soon as she arrived home. She and Tom would tell each other about their day's work. They seldom argued, or even disagreed. They spoke kindly from conviction that people should be courteous with each other, as they should be honest and fair-minded. Tom was putting far more time into the Labour Party, a fact which puzzled people when they first heard of it. What's he in *that* for? What about his family? The land that's coming to him? Those are the knives are they, Tom would ask, that are meant to trim back everything, common-sense, responsibility? He put such questions quietly, disconcerting the party people he worked with almost as much as he did family friends. His uncles pointed out that his father had been into dynamos run from windmills, into anything except straight-forward farming. It was that same craziness taking a different turn.

Tom asked her one night, 'If I had anything to do with another woman would that put paid to it? As far as you were concerned?'

'Paid to what?'

'To us.'

'No,' Monica said. She supposed he asked for the only reason that occurred to her.

'One has to tell the truth.'

'Yes,' she agreed.

'Otherwise.'

'I know.' They meant otherwise trying to live like this, civilised, considerate—all that would go in a scribble across whatever careful order one tried to make of life. And while her husband spoke she felt she was watching him again on that night when she woke to an empty bed and had gone to find him in the bright circle from the desk lamp, his pencil running along the lines of the special calendar that gave him the day and the month for a hundred years. What he was saying seemed that remote. Neither of them spoke of love, or whatever the word should be. Then quite angrily Monica thought, as though on the other woman's behalf, that it shouldn't be like that. It should be passion or being carried away or swept off his feet. It should be so he didn't give a stuff what his wife thought of it, instead of adultery neatly stacked like his old diaries, his political papers, life as ever under control.

'So it's all pretty clear then?' Tom asked. He meant, so you won't leave because of it? We won't dislocate our lives absurdly?

'It's better that you've told me, certainly.'

The next Sunday for the first time Tom stayed away from Mass. For a long time Monica had attended only occasionally, at Christmas and at Easter and the Sundays when her father was down staying with them. 'Of course you mustn't go if you don't feel you should,' Tom used to tell her. 'It means nothing if it's compelled.' She sometimes sat on the veranda, a mug of coffee warming her hands, on those Sunday mornings when he drove along the valley to church. She often put to herself whether she had stopped believing, 'given the show away' as her father would say. There was no answering even that one simply. She thought of the sentence she had underlined at university in her favourite book—'I neither believe nor disbelieve.' Yet any intelligent woman should know at least that much about herself. She considered her brother in Australia. He had turned so strongly against it all, against as he said those years out at college at Glen Innes, a memory that was nothing but the dreariness of rugby changing sheds and teachers inflicting scraps of learning as though you could expect nothing without paying for it, not in this vale of tears. But then there was her cousin too, her favourite. He was now a solicitor in Auckland, he served on political committees and carried a small scar from one of the marches a couple of years ago that showed like a strip of white cotton if you moved his hair aside. He called it his liberal's stigmata. He still believed he said because it was logical and it satisfied him emotionally. And probably, he joked, because he didn't fancy a bit on the side. He meant he wasn't like Jack in Melbourne, who had left his wife for a girl with an Italian name, and then left her for another. But now she envied Tom that between one Sunday and the next he could pull down the whole edifice of his religion and level the section and have it planted in ornamental shrubbery, as it were, exactly seven days later.

'And now?' Richard said to her. They had been talking of God, and then of Tom. They sat on the thick flokati rug in the centre of the room.

'He goes to church again, of course.'

'Of course?'

'Since Margaret dropped him.'

Rain was pelting down outside. Monica hoisted the blanket she wore closer about her shoulders. She stretched her feet towards the bar heater and the undersides of her calves gleamed as she raised them. The blanket fell back from her thighs.

'Come off it,' Richard said. 'Not trying to excite me *again*?' He took her feet and rested them in his lap, across the red Chinese-patterned gown. His hands ran along her warm flesh. 'So you got to meet her anyway?' he said. 'The woman he'd taken up with?'

'Remember I mentioned Margaret Stein? Old family friend? Bridesmaid? The one Tom asked what's a girl with a nice Jewish name doing in a church like ours? Well her. They met up again at some Labour Party jamboree.'

'And then she dropped him?'

'She pleaded conscience. Husband of her school friend and what have you. In fact I think she became bored more quickly than she bargained for.'

'With sleeping with him?'

'Even more with his politics. Margaret had jumped in the Marxist end of the pool by then and thought she could entice Tom into joining her. Radicalise him, as she said.'

'Why in bed?'

'Where better to start? One of her catch-cries was that only one in fifty women thought differently to the men they slept with. I suppose she liked the irony.'

Richard placed her legs again on the orange rug. He said, 'Let's have a drop of something to warm us up.'

'I'm not all that cold,' Monica said. She watched her lover raise a fringed cloth from in front of a set of shelves. There were postcards of various places—Vienna, Nepal, the Tholos at Delphi—pinned on their plain wooden side. It made her think of undergraduate flats, although everything else was sparse and tasteful.

He turned to her with each hand carrying a glass with an inch of brandy. He rubbed his knuckles against her cheek before she reached up to take her glass. 'Come on,' he said. 'No being sad now.' They had promised each other that after their first time together.

They met in the first place because her motor-scooter had spluttered out a mile after she left the orchard. She pushed it as far as the next drive, leaned it against a post, and walked towards the odd-ball house she had glanced at often from the road. A modest enough cottage had been added to haphazardly. It made her think of those interlocking bricks that children built with, adding crannies and half-storeys and unbalanced extensions to whatever might have been an original plan. Her old Dutchman had told her something—what was it?—some old joker years ago had tinkered on and off with the place. The side of the building that faced her as she turned from the drive was primed with pink daubs. She supposed he was some old gaffer amusing himself, 'filling in time' as one always euphemistically put it. But then she saw a man not so much older than herself walk from the shed at the side of the house. He carried a can of petrol as though he knew for certain what she was after.

'I only wanted your phone,' she said. 'If I could ring my husband?'

'You can do that too if you like. I'll just put the petrol in first.' He walked with her back down the drive. She saw that the man had not shaved that day, and that his arms, as he raised them and balanced the can against the lip of the tank, were thin beneath his shirtsleeves. She remembered then what someone else had told her about a man who lived along this stretch of road.

When they were back at the doorway to the house, the man said to her, 'The phone's up there.' Monica followed him to a room with wall-length windows and a ladder rising from the far side. She saw the typewriter and the manila folders and photographs held together with coloured plastic clips. She tried phoning home to say she would be late.

'No luck?'

'Farmers,' she said, shrugging.

'You mean you wouldn't expect an answer?'

'I mean you're not surprised if there isn't.'

Monica noticed a small crucifix on a white expanse of wall. The man picked up her glance. 'Vestigial,' he explained. He smiled at her for the first time.

'Am I being nosey?'

'Why not?' Richard took a book from the shelf behind him and held it so that she saw the gold lettering on its spine. 'I read this too.'

'For old time's sake?'

'It's the story I've known longest. Those are the ones we're supposed to like best, aren't they?'

She saw that his grey eyes were flecked with darker dots. She tapped the folders on the desk and asked him, 'Are you writing a book?'

'A local history thing.'

'Why?' she said.

Instead of answering her he said, 'An enthralling story about bigots and carpetbaggers and rip-off merchants and the lower orders scrabbling to put the boot into someone further down. It's the story of our country in miniature.'

She heard the edge cutting across her own words when she said, 'Why waste your time on people so much beneath you?'

'Because some of their descendants are paying me to do it. The local council in fact. They think if your grandfather is in a book then he couldn't have a been a shit.'

'And you'll enlighten them?'

'No.' Richard sat on the arm of a leather chair drawn close to the expanses of glass. He smiled at her again. He said that he used to be a journalist, and this was simply work he could do at home.

'Try the phone again if you like.'

She said, 'You must be the one who's supposed to be dying.'

'I know you too,' he said. 'Your husband's a Tory radical posing for the time being as a centre-left Labourite.'

'Goodness!' Monica laughed. 'Have you got spies?'

'It's called research.' He was glad that she had taken it as a joke. 'I also hear he's got journals and things I'd like to borrow.'

'I don't think he'd let you have them.'

'Never mind,' he said. He moved his hand towards a chair, inviting her to sit down. 'We've both heard things that are half true.'

Her husband had said some months after his 'openness' with her, after the honesty that had cleared his behaviour in much the same way as his no longer going to Mass had done, 'It's all over, Monica. That whole business with Margaret.'

She had thought, 'This is like the second act of some play about adultery. The audience has been out for coffee after all the pain and now it's back to see how the stitches are put in.' She and Tom were sitting as they had that other evening too, the same papers probably on his desk, she with the stack of exercise books on her knee. She cuffed them with her palms so they sat square.

'It was a mistake.'

'Everything is when it's over.'

Tom uncrossed his legs. He said, 'You know that's pretty trite.'

'So's fucking for a few months. If it's only that.' She knew putting it so crudely disturbed her husband. She felt she was like the bitches she had seen on television or read of in books, now that she had the whip hand. She said, 'It didn't take long for her to get bored with it.'

'It wasn't boredom.'

Monica set the exercise books on the floor beside her chair. 'Sorry,' she said. 'I thought ordinary old grabbing a bit would follow the ordinary old pattern of it wearing thin after a while unless there were spiritual depths I wouldn't know anything about.' Then she caught herself at what she was doing. Never mind about Tom, she was demeaning herself. She cleared her throat and told him, 'I shouldn't go on like that. It's not what I mean to be saying.'

'Well?' Her husband waited for her revision. He had picked up the ivory paper knife he used for a marker in the farm diary. It had been a Christmas gift between his grandparents before they married.

'I only mean we need to make an effort. You know, that we don't sink ourselves in brawling. I'm just reminding myself of that.' Tom put down the paper knife and walked across to her. He began to unbutton her blouse. It was not like him to step aside from habit even in a thing like sexual advance. He fumbled the catch on her bra and undid the buckle on her leather belt. He continued until she was naked in front of him, but her own hands had not moved. He looked at her and told her to sit down again and then he knelt between her knees. She thought Margaret must have taught him something, after all. She felt his head against the inside of her thighs. His hands, folded into loose fists, rested on either leg above her knees. Then he remained still like that, her own hands now on his shoulders which she rubbed at gently. She thought how behind the sex there was something even stronger. He was a man who liked being humbled more than anything else.

They remained like that until Tom believed he was pleasing her. There was the occasional distant sound of an animal from across the farm. The curtain moved at the open window, swaying out slowly across the desk, its hem whisking softly against his papers. Her hand moved across the back of her husband's neck then began to unbutton the shirt she had given him at his last birthday. She supposed afterwards that she was the one finally who had behaved like the man. She might have done anything to him, as they say about submission.

'Fourteen years!' Monica said. 'Fourteen years away from everything here and you wanted to come back!'

'You know the old saying about going back to the mat.'

'I know it but I don't see the point of it. Not with you.' Richard told her he came out of the doctor's rooms in Clapham, after the first tests had come back, and his mind was already made up. 'Twenty-four hours later I'd booked my flight home.'

They were walking on the far side of the swamp. Its level was high from recent rain, and lay still as a mirror. Richard swung at the grass with a stick. He had thought of here, he said, the minute he heard.

Monica was still puzzled. 'But throwing in all that because you hear you're not well. I mean if you get better and then you've left your life over there?'

'All that?' Richard took her up. 'A number of people I worked with, went to the pub with, walked round parks or galleries with on Sunday afternoons? That's all we're talking about.'

She shook her head. 'I'm out of my depth. If you knew what I'd give even to get there.'

'There were about a dozen of us, close friends. Some were married, some weren't. From time to time one of us drifted away from the group and someone else floated into it. We all liked much the same things and it was civilised, if you like, in a way I'd never have known here at home. I lived with one of the women for a couple of years, then she took a job in a museum in Cambridge.'

'That's not far. Is it?'

'Distance is how many people there are between two points quite as much as it is a matter of miles. In English terms it was a long way.'

'But there's no one here at all,' Monica said. 'Not ones that matter to you.'

'You can't compare either, if things are too far apart.'

'Oh!' Monica flicked a rusted can from her path with a rapid turn of her foot. 'I can't run a measuring tape over everything as easily as that.'

They said nothing then for several minutes. A horse in the neighbour's paddock ambled towards them. Monica plucked handfuls of lush grass from beside a log that must have lain there for half a century. The horse's mouth quivered along her sleeve before it nuzzled into the feed. The lips felt rubbery against her palm. Then she and Richard walked further beside the placid rim of water. The horse kept up at their shoulders, waiting, breathing heavily, until they both stooped to gather more grass for it.

'You know I see a place on TV or get a letter from somewhere and I think for a moment that I've got a whiff of what it's like, but it's not even that much really.' Monica's hand lifted as she spoke. She meant the place here, the district, the town over there and the private school in the hills and a little beyond that, her husband and the farm, the quick drop to the coast, the stretching out and out of the sea—all that for the moment was balanced on her hand. 'That's about my world,' she said. 'I don't even know enough about the rest to miss it.'

'I still write now and then,' Richard said. 'Maybe for the first pint on Sunday mornings someone says, "Heard from

Richard," and someone else says, "Christ that reminds me, make me drop him a line sometime will you?" That's about all it means once you've left.'

More sharply than she meant, Monica asked him, 'Why should any of us expect more than that?'

The man beside her raised the willow stick he carried and tapped it against her arm. 'I'm not whimpering,' he said. 'I'm not asking for special favours, miss.'

They were at the far end of the swamp. Trees grew at odd angles from the low bank above the water. It was difficult to say of some of them whether they were alive or dead. The trunks and the leafless branches reflected blackly in the water beneath them. A fantail cut in rapid bursts a few yards from where Richard stopped and Monica came up behind him, circling him with her arms and resting her head on the back of his suede jacket. They stood in the heightened silvery light, the bird piping thinly as it darted about them, and Monica thought how if they stopped like this for only a few minutes, the fantail would perch on them. But they turned to the impacting clatter at the far end of the swamp, the mirror sheered off into fragments where first one duck, and seconds behind it another three, slapped down onto the water.

It was several evenings later, back at the house, that Monica said, 'What does it give you here, then? I mean what are you after?'

Richard said, 'You're always saying "I mean", do you know that?' He stood up from where he sprawled in the leather chair. Monica sat on the floor, her head leaned back against its arm. She watched him draw his gown around him and she thought how gaunt he looked as he did that. The token of his illness. 'Token,' she thought again. For it did seem only that, a sign and not an essence; not the defining and corrupting force which of course it was.

'Don't prevaricate,' she said.

'The "gift" then, if you want to call it that. What I'm after is stillness.'

'Stillness?' She heard the slight rise in her voice that completed the statement for her—*is that all?*

'Since I was a kid, you know? The thing I've always admired because it really is so simple yet it's hardly ever been around me. Not in my family to begin with, not my marriage with Jane nor with anyone else I ever had to do with.'

It was important to her that she understand at least this about him. 'You came all the way back for *that*?'

'The only reason,' he said. He leaned back against the ghost room in the reflecting expanse of glass behind him. 'The day I heard—the *minute* I heard—what was probably wrong with me and how long it would take for this or that to happen. It was like an instinct. This place came into my mind although I suppose I hardly thought of it at ordinary times, I mean.'

'There. You're saying it now.'

But he passed over her banter. 'I didn't need to think of it much I realised later because it was always there, underneath the rest. Behind whatever else I was doing.'

Monica watched the man she loved as he hunched against the glass, one naked foot set across the other, his fists weighing like stones in the pockets of his dressing-gown. She was thinking how absurdly lives converge, strands draw together. She could see no more sense in it than that. And she remembered his telling her on one of their first days together, at the distant beginning of their friendship, how he was here at all in this odd-ball house on these few acres of rough paddocks with the swamp she looked down on now, a greyish smear out there in the night. Here as he said because a half-inebriated grandfather had met another man in a bar in Onehunga, beside the wharves, in the same November week as the first war came to an end. The man was known always in the family as the stranger. He is with an Aussie mistress who looks exactly what she is and talks of racehorses he has owned or is going to own. He has also (all this in Richard's words, his mother's words, presumably at some stage his grandfather's too) a contempt for almost everyone he knows, he sees already that the ending of the War is as much a farce as its beginning. Some years later according to the story he disappears off a ship between Melbourne and Perth in weather so calm you'd think it was part of a painting. But in the Onehunga bar, in the reek and bonhomie of Scotch, the celebrating racket of distant victory, the stranger says he's got this bit of land it's going for a song, you wouldn't find a better piece, dirt cheap. *To cut it short* Richard had said several times while he told her. So his grandfather comes here after parting with his last hundred quid. He clears the scrub and carts in gravel and digs pits in one place to throw up mounds in another, anything rather than admit the stranger might have sold him a pup. He builds the cottage and drags stumps from the swamp except for that far end where the trees still sloped above the water because he believes one day that will be an ornamental garden, it is only a matter of time which he thinks is the one commodity he's not likely to run out of. Only one day thirty years later his heart stalls and the Maori woman he has taken up with the minute he gets out from under Richard's grandmother's eye turns him from the sacks he's slumped against and he's already dead. But that is how the cottage was built and the swamp first cleared. Then a son who has never married, who the rest of the family accept as more than a few bob short, who walks always with a limp although no physical reason was ever found for it, takes over from the old man and turns his energy and inventiveness against the house itself. He runs up bits and pieces from the walls and above the roof and out at defiant angles, until he in turn dies on the afternoon of a Ranfurly Shield game because his body is found in the kitchen several days later and he's wearing the black and white woollen cap that he always wore, the closest he came to ritual, whenever he listened to a match. 'From then on,' Richard said, 'there was a string of tenants who knocked the hell out of the place and a while when it was empty, until I started coming here as a student. Because nobody in the family ever thought it worth selling any more than it was worth doing up. That was when I put the glass in place of one wall and made the bedroom upstairs you can see nothing from except the sky. At the time it was the most romantic thing I could think of.' And this talk coming back to Monica now as she watches him against the dark glass, as though the glass itself is water and the reflected objects of the room, the armchair and the bookcases and she herself sitting on the orange rug, are receding into it. We are what brings the story this far, she thinks, we shall press back as it goes on and becomes someone else's. Her eyes were tired from crying earlier on. She had decided months ago she would never do anything as crass as that, Richard must never be yoked into some awful sentimental thing because of her. But today they had sat here in the room for hours while the late sun drained off from the hills and the night had risen as it seemed from the ground, until now they floated on it. The water outside moved with quick running lights when cars turned at the corner near the Dutchman's bend. They had decided—Richard made her decide—they would not tell Tom after all. Not tell her husband she loved another man, as she wanted to do. He had brushed his hand across her hair, spanned her wrist with his fingers, talked so calmly to her until she saw how right he was to leave things exactly as they were. 'Talking her down,' wasn't that the phrase? A suicide on a ledge, a test pilot—where did the phrase come from in the first place? But down, certainly: from hope, from her fears of grief, from expectations of oneself or of others. His hand moving smoothly across her flesh, adroit as oil.

Billy Joel Her Bird

Billy Joel her bird. Betty's bird. He move along his stick in the cage, the cage swing out, Billy Joel make it swing. His whistling then all morning, afternoon. His cage on a hook over the cut-out bench and Betty talk him every little while. Sometime the other girls make Betty mad, they run the scissors along Billy Joel's wire and he stop singing. He shaking in one corner of the cage and the girls laugh. Fat Frances say or Rachel, look, where his whistle Betty? Then they hide down behind the bench because Betty throw her markers at them, hold up her scissors like she going to stab them hard, you dirty cows! Come on, Fat Frances tell her, where's a joke? So she hand over this bit of lettuce from her lunch box and Betty fold it over careful between the bars. Here my Billy, she say to him, here my darl. Betty she so pretty everyone in the factory like to walk past her. Her hair fall down shiny right pass her shoulders, over the pink line beside her ear she hate people to look at. And she got this radio nobody to touch that except Betty say to, and the tapes inside her drawer. See, everyone like giving Betty presents that how she get all these tapes. But only her favourites she ever bother to put on. There, she telling her bird, this one ours. She makes her mouth go with the song.

But I'm taking a Greyhound
On the Hudson River Line
I'm in a New York state of mind.

Fat Frances tell her, you pretend you know that Betty? Not even saying them properly. That no worry Fat, she call out.

No worry either Gunga and Frig come pass when they pick up the big bin of scraps and they touch her on the arse, Betty just flap her hand, push them off like it nothing much. It's Rachel shout out youse leave her, youse touch her tit you cop this. Rachel hold up the long weight like a ruler she keep her patterns straight with. Touch yours too had any, Frig tell her back, all drop off or something? And Rachel tell him then wouldn't know where to put it would you Frig. Frances say, not even for practice, those just two wanker. Betty not caring one way or other. She turn her tape over. Listen darl.

Sing us a song you're the piano man,
Sing us a song . . .

Betty only twenty-two. She so pretty, Betty, I think I tell that. She wear jeans every day Rachel say her mother want to hide her legs from the men. Stop men reaching up their hands. And best tits. Everyone reckon that. Should be in movies, Rachel tell her. Rachel always try to make it nice when Betty cry and her friends say don't Betty, everyone your friend, even the mongoes standing up you get on the bus, want to carry your bag. Then Betty smile again like she forgot already why she start to cry. Put her tape on, Fat Frances shout across to me, stop gawping at her. She let me touch her radio Betty but no one else. Everyone else scare to. But I find a tape I say this one, Bet? Listen Rachel laugh out he calling her Bet now. But she tell me that the one, that the one she want on. And she shove her hair back and smile. When I push the button I say that all right then? Fat Frances watch me, she say to Rachel Hey, Mister Ronnie Corbett chasing Betty's pants, you watching Rachel? Mister Ronnie Corbett my joke name with everybody. I see him Thursday night in his big chair and nice pullover and glasses a bit like mine. And I smile big like him. My hands between my knees in the lunchroom that like him too. I watch him careful, how he walk next to his fat mate, I walk like that next to Fat Frances sometime everyone piss himself. Betty some days she come right up there behind me, her hands squeeze my shoulder, she say when everyone else looking, see my best mate here, everyone? I lean my head back on her. Not on her tits, not talk like that, on her chest, that the polite way to say it. I smile so my teeth look good, I sing in a voice come a surprise to everyone,

Friday night I crashed your party
Saturday I said I'm sorry
I was only having fun
wasn't hurting anyone.

Anyway Billy Joel this morning I think of, he lie there, both his feet these little hooks, his eyes still open but sort of rubbed. I mean the shine not there, only this dull old dead eye. Betty look at him at first, just not believing Billy Joel dead as all that. She think he having a game or something. Then she turn the cage and swing it round so sudden Rachel turn her head only quick enough in time, and *thwack* the cage belt on the edge of the bench and all the wire bits make me think of straight stiff rain when the cage hanging there on the nail those wires spring out all over the place, and Billy Joel just this fucked dead yellow fluff there on the floor. Then all week, every day, Betty not even playing her tapes, her face swollen up like someone bash her. Fat Frances and Ruth make their joke after a while but not so funny now. Every day at the canteen I bring Betty back the cake she like, you peel the paper off the side and see the little ribs. She eat them all right but not as good as before. So I think what to do to make her happy then? The whole workroom different too when Betty like this. The forelady scream and carry on that the work not done right and Rachel hold her scissors until she past and shove them up and down in the air behind her, says cut her arse to pieces one of these day. So all this time I thinking what to do for Betty just across the bench and her lovely hair over her face like she inside this shining tent. Then I think well we get her another bird. I tell Fat Frances and she say she ask Rocky fix that shagged cage. Rocky her boyfriend in the metal shop, Fat say he do anything for her if every now and then she go in the storeroom with him. She got these other boyfriends too, she laugh and shout out when sometime they punch and kick out in the yard because she nice to them all. Enough to go round everyone, that her joke. Rachel tease at her, room for Mister Ronnie Corbett in there too? I hope Betty not listening when they talk dirty things. Anyway Betty only smiling, she touch my shoulder, she say out loud jealous of you, that their trouble. Anyway I make up my mind. I go into the pet shop near to Coles where the man let me watch the puppies and hold the kittens and sometime when he too busy I sweep the shop for him. One day I even mind the shop all lunchtime on a Saturday when he go down the road. So when he out the back where he keep his straw and the big lot of food for his shop I open a cage and take out a bird got blue wings on it and like someone draw on him with a pen, these little black marks. I think it all out very careful before I go there, I take this rubber band that hold his wings down at his side so there no flying off. On the bus I feel him warm and jumpy in my pocket and he shit white and runny over my hand. Then I run up the workshops before the others get there. Fat Frances there though because we plan it and she hold open the cage for me and I take the rubber band away. At first though the bird not jumping and flying like we hope, he sort of drag over to a corner and just bunch up. Fat say I reckon you half kill him Ronnie. And now he go all ruffly like he been rained on and not quite dry out. Then Betty arrive and funny enough she think it my bird, see, because no one say it a present for her, because it too sick to say that. So she hold my hand and she saying never mind, never mind, and when it stop moving about morning tea time she take it out carefully and wrap it in a piece of material they cutting from this week and when she come back from outside she say I put him somewhere quiet for you, Ronnie. And she smiling at me whenever after that. Ruth and Fat Frances look at me and behind Betty's back move their fingers rude as they can. Hey bitch! Ruth shouting at her friend, the peppermint on her tongue showing like it sit on a dirty cushion. And Betty say suddenly like it just struck her, someone fix up this cage? Then she lean over and say to me, for the first time since Billy Joel dead, because no one else ever allowed to touch it, she ask me, push that tape on for me, Ronnie Corbett. She even put her own finger on the button next to mine. And the music start again, after what seem ages. Her old favourite then, Betty's mouth talking with the words, *I was only having fun, wasn't hurting anyone*. Nice one, Fat Frances call out. We all tapping our hands on the bench in front of us like Billy Joel never die, like it was before and good as now, just about.

the snow in spain

if you could only see me the way i am now alec you'd piss yourself at the very sight. remember the way you used to love anything a bit freaky remember that. if i could work the brackets on this thing with only one hand i'd throw them up either end of this sentence and say look who's talking will you just look ha ha. i get so bored sitting here even with perth across the stretch of water there so shining and all it makes you think of oz at the end of the movie it makes you think there has to be something wrong with it, it couldn't be that lovely. the girls are off at the club and there's this other bloke standing in for me until i have the plaster off. that's in a couple of days time and in any case the show might be closed up by then, there's been letters to the papers and wowsers snooping round as it is. if only roxy had thought of it before she said i've carried this bloody portable round with me for years god knows why i don't remember when i even opened the thing. she gives her roxy laugh. thought once she says i'd do a typing course the minute i got out of the cross there but you know what those plans come to don't we all. roxy's a bit like looking across the city on mornings like this. you'd have really gone for her alec. you'd have made that little duck's arse out of your mouth and sucked your breath in and said just put my name down for a slice when that one's handed round. so i started tapping out with two fingers of my left hand because the tv is shot since mitch put his foot through it and who the hell's going to explain that to the hire people i thought i'd write alec it might be years till i get round to it another time. like it seems years ago doesn't it since those long warm evenings in the green kitchen you said just looking at it made you want to chuck, the fridge placed so you only had to lean your chair back on two legs to drag the stubbies out. we had to sit inside in summer even because if there was only one mozzie in the state he'd sniff you out the minute you opened the wire door. i'd been thinking about those times anyway before i decided to write. remember when i told you very early on about the one thing at the factory i used to look forward to. jesus the dirt used to pile up on me there. i remember i told you that and the other things the awful stink all that time from the sulphur vats. even now i can't stand the look of anything yellow not even a yellow car or a yellow tablecloth that's enough to bring back the smell, a corridor of pus at the back of my throat. and the racket of the place. by knockoff time i'd be aching with just the din of the presses and the belts slapping across above the machines. i told you all that otherwise i'd never have mentioned what i looked forward to that one afternoon a fortnight when the machines shut down at two o'clock and the sports teams from the different sections took off to the oval. at first i thought they might drag me along as a lucky charm a mascot you know how but luckily that didn't occur to anyone. no one gave a stuff much what i did. they'd yell and shove at each other in the locker room and call out to me to watch my step there samson who did i think i was leaning on. then once it was quiet i'd go out the sidedoor from one of the storerooms and there it was. yards of this deep grass and the sound of the creek. the light that was kind of dusty and red between the tall brick walls but this bloody grass alec you'd think it was painted. it was a real creek between the workshops water for some reason that hadn't been mucked up. it wouldn't have been more than a foot deep and these small ferns on the edge and moss that was plushy you know when you pushed at it. it was clear that way aquariums are in posh hotels and i'd put my hands in the water so they'd look green and different and these tiny bubbles along the hairs on my arms. and you'll say i'm boring the arse off you going on about it. you used to tell me that often enough, eh alec. if i told you what i'd read in the papers say or especially if i ever mentioned things made me think of grafton, for the love of god do you have to be so boring. probably, i'd say. and then you would laugh. you'd take the plate i gave you and not say a word until there was the sound of your knife scraping round the edges so you wouldn't lose a scrap. you'd say sometimes one thing you can do's make bloody great tucker. you'd let your belt out and raise one leg and call out duck this one, soldier, and i'd roll over making out you'd bowled me. jesus it was fun those days alec. sometimes i'd hardly be able to get up for laughing. you'd put your foot on me and pretend you were holding me down till you had another one ready to let go. you used to say yourself what fun we had. you didn't give what you called a tinker's root either for who saw us walking to the bus together, what anyone thought about anything if it came to that. you did it all so natural. and you'd have understood mitch's offer too if you'd been round, just don't give a bugger about what they think, isn't that right. well you'd love it now alec if only you'd stayed round. you'd love every minute of it.

behind everyone we call 'you' that's really special there's another you, know what i'm getting at. it makes me think of those trick ads on tv sometimes there's a man say advertising some health food let's say he's bouncing up and down, raising his arms, making you think how fit he is. then suddenly his edges blur so where there were two arms there are now four, he sort of unpacks himself one behind the other so you feel there is a line of people where at first you thought there was only one. the one in front of you at the time seems the only one, the only real mate, but there was always someone else who mattered that much too at a different time i'd love to explain it to you alec just to hear you say mother of j.c. esquire what's the wank of the day but grafton would have understood like a shot. grafton'd know alright.

some mornings i come out on the veranda and see the stretch of the river just across the street. it makes me think of some shimmery material pulled very tight and i can hardly believe i'm over here in a place like this, as if the factory and all that was just a story someone told me about someone else. when i was a kid practically grafton i heard you say you'd give anything to be able to paint or something so you could make things last and i remember i thought what on earth's he talking about, why's he want to do that. but i think that too these mornings. i think this is perth where i never expected to be and there is something i can do and i'm paid more to do it than i'd ever get from anything else. i know the names for things that i'd never heard of a month ago. roxy has shown me geraldton wax for instance and coral trees and i know my way about hay street and sometimes when i'm with her we eat pastry that's shiny as glass in a place where the waitresses dress as mountain girls and the building is like a swiss house on a calendar. you told me grafton about the spanish girl you had lived with when we were at home by ourselves until you'd get up and walk to the window and jingle the coins about in your pockets and say tempers fuckit, that's latin, old man. and when my aunt came into the room you always stood up. you were the only man she ever brought home to stay because it didn't worry you that i was there. first time you came in you saw me sitting on the sofa in that dark old sitting room and you said now if she'd told me you were here i could have brought you some toys. i remember my aunt covering her face with her hands and you realised you'd made some kind of mistake. but he's sixteen she called out. she was crying for herself though because she had had to look after me from the time i was a kid. she had said to me only a year before wouldn't i be happier if i joined some place where there were others the same. she said there were lovely clubs and social functions and i'd really love it. but this day anyway grafton you put your arms round her and patted her head against your shoulder and winked across at where i still sat staring at you both. you were letting on we understood each other, what was a bit of a mistake about mentioning toys after all. because i laughed out loud then, didn't i. i beat my shoes against the leg of the chair and my aunt thought i was going to have a fit or something. we'll get on famously, that was the next thing you said. in the posh voice i know she liked you for as much as the name she never knew could be a person's first name. after you left the next morning she was all over me. she kissed me and rubbed my hair because she was so happy. i think about that when i go into the dressing room and the girls start pawing me about. you'd be amused by that grafton as alec would. he'd have flapped that wonky arm of his and done his rooster call but you'd just lean back with your hands in your pockets and say play it again, sam. you always came out with that when you heard something you liked. all that female flesh eh grafton. those blessed sets of pliables, that's what you called them, reaching up as my aunt passed behind your chair and she would look quickly over at me and then at you, as though you shouldn't speak like that when i was there. but i'd kick this drum-roll on my chair legs and we'd all break out laughing. the jokes you could have had with this lot. and i'm thinking now as well grafton about that time it snowed. it was freezing because the oil heater had packed up and all we had were these measly pinecones to try and catch a bit of warmth from in the grate. my aunt said why are we living in a dump like this anyway, she was never out of the sight of beaches until she was in her twenties and look at her now. you had your arm around her and pulled the blanket up across her shoulders and told her there were people in spain who had never so much as seen the ocean in their lives. and my aunt was laughing and crying together and said well she had never seen a bullfight but what did that have to do with it. when my aunt became upset like that her hair fell in wisps about her face and above where her fist held the blanket against her throat was this lovely light pink colour. but this night, you can't have forgotten that. i was the first to see it. i drew the blind back from the window and there was this quick rushing where the big flakes hit against the glass. look. i ran across to the sofa and put my hand to my aunt's cheek to turn her to the window. look at this. you opened the door onto the veranda and she ran to stand behind you. she said in this quiet voice as if she were almost afraid or something, but this never happens here. she put her arm around you and her thumb hooked over your belt. then you let out this whoop grafton that startled us both. you grabbed me up and swung me in this arc so that my legs were flying in the snowing before you had left the top step. and you ran down the steps and carried me with you into the yard. i looked up at the spinning ropes of snow that fell in my opened mouth. it sprinkled so quickly over our shoulders. and you held me up there above you, shaking me at the sky. esta niviendo you were shouting out, esta niviendo. then my aunt was there beside us when you put me down and i pranced my feet up and down on the pure ground. we were all shouting to each other and i was stinging with the cold. grafton she called out grafton no as you put your hands at the top of her legs and hoisted her up. her arms were round your neck and her skirt rode right up so that through the black and white flicker of the night i could see the length of her naked legs her thighs as they gripped round you and you tried to run through the spinning flakes. then the excitement had suddenly gone from it as though a light had been switched off. i went inside and waited shivering until you came in. then we all had glasses of brandy until our fingers pulsed thick with the hurting warmth and the steam rose from our shoulders. i hold the brandy in my mouth when roxy lets me drink from her glass. we make a sort of game of it. she looks towards the door making out she's terrified someone's coming in on us if monique or simone happens to almost see us she'll toss a towel or one of her underthings across the glass and say that was a close one, perfect. mind you mitch would really throw a big one if he ever caught us. he thinks if i drink it will bugger up my flight. but he doesn't like it either that roxy's even my friend. neither of you, not you alec nor grafton either, would think that mitch was worth a pinch of shit. he's supposed to be roxy's bloke but you ought to hear how he talks to her. or to the others too, the crude talk i mean in front of her. he says he pays them more than grinders have any right to expect so the door's always open, they can piss off the second it comes into their heads. he has an eagle would you believe it tattooed across one of his shoulders and a little star on his cheek, just on the side of his eye. he wears belts with big cowboy buckles and before we go on he puts a folded teatowel down the front of his leather pants so it looks bunchy as a fist. that's the real star he grins at roxy. you said as we drove down to town once grafton when your eye was playing up and you needed to have the socket looked at, most people you said are god awful shysters know that old mate. i said i didn't know.

you have to know both of you what it's like when someone suddenly walks out. the person left thinks there's been some kind of mistake for a while, as if it's not really yourself who is feeling all this but someone else who has taken your place. then it comes home that it's going to last. just leaving that note for my auntie when it seemed the three of us were set together, that wasn't on. or just telephoning from the station alec saying there was this job in the north you weren't in a position to say no. but what about your crook hand i said. it was the only thing i could think of to say. i could imagine you see at the table in the kitchen stroking the shiny skin where the accident was. with anyone else you always made sure it was out of sight. sometimes you put a glove over it when we were out. but at home you'd stroke it the way they stroke a cat or something or even someone's forehead when they're sick. jesus you'd have hated it if i said that though eh. you'd have worked up a real snorter for that one or one of those great belches when you'd pull the front of your shirt out and look down at your gut and say who fucken invited you then. but on the phone when i said that about your hand there was this gap when i knew i'd made a blue. then you gave this half grunt this half laugh, you said there's worse things than a crook arm you dopey little bugger.

so i'm bloody careful about whatever i let on to you then aren't i mitch. one thing mind apart from work you couldn't care what i think about anything. when i met those guys at the morley pub the night we went to watch their turn one of them said you were the best thrower there is. he'd seen them at the manhattan in brisbane and the venue at st kilda so he must have known. the little abo bloke said he knew people who worked with you and they all said, he's ace. holy shit one of the others said there's throwers out there smoke dope so they don't give a shit if you go into the crowd. the abo just hung on this bloke's every word. doc's done all sorts of work haven't you doc, he said, he's done the big shows, ice, the lot. but it was then you and your mates came over mitch and there was talk then about which clubs were the ones to work and how the pigs were supposed to be going to close us down for good. the abo's thrower said there's more fucken do-gooders in this state than there are fucken people. then you told them mitch how we'd never had anything except full houses, chocker, there was a demand out there the public had a right to so let the fascists rot. i could see that vein in your forehead going bump bump. then this other bloke chimes in you've got the girls as well mate you can't go wrong. that's when you squeezed my shoulder, sort of building me up in front of them all. look you told them they can see a bit of snatch at home if that's what they're after, we're the ones they come to see that right. that's right mitch, i said. but tell you what though you said looking round all of us, the girls are what bring the women in. go on, the abo said. and you told them what roxy had already told me anyway, that the women got as big a kick out of a decent strip as the blokes did. and while you were talking i thought god knows how you've hung on to roxy, even simone and monique look trashy next to her. she walks into a place even with all her clothes on and she knocks them out. you see it's grace she'd got not just what you call the goods, mitch. you'd think i was out of my tree if i told you that, you'd think i was a sniffing little bastard like that mate you had over surfers. it was different girls over there but you just got sick you said of the way he could do what he liked with them, took their bras off in the dressing room, remember you told me that, sprayed under their arms for them. you walked in once and caught him making out one of those private things of theirs was a joint, he'd even lit up and these slags were killing themselves. you said who did he think he was woody allen and kicked his arse round the room. that was before throwing ever came in, he just strutted about between strips and cracked a few jokes so you could get rid of him just like that. it made you fucken mad to see those little mitts crawling between the girls legs and they either didn't mind or even enjoyed it, the bitches. lose respect for those you work with the show can only go downhill. you were the one told me that, same morning soon after i started and you said roxy was your bird, you'd hand out more than a warning to anyone fancied he could do alright for himself there. i mentioned this to roxy later she said he's even jealous of blind people the dozy prick. that was after i'd got to know her and i'd sit reading the paper to her in the dressing room and the girls changing their gear all round me, simone sometimes pretending to smother me to death with her jugs until i'd have to shove her away to get my breath back. you came in just as roxy was leaning over me that night you mucked up the throw. i knew by the look of you something would go wrong trouble is you're thick as pigshit that's your trouble mitch. all the teatowels you can shove down the front of your jeans won't make up for that.

the girls rent this house not far from the river. what's the point of a fucken house though when we'll be moving all round the state, mitch couldn't get the point of it. look you said unless the cops make us close shop we'll work a dozen places from bunbury to geraldton, they're crying out for us. see that photo of bloody schwarzenegger here in the paper last week, had to turn them away didn't we rest of the morley run. the photo showed me in mid-air my arms spread out my helmet making me look like an astronaut. underneath it said how i'd told them it was great people like myself were given a chance to make a living. i said i certainly didn't think it was demeaning, it was a skill there was a market for and it was a great way to make new friends. you'd wised me up mind about what things i'd better say. the crash helmet's light blue and matches the jumpsuit roxy made out of blue satin with a red triangle on the chest. the crowd love the joke as soon as i walk in, lois lane still drop her daks does she, they're shouting out things like that. that abo boy i talked to a while back said he was always having to find some new slant just to keep them off the snow white jokes, he got so fed up with a little black goes a long way sort of thing. but it's pretty good when we first go in like that isn't it mitch. i'm leading you by a chain that goes with the leather gear you're wearing and the spiked collar, your arms bare and the eagle bulging there at the top of the arm your hair sleeked down so it shines. i know you get a high out of the roar and the whistling when it looks for a moment like the freak is leading the stud. then you hold your arms up with the black leather strips round your wrists and explain how the throwing's done and although there is no chance of anyone getting hurt you say you'd appreciate utter quiet during the performance. some shows you hear of let the audience have a go but you won't wear that. it cheapens the whole thing, you say, it's just pissheads wanting to act big to haul in pussy. so when it's quiet and simone's got the drum roll going in the corner you lean down and straighten my scarf and there's that smell that tells how you're excited. it's the crowd and the noise and the smoky light when the spot's on and you're at the centre in your black gear, your face dead white. but your hands underneath my arms when you pick me up then let me sort of float there while you grip the harness must be the steadiest thing i've felt in my life. see that's the puzzle about you mitch, steady like that and mad as a snake. on the bus across when you flew on ahead i sat next to roxy all the way, that's how i know so much about you. she said she'd been with you now a couple of years. she wasn't interested in working the parlours the way monique would go back to because it screwed you in the head. or some heavy got hold of you and you tasted a bit and next thing you couldn't knock it off, they owned you once that happened. she didn't know much else she said except taking her clothes off that was the trouble, grinding her bum so the wankeroos had themselves a free fat. what's a wankeroo i asked her. every second bugger in australia, she laughed, you won't have a problem finding one if that's what you're into collecting but mostly on the trip over she'd look out at the scrub, at the red distance not changing for hours. sometimes she says to me and she's only half joking why don't we just cut loose from all this shit. when she's had a blue with mitch after one of the shows say and we sit on the veranda and look at the city reflected in the river like something massive's been killed and all this bleeding across the water. or when we're on this swinging seat thing in the mornings and one of those long green parrots with the little yellow ring round its neck slices down between the trees. just leave all that shit imagine it roxy says and settle for something like this. i think of my aunt saying one of these days it won't be like this grafton we'll be out of this dump and up the coast there where the big lights are. or you alec. it's got to come, you were always saying that, the sleeping giants, going to wake up one of these days and the bosses won't know what's knocked them. could you leave the rooster though, i say to roxy. that's all monique and simone ever call you, mitch. the fucken rooster. christ roxy says, could i what. she looks up from her knitting and she's laughing at the thought of it. come here she says, turn round. she holds the half made cardigan against my back to make sure she's measured right. and funny thing her hands against my back make me think of your hands mitch as you raise me up and i brush against the leather singlet as you begin the to and fro of the swing to build up pace. i reckon when you let me go beneath all that husky sweat and your rippling tattooed eagle you still wish you were the one with the light flaring past in this wobbly streamer and the lovely bit, never mind it's only a second or so, the bit when arms out and all i'm flying. then the racket starts up again and i thud on the foam mattresses and they're shouting out fucken beauty and terrific and did you see him go the little cunt. a few throws like that then back in the dressing room that's really just a storeroom in some places or an outside bathroom even but everything for a few minutes anyway is shiny satin like i'm wearing and roxy unbuckles my helmet and pushes her fingers through my hair. you light up mitch and you like making your eyes go narrow through the smoke and you say as the girls go out for the final number and the disco's like a hand thumping against the wall, don't give it away out there ladies there's mitch back here loves ya all. and one of the girls will ask the others as they scramble past did his mum dress him like that for spite or does he just like looking like a dork. when they go out on the floor there'll be whistling and stamping and they'll turn green and purple and yellow in the lights and the bits they take off sparkle and reflect over the walls. alright muzza are you, you nearly always say that mitch when we're suddenly left there, just the two of us. and i nearly always raise my thumb like i'm in a plane and signalling through the windscreen. i'm beaut, mitch, i'm saying. fucken beaut.

Putting Bob Down

It is usually assumed that if a man has two mistresses or two wives, then they must be physically quite contrary types. Perhaps literature has corrupted that part of our thinking irretrievably. There is always the 'dark she, fair she', as the gloomiest of English poets once wrote. Or what we drew from those books we were reared on. Walter Scott. Nathaniel Hawthorne. There is a blond girl who embodies the domestic virtues, who wears a plaid shawl, looks after an aged father, and gazes at the hero with eyes so blue that ice floating in the coldest fjords is not to be compared. Truly. And there is a raven-haired woman who speaks directly from the blood. She is Mediterranean, and behind her we see the temples of forgotten faiths, a rage for existence which that blond girl knows nothing of. She carries phials in her pocket, while the Anglo-Saxon angel has merely an address book in her reticule. Which is introductory to this simple fact: when Bob Roberts died, there were two women at his graveside. They were almost identical.

Helene, whose name had always enchanted him, said as they walked away from the dark gaping hole, 'We all get finally I suppose what we most deserve.'

The other woman was called Frith. She hated her name intensely because of that mucky story about the bird. She said, 'If only we did.'

Metaphor is something that Helene hates more than anything on earth. A plate is a plate. A fish is a fish. A plate can never be a fish, even if it is shaped with fins and painted with scales, and signed Picasso in the corner. Because there is always the irrefutable test. Give a hungry man a plate painted like a fish.

Frith does not think like that at all. To carry metaphor in one's emotional arsenal is to carry a thin stick that snaps open to a gorgeous fan. There is a semicircle of wonder as close as the palm of one's hand. Japan, as she once explained it to Bob, sits waiting in Brunswick. There is holocaust in every match that is struck correctly.

At the graveside both women stepped forward simultaneously to take a handful of clammy yellow earth. One had removed her glove while the other had kept hers on. The better dressed of the women reached out her right hand to the trowel which the undertaker offered them. The other woman took her handful from the left. Frith thinking of a cake offered on a cakeslice, Helene looking only at the clogged crumbs of earth.

When Helene threw that clutch of dirt into the grave, onto the polished wood and the freshly engraved metal plate, she knew quite absolutely she tossed dust to dust. So did Frith. But she was thinking how she knew beyond any disbelief in resurrection or anything else that she was throwing eternity onto dear dead Bob. That all of us, walking or sleeping, wear bodies which are indeed the merest tip of the past, the arrowhead that shall then lie round for a million years. She thought, I am throwing the dust of today onto the ash of stars.

Bob had said to them separately, 'You cannot expect me to choose between you. You just can't.'

Each of them had said in her own way, which in fact was very similar, 'We're not cannibals, love. We don't believe for a minute that one has to devour the loved one.' Helene had spelled it out. 'Isn't that what we've been fighting against for millennia. That old *mine, mine* nonsense?' Frith put it like this. She said, 'If we could only think of sex as an aesthetic experience too, as well as a mere tingling of nerves.' (In her mind she saw the telephone exchange her mother worked at while she herself was a child. And on some days too many bells ringing in that small town for one operator to cope with. Until mummy's hands finally across her ears with the room ringing about her and the lights flashing on the switchboard and simply not enough hands for too many wires. With mummy crying *oh shit oh dear*.) What Frith in fact was saying: 'If you own a painting I mean. You don't turn it to the wall if someone else enjoys it too.'

At the graveside she wore a plain grey suit and Helene a black frock with a cut-away matching jacket. From not very far away they might have been sisters, one of them clearly richer than the other. They had both taken a taxi to the cemetery. Neither thought it important which of them had known the corpse the longer time.

Even now, if it came to the push, Bob would not have known what woman he preferred. Thank God though there had never been anything sneaky about the liaisons. He had told Helene quite openly. He had said, 'I don't consider myself a particularly randy sort of man but there's something I'd better tell you.' It was almost as if she had expected him to say it. She had stroked his hair as she leaned across him. He had thought, I'm buggered if I'd have taken the same thing from her. But another time when he had forgotten an appointment with her, Helene threw things at him when he next came into the house.

Frith was so much milder. Yet she wore exotic underthings and said the strongest words when her breath caught and her hands fluttered across his rump.

A point to be made here is that it's not at all the same thing as looking through a doorway, although it's easy enough for writers to imagine that it is, when the figures pull back from the sunlit and lovely oblong which is the top of a grave. To imagine it is like friends going from a room. As a matter of fact the legs are absurdly out of proportion to begin with.

They are positive pillars. The heads too such disproportionate bumps above the big swinging handbags, the hands the women held together in their dark gloves rather like the mitts of boxers touching as they prance in their corners. Then when they drop those handfuls of dirt. Honestly, the way the clods come pouring in you'd think they had it in for you.

'I'm only a journo,' Bob used to tell them. 'Only run of the mill in the least elevated of callings.'

'It must be so marvellous to use words at all,' Frith said. 'With that freedom, I mean. That control. All I ever do, day after day, is hear children recite their grammar. Hear them conjugate, decline, fumble with sentences they will never know how to use. Languages!' she sighed. 'Those complicated and dreary ladders. Where do they expect them to reach?'

She liked it when he nuzzled close against her, ran his hand down her stomach and left it lying there. 'A man is like the *Zeitwort*, do you understand that? The verb. Women are so many nouns.'

When both of them stood back from the long bright space hanging there above him, he thought how lovely a patch of pure blue could seem.

The women turned away and walked for perhaps a minute in silence. Then Helene was saying to Frith, 'In the six funerals I've been to in this cemetery this is the first one it hasn't rained.'

They were cutting across the rows of the buried towards the road. A champion billiard-player's monument with its slate table, its marble cue, struck them as too absurd. 'God knows what Bradman will have. A whole oval made from brass.' They touched each other's arms in amusement. 'Imagine what Bob would think, us talking like this!' They remembered how he believed that women knew nothing about sport.

As it happened, he thought a great deal. He thought of Helene's knee on the side of his bed, her preparing to throw herself across him like the great Jim Pike across Phar Lap himself, and his telling her, 'You are lovelier than anything I know.' And her playfully putting her hand across his mouth so that he bit at that fleshy part just down from her little finger. Her saying to him, 'Never say *than*. Never say *like* or *as*. Do you hear?' Pressing with her strong knees against his sides. And his saying quite seriously, so that she roared with laughter, 'There's not a love poem I bet you in the whole of literature for that part of a woman's body. That little soft bit there on the side of your hand.' Helene would even laugh sometimes in the middle of their loving. With Frith there was either no talk at all, or those words she would never think of using anywhere else.

The first time he had ever seen them together. At an art opening he had to write up for his paper because the critic was down with the mumps. He was terrified at the thought of speaking to both of them at the same time. He leaned close to Frith as he came in and saw her by the table with the catalogues. 'There's an awful lot of people I have to nod to tonight. Or the paper does rather. Know what I mean?' He brought her a glass of wine and looked at some pictures with her. She knew the names of all of them without referring to her catalogue.

Helene said out very loudly, 'This is the most boring exhibition I have ever seen.' He had been shocked. He looked at the famous black figures against their ochrous background, the flashes of gums and flowers like gunshot in the violence of the light. She said, 'Introduce me to her anyway. She can't be worse than this.'

They had reminded him of a Moore exhibition as they peered down at him a few minutes ago. Their heads so small and distant, mere tufts on pyramids of flesh.

Helene, he had sometimes thought, liked to be with him so that she could *hone*. On anything. On politics or race or people they knew. 'Private money makes it so easy,' he would say to her. 'I could sneer at half the price.' She sat with her legs tucked under her, her glass of wine reflecting like a great coin. Folded on her knee was the paper with his column. 'What would you do if you actually had to look at something? Come into the open without your clichés? Your little images? Run like a nigger flushed from the cane-brakes, I wouldn't be surprised.' Her teeth when she teased him like that! So white and even and gleaming. She enraged him. And then so deliberately looking at her watch, declaring that her husband already had left his office, was stroking this very moment life into his Bentley. But the excitement never really wore off, because there was one lesson he learned very early. To root above one's station is the first step to the stars.

It is surprising how little it shocks one to hear that a friend is dead. It would surprise one more at times to hear that he had won a fortune or written a book or even that he had remarried. Death, when the chips are down, is a very ordinary thing to come to terms with. No sooner has one heard it than there are those meetings with other friends, the ceremonies that nudge it so easily, so gently, away from the warm place where we stand ourselves. To buy a hat, for example. How much of grief can be absorbed in that. To buy, as indeed Frith did, new black underwear for the funeral. Appreciating her own dark joke as she tried it on at home, for a moment there Bob was alive again, watching her from the bed, assuring her she was a bit of all right, bloody oath she was! That other time twenty years ago when she had surprised him with what she wore beneath her dress. The day she had opened the book that he gave her at the end of their first summer. In the tiled vestibule of the Seacliff Hotel! The dark pines on that space of lawn across the street, a solitary girl walking there in a white frock. *Munch!* Bob had said when he looked at her. One of his dreadful artistic puns. Just before he gave her the brown-paper-wrapped present and told her to open it in the car. 'I'll open it now!' she had said, and they were tussling, fooling about, people giving them the oddest looks as they passed at the foot of the big staircase. She tore the brown paper and saw that marvellous gilded face. The thick black lines on the eyelids. The cheekbones of pure gold. All because she had said once, *wouldn't you love to go to Egypt?*

After the women withdrew, there were minutes in that oblong of brilliant light when almost nothing happened. A palm frond waved across bottom left. A flight of longnecked birds that could have flown from a Russian movie flicked over very high. Then a man sat there briefly with his feet dangling down as though he sat on a wharf, and smoked a cigarette. When he stood up again he hitched his belt and shouted across to another bloke to move his arse. And the earth started to rain in. Bob tried to remember something. Yes! That quick flowing across of girths and bellybands as ground-level cameras caught the jumpers at Beecher's Brook. The clods flying out from the impacting hooves. The clods now pouring down and the blades of the shovels flashing above there like aircraft in low flight.

And by Christ to hear them now you'd think they had been cobbers from way back.

Helene said, 'You must have known him as long as I did?'

'I suppose I must have,' Frith said. 'At least as.'

Helene said, 'Did he mention me much?'

'You know what men are,' Frith said.

Helene asked again. 'Did he ever mention me?'

'Only to denigrate,' Frith said. 'To say he was chained to a cunt the way men used to be tied to benches in galleys.'

Helene said, 'Whenever he mentioned you it was like he spoke of a disease.'

Bob enjoyed their saying that. He thought how even here you could write your own column. But the women refused his script. They did not squabble as he had hoped. What Frith said in fact was this: 'He lied to both of us, of course.'

'He was a liar all right,' Helene said. 'And he wasn't even that bright, either.'

But there are ways the dead unsettle the living. There are casual remarks made long ago in the warm rooms of the flesh which become weapons in neatly cuffed and buried hands. Bob thought, it is the least I can do for them now.

'Metaphor is shit,' Helene had said to him once, putting down his paper. His livelihood and his skill dismissed just like that. He had told her you have to be well off to say that. Only the rich were content to be exactly where they were. All very well for her with her fat books of philosophy she could read all day, her picture of Bertrand Russell on her desk like a boiled chook.

'If it wasn't for imagery life would be one long walk along a gutter.' That was Frith. Her blue pencil in her hand, saying that to be able to put 9 out of 10 on a schoolgirl's work was indeed *délice*; 10 out of 10 was *jouissance*. They had a silly game in which she came to bed only after a pupil had scored the top mark. While Bob lay thinking then as now, that for a heavy smoker life indeed could be worse than keeping a gutter eye out for what his old man had called derbs. 'For every ten drowned butts there is one that lies there dry enough to light.' Not every father has that much wisdom to give a son.

He thought very hard about cigarettes, and the room where the women were talking.

In the large quiet room above the park Helene saw the walls flare sharply at her, then return to their tasteful white. It frightened her because she knew there had been no alteration in the light. She said to Frith, 'What were you thinking just now?'

Her dead lover's anterior and it seems always concurrent mistress said, 'I was thinking how life is like a rainbow.'

Strangely, for a moment there Frith had felt as though she bent back on space, her head and heels drawn towards each other, the ether as the poets call it so sparkling about her. *Arc-en-ciel—c'est moi*. Her eyelashes had seemed like the spokes of an iridescent wheel. She wondered if Bob was trying to get through to her. While Helene, because she was the cleverer of the two, thought: if that dead bastard is coming at this one . . . Talk of things like telepathy made her want to throw up. I am a single and finite mind, she told herself. I am not a bloody button in some cosmic jukebox.

From her chair on the other side of the comfortable lounge, Frith watched how her friend's hands met and laced and moved in the silvery light, the point of her cigarette so alive across there, so brilliant. *Alive*, she thought. As the dusk rinsed and dipped in the long low mirror that ran the length of the far wall.

He had quite expected the first night to pass slowly. The light coming up across the surrounding rows made him think of arriving at Kennedy airport in New York, one morning when it was very early, on a dawn flight from the West. Manhattan's blocks, its tall secular angels above their strips of narrow street, had made him think it was like a cemetery.

He thought, given time I suppose I shall remember everything. I shall get bored I suppose with this outlook as I have with every other until I remember this one is for keeps. And oddly, that quite comforted him. There would be the chance at last to find one experience that was inexhaustible. He would want to remember precisely what this sensation was like, the first light breaking of the first day. To recall it would be to continue it, to extend it and to know how this day differed from the second. And through memory living those two days as the third was added, and so on. The hundredth. The ten thousandth. To discriminate each moment, as he had liked to quote when he was a student, 'on that day of frost and sun' or whatever it was. Six crosses ranged to the right, then. A stone child dropping a stone rose. Those bloody Italian inscriptions he could never read! Then the college tower far over there beyond the fence, across petrol stench and the trees. There were some positions as he knew that had a damned sight less than this to pass the time. And in the distance there a corner of a building with the dawn smearing its upper windows behind which, had one turned directly about and walked through the lounge with its morbid mirror and its Aubusson birds, one would come to a passageway as they called it when he was a child in which a fumed oak stand protruded antlers for one's hat and a painted Victorian can waited for the winter months to receive one's umbrella, past which one proceeded clothed as a rule or dishevelled at times or on some few occasions starkers towards a bedroom where a woman now lay looking at the light which broke not only there for her but across a city, and given time, a country; a dawn into which she might walk from her own front steps with their small ornamental lions and along an empty street to the locked iron gates which suppose were opened, she might then pass through and walk on between and beneath the elaborately cut stones and the marble figures, the religious confectionery which made her think if not of the bread of life at least the cake of eternity, and so come to the mound where the flowers already wilted although some of them this time yesterday had not been cut, their binding ribbons straggling damp, their handwritten consolations already dribbled ink. From a point equidistant, say, that mound of the grave, the shape of the bed in this greyish light, were not so fancifully unalike. Only Helene tugging her covers close, hoping for further sleep before she had to rise and take her bath and dress. At which moment, Frith: that quite as loved but much less wealthy woman lay with the fingers of one hand spanning the wrist of the other and thinking of how at Père Lachaise she had stood at the graves of so many famous of Oscar of Baudelaire of Alphonsine Plessis Chopin Daudet it could have been of Colette too so she heard later but had missed her at the time. *The grave's a sad and lonely place*, who said? It is a bed it is a bed, she thought. I am running out of what-it's-likes!

When the women met at the Jewish cake-shop at St Kilda Helene said the moment her gloves were removed and lay like something skilfully skinned beside her, 'That old sod's been on my mind practically non-stop all week.' Stabbing the golden arse of a *pêche* concoction. 'Don't tell me he hasn't been on yours?'

'My mind becomes blank whenever I try to think of him.'

'I wake,' Helene said, 'in the early hours and my mind's as full of nonsense as that glass counter there of European gut-rot.'

'You go over the past?' Frith said. She peeled the paper from the *torte* she had chosen.

'Sometimes I remember the past like it's the present.' Both women noticed the unexpected word that established itself in Helene's sentence.

Frith's cheek bulged horribly as in children's caricatures of toothache. She swallowed the wad of sweetness away. 'I used to dream for a bit but now it's pure bareness. *Le néant.*'

Helene said, 'Every morning when I do get round to waking all I smell is earth.' She laughed. 'I'm starting to think like you!'

Bob remembered a cake shaped like a ship with white frosted lines of rigging at a Sea Scout Christmas party in 1938. He thought of four meringues that sounded like a gravel path when he crunched them and he had wolfed them down one after the other at the wedding of a cousin who wore a military uniform. He recalled in no particular order seedcake with aunts on Sunday afternoons kisscakes with his mother measling down icing-sugar from a flour-mill lamingtons soggy as a rained-out oval *Kuchen* and *Schlagsahnetorte* during his time abroad. Those aerated squares of pure dryness Frith dipped in her tea while she went on about Proust. He could think of every cake he had ever eaten. No two had been alike. No mouthful was identical with a following or preceding mouthful.

'I'm so sick of this already.' Helene slapped her tiny fork down on her plate. One cheek of her *pêche* remained untouched.

Frith dabbed at her lips with a paper napkin.

Back with their brandies they began to talk of God.

Helene said that when she was a child there had been a crucifix on her grandmother's wall. Two narrow strips of black wood and a grey contorted figure like a deep-freeze lizard.

Frith said she could still sing hymns quite seriously. At weddings or funerals for example. She never gave it a thought between times, mind.

Helene said she would have shot priests if she had been a Spaniard in the old days. 'I see those bastards in black I want to reach for my branding irons.' Which was not really so strong an image and certainly not a metaphor, when used by a woman who was a grazier's wife.

Bob used to joke that in any case a Christian was only a lapsed atheist. He had known so many anti-clerical jokes that he couldn't keep up with invitations to speak at Catholic men's dinners.

But Frith had perched on him once, *in flagrante*, and quoted some lines of John Donne about tuning his instrument here at the door. He had turned on her and told her not to be so bloody disrespectful.

The two women now sat in the lounge and looked over the massed trees to the black iron fence and its acres of remembrance.

'You do wonder though what becomes of one. Gauguin's great painting, *Who are we?* etcetera. Cliché that it is.'

Helene reached irritably for her cigarettes. 'Anything worth saying is a cliché.'

'Aquinas, wasn't it, thought that you couldn't use any predicate at all of God? That any statement at all was pure tautology?'

'He fucking would,' Helene said. She had hated the Angelic Doctor since her childhood, when she heard that story about a semi-circle being cut in the refectory table for his bulk to sit down to meals.

The women sat in silence for several minutes. Then Frith said, 'If He is there, it makes every moment so infinitely of value.' She was slightly embarrassed that she had said it.

'If he isn't of course,' Helene said, 'every moment must be more valuable still.'

'What?' Frith sounded surprised.

'Because there is only a straight line and not a circle. There is no redeeming time, I mean. Each act stands as itself forever.'

Bob thought, 'What if you're both wrong, you smart bitches?'

A picnic in the You Yangs. The only time he had been with them both together, apart from that art show. A busload of them during a weekend seminar on 'Responsibilities of the Press'. Frith there because she believed such questions mattered, Helene—although she would not even know the word—because she was by nature a groupie. For opera. For *The Tree of Man* during its first year out. For existentialism in its time and then for Vietnam. Only a rich woman could have afforded to care for so much. So at least Bob thought while he sat behind them in the bus, listening to an academic who had been on the same panel with him that morning. He watched the heads of his mistresses sway and bounce.

That outcrop of ancient rocks gave him the creeps. He

detested people who used words like 'numinous', or a few years later spoke of 'the vibes'. He looked at the group about him. Thirty minutes standing in prehistory, as they liked to think, then haring back to the free piss at the cocktail party. The thought of those great grey boulders, the sudden abutments and leaps of rock, depressed him enough to make him consider staying on the bus. Which of course a good journo would never do, because he would not seem one of the team. So he walked with the sociologist who he suspected could not have written a convincing cheque, while the two women he slept with followed some distance behind. Frith said, looking up at the pure blue that hazed off towards the city, 'It's like being inside a jewel on a day like this.' Helene told her she had read how you saw further at this time of year than at any other. 'You can see a candle burning at night three miles away.' That in fact was no more true than the bit about the jewel.

Someone in the group had snapped photographs as they walked along. Eighteen years later Helene handed a print across the coffee table to her recent good friend. She said, 'Remember that afternoon do you?' Bob was some little way ahead. He was turned in profile, laughing. He looked young and happy. The collar of his sports jacket, so typically, was turned up at the back. In the distance far beyond him was the thin strip of the Geelong road. A woman's head was blurred beside him, but her hair was dark and long. Frith took her glasses from her purse. 'Which one of us is that—next to Bob there?'

Helene gave that laugh which sounded so butch Bob used to tell her it reminded him of rugby changing sheds. 'I'm damned if I remember,' she said. Her quieter friend began to laugh as well. The photograph fell as it passed back between them. 'Easy on it,' Frith said. 'One of us is being dropped.' That struck them both as very funny. Helene rubbed at her eyes as though smoke was stinging them.

The women went on to speak of something else, then something else again. While the sky either clouded over or grew dark, Bob was not sure which. It may have been a week later or a month. The two furthest crosses, and the rose-dropping child, were no longer clear in any case. The lawnmower that sometimes charged past like those bloody speedboats that used to irritate him so much the summer when he and Helene lay on that perfect beach on the Tasman Peninsula, that didn't seem to bother him too much at all. He was beginning to forget the names of horses, and football players, and the meals he had once eaten. He was not quite sure any more if *Mille feuilles à la crème* was a cake or a sprinter.

They were leaving the expensive restaurant where Helene had taken Frith to lunch. The afternoon was late as they passed the proprietor who swung back the door for them. They could see the gold tooth near the back of his head. If they wished to sit on with another coffee, he was assuring them, until five, five-thirty, what did it matter? They were not customers, but friends. Frith thought how that would sound so epigrammatic in Latin. While Helene leaned forward in front of her. She heard her friend's face scrape against the man's. She thought how the dangling palm there above the two embracing humans was like a great green hoof. *I hear an army charging*, she thought. What nonsense comes into one's mind!

Helene stood in the street with her car keys fretting in her glove, looking to right and to left.

'You left it up near Parliament,' Frith offered. 'Didn't you?'

'Of course,' Helene said, 'near that little lane where the press boys play about.' Old darling Bob! she thought.

Frith felt her eyes prickle suddenly with tears. Very aware, even now in the diminishing light and the sated aftermath of food and drink and her friend's expensive brooch not turned merely but *flashing* at her, aware of the lovely drifting of the past through the present's glint and whirl, knowing there was something on the tip of her tongue, in the back of her mind, an image just dissolved: with Helene turning as they walked up the slope to the sticks of traffic lights playing their brightness against the massive building, turning and saying with a smile, 'Do you realise we went a whole meal and never mentioned him?' People were walking between them, separating them, allowing them again to come together.

'Remember this same light that time the same at where was it, do you?'

'Dreamed it,' Helene said.

A man saying 'sorry' as he nudged against them.

'Wit then,' Frith laughing, knowing she was a trifle drunk. 'Would you believe I can't get my mouth round his name?'

'Wittgenstein?' They had talked about him at lunch.

'He sounds like a capital.'

'A brand of cigars.'

'*Prestige ist eine Zigarre namens Wittgenstein.*'

'Stop it!'

Oh their voices high, high and happy, happy and so thin and distant. Voices remotely clapping, can one say that? Impacting anyhow softly. Like gloves say meeting hush so softly above there in the greying distance that first far day that afternoon, the praying over, the hands of the women palming like a singer's is it, her hands clasping under the notes, the most silent clapping?

On the pedestrian crossing Frith remembering, 'Was it Wittgenstein said can to dream have a present tense?'

Closing the File

They knew each other's names from the list beside the mail boxes. The man's was spelled out in full, so the woman always thought of him as Bruce. She thought he must be very severe. He walked with his fists closed and his gaze directly ahead. Once they stood together at the noticeboard in the foyer and inspected the array of notices and cards. She said curtly enough, tapping the pink-fringed card that advertised a discreet escort service, 'Most of them in this place would fall over if they tried.' She spoke quietly, confidentially, as though to the one person she might trust. She implied that at late middle-age she and the man she spoke to were rather healthier than their fellow tenants. She then clicked across the marble paving and through the large glass doors into the street. Bruce had not known how to answer her. Without those shoes, he thought, she would seem very short.

They stood together again, another evening, as the lift doors opened on an elderly woman who in fact was dying, but for the moment simply looked ill. She was a foreigner who lived on the eighth floor. One of her arms hung awkwardly around another woman's neck, and a man supported her about the waist. In the white glare of the lighting the group looked pale enough to remind one of wax, of plaster, of the Last Station of the Cross, a body limp between those who sustained it. Bruce held back the doors until the group had moved through. He then followed the short woman into the lift. A red light on the panel was glaring impatiently for the ninth floor. 'Why don't they jump if they want to get down that urgently?' the woman said. Then she said her name was Fran. She held out her hand, which few women of her generation did. She wore a shawl with trailing edges across her shoulders.

Fran's living room was comfortably warm. The storm thrashed against its windows, the full belt of the southerly only inches behind her head. The man stood and looked down at the orange lights of the motorway. 'It looks like everything's under the sea. The cars down there could be swimming.'

'Pull the curtains,' she asked him. 'This sort of night gets on my wick.' Then they sat with their brandies, facing each other across the room. The backs of the two large chairs were covered with vivid rugs. They spoke about the sick woman in the lift, and how foreigners were nearly always Catholics or Jews. Fran said, 'A friend of mine had this story about a Catholic girl who never did more than kiss boys quite chastely after parish dances but used to keep a diary where she made up the most lurid things. And she told the priest she was keeping this sort of dirty calendar and he told her that imagination could be a mortal sin in itself.' The wind whacked freshly at the window behind her. 'What do you make of that then, Bruce?'

He said he supposed there was something absurd and sad about it wasn't there? You wrote something down you'd never actually do then you get fried for it just as much as if you'd done something worse. He told her at school in standard six they were told to make their own Easter cards, you know how they were in those days? So they did these bad copies of already bad enough religious pictures and wrote verses to go with them. And it always surprised him that two Chinese kids who weren't even Christians, who went to the school only because of the music teacher, did the goriest crucifixion scenes of anybody. Bits like red bean sprouts coming out of the side and everything.

They could hear the storm moving away, although the gusts of rain still dashed against the glass. They agreed religion was a problem all right, whether you had it or whether you didn't.

'That poor kid with her diary though,' Fran said.

Next morning, from their kitchens which were one above the other, they looked down on a city that was sparkling and still, with the mountains sharp and pure against the sky. The whole place looked scrubbed, Fran thought, as she stood with a hand on each of the sink taps. The houses across the harbour shone against the bush.

Later as they left the lift at different times, they saw the black bordered notice that always gave one a start. The caretaker with almost morbid haste made sure the tenants knew when one of their number went. And so they read that the elderly woman in the lift the evening before, with her arms around her neighbours in that awful parody of a rugby front row, had died during the night. The notice gave her name as Mrs Roberts, but Bruce had said in fact it was something beginning with Z. For a moment Fran saw a city with avenues of winter trees, people without enough to eat, the uniforms she remembered from newsreels. She had heard the woman speaking only once, to another woman, in whatever that language of hers was.

Mrs Zelmans had looked at the two faces, so white in the fall of artificial light. She thought of the faces of children raised to watch a procession as it moved past, the look of exaltation and pity as the statue was carried in front of them. At least sixty years. But the memories keep on, don't they, even when one wants them to fade. Anders had said to her so many times that we hang onto the past, onto God, onto places we have lived in, as a dog frets and prances about a bone that has been sucked dry. Yet the only important thing about the past, as Anders would say, is that it is the past. She had been a young woman when she stood in front of the mirror in their first hotel and Anders had told her how to turn, how to bend. He was excited by her movements, and even more because she felt no guilt of any kind. She did not explain that when he supposed she took such pleasure in lubricity, she was thinking merely that none of it mattered so very much. He would not have understood that. When he was less urgent Anders sometimes looked at her across a table, across a room, as though she disgusted him. He quite missed the point that sex was in fact a shopping list. People asked for what they wanted, what was more natural than that? They were happy when they were given it, they were disgruntled when it was out of stock. It would never have occurred to her to put a black beret on her head, and a long white scarf around her neck, and quite naked apart from that, to ease her firm buttocks towards the man on the bed, had he not begged her to do it for him. Later, when his books were so much more important to him, she was quite as happy with that. But he was no longer such fun. He would talk to her about ethical problems, and she would listen quite as seriously as when he had told her how to undress. He became so cross for instance with people who persisted with God. And he said as things first began to go wrong, when the armbands first appeared and the shoving about began, that people brought it on themselves. We are all so hang-dog, he said, so compliant and law-abiding. She teased him and said when the soldiers walked past they stood arm in arm in the doorway, what did he do about it then? You keep looking at your books, she said. Anders said but books were what protected them against history, against marching feet, books were always on the side of victory and life. And she came to see that a scholar was a coward who privately insisted that knowledge might somehow answer the men who told lies, the ones who kicked in faces and burned the pages he quietly wanted to read. Anders fancied that by sitting quiet he was being heroic. She realised he was a fool. Yet she never thought of leaving him. And then once the worst part was over, she had been too busy or too anxious to reflect much on anything. Just learning the new language was bad enough. But she was glad Anders was buried quite somewhere else. And now she sat on the seventh floor and watched the lights change across the harbour. The closest Anders had ever been to all this was the eastern bank of a river where they sat for an afternoon, the year before she had come out. He wrote in his notebook about a baroque yellow-walled church they could see through the birches. The river looked clean but a notice warned against taking fish from it. A rusted tank was half submerged a little down stream. Anders was ill, and looked across the river, and said one should just keep on, heading east and further away, keep on until the deadly fish and the broken trucks that were Europe were utterly out of one's life. Then he again leaned over his notebook and put the date of the building they had come from, and the name of the man who had built it. It began to rain, and his writing ran on the page. And some years later she had told her lawyer that she would like another name. Something quite different from 'Anders'.

Those neighbours who helped her in the lift were almost strangers to her. Her mouth felt coppery and dry, as she tried to speak but was unable to control the words she wanted to say. She saw that the man was frightened at being so close to a woman who was ill. But she allowed them to support her, to decide for her. She was grateful as well as nauseous. She closed her eyes through the humming descent and opened them as the doors revealed the bright unnatural light, the faces watching her emerge. One of them was a man she knew. But by then the effort was considerable. She was attempting to concentrate, to grasp what one does to make faces seem so childish and distant, so crumpled with compassion.

Fran said, 'They're such toffee-nosed bastards in this building, noticed that?' She asked how often did people actually talk to you, had Bruce ever thought? Had he ever got so much as a nod from the air commodore's wife? But she persisted in joking to them, in remarking, 'Dreadful weather for blood pressure,' simply knowing how it embarrassed those old bundles of rags and the husbands they guided and directed like bullying little girls. She said, 'I'd suck cyanide peppermints Bruce before I look the way those old bags do.' She brushed her plump hands across her lap as her friend laughed and told her just as well she was a good-natured woman. 'Imagine what you would say if you were a bitch as well?'

For all her remarks about what she called the snots, Fran was the richest woman in the block, and the one who looked like—well, certainly not like a lady. She wore purple blouses with frilled fronts and bright patterned slacks, and in winter a llama wool poncho. She said she knew very well she looked like a tea-cosy. 'Stuff them anyway,' she said. She meant the lot of them, the array of neighbours who supposed she was a former barmaid, or a retired whore. 'Skin's too good for that though,' the air commodore said. Not to his wife, naturally, but to the accountant across the corridor who was self-conscious that he had not had much of a war. In fact the air commodore put up with him because he sometimes took them for a spin in his Rover. But both men often remarked on Fran. When the former pilot spoke with a broad wink about the little lady's bristols it made the accountant think of uniforms and air-raid sirens, all those things that he had missed. But he knew from a former colleague at least something of what she did with her shares. He kept that to himself, of course, and it made him feel he held rather a trump card.

Bruce's one real conversation with Mrs Zelmans had puzzled him. It began in the lift as she asked him would he be kind enough to change the light bulbs for her. 'I am uneasy to stand on a chair.' She then gave him a cup of coffee and a pale drink in a small glass that lifted the back of his throat.

She smiled at his efforts. She emptied her own glass and said, 'My husband said only this might make him believe in God.' And in case she was misunderstood, she said, 'My husband sometimes made the joke.' Almost every sentence she began 'My husband'. Then she and Bruce spoke a little about a hijacking that had been on the news, and the deaths in the attempt to rescue people. She said, 'My husband believes that morality is only in acts. Bad people act like this, good people act to stop them.' As she spoke she straightened over and over the square of embroidered cloth on the table between them. She looked at him with yellowish eyes. 'We do not act then we are not good or bad, you understand? My husband is always saying most of us are cushions. We are not moral people. We do not act, most of us. You see?'

Bruce had waited for her to ask him to do other jobs, but she never did. She said to him, making a quiet joke of it, 'You act for my light bulbs. I can now read again late at night. You are a good man.' As he later told Fran, she was a lovely old lady, but perhaps a touch off her head.

'Philosophy always sounds like that,' Fran said. 'You can't break wind with a philosopher in the room without him beginning to talk like that. "Was that a voluntary emission or was it under compulsion?" Jesus.'

'I've never known a philosopher,' Bruce said.

'Nor did I. This one who said he was rabbited on about Plato but he was a pure con. I mean he nicked most of his books from shops or libraries for one thing.'

'How did you know him?' Bruce said.

'I was married to him wasn't I?' She broke into the quick deep laugh he waited to hear. 'Pussy *qua* pussy he didn't mind either, let alone the ideal forms.'

'What's that?' Bruce asked her.

'The philosopher's disease as far as I can make out. Quim pro quo.'

Fran was twenty times cleverer than he was, Bruce knew that after only a few days. She also said things he hardly expected to hear a woman say. Like that just now, for instance. But she said it as if there was no such thing as words that were acceptable and words that were not. Yet he liked that in her very much. He had never expected people to be so honest. She said in the lift, when Mrs Roberts' neighbours remarked after the funeral how the minister had spoken so beautifully, that he hadn't even known the woman, so how could it mean anything? The air commodore's wife with her great tang of scent said sharply, 'I thought he was very sincere. I made a point after the service of telling him so.' Fran had said, 'I wouldn't have crossed the room to pee on his shoe.'

She liked to sit in his lounge while Bruce worked at the bench against the far wall, his protective glasses on a rubber strap drawn down over his eyes. It pleased her when he held the small curved tube and for a moment the flame sat on its edge like a moth, before it hissed into a vivid jet. He made small silver ornaments he copied from magazines, or from ideas he picked up in those dinky shops along the Quay. Above the work bench were the shelves where the little figures were displayed. Fran always took up one of them as she entered the room, holding it in her closed hand, or moving it across the arm of her chair. Once he was finished he poured them drinks and they sat above the fading city. Bruce said to her the first time she looked closely at the shelves, 'Don't ask me why I make the things.'

'You could sell them,' she said. She saw that the minute ballerinas, the Piccadilly Eroses, the dancing bears were very well done.

'No point in that,' Bruce said. 'When I get too many I just melt them down and start doing something else.' He told her, 'Help yourself if you want any.'

Fran said she wouldn't if he didn't mind. 'I don't much go on finicky ornaments.'

'Don't blame you,' Bruce said. When he slipped on the goggles-strap with its holes like a miniature belt, it pressed so his hair tufted out on either side. Bent over his set of tools, his hand steadying the slender torch, he made her think of a boy playing at his hobby. Neither minded how long they went without speaking. Then Fran suddenly might ask something that occurred to her.

'Were you ever there when they hanged someone?'

Bruce continued to work the flame across the softening metal.

'They stopped all that in fifty-six, didn't they?' he said.

'Did you ever have to do one though?'

'It never came up,' he said. 'I was never in the big cities let alone the prisons.'

'Would you have minded, though?'

Bruce put down the torch and steadied the lump of silver with a pair of tongs. In his other hand he took up what seemed a dentist's probe, scoring the metal to give it the impression of fur. 'Christ Fran, would you?'

She said wryly, 'Women never had the chance of all those sorts of jobs. So it never occurred to me.' She thought how remote something like that was. 'I still can't believe it actually happened. But then we think that don't we about any kind of death I suppose if it comes to that.'

'It happened all right,' Bruce said.

Fran told him, 'I've never so much as seen a dead person, know that? If you don't count my husband all those years when he just sat there.'

Bruce told her how he must have interviewed hundreds of people about one thing or another before he retired from the Force. Thousands. And you forget most of them he said, what they looked like and all. But the dead you didn't. The ones you helped pull from rivers and cut down from beams and found behind bushes. 'You'd only have to mention where they were found and I could tell you pretty much exactly what they were like. Tell you even now.'

Fran said, 'God, no wonder undertakers never look bored. They're thinking of all the people they've met.'

'Well,' Bruce smiled back at her, 'I'm not saying they're all I think of, am I?'

'But you do remember?'

'Expressions and that.'

Fran looked at him and then stood up to attend to their glasses. 'Tells you something about human nature then doesn't it. I can't remember that much about men I've been to bed with.'

'What in hell are these?' Fran demanded one evening. She meant the several cartons in the corridor between Bruce's front door and the living room.

'They're books,' he said.

'I know they're not bloody vegetables. I mean why are they here?'

'She asked me to take care of them.'

'Who for God's sake?'

'Old Mrs Z.'

'Mrs Z?'

'The lady who died a couple of months back. Mrs Roberts.'

'*She* asked you?'

'Her lawyer came round and asked me. She wrote it down somewhere. That she'd like me to look after them.'

The books were in several languages. He could tell some were French or German, although there was no question of his actually reading them. He had no idea what some of the others were.

'*Dieva Zeme*,' Fran spelled out. 'A lot of use to you, this lot.'

'I couldn't say I wouldn't take them.'

'You must have been an easy touch as a copper,' Fran chided him.

'I let a burglar go once because he had six kids.'

'You wouldn't have done it for a murderer. Don't give yourself wings.'

'I always turned offensive women in though,' Bruce said. 'I'd watch it if I were you.'

But the fact of the books overflowing through his flat disturbed her. Why not the public library, if they had to go somewhere. 'She must have known you couldn't read them.'

'She must have thought that wasn't so important.'

'And you'll keep the things?'

'What else can I do?'

Fran moved her hand impatiently. 'You're as mad as she bloody was.'

'I suppose that was what she was banking on,' Bruce said. He took up a book with dark leather binding and deckled edges. He liked to think they were safe here with him, safe from whatever harm the old lady thought might come to them. He wondered what sort of things a person like that fears.

His friend had gone through to the lounge. 'Here,' she said, 'let me get us a gin.' She tapped his arm and said she was sorry she sounded tetchy. Then they sat together on the sofa whose pattern tumbled overblown roses on either side of them.

'Further along, can we?' Fran asked. 'Drive further along until the road runs out?'

That morning she had come down soon after breakfast. She stood and looked at the ferry pulling out in a wide slow curve, a sickle of broadening water in its wake. She said, 'It's a day for the beach.'

'You said you hated beaches. Didn't you tell me that once?'

'I meant I hated all that exposed human meat that lolls

around on them.' Then she said, 'Those beaches on the far side, you know? There'll be no one there. No one swims in spring.' She turned from the window and smiled at him as he dried his few dishes and stacked them away. Then she came and stood beside him.

'You've had your hair cut,' Bruce said. His hand brushed lightly at her pale exposed neck.

'Come on,' she urged him. 'Don't you think it would be lovely?'

'The wind could be a lot sharper than you think.'

'You're starting to sound like the rest of those old buggers,' she told him.

Ten minutes later he backed from the garage beneath the block of flats, and Fran waited at the kerb for him to unlock the door. She made a face through the glass. Then she got in beside him and said 'I know I look like a bloody old snowball but it was your idea I wrap up.' She wore an off-white coat with a pushed back hood, and gloves patterned with blue diamonds.

'An Eskimo,' Bruce said. 'That's what you look like, Fran.'

The waves were banging along the empty beach. They walked with her arm rested through his own. She said 'Your life goes by and how many days do you really see things as lovely as this?' The sky was hazed with spray, the gulls buffeted on the upswinging air. Bruce told her he had sailed the straits once in a friend's yacht.

'It was the worst day of my life. The fish could still be living off it.'

Fran said 'I wouldn't have minded the chance to do that.' He was about to ask why on earth she hadn't then, she could have done anything she liked. But other lives are mostly silence, he considered. One has no right to break in on that. So they walked on without speaking towards the smears of yellow gorse on the crumbling slopes.

She asked him to hang on a bit while she rested against a rock. She removed her gloves, asked Bruce to shield her against the wind, and drew on a cigarette. His pocketed fists weighed down his jacket like stones. He said, 'How many questions I must have asked eh when I was in the Force. Every day for over thirty years. All that time I mean simply wanting people to tell me things that most of them didn't want to tell.' He gave a quick dismissive snort. 'No wonder no one likes us.'

Fran asked him 'Did you ever have to spy out friends?'

'Spy them out?' He repeated the words as though he found them slightly odd.

'I shouldn't say it like that should I?' She leaned towards him, her head touching his jacket, letting him know he mustn't take her too seriously. But then Bruce himself said, 'Investigation I suppose is always spying.' He sometimes thought of those years as he lay waiting to fall asleep. Cases, incidents, there was no pattern to how they came into his mind. A dry-eyed housewife who had shot away her husband's face, who then calmly handed across the gun to him, stepping down from the veranda as he walked towards her, holding the barrel in two fingers like something dead she didn't want to touch. A simple albino boy who stole motorcycles. A Korean sailor who had hidden in scrub for weeks, deserting his ship in Tīmaru. The sailor had cried in the car as they drove back towards the town. It was like flipping through a scrapbook. 'It's important how it's done,' he said. 'I didn't mind it, you know.' He was turning grey small pebbles with his shoe.

'Nor you should have,' Fran told him. She took his arm again and they turned back towards the car. She said she had known for several days there was something she wanted to do, and she hadn't realised it was simply this.

'Just to be at the beach?' Bruce said.

'To be precisely here. Walking along here with you.'

He took it that the place was important to her from another time. They walked on without speaking, across the firm reflecting sand where the tide had pulled back. He then said one of the few things in his meticulous life that took him by surprise. His hands were sweating, which surprised him as well. He told her 'I'd never try to inquire about you, you know, Fran. I mean, ever.' And for the one time, she kissed him. Not his face, now so close to her own, but his hand, which she raised and held against her cheek.

In ten minutes they reached the car. A squall like a broad grey brush came towards them across the harbour, very suddenly. Then the windscreen ticked with it. 'Beat it by seconds,' Bruce said. He would remember how they laughed a good deal as they gathered in the small bays on the way back to the city. Fran told him of her sisters, an eccentric father, aunts who looked like the Marx brothers. 'Is it any wonder I hate ugly people?' While Bruce was thinking, 'How old is she then? I haven't asked her a thing as simple as that.'

When the constable called him 'sir' he was about to object, to remind the young man he was no longer his superior, when he realised he would be addressed like that in any case. They taught them public relations with a vengeance these days. And then the questions began, the inevitable routine. He was probably the lady's closest friend then, was he, the constable asked? The one at any rate who knew her best?

'I don't know about that,' Bruce said. 'We were neighbours who got on.'

He'd have no idea then, sir, why she might have disappeared?

'We never really spoke that much about personal things.'

He knew though she was very wealthy?

'Not very. No.'

'But you knew she was seriously ill?'

'I'd never have guessed that either. Not for a moment.'

He did not say that for the three days until she was reported missing he had done not much more than sit where he was now, looking down on the city. The first time in his life he supposed he was giving what they might call deliberately misleading information. There was an actual physical elation about it, a warmth that spread from the pit of his stomach to his chest. He looked at the young man writing in his notebook, at the short hair and the frank grey eyes when he glanced up. His younger self, Bruce supposed, that really was what he was looking at. This asking questions with the vast dull patience the law believes it can afford, the faith that truth is there somewhere in the service of an ordered life. And it was as though he himself had changed sides, had joined all those who with cunning or stupidity or malice had once lied to him. For he had always known when they did that, it had been his great gift. Get Bruce onto them, his superiors used to say, Bruce'll sort them out. He was now the only one who knew that Fran was dead. There was no note, no word, which passed between them. He simply knew.

The constable's hand moved across his tie, his fingers for a moment touched the buttons of his blue shirt. Here it comes, Bruce predicted. We are at the subtle point of leading the witness.

'You mustn't mind my asking this will you, sir?' The grey eyes could not have been franker. 'There was no—no special relationship between yourself and the missing person?'

'No. Nothing like that,' he assured the policeman. He said he was sorry he could tell them nothing more than he had. He was as surprised, as worried, as everyone else in the block. He would help in any way he could.

The constable fastened his tunic pocket once the notebook was slipped away. 'Well, thank you for that anyway, sir.'

'Watch those books there,' Bruce advised as they went back along the narrow hallway. They were now removed from their cartons and stacked against one of the walls.

'Read them all have we?' the young fellow joked.

'As many as I'm going to. For the time being.'

Within minutes there was a peremptory beating at the door. The air commodore and the accountant were standing side by side. 'You've spoken to them?' the air commodore demanded. His eyes raked over the nondescript fellow he faced.

'Them?'

'The police.'

'He seemed a nice young bloke.'

The accountant said, 'We were all hoping you were the one who could help.'

Bruce said, 'I'm sure we'll hear something before long.' He felt that both the men looked at him with dislike. Then he closed his door on the rage of a world that believed its right was to know everything.

He considered would he have a gin. But no, hold that for later. He crossed instead to the far side of the lounge. He tied on the short leather apron and sat with his knees pressed against the bench. He drew the tray of tools towards him, and the curved tube of the torch. Then in two broad uncharacteristic swoops he reached up and cleared the shelves of their dozens of figurines. They thudded and poured onto the wooden bench. Slipping on his protective glasses, he drew them all into a pile on the metal tray. And with no idea of what he would make instead, he turned the brilliant thrust of the flame onto the bears and angels and butterflies, onto the ballerinas and the emus, and began to melt them down.

Terminus

There is a woman downstairs with a mask over her face. I said that to my wife when she came in from work. I said there was this woman with a black mask across her eyes, who leaned back against the wall as I walked by her into the hallway to the stairs. I said, 'There's this woman. She must be waiting there for someone.'

My wife works on the trams. She is tall and jolly and when we are in bed she makes me think of a good-natured conductor on the trams jangling her sack of coins.

When I told her about the woman with the mask she had just boiled a saucepan of water to pour onto teabags in large red mugs. She was using the saucepan because the electric jug is being repaired. When she tilted the saucepan the boiling water ran up the side of the metal, hissing and spitting out. She had no idea of what she handled, of how the rising urgent water against the tilted metal made me want to stand back, on the other side of the room.

The woman with the opera mask has been there for several days. She doesn't say a word. Her eyes that are moist and shining in the slits of the mask don't seem to move as I pass her. I look across at her but the eyes behind the mask don't ever move. But because they are moist and glittering they seem always to watch. I mention her again to my wife, who says, 'Worry about every loony in this area there'd be time for nothing else.' She is trying to say perhaps, 'Try to look at things as they look to me.' Forget that holiday in Sydney when we bought the black and white porcelain faces on their slender white sticks in a shop that was called Venezia. Forget that masking is natural and even beautiful and set the way we want things to be against the fact of how they are. When I tell her there is the woman downstairs she pours the water like that, the hot needles leaping up from the side of the pot.

There is a woman too who masks her foot. I have seen her in the neighbourhood for years, a yellow-skinned elderly woman who walked slowly because of her foot. But I had never actually looked at her feet until the day she sat with me on the same tram. She wore an old-fashioned leather coat with panels that flared it out. One foot wore an ordinary shoe but the other was built up. It was wrapped round in this kind of leather cage, a mass of straps and buckles and overlacing threads. I looked at it for some minutes, disturbed by its shape. At first I could not understand what it was that irritated me. And then it was so clear. I realised there was no conceivable injury, no possible affliction, that could *need* a boot of that kind. There was something so pointlessly complex about the thing I looked at, I looked too at the woman's face and she was watching me, very calmly. She was watching me in that way which is not concern or interest of any kind but because I was seated opposite her and she had to look at something. But she must have seen the expression of distaste on my face, for I knew I could not possibly be concealing it. She must have known that while I would sympathise with any disability she might have, I also hated her deceit, her theatrical flourish of overlay and glitter and strapping, her indecent trussing of herself. Her foot was pornographic. It was meant to excite in a way no decent woman would want, she was like an amputee with the tawdry glitter of sequins across her private parts. All this I felt instantly, from the second I realised her fraud.

The conductress that day was a friend of my wife's. She spoke about the stifling weather and I answered politely enough. But she must have found my manner with her rather brusque. Because she soon went and stood at the far end of the next compartment with her back against the panel on whose other side the driver would have been looking along the dreary old road of closed shops and small warehouses and a few figures walking past. My wife's friend had both her hands, which were sheathed in mittens, sunk in the leather pouch she carried in front of her. The pouch was supported by a strap around her neck. She moved her hands and the coins shifted beneath her fingers, an unpleasant scrabble that made me think of claws against a tin wall.

The crippled woman kept looking at me. She leaned forward as naturally as any woman would do, say, to scratch her ankle, only this old liar, this fraudulent bitch, tugged at one of the buckles on her foot. She picked at it, like a scab. It lifted away from the worn stitching that held it to the leather and she turned it for a moment in her hand, letting it lie in her palm while the little finger of her other hand prodded at it, pushed it softly with a fingernail. She was fascinated as though only minutes before the thing had been part of her own living flesh. I wanted to grab her hand and press it hard around the metal until its shape cut into her. But she turned sideways, catching her reflection as she pulled at the cord to stop the tram. She then edged towards the door. Her foot dragged with her, a parcel of straps and brass studs.

My wife said to me, 'Dulcie said you were pissed the other night on the tram?'

'Dulcie?'

'The one with mittens. Her hands are that bad with rheumatism and she isn't forty yet.'

'I know who Dulcie is,' I said. 'Of course I know who Dulcie is.'

'She said she tried to talk to you and you hardly answered.'

I said, 'The bitch stood with her fingers hidden inside her bag. She sounded like a rat behind a wall.'

'God,' my wife said, 'tone it down, can't you?' My wife's nipples make me think of eyes. In the morning she raises her nightdress and stands with their naked stare towards me before she conceals them in her brassiere, hiding them away, preventing their hard gaze that I turn from rather than let on that I see. I wonder why all this had not occurred to me before, this constant play at deception that even she is good at. There is no deliberate evil in my wife, I quite know that. But I shall have to watch her more carefully. Her breasts with the dark eyes at their centres warn me in spite of her. I shall watch her if only to help herself.

The tram I take back from work passes down that long street which at one end has tall old-fashioned villas which once must have housed the rich of the city. These days they are places of obscure charities behind their iron railings, their dry cracked fountains. There are often drunks and derelicts sitting on the front lawns. Derelicts and blacks. Then further down the street has all those restaurants, Italian and Spanish, all of them foreign, even the expensive ones. People walk towards them calling out across the footpaths, carrying bottles of wine in brown paper bags. They all dress the same, in casual bright clothes, in jeans and dirty white track shoes. Then beyond this part of the street there are shops that sell old furniture and faded books, junk shops that the people who eat in the restaurants exclaim at and pull each other back to look at carved chairs, ancient dolls, hats from the different wars. Some of the shops are now boarded up. And at the terminus, right along, there is a chemist shop whose Indian owners never close. Opposite it on one corner there is a service station lit up brightly as a stage. From there the street becomes trees and small houses. After dark it is a trail of orange street lights that go on and on, for miles. There are patches of scabby grass, sections where buildings have been demolished but the rubble not cleared away. It is there you will always see cats, and groups of young people handing around their cigarettes, and people you would cross the road rather than have to speak to.

Someone once told me that the Indian brothers in the chemist shop are also undertakers, although I tend to think that can't be true. I have stood over the road from their shop so many times, my back against a doorway that a couple of years ago was the premises for a vet. There are still advertisements for different things in the window, and a small wire wheel of the kind you see mice running in, and some of those rubbery bones people give their dogs to play with. I have stood there and never seen a sign of the Indians having another trade. There are evenings when the two brothers sit on cane stools in the doorway, sit there for hours and scarcely exchange words. I have waited for the big double gates at the side of the shop to be opened and a long black car to drive out, to see its polished sides reflect the street lights in long orange smears. My wife has never heard of it either, and on the trams they pick up most things. She knows number 470 is a brothel, although no one else has ever told me that. She has heard that the old man above the shop next to where I stand at the terminus is really a priest who was kicked out of his church. So she would have heard, surely. 'It beats me,' she says, 'where you get these stories in the first place.' When the eyes of her breasts are put away we get on as well as any married couple. She does not get angry when she thinks I am exaggerating about her friend's hands in their conductor's bag or the old slut with the deceiving foot. And I hold the newspaper motionless so she does not know how much it irritates me that she has still not collected the electric jug from the electrician's right beside her depot, and that for weeks now she has tilted the boiling water from the saucepan so that it leaps and splutters from the side. It is sometimes only inches from where I sit.

Last night one of the Indians spoke to me from his cane stool outside the chemist's shop. When I stand at the corner with my back against the vet's door I think that because my wife is on late shift it will not matter to her where I am, but now that the Indian has spoken to me of course I shall have to find somewhere else, although clearly the terminus is the obvious place. The number 11 pulls in here every twenty-five minutes. In general conversation with my wife, I find out which run Dulcie is on and so avoid the times when she will be on this route. But I know for certain that bucklefoot travels to here, to the very end of the line. I have heard her ask the conductor time and again, 'Right to the terminus,' she says. (Why I wonder did she get off earlier, that day of the scab?) Always she folds her ticket over and over until it is a sliver, and slips it beneath her watch-strap. It would open out again like a very small fan, a thing to hold up and lie behind, even that tiny size.

For the first time I have struck my wife. After all these years! While she lies in the dark bedroom and I can hear her sobbing through the walls, I work out on an envelope that allowing for the time we spent together before we were married, and all that time since, we have been been together for more than six thousand days. Allowing even twelve hours a day when we are not together—and that is too high a figure surely, if one considers weekends when we are always at home—it means at least seventy-two thousand hours we have been with each other, year in, year out. Perhaps half of that time in the same bed. And for less than ten seconds I have forgotten myself enough to act out of character, and to strike her twice across the face. That is less than one two-hundred-and-fifty-millionth of the time we have lived with each other. I have worked it out as exactly that. But I shall not try to explain that until the morning. I shall do a graph of it as well so it shows as an infinitesimal bead on the wire of our lives. I shall tell her it is like something the size of a fly between here and the other side of the earth. And I shall also say that she must know how the mask was getting on my nerves, she must see that? Understand the rage that was suddenly there in front of me, pulled down like a red blind in front of my eyes.

So why did I strike her? My dear wife who came in from a day's work carrying an avocado, which we both love, and a can of artichoke heart soup, and a french roll and 250 grams of unsalted butter. She was happy because from next week she had been put on to our own tram route. She had been requesting that for eighteen months. To celebrate with her I opened a bottle of Portuguese wine. I was opening it as my wife laughed and said to me, 'You know that woman you said you saw the other week?'

'Which woman's that?'

'The woman with the mask. You know, the opera one downstairs?'

My hand ceased turning the corkscrew. I could not believe what my wife was telling me. She was laughing and saying there were these schoolgirls with all kinds of get-ups. 'You know the things. Those long feathers round their necks and bright stockings and one of them with a blue mask across her eyes. It's a school thing they're rehearsing for.' She said that must have been the one who upset me.

I saw my wife's fingers easing the fat dark stone from the split avocado. I thought, for the first time in my life, why is she lying to me?

'The mask wasn't blue!' I shouted at her. 'The woman was as old as you are!' I could see from her shrug that she too was embarrassed now I had told her that. What was the point of her lying? I demanded why my own wife would defend a woman in a black mask, some rotten creature watching you enter your own home? 'Is that what working with Dulcie does for you?' I shouted. 'Cripples and whores and liars! Is that what it does for you?'

'Oh shut up!' she screamed back at me, without turning to look at me. She could suddenly have been any woman standing in our kitchen, her face turned from me and lying, having no right to be there, not honest enough to turn, to show the lie that stood there in my own wife's place. And that red blind, as it seemed, drew down closer over my eyes. I heard the bottle crash to the floor and my hand was falling twice across the woman's neck, and the double impact of her forehead against the cupboard door in front of her. 'Black!' I was shouting at her, 'the mask was fucking black!'

I am sorry I ruined our celebration and that what I hear, this minute, is my wife's grief on the other side of the wall. But there is only a little bruising, fortunately. There will be no mark on her face apart from this little bruising. And I shall have ready for her what I have copied from the back of the envelope onto a sheet of paper. She'll be able to see for herself the figures showing how infinitesimal in time my anger was. And the graph as well, the projection of a trajectory between the earth and the moon, and a speck which cannot be taken as more than the size of a fly's body. She will see how ridiculous it is to imagine that a perfectly harmonious arc through such colossal distance might be marred by a fly.

But I shall be watching, believe me. I shall be the husband I have always been but I shall watch the trams she is on and see if bucklefoot so much as tries to talk to her as the tram sways those last hundred yards towards the terminus and my wife goes as she always does to wind the canvas roll in its glass oblong that changes the destination, to say suddenly the terminus is not where they shall stop in only a few seconds time but the place they leave behind after the driver has drunk the tea from his thermos flask. I'll see it if she does. If the cripple talks to her or if my wife answers. I shall see it all right.

Sometimes I wait against the door of what used to be the vet's but sometimes in between the trams arriving I walk along by the derelict houses and the sections of deserted rubble that don't look quite real, not under the orange lights. There are great blocks of shadow where the world disappears. Or I walk back the other way, past the shops that at night reflect back like a mirror as you go walking past. One of them is safe to go past because he says nothing, unlike the other one who asks things. The problem is to tell the difference before you are right up close, right there walking past them. But the point is I shall be there and I shall be ready. When the tram rackets past it looks like oil is on its sides when it rushes at night and the light slips streaky along the panels. But no matter how fast it goes past you can see if people are talking, and as it slows towards the terminus I will be able to catch up with it, or watch it approach me if I am in the vet's doorway, if I am standing there at night. I shall be ready when the time is right and the strapped and buckled and laced-up old slut limps off towards the trees and the shadows that in fact are purple under the orange lights, oh won't I just. And when my wife comes in late and tired and wants to hold her hands out towards the bar heater I shall have it switched on for her, and the tea warming under the cosy that is a black cat stitched from quilted squares, and the electric blanket on, all that will be ready too.

Hims Ancient and Modern

A thousand times if it was once she had said them to her friend, those two short, ordinary, so dominating words, said in so many ways. *Oh, him*, with so little left to it, so dull an inflection, a mere flopped pancake of a pronoun, meaning, so often, her husband Don. Or in tones of such utter dismissal, a dollop of ordure as it were scraped from a shoe, which was a lover discarded, a repellent colleague, a memory from years back, repeating on her like unpleasant food. Or occasionally, once a year or so at the most, the words of anticipation or desire, *oh, him*! Placing her hand lightly on her friend's sleeve, looking across the room, glancing over the tables in a restaurant, to see the figure of the moment, a man not so unlike all others, who stood bathed for that instant in sweet challenge and potential. Her friend never knew quite what to say.

Her friend was Alicia, and she was Ros. Friends from way back, Ros declared whenever they met a new set of acquaintances, my best friend for yonks. They had shared a room together in O'Rorke, remember that dreadful old warren of a hostel? Borrowing clothes from each other, window latches left on the loose to let the other in, when that great shambling warden imposed his curfews. That's how far back they went. Further, Alicia would say, we were friends at school as well. 'Oh, but life only begins at seventeen,' Ros said. 'We were the youngest in the hostel, remember that?'

Ros still looked very good. She was proud of Don, whatever the inflection she might put on *him*, and he was very proud of her. He had been head boy believe it or not the year she was head girl. At different schools, but good ones, both of them. They danced together at the seventh form ball. They married the summer after graduation. *The Great Gatsby* was the favourite book of both of them. And they loved each other enough to respect each other's privacy. 'Ros and I respect each other greatly,' Ron explained the one time he placed his hand on Alicia's leg, and Alicia's fingers met round his wrist like a very firm bracelet and placed his hand back on his own thigh. 'As pure as the old proverbial,' he said, very good-naturedly, very appropriately, for they were driving down from the mountain towards the lodge at Ohakune and high drifts of snow were banked on either side. Alicia's husband Frank and her friend Ros were in the long-bonneted Humber a hundred yards ahead of them, because Ros and Frank were such good mates and so enjoyed talking to each other. No one was jealous in the least. Ros said sometimes, her eyes widening with admirable frankness, that she simply couldn't understand how one could cope with possessiveness. 'It *wizens* you,' she said. 'It's so demeaning.' Don thank heavens wouldn't recognise it if it was sitting next to him on a bus.

In her even, quiet tone Alicia said, 'Frank says he could quite imagine himself killing for jealousy.' Hard-working predictable Frank, his hair already greying in that distinguished legal way, had quite amazed her when he came out with that. 'As if he'd ever need to!' Ros hooted. 'Honestly!'

'Italy!' they called, almost simultaneously. On the sundeck, on a June day of unusual warmth, the blue volcano riding across the satiny harbour as seductively, Ros said, as a Tourist Department poster. The Japs would be here in their millions if they could see it now. Then within twenty minutes a grim sky trundling in from the south, raindrops the size of ten-cent pieces splotching the wooden slats of the deck. From inside the lounge they watched the spears of rain march across the entire view, the colour drained from the blur of Rangitoto. It was cold enough to turn on the fire. The electric coals fluctuated with artificial shadows passing across the ruby patches of heat, when Frank said casually, 'That trip we've always talked about,' as if the rain and cold replacing sun and the smoothest of seas made him yearn of a sudden for quite a different world. The idea flared up between them as though it had waited for this very moment to ignite. 'Yes!' Ros said, her hand and its chunky silver rings slapping quickly on the broad arm of her chair, 'Oh yes, yes!' 'A break from all this anyway,' Don put in. 'How would that grab you, eh?' He grinned down at Alicia. No months and months of planning, just up and off as the spirit moved them. And because she felt so strongly the push of expectation, the sudden stretch toward new vistas, Alicia surprised herself by drumming both her fists on her lap. 'Oh yes,' she said, 'let's just do it then, why don't we?' And without a thought between them of Hawaii or Club Med or Lake Tahoe or the Ardennes, in one voice, really and truly, before the first had time to finish the word the others were saying it as well, 'Italy!' they called, almost simultaneously. Ros sat back laughing and Alicia smiled up at the men, who slapped each other's palms like black American sprinters on TV.

The next evening they sat with brochures and maps spread on the table between them. Ros had just phoned her niece. 'You wouldn't believe it would you? They're away that fortnight so the place is ours!' They each picked a city which they said was an absolute must. Frank said Assisi although no one but his aged aunts had called him Francis for years and Ros of course said Florence because that was where her niece was on a scholarship at the Villa I Tatti and Don said ever since he was a boy he had thought about the dog frozen in ash in Pompeii. Alicia pushed about the pile of brochures in front of her, the coastlines and lakes and hills with cypresses and cities studded with domes. There was nowhere she wanted as specially as all the others did. Then a man with a dark stony face looked at her directly from a page she opened, and she caught her breath. Her hand smoothed across the page. 'Get a load of *him*!' Ros shrieked over her shoulder in mock schoolgirl shrillness. She pointed at the man in his long stiff toga although she had no idea in the world of who or where he was. They were all a little silly with excitement and Don's usual heavy hand with the drinks. 'Yes,' Alicia said, closing the brochure, opening it again, smiling in that vague way that sometimes drove Ros batty. 'I think it will have to be here all right. Is that OK?' She looked at her husband, at her friends. But there was nothing vague in the way she asked them that. It wasn't asking at all, in fact. It was telling them what they were going to do.

It was marvellous travelling together in those first few weeks—the sun, the warmth, the fun they had between them, something new at every turn of every street. Don saw his ash-embalmed dog and when no one was watching Frank crossed himself in the chapel at Assisi and Ros quite knew, at last, why the art buffs made so much of Giotto. And Alicia smiling and reading and, as Ros at least picked up, looking simply radiant.

There were days in Florence however when Ros was inclined to sulk. Her husband and Frank strolled out to the Agenzia Ippica where Don would try out his meagre Italian by placing trifectas at Palermo or Genoa, although after the one afternoon he went to the track at Florence he said you wouldn't believe they'd have the bloody gall to prop up what should be dog tucker and parade it around as horseflesh. They would stop on the way back for coffees and gallianos, a mix that seemed to amuse the waiter in their neighbourhood bar. The two men fortunately hit it off together, and at more or less the same time declared they were a bit sated with galleries, and might start giving them a miss. This, Ros noticed, coincided with their coming to terms with the local bars. Don said, sometimes several times a day, 'Should have done this years ago. There's more to life than slaving to make a buck.' And Frank would tip his glass against his friend's and tell him, 'Right on, fratello.'

In her niece's minute apartment Ros closed her copy of *Look at Me, I'm Dancing*, the fifth volume of autobiography of a New Zealand author who, for all her success, had never lost her childhood values nor the bonding example of her working-class aunts. Ros wondered how her own life of travel, comfort, and tolerably civilised men could strike her at times as incomplete. She bit on the handkerchief wrapped round her knuckle and was glad when her friend came in and offered to make them both a mug of tea. Ros knew she was on the verge of melodrama, and she simply hated that. Even in herself.

The women carried their steaming mugs through to the late afternoon haze of the apartment's balcony. Across the jumble of tiled roofs and above the stacked angular blocks either side of the river, the bells of one of the churches boomed on and on. When the bells suddenly stopped there was the delicate thread of a piano, not too far off, tinkling through the haze.

'It couldn't be more perfect,' Ros said.

'No,' Alicia said. A swallow flicked up from below the eaves, circled the women, veered off behind a neighbour's wall.

'In one way,' Ros went on. Then she was silent, assuming that what she said demanded at least a query from her friend. But no, none came. She looked across at Alicia, considering as she had so often before how it was quite beyond her even now, after knowing her for half her lifetime, to guess in the least whether that pale, pretty, insipid face concealed the deepest ruminations or simply nothing at all. But Ros picked herself up, not wanting to be unkind. She is a good dear friend, she thought, only she's too solemn for God's sake, too reticent, even to know what letter fun begins with.

Alicia's eyes were closed, her head tilted back against the canvas of her chair. The sun gilded her face. It fired her lashes, her eyebrows, to a burnished copper. She was thinking of what she had read earlier that afternoon, preparing herself for their next town. She imagined those lines of perhaps forty virgins, facing across the nave the same number of young men, fresh in their white togas after fifteen hundred years. She saw the magical green hill with its allegorical flock. But the feeling she had was not connected with art, she quite knew that. She was angry too with a woman she had never heard of until recently, as much as she was moved for the man that woman failed to appreciate. She was also very calm, and very sure. She had felt rather like this, but less so, when she was pregnant with Jasmine. She thought, my face is like a mask beneath this deliciously soothing sun. Like a face in a mosaic. A mosaic in a holy place in the ancient city of Ravenna.

'He's following me,' Ros said. 'I'm quite certain of it now.'

She and Alicia had turned right from the straw market where Ros for luck had touched the brightly bronzed snout of the famous boar. Alicia had bought a leather handbag that the young vendor fetched with a pole from its peg high above his stall. They were walking back, almost at the Piazza della Grazia, when Ros made her announcement.

'Who is?' Alicia said.

'The one in brown there. Only don't let on.'

The women turned and the man twenty steps or so behind them also turned slightly towards a wall, his head tilted above the jump of a match flare between his cupping hands.

'If you're walking behind someone it's easy for the person in front to think you're following them,' Alicia said.

Ros clucked with irritation. 'I ought to know if I'm being followed, for God's sake!'

Alicia supposed it had to happen sooner or later in Italy. It was one of the bores of travel, didn't everyone say that? She wouldn't be sorry to leave this town of too many tourists. Marvellous and beautiful and reeking with history and all that, but a town without privacy. You couldn't look at a painting or a statue, you couldn't stand in a doorway to take in the blue and white enamel madonna with its string of green leaves and vivid lemons above a doorway across the street, without lots of other people seeing you looking. Alicia didn't care for that. She said so to Frank, and Frank laughed at her. 'Just you and Lorenzo de Medici,' he said. 'That'd be the perfect town, I suppose?' Then last night the two men had quarrelled about how best to get to the station. Everyone was getting tetchy. The glamour was wearing off, she supposed. They were beginning to see things as they were, every day. She had said, 'Being tourists works so long as you remember it's only once in a lifetime.' Frank had turned to her then and snapped, 'Is that contributing something?' She never did say witty things, she quite knew that. Sometimes she said things too that quite missed the point. So she said apologetically, 'I was miles away, I'm sorry,' running her finger round and round the rim of her wine glass. Ros had then said sharply, 'Well we all are, actually. Tourists. This is Italy, after all.' Don raised his eyebrows at his wife and Alicia smiled at them both. She wished they would go back to the flat, where she could think quietly again about Ravenna. She thought of a huge round mausoleum whose roof was a single slab of stone that weighed 230 tons. It wasn't the sort of thing though you could very well tell people you were thinking about.

'I know I am,' Ros insisted now as they walked up towards the bridge. 'It's not as if at our age you don't know a thing like that.' At thirty-eight, she implied. You know about men by then if you're ever going to. Oh, there was a bit of a frisson to it, that's for sure. An Italian following you through the streets. A tad vulgar, she admitted, but still a frisson.

Next day at lunch Don said, 'What's that shady bugger in the corner there find so interesting at this table?' The man in a brown suit with the dark glasses and a folded paper tilted his head so the glasses flashed with the smear of reflected light. 'God, you're neurotic,' Ros said to him. 'How can you tell where he's looking if you can't even see his eyes?' But she looked directly at where she believed the centre of his eyes would be, and defiantly held his gaze.

That evening as they undressed Frank said 'So much for Tuscany, then. What's our next kingdom?'

In the train the others slept most of the journey across to the coast. Their last night had been a scream. They had met up with—no, we didn't dream it, Don would say later as he told it—met up with two very nice Australians. And finished up in an apartment Ros went on that she would give her eyes for, above the Piazza Santa Croce. 'Don't tell *me*,' she said, 'about la dolce vita.' Their hosts had kept insisting, 'Try this one from Friuli,' implying that until you'd sampled another you wouldn't know what Pinot Grigio was. 'Italians don't drink the way we do,' the woman partner remarked. Her statement hung there, isolated, for half a minute before anyone spoke, a kind of tombstone with its line of considered grief. And the Australian, very seriously, said with understanding, 'And look where that's got them, eh?' They sang together like undergraduates. The woman, who was blond and lovely, said they'd probably never go back. She spoke of Urbino as familiarly as Dabtoe. Alicia thought, am I really here, listening to all this? In a room four hundred years old with little painted figures and intertwining vines on the ceiling, and tomorrow—she could hardly think of *that* without pressing her knees together like a girl waiting for the curtain to go up at a pantomime.

On the balcony soon after midnight their host put his arm around Frank and nipped the lobe of his ear. 'The good thing about here,' he said, 'the great thing about here'—and he waved his other hand that roughly took in the sweep of half the city and the hills—'is that you can't only look at the loveliest stuff in the world. You can get anything you want.' There was a significant pause, as they say, above the square with Dante standing in front of the vast raw brick façade. 'Know what I mean?' the host said.

When the rest of the party came onto the balcony Frank tapped his watch and told them, 'Work tomorrow, playmates.' After they called their farewells up the echoing stairwell and came into the yellow lighting of the piazza, he broke out, 'Christ, rugby league and vino until they're coming out your ears and then he goes and touches you up. You never know where you are with Aussies.' They laughed and shuffled about on the pavements like a group of teenagers on their way back home, their voices appallingly loud as they turned into the canyon of the Via San Niccoló.

And so they slept most of the journey in the train. A man in a brown suit and wearing dark glasses passed their compartment, twice. He looked in at the three sleepers and the woman who read, glanced from the window at the rushing plains, and read again. The man put his bunched fingers to his lips, then exploded their bud to a full bloom of palm and fingers. He reminded himself of something happening in a book. A schoolteacher from Bradford, this playing at Graham Greene roles was his annual diversion from randy adolescents and sweaty gym shoes.

Alicia read slowly, and with great delight. 'A period of battle and intrigue, but also of incomparable beauty, and mysterious sighs in the passageways of civilisation.' Was it too much to imagine one might hear them still, those echoes, those sighs, hear them with attention enough to catch the very words? She looked from the pages and their visions of marble, blood, incense, brilliant stones, to the flicker of poles along the side of the railtrack, the smears of mist rising from the dark fields. St Heliers seemed ever so far away. So did the children, as did their father, this very moment dozing across the compartment from her. She looked at him quite dispassionately. In a sense she already knew. She was very calm about it.

They stepped from the train to a cold platform and a depressing fog. The two women and Don went to the station café and ordered cappuccinos. Frank, with his list of recommended addresses, crossed the space in front of the station to the dull modern hotel. This was a town that had been here since the Romans used it as a port, where civilisation rested on its flight from Rome to Byzantium, but it made him think of Frankton. You take the sun from Italy and you turn it into a junk yard. Nothing was truer than that one.

He spoke with a surly girl across a formica desk. On the wall behind her shoulder hung an overbright replica of a mosaic dove. He asked the prices, got her to write them down, and booked two rooms that faced away from the street. He then waited for the wet gleaming side of a bus to slip by in front of him, and recrossed the square. He skirted the taxi drivers who offered their services in arrogant mocking English. He said to the last one, who came up close towards him, 'Look, piss off.' And he said to the group he had left in the bar that the hotel was no great shakes but it would do. It would bloody have to.

They sat in the cold hotel bar, the only patrons. They drank two quick brandies which did little to warm them up. Don and Frank were fractious together, disputing the difference between cathedral and basilica. 'It's architectural,' Don said.

'Like hell it is,' Frank argued. 'The difference is bureaucratic.' Then Don ordered another brandy which even he knew would make him more difficult. When the men left the bar to get a guide book from upstairs Alicia said, 'You remember that man?'

'What bloody man?' Ros asked her.

'The one in brown clothes and glasses? The one in the restaurant the other day?' She said he had been on the train.

'My God,' Ros said. She rolled back her eyes in irritation. 'Him!' It was something to be grateful for, she supposed, that Alicia bothered to tell her even now. For a few seconds she hated all of them. Then she put a Kleenex to her eyes, her nose, and looked from the side of the lace curtain at the strip of sky that was like a dirty Band-Aid.

Alicia said, 'I've seldom felt happier. Isn't that odd?'

'Remarkably,' Ros said. Sometimes she could not believe what a trial other people might be.

They were close to the mausoleum that historians consider unique. They walked down the steps from the road level and its hum of constant traffic to the quiet pathways and the stretch of lawn. They purchased tickets at the booth and moved towards the tomb of Theodoric, emperor, Goth, servant of God, soldier, husband. Ros said, 'Mosaics are one thing, sure, but don't tell me people come to look at this? A cross between an outsize dunny and a concrete silo?' She was tetchy still, with the weather which kept on foggy and cold, let alone with the hotel which she disliked, the Italian men who had done nothing more than track and ogle and elude her, and with her husband who said arse-freezing temperatures or not he had no intention of pushing on towards England ahead of the schedule they had planned. And Frank of course encouraged him to drink. Anything. Wherever they could. Their combined male memories of Italy would be a series of labels and torn-up betting slips.

On the pathway to the tomb, the massive arches set so far below the level of the present world, its chunky dome rising as it had always done above whatever age surrounded it, Alicia said, 'He was here for a comparatively short time after 526. The mortal part of him.'

'What's she on about this time?' Frank said. He too was already bored with the morning's task.

'That pattern around the top,' Don said. 'They're like dentists' tongs, eh, Ros?'

'It's better to say nothing sometimes,' Ros snapped at him. 'Just effing nothing.'

'Never knew you cared,' Don said. Sarcastic now, Ros thought. Pity there isn't a door for him to slam as well.

Frank began crooning, 'What a swell party this is,' in his Sinatra voice. Getting at her, of course.

'That's it!' Ros said. 'No, really, that's it!' She clicked across the scruffy patch of grass to a seat beneath some sodden pines. 'I'll just wait over here.' There was the pattering of small drops about her and she felt the dampness already seeping through her clothes. But she had to sit it out now. She simply had no choice. She bit her lip and was determined not to cry and thought why couldn't she be more like her friend, safe in some dull little cocoon that protected her from this kind of hurt?

Alicia kept walking, quite unfussed by the squabbling about her. She walked through the black iron fence and mounted the external stairs to the chamber directly beneath the dome, the room which architects had wondered at for a millennium and a half. She took in its austere detail, felt its magnitude and bulk. She remembered all that she had read, in a flash that plucked her from the normal currents of time. She was unaware of crossing the floor but felt the rim of the huge lidless sarcophagus against her breasts. It was like a massive bath. She raised her hands to the porphyry's solid iciness and felt a change suffusing her. She walked around the sarcophagus, right around it, her fingers stroking the broad sloping smoothness of the rim. She knew her lips were moving, she heard the incantation of her breath, but had no notion of what she said or why. Then she stood at its foot, her back to the high open door, and looked into the great hollowed block of dark red stone as though she simply looked at a bed. Had she turned she would have seen through the oblong of the doorway how the sky hung dull as canvas. But Alicia did not turn. Her hands still at the sarcophagus's rim, she felt a tremor of a kind that she hardly expected. She knew it was autumn and that there was fog between the mausoleum and what surrounded it. Yet she saw a shadow moving steadily past her, a shadow in a cube of brilliant light. She was not in the least fazed by its presence. She turned and the living mosaic was within arm's length. She was surprised only that he was no taller than herself. She then asked him quite calmly, as though she spoke to her husband when he dressed not quite adequately for the weather, 'Do you think those sandals are a good idea?' She pointed to the feet of the greatest Goth of his or any time. And then, as naturally again as she might straighten her husband's tie as he set off to work, she touched the dull gold clasp with its nine surrounding white stones, the three chunky matching pendants, and ran her opened hand from his shoulder to his chest, across the prickly brown fabric he had worn now without changing for a very long time. She brushed the stubble of his cheeks, no more frightening in fact than the growth on the Whetton brothers the morning before a Test. It was though a little unexpected to see his head with only the cap of tight brown curls. She had got so used to him in his famous picture, the squashed tiered crown and the large gold disc behind his head. They were both struck enough by the novelty to laugh out loud. The funereal vault was a place of sudden fun. She asked, quite knowing how silly it sounded,

'Do you come here often, then?' She felt she must surely be the plainest woman he had ever been this close to—no tiara, no fifteen inches at least of earrings as that empress wore. She thought, My God, am I asking for trouble mixing it with her! But he was watching her with a kindly expression and must have read her mind. 'Look,' he said, 'she was always a bitch. And you've got to remember when it was. Rotten teeth. Warts. Hygiene problems of one kind or another. You don't know when you've got it good. No,' Theo summed up, 'you can forget about that one. Slag wasn't in it.' That should have sounded coarse, even in Latin. But it made Alicia very happy because she knew he told the truth. Then the brightness was blocked by his approaching head. She felt the pressure of the sarcophagus against her shoulders. She opened her lips and his tongue was as warm as you could reasonably expect any tongue to be. She bit on it softly. It tasted of cloves and Sicilian wine. She felt his calf muscle tense against her own. 'Veni, imperator,' she said very softly. His breath was hot against her ear and she heard him sigh, 'It's been so long.'

Marriage really is the oddest thing. It was nearly twenty years since they first slept together, in Frank's parents' beach house at the Mount while the oldies were off at a Rotarian dinner. Alicia was twenty-two and knew sooner or later it had to come to this. She had thought with some coolness well thank goodness it's not happening on the beach anyway, at least there isn't sand to contend with as well. And when Frank's parents came back they were sitting there playing Scrabble and his mother said, 'Why don't you two ever go out and have a bit of fun?' Mrs H., as Alicia thought of her even years after they were related, couldn't make out the young these days. 'You're such stick-at-homes,' she told them. Her husband belched so that his wife flinched, and announced 'That's all for now folks! I think I'll pile up the zeds.' She herself smiled wanly and went off to her own room. And the next morning the young ones said they would get married after their final exams. Mrs H. gave Alicia a family locket and said she'd help her choose her clothes from now on.

And now here she was, in Ravenna, lying beside one man, thinking of another, never quite so startled, nor yet quite so at peace, in her life. Marriage really is the oddest thing, hadn't she said that this afternoon? And Theo had laughed, exposing the molar broken in half by a glancing barbarian axe. 'Need a stronger word than that for some I can think of,' he had said. 'You must have seen her up there in all that fancy clobber? Talk about a cow!'

Alicia turned carefully, anxious not to wake Frank. Her shoulders ached from where the porphyry rim had pressed into them as Theo's ardour jogged at her. And the rash on her throat where his beard had rubbed like a pot-mitt. 'Amor,' he had said just before he moved back into the radiance and his shadow flowed across the floor again as though cast in front of a searchlight, 'amor omnia vincit.' She turned and winced from the long bruise on her right thigh where the jewel-encrusted scabbard had danced and flipped against her like a playful whip. She still felt the firm pressure of his grasp as he hoisted her against his tomb.

And it *does* conquer everything, love, that's the delicious thing about it. Back on the sundeck a few weeks later, the same harbour spread there in its marbling blues and greens, the scents pungent from the conservatory. Ros fanned the colour prints across the low table between them, and Alicia looked at them and nodded at what a scream it all had been. Don could be an Italian almost couldn't he, tucked under the archway with that silly leer? And Ros herself there, see, the very spot where those marvellous hillshots were taken in *A Room with a View*?

'Frank's talking about going back next year,' Alicia said.

'Back!' Ros declared. Her eyes were wide and expectant. Alicia told her, 'There's a man at Russell McVeagh with a time-share near Livorno.'

'Imagine,' Ros said, 'imagine all that over *again*!'

Alicia laughed and touched a print of a green and white facade. 'Remember your man in brown?' she said.

'Do I!' Ros declared. As if she'd forget *him*. 'After tracking me from city to city?'

'Wasn't it there we saw him first?'

'Where didn't we see him?' Ros said. 'Talk about *infatuated*!' Alicia smiled and looked at the images of what, after all, was only a couple of months back. She thought of how careful she had to be for days so Frank wouldn't see those marks. She thought, rather more apprehensively, of the little airmail packets that arrived every few days, the chips of coloured stone she simply didn't twig to until she had several dozen of them, moving them idly about one afternoon where she kept them hidden in the toolshed, and realised they formed—she could hardly believe it—a sandal, a big toe, an ankle, the hem of a toga. She laughed out loud as she had in the mausoleum, and there was the same quick echo, a fraction behind her voice. Because it came to her, that instant. That absurd dear Goth was actually posting himself to her, bit by bit! But they would notice soon, surely—there must be a wall, somewhere, a curved space in a dome, where his image was diminished by as much as appeared there, in front of her, on the bench in the garden shed. She was quite content to wait. She would manage Frank when the time came.

'His name,' Alicia said suddenly, 'his name means a special gift. Did you know that?'

'Whose, my dear?' Ros asked her. She felt so warm towards her friend since she mentioned that Latin admirer who had taken such risks to pursue her. She had thought—she was a bit ashamed of it, now—she had thought Alicia might even have been a tad envious that *she* was the one the males decided to track. 'Whose name is that?'

Alicia held up the picture Don had snapped with his Singapore zoom-lens. It showed the placid, intelligent face surrounded by the lesser figures of his rigid court. 'His,' Alicia said. 'That's what his name means.' And she said it out loud, in case Ros had forgotten it. A name that was frank and warm and took its place exactly, among colours that would hold for another thousand years.

Coasting

Brin and Fran, fortyish, academics, New Zealanders, and thus trebly anxious, drove in sudorous heavy silence while the gauge rolled over another thousand ks. It was like travelling in a clammy tin. The car smelled of food and feline presence.

The landscape intruded by its very sameness, gums flecking its edges with their archaic repetitive script. The couple looked straight ahead or to the side, but seldom at each other. Childless and bookless, although they had tried earnestly enough for both, they travelled north, always north, with their cat Palincest on a spread newspaper on the back seat. The cat they had thought a female as a kitten, an inexplicable mistake considering the close inspection Fran had given next door's litter when they were no longer a mere clot of undifferentiated fur. Yet within months it had made advances at its own mother, its gender orientation unexpectedly reinscribed. Hence pussy's playfully hypocoristic signifier. A bowel disorder, picked up in the camping ground at Noosa Head, now made it more a patient than a pal. Fran in fact detested the creature. It was Brin, anxious that all living things share his mental space, who spoke to it quietly and fed it bacon rinds at breakfast. One day, Fran thought, one day it will skulk about in the scrub and a snake will bite it to death. Good.

Fran and Brin were thoughtful enough to realise that marriages, as much as houses or one's critical discourse, from time to time demand refurbishing. This long—unbelievably long—north-eastern coast was what they hit on for refreshment. No theatres or libraries, no bright lights, but simply as close as they could come, within reason, to the solitary, the remote, to touch centre as it were and then emerge to new perspectives. Fran said, 'We're starting to talk like those bloody white male explorers used to.' Brin asked but wasn't marriage itself a site with now the flag of one empire, now that of another? *Alii alia dicunt*, wasn't that life all over? It was this alertness to linguistic slippage that now obliged them to travel anywhere except in their own country. For hadn't they been among the first, God knows, to impose self-discipline on their recognition of the word as oppressor, of vocabulary as imperialist *piège*? Adam naming the beasts, not the killing of Abel, was the first act of violence, as their students immediately understood. They refused to travel, to stay, even to cross those areas of appropriation where names had been changed, imposed, inverted, by Pākehā transgression. At least they would not go along with 'Wellington' for Te Upoko o te Ika, 'Auckland' for misplaced Tamaki Makaurau. Certainly their presence would not contribute its trace towards illicit reinscription on such a massive scale. Their absence would declare, however modestly, an atoning erasure. And more than that. They had each, by way of solidarity and protest, excised a syllable from their own given names. A simple enough gesture, sure, but at least enacting within the frame of the nominal a metonymic castration that mirrored (with all the duplicities that implied!) the larger rape of the indigene as language; that carried in their own address to themselves an imperial displacement as vivid, if not as painful, as Kafka's celebrated discourse on the colonial/penal body. While behind that too, as Fran noted, one might usefully recollect and so re-enter Nietzsche's witty configuration with crime and sin, *der* Frevel and *die* Sünde, making of Eden itself a contentiously gendered site by virtue of those rabidly buoyant defining articles. Fran, to Brin's constant admiration, could articulate things like that in the twinkling of an I/eye/auie/aye.

Brin said, 'It would prevent us being here too, if we knew enough about the place.' Two hours later he spoke again, as they drove past a tiny settlement where the First People sat on a raised wooden veranda in front of a blue and yellow country store. 'Putting Blake's drawing of a native family—remember?—still putting that in front of what the people in fact are. Imposing our semantic grid. That's what we're up to, you know. Still.' 'Piss off sometimes will you,' Fran asked him, 'darling?'

In the motels in the evenings Brin read Cook's account of sailing north, Beaglehole's monumental rewriting of Cook, Hoare's probing of Beaglehole, and the articles that challenged Hoare. History, as he well knew it, was a progression—regression?—of referential drift. But so was everything else.

Fran lay on her back at nights and smoked, and sipped at gin. Every few minutes she raised her cigarette to her mouth, its pharos of incipient lungwrack intense and brief. She thought of the real-estate salesman at last night's hotel. She thought of the fair-complexioned teacher and his obviously non-connubial companion in the lounge after breakfast this morning, and of the photographer who raised her hand to wave from a sand-dune sixty kilometres from a phone box. She thought of her own remarks on a student's narratology assignment, reminding that language at best was a makeshift net, not a containing dish; that the mind's sharpest objective perception constantly echoed itself. She thought if this ice can't last longer than that before riding into the lake of lukewarm gin, then come back referentiality, come back boredom and hang-dog fucking realism as long as ice means ice. And she thought if that cat craps again during the night I shall not even bother to wait for the snake.

In such moments, and with some minds, stories begin. With others of course, not. But as Fran and her brighter students very well knew, not to begin a story is also a story of a different kind.

> *Sunday April 1. In the P.M. had a moderate breeze at E., which in the Night Veer'd to the N.E., and was attended with hazey, rainy weather . . . At Noon our Latitude by account was 40 12S., Long. made from Cape Farewell 1 11 West.*

At a pinewood committee-room table, imagine, there are seven people. Real people. No one person likes every other person, naturally, but good manners and complimentary wine would make an eighth person suppose amity prevailed among them all. It is a Friday evening, ten minutes before sunset. Light pours across the table as a veranda door opens on the company, a sudden flag of brilliance for several seconds until the door is again shut. A clock ticks noticeably when there is a pause between words. These people, moving left to right, do not in a sense exist until they are named. Let them be named then. Charlie and Moira, Harry, Connie, Bazza, Emma and Rex.

Across a pause, Connie Batchelor says, 'I wish someone would kill that bloody clock.'

'At least it's had its strike cut out. It's been neutered to that extent.' When Charlie Ruxton says that he grins so his tongue shows grey as a calf's between his teeth. Beside him, Moira Lucas thinks how that man turns even time itself into an animal, so he can say something smutty. She sees that Harry Buchanan on her other side is drawing small intricate wheels on a piece of paper. Across from her, florid Rex Morrison, the real-estate dealer, helps himself from the carafe. He then holds it up, his glance round that table asking them all, Who else? Only his young wife Emma pushes her glass towards him.

'No,' says Bazza Forbes for the rest of them. 'No thanks.' The schoolteacher's face, a red wedge beneath straw-coloured hair, does not turn to Rex as he speaks, but he moves a finger, his middle one, so that only Emma notices.

Connie Batchelor brings them back to the business of the meeting. She says, 'We've got exactly two months until the Event. Everything looks pretty much on schedule, wouldn't you say?' Pretty Emma Morrison answers because she fears that otherwise she may not seem alert and keen. 'We all know where to go next, then, what we're supposed to be responsible for?'

Vapid bitch, Moira Lucas thinks. She smiles, however, and says, 'I'm sure that goes for everyone, Emma.' She leans across to the desk calendar in the centre of the table and rips off the leaf which shows the end of March. 'There,' she says. 'A nice fresh month for us all to start with.'

Rex says the weeks will be on top of them before they know where they bloody are.

Friday 20th April. The Southernmost point of land we had in sight, which bore from us W.S., I judged to lay in the Latitude of 38 0 S. and in the Long. of 211 7 W. from the Meridian of Greenwich. I have named it Point Hicks, because Lieutenant Hicks was the first who discover'd this Land. The great navigator was tempted to commit to his journal the observation that the baronet, brought on board at the last moment at the Admiralty's request, was for all his breeding and wealth, and his friendship with Mr Banks, a most wearisome companion at table. Yet again the gentleman had raised that his own name be held in reserve for a piece of land considerably more impressive than mere headland or estuary. The baronet's hands played constantly with his cutlery, with turning his glass and folding, unfolding his napkin. Cook noticed how Solander observed the man scientifically. He must have a word with that sober Swede. But none of this he committed to the page. Instead, he continued

> calmly, *In the P.M. saw other Egg Birds [Sterna fascata] and again, in numbers, the Gannet [Sula serrator].*

Mrs Connie Batchelor put her copy of Jung on the pile of books beside her bed—*The Interpretation of Signs, Time and Distance*, and a journal she subscribed to on reincarnation. She lay for a few moments with her hands behind her head, her elbows pointed high. From the ill-lit mirror facing the bed, she had the impression of heavy pale wings. Then she switched off the light. There was the faintest feeling, which she knew could well be unsettled Scotch, that made her think the room gently swayed. She closed her eyes and thought of the broken pattern of the *I Ching*, an arrangement which warned her of approaching change.

At more or less the same time, Harry Buchanan was moving a series of matches into lines that were not unlike the rows that Connie thought of. In fact he had picked up the habit of moving them about like this all those years ago when he and Connie were very close. She would throw the coins and say, 'Set them up for me, Harry.' He would then lay down straight matches, or broken ones, so she could take it in, as she said, rather more vividly than you could when you simply drew the lines on paper. This way the smooth unbroken sticks contrasted with the snaggle-ended halves that Harry snapped. It was how things should always be, Connie used to remark, ideas set out in objects, even a humble clutch of matches taking their place in the eternal scheme. She said it with a laugh, of course, she hated the very thought that she might sound pretentious. And her young watchmaker friend simply listened, mostly. He liked hearing her talk and he liked her size, the arms that made his own seem emaciated and the breasts when she first let them loose from her bra and the streaks of powder he could see along their sides, making him think of flour sacks. He liked it that he was twenty-four and that she was twelve years older. All girls had stayed pretty much sisters until he met Connie. She had said to him as he handed across the counter a silver clasp that he had fixed, 'Libra, am I right?' He told her what day. She said, 'Ah, Taurus. Venus on the cusp.' He looked at the handsome big woman as she laughed and tapped his wrists. 'That's why we'll get on.'

Emma Morrison said to Bazza Forbes, 'But doesn't your wife ever suspect?' 'Nah,' Bazza said. 'Not an earthly.' Emma thought of a mechanic she had gone out with once who told her life only began when you had grease on your hands, and yet he always spoke so beautifully she said to him once that if you heard him from the next room you'd think someone was talking on the ABC. And now here was Bazza who was a teacher and an historian as well and he deliberately made it sound as though he had it in for nice English.

He put his hand further along her leg.

'I can't at the moment,' Emma said. 'Aren't I a dead loss?' She pulled a sorry-for-both-of-us face that inside the dark car he may not have been able to see. 'Jeeza,' he said, 'I'm surrounded by women this week who feed me that line.' But he said it so good-naturedly Emma could hardly mind the reference to his wife.

The car rocked as though someone leaned at the side and shoved it. 'Cook got the winds this time of year too,' Bazza said. 'Blew the tripes out of him further down the coast there. Out from Sydney.'

'Sydney wasn't there then though was it?' Emma said. She knew Bazza enjoyed her playing dumb. His own ball-and-chain as he said was thick as the proverbial yet she fancied she was Mrs Einstein with her Uni external courses or whatever. 'And here's you,' he told Emma, 'You're the brightest person in this scumbag town and you make like you're the old two planks.'

'I don't mean to,' Emma said. 'I think it's just a gift.'

'That's why it's so nice.' He stuck his tongue in her ear the way he did as a kid at Towoomba High, thinking you had to do that to stir a girl up. She said, 'Settle for this then, will you?' She began to undo his belt, humming beneath her breath.

'As long as you don't sing at the same time,' he said. 'High notes make me excited.'

He watched the pinpoints of light from down the coast. The moon that had ridden out there over the sea as they drove up to the lookout was tucked behind skimming cloud. He dosed his eyes and thought, This'll do me! And on the way back towards town the teacher said to his old friend's wife, 'I've never actually asked you how old you are.'

Emma said, 'I do a nice schoolgirl, mister, if the money's right.'

In his cabin the greatest sailor in the world put down his quill, rested his elbows in their long linen shirt-sleeves on the edge of his table, and rubbed his eyes until he saw grainy spots. He thought how he must ask the surgeon to suggest some cordial for the baronet's nerves. 'It was important for the navigator to maintain a steady grip on the goodwill of his crew, as well as his own confidence in the entire enterprise, fraught with difficulties as it often was.' Two hundred and twenty-eight years after Cook pondered on the gentleman who irked him, and lay down his quill in mild irritation, a small town's historian would summarise his character in those surprisingly vacuous words, as part of the brochure for the celebration. The brochure's cover would carry a photograph of a model ship, against a painted frothing sea. A light showed at a porthole of what was taken to be the captain's cabin. A light which Cook shifted slightly before he shook the sprinkled sand from the page of his freshly written entry, and a little later blew out. He commended himself to God, praying briefly for his distant wife and their brood, and lay so that his left ear was only feet from the sea. *Stood to the N.E. until Noon, having a Gentle breeze at N.W., at which time we Tack'd and stood to the Westward. . . . A point of land which I named Cape St George, we having discovered it on that Saint's day.*

The town might be far from the largest on the Coast, but once Charlie Ruxton, who had sold them their cars for years, and Rex Morrison, the property wizard who promised he would have two kilometres of tasteful bungalows geared to the middling-to-well-off elderly at Touchdown Beach by the end of the decade—as soon, so the TV feature said, as soon as jaunty Chas who was the wheels of the town and Rex the man with the market initiative put their heads together on the project, then it was all on, believe you me, all systems were go. The first dozen bungalows on Endeavour Heights in fact would be opened the very week the little town paid its respects to the man who, after all, had made Touchdown merit that name in the first place. They might have got only a thirty-second slot on the southern channels but within a week there were more queries from suburban retirees down there in the damp and mist than Rex could have built for in ten years; and more offers of sponsorship than Charlie Ruxton's committee knew what to do with.

'There's a Japanese condom firm for Christ's sake just faxed in.'

'Snap it up,' Rex said. 'It'll make the ethnic factor think they're part of the celebration too.'

A lot of people knew Bazza Forbes at the High School had hit on the idea. But the word was put round Rotary that it came to Ruxie and Bucho on the fairway to the eighteenth. In fact, as the three men knew, but saw no reason to say, it was Moira Lucas who sparked them off. In her darkroom almost a year ago she was waiting on a seascape taken from the hill above the bay. In the odd jostling of molecules on their way to stability, it seemed for several seconds that one of the distant rollers was the sail of a ship, the crest behind it another sail again. In ten seconds however there the true print was, a stretch of barren sea.

Moira did not believe in the perfect photograph, although she believed perfection was what one had to aim for. Most of what one looked at was wank, she thought, every square centimetre of it. For the past months she had been after something that was, well, nothing actually like an Utamaro print, but would make her think of one all the same, the moment flared out in a delicacy that was also monumental, which said this is what you see for a fraction of a second, but what you see is absolute.

That quick fading of what she had taken to be a ship lingered in Moira's mind. She said, quite idly, as she chatted to the chemist in the main street, why had nothing ever been made of the fact that Cook, of all people, had touched down here, even for a morning? There was sponsorship money round, she said, for celebrations like that. She had gone on to imagine the canful of images you could have nabbed if you'd sailed with him! 'Think of a koala even,' she said, 'the most boringly photographed little bugger in world history. Imagine him looking down your lens for the first time! It would have been the one and only snap of the thing worth taking.'

She paid for the large packets of photographic paper and pressed them against her chest as she left the shop. She was a good six inches taller than the two men who stood back for her inside the doorway, and nodded politely as she passed. One was the schoolteacher who looked sunburned any time of the year, the other the car dealer who sported in his showroom Moira's portrait of him, going on life-size, inspiring confidence and trust with a wide engaging grin. The men had overheard her conversation. They knew that she was onto something. Onto something big.

At 8, being very squally, with lightning, we close reef'd the Topsails and brought to, being then in 120 fathoms. At 3 A.M. made sail again to the Northward, having the advantage of a Gale at S.W. Cook welcomed days when the seas were too boisterous for the baronet's weak stomach, for that gentleman, after all these months, had still not become accustomed to the elements. The captain tired quickly enough of the clever southern talk—Banks on native women ('more naked than Eve,' whatever that should mean), Monkhouse's speculations that the Polynesian and Egyptian tongues derived from some common source, the baronet, worst of all, who called himself a scientist yet spoke with tiresome warmth of the great Stone and the flasks, as of something verifiable. He spoke too of coincidences and spirit manifestations, until the captain at times cut sheer across him, addressing questions on tapeworms to the surgeon, or requesting Solander's opinion on cultivating rice on the terrain that now stood to their west. With flinty northern humour he remarked that flatulence perhaps accounted for his own meagre gifts at speculation. *Saturday, 5 May. I had sent the Yawl in the morning to fish for Stingrays, who returned in the Evening with upwards of four hundred weight; one single one weigh'd 240 lbs. Exclusive of the entrails.*

It amazed the small town that the first meeting to consider the project was so well attended. Few of them knew much of Cook's passing until Bazza Forbes stood up, produced an old-fashioned map drawn down from a roller, and explained to them. He said unfortunately precise details had not been recorded, although the name indeed was on the first maps printed after Cook's return to the Admiralty. As they knew, the iron hoops from a cask, presumably broken by accident and left at the freshwater creek, had been found over a hundred years ago. There was also the pewter dish with MONKHOUSE incised upon it, which could be seen to this day in the small museum on Sunday afternoons. Monkhouse, of course, had been on board as ship's doctor. 'And there is no conceivable doubt,' Bazza Forbes said, 'that the greatest Englishman of the eighteenth century stood somewhere not far from Rex Morrison's new development that does honour to the navigator's name.' He finished with the remark which so puzzled Emma, that any Englishman who wanted so desperately to get here indeed deserved such a memorial.

So the special commemorative committee was chosen with an eye to several factors: Charlie Ruxton as the man in town who spoke daily to more people than anyone else, who had been responsible in his time for public toilets, for gas barbies in the park, for the Premier's visit to the Assembly Church, and for Safari Enterprises, run by an old air-force mate who dropped 120 Nips on the town once every two months regular, which meant motel trade you wouldn't have thought possible a couple of years back. There was Bazza Forbes of course for reasons no one doubted, for if history was your bag then Forbsie was your man. And Connie Batchelor because she ran the motels, catered like a charm, and because she told them of a seance she read of in one of her magazines where a member of Cook's crew, with an accent the medium could scarcely decipher, told a Dabtoe circle he couldn't wait to get back to the North. The manifestation had given a longitude which was uncannily close to their own. Also Connie had more imaginative flair than any of them. It was she in fact who called into Harry Buchanan's shop, carrying in a brown paper bag an old bottle she had kept at the back of a cupboard for as long as she could remember, a bottle in which her grandfather, as a lad at sea, ingeniously erected a scale model of the *Endeavour*. Family lore had it that the model was by way of winning a thin seventeen-year-old girl to accept a man whose delicacy of touch and steady eye could pop history so cunningly into an aperture the size of his thumb. She said to Harry Buchanan, 'Could you build me one like that? Only life-size, I mean.'

Harry recognised the smell of the powder from years before. 'No probs there, Connie. So long as there's funds.'

She said, 'It only has to sail half a day. It's the next thing to building a stage set for *Pinafore*.'

And Harry told her again, 'No probs far as I can see.' The proposal excited him. The Sea Scouts and the Christian Youth for month after month would run up and down ladders, cart timber and patiently follow plans, as they built the sailing ship around the hull of Rex Morrison's luxury launch. Close up, Connie said, the thing looked like an abortionist's picnic, but fifty yards off it was as good as you'd see in the movies. She had in mind the *Bounty* dancing on little waves in front of a palm-treed shore. She thought her old beau Harry had come up trumps. Behind their many meetings and visits to the building area in the yard of the Scout Hall, there remained the faintest memory of the clamminess of summer afternoons, her hands running across the lithe young man who instinctively shook her watch and held it against his ear, after he removed it from her arm and before he placed it on the table beside her bed. That was what Harry had always been like. Meticulous, down to the very last tick.

Emma, because she could take shorthand and type, had been invited to act as secretary for the group. As the commemorative day grew closer she found she had more on her hands than she ever might have thought. Each day was a turbulence of letters received and answered, queries referred to other members of the committee, and matters for the various sub-committees (maritime, catering, publicity, coordination, transport and community comfort, finance, children's activities) those members now chaired. She handled the banking and wrote the cheques, endorsed by at least one other signatory. Usually this was the town jeweller because his shop was directly opposite the council chambers. She so easily popped over. Then one day Harry Buchanan gave her a tiny gold reef-knot, the logo all over the town for the coming Event. He had noticed that some days she wore charms on a chain around her left wrist. She did not tell Bazza Forbes of the gift because he would have said Harry was after her pants. But she wore the little ornament to every meeting. And she found that sometimes she was inventing a cheque just for the relaxation of talking to her new friend. She found it rather exciting, even a little kinky, when she came in on him once and he raised his head and she saw his greatly magnified eye swimming there like a kind of jellyfish behind his jeweller's glass. He pushed the device to his forehead and there he was, normal as ever. She said, 'Put it on again, Harry.' She playfully leaned across the counter and went to touch his bulbous eye. 'Ugh,' she said, 'you're like a late-night movie, Harry, know that?' And when she felt his firm fingers take her wrist and lower it to the counter, his voice telling her quietly to be a good girl and not touch what wasn't hers, Emma knew she would have to face up to it. Your pulse never lies, she liked to say, does it? It keeps perfect time.

It was Emma whom Harry intended to phone, that evening when he moved the matches on the glass-topped table in Charlie Ruxton's modern lounge.

After an expanse of island-studded water which he named after James, Earl of Morton, President of the Royal Society as well as one of the Commissioners of Longitude, Cook turned from the murky channels and the mangroves towards the open sea. A gathering southerly sat behind him. For several days he had confined his diet to biscuit and claret, and a little fresh fish. Dr Solander sat with him several evenings and read aloud from Pliny, a diversion that particularly pleased him, for the loose talk of the gentlemen at dinner rather distressed the captain, especially as young Isaac Smith, midshipman, and a cousin of his own wife's, had sat with the older men. It was unusual for Cook to feel unwell. He examined his stool and found nothing untoward. *17 May. At daylight I found that we had in the night got much further to the Northward and from the shore than I expected from the Course we steer'd, for we were at least 6 or 7 Leagues off, and therefore hauled in N.W. by W., having the Advantage of a Fresh Gale.*

One day about the middle of May Emma asked Harry Buchanan, as she would never have put it to Bazza Forbes, asked straight out was Charlie Ruxton, you know? She put her tongue between her teeth for a moment.

'A what?' Harry asked.

'You know, Harry. You know very well.'

'He keeps it quiet,' Harry said. 'The town wouldn't go much on it if they knew.'

'Then how do you know, eh?' Emma's breast flattened against his chest as she leaned across him. She ran a finger down his cheek and looked at him with arched quizzing brows.

'Charlie tells me everything,' Harry said.

Emma bit the lobe of his ear. She so liked it when you became close with yet another friend. Harry would never have told her a thing like that a month ago, not even with his clothes on.

> *Saturday, 19th. Variable Light Airs and Calms . . . regular, even Soundings, from 13 to 7 fathoms; fine sandy bottom.*

> *Monday, 21st. At 9, we discover'd from the Masthead land to the Westward, and soon after saw smoke upon it.*

> *Friday, 25th. The Mainland in this Lat. is tolerable high and Mountainous; and the Islands which lay off it are the most of them pretty high and of a Small Circuit, and have more the appearance of bareness than fertility.*

Moira Lucas had more work than she might reasonably handle. She had designed the brochure and other publicity material, and taken the syndicated photographs of the coastline, and simply spools of the *Endeavour* firming up behind the Scout Hall. The little gallery she rented from Connie Batchelor was doing a roaring trade, what with so many strangers driving through at weekends. And now you couldn't walk along the bluff on a weekday afternoon without passing half a dozen couples, the kind with orange anoraks and hiking boots, or elderly pairs sitting in the marram grass, the woman perhaps pouring tea from a thermos flask, the husband reading aloud from Cook's own account. Some of them sat with their knees tucked up, looking out to sea, to the same slanting of light, the same play of winds, that returned here over and over, since the famous captain ran his minuscule ship along a continent's rim.

Moira was out with her camera whenever she could snatch time away from town. She had been obsessed like this years ago with river gums at Overland Corner. She knew there was an image among the rest that would be that fraction finer, closer to what all the others aspired to. When she tried to explain that to her father way back in those days he had said, 'Plato, eh?' and she imagined throwing her camera so that its German fragments splintered across the caravan they camped in beside the placid bend of the Murray. But, 'Plato's arse!' she had simply shouted at the old man. Couldn't he see it was the exact reverse she was after? Not some ridiculous ideal that infiltrated particulars but a particular so real you could not imagine anything like it that wasn't already here in this. It was the last time she tried to explain anything to anyone. But as the river gums then, so this coastline now. She thought of it when she woke, and its long curdling hem of surf, its hazed penumbra of spray was in her mind as she went to sleep. She shot forty or fifty exposures at a time. She refused to crop her prints, which she knew was like cheating at cards. Every few days there was one at least decent enough to sell in the gallery.

> Cook stood at the taff-rail. The breeze boomed in the mainsheets, a halyard vibrated in his fist. From second to second, he thought, the universe seemed under control. When he held the brass sextant against his cheek, or watched the lecherous Mr Banks working so quietly at his dish of paints, giving his sapless specimens a rich second life as he transferred them onto sheets of card, it seemed a simple thing to acknowledge Providence. And then the intricate cordage would bellow with the accelerating wind. The naked feet of the crew slapped round him. He called for the alteration in tack, the ship heeling down to his command. He quite knew what the classicists meant when they spoke of the exhilaration of hubris, of facing uncharted waters through hazard and chance. He knew that he provoked destiny as his vessel took current and wind. Yet one commends oneself to God and takes no undue risk. *Winds and weather as Yesterday, and the Employment of the People the same.*

Charlie Ruxton indeed did not confide to Harry Buchanan that his sexual preferences were of a kind that Rotary would have turfed him out for, smartly. But Harry, wanting to impress Emma Morrison, had said that rather than tell the truth. For the truth was that Connie Batchelor told him on Easter Monday morning, all those years ago, when she believed in her post-coital closeness that whatever she said was safe with her young friend. She said she was distantly related to the Ruxtons, although no one in the town was wise to that one, either. And Charlie poor dear had actually gone by another name down south and only escaped by a whisker, once it got round that he dished out fivers as they were in those days to teenage louts for opening their mouths on demand and keeping them shut later on. Young Harry had been taken aback by the language the generously naked Connie employed. 'Arse bandits,' she said, 'gob-stoppers. I don't know what they see in it.' Harry would never have thought of telling a soul if Emma, her tongue wet and provocative, had not asked him at precisely that moment. Or returned to it later, on the concealed ledge of the bluff where Bazza Forbes had taken her first and she in turn took Harry. He made her promise she would keep it to herself. Hell, he said, hadn't he known Charlie for years? Didn't they watch VFL replays together on Sunday mornings? He'd never seen so much as a flicker of that side of the man. Then because she supposed that Harry, like Bazza, would think it very sexy, and also to take his mind off betrayal, Emma moved her tongue like an urgent slug inside his ear. Evening came on. The white collar of her Canterbury was the last thing that shone out against the dark.

A long time later she said, 'Time to slip your daks on Harry. My daddy man will be wondering where I am.'

From the dark hillside Harry saw, far out to sea, a light flash very weakly. 'It must be all that peering with your periscope thing in the shop,' Emma said. 'I can't make out a thing.'

A light which as it happened Connie Batchelor saw too, from her own windows high above the beach. In daylight she looked directly down on Rex Morrison's development. She thought enviously of those medieval sieges where they poured reeking ordure on those below. It was an image that gratified her, to think of Rex with his hairy fingers mining behind his spectacles, scooping them free. For Connie had just been speaking to her cousin on the phone. He thought he might leave town in a day or so, he said, perhaps even tomorrow. 'Before the Event!' Connie said. Before the replica they had put all that money into sailed round the bluff—before the re-enactment on the beach with Charlie himself as Cook and the gala party for the whole town? 'You're not talking sense, Charlie!'

'Things tend to get round, old darling,' Charlie said to her. She was meant to pick up the sad bravado.

'Oh, not the same trouble as down south?' she put to him.

Connie sat and looked at the black expanse, to the tiny winking light. Someone was leaning on Charlie of course, that was always the story. She threw her *I Ching*, which predicted great changes, a tempest of unresolved forces and broken lines. It's paying the little shits, she considered, that was the problem. Why did Charlie never click that people give it away?

Charlie Ruxton as it happened did not leave town until after the monster piss-up hosted by the committee the night before the re-enactment and the Floral Float Parade, and the various related functions on the oval behind the Town Hall. Connie Batchelor nursed her one glass of Scotch throughout the evening. She talked to Bazza Forbes's wife when she saw Bazza nip out with Emma Morrison. She then talked with

Rex Morrison when Emma returned, and left the hall again within minutes with Harry Buchanan. She decided she had seen enough of all these people to last her a lifetime. Without a tinge of regret, she told Rex she would sell him her hillside, the whole bloody lovely flank of it, that he had been chasing after for years. The figure she put to him was so reasonable that each knew without saying a word that she was saving her cousin's bacon as well. She thought with some disgust of petite and pretty Emma lying next to her unattractive husband and confiding whatever she had heard from her current lovers. She was glad to leave him, to get away from the square warm hand that continually touched her arm as he spoke to her. She moved across to Moira Lucas, who thank Christ had left her camera at home for once. Because Connie, for the first time in her life, was feeling her age. Which meant there was very little in the evening that interested her, nothing about the people she spoke to which she found charming or diverting. She closed her eyes and thought of a mandala, a white centre among frothing blues. She remembered the fractured lines of the *I Ching*, black waves that moved towards her, and Harry's hands years ago in the lamplight as he had set the matches in their squares. All patterns were like cages, weren't they? Little cubes of fate. They spoke of those deep and intricate codes that made all things possible, all things assured yet seemingly unlikely. She saw Charlie shaking hands with Rex Morrison as she tucked her sequined evening bag beneath her arm and left. Outside the hall, she took her keys and her credit cards from the bag, and left it on the low wall beside the carpark. Leaving it was her sudden gesture that a great deal no longer mattered. She had carried the thing, or others much the same, to nights like this for forty bloody years. As she turned the car towards the exit, its lights picked out for a moment the cluster of scintillations of the concrete ledge. Then the beams burrowed out into the dark.

> The baronet disappeared from the ship. His recent obsessive talk of their need for 'touching down' as he called it, his monologues with Banks on the fauna he expected to discover and whose names he was prepared for, had warned the Captain of the sudden event. Cook at once ordered a boat to be put down, and several empty casks despatched overboard, in the unlikely hope that the crazed man might cling to one of them. The ship circled for many hours, before resuming its northward set. The great sailor of his age quite took the irony of his calling the adjacent shoreline after the baronet's own repeated phrase of touching down, rather than the family name which the poor man had felt a continent could scarce do honour to. He wrote that evening: *Fresh gales between the S.S.E. and E.S.E. Hazey weather, with some showers of rain, which shorten'd the Prayers I thought fit to summon Officers and Men attend.* He did not elaborate on the missing articles reported to him during the noon and evening. One was Mr Banks's own ivory-handled magnifying glass. There was also a cooper's hammer, which the insane gentleman presumably had used to weigh himself down, and a belaying pin a sailor observed him trifle with moments before he jumped. And Dr Monkhouse's dish, with his name worked upon its rim, which the suicidal baronet seized from the medical man's hand as he dashed past, stuffing it down his shirt, bidding him good day.

Moira Lucas felt the lurch to her feelings as she watched the image emerging in the developing tray. She was tired from the party the night before, and knew how hectic the next day would be. She had driven out to the bluff that afternoon, simply to calm herself after hearing that Connie Batchelor had disappeared. It was purely out of routine then that she developed the roll before she went to bed. Her mind was vague, a screen of indistinct sand hills, the deserted beach with its fringe of trees, a couple in a passing car she had waved to. And then the picture rising to her from the tray, its sense of commanding absence that she had always wanted from the sea. She realised as she looked at the grain of indistinguishable sea and sky, that normal demarcations seemed sluiced off: a sense of neither right nor left, past nor present, up nor down, an emptiness so pure nothing might encroach on it. A photograph of Zen perfection.

> *Wednesday 30th May.* Captain James Cook writes how *I gave over all thoughts of bringing the ship a Shore, being resolved to spend as little time as possible in a place that was likely to afford us no sort of refreshment.* He glances across the starboard rail before turning in. The waves, scribbled with moonlight, are a page of indecipherable script.

'Christ,' Fran said, 'what's all this about the winterless north?' The sky was the colour of pewter. The sloping bluff, the low hills behind the beach, identical empty stretches to north and south. It was all so dull. She slipped a cardigan over her shoulders as though it were a cape, and realised Brin was droning on; imagine if Cook had landed kind of thing, imagine if he had and we didn't know, imagine if he didn't land and we thought he did, oh as if referentiality wasn't tricky enough this very minute, to know even where you were sitting, what you were looking at, what to call what you saw, let alone naïvely believe it stayed the same once you called it anything at all. Who the hell would be a historian, Brin demanded, who the hell can even write a cheque with confidence in our current foci of indeterminables? 'Pity he didn't,' Fran said. 'Cook, I mean. There might have been a tea-rooms here or anything. A pub. A library where we could read about the place instead of having to bloody be here.' She knew she was being epistemologically vulgar and simply didn't give a stuff. She moved slightly on her haunches, her sheaf of written pages ruffling beneath her thighs.

Brin sighed. He edged a wedge of chicken flesh towards the cat. Palincest nosed the gift and moved away. 'He's still off colour,' Brin said. Fran failed to answer. She was occupied in trying to flick an insect from her glass. 'Watch out!' Brin called to her. 'Oh bugger me, watch out!' The cat was close beside her, its sides convulsively heaving before a feculent gush threaded across her jeans, colonising the text wedged under her thigh.

'That's it!' Fran shouted. 'That's fucking it!'

'It?' Brin put to her. He carefully placed his copy of Beaglehole on his copy of Cook, Beaglehole and Cook in turn on Hoare, then Beaglehole and Cook and Hoare on the folder of essential articles. He slipped them all into a blue plastic carrybag whose lettering appeared reversed either because the bag was inside-out or because the bag was printed that way accidentally or possibly on purpose. 'What on earth, Fran love, can *it* refer to in a context like that?' He was amused at her ludic brio in assuming 'it' might mean anything at all.

Recital

Here it was, Easter again already. Her last Easter, Briar thought, without being too disturbed at it. It had never meant much to her in any case, apart from holidays, which a few times she enjoyed, although mostly they were days that moved slowly, time spent with others that she would rather have spent alone. And now it would be that dullest thing of all, a family that felt obliged to do her a good turn. Her nephews whom she didn't care for, their latest round of wives, the children from one coupling or another, who would be as bored with her as she was with them, if they had any sense. But there was no money worth chasing, she supposed she could credit her sister's sons for not being after that. A pity, though. She could have told them not to bother, they were never in the hunt. No, it was even worse, Briar thought with dry amusement. They were driving a long way south and staying in the dullest of motels, simply because she was their one decrepit aunt, and blood was, in their love of clichés, they believed thicker than sheer boredom.

She had phoned for someone from Hire a Hubby to come round and spruce up the section. It amused her, that name on the side of the truck parked there in her drive. She wished Janet Cotter still lived in town to share the indecencies that came readily enough to mind. Janet was a dab hand with the risqué. Then the dark young man who turned up with his shiny mower was unexpectedly charming. And Briar caught herself even as she thought it, wondering was there condescension in her putting it like that, even to herself? Why shouldn't he be 'charming'? Was it only men like her nephews, educated and overweight and self-satisfied, who worked so hard at being agreeable, that the word should be reserved for? She made the dark young man tea after he had been working for an hour, but she left the tray for him on a card-table she set up on the veranda. She remembered enough of how young men thought to know the last thing he would want was to have some old bat bailing him up. She was surprised though when she collected the tray to take inside, that he had drunk his tea without milk, and eaten the crackers with sliced tomato but left the Mallowpuffs. She thought perhaps he was a footballer with orders to watch what he ate. Even footballers these days were like jockeys, she had read that somewhere. They lived on their scales.

If only her nephews did, Briar thought. John and Stevie, one with petite Sandra and the other with anything but petite Carol. All four of them on their second marital time round. Retreads, no one has anything else these days, Janet Cotter said. It was six months since she last had seen them and would not have minded if it had been more. Should she not be grateful though that they made the effort to see her? Her only living relatives after all. No, she frankly thought. There is no reason why I should be. Those boys and their dutiful wives. Sandra who has lain God knows how long under sun-lamps and absorbed John's QC takings on dental costs alone. Vapid is as vapid does. And good-natured Carol whom Stevie already found a bore. There was so much temptation around men like that, she supposed, in the university. Jail bait by the yard, as Janet Cotter said.

Briar had never married, which made the young ones assume she could not conceivably know what life added up to. She imagined easily enough the kind of things they said to each other before the visits they must have looked forward to no more eagerly than did she. Mind you, she could hear one of the boys saying, there were rumours weren't there about men? She was a looker in her day. 'Abandon hope,' clever Stevie might say, and who wouldn't have once a man realised it was six hours practice a day, early nights to keep her up to scratch, her mother, imagine that, pushing her career like a wheelbarrow of stones. Then how come it petered out, one of the wives might ask, Sarah or Naomi as it was ten years back, Sandra or Carol now. And John kindly enough, Briar supposed, but smug as an oyster, shrugging and saying, 'We all have our hopes, don't we?' And Stevie again, thin-faced for all his bulk, putting it with more accuracy. 'Because just talent isn't enough, is it? You need a damned sight more than that to bring off what she was after. Concert pianist. Christ! What sort of life's that?'

The life Briar was now sifting through and throwing out. It's amazing how one keeps all this stuff. She dumped another pile of papers into the big plastic rubbish bag. Letters from the fifties, even earlier. Articles she had clipped from music journals. Stacks of magazines. Programmes that must have added up to months, to years even, sitting in halls, listening to those who did supremely what she managed only moderately well. Although be fair now. There were those who thought she did better than simply that. There was a man in Margaret River, Western Australia, whose letters she had chucked out the day before. He had heard her play on the ABC. He wrote to her for years. She supposed now what had never occurred to her then, that he was some remote farmer, disappointed himself after being a clever young man, and he had liked her face when it appeared in the papers quite as much as he liked her playing. He had asked her to send a photograph with an inscription written on it. They were nice letters he wrote. 'Why don't we ever hear Gottschalk!!!' His exclamation marks like a row of fence posts. But I've played him myself, she wrote back, in a competition, the *Pasquinade*, and the judges thought I had lost my mind.

Briar hesitated over the old account book, with its stiff plushy binding, that had survived in family cupboards since her grandfather's days as an auctioneer. Her mother had cut out the few pages of inked figures and brief descriptions, and used the rest to paste in cuttings about her gifted daughter. The frock that looked white in the faded newspaper photo was pale turquoise. Mr Fraser the Prime Minister bending close to talk to her, after the twelve-year-old had played in her first concert to raise money for what everyone had called 'the boys', but were really soldiers. Even the Trinity College results snipped from newspapers, her name at the top, and the dent in the paper where her mother had run a pencil line underneath. Then later the longer pieces, the approving reviews, when it seemed she was 'taking off'. Her mother liked saying that. At church. To neighbours. 'Yes. Briar's taking off.' For a moment the old lady looked at the reviews no one else would ever read. Or ever want to. She then threw the big book into the plastic bag, after the other rubbish. She thought, at least I have earned a gin, after honesty on that scale. She bunched up the throat of the bag—it was the third one of the day—and tied it with the black strip she tore from its perforated top. There were sixty years in those bags, at least. She sat back in the chair beneath the old-fashioned standard lamp, with its parchment shade that threw out what she thought of as a honeyed glaze. She allowed herself, at last, to close her eyes. She thought how so long as the odd gin was such a gift to her, and the nag of her illness for the time being let her be, she was neither young nor old nor anything else. She was content to be exactly as she was.

Briar watched the sky paling behind a ridge of pines. She had never been one for mornings. Whoever heard of a performer who was? But these last few months. She had hated it at first, this lying in bed, waiting for things to start. The discomfort throbbing on some mornings, but at least with an open-minded doctor who now prescribed for her, there was little of that. Now she even came to like the mornings. The *stealth*, that was it, the caution almost, as the world returned to itself. The surprise of it too, simply to take in the basket of pegs, say, hooked like a hunched creature at the side of the porch, that she could see through the French doors of her bedroom. And the brightness once the colours appeared, the slivers of green and pink and yellow plastic she had never really looked at before. Everything coming back like that. So ordinary, so special. She had seen a television programme where the dawn came up over a jungle somewhere, and the creatures in the trees turned to the ascending sun with the incredibly raucous carry-on of their delight. The beginning of religion too she supposed, this feeling that light was both a thing out there, and an awareness rising in yourself. Life was what went on between you and it. 'You'll be singing hymns next thing,' Janet Cotter warned her at long distance, glorying as she said in the Queensland sun, the reflections smacking off the pool she looked at from the opened sliding doors. You need to come here, her oldest friend had told her, you don't want your last years in that gloomy bloody house.

Briar did not ring back for weeks after that. Janet had never quite clicked, had she, just what you can say, and what you can't? Those months when Briar thought it would take the patience of a saint to put up with another evening of her friend's grief and complaint about Desmond who had left her, not for a woman, as she kept repeating, not for a man either, she could even have put up with that, but just left her presumably because it was *her*! Then within a year her declaring how you just didn't realise how little you'd miss a man until he actually shot through. 'I can't thank him enough.' And after Briar's flicker of rage at what had been said about her house, they were now back to their old routine, to the long weekly conversations on a Saturday afternoon, when the calling rates were cheap. As Briar told Janet Cotter about the Easter she did not look forward to, they were, thank God, their old tasteless selves. Janet had said, no wonder JC threw in the sponge on Good Friday, and there wasn't even his family that he had to put up with. After she replaced the receiver, Briar stood at the opened doors onto the back lawn. She liked the neatly alternating rows where the nap of the grass lay one way and then the other, the way you see it on cricket grounds. He made such a point of cutting so neatly, that fine young man with his strange tattoo, like thorns lacing the muscle at the top of his arm. He had leaned over the kitchen table and carefully filled out a receipt when she paid him. She could smell his sweat and his youthfulness. He handed her the small square of paper. 'To make sure we're not ripping you off, eh lady?' His frank, friendly smile. Then telling her to make sure she had a nice one when he hoisted his mower onto the back of his van, and called out to her as he slammed the door. Day, she supposed he meant. When the girls in Countdown said things like that her impulse was to ask them was it their business whether she did or not? Of course she never did say so. But she liked it when the young man said that because it sounded as though he meant it. She waved back to him when he raised his thumb through his opened window as he turned onto the street. When she had learned Latin all those years back the form mistress told them that when the emperor did that in the Colosseum it meant 'Let them live'. She liked it, remembering that now. The young man's arm through the window of his van. Whether he meant it like that or not. Let her live, it said.

She was startled by the child's voice. 'Is that the coffin?' Becky asked from the doorway. The rather ugly little girl pointed to the black bulk of the piano. She had come into the room quietly as a cat. The old lady's head jerked when she spoke to her. The question, for the merest moment, rattled her. And then amused.

'I thought you were at McDonald's with Daddy and—' What on earth, Briar wondered, did the child call her father's latest wife?

'Sandra,' the child helped out. 'We call her Sandra because that's her name for both of us. Way Carol is what Stevie and Simon both call Carol.'

'You know a lot of things,' Briar said. She liked it that the freckled unattractive girl spoke out. Unlike Stevie's Simon. The boy was three years older than Becky. Foxy, that was the word for him. He had now slunk in and stood behind his cousin.

'She shouldn't have said that, Auntie,' he said. Briar could tell by his voice, already, that the boy went to elocution classes.

'And why not?' she asked. She had told them the night before to call her by her name. Everyone else did, so why shouldn't they? She disliked the boy for that 'auntie'.

'Said that about the piano,' he insisted.

'Well,' his aunt said, 'it does look a bit like a box I suppose, doesn't it?'

'It does from here,' the girl said.

Simon then said, 'Everyone knows about the piano because she was famous at it.'

'Sometimes,' Briar said, 'if I come into the room and look at it from where you are Becky, when I can't see the keys and all I mean, I think the very same thing. I think who's put that there, that bloody old coffin.'

The children laughed when the old lady said that. Said a word you shouldn't say. Simon slipped away. Wanting to be first to tell. He knew his father would like hearing that, how she was swearing now as well, the old bat, sitting there with her black plastic bags all round her. But when the boy moved away from behind her Becky came up closer to the old lady. She stood in front of the low table where Briar piled things up and moved them about.

The child put out one plump finger to touch the metal flap of what once had been her great-grandfather's inkwell. She said, after lifting the lid to make it clatter two or three times, and looking at the way the room was so messed up, 'Is this because you're dying, is it?' The plain little face lifted towards the old woman, waiting to see if she would make her laugh again.

'There, I said you knew a lot, didn't I?' Briar told her. It amused her too that none of the grown-ups would have dared put so directly what of course was at the front of their minds. She had watched the child's pompous father the evening before, his never, she was sure of that, forgetting the letters behind his name, as he explained that it was imperative, positively imperative, that the paperwork was done, that everything she intended was written down.

'You mean in case I forget to leave things?' she had said to him. John's hand had slapped plumply, impatiently, on the arm of the settee. But then others had come in at just that moment, so he laughed in his broad engaging way, and said he was trying to get Briar here to come north with them for a break, how about Stevie adding his own persuasive skills? John poured himself a brandy from the cut-glass decanter whose level was pretty much as it had been last time he raised it six months before. Stevie smoothly assured her she was welcome any time. More than welcome. 'So long as you know that, Briar.'

She was glad the little girl was not pretty. There would be so much less fuss, less expectation, from the kind of parents she had. She would see through her father so much more quickly than a pampered child might do. Briar nodded towards the piano that had taken so much of her life, that she wished had taken more.

'Have you ever tried?' she asked. 'The piano?'

'Mummy used to play a violin. You know, Mummy before

Sandra? But Dad said to get rid of it because it was such a racket.'

'A racket?' Briar opened her eyes wide at the child. 'I can't believe he said that.'

'And when he says that now Sandra says tell me about it, she lived with the same thing.'

'Well, why don't you sit there,' Briar said. 'So you know what it feels like anyway.'

The girl hoisted herself on the swivel seat, her feet not touching the ground.

'You're allowed to, you know,' Briar said.

So Becky touched one key that rang out so much louder than she expected, and then another. Briar told her that each one had a different name, so that supposing you were in another room you could call out the name and the person at the piano would know exactly which one to touch. 'And that one,' Briar said, 'the one in the middle is called C.' All the notes begin from there, she said. This way or that, you can go on either side, like wings, until when you're good at it, you can make them move, any way you like. Sad or happy, anything you like.

'Any way you like,' Becky repeated. 'So they've all got a name as well as a sound and are wings as well.' She moved her small hands gently along to either side of middle C, barely brushing the keys. 'That's neat then isn't it? Isn't it, Briar?'

'It most certainly is,' the old lady said.

She and the girl laughed then, not because of what they said, Becky thought, but because they just liked looking at each other. She swung the piano stool round to face Briar properly. She began to talk and Briar nodded at what she said. She saw the old lady tipping something from a small bottle into the glass on the little table beside her, but her aunt kept watching her all the time to let her know she was interested in what the girl was telling her. She told her you could change the words for some things if you wanted to, she supposed, couldn't you? But there were others you couldn't, you weren't allowed to were you? Like C when you touched the one there in the middle, because if you messed up that and called it something else then it wouldn't work, the wings wouldn't work.

'No,' Briar agreed with her, 'they most certainly would not.' Then the two of them sitting there while the light drew away from the room, away from the street to behind the big hill, but the old lady did not switch on the lamp, and they kept on talking until Briar could hardly see Becky's face, and Becky could not see Briar's.

Picture Window

'Ah, the river!' my mother used to say, pausing at the large window while she dried her hands under her apron. It was a habit that always made me think, for a moment, that she was pregnant and things moved inside her.

The 'picture window' it was called, twice as big as any other window in the house. When storms banged in from the south, you could see the plate glass almost give. I'd sit and watch the way it seemed to bend and the light shake across it.

'The river's in all of us,' she'd say. She would draw her hands from underneath the apron and as soon as she'd said it, she would turn and smooth over the checked cloth on the table with her open palms, or move the vase of paper flowers on top of the wireless. It seemed that saying that was a kind of signal, a switch that threw her from whatever she was thinking as she looked down at the braids of water cutting this way and that across the wide shingle bed, which swelled and joined up and sometimes poured bellowing down between the banks, and took her back to where she was for most of the time. Which was tidying up, washing, taking down the curtains if she could think of nothing else, standing on a chair to rub a wet cloth along the pelmets.

It is amazing how *things* date your childhood, so much more than your own body even. Pelmets with scalloped edges, a radiogram where you could stack records one on top of the other so they clashed down between the songs. An electric fly-catcher an uncle brought back from Singapore, and every time a fly flew against it, there was this *pop*, so you knew the fly was killed that instant. Someone said to me once, those things did not exist back then, they were later than the time in which I say I remember them, that would not be the forties. As if I should go off at once and check whether it was true! When I remember one, I remember the other, that is the point. I remember when she paused by the window and looked down at the river, and I knew what she was going to say.

That is how I remember it. I sat inside the web of rail tracks with the green engine whose big key I could wind only six times before it held firm against my pushing thumb. You should have been able to wind it more than that. When I fitted the wheels back inside the raised sides of the tracks, and fiddled the gear levers that poked out from the back of the cab with brass screws for you to press against, the engine ran only half a dozen circuits before it had to be wound again. Of course I cannot always have been sitting like that in the middle of the tracks when my mother stood and dried her hands and looked out from the window. But that dominates my memory. It seems now that it was always like that.

Sometimes a neighbour who stood at the doorway would look across to where I sat cross-legged, my dress high above my knees, and say to me, 'What's this, then? A girl engine-driver is it?' And my mother would tell her, 'You won't catch her playing with dolls, believe me!' Or sometimes she said, 'She'd be under my feet all the time if it wasn't for the Hornby.' She smiled at me while she said it. And I would look down as if the train was more important than the grown-ups were, whatever it was they said.

There were only three wagons to the train. One was a flat-top with two slabs of balsa wood held firm by crossed red string. Another was a grey petrol tanker with a red star on its curved side. And an ordinary wagon with raised dark sides, which carried anything you wanted to put into it—a matchbox, cotton reels, buttons you could tie close together and pretend were the rolls of wire that came to the station down the road and were taken off on the back of trucks to the high country, where the pylons were being set up. My mother said she knew it had to be done, she knew you couldn't stand in the way of progress, but it broke your heart, the way those things marched out and messed the country up.

When the engine and its three wagons ran round the tracks there was a *click-click*, again and again, as the train passed over where the pieces of rail slotted together. Sometimes I sat with my chin on my drawn-up knees and watched the train circle about me, slipping by with quick streaks of light. Its journey was endless and distant even as it ran so close to where my fist lay beside the tracks. I could feel the brush of air against my knuckles.

I was not yet ten when I sat and played like that. My mother was not much more than thirty.

This has the makings, you might say, of a typical New Zealand story. If I had read over what you have just read, I would want to say, ah yes, a solo mother, an introspective child. I would say the child is afraid she may be challenged by another child, the mother feels, in those grim spaces between one task and another, the threat of icy water, rising winds. Order pants on a tight rein. I would say that, and add as we all do when we read, a few details of my own. The John McCormack records, say, the voice like scoops of honey while my mother sits and clicks her wedding ring with the tough square nail of her thumb. Her sometimes laughing in a way that isn't meant to be for anyone else, saying as she stands up from the green settee and turns the knob of the wireless, 'So, that's facing life now is it, Portia?' Until one day she puts down the telephone and turns to me very calmly. She takes off her apron and folds it in half, then in half again, and says, 'You'd better pack that up good and proper too, young lady.' When I ask her, 'What?' she sits on a chair beside the table whose sides flap down like wooden wings. Her hands are open on her knees.

She is looking down at them. Then she twists at the ring on her finger until she tugs it loose. Her finger is nearly purple as the ring comes off. 'There,' she says. She puts the ring on the table. 'I thought I'd have to put soap on it.'

'There,' she says again, and holds her fingers out in front of her and wiggles them. There's this white streak on her finger where the ring had sat since before I was born.

'There's a bump on either side like a bee-sting,' I tell her. 'There's a track through the hills after all,' she says. And she moves her fingers at me, and we both laugh.

'Money?' the interviewer says.

'Money?' I say after her.

'But she must have been a visionary. No one does what she did without—well, simply without that, do they? Without vision?'

She's a clever young woman, the interviewer. I ask her was this part of her PhD, this kind of questioning? I know that for some degrees you have to do dozens, hundreds even, of interviews like this. Then 'extract your data', isn't that what they say?

'My PhD is ages back,' she smiles. This deep fringe of hair and her open fresh face and the most delicate hands that slip one across the other, as if she is stroking someone else. She then moves her fingers up and down on her skirt. I say to her at one point, 'Do you play something? A musical instrument or something?'

She smiles back at me and the light slips across her fringe. 'I don't play a note of anything,' she tells me.

So we get back to Mother, as I always call her now. And when Sarah—that's the young interviewer, who is Doctor if she wants to call herself that—when Sarah asks me about money yet again I tell her, 'It was more than money. It was lucre.'

Sarah smiles and I know she doesn't have an earthly.

'The Bible?' I prod her.

'I did a Bible and literature paper a hundred years ago but not much of it stuck.'

I tell her that in the Bible and in the way people talk about it in church—Mr Huston, say, tall and balding and Presbyterian, his finger on the text while he looks up at the thirty or so people who had scarcely twopence to rub together—they always say lucre like it's worse than money. Money you work for and save for a rainy day, but lucre is what happens to money when Herod holds it in his hand, when a man who runs a vineyard tells the honest labourer he is not worthy of his hire, and withholds what is rightly his. Out of love for lucre.

'I've lost you. Sorry,' Sarah says.

'It is money with shine on it. The filth gives it shine.'

'But your mother?' Sarah says.

'You tell my mother the shine was the thing that gave it value and she wouldn't bat an eyelid. And then she'd eat it. The shine, I mean. If she thought there was any profit in it.'

I can see I have lost bright young Dr Sarah completely. She stops tapping at her laptop and closes its grey case very slowly, like a heavy tired eyelid. 'That's great,' she says to me. 'You've been really great.'

Sarah is writing a book on New Zealand women entrepreneurs. She's the first to admit they're a bit thin on the ground. And Mother, not surprisingly, is one of the few. It fascinates her that a woman with a ten-year-old child, in a tiny general store on a riverbank where a few hundred people each year came to fish, suddenly ups anchor for no apparent reason. Then five years later she buys out a freezing works, and five years later again is listed on the stock exchange under her own name. She had a reputation for being tough. As they come. Sarah told me and then later wrote it up for one of the smart monthlies, and picked up an award for the article as well, that when she interviewed the celebrated Sir Robert Bowen, who didn't give a donkey's toss for God or country or other men's wives or his best mate's life savings, when she asked him about Mother he had turned white about the gills. He said, 'Look here, whatever your name is.' (Sarah I think quite liked the rudeness of that.) He said, 'That woman gave me the shits like no man's ever done. So don't ask me to cluck over her for your bloody femmo textbook or whatever it is. She was a kamikaze who didn't need a plane. Only she always survived.'

I tell Sarah, 'She would have said something about his nose, for starters.' But she is only interested, that young woman, in what she wants to hear. She misses the point that Mother knew who was a Jew or a mick or a holy roller before they knew themselves. Any little thing about anyone that stood out. 'It gives you a handle on them,' she used to say.

It was because of Mr Cooper's ears her luck took a turn. Mr Arthur Cooper, coal merchant and cement carrier, a shy man whose lack of personal charm, whose enormous ears, diverted the warmer feelings he seldom had the chance to express into the grim satisfaction of hard work. And so he took on a hardness of manner that made him, as the locals used to say, coal right through. Mother, at thirty-two, won him round. Thirty-two was the age, she loved to say to journalists, or to anyone else, when her life began. When she stopped looking at the river and enduring day by day, and decided to pick up life and give it a decent shake. Mr Cooper's ears were what helped raise it up. She asked him in for tea. She laughed and leaned forwards when he stirred his tea so vigorously the milkless reddish liquid leaped over the edge of his cup, as he said to her, 'You know Davis Cement in Ashburton? Well, I've bought them out for a song.' She *kissed* his ears, and it mattered nothing whether I was in the room or not. She spruced herself up. She took the bus into town one day and came back with her hair set like a meringue, and said to Mr Arthur Cooper couldn't he see the power of good he was doing her? He laughed and ran the side of his forefinger across his upper lip and his ears blazed like two red kites.

I sat at the table with my homework and she stood at the stove, brushing the top of the semolina custard with egg yolk to make it shine. When the green Morris pulled up and she spotted him through the window she would say, 'Mr Cement himself.' When he came inside he gave me a white paper bag of Minties and she always said, 'There's no need to, Arthur,' and he would say, for some reason, 'Question not the need.' His small body in its dark suit moved smoothly as though it ran on tracks. When he died the next year, just after Easter, my mother was left the coal yard, the trucks, the Ashburton cement. Mother at that stage could not drive, so the Morris went to a nephew in Rakaia. She said to me, a child of ten, as though it were a story she told of someone she had heard about but didn't know, that Mr Arthur Cooper's family had been in the district almost as long as her own. Everyone knew his father and his grandfather before that had dicky hearts, and popped off early on. Mr Arthur Cooper's mother used to say of her son, 'He carries a burden, that boy.' And she would add, so that it became a local joke, 'It is all a matter of timing. Everything in life is a matter of timing, and setting your clock in accord.' And my mother said when he died, 'We know not the hour nor the day.' Mother it seems had no idea that it was religious, that phrase. On television, not so long before she died, she attributed it to Henry Ford.

Everyone—the ratbag journalists, cool Dr Sarah, the person in the street, as we say—everyone wants to believe there was some mystery about Mother, some inner spring they never quite define, which will surely explain her.

'How do we account for such an extraordinary woman?' the little high-heeled monkey who swings about after the six o'clock news pressed me to confide. It was my first week back after the funeral. He longed for me to parade my grief, to hold up an X-ray of my feelings for his viewers to gawp at.

'I don't account for it,' I told him. 'Why on earth does one need to?' I watched the muscles at the corner of his mouth go into their famous twitch. *Smart bitch, are we?* the little muscles told me. I explained that she was rich not because she was clever, but because she did things other people baulked at. She also had a capacity, I said, for making friends, although friendship itself didn't matter a jot. She had no friends at all before she was rich.

'You don't sound as though you loved her,' the monkey said. He took off his glasses and rubbed them with his tie and looked at me with his pale eyes like two blobs of spit. 'You didn't love your mother?'

It is not just that, I thought. He dislikes me for my own sake. I said, 'If she was here now instead of me, she would give you the answer you want because you would then warm to her. And human warmth, as she knew, is the grill on which we fry our fish.'

'So you do explain her after all?' His hands folded together, he smiled at the second camera that cut me from the scene.

'I've told you what she did,' I said, 'and what she was like. Isn't it rather stupid to think that is the same thing as an explanation?'

Let me tell you a little more about who she was. *One's own mother*. The first mirror we look into, the first means we have to define ourselves, define what we resist. So I thought of myself as a miniature version of that long but not particularly shapely figure; those clumsy, solid, Otago legs, the famously frizzy hair. When I sat on the floor, even before I could speak—or so I think I remember—I knew that other women, neighbours or visitors who came into the kitchen, or very rarely the sitting room, somehow had the edge. When the TV monkey pressed me, exasperated, 'Well, could you give her to us, do you think, in a word? Is there a phrase that always springs to mind?' I hadn't played his game. When I told him, 'No, I don't think I can', the truth was that I could have, very easily. I could have said, 'Graceless. That's us all over, isn't it? A graceless breed?' I noticed that too from when I was a child. At school picnics, women's institutes, Presbyterian bring-and-buys, how charm seemed squeezed out of the women. As though God's own choppy fingers had not quite shaped them as he should. How seldom did I see a woman move across a room, walk down a road, so that it was a delight simply to look? Before I knew the word I knew I would never see it in her. That is part of the way I would define her. Graceless. Money can't do a thing to help.

Yet she indulged me, at least in what I wore. 1956 was the first year she took me abroad. We went to the opera in Paris. My mother was fussed over by a Frenchman who behaved as though her body was of importance to him. My mother, I believe, was the first New Zealander to buy out a French company, even if it was only a minor perfume manufacturer between Nice and St Paul-de-Vence. We went down there for a week. The owner, who was also the company's *nez*, the professional sniffer who could tell you oil of roses from orange essence at a hundred yards, was the man at the opera. He fawned over her like a puppy prancing at a door when it wants to go out for a pee. When he came to visit us at our hotel he brought with him a squint-eyed teenage boy who, I am sure, did the trick. The boy sat in a white cane chair and his black hair fell over his forehead and when he believed no one watched, picked at a scab on his wrist. My mother was not sentimental about children as the rich often are, but the repellent boy somehow won her round. My mother bought the *parfumerie* and kept the same man as manager and never learned that the child was a relative's son, that the *nez* was a shirt-lifter *extraordinaire* who employed only male assistants. It was one of the few debit investments she still owned when she died. But the point is hardly that. When my mother and the man of scents walked down from our hotel to lunch near the Madeleine, a building that fascinated her because it looked as though the gods and not God lived in it, she said to the English woman who was supposed to look after me, 'Try to dress her in something that shows her to advantage, can you?' She passed the woman an envelope thick with new notes. I was fifteen. I was filled with rancour that my mother would let me spend without limit on clothes, but would not tell me a thing about what business really meant. She taught me none of what I so desired to know. What she wanted was for me to be a rich and fulfilled young woman, and so ignorant that my gratitude would never go off the boil, an eternal child gratified that the saint had provided perfect weather for her *fête*.

'The accident?' is what none of them actually asks, although the little TV chimpanzee would have given anything but his tongue to put it to me. So would clever Dr Sarah. It hovers there with almost everyone I meet, like those haloes that tilt behind the heads of saints in a thousand pictures I have been obliged to look at as my mother worked at transmuting lucre into culture, even to the second generation. They are hoping, all of them, aren't they, that whatever it was will catch the right light, some miracle will occur just for *them*, and I shall say, 'Oh, the accident, yes . . .' My mother, old by then of course but still not what you'd call frail, standing as the carriage seemed to tilt a little, as it does taking those tight curves above the rocks and their languid lacy collars. The run of one tunnel after another, sudden as a hand clapped over your eyes and the hand then lifted as suddenly again as you pour out to the blue dazzle, the promenades, the palms like tired slow spiders . . . I could say any nonsense that came into my mind. 'Accidents happen so easily, don't they?' 'Yes, we were the only two in the compartment, which is odd, isn't it, for that time of year?' Or 'Crossing a river. It was a far cry, of course, from anything that we might mean by a river.' And her eyesight? As good as mine. She could read without spectacles if she had to, if the natural light was good enough. So it's difficult, isn't it, to think she might have mistaken the door of the *gabinetto*. She was as at home on trains as you are on your studio chair, or perched there with your laptop. And you're right. She must have travelled that coast literally dozens of times. It's true, they could have asked, it's true is it she was obsessed with railways? 'Obsessed?' I would have made a joke of it. 'I think Pierpont Morgan was the only capitalist she ever envied!' But I don't say a word, and nor do they.

At the time, as everyone knows, I fully cooperated with the authorities, and the papers told over and over how close we'd always been. I continued to wear black for longer than I needed. And they want to ask isn't it a burden for me, surely, the loneliness, seeing I am not married, living alone, harbouring my grief? To be rich is provoking enough, but also to be single, to be still in my fifties, with hair that positively finds the camera without my least effort—there must be a secret, musn't there, that the world is desperate to share? There is no secret, I assure you, but as long as the safe is closed how can they ever be sure? Their rage is real enough. I hear it when I walk into a room, without their having to say a word. How dare you presume to keep anything back from us? Not tell us about your fears, your periods, your bank accounts, your thoughts of God when you wake in the middle of the night? How dare your mother, famous as she was, fall from a train above the most beautiful of little harbours, above the timeless flash of Mediterranean ease and corruption? Call yourself a New Zealander, and not let the rest of us in on that?

What they find hard to take on board is that there was so little glamour. There was lots of travel, we stayed at nice hotels, there was an endless number of men in identical suits who came to talk money while I sat in another room. While we travelled my mother opened a black folder from time to time, as though it were a timetable she checked against to confirm that yes, that is the Matterhorn, say, on time as it should be. We seldom flew anywhere except across oceans. That became part of her myth. It fitted the old-fashioned image of the solitary financial wizard, the woman who raised or brought down markets as we rocked at night across the stretch of unseen plains, or the Alps slipped by, pale as paper. This was not the way to do modern business, the *biggest* business. The press loved her for it, and her own country was at her feet. It is one thing for men to knock off mountains, to sail faster yachts. But for a housewife to come at this, to do it as though it were a hobby that began in her backyard. 'Jesus,' as Sir Robert Bowen mocked. 'It was as close as we can get to an Incarnation of our own!'

I dreamed once that she stood at the picture window, her fingers moving beneath her apron, and when she spoke of it in that way of hers, the river indeed rose. It levitated in a drift of broad silvery swirls, like an actress's scarf pouring out in a breeze. It rose and rose, this fluid living swathe, and moved towards the window where it hovered, compliant and lovely, waiting for what my mother next told it to do.

It is an impossible thing, as you must have thought yourself a dozen times. But think of yourself in the most torrid sexual moments of your life—rancid armpits, excessive promises, mouth crammed on this or that—then think of your parents doing precisely that. It will never work. The turbulence of our loins is an exclusive business, a deep innate denial that exactly this is accessible to others as well, least of all to those who begot us. I talked of this only once, to a friend who flung on one of those Japanese gowns, dark blue with bamboo leaves patterned across it in white. He stood at a window where reflection from the snow in the park outside made him seem both deathly pale and illuminated. Something rare as life and art together. And his saying, petulantly, 'You have no idea how distasteful it is, your talking like that.' But it is another story, that, the snow, the gown, the graze from his unshaven face that was like a rash on my thigh for several days. And my lying there, my arms across the sheet in the almost morning light, and my mother so large in my mind, my mother, and my father whom I have not so much as mentioned. Lying there, thinking about her, about him, as I watched my lover at the window. I did not know for years that when she stood at that other window, above the curdling skeins of water below our house, that while I sat with my train, and her fingers moved below her apron like a kicking child, it was not that view at all she had in mind, when she looked down and spoke.

Mr Cooper's cousin had been with my father in the same stink and heat. He told her about beriberi that made you feel like your insides were corroded copper, or pellagra that peeled the skin from your testicles, from inside your legs, so you looked like skinned tomatoes. At 75 kilo camp and 105 kilo camp, Mr Cooper's cousin said, at night the insects emerged from inside the framework of the bunks and were like another unbearable skin. The guards bawling 'Speedo, speedo,' while a man's guts spilled down his legs, but the baskets had to be filled with broken stones, the rivets driven in the tracks.

'They all had a cross with their name on it,' he told her. 'Somebody would say something even if there wasn't a book to read from.'

And so, 'The river,' my mother used to say, the shingle and the braided glints in front of her, the brown strong tug my father must have looked at every day, the famous river there were movies about later on, and a cross somewhere above it with his name which, apart from the 'a' that has to be added for a girl, is the same name as my own.

We never grew closer together through all that travelling. A train I might even define as a conveyance to draw mother and daughter apart. She took me everywhere as I've told you, she gave me what she believed I wanted, and her own life was in her head, in the figures shining on the calculator, jotted on the ordinary school pad that made her quaint and rather feared. My life was watching her do it. I knew the languages she never learned and had affairs with young men she allowed to knock their wings against my lamp. Sometimes we laughed together and remembered a mad stark-naked Serb who ran through our train as it came to Zurich, and how a Pole offered us vodka near the border at Opava, and we drank with him like skunks and through the night he stole our luggage while we slept. I was the human touch she liked to have with her. We dined in excellent restaurants and drank from goblets and she became rich enough for us to live like that for a hundred years. She bought into Eastern Europe ten years before anyone ever imagined that one day the East would not be there, and the pickings fell from the trees. That night they want to know about how she watched me and closed her calculator and held it like a small prayer book, and we flickered above the neat towns at the edge of the sea. She stood and left the compartment and opened the door onto emptiness and velocity and ripping wind, above the olive trees along the banks of a ravine where the stream runs only a few months or so a year.

I am looking out at water in any case. The tunnels are black and flat as a blind between the glittering bays. She looks at her watch and says we can only be twenty or so minutes from Nice. Monaco has already passed, its opera-set palace, its glimpse of casino lit up like a grounded liner. She stands and asks would I like to come with her, along the corridor that tilts with the movement of the train? I know she dislikes walking it by herself. But no, I tell her, I don't, I don't want to come. She stands then at the door of the compartment where we have dimmed the lights, her fist is closed in front of her blouse, so white against the magenta silk, and I think for some reason of a child holding a chunk of bread. Her face drifting and pale and receding as she steps back and draws the door across. I turn and look into the blank window. My own reflection faces me as a train whacks past, pelting through to Genoa. (I know the timetables that well.) There is the dash and racket of the speeding carriages, the flowing sheen of metal. And in my head, gliding by as it has for forty years, the light sheering along the grey toy tanker, along the black chassis that holds with red string the strips of balsa, along the green engine and the twinkle of its small brass rods. The three trains for that moment together, while I sit and my mother walks towards the mistaken door. And a train, a fourth, squat and black beyond the words I have to say, steaming past camp 75, camp 105, towards the tall viaduct my father watches too, spanning the brown river. I see it only because he saw it first. But I see it more clearly than my mother ever saw it, looking down from her window, drying her hands beneath her apron, the click of the Hornby whirring behind her on the carpet. While she thinks, yes, one day I shall escape from this, I will find another river in another place.

One Ordinary Thursday

'No,' John said. 'No, of course I'll not tell her that.' He moved the receiver a fraction away from his ear. The voice was too loud, too insistent. The soft clutch of the cord wound around the little finger of his other hand. Like tendrils, he thought, that's what Joy would say. 'You needn't worry then.' Once again he said, 'No, of course.' And then, as if soothing whoever it was that spoke to him, 'You've enough on your mind.'

He placed the phone back in its cradle—wasn't that what Joy called it? Where it lay, in any case. John put back the phone. Then he took up the folded paper he had been reading before the ring shrilled through the house, as it did first thing in the morning, or late at night. As it seemed to do whenever Joy slept, and he rushed through to snatch it up. Before it woke her.

It was one of the treats of the month, to read *The New York Times* a friend down the road passed on to him. Before the phone had broken in on his morning, he held the paper angled in front of him, catching the early sun. He read an essay about Berlin that spoke of the famous photograph of Russian troops raising the flag in victory above the Reichstag. The picture was there on the same page. The person who wrote the article said to look at the arms of the soldiers, festooned with looted watches. How it depressed him to read that. It was more than fifty years old, that photograph. Yet it made the marvellous fact that the killing concluded on that very day seem grubby and devious. These men who should be heroes were simply thieves.

That mood of disappointment persisted as he folded the magazine and put it beneath a cushion on the couch. He thought as he arranged the cushion to conceal its edges, why was he even doing this? He was like a child, hiding something that would get him into trouble. A broken vase. A cracked silver-backed mirror he should not have picked up in the first place. He was like a child doing that. He then stood at the big window, the one Joy called their 'picture window'. He looked down to the road leading through the gorge, and across to the hill that ten years ago, when they first came here after they married, was bush from top to bottom. The hill was now packed with expensive houses. Most of them tried to conceal themselves behind fast-growing trees, planted in clumps and angles that said the bush is still really here, it only seems we have replaced it.

It continued to nag at him, why that story had so upset him, why he now so carefully put it out of sight. There were only the two of them in the house, for God's sake. And Joy would no more think of reading it than—she'd find one of her extravagant comparisons that amused and irritated him at the same time. 'Than she'd think of marrying a man who thought a photo like that mattered.' He spoke more loudly than he intended. The cat on the corner of the sofa looked up, saw nothing was amiss, and placed its head back on its extended paws. Again, there was total stillness. A man standing at a window, watching a yellow truck like a huge toy making heavy weather of the gorge's steep rise. Behind him, a dozing cat. And through the closed door, along the corridor and behind another door, his sleeping wife. The man heard the distant straining of the truck. A fantail zagged across the lawn, and behind Joy's hedge of camellias. 'You needn't worry then,' he had said to the other man on the phone. He would like to be able to stand here now and to think of nothing.

When John woke in the mornings, in the bedroom with its glint of Asian brass and its long uncurtained window, the first thing he took in was the expanse of sky. Only when he sat up did the harbour, and the ranges stacked behind it, come into view. Sometimes the whole caboodle, as Joy liked to say, was enough to take your breath away. She said it to friends when the weather allowed them to sit on their sundeck for Sunday lunch. 'We've a Japanese friend,' she said, 'who can't get over how the island sits there dead centre at the end of the gorge and even the trees along that crest seem part of a deliberate deal. I think he's convinced we're the ultimate in Zen gardening and we arranged the lot!'

Her sister sometimes said, 'Do you have to go on so much about things, Joy?' but their friends seemed to enjoy it. It was part of her name, her exuberance, why she so got on with people, why she was dead straight and spoke her mind and if you couldn't cope with frankness, she said, then better not talk to me had you? Their friend Tony Moreno, who was near the top in arts administration, said lunch with the Lawsons was an *obbligato* for trombone and flute—a lot of Joy's blare and twinkle, the saving touch of her husband's thin, trim note.

On the way home from one of their friend's protracted lunches Tony remarked that John and Joy were the only case he knew of conversation by osmosis. His wife, who was driving, edged carefully around the orange signs of roadworks before she asked him tartly, 'What's that supposed to mean?' Their own marriage, so gossip went, was on a rocky patch.

'John sits next to her and their arms rub against each other and whatever he's thinking Joy obviously knows and so says it for him. If you knew what osmosis . . .'

Rachel Moreno said, 'I know what osmosis means as well as I do what mean-arsed and envious does. Which may be another surprise to you.'

Her husband laughed and put his hand on her knee. Tony and Rachel were in their fifties. Rachel had been at school with Joy, Tony knew Joy at university, John and Rachel had once worked together for the Wadestown Labour Party. Between them, John once said, they had almost a hundred years of friendship. A mildly pointless *non sequitur*, someone or other observed. Once John had also said to his wife, surely it would be fairer all round if Rachel was told?

'People exist one by one,' Joy said. 'The moment you start legislating in pairs . . .' Her sentence went unfinished.

'Yes,' John had said, 'I know you think that, love.'

For all the view that visitors were struck by, John preferred when he woke to look at the clouds. A cliché all right, he would say, but the fact is they *never* are the same, not two days in a row. Their utter immobility some mornings, the different densities of light they seemed to carry. On other days the streaming and ribboning and teasing out as the winds drove them north. Joy liked to say the names of painters if she saw him absorbed in the sky. Turner or Corot or whoever, even McCahon when there was a winter storm at seven in the morning, and there was only darkness, and the narrow zip of lightning across one corner of it. He could see what she meant. But he wished she wouldn't. You didn't need to talk about it, you didn't need always to slip the hood of words across things, as if that was the only way they made sense. The changes even now, he thought. At six the only sky had been a deep unmarked summer blue. And now, at not quite nine, how different that same expanse of sky and water and hills. A front moved in even as he watched, a brooding mass of rapid cloud, and beneath it, the sea turned heavy as lead. A wall of shadow was moving across the Hutt Valley when the phone cut across his taking in its dramatic change. A woman's voice spoke quickly, close to tears. He listened to her rushed words for at least a minute before he spoke.

'This morning?' he repeated after her.

'It's important,' she said.

John looked at the squares on the calendar in front of him. *Lake Furness*, he read, *popular with tourists throughout the four seasons*. The woman said the cafeteria of the National Library, was that all right, at half past ten? She had cards it was important to put on the table. She told him that twice.

'Why is that important?' he asked her.

'You're pathetic, John,' she said. He realised, as so often, that he had not said things in quite the right way. He knew he should have said there is no need to be so fussed about things, Rachel. I know about the cards.

Joy was a colour consultant who worked in some of the big government offices when the move was from small private spaces to open-plan work areas. 'Personality has to breathe,' Joy liked to say, as she took in the drabness and the conventional spatial areas it was her job to make over into warrens of a different kind. John was an engineer who had taken early retirement. As a young man he had published on wave theory and it surprised anyone who knew him professionally that he had not risen a little more rapidly. No killer instinct, Tony Moreno put it down to. He meant it as a compliment. Joy and John had each been married before, and neither had children. Forty-fiveish was a good time to put things together again. That was now a decade back. Chalk and cheese, Joy said, when it came to most things, but would you believe it actually worked? But *really*. Because they were companionable, that was it. Joy had never known a man she so got on with. She often told others how well they managed together. John avoided large statements of any kind, and particularly any that might apply to himself. Yet yes, he would say, he'd certainly go along with that. There was no reason why they should hit it off as they did, and yet lo and behold, they did. Companionable, as Joy said, was simply a longer word for sexy.

Rachel worked in the photographic section of the National Library. John arrived early, and waited for her in the big entrance area. The black leather armchairs were imposing, comfortable. He liked the marble floor, the sense of high, open space. He heard the click of her heels on the white squares and looked up from the brochure that explained to him how the Library could source almost any interest he might have.

She was taller, more elegant, than his wife, yet looked several years older, although Joy had been a prefect at Diocesan when Rachel was still, as she said herself, a brash and brazen fourth former. She hugged close against her chest a large brown envelope that had she been a nurse you'd have thought contained X-rays. John stood and removed the black cap his sister had sent him years ago from Greece. It was the kind that with its embroidered cloth and shiny peak allowed men who had spent their lives in government departments to come across as a touch jaunty. Rachel smiled slightly and said, 'That makes you look sinister, do you know that, John? That cap?'

He patted his thinning hair. 'You'd be surprised how cold it gets.'

The number of things he found himself saying recently that apologetically said 'age'.

Rachel said the cafeteria downstairs, that would have to do, when he asked would she rather the coffee shop further along the road? 'I've someone coming in for these,' she said. She meant whatever was in the envelope she held against her.

John paid for their coffees. He carried them to a long bench beneath a window that faced a street of parked cars, and a few walking figures leaning slightly against the wind. Further off, he could see the lacy front of the Parliamentary Library. When he was a boy he thought it the nicest building he had ever seen. Although those roses. The roses on the slope in front of it were blown and scrawny, not at all what should have been growing there. 'I don't think much of those roses,' he said.

Rachel drew her stool close enough for their arms to touch. She spoke quietly, as though aware of those at the tables behind them. She said, 'You know why I want to see you?'

'No,' John said. As if he had the choice of telling the truth. So she told him she had left her husband the night before. John did not say he was sorry, or that it must have come to her as a surprise, but he told her, 'I've wondered sometimes why you didn't leave him years ago.' He said it so quietly, without inflection of any kind, that it seemed he spoke of something so far off it was hardly of great concern to either of them.

His reasonableness was like a pin driven into her. She shifted her stool angrily, its legs scratching against the floor, her arm jogging her coffee so that half of it leaped the cup rim and flagged out across the wooden ledge. John's hand shot forward. He stopped the cup from tipping completely. A woman with dyed red hair and wide-winged glasses was at their side almost as soon as the coffee spilled. A black man from behind the counter stood at her side. 'I'll just shift this for you, ma'am.' He moved the brown envelope and ran a Wettex along the ledge. He said, 'Accidents happen to the nicest people.' He had a white cloth slung over his shoulder, a steward from a thirties movie on a long-distance train across America.

'I'm making a scene,' Rachel said. 'I'm sorry.'

'Only a small one,' John told her. He made her smile, that was something.

Then she said what was the hardest thing to say. 'Your wife's carrying on with my husband,' she said.

'Carrying on?'

'Screwing him,' Rachel said.

John turned his saucer several times. He looked across at the stretch of road to the straggle of roses below the old library. Then again he turned his saucer. He could tell this irritated the woman beside him. She seemed only just to control the anger that seethed in her.

'Doesn't that mean *anything*?' she demanded. She looked at him directly, disliking him, he knew that.

John looked back at her steadily. We so seldom really take in people's eyes, do we? he thought. Green with brown flecks. He had known Rachel all these years yet had never quite noticed that.

'Doesn't it?' she said again.

'Yes and no,' he said. Yes, because it was true, and it would not be natural to pretend he didn't mind. And he wished for Rachel's sake it was not true. But no as well, if he told her honestly. If Joy was an 'item', to use the word he would never say himself but he knew was the one his wife would choose, if his wife was an item with an old friend, it did not touch him in the way this agitated woman expected him to admit. So instead he said to her, 'On the whole, Rachel, no.'

She crushed the pink paper napkin in her hand and dabbed at her watchstrap. A single speck of coffee had splashed onto it. 'I don't believe this,' she said. And now it was as though John's sitting next to her was of no consequence at all. The man realised that she had pushed away, as it were, from whatever little island of interest he stood on, and she was now preoccupied somewhere else. For a moment he looked down at her hands as they smoothed out the soft paper of the napkin, over and over. He thought of the numerous Sunday lunches and their easy, leisurely talking on the sundeck as the afternoon declined. They would never be like that again, the four of them. There was something so finally ended, and yet the thought of that did not disturb him much. It was there his mind hovered, on how he should have been more moved than he was, more pitying to this woman with her dark severely drawn-back hair, her ageing skin. He knew the hollowness she must now be feeling, the fracture of an ordinary world that for now at least she could not imagine ever being restored. He knew all this, and knew he failed her as well. He said, 'There's a book I might as well check on while I'm down here at the library.'

He was at the first landing on his way back to the level of the entrance when the American from behind the counter caught up with him. The man spoke with an accent that was as much from the movies as that earlier image of the white cloth across his shoulder. He held out the Greek cap. 'There'd be a lot of takers for this one, I'm sure of that.' John noticed as the cap was held towards him that the man's arm was smooth and hairless, as if he had been sandpapered. He felt the man's kindness and warmth. He would have liked to say something more than the stiffish 'thank you' that he came out with. But that was always the trouble, wasn't it? To have the right words there when they needed to be used?

He checked the catalogue and filled in an order slip then leafed through an Australian newspaper as he waited for the book to be delivered. It was a memoir by a writer who once had been well known, and now was read by no one much, he supposed, except the kind of people who write entries for biographical dictionaries. He wanted to see the book because his father had once met the author. That was during the war, when his father was in the Air Force, and his mother still in love with a man of twenty-four in a sheepskin flying jacket in a silver frame beside her bed. The airman and the author met in a pub in the Strand. The author, who was much older but still liked to talk about Whakatane as it had been more than thirty years before, worked for the War Office and lived across the road in the Savoy. He was kind to his young compatriots and saw these 'athletes of the clouds' in a romantic haze. He wrote about one of them in the book John looked up. The pilot in the book had won the Victoria Cross and the author felt a twinge of refracted glory as he bought him a pint of Burtons amid the bluish drift of cigarette smoke, and shared the round of ham sandwiches from the servery where a woman with a wall-eye carved the thick slices the pilot adored. The young man always chatted with the woman who was three times his age, and gave her an armflash for her grandson and signed with the author's thick Waterman fountain-pen the photograph in the *Express*. The photograph showed the King with his hand on the young man's arm. The author said yes, a very decent man, because he had written the book about the King's brother that had made him quite famous, as well as rich. Dad had known the same pilot and even shared what he called 'digs' with him.

John supposed his father must have been rather like the pilot in the book, with the grin he knew from the photo in the silver frame and his flying jacket lined with New Zealand wool, and his eyes picking up the first specks in the distance as his plane rolled off in its wide sweeping arc and his gloved hand waited to press the button. All that excitement back then. He liked to think of before the famous pilot in the book ditched in the Channel and before Dad came back to the rotten years after that, boozing it up and the rest of it. There was another photo somewhere in one of the boxes under the house. John was wearing his father's cut-away leather flak-jacket. The jacket came down below his knees. He remembered the strange floating feeling against his legs, as if he wore a piece of cloud, he liked to think. Dad's arm was across his shoulder in the photo and the fingers of his other hand gripped at Mum's arm. John was a lot older when it occurred to him that Dad held onto his mother so tightly that you could see the dints of the pressed flesh, and Mum seemed to lean away even as she was held, as if the old man needed her there to keep his balance. But Dad's head was only partly in that picture and you could never tell for sure why that had happened. The big bunch of flowers on the table helped obscure him, and were blurred as well. He supposed whenever he looked at the now fading square of shiny paper that somehow the table must have been jogged, and the shutter clicked at the wrong time. It was difficult to imagine how. But there they were, forever, the flowers sliding towards the right-hand side of the picture, as if anxious to get away. And as he thought too when he looked at it, at the partially concealed man and the proud boy and the woman with the taut lines of her neck and the indentations where her husband's fingers clutched at her arm, how it was nonsense trying to guess anything about it really, that Joy was the one for fancying things. But it was deeper than fancy, he knew that too. It was all of them, at that moment when the camera preserved them and the table moved, ready to take off, somewhere or other. As they all had done.

John read the book for an hour. Then he placed it on the broad counter with other returned books. Things people read, he thought. A manual on bee-keeping. Islamic art. A dictionary of Tongarevan Maori. A girl in a green school uniform slapped down several folders of musical scores. This in one hour, he thought, the world grazing on dead facts, piling up words, images that cannot mean, can they, whatever they did for those who made them?

He went to the phone in the wide vestibule to telephone home. The woman at the reception desk glanced over to the tall man as he selected a coin from those he spread on his palm. She heard the button on the apparatus click, and his mild, even voice asking, 'What else did you think she wanted to say?' She missed his next few sentences, as he said to his wife that yes, if she thought she could make it down in twenty minutes? He would wander over to the cathedral and see her outside there. The young woman watched the man pass through the double set of automatic doors and then stand in the uneven scatter of sunlight and shadow. One moment he was bright in the fall of it and the next as drab as the walls around him. She rang her boyfriend across in Archives and said she would see him as soon as the other receptionist was back. She wouldn't mind buying him a cap like that one on the old bloke, if only she knew where to get it. He'd look so choice in that when he wore his black T-shirt and sat out on the veranda with his boots resting on the rail.

For the second time in two hours, John sat opposite a woman and watched her stir sugar into her coffee. When the spoon was lifted from the cup it wore a slippery white beard, it always reminded her of that, Joy said.

John said, 'You know I never see those things until you point them out.' Then directly, because that was the only way to keep things clear, he told her what Rachel had said, and how upset she had been. The worst of all, he said, was the surprise of it. It seemed really to have knocked her.

'Tony's been "seeing" people ever since they were married,' Joy said. She jigged the spoon against the side of her cup until John stretched out his hand and lightly touched her wrist. Her fingers then rose to move against her thick jade beads. 'I don't see why, this time. Why is it such a fuss?'

'She knows all that as well as we do,' John said. 'Only this time we're her friends.'

His wife leaned back from the table and looked through the curtained café window. The room was timbered and plastered like a Tudor take-off. Behind the curtains the windows were divided into small squares with dark wooden joinery. She said, 'I've less patience with this sort of carry-on than I used to have,' meaning the décor that surrounded them.

'You've less patience with everything.' John smiled slightly and so did Joy. She said, 'I'm spoiled by you, that's the trouble.' He supposed she meant the way he accepted the 'deal', or whatever it was. Other people would call it a lot of names. The deal of almost a dozen years ago when they sat like this, across a table from each other but in the most expensive restaurant the city then had, a chance for her to use her French with the waiter. He said that after their holiday in Rarotonga and now they knew each other pretty well and knew even more importantly that they got along, why didn't they make a go of it? Joy had said she thought that was exactly what they were doing, but she was pleased that John said it. She knew before she agreed that it would not be a mistake, she was certain of that. But she had said because she believed it was better to be utterly honest, just as she knew it was not a great risk she was taking in saying it, 'You know about that friend I mentioned I've been sort of seeing off and on for years? It's nothing that important but I want you to know.'

As simple as that. A kind of distant background murmur they did not refer to, even when five years or so ago he had guessed who the friend was. Yet the lunches went on, Tony and his wife were his friends as well. And his assuming Rachel too must have an inkling of it until this morning and Tony distraught in his early morning call, *She's left me*, his repeating that, and asking twice that John not let on to Joy. And as he assured him no, he'd not tell her that, admitting to himself—unable any longer not to admit—that his own weakness was profound, who would not think that? And yet he did not think so. He knew and he accepted it, that was all.

Joy's hands now held her cup the way a child grasps a mug, lifting it by its sides, the handle poking like a tongue between her fingers. She said again, 'You've spoiled me, that's the trouble, John. I expect everyone to be as calm. As sane about things.'

'We've spoiled each other,' John said. He took up the cake-fork and drove its side against the lamington in front of him. 'Not even half?'

'I'm close enough to shopping at Jennifer's as it is.'

He divided one half again, then speared it onto his wife's plate.

'Who's that?' he asked.

'The fat ladies' shop. Don't you ever *look*?'

'Obviously I don't.'

Joy eased out her watchstrap and her forefinger worked against the itch beneath it. John told her, 'You wouldn't get that rash there if you put nail varnish on the back of your watch. It coats the metal and the metal's what irritates your skin.'

'I know,' she said. 'I should have done it.'

They both looked through the tiny squares of glass to the sudden splattering of rain. He felt a weariness with the town, with its weather, even for the moment with his own life, although he knew enough of himself to know that his depression would pass. 'Nothing St John's wort won't fix,' as he sometimes said to Joy when she asked him what was wrong. A plastic rubbish bin caught by a turn of wind bowled and clattered on the other side of the road. Joy thought of fucking Tony Moreno, and it being found out after all these years. Intermittently, if that made any difference. It was hardly what you would call a highly passionate affair. A preliminary grope at a university party, that was how far its beginnings were. At three in the morning, while everyone else yahooed in someone's sitting room, watching a test from Twickenham. Then another time, the Saturday night it was announced the Prime Minister was dead, and parties wound down all over the country. She had gone to the car to get an address book. And as she leaned across from the driver's door towards the glove box, one knee hiked up on the seat, she felt his hand slide upwards from her knee. It was the suddenness that excited her, the forearm that was like a branch she sat on. She had said, 'Don't do that!' She moved back from her crouching inside the car, the address book held in her hand, and stood beside Tony Moreno who told her you can't go round provoking people like that, young lady. She was taller than he was, which only struck her when they kissed. She settled her skirt and could never remember whether in fact she spoke, or simply intended to. But someone was standing there on the veranda, calling out, 'He's dead. Norm's bloody dead.' That's how far back they went.

John said, 'You haven't said anything for a while?'

'Miles away,' Joy said.

'So was I,' he told her. He had been thinking, I've never asked her even that, have I? Where they ever went to be together, I don't even know that.

His wife touched his closed fist as it lay on the table beside his cup. 'I'm sorry,' she said. 'I'm sorry it's all come to this. I'm sorry I ever thought the arrangement would work.'

The next morning John watched the sky. Half an hour before the clouds had been placid, pale tufts. Now the wind came up again and all that had changed. The harbour was a raw dismal smear. He was glad Joy still slept in the bed on the other side of the room. As soon as she knew his attention was on the harbour, on the movement of sky above the hills, she would feel compelled as usual to say something about it, to do anything, he sometimes thought, except look at it, to be content with things as they were. He knew she intended well. To be impatient would not be fair. Fair. Most things come down to that. At least it saved you from sentimentality, from carrying on about things. Sentimental people so seldom told the truth, he was certain of that. Take his friend Kevin Driscoll. Kevin weeping and crying out at the graveside of his wife a year or two back, and his mistress everyone in the department knew about on the other side of the hole and the disappearing box. John hadn't had that much time for either of them but after that he had none. The humbug of it all. He and Joy liked each other—loved each other even, they must do, or they wouldn't be together now—but there wasn't an ounce of deception. They understood each other pretty well. 'No God, no sop,' as Joy had put it, ages back. Avoid those two and life's at least got a chance of adding up.

John moved about the kitchen, slicing the banana into a bowl, making sure the muesli was damp but not sodden. He took teabags from the different jars, the Earl Grey underarm deodorant that Joy believed was tea, and decent English Breakfast for himself. Not to take it so seriously, he was thinking, poor Rachel at the library yesterday. He was dragged back smartly to the world in front of him. From the dining room he heard Joy's ageing tabby begin the long-drawn coughing that was likely to end with a serious dab of cat vomit on one of the Turkish carpets. 'Out, you little bastard!' he shouted through from the kitchen. Before he reached the doorway to the dining room the creature streaked past his legs and clattered through the cat-door. And his wife's muffled calling from the bedroom, 'Are you killing my cat again?'

'If only,' John said. A phrase he had picked up from the teenagers next door, as they yobboed about on their skateboards on the concrete drive. He lifted the warm pink mess from the carpet with a paper towel, then flushed it down the toilet. He scrubbed at his hands with the nail brush that lay on the shelf above the handbasin solely because of the puking cat. By the time he carried Joy's breakfast through to her she was out to it again. He took the saucer from beneath the cup and placed it over the top. Then he took his own tea and muesli through to what Joy called the conservatory and he himself, more accurately, the glassed-in porch. The sky seemed to have lowered and frayed. The clouds now skidded along the crest of the hill across the gorge. Like a pulled rug as Joy had said on a similar day. How on earth that poet fellow on the radio got the idea that talk like that 'sharpened awareness', wasn't that what he said? And the woman who was so edgy most of the time oohing away as if someone had all of a sudden rubbed a windscreen for her and she now knew where she was going. To be fair, he supposed, that sort of talk worked for some people, but it certainly did not for him. Low cloud, a southerly of around forty knots an hour, with intermittent showers. Why couldn't people just put things like that for a change? Things looked just as good surely if you called them by their right names.

He held his tea mug to warm his hands. It was a good feeling, that. Rubbing velvet so it flowed with your touch. A warm river stone against your cheek. All those things that were good when you were five and are just as good now. Chalk under your fingernails. The screech when you took an old nail out with the claw of a hammer. Rotten sensations like that. They lasted too. Do any of them now, and it was fifty years ago as well, exactly the same. Time collapsed. Or became an accordion, more like it. The past and the present meeting, touching together. 'You make me so happy, you do know that?' Joy telling him that once, out of the blue, in a New World supermarket as he handed down tins of cat food from a shelf too high for his wife to reach. And the only other time she had told him, so frankly, on a calm June day six miles off the coast of Kaikoura, the mountains strung out above the rising green lift of coast, as they waited with a boatload of tourists. Just before the captain told them he had picked up two whales on his sonar screen, that they would rise sixty yards away in about a minute's time. There was a hush as the tourists grasped the rails and held their cameras at the ready, a waiting that was so brief, so drawn out, at the same time. Joy saying that about loving him as she leaned close against him, and the quiet wait until the surfacing, and the grace and slowness of the whale's stupendous tail lifting against the distant mountains turned the pit of his stomach with elation, as nothing else had ever done.

John sat on the settee, his hands resting to either side. It would be an hour at least before his wife dressed and came through. He felt the edges of the journal he had hidden beneath the cushion yesterday morning prickle softly against one hand. He unfolded the page where he had left off, the picture of the raised flag. The arms with their looted watches. He read on, angling the paper to catch the light. And a detail towards the end that he read over twice. About a young girl handing out cyanide sweets while Bruckner played on a gramophone. He did not know what Bruckner sounded like but imagined it as both grand and tender together. The swell and pomp of the music that made flags stream out against a breeze and men stir with theatrical belief in conquest, victory, and then at last, defeat. And the quietness, the tenderness, that other music dabbing at their souls, whatever that might mean. And through the grandiloquence and the comforting, the child walking in her white frock, a child among old men, holding out her plate of sweets, the plate for error to escape itself.

The image of the girl was vivid in his mind, the drift of her innocence through the dark uniforms and gleaming caps. He had no idea why the story so moved him, why he so wished he had never read it. In the crush of things so contradictory he felt his own complete ineptness before fact, history, whatever one liked to call it—that towering vague cliff at whose foot he saw his own figure, so ineffectual, and across it, like montage in a film, the slow moving of the girl as though down the aisle of a church, and the descending hands, the black cuffs, towards the plate she carried. He closed his eyes against the blurring of the printed columns in front of him. I must try to think of nothing, he told himself . . . I must try to think of nothing.

Photos, to Begin With

Pat Costello's hands, my mother used to say, Pat's hands, have you noticed how lovely they are? They could be a woman's. It is an old memory, my mother saying that, but not a faded one. From not so long after the war, and the men recently back, because when Titch Evans phoned from the railway station after he stepped off the Limited from Wellington, or Tai Martin called in out of the blue, there was a lot of excitement, laughing and stories that were above my head. I could tell my mother liked it, the men Dad had been away with dropping in, knowing our house was there to welcome them. I knew her excitement by the way she went to her and my father's bedroom as soon as the phone was put down, as soon as the squat car pulled up, that was almost like something Tai wore and took off like a coat, as the big man stepped out of it.

In the bedroom she would half close the door and take her make-up from the top drawer of the dressing table, with its big central mirror, and to either side of that the smaller mirrors she moved to show herself side-on. My mother leaned towards the mirror and ran the lipstick across her parted mouth. She then licked her lips so they shone before she dabbed at her cheeks with the powder puff, and let me put the lid back on the round black box. There was a small raised figure on the lid of a woman holding a mirror. When the top was pushed down there was a hushing sigh, and the faintest cloud of powder from round the edge. That is a memory too whenever I think of my father's friends from the Div coming round to see us. In memory they called in on only the finest days, when the kitchen chairs were taken out into the backyard and my mother put a checked cloth across an old table that was always out there, beneath the two pussy willow trees that were higher than the guttering. Our house was on a section that I remember as being so much larger—almost like a small park it seemed to me then—than of course it was.

All that, coming back to me, as I think of Pat Costello's hands.

I can't have been to Auckland for twenty years, and certainly not that part of Auckland, west of Cox's Creek, for almost twice as long. I met a school friend, Marie Clifton, at the top of West End Road, and we walked down to the curve with the sea held to one side, where we walked hundreds of times as children. Marie hadn't been down there for even longer than I. She had phoned me at my sister's and said, 'You won't know who this is.' But I knew at once. More than half a lifetime on the other side of the world, and her voice hadn't changed a jot, a hesitancy as though she was never sure of how one would take her. The girl who was prettier than any of us, and cleverer, and the least sure of herself in class, or on the basketball court, or when one of the nuns spoke to her in the street, trying to be nice to her, to draw her out. ('Going to confession was the only place I felt sure of myself,' she told me once. No wonder most of us thought she was weird!)

It's nothing to be proud of, I know, but when I embraced her outside the old Bayfield School, and told her how lovely it was to see her, and meant it, I knew I looked younger than she did; that I had 'weathered the years', in a phrase my mother liked to use, and I was elated.

We later told each other how we were both surprised at hitting it off so well after so long. Neither had found it so easy coming back. We had tried to pick up the old traces with other friends, to pretend the intervening years made no difference at all, but of course they did. A cousin for instance—I once had been so infatuated with her that both her parents and mine were worried about it. The Parker and Hulme business was still talked about and misunderstood, as its details emerged of murder and fantasy and lesbianism at the base of it all. New Zealand suburbia was caught between fascination and icy fear. Some families, like our own, became over-vigilant. All my cousin and I were up to after all was smoking, and looking with a flash of disbelief at a stack of *Man* magazines a sharemilker kept behind cans of disinfectant on the shelf of his garage.

I mentioned all of this to my cousin and her husband, a retired teacher, when they asked me to their home in Orewa, a huge house I thought it for only two people. There was a big window as she told me that 'commanded' 180 degrees of sea and sky and houses like their own. Her husband was a warm, amusing man who reminded me of my brother who died while I was away. He was interested in what I thought about spending my life somewhere else, and what I thought of the country I came back to, so different from the one I had left. But when he had to go off to some local committee he was on, I could tell my cousin was not quite easy with me. I mentioned the way our parents had watched and worried, and she smiled and said, 'The things the young get up to,' as though it were not ourselves we talked about, simply girls we had once heard of. I find it hard to get quite right, the feeling I had as we sat there, filling in time, waiting for her husband to come back. Too much water, as the cliché goes, had passed under the bridge. We talked families and those who were close to us, but the names we used were only that, labels rather than people. Nothing came alive. By the time her husband returned, I think each of us knew we would not go out of our way to meet again. The Christmas cards will keep on. The photos of grandchildren. The news that does not matter papering the gap that does.

Marie understood without my having to spell it out.

It was much the same with her sister, but worse. 'As if my being away,' she said, 'was an offence. Although for a foreign husband to leave one at this stage in one's life—well, that's a triumph for her. Still having her local one, I mean.' She said this without rancour, without even the irritation I held against my cousin in her too big Orewa house. Marie told personal things in a direct, unsentimental, neutral way that puzzled me. Something bad happens and emotion flows out behind it. Difficult, troubled feeling most of it. But she seemed not to mind, at least not in any angry way, that this late in her life 'the tide had turned', as she said. The phrase spoke for itself, as though it were in the nature of things that nothing was to be presumed upon.

I was staying in a house, an old wooden villa, in Mt Albert. Through another cousin I was put in touch with a woman whose work for a government department took her to Canberra for three months, and she let me rent very reasonably. Marie, who wasn't short of money, was in far more fashionable Herne Bay, sharing a smallish flat for which she paid what seemed to me a rip-off price. But from two side windows of what had been, a hundred years ago, a worker's cottage, and was now renovated and as sparkling, she said, as an operating theatre, she looked down on that lovely stretch of water towards Kauri Point, with its long tongue of yellow cliff and blue bush. Tucked down below the house was a glimpse of smooth green, Point Erin park where, I reminded her, we had walked, innocent beyond words, with boys after swimming in the salt-water baths.

Marie liked looking at what she had known so well so long ago, but had none of the discomfort that so often seemed to flood over me as I walked the same streets. She didn't mind, as I did, that the old shops had moved so up-market. A hardware shop on Jervois Road, once packed and smelling of oil and cold metal, was now an uncluttered space with expensive pottery and blown glass; a long narrow room that had been a place for shoe repairs was transformed into a restaurant, specialising in a cross between Asian and European cuisine. All this is admirable, I know, a far less stolid and complacent world than the one in which I grew up. But Marie noted none of this. She was as untouched by nostalgia as I was swamped in it. She smiled when I said, over and over, 'remember', which was a word she never used. Marie found the present quite satisfying enough. Which meant, too, that she could speak of the years between when we knew each other as girls, and now when we met as ageing women, as if it was nothing unusual, life returning her to where she began. While I always thought of us as special cases.

We met once a week, and mostly ambled at random. We walked the old streets, the old circuits, Green Street and Selby Square and Ponsonby Road, John Street and Vermont Street and the lovely tree-lined length of Jervois Road up the rich end towards Masons Avenue and Marine Parade. After an hour or so we drank coffee for another hour in a place we had become attached to, a café with cool glass tabletops, and on each table a tall transparent tube that held a single autumnal twig. Or if the weather was good, we would push further into Westmere, across the shallow arc where the water lay to one side of us, then up the stiffish climb towards the shops. What was once Mr Caddy's the butcher, Mr Cahill's the grocer, Mrs Leigh's the cake shop, were now different names for different things. A wine shop. A delicatessen. We found a coffee shop, even there. We were served by a young Chinese man who, though it was autumn, wore a grey string vest and long spider-webby mittens, which cannot have given any warmth. His hands, delicate almost as a girl's. Then as Marie and I walked up the long, sloped road towards the zoo, and came to Notley Street, I remembered Pat Costello's hands, and what my mother said about them, and how he died. I looked at the wooden State house, as plain a box as you'd ever see, and the apron of back lawn where I expected to see the garage, but that had been pulled down. Just as the family next door must, decades back, have moved on, people who, in my own family's eyes, and in many others in the district as well, were marked forever.

I could see my father at our kitchen table, the pages of the *Star* spread out in front of him, my mother at the bench, peeling the potatoes for dinner. It is a memory I could take from hundreds of evenings of my childhood. My father would read each page completely, apart from the women's fashion, then turn to the next page with a distinctive slapping of his palm on the fresh columns. My mother set the various pots and saucepans on the gas stove with its blue surrounds and white oven door. We were a family of habit. You could say to me Tuesday six o'clock, or Sunday morning, and I could tell you even now what we did, what we had always done, at that time. As I could tell you much the same for the rest of the street. When the McIntyres came home. The nights the blind twins were away at the Institute. When Mr Carpenter was 'off travelling' again, the euphemism even children saw through when the dapper salesman was doing time. We laugh at the fifties for their dullness, their complacency, the fact that most people like my parents would not know what lasagne looked like, and had never been to Australia, and overcooked their cabbage. We talk of them with the condescension we keep on hand for those who are not as smart as ourselves. All this in a flash, as one says, as Marie and I pass Pat Costello's house, where there is now a half-completed miniature fountain on the scrap of front lawn, beside a tilted trailer, and a basketball goal with its sagging net skirt attached to a side wall.

My memory flares so vividly I feel my eyes prickle, my mother coming down the hallway from where the squat black phone waited on a circular table with a crochet mat beneath it. She stood between the narrow curtains that fell either side of the doorway to the kitchen, and told my father what had happened. I was doing my homework at the other end of the kitchen table, the green and orange checks of the oilcloth beneath my books. My father leaned his head on both his hands, his elbows on the table, and it seems now—seemed then—that there was silence in the kitchen for an age. A pot lid pelted above a boiling saucepan on the stove, that was all. Then my mother came and put her arms across my father's shoulders, and drew him to her, cradling him, and made this sound above him, a prolonged soft crooning, as though he was a child who had been hurt, and rocked him to her. I was fascinated and ashamed. I didn't want to watch them. Whenever I saw them kiss it was like old friends kissing when they met or parted. I had never seen more between them, something as mild and perfunctory as that. But she was holding his head now and kissing it, crying into it, they were unaware that I was there, the two of them so close and I so distant, and I knew for a moment what marriage might be, and what children have no inkling of. I was angry that they behaved like this in front of me.

Marie was telling me about a book she was reading; she said how much there was to catch up on since she came back. She made the books she got through at such a rate sound interesting, and I liked her bringing me up to date with what people wrote about and thought important during these years I'd been away. I was fascinated by how she was driven to read so much, as quickly as she could. 'I am filling a great hole,' she said. 'I have to fill it and understand what's there.' She asked me didn't I feel the same? And again I was struck by how different we were, my interest really only in things past, rather than in what happened now. But mostly we spoke about the lives we had lived in other countries, and what had attracted us, and what repelled us. She told me she was the one who insisted on marriage, not her Irish husband, although 'oddly', as she said, 'he was the one who believed in sin.' She admitted she may have badgered him. 'He was weak in almost every other way, so I expect he was in that as well. Being leaned on by me.' She laughed though, as I did too, when I said it was the reverse in my case. I was the one who held back, even after we had lived together for several years. Even after Cecilia was born. My Italian husband was a flamboyant atheist, which he thought in itself must make him special, mistaking rarity for more than it was. But he accused me in one of our fairly frequent rows that I was an immoral woman, that I had no respect for marriage, and now none for the good name of his daughter. He never convinced me of his point of view, but I married him because I believed that if I stayed in his country, I owed his family something. His mother, who was Swiss, and was thought unbalanced in a harmless way, told me a month or so after the ceremony that I had disappointed her, although it was not her place to say so. I had set a bad example, she said, to Italian women, who made fools of themselves to pacify their men. Enrico is my son, she said, but nothing special.

Marie said she had known no one like that among her own husband's family. 'Conventional wasn't in it.' Twenty years was enough to put her off Yeats entirely. 'Romantic!' she said. They convinced her the Irish soul was only at home with ringing tills and bank drafts.

'So that's Italy and Ireland taken care of,' I said.

'Never look at pictures of places when you're a child,' Marie warned. 'I thought it would be round towers and the Kerry dancers.'

I think of a tiny packet of black and white photographs of the Italian lakes, which had been a treasure when I was seven or eight years old. Which made me remember as well walking down from school, to meet my father at Pat Costello's. Pat Costello was working in his garage, half of him hidden beneath my father's car, which was tilted up, like a speedboat rising from the water, on a platform jack. 'It's me, Mr Costello,' I called out.

There was the sound of something rolled on concrete. I saw Mr Costello's legs scrabble on the floor, and then the rest of him appear from beneath the car. His back was lying on a piece of board with little wheels beneath it. I had never seen such a thing. I laughed down at Mr Costello. He smiled up at me as he rolled to where I stood just inside the door. For the quickest moment I had this notion that the wheels were growing from his back, that this was a secret Mr Costello had kept from us all along. Then he stood up and took a wad of material from his overalls and wiped his hands clean.

'It must be awful under there,' I said. 'How can you even see?'

He told me to bend down and look under the car. 'See that?' he said.

There was an electric light bulb inside a wire cage, and a cord that ran across the concrete, then up to a switch on the wall.

'That's how,' Mr Costello said. 'All I do is switch it on.'

I asked him where was my dad. I thought this was where he was. He said he had driven up to Surrey Crescent. 'Would you believe it, there's not an inch of insulation tape in the whole place?' And one of the hands that my mother liked to look at moved in a circle that meant in all his garage, with its racks of tools, its shelves with packets and small boxes set neatly along them, and there too, beneath the bench that ran from the door to below the window, the bigger compartments where there were coiled rubber tubes and differently sized funnels and petrol cans and bits of chain. There was a float he said he attached to a net when he went fishing that glowed on a half-darkened shelf like a big orange. There was a folded-up tent in another space beneath the bench. Could I imagine, not an inch of tape!

'You mean my dad's taken your taxi?' The thought of it amazed me. A taxi seemed such an exotic thing to me, its yellow circle with 'T' lit up in the middle of it, which set it so apart from other cars. Taxis were for the posh, or for emergencies of the kind our family never had. Or, in ways I did not quite get the hang of, for things that weren't nice. Sonny Troupe in the next street came home in a taxi when, as I'd heard Dad say, he couldn't walk from the tram stop without going arse over kite. Why his wife puts up with it, my mother would say. Fascinated as she said it, because Mrs Troupe was much younger than her husband, pretty and small and blond. Taxis were for the likes of them. Or for reasons I was even less sure of, for Mrs French in Kotare Avenue, with her fur coat and lipstick like someone had cut her across the face, who went into town on the four o'clock tram and bowled home in a taxi, as often as not with company. 'Mrs is right,' Pat Costello said.

I said now I wished I'd been back from school in time for me to go with Dad. No problem fixing that one, Mr Costello said. When my father came back his friend said he'd be a while yet on the job, why not take me for a spin? So Dad said to me, 'Right then, sit in the back there like Lady Muck and I'll show you what a taxi ride's like.' We went down West End Road and up the hill on the other side and along to Three Lamps. When we drove back and passed the top of Ardmore Road he said, 'Could have bought a nice place down there a few years back if the bloody war hadn't interfered.' It was the first time I felt grown-up with my father. Always my mother became quiet when Dad started talking like that. 'Bludger had it cushy right through,' he said about one of her brothers whose farming had kept him at home. Even about

Mr Costello, once he had said, 'Landed on his feet all right, old Pat.'

'Because he knew where to put them, that's why,' my mother had said. I could tell she was angry. I knew too Dad was unhappy that his work across at the furniture factory in Blake Street was going nowhere. 'Marching on the spot,' he asked. 'What sort of life's that?' He was quiet for days at a time, especially after Mr Costello died. But all that was ahead of us, the day Dad drove me in the taxi, and talked to me like a friend. And the day became even more important to me because of the souvenir photographs Mr Costello had kept from Italy, and gave to me when we arrived back at his house.

The pictures were only a few inches square. They were in a blue paper envelope with '*La Veduta sui laghi*' in swirling lettering across the front. There were steep hillsides with houses sprinkled down their slopes, above stretches of water. There was one I especially liked taken from the top of a hill, of a lake with tiny islands, and buildings on the islands with towers and battlements. Not part of the set was another with '*Milano*' in raised-up writing across one corner, a church that seemed made from a stack of knitting needles, with little figures on the top of every needle. I could not believe such places might be real. They are the kind of places set in a child's mind like a jewel, and time will never remove them, even after the places themselves have been seen and maybe lived in. They explain decisions we later make, and regrets we can do nothing about. More than twenty years later, and six months after I met him with a group of friends who had gone to Siena in August for its days of flags and horses, Enrico asked me would I like to go somewhere for a weekend, somewhere special for me. I said, 'Would Como be all right? I'd love to see Como.' And the magic that had been there in the small packet of black and white photographs in Notley Street expanded into a marvellous lake, its slightly misted hills, and the town where we spent one night, and then the next day the enchantment of driving on to Spesa. In his last weeks Enrico joked, knowing how impossible it was, 'How about a trip to Como?'

Later, when my daughter and I were packing up the apartment, and I had infuriated her by saying I wanted to go back home for a while, that was all I wanted, just a few weeks of it, I tried to tell her of the cards I pored over as a girl, and the thread between them and the fact that she was here at all. But she was in no mood to go along with it. She said to me surely by my age, by *half* my age, I should have worked out where home was supposed to be? I told her, clever scientist though she was, that what she lacked was heart. 'You even sound like an Italian!' she flung back at me. She liked New Zealand the two times she had been there, the first time when she was six and her grandparents had made so much of her, and again at eighteen, her good looks and her accent making her much admired by everyone she talked to. How we go for it, we New Zealanders, the exoticism I liked to think I had seen through years ago. The slick of glamour that can make a man who is lazy and deceitful and rather dull, shimmer like Adam until one day—it may take no longer than that—one day the lights are changed.

I said to Cecilia, 'Your father dying. I need to sort things out.' She said, not meaning to hurt, I'm sure, as much as she did, 'Perhaps you could find yourself a new packet of magic photos, then.' But then my granddaughter, in her costume for the part she had landed in the local theatre, came into the room, her young German fiancé behind her. They looked so marvellous together, laughing, talking of their honeymoon in Thailand. I wished I had not tried to tell Cecilia. I felt a chasm between us. Yet since I have been here we talk on cheap weekend rates, sometimes hours at a time. She has even cried across that distance, saying how she so misunderstood me. She upsets me, sounding apologetic, sounding so much like myself. 'Another month,' I tell her, 'I'll be home in another month.'

'You mustn't hurry, Mama. You must take just as long as you want.' Her surprise for me, as I will find out later, is that she has had the new smaller apartment painted, and prevailed on the landlord to put new doors onto the balcony above the square. I will know when she sees me sitting there, looking across to the white and green intricacy of San Bartolomeo, that she has already pasted me across the view for the next twenty years. Cecilia has my last role planned out for me. But all that is another story. For the moment, back in Auckland, I am absorbed by Marie's collapse, and what I might do to help her.

I phoned her sister's house when Marie had not turned up for our weekly walk, and did not get in touch. Courteous, fastidious—these 'old-fashioned' qualities were so much part of her apparent calm. They were part of what made her seem wiser, more placid than I. Sometimes as I rattled on about Cecilia, or my granddaughter's impending wedding, I felt I must strike her as awfully scatty, even self-centred, considering how little she had said about the man who left her, his family, her own wanting children but never having them. And now her sister telling me, rather coldly I thought, that Marie was in some kind of home. An institution, she said. No, she was sorry, but visitors were out of the question. She could not tell me, no, quite what the problem was. 'The doctors are undecided.' I phoned several times, for much the same kind of answer. Until her sister—her half-sister, by now that at least I had learned—surprised me by saying if I could spare the time to call round? 'To have it out,' was what she said, as though there were some dispute between us that must be concluded.

I'd got the wrong end of the stick, you might say, about everything. Monica was Maori, to begin with. She saw my carefully showing no surprise, and said simply, 'Marie was particular who she told about our separate fathers.' Her house was in one of those long sloping streets off Jervois Road. It may have been Marie's rather old-fashioned clothes, or her sister's reserved tone when I had spoken to her on the phone, that made me think of places lived in fifty years ago by ageing aunts, darkish rooms and heavy hall mirrors, and the dull polish of aspidistra pots. In fact, I had not been in a more modern house in my life. One entire wall was curved plate glass. Metal studs ran across the white walls. There were bright, harsh paintings, a tall sculpture of highly polished metal, and a slack-jawed wooden head, transplanted from a ventriloquist's dummy. Monica smiled and said she couldn't help it, every penny she had went on stuff like this.

I was puzzled by everything. Monica was hospitable and warm while in fact she told me little of what I wanted to hear. Of their family, of her own relationship with Marie, of the work she did that would explain the house we sat in. She took her place close to me on a white leather couch, and sometimes touched my arm as she spoke. An hour later what did I know? That Marie disliked her father, who had died, a very old man, a few months before. Monica said, 'I think coming back was a kind of sorting things out.' There was no Irish husband, Marie had told others that story too. A librarian, all her life, in a small city in the north. There was a partner for a year or two, then another later on. 'Only Christmas cards,' Monica said, 'I never knew much more than that.' And then she surprised me, cutting through her sophistication, her keeping it all at arm's length. 'Nearly everything we guess about another person is likely to be wrong,' she said. Was it her way of saying, too, that what she had told me may not be the whole truth, but it was all I would get? There was no point,

Monica was insistent on that, no point in seeing her sister. It was too late for that. She stood at the front door and held my hand. She said, again, 'There's so much to sort out.' And the firmness behind the warmth that this was finished business, we would not bother each other again.

Cecilia, who had come full circle, now pressed me even more to stay longer. Make the most of it while you're there, she said. Her Antonio came to the phone and told me nobody missed me. I wasn't ever to think that. 'Perhaps the German does,' he said, 'the one who is marrying your granddaughter. These foreigners stick together.' His loud, good-natured bellow ringing at me round the world. The call worked of course as it was meant to, and I booked my ticket back for the end of the next week. I lay in bed that night and thought of the girl in Westmere who used to lie, her hand beneath her cheek, exactly as I did now, with Mr Costello's lakes beneath her pillow. The Italy that was more magical than real, and here she lay, half a century later, thinking again of that same place, more real now than home.

The rain started up as I lay there, the Auckland rain that grows intense within seconds, until it stalks the roof and the excitement of it shakes inside you as well. The kind of deluge my father went out and stood in near the clothesline, after my mother held him, and he knew about Pat Costello. His clothes moulded wet against his body, making him seem smaller and alone, the water pouring from his lowered head, as though being baptised by something frantic and malign. From time to time, for years, it came into my mind, so much a part of me that it would go as quickly as it came. But tonight I thought of the whole story, as I had learned of it as a girl, the story that was so simple we thought no, there must surely be more. And the horror, if that was all. Pat Costello taking the girl next door, who went to the same school as I did, in the taxi with him if he drove to the shops for cigarettes, and she happened to be standing across the fence. Her name was Gail Gatting. Pat Costello was friendly enough with her parents to listen to football tests with them in the middle of the night, when the crowds in Wales or England surged through the big radiogram, and the neighbour's wife cooked black pudding for halftime, and Pat's wife slept back at their house, she couldn't stand the mention of rugby. The Costellos so at ease with the kids their back door was always open, and the girl with the run of the house, helping herself to the cupboards. And her running in one day as Pat Costello stepped from the shower, then haring back across the shallow yard and through the gap in the hedge and yelling to her brothers, showing off to them, frantic with the excitement of it, that she had seen it, seen Mr Pat Costello's cock.

The police came and asked him questions and he was appalled at what they meant. He went to the pack completely, my father said. He cried when he told Dad what the neighbours thought, and what the police kept coming to ask him about, a cop from the Ponsonby station because the one in Richmond Road who knew him said no, he wasn't up to this one. He said, 'I don't know how much I can take of this, Jack.' He said he knew what the neighbours must think, of course they'd think it. My father told him to shift out of the place. You couldn't live with bastards like the Gattings next door. 'And make them think I scarpered?' Pat Costello said. It got too much for his wife, who went to stay with her sister, even after the police said there was nothing to follow up. My father spent so much time with his friend even my mother became impatient. 'He has to stand on his own feet sooner or later.'

Then the phone rang and it was the sergeant from Richmond Road, who had been with my father and Pat Costello in Crete, and then in Italy. He told my mother Pat had fixed a hose to the exhaust of his car. My father stood in the rain until my mother couldn't stand it, and took an oilskin from behind the washhouse door, and went and stood beside him, trying to cover the both of them. Later my mother said she couldn't face the funeral, the gawping and the talk there'd be at it. But my father arranged it, and rang around their cobbers from the Div, and shouted down the phone the night before, so my mother called out, 'What's all that?' Dad came back into the kitchen and said that stupid bastard from the undertakers, you wouldn't credit it. Did they want a flag, he had said, a flag across the coffin? He was a soldier after all, the considerate voice had said. That was when Dad had shouted. He looked at us, his eyes wild in a way my mother and I had never seen. It was the look too of a man bewildered that there were things in life he did not quite have the measure of. Then he laughed, but it was as though something had caught in his throat. 'As if Pat would want a bar of their bloody flag!'

Not Always, Mrs Woolf

Gerard read the sentence from Virginia Woolf that said 'If you do not tell the truth about yourself you cannot tell it about other people'. He liked quotations that put things neatly, ones that offered a freshness and surprise as the page of his diary was turned and there was the quotation to enrich the day. He liked them in the same way as in his schooldays he derived such a kick from memorising saints' days. There was a flicker of pride when the class looked at him, when the form master wrote the date each morning at the top of the blackboard. Say 14 August, and he would call out 'St Hippolytus', or 3 December—which indeed was today—and he would know. He had learned them, month by month, by heart. He had no need to look at a reference book tucked away in his desk. They were there the way other boys memorised sports scores, or the winners of the Melbourne Cup. Yet saints were of no particular interest to him. When he spoke of it once to Norma and said he supposed it was his lust for order, she corrected him. 'It is your passion for control.'

It was nine o'clock in the morning. He heard the clock strike from the public library on the other side of the park. It was at the same time each day that he edged his chair towards his desk, and turned the page of his desk diary. Some days the quotations were not interesting, or even meaningless to him, or not worth giving time to. Sir Joshua Reynolds saying something on landscape, which held no interest, or Groucho Marx's joke about shooting an elephant in his pyjamas, which was funny when the comedian removed his cigar to say it, but not when it was written in small print at the bottom of a page. Gerard liked it when you could agree or strongly disagree with the quotation. When he could think, yes, that's dead right, when it's put like that. Or no, you may be William James, whoever that may be, but you will not find me going along with that.

Gerard had once read a story by Virginia Woolf. This was after Norma had told him how good she was. He could see why she said so. He liked the way it seemed to be about very little and then surprised you by how much neatly fitted in. This morning though he read her sentence twice then said decisively, although he was the only person in the office, 'Well, she's wrong about that one.' Because seeing the writer's name reminded him of Norma, and hearing the hum of the air for that fraction of time after the last striking of the clock across the park, made him think of two things together, in a way he was not used to. He remembered how once he had placed his hand across Norma's on a table in a railway waiting room, his fingertips playing with her watchstrap, and cross-hatched, as it were, was a further memory still of the bumping of an ambulance stretcher against the long clock in his boyhood home, as his father was manoeuvred towards the front door and down the dozen steps, and the chiming clock thrummed with the impact. Both memories were for that moment so vivid. And there may as well have been a voice beside him saying the words he thought, 'You are wrong Mrs Woolf because I am a liar, and I understand much more about myself than if I told the truth.'

Norma left him in the spring. They had walked to the railway station in Adelaide for the train to take her east. He carried for her the suitcase he always had thought a touch tarty, an imitation animal skin of some kind, but he never told her so. As they walked under the trees along the road from the carpark to the station, small purple flowers fell to her shoulders, and he said, 'Stop for a moment. I'll brush them off.' He did not like the look of them, the pale blossom from the jacarandas. Norma laughed and kissed his cheek. She said, 'You can't brush me off that lightly.'

Spring, and yet she was wearing her leather coat. It had been cool that morning when they left the house they rented in the hills. Overnight, spiders had worked a tangle of webs that glittered across the entrance to the garage. They stood briefly and looked at the seemingly random sparkling threads. Then Norma ran her forefinger like a knife down the side of the door, and the brightness folded and crumpled, and she wiped the grey stickiness from her hand on a towel inside the door.

They had bought the coat in London while Norma was married to Harry and Gerard was living with Ismay. They spent the night in a place that was run by Spaniards, in a row of cheap hotels with double white columns and elaborate porches, and cheaply carpeted stairways that led to narrow depressing rooms. From the window they could see the tower of St Pancras Station. Norma thought Victorian things interesting, no matter how shabby. She had stood in the station's marble ticket lobby the day before and looked about as though she were in a cathedral. 'Which it is,' she said, when he teased her, 'only there's nothing here that might be mean to me.' It was her saying things like that that drew Gerard to her, and also made him impatient, because Norma knew that God was important to him.

They walked through the tangle of streets between their hotel and the playground at Coram's Fields, because Norma thought it so right, a park where adults unaccompanied by children were forbidden. They passed through the archway of the university building that was used as Party Headquarters in the film of *1984*, and through to Tottenham Court Road, where they stopped in front of a shop whose window carried the announcement 'German labels at English prices', and Gerard bought her the coat. That night they found a house

Norma wanted to look at in Gower Street and then sat in Russell Square, and all Norma wore beneath her leather coat was her underwear and her stockings. At the time he had thought they did something so unique! It was the same coat that he brushed the fallen purple flutes from as they walked to the station in Adelaide. He put his lips against the shoulder of her coat and ran his tongue on it, so the blackness shone. He said to her, 'I wish you weren't taking the train.' She placed her hands flatly against the lapels of his jacket. It was the way a woman can lay her hands so they seem within a fraction of pushing one off, or as intimate a gesture as one could want. Her body was against his own, neither compliant nor resisting, yet telling the man how yes, we are as close as this.

For ten minutes they sat in the station cafeteria. Neither did more than sip at the coffee Gerard carried across from the counter. Their hands lay beside each other's and he ran his fingers along hers. They kissed again on the platform. Then Norma, standing inches behind the long glass in the door at the end of the carriage, did one of her favourite tricks to make him laugh. She pouted her bottom lip and placed her tongue fatly across it, so her mouth appeared provocative and parodic, a bad-taste darkie take-off. They sat at the table sometimes after dinner, a night when they had drunk a lot, and he would pour more wine into their glasses and she would suddenly do that, shaking her head slightly, intoning 'Mmm-Mmm', a rising then falling cadence that was from the TV minstrel shows that had not been screened for thirty years, since they sat as kids on Sunday nights and watched family viewing. Her father had liked nothing better than those flickering chorus dances, the top-hatted made-up blacks that week after week made him say 'Al Jolson, now', his touchstone. And her mother said impatiently, 'Just listen now can't we, Frank?' Norma camping it up on the train that would take her east, her hands against the glass as the train pulled out, pressed so hard it seemed she was wearing white gloves for her final number.

He knew Harry, who stayed on in England after his sabbatical was over, was now back home and in a different job. Something of a come-down from where he had been before, the place he was at now was a former community college whose name had changed but its standards stayed the same. Gerard did not ask would she see him when she went across. She had not offered to tell him. She would phone him, she said, from her sister's at Barwon Heads. Then the call came from a campus six hundred miles north of where he thought Norma was. Her voice—he could not be sure—crying as she talked from the town where he knew her husband lived. Her saying no, she could not come back, she did not expect him to understand. He could have no idea how sorry. All the trouble she had caused. And the ringing of the disconnected line in his ear, the pouring emptiness through which all things that fell, fell towards him.

All this came back to him as the final chiming of the clock thinned out, and his office was very still. He took up a folder and tugged at the green tape binding it. He opened the first file for the day. The hardness of fact, the sureness of figures, gave him certainties he was at home with. He was irritated at what he thought of as a tiresome lapse. He had told Norma once, and she laughed at his telling her, that he did not think much, actually, of hauling up old memories, turning over what was past and better left to lie. 'I don't go in for sentimentality.' As he would most certainly call it now, this thinking back to the falling blossoms, the licked leather, her standing on the platform before the train eased away. 'It's all we have,' Norma had said, when they spoke that time of dredging the past. 'We edit out and we probably get it wrong but like it or not they're what we're stuck with.' She meant the images that hang on.

He was not good at that, Gerard tried to tell her, although that was not one of the things he remembered, as he tugged at the tape some fool of a secretary had made a hash of tying. He took the scissors from his desk drawer and snapped through the tightly knotted tape. It was his brother he now thought of. His brother the writer whom he had heard say a dozen times if he said it once, on the radio, in printed interviews, rattling on how the guts of writing was to make it *live*. 'That's not realism either. It's putting a line around something. Making an image of what we know.' Perhaps it is, Gerard thought. He always thought his brother laid it on a bit thick. It was simpler than that. He remembered the illustrations in *Principles of Geology* that showed levels of ash deposit and lava flow and whatever, one drawing in particular where the lines were straight and then a dip, a bulge, where things *have* to matter, anyone can see that. The coat and the strewn purple scraps and the fracture that leaped out at him when he thought of it. Then a decade later Norma dying 'out of the blue' as we say, and the death of a woman he had lived with for two years meaning not much more to him than if it were a casual friend he heard of, a friend's wife. Why hadn't it mattered more?

And now it was like saying 'Virginia Woolf is dead' or 'The war ended in 1945'. Both of which were true, but truth is not the same as grief. The tape was now wound to a small ball around Gerard's fingers. He slipped it free and placed it neatly with other similarly wound lengths in the drawer where he returned the scissors. Yet they don't matter, he thought, these things I am going over hardly matter. Wake at five in the morning when what we think and what we feel are so doused in each other that set a match to one and the other is in conflagration, who gives a damn at five in the morning, Gerard thought, about when a war ends, about a neurotic with stones in her pockets walking into a river? The dark at the bedroom window leaching off so slowly.

Not wanting to wake Anne and have her asking what is it? Willing it to change.

There were several appointments pencilled in on his desk calendar, beneath the date he knew the saint for, above the quotation in italics he did not agree with. The first was an appointment for nine fifteen. A woman far too young to let it bother her, wanting to discuss her will. Already he had sat and discussed it with her. Reasons given that were never asked for, doubts raised at the most obvious points. And her urge went on and on to tell, to half-tell, to cover the same ground, with the only story that for the moment mattered. It was not the thought of death that drove her to talk wills, so much as a man who may or may not have wanted to spend his life with her. She would be late arriving, the young woman. Twice before she had been late. Time is money, he had even joked with her, hoping that might bring it home. There is no need, please, she had answered him, almost haughtily. As if, Gerard thought as he waited, as if it mattered about the petals now, the hands pressed white against the glass, whatever. The shine along her leather shoulder as though some animal had run its tongue there. Norma his friend for years and then his lover and then her husband's wife again. He had heard about her illness.

Sorry, how could he not be? The slowness of it, how well she managed it, then the bad part, the ending. The evening he heard of it he had gone to an opera with Anne. He would not have liked the performance in any case. The high staginess one sat through for the few minutes, if that, of 'transport', as his brother would call it. They went on to a party where he was glad to drink until the host slowed hospitality to a trickle. A Saturday evening so that late next morning the phone shrilled on and on, a siren in a rambling dream, a cry that seemed suspended, neither coming towards him nor receding. Woken so suddenly, 'Of course I haven't,' he said. 'The news?' a friend's voice said from interstate. 'You've heard the news?' And so for the second time he heard of Norma's death. Norma standing at the closed door of the train. Walking beneath the shedding trees. The fragments of colour like torn scraps of cloth. There was a section of the park he crossed each morning where for thirty yards, each year at the same time, the same trees carpeted the lawn. How things like that, unimportant things like that, could fill your mind the way a painting packs every inch up to the frame. No room left for yourself. Time was the same as thinking about a painting.

He heard his client's steps on the stairs. Hollow, was that the word? He had held out against having them carpeted even when Anne told him, 'Let's face it, Gerard, your meanness is proverbial.' Saying it as she laughed and pressed her face against his sleeve. Walking back from the river, the mist almost like a net slung over the morning. He explained you could hear from the floor below whoever was coming up to the office. That way a client never took you by surprise.

The young woman stood on the other side of the opaque glass in the doorway. Her fist tapped sharply. 'I'm awfully sorry,' she told him. Her car keys still held in her hand. He put her at ease. He could tell she liked his kindness to her. 'There is no need to rush,' he told her. This morning she told him details he had not heard from her before. It amazed him how with some clients, after half a dozen meetings, there could be a reference to a property, an event, that should have been mentioned months ago, that made all the difference. He wrote notes on a piece of lined paper. He said to her, 'You know what today's feast is, Lucy?' She had no idea, the young woman said. She seemed almost embarrassed to be asked. He explained its importance on the other side of the world, what her name had once meant. 'Light,' he said, 'the coming back of light.' He thought as he listened to her how the straight line of the past, as we so think it at the time, becomes a ravelled knot as we look back on it. He would help her straighten it out. They came to him, these clients, because usually they had heard that he was good at telling their stories well. On the day in court when whichever truth was told the best, would be the truth that won. He said he was sorry not to offer her a coffee, but his secretary would not be in until later that morning. 'I live on coffee,' she said, 'it does me good to miss one.' He held the door open for her as she left. He heard her heels ring on the uncarpeted stairs, their diminished volleying in the large wooden hall downstairs.

He knew his client would know she had come to the right place.

Waiting for Rongo

Cards on the table then, as my former husband used to say, pretty nearly about anything. It's a straightforward enough deck I have to deal from. I was married for over twenty years, I had one 'relationship', as they say, before marrying Edward, and one after he passed on—rather than away. It doesn't sound so much, does it, one and one, making three like that over a lifetime? But I think I'm a fairly direct and sensuous woman—have been, at any rate—and have never thought a scorecard necessarily told one very much. I've liked the men I have been close to and there's nothing we did together that I wish we hadn't done. That's as close as I'll get to being explicit. I don't quite know how to put this even, but I've thought a few times when reading 'confessional writers' as they're called, that the 'confession' part can actually conceal, when of course it claims to tell all. I feel there's always a figure behind the curtain, you know what I mean?

My neighbour's name is Virginia Smith. I have no doubt whatever about the Smith, but the other I suspect may be something she plucked out for herself. I say this because a person knocked on the back door a few years ago and asked did I know Mrs Marty Smith's 'place of abode'. He gave the impression of having seen better times. ('Incorrigible,' Raymond laughed when I told him. He teases me for being a snob. As though anyone born near my end of Parnell Rise could be that, I reminded him. Q. E. D., he said.)

The man's heels in any case were worn down to the uppers. I told him I knew Mrs Virginia Smith but I had never heard of Marty. 'Close enough,' he said. Next thing I could see from the lounge window he was rat-tatting at her door and the moment it opened a cat took off from behind her leg and down the drive. 'Virginia' looked a sight but that did not seem to register with either of them. They were hugging as though they mattered to each other. 'You've got it in for that woman,' Raymond said. He said that first when we went to Fiji when the hotel rates were a song after the big dust-up the locals had together. A week in August, which is exactly when you need the sun and the rest of it. He said I should have asked her to keep an eye on the house. 'Neighbours like to be asked,' he said.

'There's neighbours and neighbours,' I reminded him. I said I'd rather pay a woman who was recommended to me at bowls. To take in the mail, move the curtains, switch on different lights on different days. You pay someone you don't know but can trust. There's no question then of asking favours.

'She's a pleasant woman,' he said.

So I told him, 'Raymond, don't take that cheery waving stuff for friendliness. It makes *her* feel good.' The way she waved if she ever caught us on the drive. Thank God the patio's on the other side.

'What would you call it, then?' He didn't often have that edge to his voice.

'I'd call it pushy, Raymond,' I said.

There must be half a dozen cats. Perhaps more. I don't mind cats myself although only once, ten years back, I had one for the summer, until it disappeared. Stolen, I've always suspected. There were children across the road couldn't keep their eyes off her. 'She doesn't like being handled,' I told them, although she brought it on herself, running across to them the moment she saw them. So it's not as though I have anything against cats. But next door makes such a fool of herself with them. 'Here, darling. Here Rongo, pet.' That kind of thing, morning and evening. Stuff from the meat counter at the supermarket, too, nothing out of a tin.

'If that's what she wants to spend it on,' Raymond said.

'As if the same cardigan practically day in day out, as if brown Warehouse trousers summer and winter, isn't a case for something other than treating cats like royalty?'

Raymond enjoys talking with her. He says he likes 'her turn of phrase'. I tell him anyone who half-made it to a classroom door speaks better than she does. Even her surgery. She tells Raymond about her surgery. 'At my age,' she had said, 'you don't go on doctors gawping at you, do you? I don't like it myself, to tell the truth. Saw myself in the mirror, the stomach like, next thing to a whipped suet pudding.' She laughs and spits into her handkerchief.

'She's vulgar but she's colourful,' Raymond defends her. I tell him you could say that about a baboon's backside.

This is starting to sound as if Raymond's right, as if I have it in for the woman. That isn't so. It is just her type, which is not mine. I said to the man who comes every fortnight to do the lawns, 'Doesn't it ever occur to her that a yard like hers lets the whole street down?' He's been coming for years. 'Your Grass is Ours' on the side of the van that carries his mowers. He looks after them religiously. Each time he takes one down the ramp at the back of the van I say to him, so it's become a regular joke between us, 'Not another new mower, is it?' He's not a talkative man but he smiles at that. A smiling workman is a good workman, that's one thing I have learned over the years. But he disappointed me when I put that to him, about Virginia Smith, if that is her name, letting the street down. He did not look at me directly I must say, he made out he was tinkering with his machine. But what he said was, 'Perhaps she doesn't think the rest of the street's worth worrying about.' It was hard to tell whether he was being offensive or not. Well, I'll be looking in the ad columns under 'Lawns Cut' was what I didn't say to him. I think he knew he'd gone too far.

*

Strange how the unlikeliest things come back to you when you're half-awake. Forty years ago Alex was halfway through his degree and lived in a rundown house ten minutes from Three Lamps, a house frankly that I told him would be the end between us and it was, although today you'd need a cool half million even to think of it. Alex had a cat that was heavy as a child when it jumped on the bed. About as much character to it as a lump of coal. The first time it hurled itself up and landed like that it frightened me silly. Either shut the door when we're in bed, Alex, I told him, or I'm calling it a day. 'He likes watching,' Alex said. He thought it amusing to twist things like that. Not that I was a prude or I wouldn't have been there in the first place. But I hadn't thought of that cat, obese and green-eyed and Lucifer, that was its name if you please, I hadn't thought of it for years and there was this thud and I could have sworn it was jumping on Alex's bed.

In fact it was Raymond putting out the bin, and the wheel had caught and the thing banged into the side of the house. But when I woke I could hear a cat and I was forty years back, and happy, that is the odd thing. It was as though the mood I must have had one morning back then still continued now, and everything in between had not taken place. And when it came in on me where I was, and how much later it was, I cried for five minutes in the bathroom. That kind of thing, it's completely out of character, I can tell you.

Later, Raymond said, 'There's coffee on the patio, when you're ready.' I looked from the lounge window before I went out. Virginia Smith was standing in her yard with grass up to her knees. She was laughing as she tried to drag from her the cat that was climbing with its claws at her cardigan. I knew by now the creature was her favourite, its irregular head like a closed fist, an ear half-missing, its body an ugly reddish colour, until a broad dash of pure white ran down its back legs. I thought, this is unreasonable, I know that, but how can one not detest that woman?

'You're all right, are you?' Raymond asked me, when I joined him in the early September sun, and sat in the canvas chair and raised the coffee pot above my cup. His car keys were beside his own cup.

'I think I might just read today,' I said. 'I wouldn't mind a quiet day.' Mondays we usually drove around the bays, and had lunch looking across the harbour. My friend Linda, who is always hoping to improve me, has given me the life of a writer who ended up killing herself. I don't quite see how knowing the details of that will improve me. But I have kept the book for a fortnight as it is, and Linda will quiz me as she always does. I don't like the photograph of the woman on the cover, which is a bad start. She is leaner, mind you, and Caucasian as they come, but there is the same lank stringy hair, that same curious sense of certainty about herself, as Virginia Smith. Who would not, of course, know the first thing about the woman whose picture lies on my knee, looking straight through me.

'Those cats,' Raymond said. He is standing in the lounge at the window, watching the carry-on next door.

'Draw the curtains at least,' I tell him. 'She'll know you're looking.'

It is as though he has not heard me. He says instead, 'It's remarkable, isn't it? The rapport, or whatever it is she has with them?'

'Give it a rest,' I tell him.

An hour later, by the end of the first chapter, I know I will not be going on with the book. Linda can say what she likes. It's the woman, an American, thinking she is so special, feeling miserable all the time. As if I want to spend another 200 pages on that, to get to the ending I already know.

*

There is a programme on television on Friday nights about people looking after animals. Pleasant young women in uniforms go round to old people's houses checking their pets. Sometimes they are telephoned to pick up stray dogs, or take damaged birds to volunteers who nurse them back to again facing storms and skies. I said to Raymond, 'I know one address I wouldn't mind passing on.' It must have been one of the last evenings. He handed me a G and T with the lemon cut too thickly, but I told him, 'Thank you, my love.' Raymond was about to go to his daughter in Queensland for a fortnight. The last thing I wanted was to have an awkward moment before he left, so I said nothing when he said, as he leaned across and brushed his lips against my forehead, 'I'd look out another window for a while if I were you.'

So I tried. I spoke to Mrs Smith when we happened to be at our letterboxes at the same time. When she said she was dog-tired, this traipsing backwards and forwards to the hospital a couple of times a week, I offered her the opening I thought she would jump at. I said, 'Something they'll sort out for you pretty soon, I hope?' But she said oh you know what public hospitals are like, five minutes with a doctor and two hours of waiting. She looked at me so steadily I felt uncomfortable. I can say that now. At the time I thought it simply rude.

I saw her as usual after that, but avoided if I could more than having to nod to her. And of course I heard her calling her cats. Then a week after Raymond had left for Queensland there was a tap one evening on the back door, just after the news had started.

'I'm sorry,' she said. 'I didn't realise the time.' She glanced past me to the television. I told her not to worry, it was not my favourite she interrupted. Irony was not in her repertoire. She stared at me for a long moment and then said, as though there were some effort in finding the words, 'I want you to do something for me.' She said the SPCA people had been that afternoon to collect her cats. I had been across to Linda's with the book I couldn't read, so I missed the scene I could easily imagine. Virginia Smith did not say why she had asked the van to come round. 'Sergeant,' she said, and paused again. 'Sergeant wouldn't come down from the top of the wardrobe so they had to use a net. You know that big net they use?' It took ten minutes, she explained. She could hear him crying from the van. Then the favour she was asking me was that she didn't have the heart, not after this long, not with his eyesight going and his always being timid anyway, she couldn't bring herself to send Rongo off as well.

'Away?' I asked her. For a couple of weeks, that was all. Up north, she said. I could imagine her at her sister's, some modest house facing a beach. She could just walk across the road and there she would be, close enough to the sea to dip her feet in. Odd, isn't it, how that came into my mind? I suppose it was from seeing pictures of them on television, those scruffy little settlements that somehow struck you as idyllic. Virginia Smith then picked up the plastic bag she had set down on the porch before I opened the door. It was heavy with cans of cat food. 'Not what he really likes,' she said, 'but it will do.' Once a day, she told me, on that bit of concrete near the under-house door. I needn't call him because he probably wouldn't come anyway, not so long as I was there. 'But I don't think he'd manage by himself, you see. Otherwise I wouldn't ask.' Then she said—as if I might have designs to keep the thing!—'Just until I come back.' She became insistent. 'You will do that, won't you?' The fatigue drawing her face. It embarrassed me. I promised because I wanted her to go, when I knew I should have asked her more. About herself. About her sister. 'Rongo,' she said. 'You'll get to like him all right.'

It was a bad time, the next few weeks. Raymond rang to say his daughter was twisting his arm to stay on. When

I repeated that, 'Stay on?' I expected him to say, 'For a bit longer, love.' But what he said was, 'I don't know if there's much more mileage in it, do you? In us?' Which brought it home, with rather a thud. That he had known before he left that he would not come back. I then saw how little in fact there was of him that was still in the house. I realised how carefully, over weeks, he had moved so much back to the flat he had not properly lived in for over a year. I don't know why I hadn't noticed. The only jacket in the wardrobe was a herringbone, old-fashioned and I expect now too small for him, that I had never seen him wear. The trousers on the hanger next to it were a pair he wore when he took the clippers to cut the hedge. A few razors, a few jars of unimportant pills. The only things—the deceptive things—that lay around were books. So long as I saw those, the stack beside the bed, the papers on the window-seat in the lounge, I would think he was on holiday. Between the time I placed the phone down, and three minutes later when I had checked the house and it all came in on me, I had turned him as surely as one might turn a chair to the wall, and the man I had liked, at the very least, became the man I knew I would detest for a long time. It had happened before, and I had tried to joke when I told Raymond about it, how deeply one resents it, the betrayal, the emptiness one sees in oneself. Until one believes, at last, what a trivial thing it was.

Nor did my neighbour come back. She did not go north, and did not have a sister, but died in the local hospital, and only the names of two nieces, in a town two hundred miles away, were in the notice in the paper. And a brother, who I suppose was the man with worn heels. But Virginia was real. That was the name in the notice. And here I am, on a late summer evening, standing in her backyard, the grass stalks rubbing against my legs. And my calling to him—'Rongo'. Saying it quietly at first. And then louder, too loud, so that other neighbours may even have heard me. 'Rongo. Rongo, pet.' Wanting so much for him to come and take the food I have for him. Wanting his torn ugly head, his skinniness and rasping, wiry cry. Wanting him to watch at least from the corner of the house. Wanting him to know it is better here than anywhere else.

Still Life

Margery Sutton was reasonably clever at the good school her parents sent her to, and reasonably pretty among the girls from good suburbs who asked her to their parties. This was the groundwork for making her the woman she later became. That, and the fact that she believed 'reasonably' was a word for others, but never likely to be applied to her. It was not a disadvantage that her father, a successful scientist, was frequently referred to in the national press. And it was an important fact in her *Gesellschaftsklasse*, as Rick taught her to say, that her brother who was three years older was very clever indeed, and good-looking, and adept enough at sport not to be dismissed as a mere scholarship swot. All this was in the 1950s. Hers was a small world in a provincial city, where a well-connected and personable girl might cut a dash, and believe she filled rather more space in the eternal scheme of things than may have seemed to be the case from any viewpoint other than her own.

Her Latin teacher in Form Six was Hamish Forbes. He spoke with an accent that those who mattered to her tended to be thrilled by. It was 'the real thing', as Margery's mother said, the finest compliment in a community that considered itself as close as one could get, without actually being it. The fantasy had hardened for over a century into an article of faith by the time Margery heard her mother use the phrase. Her parents were kindly and intelligent people, who nevertheless would not have thought of questioning certain verities. One was that you could trust most Englishmen as a matter of course. And you could trust your daughter to quite recognise what it was you trusted in them. So they liked it when Hamish Forbes came to play tennis with the boys at the weekend. They were grateful that he made such a kindly fuss of Margery. And they were amused—what parents would not be?—that their sensible daughter was just a little head-over-heels. A 'crush', as they referred to it. Their friends were diverted by it too. '*My* crush,' her Aunt Elizabeth said, 'was a brute in a shearing gang when I was her age.'

'Mine was a new young bishop!' Margery's mother said. 'Remember him?'

'Mother didn't mind my mooning it over the shearer,' Aunt Elizabeth said, 'but she was furious, I know that, when you pinned up the bishop's photo on your wall.'

Margery heard them talking in the next room. She despised their condescension. If they half-knew it would be a different story wouldn't it? If they knew that when they were working on the *Aeneid* Book Six, when she had stayed behind to ask Mr Forbes how he would explain the use of the ablative in a tricky line, her teacher had leaned across and not even kissed her, but put his hand under her school tartan, and next thing his finger had wormed inside her navy knickers. He was breathing so heavily, and whatever he put on his hair was rubbing against her chin as he leaned across her. She did nothing, she knew that, she did nothing to deter his eagerness or his stroking but she hated it. For the rest of her life she remembered hating it. The fact that *worming* was the word she kept thinking over and over. And all that came to mind to say was, 'That word there just doesn't seem right though, does it? Or was Latin different then?' But his finger remained there as neither said anything more, and she slid a little bit forward on her chair because otherwise the elastic was so tight. She knew later that Hamish would never do that again, he had been so apologetic about it. But he would be in thrall to her, like the knight in the Keats poem, and when he came to play tennis with Rick she would hand him his Rose's

Barley Water to let him know it was all right, goodness, he mustn't think she bore grudges.

And after Mr Forbes the excitement, imagine, the disgust, not more than a few months later when her father's old friend was chatting to her in his study with its high dull bookcases and the oar from his Cambridge college stretching the length of one wall. She sat on his desk as he talked to her, her skirt not quite covering her knees. 'This is one of my treasures,' her father's friend told her. He opened the old black leather cover of a book he had picked up by pure chance when he was a student on holiday in Geneva. 'It may be theology,' he said, 'and you'd find it very dull, but what a beautiful thing!' His flattened palm ran over the title page, and Margery put her own hand beside his, feeling the strange rough flow of the paper beneath it. Then he had touched her knee and let his fingers lie along the plump inside curve of her thigh until that hand it seemed was mimicking the movement of the other across the book. Only this time, in a phrase she hated when she heard it later on, it was rather more than with Mr Forbes. It had been pretty near the whole hog.

Thirty and forty years later she admitted, when she thought of it, that this was most certainly what one meant by a defining moment, as she confided to whichever woman friend was closest to her at the time. There was something a touch emblematic about the whole rather unpleasant episode. What she meant, Margery said, in a nutshell you might say, was that most of her relationships with men were already there in miniature. But keeping males as friends afterwards, she knew she was good at that. Which surely was the hardest part, to be generous after the event? Not to gossip. Not to judge. It was a thing that needed to be said. As preface, as it were, to her saying how she had seemed fated, that was not an inappropriate word, fated to get caught up in the troubled, exciting, territorial world of the Charles Goodfield estate. By now of course her name was as good as synonymous with his. When a new picture came to light wasn't the first thought with buyers, with the press, to get in touch and see what she said of it? Then with those who had a taste for blood sports, what did Ormsby think, once he heard what Margery had said?

The story was a complicated one, although it was possible to give a pared-down version that in essence was more accurate than either Margery or her former lover would have favoured above their own accounts. This is the shorter version. Ormsby and Elton were the closest friends, before Margery, soon after graduation and halfway through her library training, surprised everyone she knew by marrying Elton, who was quiet and conservative and had been married before, and had no great interest in painting. That was Ormsby's line of country. But Elton's father was a friend of Charles Goodfield's before that awkward, angular, driven man became a household word. He had bought the six canvases that became famous as the 'Kahikatea series' for twenty quid just after the war. He did so simply to help out an old mate. It was a kindly act, from one who was bringing up a family on a post-office worker's pay. And so through Elton the young Ormsby came to know Charles as well perhaps as anyone was ever to know him, and Margery became something of a favourite with the painter who, to generalise for the sake of brevity, had not much use for women. For a while—for many years, in fact, after Elton's early death—the three were pretty much inseparable. 'Keep them,' Goodfield told Margery, more than once, 'keep those daubs I lent you young ones years back. It's the least I can do.' Although that detail is not so important, as the next most certainly is.

Goodfield owned what was little more than a shack twenty minutes' drive from Oturehua. A cramped dining room that was also a kitchen, one bedroom with several beds, and ten yards away a big draughty shed with a tiny window where he painted in light most painters would have found inadequate.

'If you can't keep outside in your head for that long,' he said, meaning for long enough to do what he wanted with it on his canvases, 'then you shouldn't go outside.' And after the artist died in an accident where drink, so everyone claimed, was surely a factor, his closest friends forced a small locked door at the end of the shed, which Charles had told them held nothing but junk. And there they found the most celebrated paintings of all. The erotic 'Pasiphae' sequence, a brooding set of defiantly religious motifs, and the 'Waimarama' triptych that finished up in New York.

A few days later the papers carried a photograph that in a sense became notorious, at least to art critics and close friends. It showed the folding screens Charles had picked up for the price of removing them from a Chinese restaurant that went out of business, and scored across with a mix of colour, and lines scratched in the dried paint with the double points of scissors. As scholars would later say, you could note the eclectic referencing even there in the grainy newsprint. But what later became a source of such regret to Margery and Ormsby alike was that from either side of the shoulder-height screen they smiled broadly at each other, and their hands met, one on top of the other's, along the thick wooden board at the top of the painting. After their years together, then the awful public brawling over, of all things, their interpretations of Charles, the photograph brought home to them how much they detested having ever been so close.

Yet their names, to some extent, are still inseparable. In those years together each made rather a thing of how sexually they got on. They sometimes embarrassed friends with uninvited frankness. But as well as their 'rejoicings', as Ormsby always put it, they collaborated too in dating Goodfield's oeuvre. They gathered in a remarkable number of the artist's letters, which he wrote in vivid inks, and fired off to near strangers as much as to old friends. They interviewed and recorded many of those who believed they knew Charles well, and nurtured an ever expanding archive. For Margery and Ormsby saw what few others at the time quite comprehended. That their friend was not simply good, or very good. He was as close as we'd yet got to the real thing, to a vision that could not possibly have come from anywhere but here, yet was like nothing that had happened before. The curators and the backers, as Ormsby loved to point out, were not really in on the act for several years. 'The lassoes of their prose,' as he wrote in his first catalogue note, 'which could bring down anything, were mercifully uncoiled until they got wind of where the stampede was.' He and Margery discovered and promoted and anticipated the lot. And then the partnership was over.

'It was my breasts, basically,' Margery explained to women friends. 'They weren't quite up to scratch.' This she said when Ormsby, emotionally speaking, had long been out of the picture, and she was the *other* expert in all things to do with Goodfield. 'He met Jane, does anyone actually remember her? Even Ormsby knew there wasn't much else going for her. He said to me once, now your head Margery and Jane's body, there's a fantasy for you. Heads lost, which won't surprise you.'

Not that Margery brooded. She moved north, to a less oppressive city. Keeping men off, as she said, that was the problem, not bringing them on. Humour as she found could be a saving grace. She also began to be considered wise. You could always confide in Margery, her best friends at the time would say, because she never holds back about *herself*. There was a certain aura too in being the Goodfield expert. 'Charles,' she would begin, and of course attention was assured. People like an expert, and one who could hint at intimacy was better still. Her life was sociable and diverting and overseas scholars—that's how seriously Charles was now taken—came to interview her. She was acknowledged in prefatory notes and appeared in appendices. The children she had with Elton grew up and did well and only Fran gave her what after all was no more than the faintest concern, when the girl became engaged to a nice enough boy who could not have treated Margery more courteously. He painted the two front rooms for her and liked her slightly risqué stories about well-known people she personally knew, writers in the sixties, university names in the seventies. She visited his parents once, and that of course was that. It was years ago mind, heaven knows what they'd go in for now, but in what they called the sitting room the ceiling was that kind of stippled plaster with flecks of glitter worked into it. It reminded her of the Christmas cave that had been a children's favourite all those years ago in Ballantynes. Fran fortunately decided to drop the boy quite off her own bat.

But again to the Ormsby factor. Presumably something even more pneumatic than Jane had come along, for by the time his much-praised Goodfield biography was on the shelves he was with some smallish university in the States, and with another wife. Although this one actually had a degree in something or other, it may even have been a language. Something anyhow to divert her, as Margery said, between the kitchen and the bedroom.

Margery did not come well out of the biography. It was all of course done by hints and mirrors, for Ormsby was nothing if not feline. Behind an account of her kindliness that Charles had warmed to, a slur was then cast on her flirtatious little notes to him, the suspicion that had he not been set for immortality, Charles may have interested Margery rather less than he did. It was told too that soon after Elton's death, Margery sold the famous panels his father had bought for a song, without informing Charles that a banker now sported them on his walls. There was an ensuing sharp exchange in the press about the dating of one of Charles's rare portraits. A cynical friend from the days of their love affair spread the phrase 'scholarship interruptus'. But the battle lines publicly hardened when it came to interpreting a dark figure in three successive resurrection paintings. This figure was hooded, reluctant, yet the balance of the images—balance was big with Goodfield in the Vietnam years—made it a necessary presence. An elusive communal conscience, Ormsby argued in an elegant essay. Margery's counter was that this, surely, was the indigene, the obligated witness, yet excluded from full presence? As the critical tides turned, Ormsby's reading came to be dismissed as shallowly Jungian, predictably Eurocentric. Margery's was *de rigueur* for any intelligent teacher. Nick Forman of Central Galleries, in his preface to the first major retrospective, noted approvingly that 'she was onto the semantic grid before her contemporaries even knew there was one'.

Margery revelled in so much attention this late in the day. It was almost twenty years since Goodfield had died, more than ten since Ormsby. Young people came to ask her about both men, about the artist primarily of course, but also a few who were interested in biography. ('Supposing,' a bright chit of a thing from an English Department put to her, 'supposing biography is any longer a viable genre, that is.') Margery believed she made their visits worthwhile. Certainly they left with the conviction that she had brought them closer to both men. They liked it when she put them so at ease and began to speak quietly of 'Charles', or said, 'Now I really don't know if I've ever touched on this before.' And some detail, some little characteristic of the man emerged, which they departed with like bearers of a relic. How precious their time with her seemed! As the colours receded from the expanse of water below them, and the room they sat in high above the harbour took on a silvery floating ambience, she would suggest, with just a hint in her voice that this was rather pushing a special occasion,'Why not a little gin?' An hour or two later, as they sat in near darkness, it had become 'drinking by braille' as she said, guessing the depth of what she poured by its splashing, and the weight of the glass. Then in no time she was saying, 'Be a darling there and light those candles, will you? The matches are beside them.'

The candles burned back from the big mirror above the polished table. The scent of flowers that were always somewhere in the room seemed suddenly more present. The two Goodfields on either side of the fireplace were dark brooding fields. And much later as she nipped out to what she coyly called 'the girls' room', knowing exactly how her guest was utterly held by it all, by the confidences, by her frankness about sex, and her interest too in whatever confidences might be given in return, Margery would flick a switch near the door, and the lighting that Ormsby advised her on decades ago leaped out from behind its opaque shields, and the paintings—two of the *famous* paintings—were living and vivid and suddenly on the walls. One with its diagonal rush of ochre, a colour only there in the painter's last twelve months, and the companion canvas from almost half a century before, its dappled chunky planes tilted and stacked as though light and shading cascaded towards the viewer. When Margery came back with a plate of crackers and gherkins (part also of these legendary visits) she said, 'Odd that there is so much figurative work between these two yet not a flicker, is there, of "reality" so to speak hinted at in either of them?' Alpha and Omega, she said, was what she called them to herself. 'The whole of Charles pretty much comes between the two.'

Only very occasionally did her charm, her openness, not quite come off. A sharpish Australian curator believed he saw through what was simply an elderly woman taking herself too seriously as a cultural event. 'And what did it come down to?' he said, diverting friends back home in a wine bar on North Terrace, 'but gin time with Alpha and bloody O and her story about Goodfield's inept grope in an apricot orchard in Otago or wherever it was. She believes she is opening the doors of perception but she might as well call it cock-tale hour.' Most showed more respect. Margery was an indispensable link with so much that interested them. Clive Evans was one of a group who once heard the Australian sounding off, and had put him in his place. Clever Clive Evans whom few people cared for. He quoted Wittgenstein's advice on keeping silent when understanding is beyond us. He said it with the wide thin smile that made people wary of him, his head tilted so the light skidded across his small circular glasses.

Clive had served notice of what was to come with his early monograph on South Island landscapes the year after he left art school. The sixty pages were perceptive and informed and brightly written, which was bad enough. It was also a merciless dismissal of the art historian who had taught him a great deal, a now-retired professor who had insisted to anyone who attended to him that if there was going to be a new critical voice to make them all sit up, then here it was, young Evans. The jokes in the book, rather cruelly, were in the curt, dry style of the man who had sung his praises.

He was now working on Goodfield. 'Great in spite of almost everything he tried to do,' a further declaration that cosiness was not to be his thing. 'He liked painting religious after-death scenes,' he told a Wellington conference. 'He liked the formal rigidity of depositions, because the female figures obligatory in that tradition served as a protective mask. Because he did not have the courage to paint the scenes in gay saunas that the natural secularist in him would far have preferred.' He tapped the control of the slide projector and the screen at the front of the lecture room lit up with a near-naked male body on a cloth whose design suggested tapa cloth. The grouping of the figures was traditional yet disconcerting. A long beach curved away behind the set piece until it spread, a flat Byzantine gold, to fill the back of the canvas. 'Notice,'

Clive Evans said, 'the cadaver's head on the lap of a figure you cannot be certain is female and yet we presume, because of tradition, must be. A conjunction heightened by two standing and clearly male figures, needlessly undraped should you consider the actual occasion. This is beach boy fantasy at Club Golgotha. A brilliant painting not only technically but because it *hovers* between what we see and what we know we almost see. As soon as we realise that *almost*, then of course we are seeing something else. What the picture actually is.' He enjoyed the discomfort as he went even further. 'All this Yeatsian highfalutin "holy fire", this high art iconic moment. And yet at the same time its deliberate indecency. Look carefully at those folds, those angles.' The little red light of his pointer ran across the loin cloth of the dead figure. 'A badly concealed hard-on covered by a tea-towel.'

Margery joined the herd and thoroughly disliked what she had heard of the young man. When he phoned and then came up to speak with her, he sat without being invited in the Morris cretonne armchair she had for years regarded as her own. This meant his head, instead of hers, was silhouetted against the dying of the light, his face impossible to read. Clive Evans, who of course had heard of her hospitality, her conversational largesse, also refused the gin she offered him. He told her, 'Life tends to jump around with alcohol. I prefer to respect my critical eye.'

'I've looked at Charles's work for so long,' Margery came back at him, 'I'll begin with my usual double.' But Evans was not here for pleasantries. He did not waste time. The ice still chinked against the sides of her glass as he homed in on what, after all, was his only business for sitting there. He put it to her bluntly. 'You don't like what I write?'

'I haven't read it carefully enough,' she said. She thought it a reasonable evasion.

'Of course you have.' Evans even laughed, quite pleasantly.

'We always read carefully anything that threatens us. It's possibly the only thing we're not tempted to skim.'

Margery felt the chill of what she was up against. Yet she understood with an instinct that curiously upset her that the young man was not here to hurt her. It was something colder than that. He would not care if he did, but that was not his intent. Which meant her own weakness came in on her. She was aware of herself in a way she did not enjoy. She heard her little evasive parries, the usual trotting out of remarks, some coy, some risqué, that for years had amused and drawn out and edged those she talked with towards their own confidings. She saw herself as a conniving ageing woman with a glass in her hand, imagining she cut something of a figure. Girlish, decades too late. She was unsettled as she thought of it, at being *made* to think of it. She found herself saying, 'I used to smoke.' She smiled towards him, letting him know she was nervous. 'It hasn't helped, has it, giving it up?'

The young man told her, 'My mother smoked too. Only she didn't give it up.' But his statement, personal as it was, did not have the effect of bringing them closer. He is even worse than I thought, Margery considered. There is nothing that will touch him. Then as if picking up the drift of her thinking, he told her, 'There is nothing personal in this. But Goodfield interests me because he was so brilliant in one way and such a fraud in another. You and Ormsby were his closest friends.'

'Only at one stage,' she said, 'were we really close.'

But Evans was not interested in what she said to him. His interest was in telling her how 'Ormsby I expect he liked because he was handsome and because intellectually he understood to some extent what the paintings did as distinct from what they attempted to do. You offered him something else. A mirror for the side Ormsby didn't know and didn't need to know. Like that thing you wrote on the hooded observer. The muddled side. The fraud in him.'

Margery knew she was good at least at appearing self-possessed. She said, 'That's a novel insult.'

Evans seemed not to hear her. He kept on. 'You don't really look at a picture, do you? You think of what you should say about it. Words not paint. Goodfield did that too, oddly enough. But with him it didn't matter because he'd already done it, got the painting over with before the saying. You only had the talk. Which disgusted Ormsby, incidentally.'

Margery said, 'And you know all this, do you? Some rare gift to proclaim what people you never met in fact thought about things?' A vein in her neck thickened with irritation. She hoped her voice did not give away quite how much he had rattled her. For a long moment that made her think there, he will have to admit his conceit if nothing else, Clive Evans said nothing. Then he told her, a certain roughness in his voice that might be contempt, or simply a catch in his throat, 'I know all this for certain because I have Ormsby's diaries.' He then sat there, adding nothing by way of explaining how, how and where, for God's sake, they had fetched up from.

Margery knew Ormsby used to write in school exercise books he carried about with him in his canvas haversack. She had assumed that he jotted drafts for articles, notes for his lectures. Or wrote down perhaps what Goodfield said to him. He liked drawing the artist out on politics. On childhood. The biography must have been in his mind even then. But she said now, 'Ormsby had a gift for fiction. A gift like that doesn't just come out in novels.'

Clive Evans began to recite. 'It is eight o'clock and the light across the Hawkduns so vital, CG says, to the point one waits to hear the hillside pant. In comparison M, semi-naked at the window, her breasts flaccid plates, is an ensemble he calls, when she does not hear him, "mildly repellent". He began to paint her but grew bored. She likes sitting like that, in front of both of us. Thinks nakedness a personal attribute, which makes her in some way special. No, CG says . . .'

'Shut up,' Margery demanded. What surprised her was her own feeling. Not anger. Not outrage. What was it then—a kind of boredom at the memory forced back on her? Not even that. A boredom with herself, suddenly, a dry deep nothingness as she thought, what is it I feel? Irritation, too, as she looked across at the young man watching her. But that was of the surface, that hardly mattered.

'There's more,' Clive Evans told her. The slight alteration in his voice told her he was again quoting. 'Later in the evening. One woman. Two men. Even though one was gay.' And his own assessment. 'Ormsby wrote concisely.'

Margery said, 'Goodfield's dead. Ormsby's dead. Isn't that enough?'

Her visitor smiled. 'Voltaire said only the truth is good enough for the dead.' Then, in the closest he could come perhaps to speaking placatingly, Evans said, 'You asked me how I know, Margery. I was telling you how. So you'd believe me.'

It was several minutes then while neither spoke. Clive took off his watch and placed it on the broad rounded arm of the chair he sat in, and rubbed his wrist as though the strap had been too tight. Then after some time when his hands lay in his lap, he picked up the watch and returned it to his wrist. 'It is a matter of being reasonable,' he said.

Margery did not much care what he meant. Her mind was back in the wooden hut, in the landscape whose expansiveness oppressed her, although it came at Charles so differently. 'The elation of the place,' he kept repeating. He told his younger friends to sit there, by an outcrop of grey rock, or to move into the shadow of a boulder, as he used their bodies, their mass and outline, to give him perspective, weight, whatever it was he required of them as he tore through one after another of the Hawkdun sketches in which no human figures were apparent. When the young man spoke to her now across the quiet, fading room she was brought back, abruptly, from the memories that had stayed with her from those weeks together, the arid unsalvageable spaces of the country, the men's bodies in the blue half-light. The feeling then of emptiness came over her more strongly, as though something had tilted and her life was pouring from her. It was as though she dreamed while still awake. She imagined the shallow glitter of water move over featureless expanses, but what the water brought was not fertility but simply fear. As she watched the dark smoothness of Clive Evans's shaved and almost perfectly circular head against the sky behind it, she felt not even mockery directed at her, but something deeper sweeping to her like some natural and inevitable force. *That Ormsby had felt sorry for her.* All the time he had thought that.

Evans was speaking again. He said, 'Of course, apart from the sections directly to do with the paintings.'

'Yes?' She startled at his voice, as though their silence lasted so much longer than it had. He wrongly took it for affectation, her sudden exaggerated movement. He disliked that in her as well. He repeated for her, 'Apart from the bits to do with Goodfield's paintings, I've destroyed the rest.'

But surely, the power he held if he owned the diaries? The importance of the things to scholars? She was confused and misunderstood him. Should she offer him a painting? Everyone has his price. But Evans was ahead of her. He said, 'Who on earth did you think details like that would interest?' His tone diminished her. It asked as well did she take him for a mere biographer, a hack of some sort scrabbling to recover what long was past? In his interest in Charles she had not even a minor part. And there Margery had her first glimpse of understanding Evans. He was the zealot who would purify, who would burn away the dross. She was part of that, part of what stood in the way. But in the way of what?

He was now explaining to her. 'The way we look at art,' he said, 'the way we've talked about it since Vasari, since whenever. Anecdotes, laundry bills, school cert marks. The human muck that stops us *looking*.' She understood his searing clarity. The aesthete as killer. The destroyer of frames so that only the naked canvas flared in its own existence. As he spoke he was looking beyond her to the painting on the wall between the fireplace and the door.

Margery said to him, 'You don't believe in anything else?'

'No,' he said. 'I don't. Not even what I say about them myself.' He stood and smiled at her, but it was a little like imagining Calvin smiling from one of those portrait illustrations at the front of ancient books. Evans expanded. He said, 'What I write. What I say. That's dross as well. But mine makes people look in spite of themselves. What you say is to make people look at you.' He walked towards the door.

She called to him so he turned. She felt his hard impatience with almost everything that confronted him. She noticed how his fingers opened and closed in his jacket pocket, although the rest of his body was still as though carved in the door frame. She asked him, 'Why then?' She meant why tell her then? Find evidence and then destroy it? Hurt so much, and then assume the hurt did not exist? She repeated, 'Why?'

Clive Evans told her. 'Goodfield,' he said. 'To leave only him.' As though the lives that touched the painter were nothing now but ash.

Margery waited to hear the front door click behind him. Nothing she supposed could be pared back further, nothing restored. She stood and crossed the room and touched the switch for the carefully angled lighting beneath the pictures that had been a talking point, a starting point, for years. She came back and sat in the chair which until tonight had been only hers. There was nothing for the moment she wanted to look at. Charles least of all.

Family Unit

Life changed at the Mokau River. Tribal boundaries as much as geography and local customs. 'History so often altered tack at rivers,' she said. Bernice Irwin spoke as the forest-green Volvo was obliged to slow down behind a stock truck with viscous calf shit dribbling from beneath its palings. At the same moment she glimpsed the big stone embedded in concrete behind stumpy pillars and painted chains. 'That's the Tainui anchor stone.' Declared, rather than said it. This was her territory, history, after all. Such details were hers to announce.

'What's Tainui?' Stevie asked.

'The outfit behind the worst rugby league team in the history of the game,' his father said. 'I thought that stone was tied round the entire back line but I've got it wrong. Someone must have hocked it off to help pay for the corporate box.'

'Do you have to Ted?' Bernice said. Not even anger in her voice, simply a weariness that he boiled over so easily.

A girl spoke from the back seat. Lily was fifteen. Her voice was confident, mildly dismissive of those she spoke to. This surely was her right now that she had found the Truth. Her best friend had taken her three months ago to the Assembly of God. She had been inundated with warmth and a spreading shimmer that her father, watching the mudflats from the veranda above Cox's Creek, described to his wife as tidal. 'It will go out as quickly as it came in.' For the moment, faith was on the flood.

Lily said, 'We ignore history at our peril, Father.'

Her eleven-year-old brother had come to swearing at much the same time as her own conversion. He loved its disruptive power.

'God,' he said, 'friggen wanker,' not bothering even to raise his voice.

'Mum!' Lily shouted. 'Don't you even care he talks like that!'

'Don't show off, Stevie,' Bernice said.

'Only the second commandment,' Lily said. 'Not that God's word matters, does it? Not if it's Stevie.'

The car lurched as it took the long bridge across the river.

'I meant the Warriors,' her brother defended. 'The whole world knows they're wankers.'

'For Christ's sake,' Ted said, 'how do you expect me to drive with this zoo?'

'That's the second time,' Lily said. 'In thirty seconds!'

'Twenty,' Stevie said. 'Can't even count.'

'I told you not to show off,' Bernice said. She turned and leaned across and her hand slapped down at her son's white skinny thigh. She clipped him harder than she intended. But Stevie rallied and shoved his sister hard on her chest. Thought she was so cool, didn't she, just because she had tits. As if the rest of the world had never seen them before. 'Slag,' he told her.

Bernice's hand slapped on him again. The stone in her engagement ring flashed like a drop of falling water.

'Leave him, can't you!' Ted said to her. His own voice now louder than he liked to hear it. And saying it again. 'Christ!'

Lily said quietly, 'That's it. That's it then, Dad.' She scrabbled at the lock of her door and had no doubt, at least for several seconds, that she would simply rather get out. She didn't care how fast they were going, she would not ride with blasphemy.

'Lily!' As Bernice turned yet again she glimpsed the smear of moving roadway as the back door opened. Ted braked as the car left the bridge and swung in towards the grass verge. There was a moment of what later Bernice called 'cluttered' silence, the car lurching onto uneven ground and rocking to a halt. No one spoke. Even Lily knew not to push her luck and invoke the Lord. The car had turned half-circle and the family, at the beginning of their weekend away, looked at the dull brown stretch of river. Stevie snivelled and leaned his head on the back of his mother's seat. Bernice's hand stroked his hair. Ted looked in the rear-vision mirror at his daughter's pretty, frightened face. 'You all right?' he said. 'Lily?'

'Yes, Dad,' she told him.

He turned the car back onto the road. 'Then if no one minds,' he said, 'we'll push on to Morrieson's, shall we?'

The motelier glanced at the form his guest had just filled in. Ted held out his hand for the key with its black plastic tag and embossed number eight.

'A "T" is that?' the nuggety man put to him. As if there was no holding out here, believe you me.

Ted already dreaded the thought of it, the two days in what looked like a State house with a tip about itself, the red brick hoop of units around its patch of grass, its trampoline, its pint-sized pool two adults could scarcely splash in at the same time. Bernice had picked the place out of a brochure. 'Matrimony,' that's what she had said, serious-jokey in a way that irritated him. 'Matrimony needs the odd brush-up, don't you agree?', which meant she had phoned three hundred kilometres away, booked the motel, informed the children, and then told him. The enormity of it came in on him now, as he saw the owner of the place eyeing him with what, he supposed, was meant to pass muster as shrewdness. To think all this was actually planned, four bloody hours in a vehicle with a wife who thought premeditated flirting with her own husband was a cure for middle age, four hours with a foul-mouthed child whose intellectual horizon was to sit at a computer downloading songs and an adolescent driven by God knows what to sing hymns, non-stop as good as, between Pokeno and Te Kuiti. Until he could not take another verse and had bellowed out to the same tune as she herself was singing. 'What a friend we have in hormones.' Even Stevie, the little turncoat, had shouted at him, 'Shut up, Dad.' While Lily, milking the drama of it, said in the mild voice the Master may have used when reprimanding Peter for cutting off a non-believer's ear, 'It's better if you don't go on like that. It only shows how *small* you are.' Certainly he was in no mood now for chat with this chirpy bugger whose finger prodded at the form lying between them on the counter. 'T?' asking it again.

'Ted,' Ted said.

'Clarry,' the other man told him. He rubbed a thick forearm with his opened hand. It sounded like sandpaper. Ted was aware that his own hands were office-soft.

'Tell you what,' the amiable Clarry said. 'I know what it's like driving with a carload of kids on a warm afternoon. Drop the good lady off and you'll find the bar within crawling distance.'

'Thanks,' Ted said. This was only Taranaki but it made him think of their honeymoon in New Caledonia. Even when he had thought of something to say to the locals he was unable to say it.

Clarry took his guest's courtesy for acceptance. He looked across his shoulder through the office window. He saw his wife crossing to unit eight with a carton of milk and said, lowering his voice simply for the effect of it, 'Pity Lisa's not on this arvo. That would've been another reason to quench the thirst.' He winked, conspirators together. 'Two good reasons, matter of fact.' Then, because he may have come on a touch too familiar, Clarry looked past Ted to the sleek dark car where the family waited. 'Nice to drive, like the ads say?'

'I'll know one day,' Ted said. 'When I don't have to think about something else.'

Clarry clicked his tongue, which Ted guessed was dialect for 'You needn't tell me about that one, son'.

Ted closed the car door, switched on the ignition, and placed the key to the unit in his wife's opened palm. 'Number eight,' he said.

'You were long enough in there,' Bernice said. 'These two are at it again.'

'If she'd just lay off saying the Bible at me,' Stevie complained.

'See?' Bernice said.

'Yes, love,' Ted said. He eased the car round the drive towards the far unit. Clarry stood at the top of the steps, taking in the car's purring movement. He raised one thumb and jerked it slightly.

'I will bet you,' Ted said, 'any money you can think of, Stevie, that that man just said "Nice one".'

'I don't even know what you're on about,' Stevie said. And Ted did not know either that Clarry turned back into the office with the frowzy cat he'd have had put down years back if it hadn't been for the wife, and said, 'Aucklanders. You can smell them a mile off.'

Bernice said, 'You two bring in whatever's in the boot, OK?' and slid the unit door along its metal grooves. There was the faintly acrid smell of a newly cleaned carpet, before she took in the sky-blue duvet on the double bed and the matching settee that was another bed in disguise, waiting to be found out. There was a television so much smaller than the one at home that she anticipated Stevie's whine of complaint. The pale lemon walls were broken by the big square of a print, sailing boats flat and toy-like on a sea as blue as the divan. The carpet, thank heavens, was a neutral grey, what Bernice sometimes called 'family shading' because Ted's rellies, collectively, had much the same effect—inoffensive, colourless. As she stepped towards the kitchen area, the generous figure of the proprietor's wife rose from where she had placed the complimentary milk in the colour-coordinated lemon fridge. The woman turned and started. Both women shrieked together.

'Betty!' Bernice cried. 'It's Betty Benton!'

'Bernice! Someone pinch me will they!'

The women threw themselves together with the force of twenty years gone by without clapping eyes on each other. Ted heard the racket as he unloaded the boot and handed carry-bags, a chilly-bin and a carton of walking shoes to his reluctant children. He stepped to the door, tugging back the lightweight curtain so forcefully he heard the rip above his head as the material went limp in his hand. He saw his wife's arm around a dumpy woman's waist, while the stranger's hand, like a busy white crab, brushed over his wife's shoulders and along her cheek. Bernice beamed across at him. 'Training Coll,' she called out to him. 'Can you imagine that? We even flatted together in Glenmore Street.'

'Flatted!' the other woman said. 'Slummed it, don't you mean?'

Ted strained to show interest. 'You must be Linda?' he said.

The women shrieked again, their arms flailing, swimmers in distress. 'Linda Donovan!' Betty said. 'You'd need to bundle six of her together to make one of me!'

Ted thought, unkindly, how could a woman get such a kick out of looking like that, then joking about it? It was Joan of Arc lighting her own faggots.

'Betty,' Bernice repeated. 'Betty who would have been our bridesmaid, Ted, if she hadn't been leering it up in Sydney.'

'Less said about that lot the better,' Betty said, her eyes big and rolling towards the office and a presumably unenlightened spouse.

'Clarry's wife?' Ted guessed.

'Got it in one.' Betty smiled back at him. He thought what a bastard he must be to see his wife enjoying herself so much while he resented everything about it. He tried to look jolly even as he realised that he had never used that word in his life about anything. *Jolly* for Christ's sake! He'd no more use it than Bernice would say 'leering it up', and yet that had happened too. He disliked everything about what was going on.

A moment later they all—Bernice, Ted, Betty, the kids—looked towards the tall shape who eased back the sagging curtain and stood outlined against the afternoon sky. He was like a stick figure. He wore nothing but black, with two startlingly pale bands of naked flesh in the inches between the sleeves of his T-shirt and the top of the long mittens that stretched to above his elbows. There was a small silver skull on a black cord around his throat. His jeans tapered down to leather boots, where the skull motif was echoed in metal buckles. His hair was a dark stubble above a face preternaturally white. A nose stud glittered as his head turned and he took them in, then attended only to Lily. Very slowly his tongue emerged between his black lips, until another metal stud, the size of a ballbearing, popped into view. He looked at Lily with what he believed was a transfixing beam. 'Boris,' he said, his voice husky, irresistible. He then hitched at the rim of one of the high mittens so the bands of exposed pale flesh matched as exactly as bangles.

Ted was the only one who reacted. Almost as quietly as the Goth, he said, 'I'd get that pathetic arse out of here, son, before I boot your ring through that black gob of yours.' He was amazed at his own vehemence. Never in his life had he spoken so rudely to anyone. Was this part of the stress, he wondered, that Bernice insisted was getting him down? The stick figure backed out and slid into the afternoon. Betty shrieked yet again, tapping at Bernice's arm. 'Celeste Boddy's youngest, would you believe that?'

'Celeste's here too!' Bernice said, her voice higher, more girlish, than her family had ever heard it.

'Brilliant, apparently,' Betty confirmed. 'Band of his own. Drums like an angel.' She went on to say how Celeste had married into *old* Canterbury money although her husband apparently had let a sheep station turn to custard so to speak and had no definable interests beyond breeding birds.

'Birds?' Bernice said. There was too much coming in—wasn't that the phrase her psychologist friend used about stress, about not quite being on top of the information swill that was modern life? 'He what?'

'There's a convention in town this weekend,' Betty said. 'Bird fanciers of the world unite,' which set the women off again, swathed in killing nostalgia.

Lily looked with contempt at her mother and her mother's friend. She opened the small-print Bible she carried with her most places and found the Song of Solomon, which she had never heard mentioned at the Assembly of God but decided she didn't half mind reading as her very own discovery. She had thought the stud on the tongue something special too. 'You always ruin things, Dad,' she said. 'Do you mean to do it, or is it just that you can't help it?'

Ted sighed, jangled the change in his trouser pocket, and turned from the unit. He leaned against the door jamb, looking out at the carpark. Two men stood at the back of a four-wheel drive, lifting with almost exaggerated care a large box from the vehicle on to the ground. When it turned side on he saw the wire mesh and realised it was a cage of cockatoos. There was a quick panicking flutter of wings as the cage tilted and then settled on the ground. He could feel for the birds. For some reason not apparent to him a quote from Stage II English more than twenty years before came into his mind. 'Most men'—wasn't that how it went?—'live lives of quiet desperation.' He couldn't remember who said it.

'What are you saying?' Stevie asked him.

'Muttering,' Ted said, 'that's all.' He was surprised that the boy edged in against him, leaning on him as he used to do until a year or so ago when the idea of affection towards his parents turned overnight to anathema. But he pressed against him now and his father was grateful for it. He touched his son's rough, tangled hair and said, 'All right there are we, cobber?' Stevie looked up at him. He said, 'That was wicked what you said to him, Dad. Telling that dick to piss off like that.'

Ted walked around the town. The tall concrete water tower seemed to loom over him at every turn. But he could see why his wife liked the place, and he hoped the long drive, the couple of idle days, would do them good. The town was compact and neat. It was laid out. It didn't come by chance. He thought of Huntly, of Levin, the towns of his own childhood, which he loathed in memory. This was pastureland and immaculate paddocks that became a town for a few hundred yards, then again turned back into pasture and paddocks, after the interruption of asphalt and clumped commercial buildings and ordered streets. He walked along a side road, past Cudby's Family Funeral Home and a second-hand shop with high, old-fashioned hospital bed-ends stacked along one wall.

Ted pondered, in a vague way, how he quite liked the idea of order until it took him over and then he hated it. Well, grew bored with it anyway. Bernice, on the other hand, loved it more than anything in the world. Which is why she made lists of tasks for the family to do and attached them to the front of the fridge with magnetic sunflowers; why she told you her schoolteacher titbits as you drove through the country, because that put the past in order as well. Sometimes when they visited friends he yearned for the mess he glimpsed through half-closed bedroom doors or saw kitchen shelves where neatness had quite broken down. Yet the thought of Bernice not there to do it, not ordering the sun and the moon, as he put it when they argued together, was inconceivable. That was looking into the gulf. He now sat at a pavement table in the neatly cobbled main street and thought of his panic last year when she was sick. He thought, thank God I don't need to think of that. Not any longer. A basket of geraniums bloomed above his head. He smiled at the friendly girl who told him it was cappuccino or nothing when he asked for a latte. As he waited he watched the groups at the other tables. Bernice's being ill had brought home to him what mattered and what did not. And her back teaching again and as good as cleared by her specialist, and yet this gloom, so often, even now when there was no need for it. Here he was within spitting distance of a partnership in the firm, and both the kids were certainly brighter than he had been at school, even if Lily drove him up the wall at the moment and Stevie had a tongue like the inside of a sewer.

'There we are,' the girl said, putting the coffee in front of him. The cinnamon froth had spilled over the side and ran in streaks towards the pool at the bottom of the saucer. 'That's perfect,' Ted told her. The girl moved back and the geraniums swayed their bright red clots as her shoulder nudged against them. He felt a touch sorry for himself, drinking coffee alone like this. Because Bernice, when he had asked if she fancied a walk, said she would read her novel for a bit, did he mind? 'Remember I was brought up round here,' she said. 'Stratford, anyway. I don't *need* to see it.'

'It was your idea,' he reminded her.

'To come here,' she said. 'Not to have to gawp at it.'

She would have the unit to herself for an hour or so at least. It was odd, she supposed, how she liked motels, yet she was hardly ever in one. Ted was so convinced the family bach where he spent his own boyhood was everyone else's idea of a perfect holiday as well. She disliked the sea, in fact, although that wasn't something she let on even to Lily. This was as close as you could expect to get to bliss, she supposed, after a certain age—or was that too sardonic? A room that wasn't your own, dishes you didn't have to do, a story to slip into when no one else was around. Those car trips too—she wondered why they gave her such pleasure, especially since her illness, simply sitting there, thinking of nothing in particular, watching hills rise and recede, the coastline running its scribble on and on. Safety and distance and hints of infinity, so many things rubbing together and yet no compulsion, no desire much even, to untangle them, to sort things out. Simply to think, this is all happening, I am the centre of all this.

How she loved it, for instance, even this afternoon, when they first saw the mountain. She had seen it almost every day for the first twelve years of her life, before the Power Board shifted her father south. She had liked those nights when her father and a group of men in oilskins and heavy boots stood in the kitchen and drank whisky from small thick glasses and said they'd start the search again at dawn. She would lie in bed, while the wind shook the house like the dice box when they played Ludo, and watch the skinny strips of light beneath her bedroom door and hear her father's boots clunk on the floor in the next room. Two or three times a year someone would be lost on the mountain. Most times they were found, and her mother would say how an experience like that aged them. Young men looked middle-aged if they'd been up there for days, 'battling the elements'. Her mother always said that. And once or twice the lost were not found until they were dead, and there was an English woman called Phoebe who was never found at all. Bernice had thought of her this afternoon. Still somewhere up there, she supposed, as she had supposed when she was a girl and tried to imagine it,

Phoebe, whose name made her think of fluffy pale hair, lying against the ugly scoria, the English coins from her dropped purse sprinkled around her. Even now, that's how Bernice visualised the bones that were never recovered, the sixpences and shillings that would tell you, the minute you picked them up, where the bones had come from. 'Your heart goes out,' her mother had said, when she unrolled the paper from New Plymouth and the young blond woman looked straight at them. 'Your heart goes out to her parents, God help them.'

Bernice let the novel lie open on her chest. Even those pictures, she thought, even motel bedroom pictures she quite liked for a night or two. Lion Rock rested on the sea like a chunk of blancmange on a plate. And another picture that up close said 'View from Fanthams Peak', showing a swirl of competing greens across a shoulder of ash. They were art class stuff, but she liked them. Someone had taken the trouble. It was real paint; you could tell if you licked your finger and prodded them. It was one mind, one gift, however limited, taking life in on its own terms, then trying to put it down for someone else to look at. 'There,' the pictures said, 'this is real because it is mine.' Yet she'd have hated them at home.

'Minimalist,' she had said to Ted when she bought them their joint Christmas present. 'It soothes, doesn't it?' 'So does aspirin,' Ted said. They laughed together and knew they would never see most things the same way. And he made love to her on the sofa beneath the exquisite black picture she had looked at over his shoulder while he lost his breath, and 'Yes,' she had said to him quietly, 'yes,' and held him against her. They would never be closer than that, although this was something Ted failed to understand. It was never enough, wherever he was. At work. With the children. With her, especially. What more could she give him, what else was there for her to declare? And yet his feeling, she knew, that she was somehow holding back. As if there were something to her beyond his knowing, beyond what she gave. If only she could make him see. He looked at life as that painter there tried to look at a view: there were demarcations and blocks, this part so different to that, and over it all there was *placing* things, there was control. But it couldn't be like that. You walked through the dapple of so many competing things. It was the flow of them, not the pattern, that made this day real and the next quite as real again. And it was so hard to put into words. You said what you knew, the way the poetry she taught to the bursary girls said as much as it could, but then there was the point when it could say no more—the flow kept on, but you were here. That's all you could say.

'Mum?'

Bernice turned to Stevie, who stood at the bedroom door. What on earth was the boy carrying? She raised herself on her elbow, and her book clattered to the floor. 'I was completely out to it,' she said. 'Sorry, love.' Then, taking in the solemn moon face level there against her son's, 'Who on earth have you got there?'

'Charlie,' Stevie said. 'Charlie belongs to Lisa.' He jerked his arm so that the child's weight was more easily managed. He laughed. 'See him?' How long was it since she had heard him laugh like that, in sheer good humour, the surly foul-mouthed yobbo that so distressed his father quite discarded.

'And who is Lisa?' Bernice said.

'She's in the kitchen,' Stevie told her. 'She's cool.' A word that could not carry a fraction of what was in the boy's mind as he said it.

The woman had turned from bending at the stove as he looked in at her from the corridor. She wore a green dress that went almost to her feet and as she stood up, he could not believe how lovely the long fall of her hair looked as she flicked it back; and her arms, which were this colour like honey, rose and scooped great handfuls of her hair and settled it behind her head. As she turned from the stove the front of her dress had fallen forward and there was nothing underneath, only Them, big as grapefruit. He felt his face flare as though someone held a torch beneath it, because she'd seen him looking; but she just held his eye and smiled at him. She did not even ask him who he was or what he was doing there, looking down her dress. Instead she said to him, as though she'd been talking to him already and was carrying on from there, 'Twelve people in for dinner tonight, the chef's late and now the stove's on the blink.'

A baby in a high-chair behind the kitchen table clattered a plastic plate onto the tiled floor. 'Don't you start,' she told the baby, smiling still, not raising her voice in the least. Stevie bent to take up the rolling plate that ran towards him like a hoop. His fingers scrabbled the dab of mashed whatever it was from the floor and flicked it at the edge of the plate.

'You could get Clarry if you like,' the woman told him. When she talked to him her eyes were right on his, holding him as if she'd set him there until she decided to let him go. He looked back because he knew she wouldn't mind. And he still said nothing, glazed with an enchantment he had no idea of defining because he had never known such a thing before. She told him, 'That old guy with hair like a dunny brush? Reckon you can find him?'

'Reckon,' Stevie told her. He found the man she wanted, who was tightening the canvas on the trampoline.

'Only children up to ten,' the man said, when he saw the boy beside him. 'Can't have you big jokers bouncing on it.'

Clarry was unaware how he withered in the boy's contempt. 'She wants you,' Stevie said.

Clarry seemed amused. 'She's the cat's mother,' he said, 'haven't you ever heard that?'

Stevie—taking in the bristled hair, the fat nose, the grin

where one tooth was such a different colour from the others—thought, you dopey old dork. But for *her* sake he said politely, 'The lady in the kitchen. She wants you right away.'

Stubblehead winked at him and said, 'The trouble with ladies, that, take my word for it.' He slapped one hand against the edge of the trampoline and hooted. Stevie thought, have I missed a joke or something? And why wasn't shitface here jumping when she asked for him? 'The stove,' he said. 'It's on the blink.'

'That's news is it?' Clarry said. He seemed amused all over again.

Back in the big kitchen the baby was bawling and smashing a spoon against the tray of its high-chair. The lady, who was lovelier than anyone Stevie had ever seen, looked as though she might cry. Her hair had fallen forward again and covered half her face. Clarry grunted and crouched and looked into the oven—like some old perv looking in a window, Stevie thought. He pulled at a lever at the bottom of the oven and pressed a switch beside the dials. There was a 'pop' where the gas jet sprang up and the old joker's face turned blue in the light. He said to Lisa, as he grunted again and stood up, 'I'll send Betty across to help out. That bird mob can be a handful.'

'Quiet, Charlton,' Lisa said. Stevie hated to think how upset she was, how frazzled, as his grandmother would say when someone got bothered like this. Then he thought of something brilliant. It was like those drawings in comics when 'Wham!' is written in big letters and there's a splashy flash over everything. He saw Lisa bending over near the high-chair to pick up the child's furiously thrown spoon. Her dress fell forward again. Even more than before. He said, 'I could take him for a walk if you like. I wouldn't scare him.'

'Oh, would you though?' Lisa said. She hoisted the child from his wooden cage, rubbing his face with a hanky she wore in the puffy top of her sleeve, before she handed him across.

'He loves being with men,' she said. Stevie felt the pelting in his chest. Then the most extraordinary thing happened. After he had taken the boy, who had stopped his racket just like that, Lisa said, 'Oh, you don't know how sweet you are doing this!' and kissed the top of Stevie's head. He would look after the baby for a year if she wanted him to. Then she said, 'Talk nicely to him and he'll be good as gold.' Talk nicely, is that all it took? He'd show her what talking nicely was.

'So I'm taking care of him,' he told his mother when she looked up. He'd never seen her so surprised. Or Dad, if it came to that, who came into the unit behind him. 'It's five o'clock,' Dad said. 'I've walked around for two hours and there's nothing else to see.'

'I reckon I'll take him for a walk by myself,' Stevie said. 'I've got his pushchair out here.' Charlie, delighted at hearing his favourite word, jigged on Stevie's arm and tugged at his hair. His minder laughed and grabbed the fat jerking wrist. 'Come off it,' he said. 'You'd better behave or you'll know about it.'

'My God,' Bernice said, when her son had left the unit and the wheels of the pushchair crunched on the metal path outside the window. 'Are there miracles, Ted, are there?'

'There's worse than miracles,' her husband said. He had seen one at the last corner as he walked back from the main street. High up, where you'd expect visions to take place, he had spotted the concrete tower and Lily standing on its platform, her arm flung out to whatever it was she saw. Beside her, thin and black as a tarred broom, stood the Goth he had ordered from his sight. Ted was appalled and puzzled. He experienced, as he did quite often these days, the sense that certainties wobbled, that the ground tremored beneath him. His fastidious God-bothering daughter against the skyline with *that*!

'The young like being together,' Bernice reminded him.

'No one's choosy much at that age.' She put her hand across his. 'It's not the end of the world.' Which Ted may not have conceded had he heard his daughter say, her arm flung towards Mount Taranaki, 'I lift up mine eyes to the Lord, the Lord who giveth joy to my youth.' Or seen the emaciated young man, who had booted in the door at the back of the tower for them to get in, lean towards her and ask, 'How come you talk like that? Are your family foreign?'

Lily had said, 'It's God talking. I'm simply passing it on.'

'He's more of a dude than I thought,' Boris said. And she began, half-chanting for him, the verses she recently had learned.

'Can't you hear that with a decent backing?' her new friend said. He told her to keep going, this jasmine stuff, this flesh like lilies gig, it knocked the shit out of Marilyn Manson. But she stopped when she was halfway through a section she really liked, and looked at him. 'Show me,' she said. 'Show me your tongue, will you?'

He let it emerge slowly, like something that had not seen daylight for a long time. The stud was even bigger than she expected. It looked so bright and silvery and mean. Without asking him even she raised her hand and one finger outstretched, as in the famous ceiling, almost touched its glittering hardness.

'It licks like you wouldn't believe,' he said.

'Shhh!' she told him. Their hands were now very close together on the concrete ledge. She turned from him and said in a voice that made him think she was talking to someone else, but knew he would get a buzz off it as well, 'My love, my dove, my beautiful one.'

And so life in Taranaki seemed to have taken on a fresh glow for the family. It may even have bathed it in a beam that lasted into the next day, had it not been for dinner that evening in the motel's pastel dining room, whose pink table napkins had been folded into upright semicircular fans by Stevie after he'd returned Charlie to his mother. 'You could do something else to help me,' she had said.

Boris the Goth sat at the next table to the Irwins, with a mother who leaned across and joked with Bernice because she too had been at Training Coll, would you believe it? They reminisced about Jack Shallcrass and Jack Lasenby, with whom Celeste had been in love and never dared let on. 'And so I married into Birdsville and Jack wrote upsetting books about teenagers.' She meant that she had married a man whose passion was breeding cage birds, whose study in upper Wadestown would tinkle in an earthquake as the rows of medals swayed on their velvet pads and the trophies jiggled on their shelves. She was waiting for him now. 'The rage he gets in when he doesn't win!' Then the restaurant doors swung back and a dozen enthusiasts, that moment back from the Mokoia Hall where the bird convention met, poured in to take seats at their tables. 'Drinks all round!' Celeste's husband called out. His name was Cliff Macdonald. Elated at having cleaned up for the third successive year in several categories—the Timnek African grey, the green-winged macaw—Cliff now stood behind his wife's chair, his hands on her shoulders. He grinned at the next table as he was introduced, and told Bruce—which was Boris's real name—to shift his uneducated chuff and bring in the bottles from the boot.

A tall man at the doorway balanced in front of him a cage almost too large for him to manoeuvre. In its semi-darkness there was an agitation of wings and shrill avine cries. The milling bird people, still finding their tables, paused in their exuberant chatting. Ted heard a woman in heels so high he expected her to lurch at any moment say beside him, as if to herself, 'Oh no. Not this.' This being, he supposed, what the tall man with a thin sliver of spit glittering across his chin now did. He dropped the cage to the floor and with a wide exaggerated sweep brought his hand round to the catch on the front, and tugged the hook free from its staple. As the man called out, 'You and your birds, Macdonald!' three cockatoos swooped into the dining room. The creatures zoomed across the tables. A sauce bottle twirled and smashed to the floor. One of the birds rose to perch on a curtain rod above the diners, another clawed at the shoulder of a Japanese tourist.

'Sprung,' Bernice's friend announced with enormous coolness as she looked at her husband. The woman in the high heels pushed through the confusion to the tall man behind the grounded cage. She raised one foot behind her, reached back to remove its shoe, then used it to beat the man whose chest she barely reached. He made no effort to stop her, even when the heel ripped open his neat striped shirt. There was a look of great fulfilment about him.

Stevie leaped from his chair, beside himself with the shambles. He shoved at his sister's shoulder, telling her to look, couldn't she, Holy Ghosts all over the fucken show! But Lily was caught in a different drama. She could not believe it and yet there it was, a few feet in front of her. Boris who had lied for her sake about his name now slipped a stiletto from the side of his boot. The blade was not much wider than a nail nor longer than the kind of hatpin you could buy at the Victoria Park Market. One of the birds, perhaps recognising Macdonald, swooped above the next table then whirred, braking, its wings spread wide, balanced in mid-air. A half-second in which the black-mittened arm shot forward. The stiletto flowed with a quick slick of light and there the bird was, impaled, briefly shrieking, then dead, a white heavy rag at the end of the Goth's upraised arm. He tilted the blade so the bird slid onto the pink cloth in front of his father. 'That's from Mum,' he said.

'Jee-zuz!' Stevie said. Before one woman shrieked and

Bernice's friend Celeste from Training Coll, who had been in love but never spoken out, stood up and walked between the tables. Poised and unfussed, she stopped in front of the woman with one shoe who now sat sobbing on a chair just inside the door. She stopped and said to her, so the entire room heard in the now extraordinary hush, 'It's not Macdonald's cock I give a damn about. It's his rotten taste in birds.' Her son walked out behind her, the silence ringing with exhilaration. Then Clarry clapped his hands and said, a touch absurdly, 'Dinner will now proceed as normal.' Already, the efficient Betty was wrapping newspaper round the dead bird that lay, oddly serene, in Cliff Macdonald's lap. There was the sense of order restored. The Japanese addressed their steaks as though such events were local custom.

'That was one choice thing last night,' Stevie said. No one had spoken for a hundred kilometres, until the change of tempo as the tyres left the normal highway for the long Mokau Bridge. The brown placid expanse of the river lay to the right of the car, while over there to the left, Ted imagined the turmoil of the river water meeting with the sea.

Lisa had given Stevie a photo of herself and Charlton, and told him it was a long time since she'd met anyone so helpful. 'You'd be perfect,' she had told him, 'if you didn't swear.' He helped her again in the kitchen that morning, while his parents stayed in bed longer than he'd ever known them to—were they sick or something? Lily was at church with her new friend. Stevie heard Clarry snorting and telling Lisa how that rooster with the god-awful missus had asked him at seven o'bloody clock where the police station was, would you believe it, he needed to report two missing cockatoos?

Then, 'Thoreau,' Ted said suddenly.

'What about him?' Bernice was patting Stevie's hand where it lay on the back of her seat.

'I couldn't think of his name. Yesterday. "Most men live, etcetera". You must know the quote?'

'Most women too,' she said. Ted's fingers spanned just above his wife's knee, as he moved his hand across from the wheel. And risking a joke that might not come off, he half-turned his head to ask Lily, 'What's happened to the Bible there? We haven't heard a quote since the motel.'

'He asked me for it,' Lily said. 'You can't say no to someone who asks for the Word.' And taking in the cosiness between her parents and Stevie sucking up to them, she said, 'No one minds if I get my nipple pierced? No one minds that, do they?' She shoved a hand between her parents' heads and opened her fist. A silver stud, the size of a ball bearing, lay on her opened palm.

Ted surprised himself by quoting what he had read in bed last night, in the Gideon from the bedside drawer. 'Thy breasts are as the fruit of Lebanon, as globes of alabaster.'

The car had taken the diversion out of Awakino and was entering the rugged narrowness of the gorge before Stevie said, so quietly the others hardly heard him, 'That's right, Dad. Lisa's. That's exactly what they're like.'

Pictures by Goya

It is a thing one doesn't easily admit. Which is why I have never spoken of it, not even to my sister before she died, nor to Tom, who by now knows pretty much all there is to know about me. It is not a burden, even though it is the kind of thing that is stamped Top Secret. But this is the gist of it: the man I am married to and have cared for now in three countries for half a lifetime is so physically unattractive to me that I have not really *seen* him now since—I cannot remember the last time I wanted to look at him. When he is not away on one of his business trips I eat with him almost every evening; I sleep beside him each night; he is hardly ever not in my mind, one way or another. He is kind, as he always has been, and assumes that I still get something from what, too delicately I suppose, I am going to call 'our intimacies'. So you see why I cannot speak of this to anyone. Especially now.

Everyone says I cope superbly. There is a picture that is relevant to this. My father used to keep it in a folder where he saved stuff he cut from newspapers and magazines: events and episodes he said that told you about 'the human condition'. I haven't seen what even then was a faded piece of paper since I was ten or eleven. I think it was from a generation before my father's time. In any case, what it showed was a human sliver on a thread-like piece of cable, above the tumble of Niagara Falls. A high-wire walker balancing himself with a long pole, delighting the world with pure risk. With what he knew would work. The tiny figure above the pouring falls became for a while a kind of mascot in my mind. He copes, in any case. You see why I think of it.

You'll need to know more. I was forty-four last June. My daughter is half my age, and lives in Battersea, in what she says is one of the truly exciting apartment blocks in London, with a view of greasy water and a dead powerhouse. She is a dear girl and we get on, as her partner says with his gift for banality, 'like a house on fire'. He is a mildly successful journalist who writes copy for the Liberal Party. I asked her if he is what they call a spin-doctor. Juliet, thank God, has sense of humour enough for both of them. 'That may be overstating it,' she said. 'Shall we settle for spin-orderly?' Her father thinks it was wrong of her to say it. But my daughter does not have much to do with this story, which is mine as a possum trap is a possum's, you might say, to take an imaginative turn that in fact is rather out of character. People who know me well tend to say I'm level-headed, focused on what needs to be done. Ways of saying, nicely, prosaic and unimaginative. As a rule I'm most certainly not one for comparisons like that. I've even argued with my husband, in our good-natured way, about the metaphoric mind. I tell him it is like our prehensile toes—essential in their time but really something of a left-over, surely? Surely, he says, mimicking my way of winding things up. For someone with such a gifted business mind, I tell him, he is oddly sentimental. These little lunges towards poetry, without knowing what poetry is.

I noticed, after he became sick, that the pile of books between our beds became more varied, muddled—faintly panicking, perhaps? *Granta* short stories on top of D. H. Akenson's *Saint Saul*. Does that give you some idea? He leaves off most of them halfway through. He gets impatient that wisdom doesn't drop from the pages in the precise chunks he would like, that he's paid good money for. If I might be flighty for a moment more, I expect my father's man walking Niagara would step down on the other side and think, 'There is no more roar. There is no more tumble. Everything is in its place.' Only that isn't how life happens.

Richard was handsome when he was in his twenties. He was not athletic, but his body was naturally lithe. I saw a photograph not long ago in a theatre programme of an Australian boxer from ages back, who apparently died young and became a legend. His skin in the photograph was so white it seemed to shine from inside. Richard was like that. I couldn't see enough of him. Sex was part of it, the way it is between women and men at any time. But it was not that, not just that. There was another pleasure, a simple unsophisticated one, simply from watching him at the beach or walking to a bus or his standing naked, in the mornings, his back towards me, as he drew the curtain and looked down from the house we lived in then, in Perth, in Cottesloe, above the sea. 'Great, isn't it?' he would say. Or sometimes, 'The bloody Indian Ocean, imagine.' He was still excited at our living 'overseas'. It was his first job after we were married. He had such ambitions. Juliet was conceived in the Cottesloe house, perhaps one morning after Richard turned from the big window and I drew the sheet off me. That's what we were like.

Tom for a time was Richard's doctor. He was also mine for a few weeks, although the only time I saw him professionally was for a verruca on my heel. We were not long back from nearly six years in KL, as excited—or at least I was—about settling back as once I had been about anywhere that was somewhere else.

'You swimmers,' he said. 'You'll have picked it up in changing rooms, that'd be my guess.' I was sitting on a high bed in an alcove off his consulting room, and he was crouched in front of me holding my foot as though he were the assistant in a shoe store.

I said, 'It's my husband's sister who used to be the famous swimmer. Her name's Patricia as well.'

'I know who Richard's sister is,' he said. 'There were glamour shots of her on my wall when I was a teenager. I was too shy to speak to him at school because I knew he was her brother.'

'She loved all that sort of thing—attention, interviews.' I was not much interested in small talk about Patricia.

'But I've seen you at the baths,' he said. 'I've seen you there, haven't I?' I did not say I was at the pool only because I took a neighbour's girl for her coaching when her mother was away.

He released my foot and rested it on the little platform used to assist one down from the bed. He said, 'It's nothing so much to worry about.'

It irritated me that he seemed off-hand. 'In the case of one's own foot it is,' I told him. 'When it begins to throb.'

Later—years later—he told me he guessed at that instant I was unhappy.

'It's more than I did,' I said. 'At the time.'

'You don't need to be Freud,' he said. 'If a woman's attractive and comfortably off and has what most women would give an arm for, and she's snappish with her doctor, the chances are.' Teasing me, as he liked to do, to see my bridling at what he said. 'I only said the chances are.'

Marriages, if I can get away with one of these generalisations that drive my scientific daughter crazy, marriages do not go off overnight, like a bottle of milk. There is a New Year's party, say, when you cannot wait to get home to make love. There is a New Year's party two or three or five years later when you joke with your friends about pouring him into the car, when you have been sipping lemonade for hours, so you can drive home a snoring hulk. And again, after that, there are times when you sit there across a table in an expensive restaurant, guessing at the time; or at home while he expands on some deal he has brought off, and he raises both arms and his fingers lock behind his head, and you see the two great saucers of sweat on his Yves St Laurent shirt, with a button open at the waist where his gut declares how much the world is his, by right. He assumes that you are as involved in what he tells you as he is himself. There is no doubt that he is fond of you, and fond partly because you listen. For he knows how much you've chalked up from this as well, although it would shock him to think of it like that. The pale-blue Audi a dozen yards from where you sit and smile and encourage, next week's post-conference resort, the parties where you speak with other expensive dresses: all these are because of his success, and part of that, again, is that as a couple we succeed. This is the case, even as I know I overstate it.

Juliet tells her English friends she has a marvellous relationship with her mother. There is nothing she cannot tell me. There is nothing, no matter how immature or provocative, and I do not argue with her, so it is natural enough she thinks we are great mates. She also condescends to me, just a little. She tells me, honestly Pat, you've got life on a plate, I don't know what gets into you sometimes. I once made the mistake of telling her I was not particularly happy. I thought how fine it would be if I could confide in her, which shows how naive mothers can be. She said, before I had even begun, if life's good, Mum, just make the most of it. As though it were a restaurant we were talking about and not a marriage where by *choice* the menu seldom changed.

This?

Which is infidelity, disgust, obsession, to begin the list. Because there is no one I can talk to completely—talk to even partly. I have even found myself buying those magazines that run columns of advice for women who cannot sort things out for themselves. I buy them and hide them between the *Listener* and *North & South*, even though no one else is ever likely to see them. I am amazed at the kind of advice one can so easily find. Can one be contented with a man with a small penis? Can you ever get over sleeping with your husband's brother? Is celibacy a viable option? I have not seen a question, though, and so obviously not an answer, that can be of use if your problem is this: your husband is kind and providing, and has no idea you are with him because that is where you have always been. He then becomes seriously ill, and does not know that you are what *Woman's Day* would call in love with, and *Cleo* would call fucking, a man who was once his doctor, who is also his friend.

My sister-in-law, my namesake the famous swimmer, who seems to manage men as deftly as she does her business in importing textiles, has often put it to me, about this or that affair she is having, that she *loves* her husband, of course she does, but she is *in love* for the time being with X or Y. This means what she feels is more intense, yet she knows more transitory, and so less valuable, than what there is between her and the man who waits at home. The first time she told me that I believed it was a perceptive way of putting what must, after all, be a dilemma for a lot of people. But the moment I tried to make them mine, the phrases rang glib and insincere. I still love Richard as I love Juliet, as I loved my sister who died, as I almost love one or two friends. But ah, I am in love with Tom and love him too, as I have never done anyone else. And yet saying that, what really have I said? That my love is as obvious as the lawn is green or the sky behind the neighbour's roof is blue. It is true but where does that get me? It does not help me *decide*.

Any affair, I expect, except one's own, has something a touch tawdry about it, or mildly comic, or often enough pathetic. Even before I knew Tom I condescended to Richard's sister, whether I admitted it or not. She would telephone after getting back from a buying trip, and I knew, when she said she needed to see me, that none of it had to do with me.

What I gave her was the chance to talk about her life as though it were a movie. I would make her coffee, or take wine from the fridge, and know that she was about to enjoy herself immensely. She believed these periodic dippings in romance made her special and rare, as a new lover told her she was. I thought she was a fool and tried not to show what I thought. I was a cut above thinking a new man in your bed made the night sky palpably brighter. I thought most of it was stagey and posed. Until I found myself, at my age, scrambling at sex in a school play-ground after a meeting of decent, earnest people trying to get the BBC restored to local bandwaves. The project meant writing to ministers, negotiating for frequencies, corresponding with London. Tom took the minutes, did the sums, made the phone calls rustling up sponsorship. He was an enthusiast where I was only lukewarm. We were amused by the same things and—what an innocent phrase—believed we hit it off. We liked to talk and joke when halfway through the meetings we broke to drink bad instant coffee.

Richard and Tom already were friends. They played bridge together on Wednesday nights in the weeks when Richard was not away, at clubrooms above a bowling green. Tom advised him to cut down on what he ate and arranged for cholesterol tests, and came around to watch the Super Twelves, and although he was not upfront about it, I knew my husband's expensive wines were an incentive in themselves. We had never so much as kissed, or even thought of doing so. Then on the fifth of November we were the only ones who turned up at the committee room at the back of the school hall. 'Someone should have thought of this,' Tom said. He meant most of the others had youngish families or grandchildren, of course they wouldn't show up at this hour. It was not unusual, in any case, for there to be as few as four of us instead of seven. One was a musician who often played in Christchurch, another a civil servant whose beat was the Pacific. But this night there were only two.

The school we met in was high above the city. Guy Fawkes was being dealt with wherever one looked—the quick incandescent rockets, the slow hanging flares that made me think of men in trenches. There were long bursts of crackers like gunfire. I was the one who said, 'They'd look better with the light out.' And then we were kissing, and fumbling, and I considered, even as it happened, why do I not feel bad about it?

Tom was the one who said we had better head home, for God's sake. Between the door at the side of the hall, and where our cars were parked, twenty yards off, we did not kiss again, nor even really undress. We leaned against a low brick wall beneath a dim barricade of trees. I helped tug my clothes aside. I told him yes, before he was sure. The kind of vocabulary I am used to, that I was reared on, would have me say we then went about betraying Richard. The remnant of a vocabulary we don't even know we have lost.

I speak, I suppose, as one of thousands when I say how bored I am by the hours you can't get out of, watching sport on television. I think of the way the most inactive of men, the most intelligent of them, get that gladiatorial rise to their voices; who believe, especially if women are within earshot, that there is something roguishly fetching in their carrying on. Tom and Richard are masters at it: Richard who cannot pick up a ball the children whack over from next door without losing his balance; Tom who is fit without making much effort to be so, but the one time we fooled about on a tennis court he was surprisingly inept. They were good simply at being together, Richard and Tom. They liked each other and one felt the goodness of it. It was wrecking that, I know, that so upset Tom. That I was also, as a tribunal would no doubt see it, the wife of a patient was nowhere near as important as that.

As I told him once, he did not have much of a professional conscience. It's because, he told me, what we did had nothing to do with his being a doctor. I must clear that word up too: 'patient'. Apart from how he looked, Richard kept good health. The odd Synflex for gout, Daktacort for a summer rash. Tom was his doctor for nothing more than that. It was almost luck, however tasteless it is to say so, but luck, yes, that Richard became sick at the time he did, and Tom could insist that he see a specialist at once, that they were too close in any case. Yes, Richard could see that. And it put us in the clear.

I think of our last week before the illness began. We were sitting with brandies after dinner. It was early summer. The candles burned on the table, and it was not quite dark outside. The French doors were open. I sat between the only two men who had really mattered to me in a lifetime, but only one of whom I loved. The other had provided me with everything, a man I tried not to look at when he came in from the bathroom in the mornings with a towel around his waist, and leaned over me and brushed his lips across my forehead. He would say, wide awake and super-charged for another day, that I couldn't be that tired, surely? And my murmuring back, 'What's that?', in fact as awake as he was, but not letting on. And I thought of his friend, whom I so wanted to make love with again. I thought it impossible that Richard would not see. I may not have liked myself much either, yet I hardly cared. My sister-in-law going on about openness to life, about the ripeness of experience, whatever it was she called it at different times, explaining herself, justifying herself: I had always thought of it as so much hogwash. And now here I was.

I could think of nothing much but Tom. I rang him the morning after that dinner, our sitting in the almost faded light, the candles still between us, the three of us hovering, floating as it seemed, on both luminosity and dark. I rang and asked him could he go away, surely he could think of a reason to go away? A refresher course in London on social medicine—wasn't he often talking about how he would like to do that? You've no commitments, I urged him, no wife. He joked and said he had a wife, she just hadn't been here for a long time. But I said as calmly as I could, 'I don't know what will happen if you don't. This is out of hand already.'

Then it all happened so quickly. For a while it seemed that Richard might even die. At least I can say that I refused to think of that; I held back the hope of that as a way out. I refused, I suppose, to think of anything much beyond day by day. Tom and I, without ever explaining why we thought so, both knew we could not go off to a motel, that we would not put ourselves in the category that placed us in: the circle of deliberate and cold adulterers. Which was nonsense, of course, because already we were that. But we were good at making out it was beyond our control. Like teenagers, we found a place we kept going back to, an off-road, a mere track, that led down towards the river. The willows were so low above us they swept against the roof of the car as we drove through, like the ending of a car-wash. Tom said Richard had shown him the reports from the specialist. He was the one to say what I knew I should have said first. He said, 'We have to stop until we know what's what. We have to.'

What's what, for God's sake. All we meant by that. But I said, 'He says he'll keep on as normal, as long as he can. Work, I suppose he means. Until he can't.'

'That's good,' Tom said.

I wondered if he meant, 'That's good for us all.' But for the moment, tapping the windscreen in front of us, he said, 'Not much of a spot, is it, this? For romance, I mean?' There was the glint on bottles thrown at the side of the bank, the white smear of discarded McDonald's cartons. 'Where's the moonlight on the river?' We smiled at each other, and I thought, Obsession without fun. Without style. But even when we could have, we did not go back to my house, although so often Richard, in the first month or two, was away for several nights. We did not go back to Tom's place either, where his twenty-year-old son showed up one night out of three. I don't know what we thought we were guarding: our meeting in uncomfortable places; making love on a scrabbled blanket while we hoped no one would walk along; grasping at each other as though furtiveness was something we actually sought—did all that actually redeem something in us? Did we think in some way we were protecting Richard from a worse betrayal than the one we inflicted, nevertheless?

It is the story of so many nights of my life. You wait for your husband to arrive back on his flight from Christchurch, from Sydney or Canberra. You realise, now they are over, how good these few days have been with the house entirely to yourself. Without having to try. There is something almost trance-like in that feeling, to exist only for oneself. The most natural thing, and yet what luxury, what a rare gift. He will have eaten too much for lunch and drunk too much in the hour after his meeting while he sat in the Koru Club, watching reflections run and distort in the wall of plate glass, watching a distant sky paling or growing dark. As he has told me often enough, it was while sitting between flights, while waiting for boarding calls, that he had the chance to think things through. He would belch while we sat and drank coffee together, and say, like a schoolboy, 'Pardon me.'

Then, 'Drambuie?' he asks, standing, expansive, in mid-story of the day's success. He says, 'Just tell me to stop when you're nodding off.' I laugh as he says it, as anxious not to hurt him as he works at being kind to me. ('You're such try-hards!' my daughter teased me last time she was out. 'I've never heard of people dolloping out politeness the way you two do!' The way your father does, I corrected her.) He tells me about that little runt down south who tried to spike the new expansion plans. He brings me up to speed with the earth-moving shambles at the Gosford site. He explains how confidence is built up and smart bastards are put down. He says he doesn't work that hard just for himself, I know that, don't I? I like to see him contented with what he does. And we are like actors in a record run. We amble through our parts. The lines are less important than—less important than what? You know you are reaching towards something you cannot answer, that you cannot define. But there is a meanness in me too, a desire I know will never come to anything: to tug the curtain down, take an axe to the stage, make him look at me appalled, pleading, 'But we said it was so real!' I know Richard is looking at me, waiting for me to meet his gaze, to smile at him. It would be so little to give, and yet I do not give it. It has been like this—I cannot remember for how long. I try to think about it rationally, as we say to assure ourselves that there is an answer to arrive at, if only we put confusion, muddle, aside. But there is nothing much to put aside. I simply do not want to meet his eyes when he is waiting for me to look back. He does not have any idea of what I think. 'God,' he says to me sometimes, 'it's just so good having you here to come back to.' He puts his hand on my knee.

'Here's the news,' I say, and turn up the volume. But I put my hand lightly on his. I feel his fingers lace into mine. I am a liar, whatever I do.

All this is in my mind as I wait for Tom to carry across my gin and tonic, his own bitter lemon. Neither of us is much at home in pubs. A rackety song subsides, and is replaced by the rapid-fire inanity of rap. 'Look what we are doing to each other,' Tom jokes, his head nodding to the box and its sequence of flashing lights where the noise pours out. I hate the thought that in an hour he will drop me off, and I will not see him for days. The grey dull feeling of it washes over me, through me, roughly as a wave that knocks you off your feet. It was not even just wanting him. It was beyond desire—does that make sense? A feeling of desolation that swamped me so that sex as much as common sense or what grandly we call our moral perspective was swept away, a rush that seemed to wrench me away from myself, and what was it that was left?

It came home to me how little we had ever done, except to be alone together furtively, or to be with Richard, the three of us. We had never gone to a restaurant, or a film, in case we were seen. If you asked me what we did do together, it would strike us both as trivial when I told the truth. 'Apart from being lovers, hardly anything.' But the bitterness of my saying that would not convey how important it was, our doing nothing, our talking as though we could never know enough of each other. We were avid just for that. About places we had been, about experiences we didn't like. Small things that often were odd in isolation, unconnected with anything else we knew. And bigger things. Tom had a flatmate in Toronto, when he was an intern in a hospital, a black from Baltimore. Tom had gone to bed with his sister after a Thanksgiving dinner where he felt privileged to be asked. There had never been a white man in their house before. They were lovers for a summer until the girl went to Africa to work as a teacher. I said I had no romances to match that. One of my boyfriends was now a judge. Another had come out, after he was ordained, and was now a thorn in the side of his church. And Tom surprised me when he said, 'There are never two people in bed together. There are always four.' He said he was quoting from an author whose name he'd forgotten. I said I thought that was glib. Well, that depended on what you thought mattered most, he said. What happened now, or the memory we sometimes carried in us like a splinter that couldn't be removed. He was talking about ghosts. I misquoted Dylan Thomas, trying to cover with irony what I feared more deeply. *After the first love there is no other.*

'If that's not true,' Tom says, 'why are you still with Richard?'

Six months later, after Richard's worst times, I could tell when he came out of the specialist's consulting rooms and his eyes sought to hold on to mine that he was going to be all right. 'Thank God.' I remember so clearly saying that. And I must have said it out loud, because an elderly woman beside me, an old-fashioned and scuffed handbag held with both hands on her lap, smiled shyly across at me. 'I'm glad for you,' she said. So that it was shame that flooded through me at that instant, and my pity for the woman who sat in a room waiting perhaps for her own bad news, but could put on hold her worry to say she was glad that someone else's life was luckier than her own. Yet by the time we were in the parking lot at the side of the building, and Richard had told me what his doctor said, I felt a flatness that smeared everything. I closed my eyes, which Richard saw as he glanced across me at the end of the drive to check for traffic. He mistook what I was thinking. I felt his moist palm across the back of my hand. 'It's over now,' he said. 'All that worrying's over.' And his laughing by the time we reached home, his slamming the door and bounding across the lawn to move the sprinkler. He walked back to the tap at the side of the garage. There was a quick lurch as the water pulsed through the hose and the sprinkler turned in a whirl of sprayed diamonds. 'I'm ringing Tom this minute,' he said. 'He can bloody bring around his own wine for once.'

And it was, can you believe it, a happy enough dinner. I believe we all knew something was changing, yet none of us was sure what. When Richard went to speak on the phone to his sister about what the specialist had said, Tom put his fingers on mine. Neither of us spoke. When Richard came back he said, 'Family. They're the end. More interested in her new Indonesian batik deal than whether yours truly lives or dies.'

Richard was not going to die. Although his nights could still be uncomfortable, even when he seemed to sleep. Sometimes his breath catches in unexpected gasps. I lie and wait for the sound to become easier. I lie with my hands behind my head, watching, if it is light enough, the stillness or the movement of the leaves outside the bedroom window, my elbows spread, so Tom tells me, like wings. A joke of his from months back. 'Like those paintings, you know?' he says. 'The Spanish ones? Her clothes on in one and not in the other?'

Goya, I tell him. The paintings are by Goya.

'That's the man,' he says.

Tom and I said goodnight, after Richard's homecoming dinner, as we so often had done, kissing on the porch like friends. But he had left his hand quite openly on mine when Richard came back from speaking with his sister. Richard looked, without surprise, and said, 'I think we should drink to all of us.' And we did. And then we drank again, as Richard this time said, 'And to whatever there is that's left.' But we laughed before we could become maudlin. We laughed and were quiet and then drank again, to whatever it was that moved behind and through what Richard said—the other things it said—that none of us put into words. There was another moment, though, as Tom left, when we found ourselves laughing again. Richard and I stood on the top of the steps at the front door. Tom swore from where he stood down on the darkened lawn. He had dropped his keys, and his sleeve swept like a pale scythe as his hand sought for them. Then he stood again and jingled them at us before the car door closed and the engine sprang into life. And the distance began.

The Families

Dad said, as he always did, that of course he would drive through to pick her up, and she, as he quite expected her to do, said no she wouldn't hear of it, it was so much easier for her to get a rental. She told him she would drive through in no time. It was his being there when she crossed the bridge and drove into Knighton Road that made her know she was really home.

Kirsten guessed the hardest time would be the first weekend back, her father looking at her with that quiet, assessing sympathy that he was rather too aware of, and her mother's blunter questioning. Dad was good to have a cry with, if that was what you needed, but with Mum it was frankness after the first ten minutes. Life's not just a nice red apple, as she used to tell Kirsten and her sister when they were children, waiting for you to come along and do it the favour of biting into it. That was the way it had always been, Dad for sympathy, Mary, as Mum was always called from the time the girls were in their teens, the one with suggestions about what to do.

She was struck, as she always was after flying in from Melbourne, by that sense of the mildness of what she came back to. It was not only the weather, which was so much less pressing than the summers she still found a trial. It was the mildness of the people too that came back to her, the quieter voices, the hesitancy, the sense with her family perhaps especially that there was the slightest distance between them. Intimacy was something you worked at, that could never be assumed. 'You mean good manners?' Gail had once said to her, when she tried to speak of it. She thought of it now as she waited in the queue to have her passport checked. The woman looked at her and down at her photograph and then up at her once more. Sammy had told her how much you could read into that moment as you passed through Immigration. The woman handed her passport back and hoped she would have a nice stay back home. For a moment Kirsten had in mind her senior class before she left on the Friday afternoon, wishing her the same thing. Clever, good-natured girls, and all of them shocked, amusingly enough, when they first read together the final section of *Gulliver's Travels*, appalled at Swift's being so destructive about mere reason.

She liked the drive into the green casual country. There was that same expectant lift she had known since she was a child, when they were driving back from Auckland and you first saw the long glint of the river, the far spread of the Waikato, the high distant smokestacks at Huntly. Dad would tell them about places as they passed, point to where the battle had taken place at Rangiriri, the sacred hill at Taupiri where the chiefs' bodies were carried up the slopes, and the piece of riverbank they waited for, where heads had been raised up on poles, waiting to say in chorus, 'Yuk!' There were stretches when the river disappeared behind stands of trees, or the elevation of the land, and it seemed rather dull country you were driving through. Then there it was again, the river, sometimes close enough to imagine throwing a stone at, and at one place she waited to come to, where there was a little island in the middle of the river, and the current divided then met again. The river changed colour with the sky. It was brown and wide further back and under cloud, and now, as she came towards the city where she had grown up, it narrowed, bluish-grey like an old blade. She wished she could look at things without that intrusive 'like'. Look at them plainly as they were. She advised her classes to watch out for that. The simile trap, she called it. There was nothing wrong with describing something as it was.

*

Riley hurled himself at her even before she stepped from the car. He pawed at her door and when her father called him back and gripped his collar his tail whacked against Dad's leg, almost making him lose balance.

'One fan you'll always have,' Dad told her.

'He does the same with anyone,' Mary said. 'He knocked your aunt over a week ago.'

'I know, I know,' Kirsten said, pushing against Riley's enthusiasm, her lips tingling as his tongue came close and she tilted back her head to avoid his slobber.

Then, 'You've lost weight,' Dad said as he embraced her. Kirsten let herself sink against him, his warm hands spread across her back. The feeling of being home.

Mary too hugged her. Kirsten felt the lightly pressed lips against her cheek. 'You could do with losing a bit,' her mother said. Yes, she knew she was home.

Dad picked up on what passed through her mind. 'What it is to be appreciated.' She knew he was glad the dog still bounded around them, excited at her return. It allowed him to say what he may not otherwise have said, laughing, telling her, 'The house will be jumping at you next, Kirsty. Everybody's darling.' He pressed her arm and took her suitcase from the boot. Her mother stood back and smiled. Their daughter raised her hands to the side of Riley's head, ruffling his ears, feeling the little knuckles of gristle where they folded against his head. 'And Mum,' she said, 'you've dyed your hair!'

She was home without really wanting to be, which she knew they understood. Riley was doing them all a good turn, carrying on like a fool, telling them what fun it was, having her back home.

Dad said, 'I think he's got the hang of things.'

Kirsten linked her arm through his as they walked the dozen yards to the back patio. Last year it had newly been added on and its timbers raw. Now it gleamed golden-white. She pretended to shade her eyes against the glare of it. 'My!'

'All things bright and beautiful,' Dad said.

Dad liked to walk. When he still taught at Boys' High and if the weather was right for it, he would leave half an hour earlier than if he drove, and walk along Grey Street and over the bridge at the other end of town, and walk back in the late afternoon. These days he would sometimes ask at ten in the morning if there was anything needed at the shops. He would saunter up to Hamilton East in any case, walk twice around Steele Park with its trees marvellous at any time of year. It took heavy rain to break his routine. He would walk again in the evenings. Mary said, 'I'd come too if it wasn't for all this,' which they both smiled at. There was always something she was working at, the accounts she did for the café in the Gardens, the Drama Club, the schedules for bridge. 'The only time I have to think about anything,' Dad liked to say about his walks. 'I can't do that just sitting in a chair.' Kirsten wondered if that was true. Think about what? She knew it sometimes irritated Mary, with her Zonta and her volunteering and what Dad a bit sharply called her 'missionary work', the hours spent with the Somalis in Claudelands, finding them furniture, helping the older ones whose English scarcely existed. 'Walking and reading,' Dad said, 'your mother seems to think they're not quite what an intelligent adult should do.' But that was the way things were, from the time Kirsten and Gail were children. Mary got things done, Dad watched from the sidelines. All's right with the world.

'So?' Dad said the next morning when Kirsten insisted yes, she really did feel like a walk herself. The sky was overcast but the wind was warm. She supposed he would wait for her to talk. They had been considerate last night, her father and Mary, neither for a moment pressing her to explain. She had telephoned a week ago to say there would not be a wedding after all, that the plans for November had been scrapped. All she had told them over the roast lamb that Mary knew was her favourite was that it had not thank goodness ended in any kind of row with Sammy; they had come to see it at pretty much the same time, seen that it was simply too hard. They left her to say what she wanted, in her own time. How reasonable they had been too, earlier on, though she had guessed they were disappointed that she decided to marry over there and not at home, with the kind of wedding they had given Gail. Far more sensible, Mary agreed, to marry where Sammy's family was finding its feet. Yet how odd it was too, that feeling Kirsten knew from when she was in her teens, the feeling that her mother understood her, that Dad did too, yet as one, and as the other, rather than both of them together. She was unsure quite what it was she meant. She could not have explained it, had she needed to make it clear to someone else. Even to Gail. But she knew there was something more than mildness behind Dad's careful calm. She had read a sentence once that had struck her as saying what she herself could not have said. 'Happiness is a matter of a well-conducted truce.' When she found it in a notebook ages after she copied it, she was embarrassed at its triteness. In a book with scraps of Leonard Cohen and Borges, when the South American was all the rage.

At the end of the meal Mary had asked, 'But you'll stay on over there?' And before she answered, her father surprising her. 'As if she wouldn't,' he said. Pouring the last of the Te Kauwhata chardonnay into her glass. As if it was important that he said it before she did.

'I feel such a fool,' she told them. She left it there. Whatever more she meant by it she would tell them in her own good time. They both knew that. She loved them for it, their giving her time.

*

Her father liked Sammy when they came across last Christmas. They talked together easily. 'We science teachers,' as Dad liked to say. And Mary carefully practised tact as though it were her way of life. Kirsten had not yet met his family. That, as Sammy said, was the treat in store for her when they went back. They used distance as their excuse, which was easy enough to do. A four-hour drive, there and back. 'But we'll have to sometime.' Have to visit his family, which he told her she might 'find a bit tricky'. She guessed he meant it came down to the language problem. If you heard Sammy across a room you would assume he was Australian. But his mother, even now, was unable to shop unless one of his sisters accompanied her. Both the girls were older than Sammy. One sister was married; the other, the one hurt as a child, lived at home. Sammy sometimes joked about them. 'These women who believe they own me.' Yet she knew he spoke with them at least twice a week. There were times when she was at his flat and he would smile and hold his finger to his lips when his mother rang, sometimes at ten or eleven at night. Kirsten guessed he spoke placatingly to her. But there was no mistaking his patience, his respect. He seldom told her what they had spoken of. 'We'll have to go up there one day.' 'Up there' was practically South Australia.

Gail, who was closer to Mary in temperament than she ever guessed, sometimes asked during the long calls they made every few weeks, 'So it's still OK then, is it?'—as if sooner or later there would come a day when Kirsten would say, 'No, Gail, it's not.' Her younger sister had married at twenty, and now at twenty-six, two children later, had moved into a dream house on the Raglan road. The elder child would start school next term and already could read. Although Gail never skited. She just delivered facts, which almost always were ones to be proud of. And as she said about their parents,

'I'd shoot myself, honest I would. If Gavin and I ever got to that. They can go a week and hardly say a word.'

'They don't fight,' Kirsten said. 'We've never heard them fight.' She was unsure why she so needed to defend them. And Gail said, the shrewdness of it surprising her, 'Who said you have to fight not to get on?'

Gail was a quiet child and attractive, but her big sister was the clever one. Kirsten was the one her parents told friends about first, when asked, 'How's the family?' Yes, finished her degree. Yes, a good school in London, they love her there. No shortage of boyfriends from what we hear. Yet next thing she was thirty. Mary mentioned Gail rather more often. No, Kirsten's Italian engagement didn't quite work out. Yes, Melbourne now. Had her fill of Europe, Mary said, it was nice being closer to home again of course. And no great surprise then if another engagement now didn't go to plan. The cultural divide can be a big one. She'd know more once Kirsten came back for a break. 'She'll tell us in her own time,' as she said to Gail. If being civilised meant anything it meant that. You didn't lean on people. You gave them space.

It was nice, in its uneventful way, to walk along the old streets, to speak with the neighbours she had known for years. If there was a world contest for suburbia this would have to be a finalist. The neat sections, the modest, decent houses, the cars in the drives. When she was a teenager Kirsten had thought, if God meant you quietly to smother in the blandest way he would put you in a place like Hillcrest. A week back now and she knew she would find it as stifling again. But walking those streets with Dad at this moment, the sparkle on the early morning verges, the trees vivid and dead still—how nice it was, how nice to remember even what it used to be like! She could have managed to walk here blindfolded.

'You're lucky, Dad,' she said, 'to know what you want.'

She knew her father would be waiting for her to confide. She must tell him a shortened version at least. Calling off a marriage is serious business. The clock keeps ticking, we all know that. She could hear the whirr of the old clichés. But not now.

Her father broke the easy silence between them. 'So you don't hate it too much? Spending time back here?'

'Dad,' she said. She leaned towards him, touching the shoulder of his jacket with her forehead. 'I wasn't that bad, was I?'

'Standards vary,' he joked at her. She could never feel this naturalness with Mary as she did with Dad. There was simply nothing that came between them. Each took the other for the private person they were. That was the ground they stood on. It had saddened her last night, sitting in the lounge after dinner, sipping the Dubonnet she knew her parents had bought especially, their remembering her telling them years ago it was her favourite drink while she was away. Saddened her at how he had aged, even in a year. That fraction slower, that thinning of his hair, which those who were close to him each day would not have noticed. She had crossed the road in front of the Catholic cathedral, walking down towards the bridge, towards the long gardens along the river's banks. She went over what she would tell him, how she would account for calling the wedding off, without ceasing to love the man she had intended marrying.

Dad would be on her side. He would try to understand. He would agree with her in any case, even if he did not.

Sammy's mother stepped back as Kirsten made the mistake of leaning towards her.

'I should have told you,' he explained to her later. 'We don't kiss first off the way you people do.' Yet not quite saying it as lightly as she might have thought.

The lunch had been a disaster. His sister who was married to a timid Australian at least had called her by her name. And, 'This is Rob,' she had said, without turning to her husband. He was a lot older than his wife. Sammy had said on the drive through that his brother-in-law ran a small electrical appliance store, and Jenny as she now called herself had worked for him. He believed the community should do what they could to welcome new Australians, and a year after she began there, Jenny and he had married.

'But your mother didn't mind that?'

'She was a girl marrying a man with a nice house and a shop in the main street. There was nothing too much to mind.'

Kirsten tried not to make too much of it. She laughed, touching Sammy's knee. 'If I put in a pool and bought you your own car do you think that would help?'

'And make me lose face?' He put his hand on hers, leaving it there for several minutes as they covered the long flat road towards 'the Family', as she thought of it, the word drained of any warmth it might be expected to hold.

'Rob isn't a drinker and he doesn't expect Jenny to cook steak and chips. How can we compete with that?' She smiled to show she was up to whatever the Family might throw at her, but was apprehensive. Sammy was part of the Family too, as deeply a part of it as his sisters and far more important than them, of course. He was what his mother was proud of, he was what they had achieved. The girls were minor players.

On the way back home on the Highway, ten minutes after they had left the house, Kirsten said quietly, 'You didn't warn me I'd be treated like shit.' Her cheeks burned. After that first gaffe with the attempted kiss, Sammy's mother ignored her for the longest two hours of her life. Kirsten was seated at the end of the table, Jenny to one side of her, Rob on the other. Both spoke to her, but sparingly, as though Rob's now being one of the Family obliged him to behave in the same way. All attention was turned to Sammy, who was next to his mother and elder sister at the further end of the carved heavy table, with its red embroidered runner and elaborate arrangement of dishes. A big jug of lemon tea was poured by Li, who was pretty, but walked with one foot shuffling from her injury. Jenny occasionally looked towards their guest and asked if she liked the food. Her mother placed dishes in front of the others, but left it to her son-in-law to attend to the woman her son had brought with him.

Kirsten looked at the large vases of artificial flowers on their low black tables, at the figurines on the mantelpiece that may have been religious. A jar with blackened joss-sticks stood between them. A large hand-coloured photograph of a middle-aged man hung on the wall above them, with two miniature crossed flags beneath it. Sammy seemed not to take in how wretched she was. Towards the end of the meal Rob broke ranks and began to ask her about Melbourne, and when she said she lived a stone's throw from Central he said he supposed there would be no point having a vehicle that close to the centre, even supposing you had a place to park it. No, she said, there wouldn't be much point. He seemed not to mind when she said she hadn't given it much thought.

Jenny too began to speak. 'An Audi, that's what we have,' she said. 'An Audi, Rob?'—as though he may not have heard.

'I like a European car,' he said.

Sammy's mother looked down the table and said to her son, who translated and passed on to Rob, that his mother-in-law thought that in a flat city like Melbourne, it was ridiculous how few bicycles there were, or even mopeds, how every Australian seemed to want a car first and then only after that a wife.

Kirsten forced herself to smile, guessing the mother may have made a joke. But Sammy had translated what his mother said seemingly dead straight, and Rob too appeared to take her opinion as worth attending to. And he said quietly across to his wife, that the fish was OK but you could tell it had been frozen longer than was good for it. They'd have to give that new place a try, did she think?

Jenny agreed. She said, to no one specifically, that was the trouble living inland. You could never be certain, whatever the shop people said.

It was inevitable there would be a row on the long drive back.

'Not a word,' Kirsten said, 'you must have noticed that? Not one word the whole time we were there.'

Sammy tried to tell her, 'Nothing else much matters when she's cooking. She's the generation where cooking is everything. Getting a meal ready for people. She went to a lot of trouble.'

'Ready for people? Well I wasn't one of them, I can tell you that. If she and your sisters had their way they'd have starved me to death!' She felt the stinging shame of not being able to keep her anger to herself. She knew Sammy must have hated it as much as she did. He said, 'We had to get it over. Now we have.' And as if grasping for some small thing that did not offend her, 'Jenny was nice to you, wasn't she? Jenny was nice?'

Thinking of it now, knowing somehow she must explain to Dad, Kirsten blinked back tears. The humiliation of it all. The message there in every moment she had been in their home, You are not what we have in mind. As they left, Sammy had leaned forward and his mother and his sisters kissed his cheeks, ran their hands along his sleeves, gave him round bamboo boxes which were treats they had made for him to take home. Jenny relented enough to say, when the others were still fussing about him, that Sammy looked so like their father, that was why their mother cried, why they all spoiled him. But Rob, she noticed, did not say anything to encourage her, to make her think time would improve anything. And yet she said 'Thank you' to him through the lowered window as they left. His mother and the girls were on the driver's side, still grasping at his hands as he drove off.

'But I told you,' he said, 'I told you it would be like that. It isn't you. They would be jealous of anybody. Now we can forget about it.' Because he had expected it and it was even rather amusing to him, he thought it might be so for her as well, something surely they could see in perspective? It would prove how close they actually were, how they saw things in the same way because, in that stupid phrase he had picked up somewhere, they were soulmates. Well, weren't they? 'We are soulmates, Kirsten.'

'I was shocked at myself, Dad,' Kirsten now told him. 'That was about the worst part. That it mattered so much to me.'

They were walking down to the dark broad tug of the river. It ran close in against the banks. 'It's high, isn't it?' she said. When she was little she had always been apprehensive when they walked this path that the level of the river would suddenly rise and lap around them and push them downstream with the driftwood and scraps of pumice you saw floating past, so much faster than you'd ever expect. An older cousin knew how much the river frightened her. 'It's coming up, it's coming up,' she would say, very close against her so that only she and not their parents might hear.

Now she had started, she went on. 'I never thought I was like that, you know, and here I was hating them. Really hating them.'

'You'd have felt the same if they'd been Kiwis,' her father said. 'It's not what they look like. It's what they did.'

They each knew there was not that much more to say, but it was good even to talk like this, as she never would with Mary. It had always been like this. When she was a teenager, when girls were supposed to be close to their mothers, it was Dad she found herself talking to, telling him about her boyfriend even, about Ron Dowse from Tirau who had said if she didn't let him do more, let him undo her blouse anyway on the long summer evenings when they and some friends drove up the sanatorium road to Maungakawa and watched the bands of gold and shadow across the river country, well, he had said, that was that. Not that she told Dad exactly, about having to deal with Ron's hands as if they were huge insects that she constantly slapped at. She supposed now Dad must have guessed anyway. He had told her, 'Remember you're always in charge, Kirsty. Your friends can't make you do anything. You're always in charge.'

Sammy just couldn't understand, she said. It came down to his expecting what happened. 'And so he thought I would too. He knew they wouldn't like me. Wouldn't like anyone who wasn't one of their own. Ever. He had taken it for granted I somehow wouldn't mind. That I'd pretend it was OK because he believed himself that it shouldn't matter.' Dad touched her arm but thank goodness didn't come out with what she had heard enough of already from friends in Melbourne—that people change over time, that getting on with in-laws wasn't everything.

They walked slowly along the path to the low hulk of the old gun-boat. She knew Dad's silence told her he agreed. You know in your bones what you think is right. Although he did say, 'When that first lustre wears off, that's when you see problems for what they are. It's a lot harder then to put things right.'

'Once we get used to each other'—she had gone over that so often too. For the week after the visit to his family he came round to her flat and they made love and he told her what she meant to him. But even then, with the comfort of his breathing beside her when he slept, his back warm against her arm, she thought of that, and feared it. When we are used to each other, I am the one he will think differently about, not them. She knew how bad it must have been for them in the war, how, once his father died, his mother had starved and lied and even killed, Sammy had hinted at that even, to get them through, to bring them here. He will not become unkind, Sammy would never be that, but what he grew up with cannot go away. There will be a veil between us, and then at last perhaps a wall.

They walked up the grassy slope and sat on a bench beneath a tree whose name Kirsten did not know. Mary would have, though. Mary could have walked to the coast and told you about everything they passed. But how good it was to sit here. The peacefulness of it. The last few weeks had been so wretched. Sammy had said, over and over, 'Perhaps we just need time. If we love each other we'll get through.' She watched a sculler skim across the taut dark water. On the other bank a group of rowers were carrying their boat down to the river. Kirsten said again, 'I'm sure the river's higher than I remembered it last year,' and Dad said there'd been so much rain, weeks of it in fact. Then he said, 'You mustn't regret what was good about it, though. That always stays as it was.'

She could have hugged him for saying that! She put her hand on his and he took her fingers and pressed them, before they stood and walked back up to River Road. He said, 'I think your mother wants to drive you out to Cambridge after lunch. To have you to herself.'

Which meant, Kirsten supposed, her wanting to say something without her father there to hear.

On the way they drove past the house near Hautapu where they had lived when Dad was at the country school.

'We must have been so packed in!'

'We were,' Mary said, 'but we seemed not to know at the time.'

It was the first home Kirsten remembered, before the later years after the shift into town, years when Mary did the accounts at the dairy factory, and the arguments when Dad said he was content where he was. It angered her mother, his having no desire in the world to apply for something more. He was an excellent teacher, wasn't he, a school of his own would have been his for the asking. 'But I like what I do.' It must have been said so much the sentence stayed in her mind, as did Mary's silences. The house was a roughcast, white-painted box, with blue sills and a door that made it look oddly like a Greek postcard.

'It doesn't look lived in,' Kirsten said. The lawns were uncut, a trailer stood in high grass.

'The school closed years back so there's no need for a teacher's house. The dairy factory too. That's closed.'

'And the big tree. It's not there.' The copper beech that flickered across the windows at the side of the house, its leaves looking as though it was an ordinary tree that had been scorched. She thought of the fat, round cheeses, so heavy you could hardly hold one, which Mr Prendergast the manager let their mother bring home. Kirsten did not remember ever seeing him, Mr Prendergast, but knew they were a present from him. The deep sides were curved and lovely to run the palms of your hand across, but if you pushed at the cheese before it was cut it made her think of trying to push against hard rubber. There were some nights too—not many, but how they stayed alive!—when she and Gail lay in bed and her parents argued in the kitchen. Dad had closed the door so what they said was not loud enough to hear. But you could tell just how angry they were. Gail had said it was like when a kettle begins to boil. But once when they thought she was outside and Dad was marking at the table he joked about and called his office, she heard Mary ask him, not sure of what her mother meant, what sort of man doesn't want to get on? Surely he owed her that?

'You wouldn't remember much from when we lived out here? Before we went into town?'

'Not much,' Kirsten said. 'I do remember how empty it all seemed, though. The paddocks. How big they were. How few houses. And now they're everywhere. New and ugly.'

'Not all of them,' Mary said.

'I suppose not. Just big and ostentatious.'

'So Marx isn't dead,' her mother teased her.

'Not as dead as that,' she smiled. How they argued about all that during her last year at school! Not even argued, that was the problem. Her parents, who voted Labour anyway, had been amused at her vehemence, at her defending Trotsky as the lost leader.

Just before coming into Cambridge, a stone's throw from the watertower that once seemed so exotic to her, like something you saw in books about foreign places, they passed a mock Tudor mansion where a cousin, the town's plumber, lived in style. His wife grew orchids in a long glasshouse at the side of the house. There was talk of his standing for the local council on a Ratepayers' ticket. 'He's that overweight,' Mary said, 'I doubt he'll last till Christmas.'

Both women laughed at what occurred to them together, the thought of his bulk clambering beneath houses to attend to drains. 'You never let up, do you?' said Kirsten.

'Not with a prick like that, I don't.' It brought them together, her saying that. An easing of tension, Kirsten supposed that was it, their shared mockery of a relative they both disliked, her mother using a word that took her by surprise.

Then, 'Let's live it up,' Mary said, as they passed the war memorial and she turned to park facing the green expanse where over the years they had come to heaven knows how many occasions, candlelight carol services, athletic events, even cricket matches, when Gail had briefly played for a first-class team, and then gave up a month after she met Gavin, when she might have been chosen for the national squad. They walked back past the Town Hall, to the gable-roofed church that was now a coffee shop and painted lolly-pink.

'On me,' Mary said.

Kirsten felt she was at school again and being taken for a treat. They sat at a table made from recycled wood, with koru patterns roughly incised in the surface. There were equally rough paintings with pioneer motifs on large hardboard panels attached to the walls. When their lattes were brought to them, with fern-leaves patterned in the crema, Mary said, 'If I ran a place like this I'd put something offensive on them. Swastikas, say. I can't stand this way we have to play at being Kiwis all the time.'

I suppose this is it, then, Kirsten thought, she will want me to talk. Mary began head on. 'You miss him, do you? Sammy?'

'I hoped I'd be over the worst of it. But yes. All the time.'

Her mother tore at one of the narrow paper tubes of sugar stacked in a bowl in front of them and tilted it over her cup. 'Good,' she said. 'It shows how deeply you've considered what you've decided to do.'

My God, Kirsten thought, what she wouldn't give to live as neatly as Mary managed to. Life clipped into place. Hedges trimmed at the same time every year. Essential things logically done. There was no condescension in her thinking this, nor envy either. She could not imagine herself being further from her mother, that was all. In temperament. In what she wanted from life. And then what in a week's time would so come back to her, in the high tidy apartment in the renovated Drewery Place factory, with the noise from the nightclub across the narrow lane starting up at midnight, and lasting sometimes until four o'clock. Her mother now asking her, 'You've talked with your father then?'

'When we walked down to the river. There's not much really to say, is there? And you know Dad. He's not one to lecture. But he was kind and listened. It was good to get it over.'

'No, I mean about us,' Mary said. 'He didn't talk about us? He didn't tell you that I'm leaving him?' She folded in half the empty sugar packet she took up from beside her cup. Then she said, 'No, I suppose it's fair enough that I'm the one who should tell you.'

Kirsten began to cry. Her mother passed her a tissue that she took from her purse, then sat holding her daughter's hand, running her index finger along the cuff of Kirsten's shirt. 'My dear,' she said, 'I know, I know.'

'The worst thing,' Kirsten said later in the day, when she walked to the end of the back garden and stood against the small glasshouse with its neat shelves of potted herbs, its staked plants, the things she did not know the names for, and talked to her sister on her mobile. 'The worst thing was the moment I heard her say it, I knew it was right. It would never have occurred to me that they might break up. But as soon as she said so I was thinking, yes, they're right to. I cried but it wasn't for that, it was because they had left it until now. And for her too. That she was the one who had to see it.'

She felt her sister's anger surging at her. 'I think you're talking shit,' Gail shouted. 'You've become so bloody selfish over there you can't think of anyone else. Have you thought of Dad? Have you?' There was the interruption of one of the children hectoring its mother, a whining that made Kirsten impatient. But Gail was the one to say, 'I'll talk to you later.' Although before she put the phone down she found her final shot. 'I'd get myself sorted out marriage-wise if I were you, Kirsten. Before working it out for others.'

On the way back along the Cambridge Road Mary had

said, very calmly, 'I expect it was like that with you. You just know a point's been reached. There's nothing very dramatic about it. It's not there in big lights. You just know.'

Kirsten did not say, as she might have, 'No, Mum, it wasn't like that with me at all. We were at the beginning. Sammy and I had hardly begun. You are at the end.' She was glad she held back from saying it. They were passing the old farmhouse with an enormous Norfolk pine at the end of the drive. How many dozens of times they must have driven along here, from the time she first remembered, she and her sister strapped into the back seat, Dad sometimes singing and turning to call back to them, 'Come on you two, you know this song don't you? Right? *Row, row, row your boat,*' and Mary telling him, 'Watch the road, can't you, John?' But she would join in too, her voice thin and sweet, Kirsten liking it so much when they sang like that together, '*gently down the stream.*' Their grandmother had lived in a house dark as a cupboard. She got their names mixed up or sometimes called them by names they had never heard, names of people in other places and some of them even dead. The house was a box of shadows, and smelled of medicine and dust. The curtains were drawn in the room they sat in while Dad was outside running a mower across the lawn. When he came inside he left his shoes on the steps, sprayed with grass that looked like clipped green paper.

Kirsten said as they passed another villa set behind a wide swathe of acacias, 'They were horse trainers, weren't they, the two men who lived in there?'

'Something odd about that set-up too,' Mary said. And their laughing at that, as Kirsten noticed the glazed streak on her mother's cheek. 'Oh, Mum,' she said, touching her arm.

'Those tissues are in the glovebox,' Mary said. 'I don't know which of us needs them most.'

*

Kirsten switched on voicemail messages as soon as she set her bag down inside the bedroom door, and threw her jacket across a chair. It was late afternoon. The apartment in the converted printing works was cool enough for her to slip on a sweater, although when she stood at the large window of the lounge and looked up the sky was bright above the walls of the lane. A friend from school had phoned to say ring back if she felt like meeting at the usual bar in Carlton. 'Tuesdays are good,' the message said. 'We can hear ourselves talk.' She knew it was a sympathy call, her friend thinking she would need cheering up now that she was back to an empty flat. There was another message from the telephone company, with details of a new deal that ran out at the end of the week, and a curt reminder from the caretaker that garbage collecting had moved to another day. She then counted seven calls that left nothing but the click of a phone disconnecting. For those last few days before her trip home she had sat while the phone trilled, unwilling to have another conversation, not wanting to cover the same ground again. It was the hardest thing not to ring back. She sat now with her hands in her lap, looked through the squares of the big divided window at the brick wall of the nightclub across the lane. She had felt exhausted the minute she boarded the plane, and slept until they were crossing the coast. She looked at the stretch of land beneath her, the vastness of it, until it was lost in a bluish distant haze. Her mother had said to her the other afternoon, as they came up from the dip and into Hillcrest, 'You're the tough one, Kirsten, you'll be all right. Your sister's the one I worry about. I don't know if Gavin's all he should be.' I'm not, Kirsten had wanted to cry out, no, I'm not! But with Mary there was a point where you drew the line. And later Dad said only, 'It can't have come as such a surprise?' And again she had not said what she thought, 'There was nothing in my life, Dad, that surprised me as much.'

Luckily, he said, money was not an issue, they certainly wouldn't be arguing over that. Luckily there's the bach at Raglan, in fact he quite liked the idea of living out there, years of reading, he said, to catch up on. There'd be no problem with Riley. There wouldn't be the least problem with the dog.

'Don't keep saying "luckily",' she had said to him. And then they talked about teaching, how he knew he had been good at it but had not missed it for a day. That had surprised him. She told him about her own classes, how fortunate that most of them were French, she didn't have the problems that drove some of her colleagues up the wall. It had been the same with Sammy and senior maths, she said. They didn't get the yobbos. They didn't get the thugs. Luckily.

When the window darkened she turned on the lamp that stood on the small carved table Sammy had given her, the Tiffany panes brightening the room. She looked at her watch and saw it was eight o'clock. The phone began to ring. I won't answer it, she said, I won't answer it, as she stood and walked towards it.

On a Clear Day

I don't quite know how one is supposed to tell something like this. Stories about husbands falling out with friends who become keen on their wives are two a penny, to use a phrase my mother was fond of. There are husbands apparently who get a kick from such a situation, which I suppose is a combination of flattery at one's own good taste with a dash of perversity thrown in. I imagine the ways of responding are considerable. I don't read much fiction and don't talk that intimately with male friends, so I'm limited in assessing such things to the odd scrap of gossip one can't help but hear, or to what I've seen in movies or on television, things which in any case I usually forget within a few days. So you'll appreciate my saying that: 'I don't quite know.' I have no other experience to base comparisons on.

'Nothing new under the sun'—yes, I know how casually you hear someone remark that what we think so unique to ourselves isn't so at all, if one knows a little about the way the world works. Well, I don't, that's the point. This is the situation. One of my friends was blind, and in love—or was he?—with my wife. And I don't quite know what to do with it, now the story has come to an end.

Claire used to think it was something of a joke, in her easy-going way. She liked Peter far too much to condescend to him, so joking all round was the way to cope when he flirted in an obvious, good-natured way. 'If dear Peter could actually *see* me I doubt he'd last until tea-time.' Or a little more seriously, she said, 'I simply can't imagine anyone without having some picture of them. How can you like someone you've never actually seen?' Another time, soon after the four of us had been at a play, she thought, 'It's amazing apparently what words can do, if that's all you actually have. Words and tone of voice. Expression. Even saying nothing at all. Silence can do a lot.' But all this, you might say, is *post hoc.*

To go further back. She said an odd thing early on. It was a Sunday afternoon after we had drunk a bottle of rosé at lunch and I stood behind her as I hadn't done in quite some time. I leaned down and kissed her hair and slipped my flattened hands across the front of her blouse. She said that afternoon as we lay in bed and the half-tilted slats of the blinds barred our skins with strips of light and shadow, 'Close your eyes. Make love to me with your eyes closed.' Then afterwards she asked me, 'Was that more intense?'

'Than what?' I said.

'Was it? With your eyes shut?'

'No,' I said. 'It was just as if the light was switched off. That's about all.'

Peter was tall and good-looking in so far as one man can judge another, and clever, which was obvious from everything he did. If we were in a restaurant, or anywhere else for that matter, he was the one who handled the figures. He knew French. He played the piano. He remembered the names of characters in the books he liked Rose, his wife, to read to him. And—a strange thing perhaps to say about a blind person—he was elegant. He was so sparing in his movements when we ate together, for example, which we often did. I don't mean he was careful, which of course he was, or practised in the long habit of sensing where objects were. At least I understood that blindness atones with the sharpness of other senses. I've noticed that time and again. His awareness of someone, a waiter say, entering, no matter how quietly. His memorising a room, the placement of furniture; the caution that somehow never seemed so direct as that. It was an apprehension taken into himself, and returned as poise. You might even think, as I did, it was *as though he might see but chooses not to.* That phrase surprised when it occurred to me. Claire is much sharper about such things than I am. 'But that's exactly it,' she said when I told her. 'I've never thought of it but that's the impression he gives. As if affliction is a choice.'

It is three years since we met. It was the kind of coincidence that occurs when you are in another country. Peter and Rose were across at a niece's wedding; we had been to a cousin's fiftieth. The Monday after these occasions the four of us, two couples who had not yet met, stood at the stone wall at Katoomba and looked out to the amazingly blue distances, the exposed escarpments and the ravines, the valleys and slopes with their million on millions of gums. It was late afternoon. The shadows were deep, the cliffs still alive in light. Without at first paying much attention to it, I heard the middle-aged man beside me explaining how the air for as far in the distance as one might see was packed with infinitesimal refracting particles of vaporised eucalyptus. It was this that explained the famous blueness that tourists came to see. By now I was interested in what he said. He told the woman beside him about other things. He spoke about Darwin the great scientist coming up here when he visited the continent he found compelling, but disliked. He said, 'He wrote as he sailed out, "I leave you without sorrow or regret."' There was a pause then when the man said nothing, and the woman with him spoke too quietly for me to hear. But I heard the man laugh, and tell her, 'I agree. He must have hurried when he hiked up here.'

Claire too was listening, although the man was not speaking in a raised voice. Yet the afternoon was so still, the air so laden with blueness, that he might well have been addressing us. Then two coaches pulled up not far from where we stood, and in the babble and shouting and herding towards a vantage point, the couple near us moved away. We saw them again later that evening, in the dining room of the hotel. We looked at them and nodded and the woman, who was short but rather lovely and wore a peacock-shimmering frock, smiled back at us from the other side of the room. We were seated near a window, the other couple some distance away, beneath a huge Victorian sideboard you see in advertisements for the hotel. Towards the end of the meal Claire said, 'I simply do not believe it.' She had been glancing across the dining room for some time. I should not have taken a Drambuie with the black coffee I ordered after our dessert. All I could think about was falling into bed. I was dog-tired after the day's long drive, the walk down from the hotel to the mountainous waves of blue towards the descending dark, and then back.

'What's that?' I asked. 'What don't you believe?' And she told me the man whose talking at the lookout area had made me see the country with a clarity I otherwise would have missed, was blind. She said, 'You'd scarcely think so until you watch carefully. His wife touches him differently. Odd how that gives it away.' Which I understood as I later took it in, how Rose's hands would hover and lightly rest and discreetly direct. I am still surprised when I think of it, how intensely close she and her husband are, the ease that is not predominantly one or the other, but the quiet pooled intelligence of both.

We live in the same city, and so later on saw a lot of each other. I used to read aloud for Peter once or so a fortnight. Rose reads to him every evening, but she preferred biographies and novels, rather than the military history books he also likes to hear. In the eighteen months we were close, when the four of us were friends and went to concerts together and drove up the coast in summer, I became quite interested in what otherwise would not have come my way—Blunden's and Graves's accounts of life in the trenches, Massingham's and Montague's essays, Davin on Crete. I once asked him why he was drawn to such books. 'It's what people think,' he said, 'under duress. I don't mind Rose's novels but of course for all the puppetry they're only one person's take on life. I like those parts of books where people can't lie. When what they say has to be the truth.'

'The facts?' I say.

'Even if they're lies they become facts,' Peter laughs. 'That's why wars hold us even though they're vile.'

I don't quite understand him. Nor does Claire, when I repeat what he said. This surprises me, as she is far more at home with thinking about such things than I have ever been. After all, she teaches teenagers about books, how to read them carefully, how not to be taken in; how to imagine further than you'd ever go alone. She sometimes reads to Peter as well. Historical novels that would have bored me stiff. He asked could she find another one like that, after she read him *Wife to Mr Milton*.

There were other friends we shared. Peter's cousin Kevin, a solicitor from Masterton, whose passion I believe was grafting roses towards shapes and colours they would never arrive at without interference; Rose's unmarried sister from Silverstream, who taught at the same school as Claire. There was another friend called Rory who worked at the Foundation for the Blind, a volunteer who visited homes and made what he called 'talking letters', tapes that could be sent to friends overseas. Peter and this friend went jogging in the park above Newtown. They ran side by side on the footpaths there and back. Claire had passed them more than once. She said you would never have guessed. Rory ran on the outside, and she saw that he was talking as they ran. She supposed he kept up some kind of commentary on where to turn, what to look out for, kept an eye out for dogs. But no one would guess, Claire said, from looking at these two men running side by side, that one of them was seeing for both.

Claire from time to time read to Peter on Saturday mornings, while Rose played squash with her sister before lunch, as she did on the morning I come back to. I had been to see the exhibition from Pompeii. Our son in Melbourne insisted it was not to be missed. Claire visited twice with groups from school but I had left it to the last minute. I couldn't face telling Rob that I'd not got round to looking at it, although when I did go with the crowds on that last weekend I found it unpleasant. You don't live where we do, in a pole-house above a cliff, and sit through a vivid presentation of earthquake and destruction, then join the crush attending to the scraps that survived, and walk out as though you'd just watched *Shortland Street*. When I handed back the special glasses one wore through the fifteen-minute film with its fractured pillars and its piling ash, I found myself three-deep with those taking in the ancient oven and its carbonised bread, the oxidised mirrors, the figures of votive gods whose names no doubt were appealed to as the roofs cracked and the air thickened to paste. The casts of bodies in their final throes, the half-naked young woman with her fists clenched, her clothing dragged over her head, the contorted dog wrenching at its chained collar as its lungs burned—you could see why queuing Wellingtonians were absorbed. I moved quickly through the exhibition. I was glad to get back to the push of the southerly as I left the big cavernous building. The wind whacked the cord against a high metal flagpole. I needed to clear my head.

Instead of going through to the car park beneath the museum I decided to enjoy the pelt of the wind. It was twenty minutes to Peter and Rose's along Oriental Parade. I kept to the harbour side of the road. The spray rose and its saltiness was flung above the railings. The gusts lifted the collar of my jacket and whirred it against my cheek. I felt the elation of it as I had when I was a boy and the winds came up and rocked you in a life bigger than your own. I had forgotten Pompeii, the thoughts that inevitably come to you as you stand above a crouched contorted man, his cloak muffling his face, or another with iron brackets on his feet, unable to run with the rest. They are good things to forget.

Peter and his wife lived halfway up a hillside you come at by a zigzag from sea-level, following ribbons of white-painted railing through trees that seem almost black as the wind tugs and belts them. But from the house you looked over them to the harbour and the hills. 'We're here for the view,' Peter liked to say. The path from the gateway to the house cut through branches tangled overhead so you walked along a green tunnel to the white side of the house. If it recently had rained your shoulders were soaked by the time you reached the porch with its swathes of fuchsia in huge Aladdin pots.

'I hear everything,' Peter would joke. 'I know when someone's even thinking about calling in.' But not this morning, Peter, as the wind dashed the trees against each other and there was the sound of a loosened iron strip banging on the fence between our friends and their neighbour. I opened the back door as I always did and walked through the kitchen to the lounge, towards the glassed-in porch where Peter sat when he was read to. How strangely still it seemed for a moment, as I stood on one of the handsome Persian rugs. As the gust lessened I heard Claire's voice as I moved towards the porch. There was nothing dramatic in the way she read, nothing of the exaggeration that I dislike at times when a story is heard on radio. There was an attractive modulation as she followed the meaning through, the merest lift and fall as the words demanded—a sense of rhythm, that was it, not imposed so much as taken from the sentences she read. You could tell one voice was guided by another, the reader by the writer who had set how it might sound.

Peter stood behind her, bending over her, his shape dark against the hurl of the sky and the veils of rain. He turned, and I remember thinking, if he hears everything, as he says, why has he heard me only now? As he stepped aside Claire's head too turned, and Peter's hand withdrew from her breast, which she quickly covered with her lowered sweater. I assumed Peter thought I had seen nothing, although how could I know?

'Odd' is a word I later kept saying to myself, that I've said several times to the marriage counsellor when she insists I need to talk it through. 'Odd', when of course I meant I had not been so startled by anything in my life as I was by the feeling that I interrupted some deep moment of privacy, that I was the one who needed to excuse myself as I saw the white scoop of my wife's breast released, the dark uncovered nipple. I in fact had said 'Sorry' from the half-opened glass door. The memory of that sears more than what I saw. Then Peter was facing me with the eyes that took in nothing, and asking, 'Pompeii over already, then?'

Claire closed the book she had been reading from, took her cellphone from the small table beside her, and stood up. 'I was going to phone but the story was longer than I thought.' Then her embarrassment only then, her shame at that, I think, at saying something so inane. 'Odd,' I said to the counsellor. 'I'm convinced that was it. Far more that, than that I'd seen our blind friend touching her.'

'You've asked her about it?' the counsellor said. 'Talked about it properly?'

'I don't think either of us would see much point in that.' I could see that Toni, who is the woman I talk with, did not think much of my answer. I expect it failed to tick the right box, seeing as 'talking a problem out, frankly' is pretty near item one of what they call essential advice.

I'm not sure about this counselling business. I am usually sceptical when I hear that kind of thing, grief counsellors being brought into schools when something unfortunate happens, soldiers even, can you credit that, needing psychologists when war turns out to be exactly what the word 'war' means. Odd, too, that my walking in on whatever it was I interrupted seemed not at first to bother either of us as much as you might expect. Neither Claire nor myself, that is. We are not the kind to shout and throw things. Not surprisingly, though, neither one of us was in a rush to get in touch. I can only guess that Peter must have spun Rose some line. I've no idea. It seems so obvious to me now, although it had not entered my head before, that all this talk you hear sometimes about the mystery of another's personality, the unlikelihood of truly knowing even those close to one, really does stack up if it means a friend who has never in fact seen you, but the darkness of that, as it were, is transferred from him to you, he is the one you have never seen.

I said to Toni over our herbal tea—there is always that, a Chinese-patterned teapot and two handle-less cups we drink from as we talk—I said, 'Thank God that Claire and I don't use phrases like "We need to be grown up about this" or "It simply looked worse than it was". We at least don't play games like that.'

'Better to say nothing, then?' she asks.

'In our case, I'm sure, yes.' I tried to explain that Claire and I, after all, we both knew exactly what it was, and it is nonsense to make out it was anything else. It was a woman letting a blind man fumble her tits, while the spouses of both believed that all that was going on was reading a book, another man's wife reading a book out of the kindness of her heart, and another woman's husband grateful for the kindness. I tried to get Toni to see. What is the point going on about confusion, when clarity is already there?

The next morning was stunning, one of those autumn days when you feel you are in a hollowed diamond, everything calm and sparkle. It seems wind is what you once heard of, but scarcely remember. I stood at our kitchen window watching the small boats in the bay, the kids in their yellow lifevests ducking as the sails swung slowly across them, although there was scarcely breeze enough to puff them along. I heard Claire come into the kitchen and open the fridge door, the muesli shaken from its packet, the scoop of her spoon against the plastic container of yoghurt, then the pouring of milk, almost a whisper. The images from yesterday, my walking back through the swathes of sodden fuchsias after the absurdity of my 'Sorry', the inanity of what she had said, and my leaving without speaking to Peter, not waiting for my wife—these ran over and over in my mind as I watched the drift of the little boats and the children leaning forward, as though that would somehow edge them ahead.

I said, 'It doesn't bother me as much as you might think.' Then for the first and only time in our marriage, Claire turned and physically attacked me. Her closed fist came down sharply on my collarbone. I guessed that in her quick rush of anger she had not quite lined me up. I had thought before I said them that she would find my words placating, but it seemed not. It took me some time, with Toni's help, with the constant raising of her Chinese teapot and the refilling of the little cups, to appreciate why Claire was so enraged.

'It's because your friend is blind,' she wanted me to understand. 'What a woman *looks* like is hardly to the point, if the man who wants to seduce her has no idea how she appears. Which in turn means that from *your* point of view, so far as Claire understands it, it didn't much matter to you because it didn't count so much if Peter couldn't see. Both belittle her, don't you see?'

I didn't answer because I was not convinced by Toni's earnestness, her coming down on certain words with such emphasis as if that was where the truth lurked, and needed to be flushed out. And I thought her explanation a touch too clever, which she must have picked up.

I saw no point in making more of it. I told her, 'Thank you for explaining it. Thank you for that.'

'Explaining is one thing,' she smiled back at me. 'Accepting what is explained is another.' I suppose people talk like that because that is how they are trained to talk.

She dresses rather badly, Toni, and I can only assume she attempts to cut her own hair. She is oddly attractive for all that. Dark skin, grey eyes, a distinct vivacity when she talks, as well as what I guess is priceless in a counsellor, the ability to seem sincere at every moment. But 'slatternly' is a word which is also spot-on, and doesn't do her the harm you might expect it to. The elbow worn thin in the same jersey she wears at each of our meetings, the scuffed caps to her shoes. I'm not good at guessing a woman's age. When Claire asked me that I said, 'Could be anything, really. There's two children at secondary school, if that helps.'

I think Claire believed I was rather taken with Toni—almost wanted me to be, I sometimes thought. I didn't tell her that early on the counsellor had told me her own marriage had 'foundered', a clunky sort of word to choose, and that now she lived with another woman. 'Although we're hardly hammer-and-tongs lesbos,' she said, which made me like her. I liked her quickness too, her knack for explanations even when they did not convince me. And I was fascinated by the self-centredness of counselling. The whole business took off and returned to you alone, it was hearing yourself told as the central character in a story. Toni, I used to think, became a character too when she talked, at a remove from herself. It was a bit of a performance all round. I've never played chess, but I imagined more than once that what we were doing must be a little like that, yourself divided into these ranks of moves and defences, the black-and-white ploys that can never really bring you to a conclusion that will satisfy both sides.

It had been Claire's idea that I take these sessions she saw advertised on some women's website. 'Marital problems may simply mean you fail to talk.' There are it seems quite a lot of encouraging messages along those lines, once you go looking for them. I said, 'It doesn't seem to me, Claire, that I'm the one with a problem.'

'Charles, love,' she came back at me, 'don't tell me you're not devastated.'

'Am I?' I'm not much good at doing sarcastic, doing irony, although she thought I was attempting both. There was nothing more to my asking that than was there on the surface. I was simply puzzled why she would think I needed to sit with Toni, or felt the moorings of our marriage were slipping away. Then she had said, almost peevishly, 'You've hardly said a word in a fortnight, for heaven's sake. Doesn't it mean a thing to you?'

'Claire,' I said, 'is that being reasonable?'

'You're the one,' she said. 'You're the one behaving as though there is absolutely nothing to get over.'

It was simpler to agree then, as I did, to go once a week to 'engage in useful discussion' with Toni, whom I first warmed to because she knew there was something rather silly in the language the encouraging brochure used, and even in Claire's trundling me along as though, as I said, I was some kind of difficult child who had become too much for its parents. Although, professionally speaking, she did insist that my being willing to talk with her in the first place was a positive step. 'It shows goodwill,' she said. Then a touch too dramatically for my taste, although I realised this was the kind of thing she was paid for, she held my eye and said, in a tone I hadn't quite heard since school, 'I think we can pretty much say, Charles, we'll all come out of this a darned sight better than when we went in.'

Claire—I am sure of this, although she would never have said so—felt let down that this was all that had come from it, from that morning of plastercast corpses and a savage southerly when I walked in on them. I had turned and left Peter's house, back through the tunnel of trees towards the gate, down beside the white railings of the zigzag towards the Parade. The heft of the wind was what I needed. Had the afternoon been still and the harbour placid, I expect it would have enraged me. But the elements, if I can put it in such old-hat romantic terms, matched what I felt, my confusion and blunder and surprise and then that curious floating feeling, which is difficult to admit, the feeling that I should have felt something deeper than I did, the excitement we don't admit to when things are bad.

I was at the bottom of the wooden rails when I saw Rose walking towards me. Her blue Fiat was parked a few yards behind her, in the area marked 'For residents only'. She carried a string kit fat with shopping. She cheerfully called to me, 'Aren't you heading the wrong way?'

I knew as I answered her how oddly I must sound. 'Why don't you park up there, at the other end?' I looked back to the winding path behind me, to the distant run of railings at its further end, the road so much higher than where we stood. Her and Peter's house was pretty much midway between the two.

'I'm out again later in the day. Parking up that end can be hell.'

She smiled with the openness I had found attractive that first evening while I watched her in the dining room at Katoomba. One of her front teeth lapped slightly across the other, reminding me of a movie actress who enchanted me when I was a student. My first thought, I must admit, when I realised back then about Peter, was 'what a waste', his never being able to take on board what a handsome wife he had. But that now seemed a very long time ago as I walked back beside the wall above the heaving sea and the lift of its spray, to the museum car park.

*

How we generalise, as Toni reminded me, from what happens to ourselves, although I don't see how that is to be avoided. We have nothing else, after all, to consider as absolute, as rock bottom. Who else can we say is typical if not ourselves? Toni asked me once, quite unexpectedly, was I in what one of the brochures called 'emotional distress'? I told her, 'Talk like that strikes me, has always struck me, as just a bit stagy.' Then, without really meaning to, I said, 'It rattled me, that's how I'd rather put it.' Rattled me that I was wrong about a good deal I thought I knew.

That same evening after a blind man fondled Claire, we had to attend a twenty-first. The girl was a distant relative. There was a lot to drink and a lot of noise, there was an important rugby match on TV and half the party crammed into the 'games room'. (They were the kind of people who relished words like 'patio' and 'master bedroom'.) The big screen covered half a wall. It came home to me how few of these people I gave a damn for. I had been to the weddings of half the older ones; I expected I would go to the funerals of some of them as well. Always assuming, that is. How mordant my evening had become! Then after the rugby the younger ones took over the real partying in the big lounge and those our age were in a smaller sitting-room or the host's expansive office. But they were kindly enough people, and the girl's parents insisted as we left towards midnight that we mustn't leave it till the next big occasion to see each other again. There was a lot of kissing and embracing. Then we drove home.

By the time we came to our side of the harbour the wind had dropped completely. The city across from us was a bright swathe of lights across the hills. Claire was asleep. Her head tilted onto my shoulder. I had noticed her glass was full most of the evening. Now I said, as we took the tight run of curves before Mahina Bay, 'You'd hardly believe how calm it's become.' I meant, considering the battering across the harbour that afternoon. She said, without looking at it, 'I know. It always is.'

Toni asked me at our third or fourth session, now that several weeks had passed, now that vivid image was not returning to me, waking me, as it had in that first week, did I think I really *cared*?

'Oh, yes,' I said, I cared.

So could I understand then, she pressed me, why I wasn't more angry as well? I had told her at an earlier session how I woke some mornings and in that brief sliver of time when it was not night any longer, and not yet quite day, Claire lying beside me so close I felt her hair brush against my mouth, and for that fragment a rush of *gratitude*—yes, that *is* the word I'm after—before the detail of Peter's hand flooded back into my mind, his fingers a bleached flexing sightless spider at my wife's breasts. Then I was fully awake. Claire pretended to be asleep, her rump pressed against me. The erasing of so much, as desire begins.

'You're so certain,' Toni says, 'that Claire *pretends* to be asleep?'

'After this many years,' I told her, 'you know all right what pretending is.'

Toni of course asked the obvious question. It was her professional right to do so. There is no such thing as an impertinence if your bread and butter is to pry into another's life. 'Sex?' she said. She filled both our cups with pallid tea. 'You know I have to ask that?' She assumed I would feel embarrassed.

I said, 'Who knows what is normal or usual with anyone?'

'Give it a try,' she said.

So I told her, 'I expect we're pretty much both of those.'

'No problems, then? That you know of?'

I laughed, and then Toni laughed as well, a few seconds later, when I said, 'If I don't know, who would?'

So that was settled. Claire and I apparently were not too much this side nor the other on whatever graph Toni had in mind for the human norm.

Then—also inevitable, no doubt—her asking, 'Neither of you have had affairs?'

I knew my answer could only ever be a half-answer, but I said, 'Not so far as I know.'

'Or suspect?'

I said that Claire and I talked with utter frankness in a superficial way. 'If we can't laugh about it we don't talk about it.'

'Go on,' Toni said.

'She was attracted once to a bank-teller, she thought possibly because there was an iron grille between them. There was a phys ed teacher once in one of the schools where I did the accounts with whom I'd have most certainly been unfaithful but her fiancé was the history teacher at the same school. Bald as an egg. You knew if a woman loved someone as unattractive as that it had to be for real.'

Toni crackled a packet of wafer-thin Japanese biscuits, She looked at me a moment then asked me directly, 'Are you taking the piss?'

I said, 'It may sound like that. It's not what I intend.'

A long time later, when Peter and Rose had gone to live in Australia, Claire said, as though it were a thing that had been on her mind some time, and sooner or later had to be declared, 'A thing you know I've never quite worked out. You'll see why I have to say this, love. That time when it was so awkward there for a while between us, so tough for you I do know that. When Peter took me by surprise. One thing puzzling me I could not work out and never have. And that evening later on, that too of course. You've never said what you thought. Not really.' And then, although there was no logical step towards it, she suddenly said, 'He took his ring off, his wedding ring. I suppose I should have known from that. I heard it chink when he put it down on that glass-topped table, remember, with a kind of patterned doily between the glass and the wood?'

I suppose that was my chance to ask what I never did. 'Good manners will kill you!' I remember Toni teasing me at one of our sessions. There is that curious point in marriages, I suppose, when the chance to clarify something, to clear up a confusion, to press a little further than at least some of us are prepared to press, is within a hair's breadth, and we let it pass. As I let my chance go then, not to ask more about that afternoon of the high wind and reading aloud, and the chink of the wedding ring on the glass table, now that I knew of it, but to say to her, 'What did it mean, that last time, that other time, we were all together?' It is absurd, to think one can sleep with a person for a thousand, five thousand nights, and yet there are these few minutes of embarrassment one does not refer to.

The last time we spent with Peter and Rose was the evening before Queen's Birthday. There was no significance in that, beyond it being a holiday next day, with neither Claire nor I concerned about time or the long drive back round the bays. It was only weeks before they left for Australia. It seemed a long time since we had seen each other, my leaving the house and the fuchsias brushing against me, and then bumping into Rose at the bottom of the zigzag. Peter was the one who seemed the more excited about the move. He said the climate meant rather more to him than it might to us. 'Seeing things distracts from weather,' he joked. 'Take my word for it. When there are no distractions weather is absolute.'

Was I imagining it, I thought later in the evening, the hint of patience I picked up on Rose's features while her husband spoke? I supposed she had heard it all so often, which might be said of any spouse. For a moment I had this curious picture of marriage itself being like sitting in a room as a blind person might sit, your picking up—trying to pick up—the merest shifts, the subtlest alterations in tone, the brushings and movements of the slightest kind, which others almost certainly would miss.

I don't often think of something that I consider amusing, yet that occurring to me did, a slice of comedy that was entirely mine. In its way it lightened the evening for me.

Rose broke in through our talk about the weather. She explained that her other sister ran a successful business not far from Brisbane. She was widowed a year ago and lonely. 'We're not lonely,' Rose said, 'but we're not rich either. She wants me to go into the business with her as a partner. She caters for weddings, anniversaries, what have you. Bringing style, as she likes to say, to the outback. Sometimes she'll travel for a day—even fly sometimes—to put on these posh dos. Peter will play the piano. She says the novelty value of that can't be underestimated either.' That was another obvious picture that came to mind. Peter in a tuxedo and dark glasses, handsome at the keyboard, women high on Hunter Valley wines demanding the Beatles, the Beach Boys, the songs that had hustled them into romance a lifetime before.

Rose had gone to trouble with our dinner. Now we sat again in the house I had entered under cover of a southerly and innocence several months before. Tonight the weather was so different. Its stillness made words like 'exquisite' come to mind, the harbour's blackness running with reflected lights, the cars along the Hutt Road like a stream of moving pearls. That is how Claire would describe them on the way home. I knew the women had worked discreetly together for us to have this evening together before Rose and Peter left for their new life. There was not a note of bitterness between us. No more than the closeness we used to share.

The CD of the Tallis Scholars had come to an end. We sat in silence in the lounge after dinner, our brandy glasses like fragile bubbles in our hands. The only light was from the candles burning on the table. I felt we all knew there was something of a charade about our being together, however much the afternoon of Pompeii now seemed a ghost at the door. The faintest scratching behind a wall. Of course I have no idea—how could I?—what really passed in the minds of the others.

I was looking into the bronze smear of the brandy tilted in my glass. I heard Peter clear his throat, and the faint clip of his glass on the small table beside him as he placed it down. I heard Claire's breathing alter slightly. I looked up to see Rose's arms crossed above her head, as she drew up her dark sweater, shaking her hair free as for a moment it caught the garment's neckline before it was removed. Her breasts were suddenly unconfined, as though somehow independent of her. The candlelight and its shadows both concealed and enhanced. When Rose turned to drop the sweater on the floor beside her, they were momentarily in profile, the nipples black in the play of light, as large as thimbles. No one spoke for some time. Peter sat with his hands on his crossed knee. And that was all that occurred. Then Claire stood up, and so did I. I have no idea of what it meant to the others, that tableau that puzzles me, as I think of it, yet I knew it was significant to each of us. Absurdly, I thought, the only way Peter—perhaps Rose too—could think of to atone. Thelonious Monk picking out the first few notes of regret.

It was the way our day in the Blue Mountains finally came to an end.

Mrs Bennett and the Bears

The first time he tried to phone there was difficulty getting through. Ten minutes later the line was clear as glass. Jackie picked up the phone and shrieked, 'Edward!' She raised her hand to hush the women at the table behind her, on the other side of the two bottles and the plates with their scattered shells. 'Have we had a night, believe me!' Jackie said.

'Who's there?' Edward asked her.

'Your sisters,' Jackie said. 'Who else?' And Shirl called over his wife's shoulder, 'Ask him how the little Nip ladies are!'

Edward was fifty-six. It still surprised him that he was in Japan at all. The director had come through into the smallest of the three divisional offices and said, 'We have to send somebody up there, and I'm damned if I want to face that lot again. Intestines of sea-slugs for breakfast. Not on your nelly.' He turned to Lucy, the administrative assistant, who sat a few feet from Edward's desk. She laughed and knew exactly what the director meant. 'Emetics aren't in it,' she said. 'So I've heard.' So Edward had said all right, he'd go then, it was about time he took one of these information jaunts. Making it sound casual. In fact he had felt—not his word, true, but one that Jackie had used on his behalf—he had felt more than a tad excited at the prospect. A conference in Sapporo on the care of the aged may not sound quite the most exciting assignment, but Japan, after all . . .

He would not have admitted it to a soul, not even to Jackie, but when he thought of the place it was pretty much what his father would have thought. Which meant, seeing Dad had never been closer to the war than training on Motutapu, it was a view based almost entirely on the movies. The deck of an aircraft carrier far below with a pilot's face smooth as butter, a white scarf fluttering from his throat as he tilts and aims dead centre. A sword flashing down above a bowed neck. Less nasty things, of course. Olympic gymnasts arcing back from the rings, rice rolled in seaweed, a woman with her face whitened with flour. Yes, he was glad he said he would go. Jackie and his sisters thought it an absolute scream, Edward off to Nippon at his age when he'd hardly been out of the North Island! Shirl, who always talked to him as though he were on the end of a distant telephone call in any case, now clinked the bottles behind his wife's head and called down the thousands of kilometres, 'Tell him just listen to what he's missing!'

Edward put down the receiver and stood at the window, fifteen storeys above the long artificial lake. Scullers in bright jackets sliced the dark water, their wakes spreading out and intersecting. It was his first time away from home for years. And if what he now felt was loneliness, then that was all right too. But it was a strange feeling. Then he stepped back to the window, startled. A large wide-winged bird, a hawk it must be, swept in to within feet of the plate-glass he stood at. It was the air currents, he supposed—the warmth from the huge hotel that towered where natural cold should be, and the birds rode the comfort of it. Or perhaps that had nothing to do with it. He turned and went to the sofa in the most luxurious room he had ever spent a night in. They told you that, didn't they, that Japan was luxury. Billy Collett in Policy had said to him before he came up, 'I've been there three times and I don't pretend to know the first thing about the buggers. But they do know what a hotel is. You'll see that soon enough.'

He sat and took off the new shoes he had bought for the conference. He had not liked it when he phoned just now. He had not liked hearing his sisters—Bernice who was married and Shirl who was divorced—both trying so hard to show what fun they were having. Perhaps they were. Perhaps they were as happy as he and Jackie were most of the time. He had been elated all day, and the phone call made him feel so flat. Visiting the hospital especially, now that was something. The quality of the place, so much finer than anything he knew at home. He had taken careful notes. The young caregivers who trained for two years and wore long blue aprons as they moved cheerfully among the aged patients—their good humour and dedication that so struck him. The few old people who tried to speak to him and shook his hand. The large Impressionist prints on the walls, the cages of bright singing birds. He had talked with a physio from Christchurch, brought up here for a year to work with local staff. The young woman told him not everywhere was like this, of course, but there was nothing back home to touch it either.

He returned to the window and placed his forehead on the cold glass. The air outside was grey; lights twinkled in moving streams on a distant motorway. Another of the large birds swept in. It levelled out and hovered so close to the glass that the darker markings of the feathers stood out as clear as writing. Then the bird tilted and flowed down towards the sheet of now blackened water.

The phone shrilled on the bedside table. Mr Tanaka said he would be in the foyer tomorrow morning at eight o'clock; would Edward be so good as to meet him there, promptly? Seeing it was their free day. Mr Tanaka was youngish, handsome, connected with a string of hospitals. He had given a paper on financing care for the aged. He referred to flowcharts and the economies of several countries. He said, 'What we do for them today we do for ourselves tomorrow.' He would drive Edward to the country to see the bears. And Mrs Bennett, he said. She had been a student with him and now lived in Sydney—perhaps Edward had met her already? He said he thought so. A tallish woman with high-piled hair, she must be the one Mr Tanaka meant.

He was quite wrong. Mrs Keiko Bennett was—well, dumpy, Jackie would have called her. Her hair was short, with a shiny fringe across a roundish, middle-aged face. She spoke English and once had an Australian husband. She smiled when they shook hands. She was the first Japanese he had met in two days who did not bow and make him feel the awkwardness of his body.

Mr Tanaka sat in the front seat, next to the driver. Edward and Keiko—she asked him to call her that—sat in the back. We are like a bridal party, Edward thought, these white antimacassar things across the seats, the lacy fringes, the white gloves the driver wore. Keiko broke the ice. She said, 'I have never seen the bears either.' Mr Tanaka told them the animals they were going to see were called higuma. For all other bears there was a different word. This was only for those in Hokkaido, which were almost the biggest in the world.

It surprised Edward that he did not feel awkward with her, not in the least. Women, as Jackie sometimes teased him, were hardly his thing, were they? 'Forty before he tried one!' she said once to Bernice. And Bernice had slapped her hand and said, 'That's my big brother you're talking about, you wicked widow!' Later Edward told her, 'I wish you wouldn't joke like that.' It made him look, well, stupid, didn't it? Then Jackie lifted her cashmere sweater and crushed him in against her breasts and tousled his hair and told him there, if they couldn't joke among themselves, the family, then who could they joke with? She had held him so tight her nails hurt his shoulders. She called out, 'My God!' and when she got her breath back she said, 'Doesn't that tell you something, now, doesn't it?'

Mr Tanaka said a friend of his was once playing golf not far from the hot springs where they would park the car and take the funicular several hundred metres into the densely wooded hills. His friend was teeing off when a cry went up along the links. A bear had come out of the woods and was ambling along the course. Players ran in all directions, tossing their American clubs and their expensive Italian leather bags all over the greens.

Keiko laughed for the first time and Edward thought, how good that sounds when she laughs. Her face was lit with the thought of it—the running golfers, their dignity dropped as quickly as their number eights, and the slow, lumbering, casual beast. Her teeth were even and small; she looked ten years younger when she laughed. Edward was laughing too. She held his glance when he looked across at her. And then he remembered she was Japanese, and how foreign she was, after all. How foreign their whole excursion was. But there was a warmth between them.

It was two hours later, after they had eaten buckwheat noodles off heated black tiles, and Mr Tanaka had dropped them at the funicular, whose small red cabin gently swayed them away from the dock and out over the steeply ascending forest. Keiko pointed to where the sun broke from the afternoon rainclouds and the distant sea flashed out its great sheet of foil. 'See that, Edward?' she said. And when they were through the gates of the park she said, 'Here, hold your hands like a cup.' She poured the round toasted pellets from the bag she had just bought. She tilted the bag and steadied his own hands with one finger. It was as natural as a mother doing it to a child. But her touch surprised him, and pleased him greatly, and she smiled when he looked at her.

They walked in silence to the parapet and she said, 'Ah!' as she looked over. 'You think so too?'

'Yes,' Edward said, 'yes.' He did not catch what word she had actually said. But yes to whatever it was, for when he looked down and saw the bears he felt the catch in his breath. They were magnificent and poised and huge. Directly beneath him one hoisted itself up from where it rested on all fours. It rose and expanded and its sheer presence came up to him with the rough, tangy stench of the pit. It held up a soft black paw beneath the sheathed curve of its claws, a kind of benign, slow, imploring wave as he threw pellets down to it, then the quick easy movement of the massive head as it snapped at the flying scraps of food. There were dozens of them in the huge concrete pit. 'See the necks,' Keiko said. Her hand lifted, then fell back beside his own on the iron rail in front of them. She meant the wounds slashed in long red trenches on the shoulders and chests of several of the bears. 'They fight because of the space.'

They watched for almost an hour. Edward said, 'I feel like a child, watching these.'

'They would kill you like that,' Keiko said. Again her hand raised slightly and fell back to the iron bar. 'They are very beautiful and they would kill you like that.' And they laughed together, although there was no particular reason to. Then she looked at her watch and said, 'The Japanese are never late.' And as if to place herself a little to one side, she smiled at Edward and told him, 'I have been in Sydney now for as long as I was Japanese.'

Mr Tanaka's driver asked if they would like to sit in the car or walk a little while they waited for their host to return from one of his hospitals down the road.

'We'll walk,' Keiko said. They walked for ten minutes, passing beyond the public buildings to a small park and a few trees. The first drops of rain were sudden and big as coins. The downpour pinged off car roofs and hissed on the open ground. Edward put on the light raincoat he had carried all afternoon. 'Mr Tanaka will drive down this way,' Keiko said. 'He's bound to.'

Edward held open the sides of his raincoat in what he knew must seem a comic enough gesture. He said, 'I'm afraid there's nowhere else.' The woman stood in close against him. She put her hands just above his own and drew the coat as best she could in front of both of them. The rain ran behind Edward's glasses and inside his collar. He could smell the rain on Keiko's hair. She stood close against him, her head beneath his chin. She laughed and her hair moved against his throat and she said, 'We must look very strange.' It was only a minute. The black car eased down the street towards them. The driver's whitegloved hand rose and beckoned them to the kerb. That was all there was. They had stood in the pelting rain, their bodies close, as at ease, Edward thought, as he had ever been with anyone. 'Thank you,' Keiko said. Then they scrambled into the car.

Keiko rubbed her face and her hands with a towel Mr Tanaka handed back to her. She then ran her fingers through her hair and held the towel towards Edward. Mr Tanaka and the driver were highly amused. As they dropped Edward back at his hotel Keiko touched his hand and said, 'Next time an umbrella!' He stood at the hotel entrance and raised his hand. She waved back from the other side of the rain-dotted window. She was leaving the conference early, to visit a sister in Kyushu. She kept her hand flat on the window until the car turned into the main road.

Edward sat in the huge lobby, where a man in a white suit played a grand piano on a dais between ten-metre artificial palms. High above, in the fifteen-storey atrium, life-size models beneath brightly coloured hang-gliders swooped forever in the same place. He ordered a brandy and watched the capsule-shaped lift, beaded with tiny lights, run up and down the enclosed wall of the hotel. He knew Jackie would phone his room as arranged at six o'clock, but he preferred to sit down here.

He knew it was love, and knew it was absurd even to use the word. He knew that in a day, in two days, this elation would pass, and he would never know it again. Never. She had felt it too. Pressed against him. Laughing. Knowing as well as he did that it was a splinter of time that never should have occurred, a pure gift. He took a mouthful of brandy and held it without swallowing, prolonging the pleasure of its taste.

Twenty minutes later he signalled to the waiter for another drink. He smiled at the young man in a strange operatic uniform who carefully set the balloon glass on a coaster. Edward would have liked to joke with him, but he knew he did not have the knack for that kind of easy rapport. He thought how he would tell Jackie about the conference, about the marvellous geriatric baths he had seen yesterday, for example, whose sides rose from slots in the floor to the level of a metal stretcher wheeled above them, the bath literally coming to the patient. He could hear himself saying it: 'Geriatric care we've never dreamed of at home.' And Bernice rolling her eyes and Shirl passing another glass of pinot all round and Jackie joking, 'You don't have to be so interesting, pet.'

Of course he would never see Keiko again. That seemed not to matter. Her hair wet and scented beneath his chin, her hands resting on his where she held the sides of his coat together. They would never know about that. He would not even tell them about the bears that rose up as tall as in stories, their questing muzzles lifted, their eyes small as currants. There was no sadness in his thinking: this is the last secret I shall have in my life. He picked up the glass and looked again, up to the vast shadowy atrium, to the figures on the hang-gliders like high stalled hawks.

Fainting and the Fat Man

The voice was bellowing down at him before he knew whose it was, or where he lay.

'How many?' the bellow said. 'Count them for me! How many can you see?'

Robin wondered what he was to take them for—a distant view of skyscrapers, a cactus as you used to see them at the beginning of cowboy movies, its stalks filling the screen? Or a hand was it, just a hand, with the finger puppets whipped off?

'How many?' the voice continued to demand. 'How many?'

The questions made him angry. He knew what it was up to, that distended face way beyond the fingers, as though beyond the bars of a grille. The features shook into focus. The bulbous eyes, the red web of veins showing in their whites. The wings of the ears. He said, 'Five. Five fucking fingers. Now let me sit up.'

He knew now that he had slipped, slipped stepping up to the urinal. He had tilted back and lost balance, and hit his head on the tiled floor. He must have been out to it for half a minute, a minute, how could he tell? And now this shape looming over him, going through his first-aid routine to test him for a stroke.

Robin sat up and took in where he was. He felt fine. Strange, but fine. He raised his hand to feel behind his head. He took the folded magenta handkerchief from his blazer's breast pocket and dabbed it at the swelling. He examined the stained square, the circle that showed black on the coloured cloth. He looked at the fat man who still knelt beside him, who appeared disappointed, who had expected the fallen stranger to be much worse.

He said, knowing it would irritate this heavy man who so wished to test his reactions and who now stood with two soaked knees from the recently mopped men's room floor, 'The Japs, do you know that? They liked wearing dark blue because it was harder for the blood to show. It stained but it could have been water. Could have been a cup of tea.' Surprised at how his words just tumbled out. He had spoken them before understanding what they said. He knew they were not the right things to say.

The fat man stood there above him. He made no attempt to help him stand. But Robin could hear him breathing hard, as though what he had done, kneeling down and calling to him and standing up, had been an effort. He looked ten feet tall, tugging at his cuffs, then both his hands like flippers, their fingers joined, brushing across the front of his suit. Robin raised one hand to the porcelain basin above him, to assist in drawing himself up. Nothing to write home about there, he thought, seeing his reflection in the mirror above the basin. There was a bright thread running from behind his ear, onto the collar of the checked shirt he had never liked, but what could you do with a Father's Day gift if you're not to offend people? He dabbed the handkerchief against his neck. The bump at the back of his head began throbbing now he was on his feet.

The fat man continued to watch him. Robin was damned if he was going to thank him. He thought, you can *smell* his disappointment. Helped this fellow with a stroke, that was what he hoped to be able to say, making a thing of it, loving the drama. The way people did who had the luck to witness an accident. Not much older than I am, that'd be my guess. Hadn't been drinking, no, simply keeled over. Happened that quickly. Well, the fat man wouldn't be trotting all that out, not this time. 'Five,' he had said, almost immediately, and, 'My name is Robin.' He had given his address, his telephone number. You need me, sport, he wanted to tell him now, more than I need you, surprised at the nastiness of what he thought. The fat man left without another word. It was not a good feeling between them. The empty men's room now rang with it.

As he later thought on it, he was a little ashamed of his tetchiness, of his resentment against a stranger, but defended it. His wife told him, 'The poor man was trying to help.'

'He was intrusive,' Robin said. 'He took advantage.' That Pamela was right was not the point. In fact his distaste grew for the man who had loomed over him, his breath wheezing at him, his stubby fingers raised.

'My God,' Pamela said, 'what a nasty piece of work you can be if you try.' Serious behind her joking tone.

Robin too not wishing to sound pompous, although he did, as he told her, 'You don't usually bother to say "when you try".'

Little skirmishes was all they were, these occasional *contretemps* between them. They were contented enough together. Rubbed along. Sometimes he told her, 'We're luckier than most of those we know. Our kids like us. We like each other.' We're lucky in the long run, was what he meant.

'You're fortunate,' Pamela told him now, 'that it was only that. Just a slip, I mean.'

'I know, I know,' Robin said. But it stayed with him, the shock of it, his coming to on the tiles of a public lavatory. There was more to regaining consciousness than just taking fingers for fingers, than counting up to five. A shadow there, somehow, behind it. That was what he blamed the fat man for.

There is so much to occupy one in retirement, another thing to be grateful for. He had little patience with friends who went on about boredom. As though having time to yourself was a complaint. Jack Kelty now, one of the smartest men he knew. Stacked with talent. And his wife. As those who knew them years back before they married used to say, he's got himself a looker there! The most fascinating smile Robin had ever seen. A Jean Allison lookalike, which meant next to nothing if you mentioned that to anyone under sixty. Then their boys, both of them making a mint in IT. Last year they shouted their parents a Greek cruise. Yet Jack would drop by as he had most of his life but sit there now and whinge, the complaints ticking over as though some little motor had been switched on. Politics. The young. The programmes on TV. Even the tonic water he found fault with, not the fizz in it there used to be. Robin said after he left, after their two customary gins, 'Jack's become a bore.'

Pamela said, rather sharply Robin thought, 'He's not content to sit there reading half the day.'

'Hardly fair that, is it?' He looked up from his armchair. Impossible to mind too much, whatever she said. They weren't together because of words, they weren't going to be divided because of them. She brushed back the greying hair that fell across her forehead. As if he'd want to be anywhere else, even if he was being ticked off. In spite of, it always came back to that. For her too, he knew that. He thought of the heap of things that went against what she just implied—the walking club they went on every Wednesday, the season concert tickets, of course she knew all that. But no, he could not help telling her again, she was hardly being fair saying that.

'I was talking about Jack,' his wife said. 'How he hasn't resources the way you have. You've become so touchy.'

'Touchy?' But leaving it there. Pamela took the two empty glasses from the table beside the chair, their slivers of lemon making him think of small exhausted fish. She turned at the door into the kitchen. 'I'm outside for a while if you need me.'

'Need you?'

'The phone or anything.'

He wished he was not so aware of her—what was it since that ridiculous slip? Her *vigilance*, that was it. And that image coming back to him, the raised insistent fingers, the breathy demand, 'Can you say how many?'

He took up his old copy of Xenophon, its pencilled notes going back to the prefab where the flash library now stood. Back fifty years pretty much to Mr Minn turning his sallow, celibate face to the three students who sat in the confined room, stuffy with the smell of ageing books and papers, black-and-white photographs of sixth-century vases pinned to the walls above the shelves. Chapple began reading with such ease the account of the mercenaries' trek down to the sea, the chapter Butler, who became a cleric, so stumbled over. Chapple the one real scholar among them, killed ten years later in a car crash near Heidelberg. But as Robin now remembered him, opening a page at random and reading it as though it were a newspaper. In summer the light sifted down through the big trees in Alfred Street into Mr Minn's office. You sat in the shifting dapple of the afternoon, the fluid shadows and the patches of light, with old Minn wandering off into reminiscence, then embarrassed he had presumed too much, and tapped the text in front of him, 'If you would, Chapple?' No more than middle-aged, but 'Old Minn', as ancient to them almost as the lines he had them read about the Persians. None of those in the room really friends together, but a warmth, there'd been that, hadn't there, in the old grey prefab? 'Red figure vases,' Minn sometimes shyly confiding, 'the acme, in my opinion.'

But now Pamela calling him back. Shouting, actually, so that he put down the book and flung open the conservatory door, joining her on the loose metal path rising to the palisade of roses on the ridge at the section's end. She lurched angrily at the wheelbarrow that failed to budge.

'I've been saying,' Robin told her, 'I've been saying we should get a new one, haven't I? How many years have we had it?'

'Oil,' Pamela said, 'that's all the damn thing needs.'

He knelt on the edge of the lawn and poked with his finger at the angled wheel. 'If you think oil's going to straighten that out you're in for a surprise.'

And the mower, she said, the bloody mower had packed up on her too. Robin tried to make light of it, to draw her back from one of those flare-ups that distressed her more than they were worth. He asked her, why not drive down this minute to PlaceMakers, why not do that? They had been talking about it for weeks, what better time than now?

Pamela said, 'We could ask Ted Pike.'

'Ted'd say the same thing.' And then, 'I'll put these away and we'll drive down.'

From the door of the wooden garden shed he called across at her, 'Come on, I'll get the keys.' Calming her down, that was the story. In half an hour's time she would tell him she was sorry for her rage, and he would assure her nothing was more justified, one paid a fortune for stuff and then it packed up on you. He would tell her he'd be worried if she wasn't upset. She now walked back towards the house, pulling off her gardening gloves and slapping them against her leg. Her lips for the moment, though, still pale as though she'd been eating chalk.

Ted Pike was the neighbour people longed to have. On call to help carrying in a new piece of furniture, sharing a skip for rubbish when the underhouse was cleared out. He had worked for years in the office at PlaceMakers, a source of catalogues and advice and if he couldn't come up with an answer to a query offhand, he knew a man who could. Pamela phoned him when she went inside. Wait a week, he advised her from behind the big picture window where she could see him, across their dividing hedge, holding the phone, raising his other hand to her, his thumb raised in assurance. Wait a week he told her, a new shipment of barrows was due in from China, 'never seen anything more stylish'. But pop down now for the mower, he said. He knew Evans was on this afternoon. Evans was your man. Before he rang off Ted joked, because joking was expected of him, that they wouldn't see much of him in his own garden over the next week. 'In-laws,' he said, knowing how to come across laconic. As if the word he had said was 'plague'.

Whoever the hell Evans is, Robin thought, as he backed from the garage and Pamela reported what Ted had said. And ten minutes later saw for himself.

'You go ahead,' he instructed Pamela. He must keep his voice steady, he told himself, he must not let on. 'You're better at explaining,' he said, 'you're better with people like that.'

Better that she went up to the counter alone to speak with the big man who leaned above the counter filling in a form that was spread in front of him, who looked up and smiled at the woman approaching him, his immediate assurance that he was here to assist, in any way he might. He exuded service.

Robin was uncomfortable even before that. He sat on in the car for a moment after Pamela opened her door and stood waiting, his mind on nothing more than leaning forward a little to check the date on the warrant of fitness on the far side of the windscreen.

He had not heard when she first spoke, until her stooping to see him more clearly, asking him was he all right? Did he feel all right? Then 'Sure?' she insisted. Since the fall, how much more watchful she had become, more powerful, as a spouse inevitably does when there is the least suggestion there is something that must be watched. Only there was nothing to be alert for, why couldn't that sink in? There had been a run of tests and X-rays, there were tinkerings with diet, there was the advice to walk when it was not essential to ride. No more in fact than you'd suggest to a person half his age. Common sense, as he told his wife. It had nothing to do with the simple fact of slipping in a public loo, Christ, couldn't she take that in? Even his doctor, who ran marathons until his knee gave out, said, with his stethoscope dangling round his neck like some kind of bloody snakecharmer, 'Chances are you'll see me out, Robin, I can tell you that.' Yet he knew the ground had shifted, at least a little. Pamela made sure that it did. As he had quietly told Jack Kelty as the women looked one evening at carpet samples in another room, 'We have entered the age of surveillance, know that, Jack?' There was no way of getting round it, the sense that Pamela felt it her duty to observe. To pick up the signs. He would have said, only Jack was a left-footer and he would not want to offend, how the only important woman in his life had turned into Mother Teresa.

'You know I hate shopping,' he said. 'You know I hate the small talk,' and so his wife went up alone to the welcoming assistant, who smiled again as she mentioned Ted, their neighbour, who worked in accounts.

Robin told her, 'I'll look at this stuff here.' The enormous shelves of home appliances.

The range of Black & Decker drills. The toolkits in their bright yellow boxes. He picked up a miniature saw, unsure what on earth one would use it for, but Pamela thank God had left him where he could step back and not be seen. He felt the sweat working inside his shirt, his blood surge in his ears. The fat man Pamela smiled back at brushed at his lapels, the fingers together as though the hands were flippers.

He was unsure if he was angry, or was it upset? He placed his own hands against the deep wooden shelf in front of him. A nerve in his kneecap began a wiry twitch. Small objects on the shelves about him appeared to jitter. He bent a little to peer through the wooden slats. He saw his wife speaking and the man nodding at her while one hand moved with a slow circling between his jacket and his shirt, as though he were in some way favouring his breast. The thought of it disgusted. Robin walked down to the gleaming line of barbecues along the wall at the end of the shelves. He touched the flank of a metal lid, large enough to conceal a body. It must be meant for a restaurant, surely, something that size? He glanced back along the aisle. Pamela was grasping the shaft of a new Flymo, testing it for height, for comfort, angling it so it touched the ground, as though she were about to mow the concrete floor. The fat man stood very close to her. He took the machine from her to tilt in against himself, to make some point about its use, cradling its long handle like a broom. For one moment, as he moved in his demonstration, his bulk obscured Pamela entirely. She disappeared as though into it. And then she was there again, smiling, as was the man himself, at some remark he had made.

Robin's palms were wet, as if he had passed them under a tap. He went to an open door in the side of the huge barn-like building, standing back as two young men efficiently unloaded a van and added cartons to a stack inside the door. The breeze was welcome against his forehead, his throat. He waited until he saw his wife carry the long cardboard box towards the checkout. She talked gaily to the young woman who took her card and entered it in the Eftpos machine, but said nothing to her husband as he came to stand beside her and carried her purchase back to the car. It was necessary to lower the back seat before he could angle the mower through from the boot. With Pamela already sitting in the driver's seat, waiting to turn the key, her features set as stone, he thought, 'I am too tired for this. To care whether she is angry or not.'

The car jerked rather than backed from the parking bay. Her resolve to say nothing quickly passed, as he expected it to do. Before she turned from the car park into the traffic streaming back along the Quay towards the city, where had he got to then, she was demanding, might she ask? Leaving her to lug that lump of a thing the length of PlaceMakers before he deigned to come near her?

'I don't think you know quite how I felt in there. I needed fresh air.'

'You mean you're ill?'

'I felt I had no freedom. That the script was written for me.'

'You're talking nonsense now,' Pamela said. But his admission seemed to calm her. He supposed his words had slipped into one of her pigeonholes, 'Inexplicably upset' for instance. Once it was named it could be coped with. 'Best thing you can do,' she said, 'is lie down the minute we get home.'

'That isn't what I need.'

'It was an episode,' she said. 'Isn't that enough?' She placed her left hand for a moment on his right sleeve. She thought of the sales which started next week. Decent material this time, though, she'd make sure of that. The last jacket he had bought without her being with him, the cloth brushing into small tight tufts that needed to be picked off. Something a bit livelier too than the greys and fawns he chose if left to himself. Brighter colours suited him. She glanced across at him as they waited at the Tinakori Road lights.

'Better now?'

'Nothing to be better about.'

'Oh no,' Pamela laughed, 'I'd be the last to notice, wouldn't I.' Amazing, she thought, even now, how quickly their occasional spats blew over. Love, she supposed, although amused a little at how trite it sounded, said as starkly as that. A tricky word at the best of times.

*

Then with no more warning than if he had been clipped on a pedestrian crossing, Ted Pike next door, who had only that Monday confirmed the order for the wheelbarrow, came in from playing squash on the Tuesday night and was dead by the time his wife had taken down the teacups. The crackers and cheese were already on the table.

The funeral was three days later. Most of those in the church were from the same age group as the dead man and his wife. Friends spoke sincerely, and some found it difficult to end what they wanted to say. There were also stories one was meant to laugh at, which these days seemed *de rigueur* for funerals. It brought home to Robin how out of touch he was with how fashions changed. He disliked it too when the woman minister thought it obligatory to smile as if to jolly things along, and mentioned God as little as possible, out of deference, was it, to the dead?

Robin had looked down at his hands while waiting for the service to begin. He thought, am I a hard-hearted person? He would be sad if he was. He could not, however, line it up quite satisfactorily, this sense of indifference, of embarrassment even, sitting here among mourners, and the warmth he had always felt for his neighbour, now lying there a few yards away. How many dozens of times had they chatted, shared their delight when the Blues were beaten, collected each other's mail during holidays? Done the odd good neighbourly turn?

It had occurred to him, pretty much from the moment when the phone call came to tell them of Ted's death, that the fat man would be at the funeral. Bound to be. He and Ted worked together, after all. How familiar Ted would have been with that chesty breathing, the clump of fingers, the brushed lapels. The man to put you right, Ted had called him that.

Robin knew he was afraid, that was the only word. Afraid to see him again. But never imagining it quite like this, not with Pamela instructing him quietly to move along the pew, the man lowering himself next to her at the end of the row. The nonsense of it, even as he felt the vein beating in his forehead. A thin voice coming back to him, a teacher's voice, Mr Minn's dry informing on the beginnings of religion, mere objects becoming presences, the irrational fear that accrued to a figurine. Robin sang loudly to distract himself. He approved of the mourning family in their decent suits and frocks. He had been to a funeral earlier in the year when the deceased was carried by tieless men in jeans, followed by females wearing cardigans. You could not have dressed more casually for a barbecue, which he supposed to purely secular minds it was halfway to being. Two of the hymns he sang he knew, a third he had never heard of. There was a kind of pop song in there as well, for the grandchildren he supposed. Nietzsche would have made a fist of it, proclaimed Taste was dead as well. Made a total sweep. 'As the casket leaves,' he read. Christ, he quietly seethed, why couldn't they call it a coffin! Why not put advertising on the outside as well, to show how American we've become? The Lord's Prayer, the familiar lines. *Forgive us our trespasses, as we forgive them.* Pamela's attractive voice, her careful emphasis on the important words. The total quietness while good things were said by the minister, things that are always said of the departed, sometimes justly, sometimes not. Robin was glad 'beyond all telling', as one of the hymns declared, that it was his wife there, next to the fat man, rather than himself.

Then there he was—there they were—joining those who followed Ted down the aisle of the church. The fat man bulked in front of them, some discreet male deodorant wafting back from him. The woman minister stood to one side of the door, still smiling as though it were a wedding she was leading. The undertaker, with professional deftness, moved between the figures in the forecourt where the hearse was parked, offering a basket of carnation heads to be laid on the coffin as it slid snugly to its shining space. Time passed. The little bit of time before Ted would be driven off. Robin stood at the back of the crowd. Pamela was talking with a neighbour from the house on their other side. He was aware again of the faint deodorant behind him, the voice saying too loudly, although thank heavens not to him, saying to another man who shared perhaps the professional eye of PlaceMakers, 'Lovely wood,' he was saying as the hearse moved off, the light glinting along the varnished box. 'There's lovely wood for you.'

Daddy Drops a Line

My father used to say . . . I intended to begin that sentence, '*Our* father used to say,' but the phrase is now too suppositional, too much what the boys at least are so trying to get away from. So back to what is really a second shot to let nothing stand in the way of what needs to be said.

My father used to say if there was truth anywhere, we had to make it for ourselves. A dubious enough thing to tell children, who want certainty from their parents, not that proviso for self-discovery. As children we want absolutes we can later move from with a sense of victory won, and feel maturity is the reward for breaking away. We most certainly do not want *relativism*, not as five-year-olds. (My brother the journalist has said to me time and again in his peremptory emails, 'For Christ's sake do not put stuff in italics!! You sound so tentative about *everything*!!')

My father used to say there would come a time when we thanked him that he never told us what to think. That he never imposed his certainties on any of us. Daddy—the boys hate my calling him that—Daddy was constantly in a state of self-revising. Their view of him now is clear-cut, a picture of sad confusion from day one. I want to say to them but in fact do not that he is more like half a dozen profiles drawn on separate sheets of transparent paper that do not align exactly. Placed one on another there is a blur of lines, and the truth is in the blur.

Joel is the journalist. Frank, my other brother, is a teacher, who once fancied he would write history books. Each has a family of teenagers and is, I'd say, maritally a mess. I am the one who married at an early age, to a considerably older man who is richer than either of them. My brothers, at the time Roger and I got together, referred to him as a sexual property developer. The jokes kept up over the years, not altogether malicious, but certainly with an edge. Joel's first wife opted out for a farmer she met at a Rotary luncheon her husband was speaking at. Frank's wife simply moved in with a mother of two, a mild Maltese woman, a few streets from where they lived. I keep in touch with second-string sisters-in-law who are better adjusted to contemporary mores than either of my brothers, both of whom seem angry a good deal of the time. My own marriage is childless but contented, sidestepping whatever ravages the boys once assumed it was in for. 'Whatever *successful*'s supposed to mean,' I can hear Frank saying.

Joel lives in Dunedin and Frank in Sydney. Maori Hill and Paddington. Roger and I 'reside'—another of Joel's loaded words—in Epsom, 'leafy Epsom', he'd say. Both brothers of course believe we are far-right stormtroopers, responsible for letting the little monkey-man swing into Parliament, feeding him our votes as though they were nuts. I say very little, as nothing I say could let us off the hook. Roger's first wife way back—I wasn't yet in Standard Six—was Italian, a well-off communist from Milan, whose father published incendiary books. Her outspoken politics went with what Roger's sister recalls as 'Junoesque jugs', which, as again my brothers believe, makes my husband not a difficult man to explain.

But to my/our father. He invested in New Zealand Breweries, and Fletcher's when they built State houses, decades before the rot set in. That was aside from his own business. He was loaded, an expression used by all of us at different times, and, on occasion, by us together. His solicitor was a life-long friend and so surely must have been complicit, although it is in the nature of his profession to deny it. Nalden even has the gall to say he was surprised. 'He was never one to *confide*. Did he confide in any of you?' A guarded truculence in his voice. He had opened a drawer in his old-fashioned legal desk and placed an envelope in front of him. His chair swivelled in a semicircle, as he looked to each of us. Yes?

Frank nodded on behalf of the family. Nalden slit the envelope with a paperknife shaped like a dolphin. We could see the paper bore a single typed line, our father's signature beneath it, and another signature to the side, witnessing it. Nalden then read in a voice trained in neutrality, a voice to offend neither the living nor the dead, 'At last everything is clear.'

There was a long pause. Then Joel said, so quietly it was a dead giveaway that he was prepared to kill, 'That cannot be all.'

'I'm afraid it is, Joel.' Nalden pinched his lower lip to a little rosebud between his forefinger and thumb.

'Then what does it mean?'

My other brother shouted in the quiet, almost sepulchral office, 'It means, "At last everything is clear."' Frank had studied philosophy as well as history. He hated imprecision even as a child. For years he had corrected Joel and me if we lost the thread of a story or strayed from the point. He was now the first of us to stand up.

The solicitor again looked from one to the other, and allowed his eyes to slide back across each of us. He said, 'There are various lines of approach that might be considered.' His voice, I thought, purred with caution, reservations, the hint of protracted submissions and challenged judgments.

Joel, a touch dramatically, placed an elbow on each knee, to support the weight of his head lowered on to his spread hands.

Frank was the one whose coolness won out. 'The problem we have here may be so intractable one cannot easily confront it.'

It was the kind of remark that appealed to Nalden. 'Point taken,' he said, 'point taken,' misunderstanding my brother completely.

Frank enlightened him. 'The point I am making,' he said, 'is that your client was a prick.'

'Your father?' Nalden uneasily tapping the bridge of his glasses.

'Total,' Frank told him.

There were various factors that rubbed salt. Our father had left an earmarked fund to pay for a more ornate headstone than, in all honesty, any of his offspring considered decent. Daddy had no more religious conviction than a bar of soap. Yet there was to be not only one of those old-fashioned marble mortuary angels that always intrigue children obliged to visit cemeteries, but the angel was *to be playing a mouth organ*. 'In the desert,' Nalden offered. 'In the desert in '43 your father was what the boys called a dag with his mouth organ. Hymns. Off-colour songs.'

'What a friend Eskimo Nell has in Jesus?' Joel said, never one to rein in his bile.

Nalden said, 'You're rather missing the point.'

I said, 'It's nice to think he was sentimental about the good times, surely?'

'Christ, Sophie!' Joel shouted, across the lounge in our home, when I repeated it later that evening. Roger was irritated but for my sake said nothing. He took their emptied glasses from my brothers and carried them to the bar where he refilled them and swizzled the ice until it chinked in the awkward silence. I stroked Monty's lovely coat. Monty is our miniature schnauzer who so often is my distraction in awkward moments.

More temperately, Frank repeated the phrases Daddy had drawn up and given to his solicitor in a separate document, to be run in the papers for *three days*, in Sydney and Dunedin as well as up here. 'Deeply grieving children.' 'Truly beloved father.' 'Bereft for ever.'

'If that's not taking the piss,' he said.

'Not many people you know will see them,' Roger tried to console. My brothers had too much contempt for him to answer. Then my husband said he had phoned a QC friend of his who said there was no compulsion—.

Frank cut across his brother-in-law. 'You cannot prevent a man saying what he likes in his own bloody death notice.'

Then Joel: 'His children can't deny all that grieving stuff without sounding like ungrateful nasty shits.'

I said, 'Which of course we are.' Frank looked at me, witheringly.

There was more, though, to how our father planned to hurt us. His one-liner was witnessed by a woman we had never heard of. Then Roger enlightened us, telling us what Daddy's friend Nalden had conveyed to him because he couldn't bring himself to tell us directly. He said, 'This isn't easy.'

I said, 'As if any of this is, Roger.' So he told us bluntly that the woman whose name was Serena was actually a freelance sex worker: I heard Frank's tongue click in a way that made me imagine a gun with a silencer going off, although of course I have no idea if that is the kind of sound it makes or not. At the same moment I realised with surprise that my brothers' indignation seemed quite beyond me. By now I could not have deeply cared had Daddy been knocking K Road from one end to the other.

'You're missing the point,' Roger said, meaning all of us together. He said he had taken the liberty to get an investigator on to it. He said our father had simply phoned the woman from an advertisement he had seen in the *Herald*. He phoned her from the retirement village with its expansive view across the spread of the harbour. He told her he would pay her double her fee to meet him up the road in the Rose Gardens where she would sign a piece of paper, and walk off with the easiest haul she had earned for a long time. As she joked with the investigator, she thought there might be a God after all. 'I can see the dosh just raining down, can't you? I'll say he was a regular if that's any use.'

Daddy had then taken the envelope and left it with his solicitor, who spoke to him, as he had year in and year out, about leaving a will. 'It throws a family completely if you don't.' Nalden was insistent he told him that.

Roger left it there. None of us needed it to be explained. If we took anything to court it would hit the front page—family challenges a last statement witnessed by a whore, who might even claim to have been a close friend for years. Joel changed colour as he said any slag these days was believed before an upright citizen, that was one thing observing the courts in Dunedin for twenty years had brought home to him, Jesus, hadn't it just! 'Ever seen how judges drool?'

Then my husband, for the first time I believe in our married life, said something that hurt me rather a lot. He said, 'He may have been mad as a snake, but my God there must have been something he wanted to pay you lot back for.'

Monty heard the cat's bell from up the road that drives him mad. He flung himself yelping from my knee and clawed at the door to be let out.

Joel was in a rage for the rest of the few days he stayed with us.

'It means nothing,' he insisted. 'What he wrote means nothing as soon as you really think about it.'

Frank told him coldly, 'It means nothing whether you think about it or not.'

'What is that supposed to mean?' his brother shouted at him. He was holding his mobile close to his ear, waiting for a number to ring. He slapped his hand across it as he heard a click at the other end and swore. 'I don't believe it,' he said, 'I just don't.'

None of us encouraged him to confide.

Frank continued on his own tack. 'It is all the same whether it means anything or not. Isn't that so? From our point of view as heirs? From our perspective?'

Roger missed a beat as he came in from a wrong tangent. 'A dead man can say what he likes, I suppose.'

'He wasn't dead when he said it,' Frank wearily reminded him.

I said, 'It's like he made a joke at our expense and laughed at us before it was even told. Even that's indecent.'

I thought of an angel about to play, or having just played, a note on a mouth organ, a slab of stone that *implied* music for ever. There isn't much decency in that either. Although, as with Daddy, religion rings no bells with me, it still offended me, the cheapness of it. The *marbleness* of it, I suppose. The quiet little joke sounding on and on, whether we hear it or not.

I have taken to driving out to him, once or twice a month. I have not told Roger, let alone my brothers. I park near a row of pines and look along the paths of concrete and marble confectionery in the old part of the cemetery. I can see my father's memorial, white as a bottle of milk, standing above the lower graves between it and the car. I sit there for a few minutes, *thriving*, odd as the word may seem, on the deepest silence of the week. There is nothing morbid in this, nothing you might describe as grieving. It is *comforting* even—yes, I'd go so far as to say that. At ease.

I'm not one for *deep* introspection so I don't try to explain it. But I am glad that it occurs. I sit there and think things over.

What we got from Daddy in the long run was as much as would have come our way without that silliness of his note, or the fury of my siblings. Yet another letter was delivered to Mr Nalden from Oak Park, the rather nice home where our father spent his last two years. It was found in a book he had been reading in his last few weeks, part of his 'effects' which we said might be sent on, with his clothes and alarm clock and a few souvenirs from his time in the Pacific, to the Salvation Army whose motto 'Blood and Fire' had amused him. I remembered that fact from the time we were children and the band played carols at our corner the week before Christmas. When a young and very serious woman raised her arm and shook her tambourine and its trailing ribbons flickered, he would say, 'Blood and fire, Sophie, there we go.' The letter between the pages of his book was witnessed this time by the Matron and set the world back on course. It was, as the solicitor said, 'in the nature of an acceptable will', but carried beneath the signatures, as though as a last-minute and important reminder, the declaration that 'not withstanding this present testament, the sentiment of my earlier note I would also like to stand'. Even Roger said, 'God knows what went on there in the old bloke's head.' Then he and my brothers thought of other things now that the estate had dropped their way, and I expect I'm the only one who doesn't let go of what Daddy had thought it important enough to say.

His room at Oak Park was always stacked with books. The local library couldn't keep up. I said once to the Matron, 'Yet he scarcely opened a book earlier on.'

'Well, you could have fooled me,' she said, jolly, super-confident, scary. The kind of woman I try to avoid.

There were a couple of other men in the home he liked spending time with. One was a retired cleric of some sort, the other a less talkative man who had made a name for himself as a painter until Parkinson's struck. The one time we said more than a few words to each other he made a joke. Telling me of his affliction, he said, 'Some painters *start* with it. When mine gets bad enough I'll be back in fashion.' Daddy did not say a great deal about the friends he had made. Yet they spent time together every day in a little alcove overlooking the garden, while along in the community lounge rows of heads bobbed and floated in front of the big television screen. As I passed through the lounge on the way to our father's room, and passed through again as I left, I thought of rows of schoolchildren covered with ash in a schoolroom in Pompeii. Our father said, 'My friend the clergyman can't walk through without quoting Dante.'

I said, 'I don't quite know what that means.'

He looked at me with the direct gaze that sometimes unsettled me in those last couple of years. He said, 'I suppose it means that Italian bloke must have passed through here too, and mentioned it to my friend.' Knowing I knew he was having me on.

I don't read poetry, although Roger sometimes reads out to me something that strikes him. I quite like that. When I hear it said I can make sense of it as I wouldn't were I reading it for myself. Although if I still don't quite catch the drift of it, he tells me I shouldn't bother too much about it. 'It's not meant to be a quiz,' he says. He read me one a few weeks ago about a man who was an accountant or such, who once he retired really packed it in—let his garden run riot, refused to go to the church where for decades he had done the parish's annual audit for free, began swearing at his children. Roger thought it quite amusing that I was a touch shocked. 'Poetry is never predictable,' he said, 'nor is anything in it.' Always waving a flag about itself though, poetry, is what I wanted to say, but Roger would have taken it amiss. Yet this time what the lines were on about stayed in my mind. The story of the man in the lines. Then it came to me one morning at breakfast as I handed down a treat for Monty, which lesson one at kennel club instructs you never to do. But he lies along the back of the leather couch as if my breakfast is of no concern to him whatsoever. Then the moment I touch the paper napkin at my lips he's down like a shot and next thing his paws are at the side of my chair. I haven't the heart not to hand him the scraps that are left. It struck me as suddenly as that, while Monty's wet snout dabbed at my knuckles as he snapped the corner of burned toast. It came to me that of course the man in the poem was Daddy, that the triumph of his reversal was the shame inflicted on all of us: our father who made a modest fortune from hard work and a franchise for top-of-the-range vacuum cleaners exulting, in his last few months, in a late run at confusion.

Our father's middle name was Knox, after an important person in history. It meant little to my father, and nothing at all to us, to Joel and Frank and myself. But to our grandfather it had meant so much. It meant he was Scottish, and had no intention of foregoing what for generations had sharpened the family until it reached the fine point of his own life, narrow and hard and ready to make its mark. But as far as all that refining of history went, our father in his own words 'tossed in the lot'. Though not the capacity for work, not the urge to do well in a world that favoured effort. The fruits of discipline, rather than discipline itself, were where Daddy and his own father parted ways. He smoked panatellas, which I have always thought romantic, and drank light rum like a clutch of molten sunlight in the glass he drank it from, with nothing but a twist of lemon.

My mother died early—I was only eight—but he did not remarry. Sometimes he would bring a lady home before they went out to dinner or to a musical. The boys will squabble even about such memories as those. Joel said to me on one of those awkward evenings after the funeral, 'Where did you keep your head buried all those years, eh, Sophie?' Once started you could not stop him. 'The old man was a root artist to beat the band.' Although it was to Frank rather than myself that he directed his venom.

Frank will argue *au contraire* that his father was 'uptight sex-wise', words he says with that infuriating habit of hooking the fingers of both hands in midair to show he is not altogether owning the words he has just come out with. Then directly to me, 'I don't know where your brother gets his fantasies from.' But both question my certainty about the two or three women I clearly remember politely talking with, women in long frocks with carefully arranged hair. I remind Joel that he was at boarding school in the years I'm talking about, and then he was overseas. He was scarcely ever at home. 'Dream on,' he said the last time we talked of our father's 'squeezes', that revolting expression he has picked up from a wife who fancies that to use whatever lingo is up with the play in Dunedin makes her somehow more interesting.

Since Daddy's death, then, and the confusion afterwards, it is difficult to speak with either of my brothers without something unpleasant flaring up. Joel, whom Frank reports is drinking too much, remembers so little with accuracy yet wants to query almost anything I say about the past. He claims in his insistent sentimental way, for example, to remember Mother crying over Christmas dinner as we children squabbled about the trinkets inside our crackers. I tell him we hardly ever had crackers in those days. I say there was only once not long before she died when we all sat at the table with crêpe-paper hats on our heads, and I remember how jolly it was. Daddy had a tiny trumpet from his cracker and Mother handed me the ring that fell from hers when he leaned back tugging at the other end of the shiny green tube they held between them. I mentioned this to Frank next time he phoned and he said, 'That's utter nonsense, both of you.' He could tell I was angry with his saying that, because I thought there was something spiteful in his dismissing what I said. I thought at least there is some excuse for Joel, who has so little from those years that he desperately wants to make out he has more than he does.

'I wouldn't give it too much thought,' Roger says again. But I do. I say there must have been a great disappointment for both of them somewhere along the line for them to go on like that. Things aren't right somewhere if you want to distort the past the way they do. I tell Roger, it's as if they want to crush anything nice out of our lives completely, and make it nasty for all of us. Joel has taken to sending me the curtest emails every month or so, taking me to task for getting on so well with Daddy for most of my life. He hints with some twist of reasoning quite beyond me that I am to blame for what he calls 'the fracas at the end'. On the other hand Frank has as good as cut all ties. He says sardonically, 'By Christ, did Tolstoy ever get it right about unhappy families!' He leaves it there, enigmatic, bitter. Roger is far too conciliatory to advise me to forget about both of them. But he knows I am hurt. He says, 'It's because you're the only one in Auckland. Every bad memory of the place they pile on you.' Although Roger has reason enough to feel hurt as well. The last time Frank rang he said to him jokingly, trying to end the tirade that still went on about the gravestone, 'It happens sometimes, Frank. An intense desire to do something out of character. "How could old men not be mad?" Remember that line of Yeats?'

'Yeats be buggered,' Frank came back at him. 'You know what I think, Roger? I think you're as full of crap as your wife.'

Roger smiled at me as he put down the portable phone. But he said, really rather put out with himself, 'I misquoted that line terribly.'

I've always disliked that big dip as the road swoops down into the valley where so much of what once was Auckland lies. As I see the big sprawl of the cemetery, I think of the figures in those old photographs blown up on the walls of bars and restaurants in the eighties—images of early Auckland, men in dark suits and round black hats, women in long skirts and white blouses stepping across a Queen Street of horse-drawn trams. Or those pictures of picnics at Devonport or St Heliers with their quaintly togged-out children, the fleet blur of running dogs. That to me is Waikumete, the erased figures who stopped along pavements and walked the wide streets, their faces tilted into shadow. I turn from the main road and drive between the mottled stones and sombre concrete and sculpted marble in the old section where our father's family plot was bought for a song by his grandfather, before many of those in the photographs were even born. A bargain when he bought it, a bargain even now, when you think another three or four of us could yet be accommodated. (Likely story, as my sister-in-law might say.) And I find this unfussed sense of peace as I park for twenty minutes and sit there in that silence when you turn the motor off in a very quiet place, and hear only the ding and pop of cooling metal. Monty, his collar attached to the red strip of leather that locks him into the seatbelt, sleeps on the passenger seat. Even peace isn't quite the word. I sit in the warm metallic silence and look at the monument Daddy wanted, or the one he *almost* wanted. The idea of an angel *playing* a mouth organ was really asking too much. Daddy's old friend Mr Nalden agreed that the slight change to our father's instructions preserved the *spirit* of his wish. And so there it stands, a conventional clean-lined angel. Its head *nods* towards Daddy, I imagine, rather than towards eternity or God. In the hand held against its side, you see what is possibly a mouth organ if you look with attention, which will not occur often in this far corner of the cemetery. It might at a casual glance as likely be a purse that it is holding, or a packet of bloody condoms, Joel emailed back to me, when I sent on the stonemason's final sketch for the boys' approval. Frank did not so much as answer.

Some days, if the weather is damp or too cold, I don't even get out of the car. Other times I walk the thirty or so yards and stand looking at the grave that amuses me, actually. Amuses in a nice way. I know the boys will never see it, nor will Nalden the solicitor, so there is no one to take me to task for deciding at the last minute on that line he wrote to us all, inscribed on the sloped ridge beneath his name: '*Now everything is clear*.' I think as I look at them how words wobble and change as you move them from one place to another. I'm not much given to irony, but I do think at times, looking at the black paint picking out the incised grooves of the letters, that they are like a stone Daddy heaves back at us, at the pond he's left, the spreading circles of certainty for one, of uncertainty for another.

I always sit for a last few minutes before I drive off. My hand ruffles Monty's woolly scalp. I like to think of the lift our father must have got from deciding what to write, before jacking up his dodgy witness then sealing the envelope. His knowing how it would have us all in such a tizz. I'm so glad he was able to have a crack at something different, after a lifetime worrying about the rest of us. And if you can't say it how you want to when you're dead, then when on earth *can* you say it?

Pieces

Mandy has a flicker of what may be going on in Weston's mind. Although how could she be sure? Hadn't already she been wrong about jewellery, that first visit? At each subsequent meeting the lawyer was wearing one piece or another. Today it is a broad close-fitting copper bangle she goes to turn then realises the metal clasps her wrist too tightly for it to move. She had said, as Mandy handed the few handwritten pages across to her, 'I didn't mean you to go to that trouble.'

Mandy likes it that they don't say things to each other except when something needs to be said. She tells her, 'I wish I had something to hide. Then you could feel you earned your keep prising it out of me.'

Weston ignores the little attempt at levity. 'Are you saying that what you did saved you from something worse?'

'From taking "something worse" too seriously,' Mandy corrects her.

Weston raises her eyebrows. She is not into theatrics, which Mandy likes in her, so does not do this for effect. The older woman wonders if this is her lawyer stopping a touch short of a smile. 'It would take more skill than mine, Mandy, to convince a jury of that.' She then returns to a sheet of paper inside her opened folder. She asks, 'You checked those *Listeners* I left with you?'

Mandy moves several copies of the magazine across the table. Her own hand, now ringless, and Weston's plumper, younger fingers, touch by chance. 'I told you I never watched much. Apart from the news. A few documentaries.'

'But you have marked those?'

'What I remember.'

'These past few months?'

'You'll see there aren't so many.'

Mandy fills the plastic cup in front of her from the jug of water that is always placed there before the interviews began. She says, in a voice not quite her own, 'A line of behaviour which is not admirable but is not therefore inexplicable.'

'Which means?' Weston is again attempting to move the bracelet which she forgets is fixed. 'You don't need to invent a defence. A scenario. That's all I'm saying.' But of course it will be invented. As it is already, as she knows.

Weston's hair has been dyed, the tracings of grey at her parting quite gone since Tuesday afternoon. Mandy watches her look at the list she had written on the cover of the top magazine. 'What you wanted. They're written there.' And then, when her solicitor looks up, 'Enlighten me,' Mandy smiles. They both know there is something of a game in all this, although she would not offend Weston's professionalism by winking across at her as they say their lines.

'It's not you I have in mind, not this part of it. It's those I shall read it out to.' Yes, she would read the programmes in court a little later, making the most of them. The documentary on honour killings in Pakistan, the witnesses speaking from behind veils not in this case to meet the customs of their place but to cover the features where acid had disfigured them. Another was on zoos in China. Parents buying live chickens for their children to throw to carnivores. Buses driven into lion enclosures so those on board, as birthday treats, as party fun, might watch up close as living mules were tumbled from the backs of trucks.

'You can leave it there,' Mandy instructs. 'I can see the drift.'

'More than drift. The key to your defence.'

There is a pause between them. Then Mandy says, 'There was one I couldn't find in there. It must have been on some channel I happened to come across on Sky.'

Weston's pen is ready to note it down.

'Africa this time,' Mandy says. 'There was civil war. There was an interview with a woman who saw her husband shot, after he was made to watch the soldiers have sex with her. Her relatives are also forced to have sex with her and then they too are shot. Her daughters are raped in front of her then disappear. The woman said she still believed in God. You should add that to the list. Exhibit A.'

There is a longer silence until Mandy asks, without irony, 'So my defence, as you see it, Weston? I didn't know what I was doing?'

'There's a point,' her solicitor reminds her, 'when your opinion isn't the compelling one. Which is why we have expert witnesses.' And again, the big clock ticking above the door.

'For goodness sake take it off,' Mandy suddenly tells her, watching her fiddling at her wrist. 'It's not good for you, metal that close against your skin.'

So the bracelet lies there beside the magazines, a three-quarters shiny crescent on the table between them. Mandy's finger touches for a moment the thin-beaten copper that is warm from Weston's forearm.

'Leave that,' a voice sharply orders her. The female warder who watches through the opaque glass has opened the door.

Her counsel—'the defender of my insanity', Mandy would come to call her—is a slightly overweight, soberly dressed woman in her early thirties. A good swot, her client guesses, but not the clout, not the connections, to be one of the bright young things with a big-name legal firm. You can read as much from the card she left on the table when first they met. Her own name, and that of another woman, an office of only two. Ambitious then, presumably good at her job. She is also direct. She holds out her hand on that first visit and says simply, 'Weston.' Mandy is for the moment unsure if that is a first or second name, but as the solicitor addresses her at once as Mandy, she calls her Weston in return. After talking for twenty minutes, a matter mostly of questions and replies, the young woman admonishes her. 'You are not helping your cause.'

'I don't have one,' Mandy corrects her. 'Nothing so grand as a cause.' What is the point, she thinks, in playing games?

'These are serious issues,' Weston says, then clarifies what she has in mind. 'In terms of sentencing.'

'I was hoping,' Mandy says, 'you were speaking in terms of something decided on carefully. I would agree with you about that.'

Weston has placed a tape-recorder not much larger than a matchbox on the table between them as they speak. She taps it rather than switching it on and off. Soon she reprimands again. 'We are not getting far.'

'I don't think of this as a journey,' Mandy says. She smiles. She does not intend to be difficult. She realises her words may come across as both silly and glib. She then tells the young woman facing her in the dull green-painted room with its metal door and ugly table, and the square of clouded glass through which they can be observed, 'I know you mean to help.'

Weston would like a little more co-operation. She would appreciate her client recognising the gravity of the situation. She says, without raising her voice but with a discrete emphasis on certain words so there is an almost admonitory rhythm to what she says, 'You have, so far as most would see it, Mandy, acted savagely against your husband, destroyed property, inflicted damage on your son's professional and emotional life. What I therefore have to do is to explain this behaviour in a way that does not excuse it but attempts to relieve you of responsibility. And that is how I can help you. You do understand that?'

Which is when Mandy tells her, 'I was never more lucid.'

Again the younger woman taps the recorder. She is like a nun, that is what she reminds me of, Mandy considers. Her patiently folding her hands. Her face not altering expression. Only God presumably knowing what is in her heart. Mandy accepts she must help if she can. So she says, 'It may seem at first blush,' then surprised that she put it so oddly, rephrases, 'It may seem to the casual observer, which of course we all are most of the time, that I deeply dislike my husband and Gareth. If defence is clarity and righteousness, we had better get it right. Of course I did.'

Weston closes her folder, with a name embossed on the leather cover that Mandy is unable to read, upside down as it is from her side of the table. Then, 'What century are we in?' her solicitor puts to her bluntly.

Mandy tells her, 'As if doing something right at last is confined by temporal boundaries.' For the second time within minutes, Mandy knows she is being difficult, and now pretentious as well.

Then Weston surprises her by smiling slightly. 'We'll get somewhere,' she says, 'sooner or later.'

She stands up. She cannot be much more than five feet. She stands and holds her hand across the table, as she had done when she first came into the room. The guard or whatever she is has her back against the door to prevent it swinging closed. There was no sign, no ring, no paler strip of skin, on Weston's fingers that hinted at a private life. Nor earrings in her ears. Perhaps lawyers, like surgeons, removed jewellery as a first preliminary to carrying out professional tasks?

Turning from the door, Weston says, 'I won't insist, Mandy, that you put anything on paper. But think about what you'd say, just to me, in confidence, I mean, about thinking of suicide "academically".' She said it as though the way her client had used the word rather amused her.

Mandy is not quite sure of her tone. How can 'in confidence' come into it with the law?

'Will you do that for me?' Weston says, before she steps through the door, and the woman in uniform closes it.

Someone official attempted to talk things through with Tom. First a woman, then a man and a younger assistant, none of them wearing the white jackets he expected them to get about in if it was professional business they were on about. 'The psycho mob,' as he later told Gareth, 'paid to enlighten us as to why your mother's completely off her head. As if talking to us was supposed to tell them what they should have known from day one.'

'The police know this?' he had asked them. 'That you're talking with me?'

'They think it a good idea.'

The woman said, 'The cause before the effects.' He had told her to fuck off, which was when the male white-coat even if he was in mufti had replaced her.

He did not trust any of them. The male, who wore a bright floral tie as if he was entertaining at a kids' party, asked him, 'You obviously thought family life was ticking along OK?' What sort of condescension was there in that to begin with, *obviously*?

'Am I supposed to feel guilty about that?'

White-coat number two, a boy assistant by the look of him, piped in, 'Guilt is not what we are after, Tom. We want to understand the situation as much as you do.'

'Lie awake worrying about it, do you?' Tom said. He knew he had to rein in. 'All right,' he said, 'you can bring me that coffee you offered a moment ago.' And he tried to tell them. He had no notion in the world what his wife thought. How could he? He wasn't a criminal to begin with, was he?

Take your time, he was told, as if that was some kind of

privilege, as if time was theirs to bestow. And amazing how little really there was to tell. They had children. He gave her a home most women would kill for. They travelled. He let her spend more on paintings than most people spent on a house. There was nothing she might have wanted she didn't have.

'Emotionally?' The man's hand kept moving over the floral tie. He leaned forward a little. You saw it often enough in the movies when they wanted you to confide. Tom knew this was tricky now, the sort of thing a smartarse could distort. He said directly, 'If it's sex you're on about there was nothing wrong with that. Nothing special but nothing wrong. OK?' The boy assistant even made a note of that, as though his answer was too complicated for them to remember without writing down. Then oddly he found he was close to tears, talking about something else altogether, telling them about the boys, about Jeremy on the other side of the world, lucky if they heard once in three months, but Gareth, the boy who was here, the boy who was at home, how did they think he'd come out of this? 'He's been on the verge of I don't know what ever since. He keeps asking me, "Do you think April wants to be tied up with someone whose mother's raving?" He tells me I have to forgive, maybe because I don't have the choice but he doesn't, does he, he says, he fucking hates her.' He dragged a handful of tissues from the box already there on the desk, ready for losers to break down like this, Tom thought, as if we're the ones supposed to confess, as if we're the ones who have to explain. He said, 'He's wrong about that one though, Gareth. I don't have to forgive her any more than he does. I don't know where he got that from.' Hating hearing himself say it though. Hating it. Everything about it. And then, 'You don't expect so much, do you, after all these years? Remoteness and the rest of it. You expect that too.' He looked across at them again, the younger man and the older one, watching him as if he was something in a zoo. Pleading, he thought, that's what I'm doing now, what else are you going to call it? Although neither had spoken he cut them off. He said, 'I don't have to keep listening, can I remind you of that? That I'm the one who's actually free?'

Back home he sat in the big lounge, watched the massive totara a few yards away absorbed into the dark, its leaves losing definition against the late sky. The house had been designed around it. God knows, he thought for a second, why we're building another one. And at once corrected it. Why we *were*. Mandy had loved where they now were the moment she walked into the room and saw it there, the tree, within touching distance it almost seemed, through the great plate-glass wall. 'That at one end and the dark picture at the other,' meaning the outsize canvas he bought her the year before, what he had always thought of as the grim melancholy picture of forlorn life-size birds standing on a shoreline, on a chunk of coast, apprehensive of whatever it was they picked up on the horizon. He was drawn to it even as he disliked it. Mandy said you didn't have to make it mean anything, stand for anything else than what it was, when it was first placed up there, covering almost the entire wall. Visitors guessed at how much the picture went for, and felt they had to praise it. Gareth was pacing in front of it now, the palm of his raised hand glowing then again becoming dark, as he drew on his cigarette. April had left an hour before.

'You're getting on my nerves,' Tom said.

'Jesus!' Gareth hurled the mobile from his other hand. It slid across the highly polished floor, now black as tar, its panel flying loose as it hit the skirting board beneath the painting. There was his pounding on the stairs down to the garage, the slamming of a door.

Tom stood at the glass wall. The tree was still enough to have been carved from stone. If he shifted slightly, lights from the hill across the sloping park stirred through the mass of foliage. He thought of how Gareth had been the one close to him, and now he too was gone. He could be one of those birds watching what was leaving, fearing whatever it was about to arrive. Jeremy, the pale boy like a Botticelli angel as his mother used infuriatingly to say, had dropped over the horizon a long time ago, with his London airs and his fruity boyfriends. But not Gareth. Yet life was like that, hadn't he always tried to face things as they were? Give and take, good things one day, not so good another, but knowing there was something certain, something he and Mandy had, behind it all?

He hears the door of the garage rise, Gareth gunning the motor far more than it needs, and the screech a few seconds later as he takes the turn at the top of the street. The room now is close to total darkness. The big picture as he turns from the glass to face the long room is a square of black. Then the mobile on the floor beneath it begins to ring. The lighted panel, face down, illumines the few inches of wood to either side. The vibration of the ringing moves it slightly, a kind of science-fiction creature, edging across the polished boards. Tom crosses the room. His heel crunches down on it until the ringing stops, the light goes out. He thinks of himself, as he does so often, almost as another person, following the stage instructions of a play.

It had been a marriage made, if not in heaven, at least as if more than luck had some say in it from the word go. She had been affectionate, a lot was made of that. ('A goer if you ask me,' one jury member remarked to another, before the case was concluded.) She had been attractive, focused, an excellent mother. A lot was made of that. It was such a distant story, Mandy thought, as she heard parts of it being told. The bodies we had, she remembered, from swimming and tennis and hiking, although no one spoke of that. The way we kept sex as the last apple on the tree. She was clever as well, her family on the Herne Bay side of Cox's Creek. Tom's people in that border zone between Mt Eden and Epsom adored her. Tom from the start had a knack for doing things right, doing them sensibly. If he did very well, as the saying goes, it was because he deserved to. It was not a matter of luck. Kindly. Level-headed. The Crown came back to that, making much of it. As it did of family, which was flashed in big lights. One son running a gallery in London. In Cork Street, it was noted, which those who knew such things would tell you meant a lot. The other boy completing his business degree, a Masters, in a few months' time. In a serious relationship.

Mr Bates, for the Crown, knew he looked the part, as Tom knew he was the man for the job. He understood his brief was a straightforward one. He clasped the edges of his gown at chest level, he spoke without notes as he sketched the family circumstances. They travelled together, husband and wife, at least every second year, mostly to Germany for business reasons. The business showrooms in Parnell, he said, would tell you why. Wasn't 'style and quality' the phrase that rang in its advertising, on the company's website? The firm imported from the top of the field. There was, of course, a holiday element as well, last year to South Africa, the year before to the Aegean. A contented, considerate life. Mr Bates, Mandy thought, might moonlight as a marriage counsellor, should he ever hanker for an alternative career. As he eloquently pointed out, by now the city—the entire country—knew behind every occasion of generosity, of family largesse, of apparent marital rapport, that ravening beast, ingratitude, already prowled, more vicious than mad, make no mistake. So this, Mandy thought, was what my life was like? For a moment, there was the image of a woman flipping the pages of an inflight magazine, the glimpses of mountain resorts and beaches, cruises and safaris, the brand names less fortunate women burned for? How she was seen, by those who followed the case.

Then Weston spoke. She was smarter than Mandy had given her credit for. The story she told was a variant of what the court already had heard. It was of the golden wife, with Tom as Midas, gilding what he touched. Again, the gifted sons, the word *family* shining through. To be admired. To be envied. It was impressively done, but with a different logic, a different pitfall at its end. Another image now flickered in her mind. She was back at school. There was a picture on the library wall. The librarian had not long returned from a trip through Europe. Most of the prints she brought back were Impressionist favourites, easy for the girls to like, a sloping field with splashes of red poppies, a handsome couple dancing at a *fête du jour,* the famous sky with whirling stars. But there was another print of quite a different kind. Dutch, it must have been. A very formal family, undemonstrative, rich. Mandy had loved to look at it. She had never seen anyone quite so confident as the bearded father, so plain as the mother with pale hands, so provided for as the children who held the painter's gaze and saw through him. All the family were wearing black, with white collars broad as plates, the finest loops of lace along their edges. There was a cross with dark red stones at the woman's throat, to let you know as you looked that God had been good to them, that they would never say so, but they owned God too. That is how Weston is painting us, she thought, but she has left out God.

She was struck not only by how seriously everyone attended to what Weston said but also how their faces were tilted at the same angle as they listened: an artist could have suggested them simply by a row of sloping strokes. The young woman was oddly vital, as she had never seemed in their interviews in the room with its unpleasant green walls, its spying window. And how she drew them in, even more than the handsome man she opposed, who told the same story to such different ends! She sets us in a frame, Mandy thought, so others can only look at us and wonder at good fortune. Of course she already knew, as did no one else at this stage, where Weston would take them, to the moment of the disappearing family.

She will sweep it away like a magician, as if she raised her arm and flung out the dark wing of the gown she wore, and the cards will fly in all directions. This, she will say, this I am afraid is what the accused has already done, before I explain it to you. What normal woman, what *sane* woman, would vanish from a world you and I would envy? And one day, later in the week, she will leave it to each and every one of you, to find a more accurate word, if you might, than the one she is obliged to use. Mad, as we colloquially say, when someone does something we find unaccountable, out of character, damaging to themselves and those they love, that no one who knew them would ever assume they might do? Insane, when we speak of it more technically, as those who are expert will assess it, all the evidence to hand?

Mandy was fascinated to follow how her life emerged. She leaned forward, her hands together on her lap, watching Weston tell the story that was of quite another time, quite another woman. It was amusing even in a restrained way, this drawing together and then drawing apart of competing lawyers, one behind his banner of 'vicious', the other with her placard of 'insane', neither allowing as a possibility the words she herself so stood by, 'lucid' and 'in control'. Poor young Weston, she thought, going to such trouble to arrive at where I have never been! Poor pleased-with-himself Bates as well, his insisting how somewhere I have a secret motive tucked away, like a diamond in the hem of a dress in those Georgette Heyer stories I sped though in my teens. The diamond that will tell him so much. And the one fact that will never occur to him, that there is no mystery, no hidden spring, no evil wand. It is all so much more straightforward than anyone wants it to be.

*

The 'snap' as Weston calls it and so carefully argues, or the line, as she also puts it, where her client crossed into that abrupt terrain where a normal wife, a normal mother, becomes capable of what she did, occurred so far as one might time it between the main course and the decision to waive dessert and go for a cheese platter. She is at pains to point out it had been assumed all evening that her client was the one who would drive them home, while the others, as Gareth had put it when questioned, 'had got into it pretty seriously'. He was the one who liked to consider the lists, order the wines, who knew almost as if he had walked them the various slopes of the Gibbston, assessed the pebbly, flinty whites of the Wairarapa. It was the same when it came to looking at the cheeses, his pointing to the trolley, his assuring April that no, he most certainly would choose nothing heavily peppered, what did she take him for? The mood at the table was more than relaxed—hadn't Tom already said it was better than that, it was a family having a good time? He liked listening to Gareth take command, his showing off just that bit in front of them all. As if he'd have known where to begin, when he was that age! He had teased him earlier on, while they horsed around at home and before deciding on the Viaduct, and Gareth was into one of his riffs on the city that April was going to, where he would join her once his finals were knocked off, dropping the names of bars and restaurants and clubs as though the town was already his. 'Rushcutter's Bay,' he said, 'we both like round there, that right, sweet?', leaning forward to put his lips against the gleam of her hair while she raised her fingers to his cheek. Christ! Tom thought, lucky, lovely, where do you begin? But telling his son, in that easy way they both knew was something of a put-on, 'You've the makings of a right tosser, that ever occur to you?', and Gareth telling him back, 'Genes will out, ever thought of that?'

She had watched them, their joshing, wasn't that the word she had read for what they were doing? Not being father and son together so much as playing at it, acting out the bond she supposed they had seen in movies and on TV, even the physical moves that went with it, Tom's fist lightly punching on Gareth's shoulder, Gareth's exaggerated feinting, as though a boxer facing the real thing. And now, while they waited for the wine to arrive that would accompany the cheese, the boy covering his face with his open-fingered hand, his muttered 'Oh God, you don't really!' when his father began on his sincere, slightly drunken praise of the young woman he, he and Mandy, would be proud to welcome into the family, he knew he spoke for Mandy as well, as if that needed to be spelled out, how proud they were of both of them. As he spoke she watched the girl's own mannered pose, her elbows on the cloth, her chin on her folded knuckles, a forefinger along one cheek, her eyebrows arched, appreciative. 'I am not greatly surprised,' her posture said, 'but I am touched, believe me, I really and truly am.' It was what the moment demanded. What the occasion called for. That hollow phrase, Mandy had thought, that perfect phrase. She raised her hand and pinched the bridge of her nose, so that Tom asked her was she feeling all right, not one of her migraines coming on? He and April and Gareth, each remembered that, their asking her that. How intense and remote it was, she remembered that, the moment they sat in, like figures in one of those souvenir glass domes, small and distant figures, where descending flakes so easily were stirred. The image coming back to her as she watched, as though from a similar distance, the little drama of the court proceed around her, the figures both close enough to touch, as distanced as the moon.

She watches the young woman who speaks for her. She hears the words she was forewarned of in their meeting yesterday, Weston's assurance that this line of defence truly is the one to take. 'The unstable,' she had said, as they sat where they always met, 'are never guilty. Not in that worst sense.'

'Unstable. Lucid. They hardly go together,' Mandy had said, going back to the word she so insisted was hers. And then, 'So you've definitely opted for "snap"?'

Weston was allowed to bring her client flowers. This morning, a bunch of violets in a twist of purple tissue. 'They grow wild,' she said. 'There's a sycamore in my back yard and they grow there, beneath it.'

'Thank you,' Mandy said, when they were laid on the table between them. She thought how there is always another life that goes on, that we never guess at. Fancy Weston having a back yard.

Among other things Mandy also explained to Weston: 'Sometimes I would take the car and drive to one of the west coast beaches. I would try to find somewhere to stop where I would have a view along the coast. Or pull up in one of the car parks, level with the sand, with the sea as much something I listened to as saw. Some days there was a haze of spray above the beach from the breaking waves, the marvellous smashing down of them. Some days the bush on the hills was almost black. On others, depending of course on the weather, on the time of day I was there, it might seem to glow, as if light was given out from it as much as falling across it. I was content to sit there for hours. I had no desire to walk along the beach. I would sit in the car with the window wound down to hear the banging of the surf, to feel the wind, which was almost always there, some days cold enough for me to draw the zip of my jacket as high as it goes, and sit there with a woollen hat to the tip of my ears. If I angled the car correctly, even in winter, the sun might fall across me, warming the car in even the sharpest wind. Always I took a Thermos with me. I poured the tea into a plastic lid which served as a cup, and held it with both hands. Although very often I might think about death—I don't see how you can sit for long at a beach without thinking of it—this did not stop my feeling contented in a general sort of way. It was clarity making me think of death, not despondency. Which brought home to me that any idea becomes tolerable if you are left to think of it on your own terms. Although I know I do not believe that *utterly,* even as I say I do.

'I could sit like that for hours. Although it was usually winter when I drove there, almost always there was someone within sight along the beach, single people jogging or couples walking together, or a man carrying a sack from around a point. Or a vehicle moving across the wet sand, its tracks laid out behind it. At one beach, when the wind was right, there were young people on what looked like surfboards with wheels, and a sail that carried them along at a surprising pace. The sails were red or yellow or blue. The movement was so graceful you felt something of the joy of it, even sitting in a car with a plastic cup between your hands. Again depending on the wind, I might hear the hiss as they skidded past.

'But I have not put it quite correctly, saying it like that a moment ago, "thinking of death". Rather, it was the hovering presence of it as an idea—like another beach, say, that you knew must stretch there along the coast, beyond the dark high point at the end of the beach where one sat. It was like a tune playing at the back of my mind, whatever else might be occurring to me, taking my attention—the light, the cliffs, the sea coming in, breaking, breaking over and over, and beyond that, always again, so that thinking of death was the same as thinking of life. What is the point, Weston, of trying to say more than that? That programme I was watching the evening before Tom and Gareth insisted we go out to celebrate April's new job comes back to me. I wonder at those people in the programme, those men and those women who so wanted to step aside, to step further than the limit of where we are told we may think, and I wonder at what point their thinking cuts across the repetition, the thudding rhythm of one moment and then the next, as they decide, quite reasonably, *I would prefer this to stop.* As Tom and Gareth and April decide each minute for something else entirely, this is where and only where they shall ever choose to be, inside their thin wave whose glitter is all there is.

'And for an instant there, when the waiter stepped back from the table and the bright light fell against the white cloth, white as places you see in photographs taken by people trekking the Antarctic, the light running too across the cutlery and the knife I held tilted by chance and leaping with it as though I was holding a sliver of lightning in my hand.

'I am trying to describe this for you, Weston, not exactly as it occurred of course but in a way that I hope you will understand; that you will see how, with the greatest goodwill in the world, nothing could be the same, not after that.'

She pushes back her chair, her hand resting lightly on her husband's shoulder, before she moves towards the restrooms, the words 'Tane' and 'Wahine' for tourists to believe that was what Aucklanders usually said. Instead of entering, she keeps on to the end of the corridor, to an emergency door that leads to the car park. She hoists the light metal bar and steps into the evening. Tom's car looks almost immodest among the elegant but still lesser makes. She passes an arguing couple at the bottom of the steps. She adjusts the rear-vision mirror, eases the driver's seat forward. She waves back to a young man on a skateboard who stops inches from the exit drive, heeling back on the board so it rises and flips into his hand, and he touches the peak of his baseball cap without seeming to send her up.

It takes her twenty minutes to drive to the new house. The harbour, quite dark now, stretches out from the bottom of the cliff, where the section ends. 'This time next month,'

Tom had said two hours before. Meaning they would have moved in, that the house he had dreamed of for years, the biggest name in architecture having told him, yet again, just how pleased he was with how it had turned out, the best site perhaps he had had the luck to work on. Grimsdale had told him that. The harbour as far as Rangitoto, as far as Coromandel, the Barrier—you name it—would be theirs. The ancient pohutukawa angled from the yellow cliffs, those too would be theirs. At Christmas they flared fifty metres to either side.

Mandy feels for the switches inside the front door. The big sheets the decorators spread as they worked are folded and stacked in the hallway. An expanse of glass, divided into sections of different colours that, this time of night, seem so similarly dark, leans in a wooden frame against one wall. She moves efficiently, but without haste. She prises up with a spattered screwdriver lying beside them the lids of one can of paint and then another, before she tilts them. The thick paint pours slowly, folding across itself in smooth spreading swathes. She brings in several old newspapers from a stack on the kitchen bench. She loosens the sheets of newsprint, crumples them, places them in a row along the walls of the lounge, which seems so large and echoing as she walks on its parquet floor and through to another room, where she opens another can of paint. She is fascinated by what she does, aware of its enormity, knowing she has no choice. But there is no emotion as she does so. It is as though there is a script, and this is what she is assigned. It surprises her, how an empty house is so very bare, so echoing, so large. How it is like a garage in fact, rather than a house. She thinks too how obvious, how final, each action is, now she has got around to doing it. Perhaps, she thinks, they are wondering why she has been so long away from the table. Perhaps they have already noticed the car is gone. It surprises her that an image comes into her mind of something running smoothly on rails. The man with the narrow face had been interviewed at one point on a train, between one Dutch city and another. Not that it stopped his talking sense. Truth is what it is wherever one finds it, Mandy thinks, her own mind so level, her hands so steady, as she watches the heavy buckling of paint fall across itself: it is like watching brocade unfold, before she again crushes the paper and places it around the room. She dislikes how bare they look, the rooms, how they ring as she walks across the floors. She takes the first bottle of turpentine from where it stands in a corner of the kitchen with its gleaming benches, its brilliant taps. She removes the cap and lets it drop, then flings her arm out in a circle, the liquid descending like a jagged cape. That too is how she thinks of it. She finds a second bottle for another room.

It has taken no more than ten minutes. She then stands at the front door, looking back into the house. She holds the box of matches she has taken from the bench in the kitchen, where the workmen must have left them. She had seen four mugs on the counter. She was glad the workmen felt at home, that they felt free to use whatever was there, although the mugs of course must have been their own, as nothing for the kitchen had yet been moved in. She goes down on one knee, as she remembers seeing people do in church, and sets the tiny yellow smudge of flame against the twists of paper that lead towards the spreading pools of paint. The flame edges to where the paper is wet with turpentine and springs up higher. She turns off the switches inside the door, and now as the fire leaps the walls shake with orange light. She closes the door but leaves the key in the lock. It was not hers, the house. Locking in or out was not for her to decide.

There is a garden seat, dark green if you look at it in daylight, at the far end of the lawn, above the now dark cliffs, and the heavy presence of the ancient trees, leaning out towards the water that glints in tiny jigging points of light. It is a warm evening. She knows they will argue about all this, whoever 'they' will be, and it will be expensive. The wisdom of the law does not come cheap, any more than freedom. She hears the first loud crack behind her. A little later, as she sits and looks out across the harbour, she feels as though she is in the centre of an amphitheatre of circling distant houses, with herself at the centre of the darkened stage. But the light is growing taller, surely, behind her? She does not turn, but sees that her hands, lying in her lap, are wearing pale, flickering gloves that are becoming brighter.

Then the voices, calling out. She stands as they approach her, shapes growing against the glare. They seem almost shy, hesitant, speaking carefully, as if to an animal they are unsure of. What on earth do they expect – that she will run away?

'This is where I live,' she assures them.

He did not tell them, there was no point in telling them, how there were times when he turned from the drinks bar with two glasses in his hands, looked across to his wife on the long Swedish couch, to see her silently shake her head, although it was only minutes since she had said yes, a gin was the very thing, and he turned back and placed them down. Or tell them of times when he would stop at the bedroom door, without her being aware of him, and turn and walk to one of the spare rooms. Only a week before he had stopped the car as they drove through the Domain, when he had said to her, more puzzled than angry, 'You have to tell me. Whatever it is, you have to tell me.' She had said to him, as she had said before, 'I'll tell you, Tom, if there is anything to tell.'

They were pulled over against a grass verge, only yards from the white marble statue of two quarrelling men, a relic of the city's once Victorian taste. For most of his life Tom had thought, one day they'll get rid of it, for God's sake. He had said to her, in the curious stalled silence of the car, 'You know that's not an answer. What you have just said.'

Yes, she knew that. The unfairness of it even, she had said, her being unable to say anything more definite than that. But how was she to tell the man she had lived with for most of her life, how to explain without offending him, that she was walking across a plain, like figures in some story in the Bible, the plain of unbounded boredom, he must not for a moment think he was responsible for that, she couldn't bear his thinking that. She could not tell him, 'It is the fact of ashes.' What a melodramatic way of putting it! But how too might she explain, that melodrama need not destroy the accuracy of the story it tells? Tom would never understand.

As she sat beside him in the warm bubble of the car, his head turned to the marble figures, the ring on his finger tapping against the wheel he continued to hold with both hands, she thought of the documentary with the quiet man with his tapering face, and an attorney who argued against him, who brought down his opened hand on the studio table and shouted, then attempted to laugh at the silliness of what in anger he may have said. And the thin-faced man had brought tears to her eyes when he said, 'It's because it *was* my mother that I am willing to be jailed for it.' As she had watched Tom left the room to go into his computer and Gareth came back to his favourite line as he saw his mother absorbed in yet another documentary, 'Try getting a life, can't you, Mum?' They were miles away from the plain, from the distant fires burning companionably in the night, where those who crossed it camped. Yet how comforting faces were, when they smiled in the light!

'I'm sorry, Tom,' Mandy said. Then lamely, as she knew, 'Time will take care of it.' She felt his quiet anger, and his patience too, perhaps even what was left of love, before he said, 'You'd better get over it soon, I can tell you that.' And not wanting to hurt her, to leave it there, he said, patting her arm with the hand he took from the wheel, trying to make some kind of joke of it, 'Otherwise we're on the skids!'

When something appalling is done, we like to believe that only an aberration might account for it. The word 'unnatural' becomes our saving grace. It preserves us as the people we like to believe we are, from the contagion of similarity. Our ploy to excuse us for ourselves. So Weston thought, almost falling asleep with the dullness of it, these little forays into serious thinking as she lay in the no longer steaming water. A lawyer thinking outside the law, hadn't one of her first tutors who rather fancied himself insisted to his first-year class, is on the verge of making a fool of herself? He was a smug little prick with his so carefully modulated pronouns, and for a term she had thought him marvellous. Romance, that had been another of his sayings, Romance, and then life takes over. He had died in a car crash with someone else's wife. My God, Weston thought as she stood and reached for the big purple bath towel on its warming rail, I'm not old enough to be a cynic!

She had lain in the bath so long that her fingers were puckered in that way she had believed, when a child, our skin goes after we are dead. At least dozing off in the hot water took her mind from the case, from the woman who still puzzled her, from the law she more and more thought of as a kind of brace that some of us walk in more comfortably than others. She had watched the TV news and the quick panning across those on the steps in front of the court, the reporter sweeping back her blond hair from a sudden push of wind as she read from her pad and summarised the day, the court's decision, the reaction of some of those involved. The son spoke angrily, saying his life was in tatters, he had his mother to thank for that. There was a glimpse of the husband, but in the distance. Weston saw herself for a moment, her gown flapping as she turned into the breeze. She already had said there was nothing more to say beyond being pleased with the verdict. Russell Bates, tanned and poised as an actor, said that all things considered the outcome was scarcely a surprise.

Weston knew she had made, as they say, a good fist of it. As she walked through from the bathroom, she saw herself reflected in the ranchslider, her towel swathing her head, her knee-length Tahitian wrap, before she quickly drew the drapes. She sat in the deep leather armchair her father had given her when she graduated. A place he had told her to help forget about work. She poured herself a glass from a newly opened bottle before she took the envelope from where she had placed it on the table, and tucked her legs beneath her in the chair. A good fist of it, if not quite one that she believed. She closed her eyes, held the first mouthful of the wine to savour it. Then she looked at the watch she had put back on, as she always did, before she dressed after her bath. There was something oddly sensual in that, to stand naked for that half minute, with only the thin metal strap against her skin.

The phone would not ring now, it was too late for that. Or perhaps it would. It depended on so much, although she was beyond it mattering too much to her, beyond its distressing her as it might have a few months before. She set the glass on the low table beside the chair, and again slipped the card from its envelope. She had read it several times. Mandy had passed it to her before the closing session, before the jury returned. She had said, 'Nothing to do with the case, I'm afraid,' smiling slightly as she said it, her face calm, as it had been since the start, a calmness that itself masked whatever it was that mattered more to her, her indifference, was it, some deep fierce certainty, an attention to more important things, although quite what she had never said. Hinted at, but never actually spelled out.

It was a plain beige card on which she had written, 'It was good of you to pick them for me that day, and to bring them in.' Which Weston knew was not the truth, and that perhaps her client had guessed that too but wanted her not to think she had seen through her. For Weston had no sycamore, and no back yard, but remembered from ages back, from the long section above the river in another city where she had been a child, that one was likely to find them there, in the long grass beneath the rust-coloured tree, and sometimes snowdrops there as well, growing close by. She had bought them from a florist's but rearranged them, removing the wisps of fern and crumpling the paper so it looked as if already used, so Mandy would believe they came from home. That she had picked them for her, that morning.

Getting It Right

I knew Alice, my mother, was dying, which could well begin a much longer story than this. But the shorter version is about as much as I can bear. So I begin with her telephoning only a week after her last call, which was quite unlike her. She was not one really for 'keeping in touch'. Emails of course would have been as unnatural to her as smoke signals, although my brother Robbie had bought her a computer more than a year before. In the usual run of things, she wrote to me once in three weeks or a month, in her rather lovely flowing script on squares of plain linen paper. Croxley Bond, which she once had bought in bulk and never ran short of. When our father was still with us he wrote less often, on hotel paper he saved from when they travelled. He put a line through the embossed name, the Grand Plaza in Hong Kong, the Rembrandt in London, the way authors score a stroke through their names on the title page of a book they have been asked to sign. This meant his letters carried a whiff of the exotic, even when they were not. But then Dad, as the family liked to say, was the romantic. He was the one who sang carols at Christmas, and when he went to the opera, which he said he did not really like, he was the one who left with tears in his eyes, although Alice understood the music and read up on the story before going to see it.

When I answered the phone the dog was barking like crazy at the new people next door. I said, 'I'll have to get him, sorry.' By the time I'd dragged him inside and shut him in the conservatory I thought she would have hung up. But she was still there when I came back. She said, 'Is he all right then?' A strange thing to ask about a dog that was behaving badly.

Alice came to stay with us for a few days the next week. I worried about Chelsea with her moods and her swearing and her walking around the house in her underwear, her navel stud glinting as the light caught it, so the school trip to Melbourne did us all a favour. 'You might as well live with a nun,' she had said once before about her grandmother. Not her narrow-mindedness—Alice was never like that—but her frugality, her not needing to chatter for its own sake, was more than a teenager could take. But Chelsea wrote a card that she said she would leave in her room. 'Love you, Gran,' it said, with little stars stuck over it and shiny gold specks sprinkled across the glue stick where she had written her name. 'If that doesn't grab her,' she said, 'just tell me some time what does, OK?'

I'd hoped that Ross would be at home when she visited. But as he said, quite reasonably, 'Every third week, you know how it goes, hon.' With the new Taupo shop not quite in its stride he needed to keep a close eye. The young chap down there was sharp and put in the hours, but an older head, Ross explained, it would come with time, but you couldn't assume. Just a pity it was that week. I know he meant it too, as he and Alice rather hit it off. Cryptic crosswords, for one thing. He could never get over how she knocked them off so quickly. As he teased her with language he knew she detested, he complimented her that she was in the top bracket crossword-wise. And at least for the brief holidays she spent with us, she seemed quite happy to sit with him watching sport.

'I draw the line at kick-boxing,' she told him. She even had—I have Ross's word for it—intelligent opinions about rugby, although her grasp of rules was shaky. She liked this winger, disliked that, wouldn't trust the little Australian halfback as far as she could throw him. The one time in her life, I suppose, she bought the *Woman's Weekly* was for its cover story of an All Black whose child was dying of leukaemia. She said, 'The man's such a decent soul he'll never get over it. He thinks all this public attention helps and then he'll find out that it doesn't.' Ross told me she had written a letter to the man and his wife, which surprised me as much as anything I ever knew about her.

She travelled so lightly, my mother. I met her as she came through the gateway, where we half-embraced and touched cheeks. Her skin was so soft, and she must have been to the hairdresser's the day before. Her hair was fluffed to disguise the thinness since her treatment. My cheek brushed against it as we drew apart. We've always been a family to indicate feelings, without too much carrying on. Her right hand had not let go of the handle she grasped, one of those suitcases you drew along, yet still compact enough to get by as cabin baggage. When I said the claim area was a little further along, and lightly touched her arm to direct her, she said, 'It's only a few days. As if I'd need more than this.' She turned and smiled up at me as the escalator lowered her head level with my chest. Her frank smile, lovelier because it was a rarity. I would give anything for a photograph of her like that. How envious I am when I see the photo albums piled at a friend's house, or hear of the way some families stash away images on their computers. We had never collected that many snaps anyway, and those we had were lost years before Dad died. He and Alice were on a trip overseas. And almost unbelievable, the next bit. When the house burned down completely in a couple of hours, when the investigator brutally told Robbie you might as well have an empty house gift-wrapped when an arsonist had been working the suburb for a year, they decided what was the point in rushing back home, why miss the Colosseum and the rest of it to see a few charred sticks and a scorched section, now the damage was done? By the time they arrived back the bulldozer had been in and the new grass planted and the land ready to be built on again, although the lingering stench of ash was still there months later, when the framework of the new house stood against the sky.

I had said to her on her last visit, 'It's such a pity there are no photos of the family.'

She reminded me, 'Your father never took that many anyway.'

I said it was not many that was important, it's the fact that there are none.

'Well, that fire,' she said offhandedly, not taking what I meant.

'Not even one photo of you and Dad together. Seeing you didn't bother even when you were away.'

Her eyes held mine with their striking Scandinavian blueness that had men running all over the place, so the story goes, when she was young. She said, 'People look at photos properly what? Once every few years? Your own memories do more than that.'

I smiled but was exasperated as I told her, 'For heaven's sake, Alice.'

I had called her by her first name like that since I was a teenager. Some people thought it a sign of intimacy between us, which it was not at all. A kind of fencing-off rather.

'Sentimentality,' she said, not leaving the matter of photographs alone.

I said, 'I hope I don't get as blasé about things as you are.' But it was impossible to provoke her. So we sat as we had so many times, so many years, seemingly at ease and close, yet each of us knowing how much closer and easier we might have been. She went on, conceding, 'People feel things in different ways.' Too intelligent not to know she sheltered behind a cliché, as I did myself, although mine was compliant silence. Until I said, to change tack, 'Chelsea's eyes must have come from you, have you noticed that? I never really thought it before but now that she's grown up—.'

'There,' my mother laughed, 'why worry about photos, then?'

I knew for several years that my father pursued an affair with a woman who worked at the school office. 'Pursued'—how odd, now that I consider it, to use such a genteel phrase for his cheating on my mother. 'Had a relationship with' is how Robbie still puts it. That amuses me, a bohemian and a homosexual refusing out of deference to his dad to say 'bonking' or 'having it off' or 'feeding her a length', phrases he will fling about of anyone else! Ross, of course, can be quite cruel about that. He says he understands perfectly his brother-in-law's delicacy. Once an arse-bandit starts calling a spade a spade, even his own father's, he'd have such a gob-load of filth he'd never be able to swill the wines he pays an arm and a leg for. Ross in fact has few moral scruples about anything. It simply irks him that Robbie splashes his pink dollars about as a married man cannot. I try to say a successful artist naturally has more to come and go on than someone running small-town bookshops even if one does it well as Ross so obviously does. My noting the obvious seems to spur him on. Have I ever looked at who swans about at his openings, he asks, *les garçons du vernissage*, have I? Aston Martins. Beamers. Ever seen a rich pansy arrive in a Toyota? I tell him, 'I don't think that's a real French expression.' But then we laugh together. We don't allow Robbie to come between us. We are good mates, make no mistake, Ross and I.

The woman's name was Beatrice. Dad's bit on the side. On her previous visit I had raised it with Alice for the first time. It was almost perverse, I suppose, to do so, knowing it was so long ago it could hardly matter to her, and I should have let it lie. It was the second morning she was with us. The sun flooded the kitchen table, the marmalade glowed as if it was lit inside like a lamp, and she picked at a piece of toast without really eating much at all. I asked, 'Did you know about Beatrice? From the start, I mean?'

'But of course,' she said. 'And Dad knew I knew.' She answered me so directly I knew I should not have asked. But she left it exactly there. I admired her for that, even as I knew that it was putting me in my place. For she must have known I wanted more from her than that. I was entitled to know more. She would have known as well my less-declared reason for asking, my hope that now, this late in the day, we might talk frankly together. About anything. She must have known but felt no compulsion to oblige me. We speak of the past as another country. Yet what about one's parents? She said nothing more of that even more distant place I longed to hear about.

What I know—how meagre it now seems—is that my parents met at a church social soon after the war, although both were too young to have been overseas. Neither Alice nor Dad was religious, any more than they were against people believing. Churchgoing just didn't, to use one of Dad's favourite expressions, 'add up'. Each of them had gone to the social with someone else, but they danced with each other, and met later that same week. They were married a few months later. 'The war had rather distorted one's sense of pace.' Robbie and I were born in less than three years. My father quickly became a senior teacher and my mother was trained to teach as well, although she preferred to stay at home, as most women then did, to be with her children. Robbie sometimes teased her, 'Tough-minded as you like but definitely not a feminist are you, Ma?' It was Dad, as she said, who carried the flag. She meant in later years, when even in winter on Lambton Quay he would don a knitted beanie and shake a tin for any women's group that asked him to lend a hand. 'I was belted and so was my mother,' he used to say. 'I know what I'm collecting for.' Once his fingers swelled with chilblains from standing out with his tin. Most of us hadn't heard of chilblains for years.

Alice encouraged him and said how she admired his social conscience, but preferred as she aged to do little apart from voting Labour once every three years, and reading in between. She said, 'I'm too healthy to play sport and frankly everything apart from reading bores me.' She said it in her rather bemused offhand way, so those she said it to thought she was not as serious as she was. She managed to read through libraries while she did all a woman of her generation also did to keep her house shiny as a pin and her family contented. And she was quietly sardonic. Abovc the fridge in the kitchen hung a framed, beautifully embroidered cloth she picked up at a garage sale, with a sentence in German declaring that 'Cleanliness Is the House's Jewel'. She liked to explain—although very few quite got her point—that she believed it had been brought back by a soldier after the war, a souvenir from a bombed house. Yet what did it mean, Robbie used to wonder, having a thing like that on the wall? Did she want people to think she was a moron?

I think my father was disappointed, once Robbie and I were at secondary school and so in any real sense off our mother's hands, that she showed no interest whatsoever in taking up the teaching she had been trained for and then put aside to rear us. Knowing she had to say something, she said, 'I'm too out of touch.' I remember it being broached several times. Dad slowly stroked the side of his face over and over, a curious, disciplined gesture that told those who knew him well that he was on the verge of anger. He told Alice, 'It needn't be at my school. That goes without saying.' She was puzzled that he might think that could be the reason. 'I'd happily work with your Dad,' she said, 'Supposing I wanted to work.'

'They simply sail past each other,' my brother used to say, 'and they think they've had a conversation.'

In fact, Alice was left a little money by an aunt in Port Adelaide, which allowed her the luxury to make a choice. As she said, 'Comfortable, that darling middle-class word!' She and my father—another point when Ross wants to score—never lost their zeal for socialism, so I suppose that remark too falls under 'sardonic'. One year I remember she read almost everything written by Graham Greene. She said, 'It's all so deplorable you just have to believe in it!' She explained, as she came to the last of the novels, 'I could pass an exam on slippery theology, let alone squalid love.' My father, who usually was the kindest person you could imagine, once hinted to me that she gave herself up to enthusiasms like that because nothing in 'real life', as he called it, actually interested her, which is why books mattered so much. Robbie took the argument even further. He said Alice couldn't really be happy. If you had her temperament and were as intelligent as our mother, you knew life was a void and that's that.

Ross, though, thought Robbie and I talked up a problem that wasn't a problem at all. 'Most people wouldn't work if they didn't have to. I know I wouldn't. She's the sanest of us all and that's what we can't cope with.' As for Alice's bland reluctance to talk intimately of anything, about that Ross simply said, 'Why do we resent it so much when someone insists on being private?'

Well, whatever the spring one wanted to source her back to, my mother, in that unsatisfactory phrase, was 'her own person'. She could be kind, and was amusing, but we did not easily forgive her that elusive core she so guarded as her own. Ross may even be right. There was no great mystery to it: we just don't care much for those who live on their own terms. By the time Robbie was gay beyond concealing, and my husband was my first and almost my only lover, Dad had taken up with the vulgar woman who did the accounts at his school. 'Vulgar' was my way, my brother's way, to dismiss her good humour, her high, spontaneous laugh, her frilled blouses, the little diamantes at the side of her winged sunglasses. She just too blatantly declared that life, for all its ups and downs, was a bit of a hoot, that 'gather ye rosebuds' or whatever was as close as we're likely to get to wisdom. They made no great effort, my father and Mrs Beatrice Nesbitt, to conceal their closeness. The lovers believed their partners, both quiet, self-sufficient people, were not the kind in any case to be irreversibly hurt. Robbie told me much later, after Dad had died, that Beatrice's husband was an old hand, you could say, at a male sauna in Victoria Street that had to be closed down. But none of this explains my mother as I want her to be explained.

Had I sensibly thought about it, I would not have asked an even closer question this last time she came to stay. The evening before we had watched a Fred Astaire movie on Sky. While Alice was with us I was always on the lookout for something to kill time. I flicked through the *TV Guide* and remembered how she liked old musicals, which the rest of us used to think rather a joke. As the dancers swirled and cavorted she sat in the too-big armchair, leaning forward a little, her hands joined on her lap. 'I had no idea you got films like this on television.' But by the end of the movie, as elegant coattails flared out and the tall handsome woman stepped so beautifully beneath her billowing dress, Alice had slumped into the cushions behind her, her mouth opened, an old exhausted woman. What I still so regret asking was at breakfast the next morning.

Already I had done with her several of the things Ross and I knew she enjoyed. I drove her through the park where at this time of year the long grass on the side of the hill was the colour of straw, and against the blue sky the grey glinting olive trees, two colours in one when the wind turned them, made you think of another country. We parked for ten minutes on the rim of a volcanic crater and watched the business of the harbour, although as Alice said, in her day it had been the North Shore ferries, distant and small as toys, she had so liked to watch. She said the outline of the big buildings in the central city were like a clutch of up-ended knives. She at once apologised for being so fanciful. 'What a nonsensical thing to say!' Then another morning we drove to the café in the Rose Gardens, with their bed after bed of brilliant blooms, although half of them, she said, were more than a touch blowsy, didn't I think? But each day by early afternoon she would need to lie down. 'Too old for playing at tourists,' as she went off to the settee in the conservatory, then read in the lounge after she had slept, read until the news came on at six o'clock.

I'd have given anything, especially as I think of it now, for us to have sat together at the kitchen table, confided as mothers and daughters are meant to do. If one of my friends called in she would chat for ten minutes and then say, 'I'll let you two get on with it. You don't want an old crone hanging about.' My friends of course fell for her, smiling as she quietly moved off. As she read one hand moved absently in the dog's grey, shaggy fur. It too trailed after her, content to lie there for as long as she wanted.

It was like this each time—the three times—that she came in the two years since Dad died. Ross said after the last visit, when I was in tears, 'Some people are simply like that. It doesn't mean you don't matter to her.'

'Your *mother* can't be private!' And I insisted rather stupidly, 'She's no different with me than she is with anyone else.'

He was patient, missing the point completely. He repeated, 'If you just accept the way she is, perhaps there isn't a problem?'

Ross once asked me a strange question. He said, 'Did Alice ever tell you about sex?' He then said, as if to cover the oddness of it, 'I mean, my father never did.'

'When I was twelve. She gave me a book and talked to me about what was in it. She couldn't have done it more efficiently, more kindly, if I was a pupil and she was paid to instruct me.'

'Perhaps that's the way it should be,' my husband said. 'No big deal, I mean.'

'No shattering of innocence?'

'Ignorance,' Ross laughed. 'Better to use the correct words.'

I said, smiling back at him, 'She made love sound a bit like a Meccano set.'

'But she did say "love"?'

'She said it, I think, but not the way it should have been said.' Yet I knew as I recounted this to Ross that it was not quite that way, and why I told it like this was something I could not explain. She made clear to me what I had half-guessed anyway. She spoke carefully, considerately. She had not given me a book. I didn't say to Ross that soon before our talk, Alice's and mine, I saw my father in his headmaster's office with his hand on Mrs Nesbitt's breast. She was sitting at the typewriter and he was standing behind her. Her hands were moving over the keys, I could hear the machine's clacking as I opened the door, and he stood behind her with one hand across her shoulder, feeling her. It was a strange memory. My father's hand seemed so large. I thought at first he must be wearing a padded glove, and Mrs Nesbitt's breast, so it struck me then, was pitiably small, so why did he bother? Yet I knew exactly what they wanted to do, that this could not possibly be all that their behaviour, their secrecy, arrived at. When Alice later talked to me and ever after I invented the detail of her giving me the book which did not exist, I resented her for telling me at all, for confirming what she must have known they did.

Four days is a long time to fill in with someone you feel ill at ease with, no matter how much you love her. My mother was always polite and grateful but, I felt, not especially interested in anything we did. When we stopped in Princes Street to look at the floral clock that I thought might amuse her—that kind of civic silliness usually did—she said, 'Begonias are detestable really, aren't they?' I knew what she meant. Those cramped speckled leaves, the nothing pinkness of their flowers that made me think of children's toothpaste. Yet it irritated me, her saying that. The begonias were not my fault. And when we had driven up the ridged hill to its sudden scooped-out cone and scatter of loose rocks, the day turned suddenly dull, rain pocked at the windscreen, and Alice asked me, 'Is this where that unfortunate man drove over with his children?' That too irritated me. I said, 'That was the hill over there.' I pointed through the veil of rain thickening towards us. 'I can't see it,' she said, 'with this Auckland weather.'

On the way home she asked me to stop at the dairy at the end of the road. I said I'd pop in to get whatever it was she wanted. No, she insisted, humour me. She moved slowly from the car to the shop, and as slowly walked back. She carried a plastic bag with two tubs of ice cream. I said we had stacks of it at home, she need not have bothered. A fact she ignored as she said, with a kind of embarrassed frankness, 'I just had this craving.' I thought of when I was seven or eight, when Dad had brought home pineapple ice cream as a treat. Robbie ploughed through his as though it were the last he would ever taste. When I was halfway through mine I edged the plate aside because I did not like pineapple, and said, 'That was marvellous, Daddy.' My mother said, 'But you haven't finished.' She said, 'Daddy will think you don't like it.' Then five minutes later I was sick as I ran from the table to the bathroom. I knew something had been proved, yet whatever it was, I scarcely understood. I watched Alice slowly moving back towards the car, then easing the plastic bag down beside her feet after she closed the door, before she told me about her 'craving'. How I disliked her using that word too. I thought how is it that something that sears into you as a child, someone else who should remember so casually forgets?

I said to her next morning, 'I know you are here this time, Mummy, because you're dying. So why can't we talk?' I don't know what she thought when at last someone compelled her to speak out. And so I watched her, a frail, declining woman, as she turned her cup several times on its saucer. She then looked up, not at me but through the window beyond me, at the gently sloping lawn that Ross kept as smooth as his own cheek. ('If a blade of grass is out of place it's like a fish bone in my throat.')

She watched beyond me for so long that I thought, this time I have gone too far. This time I have hurt her. Then she looked at me directly. She said, 'I'm taking so long, I'm sorry, because there isn't any answer I can give you that will satisfy you.' Her thin hands—more twigs than hands, I thought, with a kind of shame at how glibly comparisons like that jump at one—were around her cup, as though she hoped to draw in its warmth. She began again. She said, 'I'm not here because I want to be. Next to not dying at all, I'd prefer to do it the way a cat does. Just slope off quietly.' Smiling, knowing I suppose that what she said was ridiculous. Yet insisting, 'You know I don't like fuss at any time and I like it even less now. Which is why I've not told you outright, although I know that I owe it to you. So I'm glad we've had our talk. I'll go back home and everything's very clear. There'll be fuss, I suppose, but I hope not too much of it.' Her hand left the side of the cup and was warm as it ran along my forearm. When she said 'fuss' for the second time, it was apparent that it meant her death, and everything that surrounds it: family, regret, fear, goodbye, all trimmed back to four letters that attempted to contain them. I took her hand and thought how much larger, clumsier my fingers seemed as they closed over hers. I thought, not of Alice only, but in a broader, general way, that human beings ought not to be like this, that dying was too vast a tract to cross alone, and yet we have no choice.

I said, 'Of course I'll come back with you.'

'There's months yet,' she said. 'Leave it a few weeks and then come down. That's what I'd really like.' She said there were things to sort out, not many but a few, so to come down then. 'It will be Easter, the weather's always nice.' She made me promise that for the moment I would not mention it to Ross. 'It's a dreadful thing to say, but even the kindest people can't always help.' I thought of the tugs we had seen yesterday on the harbour. They were too far off to be anything but tiny shapes, so I must have been remembering something from when the family sometimes walked down the waterfront when Robbie and I were children. We watched the thick buffers on the tugs that were like rubbery lips, that made it safe to nudge against other boats, cushioning both against each other. Her hand stayed resting on my arm.

A fortnight later Ross was down at Taupo again, checking out the new mall. He rang to say he would take another day, he couldn't be this close to the lake and turn down the chance to go fishing—well, could he, hon? He is so matter-of-fact about fishing, that is when I know that he lies. Yet we enjoy being together. He still amuses me with his stories about his partners, his employees, his incisive phrases that set them up like ninepins and then good-humouredly knock down. To laugh together after twenty-odd years of marriage isn't a bad platform for getting on. He is generous and people like him, he's as outgoing I sometimes say as I'm indoors, you'll know what I mean when I say like the figures on those Swiss clocks? But I knew he meant it when he said he'd definitely come with me to see Alice at Easter, he said he'd make sure that Chelsea came too. But before Ross was home from his fishing she died, as they say, 'like that'. I could almost hear the neighbour's fingers snap as she told me on the phone. Yes, the neighbour said, while she was watching telly.

'She loathed television,' I said, 'except the news.'

'That's why I mention it,' said Jo Kavanagh from next door. 'We saw the light through the curtains just after it got dark, that's why we went across. We both said it wasn't like her.' I could see Jo's sandpapery skin, her throat flushed above the girly collars she had worn for as long as I had known her, since Dad and Alice moved down there for the sun.

She said, 'I'm sorry I'm the one who had to ring.'

I put down the phone and went into Chelsea's room. She was lying on her bed, turning the pages of a brochure that advertised cheap rates for Fijian resorts. Her father had told her it was beyond him, how anyone could take advantage of a hijacked democracy so underpaid Fijians could cut up your pineapple for you. Although he smiled as he teased her and she told him back, 'Fuck off, will you, Dad?' As I now opened the door she said without looking up, 'This is unbelievable you know, this deal?' her hand patting the page in front of her. 'I've got to let Trish know about this one.'

I said, 'That was Tauranga. Alice has passed on.'

Chelsea swung her legs from the bed and looked down for a moment as she flexed her toes. Then she held my eye and said, 'She didn't even open that card I left her, know that?'

And then I was beating her. Not slapping her but actually

beating, my closed fists flailing down on her, pummelling, wanting her to cry out. She drew up her knees and crawled close against the wall, her body folded small to get away from me. A rage I had never known in my life came over me, a wave, I kept thinking, a wave so high of anger and regret that it had nowhere to go but here, Chelsea was the beach where it broke and threw us both aside. 'She did, she did, she did!' my words too hammering down on her in a gasping rush that appalled me and that I was unable to stop, as she writhed and began pushing against me, her raised foot catching my hip and thrusting me back against the windowsill. My anger gone as quickly as it had struck, a sense of exhaustion flooding me to fill where it had drained.

My daughter pushed past me to wrench at the drawer of her dressing table. She threw the pink envelope onto the bed. 'You can see it,' she screamed at me, 'even you can see it isn't opened!' I picked up the envelope and turned it and ran after her from the room. I called to her as she pelted down the stairs, but my words were lost in the same garbled sobbing that disgusted me, as if they foamed from a person I despised. 'It was me, darling,' I was trying to tell her, 'I forgot. I forgot. I just forgot to give it to her.' I stood now at the top of the stairs. A string of saliva had leaped across my cheek. But the front door slammed and in the silence I slipped to my knees and held in each hand one of the round wooden supports of the balustrade above the hall. I was like a prisoner against the bars of her cell. I kept saying in the same catching sobs, 'My darling!' I knelt there for five minutes, perhaps longer. I heard steps and a key scratching for the lock in the front door, Chelsea coming back. But the door opened and Ross stepped inside. He glanced up at me. God knows what I must have looked like. His hand jangled his keys that were on a key ring I had given him years ago, the coat of arms of a city where once we spent a week in Italy. From the bedroom window the sea had been blue beyond belief. He placed the keys on the hook inside the front door and put down his briefcase against the hall table. He then walked through into the living room and closed the door. I leaned my forehead on the cool white wood of the railing. I began again to repeat the words as though I was unable to stop, but quietly, you would not have heard them from the bottom of the stairs. Not sure even which of the three, which of the four of us, I meant.

Luce

Luce did not believe Bang when he told her that was his name. But if someone says that is what he is called, even if you think he is telling a lie, it is still the only thing you know to call him, so you have to. So she called him that. Although she did tell him, 'That's a funny sort of name.'

The boy said, 'It's what I'm always called.' He picked up one of the red clay marbles from his side of the board and moved it across the other pieces. 'Yep,' he said. He was not very good at the game but he kept making out he was. When it was his turn again he at once picked up the clay marble that looked like a nearly black Jaffa. But before he put it down again on one of the holes on the board he fiddled it between his fingers, as though he was thinking hard about where to place it, as though he had these different choices of what he might do next. Luce had thought when they first played that he would beat her easily. Then after two games she knew she was better than he was and Bang knew that too. Although he still did this thing with the marble moving between his fingers.

Luce's mum thought that if they were playing checkers together then they would have to become friends. Luce had asked, 'How long is he staying with us?'

Her mother said, 'Until things are sorted out.'

That was the kind of answer the seven-year-old hated. It was another way not to tell her a thing. So she had said, 'Until they know about Lola?'

Her mother ran her hands back through her long hair, smoothing and lifting it at the same time, so for once Luce could see the back of her neck, so white it was like she had put chalk on it. Then she said while she made out she straightened Luce's collar, 'You have to be nice to him, remember? Things are so sad for him at home we have to be nice to him.'

Luce said, 'I don't always have to win.'

And Luce's dad said from where he sat at the table with the newspaper spread out in front of him, 'No need to lay it on, Janice.' That was the way her dad talked when he didn't want her to know. But Luce did. She knew something very bad had happened to Lola. Bang was Lola's brother but was at another school along at Carterton because his mum and dad didn't live together. And Bang's father was the man the police wanted to talk to about it. The whole school knew that. Bang was staying with them now because her dad and his dad were friends.

Bang didn't like it that once the light was put out they had to go to sleep. It was never like that at home. But since he had come to stay with these people it was hard to know what was going on. He knew, though, he had to try. He had promised when he was getting into the back of the big car with another man, and his dad had leaned down and put his mouth on his head so he had felt how hot his breath was, and he had said quietly so no one else could hear, 'Be good as you can now, won't you, mate? Whatever Janice tells you.' Janice who was Luce's mum and had stood with her hands on his shoulders until he had moved away while his dad got into the back of the car and the other man closed the door. He had squeezed his dad's hand when he leaned over and said that to him. Then the second time Luce's mother drew him back in against her and crossed her arms over his chest he just let her do it. He was watching the car move slowly to the corner, where it turned into the bigger road and the cars that were always going fast along it, on the way to the big town across the hill. The windows were dark in the car his dad was in. As soon as it turned at the corner and flickered away behind the trees the boy took her wrists and moved them away. Luce's mother called him Thomas though she must have heard the last thing his dad said to him when he leaned from the lowered window just before the car had left, when he raised a thumb and pointed two fingers and said, his mouth moving quietly so only the two of them would know when he said it, 'Bang.'

Luce would have liked him to be her friend, but you can't just make people want to be nice to you. Mrs Kavanagh had told them that when the Corby twins first came to the school, the girls who were so pretty with long hair you wanted to run your hand down, so different too the way they talked and everyone wanted to be their friend. But the twins only wanted to be left to themselves and sat together at lunchtime and held hands. You just can't do that, Mrs Kavanagh said. If friends were real it was like a tree growing carefully and slowly, you don't say 'I want to be a tree', 'I want to be a friend', straight off like that. So Luce knew she and Bang played checkers together only because her mum told them to, and he told her, 'I could be good at this game if it wasn't dumb,' and asked her had she ever killed a rabbit. When she said no, not really, he said he had been out shooting with his dad so many times he couldn't remember how many he must have killed. But if they weren't really friends there was one thing Luce could do without anyone knowing about it, she could keep a secret for him. When he first went with her to school and their teacher said he was coming here for a while rather than his own school in Featherston, Janey Baker of course who asked everybody everything said, 'What's his real other name? It's not just Thomas.' Luce said, well that was his name most of the time, but there were other secret names his father called him, although she was sorry, she couldn't tell Jane what they were, Thomas had asked her not to. She knew that was a good thing to do, to tell it like that. Bang would have liked her saying it like that. Only by the end of the week he had to stop going to school because everyone knew, everyone said, 'His father killed her, killed Lola, who doesn't know that?', the way they pretended too they had been friends with Lola, who was in one of the big classes and Luce bet she wouldn't even have known their names.

Bang didn't go to school after that and Luce's father said, 'You know, Tom, I think it would be more fun if you helped me round the farm for a bit, don't you? Rather than school?' They were all sitting having breakfast. Luce thought, he's got the fluffiest hair I've ever seen on anyone. The sun came in through the window behind him and his hair was *frothy*, that was what it made her think of, all light and thin and shiny where the sun touched the edges.

'Yes,' Dad said, 'this time of year I can always do with a bit of help.'

'That's all right,' Bang told him. 'I'm good at different things.'

Then there was her own surprise the day after Bang began to stay away from school to help round the farm. 'Fencing,' Dad had said that night while they were having tea, 'never got that much done in a day before, know that? Comes from having someone to help who knows what he's doing.'

'Sort of,' Bang said, very quietly, bursting with what Dad had said. Someone at school had told Luce he only lived in a box sort of house in Featherston, right in the dark bit under the hill, so no wonder being a farmer was such fun. He didn't ever look straight at Luce when he said anything. But she knew he liked it when Dad touched his head for a moment while he walked across the kitchen to take another tinny from the fridge. He didn't move away like he did if her mother touched him. 'So,' Dad said when he came back and sat down and ripped the top of the tinny with its little ring you had to flip up first, 'done your packing, have you, Luce?' She went to make sure again, although she knew everything was there in the suitcase on the bed. She had checked it three times already.

Because that was the surprise. That morning her mother had said to her when Bang and Dad had gone out to the shed, said it as though there was nothing so special about it, 'I think you'd enjoy having a holiday with your Auntie Lois, what do you think of that?' Auntie Lois was her mother's sister but Luce could think of no one who was more different. Auntie Lois didn't care that there were grey streaks in her hair and wore long dresses that were so light they lifted when the wind came up and then stuck against her as if they were wet, so you could see what she had on underneath. She walked round the house without any shoes, just her bare feet slap-slap on the lino. Her father said hardly anything when Auntie Lois stayed with them, that's how Luce knew he didn't like her. But she liked Auntie Lois because her auntie laughed and sang bits of songs, started and stopped singing just because she felt like it, and said words her mother and father would never say. Last time she was here she had said 'Fuck that for a joke' when Uncle Tim had phoned and said would they like to go across to see him in Greytown, and Mum had put her hand across the phone so he wouldn't hear.

'Yes,' Mum said now, 'I thought you might like to go right down to the South Island to stay with her, wouldn't you, Luce? Now it's nearly holidays anyway?'

Luce said, 'But isn't it so far? That's why we've never been there.'

'If you *fly* it isn't far,' her mother said, as if she had only thought of it. Because that was something Dad used to say a lot, when her mother talked about Auntie Lois, 'We'll get round to it one of these days.' But now Mum was saying it was a nice idea, for her to go to Auntie Lois's where there was snow in winter and now when it was getting on for summer it was hotter than you'd ever credit if you hadn't already been there.

'How old's my cousin?' Luce asked.

'Thirteen,' her mother said. 'She's very nice. She'll look after you.'

Feilding was sitting in the car when Luce arrived. The mountains had come in so very close when the plane turned to land she had closed her eyes. The nice man in the seat next to her put on his 'specially for telling children' voice that made her feel prickly and wish that he wouldn't as he told her when the plane gets too close to them, the mountains always manage to get out of the way.

Her cousin didn't like her, she could tell that right away, although Auntie Lois gave her a big hug when she came through the door to where people were waiting. She felt herself folded into her aunt as though she was the biggest cushion. She held her hand after they had waited and taken her suitcase from the piece of black floor that kept moving around and went out to the big car that was like half a bus and looked like it had never been cleaned. It was hard to tell what colour it was beneath all the mud. There were pictures and bits of writing drawn in the dirt. And there was a man high up in the driver's seat, his hair pulled back into a black ribbon and then falling in a ponytail like a girl's. Auntie Lois said, 'This is Gentry.' He touched the side of his hat with his finger. He nodded his head sort of on one side and told her, 'Don't expect everyone to be as nice as me.' Then he laughed and coughed at the same time, his voice like something was being dragged over bumpy tin. But Feilding didn't say anything when she climbed up into the back seat and sat beside her, and Auntie Lois said, 'Fee, honey, this is your cousin Luce.'

The older girl was texting on her mobile. She didn't look at her cousin, not once, although it was nearly the longest car ride Luce had ever been on to get to where she would stay until Mum rang up and told her it was all right now, it was time to come back. There was a lake on one side of the car that was big as going to the beach. And on the other side a mountain with snow near the top that made her think of spread-out sheets. Feilding kept looking at her mobile and moving both her thumbs very fast. When Luce asked, 'What are you doing?' Feilding said, 'Knitting. Isn't that what it looks like?' and Auntie Lois said from the front seat, 'You can be nicer than that now, can't you?' They were all quiet then for a long time and drove on and on. Once Gentry put his arm across her auntie's shoulder and pressed his fingers into the top of her arm and Auntie Lois put her own hand up to his to stop them moving. Then she lit a cigarette and smoked it herself before she passed it across to him. When he sucked on it Luce saw part of his face in the little mirror turn orange from the bright light it made. She was asleep when they came to the house and the shed beside it that was even bigger than the house. When she stepped down from the car and waited for Gentry to get her suitcase from the boot it was so cold her teeth were knocking together. At the edge of the sky it looked as though someone was burning something, but too low down for you to really see.

Luce could not believe how messy the house was. Some of the cupboards didn't even have doors on them and everything just jumbled up on the shelves, bottles of sauce and things lying on their sides, or if they were standing up they sometimes didn't have tops. Mixed-up clothes and things were just piled up on a sofa, and the vacuum cleaner was still there in the middle of the room, not even put away. But when Auntie Lois did things she moved so quickly and there was dinner on the table before Gentry had lit the big stove that he lifted lumps of wood into. 'But better see where you're sleeping first,' her auntie said.

There were two beds in her cousin's bedroom. Luce stood at the door and said to Feilding, 'What bed is yours?'

The bigger girl told her without really looking at her that sometimes it was one bed and sometimes the other. 'Like what I feel like. I never know until last thing.' But Auntie Lois was standing behind them and said, 'Don't be ridiculous, Feilding. You'll sleep on the floor if you talk like that.' But said it without being angry. Then, 'That's yours there, Luce,' she said, 'the one with the big duvet to keep you warm.'

When they were sitting at the table that didn't have a tablecloth on it, and the knives and spoons were put down jumbled in the middle of the table and people reached out and took them, Gentry looked at her and asked her, well, did she have any news from up home or was she just going to say nothing the way Feilding did, entertain them with her silence?

'Don't tease,' Auntie Lois told him.

'It's not teasing, is it,' Gentry said, 'us just having a conversation together like this?' He picked up this strange-looking loaf of bread and held it right against his jersey while he cut slices from it so when he put it down he had to brush the crumbs off his clothes. He held out a thick slice on the end of the knife towards Luce.

'Thank you,' she said. 'Thank you very much.'

'I'll butter it for you if you like. I've seen visitors in this house lose an arm trying to butter bread. That's how sharp our knives are.'

Auntie Lois said again, 'Don't tease, Gentry,' and when Feilding made this rude noise with her tongue Gentry said what Luce had never heard a grown-up say on purpose, 'No idea how delicate that cousin of yours is, Luce. Even breathing pisses her off.' But he laughed as he said it and Auntie Lois smiled across at her and Luce said, remembering what Mum had told her about being polite, 'I'm not scared being here, you know.'

'That's very good, then,' he told her. And she couldn't believe it happened when he raised his hands and unwound the band that held his ponytail tight and flicked his head so the hair flung out and spread over his shoulders. 'It's longer,' Luce said, 'than a lady's is.'

He was ladling out soup from a big bowl into the plates he leaned across and put in front of each of them. 'Yes,' he told her, 'I hate the way men have no hair, half of them. I had to make people see how good I look.'

'I don't know what you're saying,' Luce said. She moved her big spoon around in the soup the same colour as mud and the steam from it came up into her face. She did not look up when she said that but she laughed so he would know she liked him, liked him because she had never seen anyone who looked like Gentry or talked to her the way he did, like he already was her friend. Auntie Lois came then and stood behind him and put her arms round his middle so her arms were like another belt. Yes, she liked being here, Luce decided, and her auntie said tomorrow or the next day they might go and look at some real mountains. But when the morning came they didn't go because it was so cold, and the rain beat against the window not like ordinary rain but thick globs of ice in the middle of it that slid slowly down the glass. At breakfast Gentry said when he came and sat at the table and Auntie Lois put this mix of stuff in her bowl, all sorts of bits stirred up together, 'Looks like we're in the cage for the day, doesn't it, crumpet? Mountains'll be there tomorrow.'

Some days there were nice things to do and Auntie Lois and Gentry were fun. They joked a lot more with her than Mum and her father ever did at home. It was awful, though, sitting in the bedroom with Feilding when there was nothing else to do, and they weren't allowed in the picture room because some of the paint was still drying. Her cousin kept flicking her thumbs across her phone or talking very quietly into it so Luce wouldn't hear. 'You must have lots of friends, Feilding,' she told her, but the older girl just looked across from her own bed where she still wore her pyjamas and said, 'God!'

But then one morning the sun came out after Gentry had decided the weather was bad enough to go to work, and Feilding came and sat on Luce's bed. She said, her voice all changed and friendly, 'You want to go somewhere for a walk?'

'I don't know,' Luce told her. 'Where to?'

'You'll like it up the hill.'

'Is there snow?'

Feilding said another of her bad words before she breathed in deep and said, 'I said a *hill*, didn't I? I didn't say a *mountain*.' Then when it seemed this brat she was landed with might start to cry, she said again, 'You'll like it.'

'I don't know,' Luce said.

Feilding put her hand on her cousin's knee. 'We'll take you to see the bride,' she said.

Luce said nothing for a moment because it was very confusing. Then she said, 'There's no bride. I don't believe there's a bride.'

'Oh yes there is,' said Feilding. And then they talked very quietly, because that is one of the ways you know if a secret is true. 'That's what we'll see but you're not to tell them. Tell Mum and him.'

So at lunch the next day when the sky was blue outside the big window, Feilding said, 'Me and Luce are going for a walk, aren't we, Luce.'

Gentry took not much notice because he was looking at a newspaper he had spread out right across the table. Then he said, 'I thought we might go across to Omakau. I got something to drop off over that way.' But Auntie Lois said that could wait, surely? She laughed and said it wasn't as though they had nothing to smoke over in Omakau until they dropped it in. 'And it's lovely Feilding wants to take her out. Don't you think?'

Gentry looked up to see Auntie Lois standing behind the girls, a forefinger of each hand pointing down at their heads, while she nodded quickly at him.

'Whatever,' he said.

The rocks up the big hill behind the house looked as if they'd never stop, and the path between them was so steep it hurt Luce's side just trying to keep up. 'It's so far,' she said. She wanted to stop and lean against a rock.

'You'll be all right,' Feilding said.

'You're so much bigger, remember,' Luce told her. 'You must have done this lots.' She nearly wanted to cry but that was the last thing she must do. Feilding would hate her even more. Then they came to a small bridge for walking across a high narrow place where it scared you just to look down. It was on the other side of the bridge that Dougie came up to them and Feilding said, 'This is Luce, the one I told you about.'

'Hi, Luce,' Dougie said. When he grinned down at her it seemed to cut his head nearly in half. He was very skinny and tall and his face made her think of an axe. Then he and Feilding walked on very fast in front of her so it was even harder trying to keep up. Dougie and her cousin were holding hands. When she did come up closer to them she said, 'Is it very far to the bride?' Neither answered her but Feilding pushed her face in close against Dougie's. He turned and looked back at Luce and his skinny face cut in half again when he grinned. Later when they sat down near a rock bigger than a house he said to her, 'Feilding says you know all about that girl who was killed and her father done it. It was on TV.'

Luce thought, what do they know about anything? She tugged at a clump of long yellow grass beside where she sat. Pulling it, though, was like pulling wire and it hurt her hand.

'Shut up, Dougie,' Feilding said. Then to Luce, 'You just sit there because you're puffed and we'll go over here for a bit.' They went to where there was another giant stack of rocks and left her by herself.

Luce sat and looked out across the flat spaces way down in front of her, and the road where a truck moved along like a toy, that's how high she was. They must have climbed so far. Auntie Lois's house she could only just see, behind a row of black trees, and the two sheds where Gentry kept another old car, and there were bundles of hay in the other one, piled to the roof. Only from here the sheds were like toys as well. The football posts in the paddock next to them were small as matches. And the road that went on and on, because this was further from anywhere than Luce had ever been.

The wind was cold when it moved around the rocks. She was glad Auntie Lois had made her wear a jacket that was too big for her, the sleeves folded back halfway across her arms, over the top of her jumper. She didn't care how long that stupid Feilding and Dougie were away. It was nicer just being here by herself. And she knew what Dougie had asked her was something he should not have said. It made her wonder about Bang. But back home and everything about it was so far away. She screwed up her eyes and when she opened them again everything down there, the road and the houses and the long black rows of trees, had become fuzzy to look at. She couldn't even see the little sticks of the goal posts. Then a long time later her cousin came back and told her, 'You just say we were walking all the time, all right? Don't say Dougie was here.'

'What about that special thing, though?' Luce asked her. 'What about that?'

Dougie stood behind Feilding and said, like he was angry about it, 'What's that bull?'

Luce's lip was shaking and she couldn't stop it.

'God!' Feilding said as she turned to Dougie and told him it wasn't her fault, the only reason she could get away in the first place was because she told Mum she was taking the kid with her.

Then Luce said, 'You'd better show me, Feilding,' surprised she was brave enough to say it like that.

'We'd better then,' her cousin said, but saying it not to her but to Dougie who still looked as if he was angry now with both of them. So she walked ahead again and Dougie was behind her, not holding her hand any more, and Luce still trying to keep up with them. Once she slipped where the path was steep and the little stones were loose and her knee really hurt where it banged against a rock. She cried out 'Ouch!' even before she knew she was going to say it. She was glad they didn't hear her. Her knee was bleeding when she looked down at it. Then they were at the top of the path where it crossed over a ridge and went down on the other side. Feilding didn't even look round, she just stood there with her fists deep in the pockets of her windbreaker and her hood pulled up. But Dougie came up to her and put his hankie against her knee and said, 'You'll be all right. Everyone falls over sometimes when they walk up here.'

Luce put her hand where the material on her skirt had ripped. 'I think the rock did that.'

Dougie said, 'It's not much, though. She'll be right.'

'I don't care about that anyway,' Luce told him.

It was not much further then to where the path was smoother and it was so much easier to walk, a flat place where a small creek that even she could step across ran between the tufty bits of grass. The wind had gone very still and she could hear the water running like someone had not turned off a tap. Then she saw past Feilding to where there was an old tree with hardly any leaves, and Dougie was standing next to something she could not quite make out. It looked at first as though someone had tipped out dirty pieces of wool in a pile that had spread out flat, and things were mixed up with the wool. Then she saw the head that was mostly bone and eyes that weren't there, and the shiny teeth with black stuff at the top and bottom of them, it was like they were trying to grin at her. It made her sick to look. And the wool was pulled up round it, like something that it wore. Feilding said to her, 'There, you've seen it, all right? So can we go back now?'

'You're like ice,' her auntie said when they got back to the house. She put the back of her hand against Luce's face. It was so warm the girl grabbed it and held it there while Auntie Lois laughed and said, 'Cocoa, I think that's the story.' She made it for them in big mugs that were rough to hold, like they hadn't been properly finished, and they sat together on the sofa in the room that didn't have walls like other houses but pictures painted all over them, trees and people with hardly any clothes and a horse with a horn growing out of its forehead and other animals that weren't really real. Some of the birds had faces like people and one man with wings was halfway across the sky.

'Paradise,' Auntie Lois had said the first time they came into the room and turned the lights on so they could see them better, and Luce couldn't stop looking at the pictures that had so many things in them, and where the colours weren't always right. There was a green dog and two of the ladies had blue skin. And there was Gentry in the middle, with a tree in front of him instead of proper pants, and Auntie Lois was sort of higher than him, and smaller, but there were two of her, one on either side. He had asked her if she liked the paintings and she said yes she did, she thought they were lovely, and he said,

'Well, I'll paint you too if you like before you go back home.' Feilding made this sort of rude noise through her nose when Gentry had asked Luce that. 'Paradise is right,' she said. But now while Luce and Auntie Lois drank their cocoa Feilding sat in front of television in the other room until the phone rang and she went into her bedroom and slammed the door, leaving it for her mother to answer.

'It's for you, miss,' Auntie Lois called to Luce. It was her Mum, all the way from home. Yes, Luce told her, she was having a nice time, yes, there were all sorts of interesting things to do. Into the mountains, yes, she said, they had been there too. And a fair they had gone to at the end of a lake. And the hay bales. Well, Mum said, it would be so good when she came home. 'You've no idea how we miss you, Luce.'

Luce swallowed hard and asked was he still there, was he, was Bang still there?

Thomas? Her mum said. No, he was up in Hamilton now, he wouldn't be coming back, now his father had gone away.

'But if you see him,' Luce said.

'Well, I don't know if we will,' Mum said. 'Not for a while.'

'But if you do.'

'Yes, if we do,' her mother said.

'If you do see Bang,' Luce said, 'tell him I saw the bride. Say I said to tell him.'